PENGUIN BOOKS

THE PORTABLE CHARLES LAMB

Each volume in The Viking Portable Library either presents a representative selection from the works of a single outstanding writer or offers a comprehensive anthology on a special subject. Averaging seven hundred pages in length and designed for compactness and readability, these books fill a need not met by other compilations. All are edited by distinguished authorities, who have written introductory essays and included much other helpful material.

"The Viking Portables have done more for good reading and good writers than anything that has come along since I can remember."
—Arthur Mizener

John Mason Brown, who died in 1969, was drama critic of the *New York Post* and of the *New York World Telegram*, associate editor of *Theatre Arts Monthly*, and conductor of a weekly column, "Seeing Things," in the *Saturday Review*. He was the author of many books, a member of the Pulitzer Prize drama jury, one of the judges of the Book-of-the-Month Club, and was well known as a lecturer.

The Portable

CHARLES LAMB

Edited by John Mason Brown

PENGUIN BOOKS

Penguin Books Ltd, Harmondsworth,
Middlesex, England
Penguin Books, 625 Madison Avenue,
New York, New York 10022, U.S.A.
Penguin Books Australia Ltd, Ringwood,
Victoria, Australia
Penguin Books Canada Limited, 2801 John Street,
Markham, Ontario, Canada L3R 1B4
Penguin Books (N.Z.) Ltd, 182–190 Wairau Road,
Auckland 10, New Zealand

First published in the United States of America by
The Viking Press 1949
First published in Canada by
The Macmillan Company of Canada Limited 1949
Paperbound edition published 1964
Reprinted 1967, 1969
Published in Penguin Books 1980

LIBRARY OF CONGRESS CATALOGING IN PUBLICATION DATA
Lamb, Charles, 1775–1834.
The portable Charles Lamb.
Reprint of the 1949 ed. published by Viking Press,
New York, which was issued as no. 43 of Viking portable
library.
Bibliography: p. 593.
I. Brown, John Mason, 1900–1969. II. Title.
[PR4860.A4B7 1980]   824'.7   80-99
ISBN 0 14 015.043 9

Printed in the United States of America by
Kingsport Press, Inc., Kingsport, Tennessee
Set in Caledonia

Parts of the Introduction appeared in articles in *The Saturday
Review of Literature*, to which acknowledgment is made.

Contents

PART TWO · HIMSELF, HIS YOUTH, AND HIS FAMILY

PART THREE · LONDON

PART FOUR · FANTASIES AND TALES

PART FIVE · MEN, "CHARACTERS," AND PLACES

PART SIX · BOOKS AND PAINTINGS

PART SEVEN · IN GENERAL

Editor's Introduction

AMONG the tantalizing "ifs" of literature is what Charles Lamb might have been like as man and writer if, in a fit of madness, his sister Mary had not slain their mother when he was only twenty-one. The "gentle Elia" the world loves was the product of ungentle and terrible events. He was the stepchild of a calamity as bloody as any to be found in the most bloodstained Elizabethan dramas of which Lamb was later to become a champion. To a tragic extent Lamb's life, hence Elia's character, was carved out for him by the case knife which poor deluded Mary drove straight and deep into their mother's heart.

Surely never in the strange annals of authorship has the world gained so much in pleasure or an innocent man lost more in freedom than in the instance of the catastrophe which resulted in Lamb's becoming the most beloved bachelor of letters literature has produced.

When he quit his desk at the East India House on the afternoon of September 22, 1796, and started to walk home through the London he loved, Lamb was not without his worries. His sister Mary, ten years his senior, had already shown symptoms of insanity. Not for the first time, either. As a person who had himself been confined

1

the previous year for six weeks in a madhouse at Hoxton, these symptoms may have had a special meaning for him. In any case, Mary's condition was sufficiently disturbing to have sent Lamb, on his way to work that very morning, in search of a doctor who was not to be found. Aware though he was of the gathering clouds, Lamb could not have been prepared for the violence of the storm which had broken out in the house where he lived with his old father, his invalid mother, his sister, and his Aunt Hetty.

The sight he beheld when he opened the door was of tabloid gruesomeness. Above the bustle of Little Queen Street, he may have heard the cries of his father and the shrieks of Mary and her apprentice as he approached his home. If he had not, the landlord's presence was in itself a warning. Certainly his eyes must have disbelieved the nightmare of reality which confronted them. The room, in which the table was laid for dinner, was in a turmoil. Charles' aged aunt was unconscious on the floor, "to all appearance like one dying." His senile father was bleeding from a wound in his forehead. His mother was dead in a chair, stabbed to the heart by Mary, who was standing over her with the case knife still in her hand. Lamb arrived only in time to snatch the knife from her grasp.

What had provoked this scene no one knows. Perhaps, as a professional seamstress, Mary had been overworking, and the stress of a dependent household had become too great for her. Perhaps the final straw had been the additional cares which had come her way because of the leg injury recently suffered by her brother John, her elder by a year and a half. Perhaps, as moderns have hinted, an ugly, long-suppressed animosity between her and her mother had at last erupted. In any event, Mary had had an altercation with the young woman who, in her mantua-making, was her helper.

Mary had reached for the knives and forks on the table, throwing them at this frightened girl in the hope of driving her from the house. It was one of the forks thus thrown which had struck her father. Her mother might have been spared had she not attempted to intercede in the apprentice's behalf.

"I date from the day of horrors," wrote Lamb to Coleridge soon after the disaster. Although by this he meant merely to place in time events described in his letter, he unwittingly summarized the rest of his adult life. To these sensational occurrences which cost him dearly, we owe, in part at least, the writer we cherish as one of the least sensational of authors. For the next thirty-eight years Lamb lived a gallant and, on the whole, a cheerful prisoner to the happenings of that fatal afternoon. In no sense of the word a tragic hero, he emerged as the hero of a tragedy. We pity him the more because he was without self-pity.

There are people, luckless mortals, who by the injustices of circumstance or because of a certain granite in their character are doomed to be caryatids for the suffering of others. Charles Lamb was one of these. He could have fallen back on the law and allowed his sister to be committed to a public insane asylum. He could have walked out on Mary. In other words, he could have done what his older brother John did and wanted him to do.

Yet even when John washed his hands of the whole problem, Lamb was able to rise, "not without tenderness," to his brother's defense. He knew John to be "little disposed . . . at any time to take care of old age and infirmities." Charles went so far as to persuade himself that John, "with his bad leg, had an exemption from such duties." He was well aware that John would make speeches about the money needed to maintain Mary in a private institution. But Charles and John, though

brothers, were made of very different stuff. Young and
poor as he was, Charles faced without complaining the
fact that "the whole weight of the family" had been
thrown upon him. From the outset he was determined,
regardless of the sacrifices, that Mary should not go into
a public asylum.

Nor did she. Instead, he assumed full responsibility
for her. More than that, he devoted his life to her. Because of this utter devotion his own life was altered
inescapably. Had it not been for Mary, age would not
have fallen so suddenly and engulfingly upon him. Without her, we might be able to imagine Lamb as a young
man rather than always picturing him as a smoky and
eccentric oldish fellow, settled in both his habits and his
singleness, whose youth had come to an abrupt end with
his childhood. Without Mary, Charles' dream-children
might have been real. The "fair Alice W——n," she of
the light yellow hair and the pale blue eyes for whom
he claimed to have pined away seven of his "goldenest years," might have been the "passionate . . . love-
adventure" he once described her as being instead of a
reference, true or fanciful, which biographers have been
unable to track down. He might not have waited so many
years to propose to Fanny Kelly, the actress with the
"divine plain face," and Fanny might even have accepted
him.

Without his "poor dear dearest" Mary, Charles might
have continued longer to try his hand at poetry and not
so soon, as he put it (with wonderful inaccuracy, in his
case), have "dwindled into prose and criticism." His
spirit would have been gayer; his laughs less like sighs.
He might not have been so "shy of novelties, new books,
new faces, new years." The present, not the past, might
have been his delight. He would not have been driven,

as driven he was by the events of that appalling afternoon, to find happiness by thinking back to happier days. Retrospection would not have become his refuge. The "boy-man" that he felt himself to be would not have clung with such tenacious affection to his own boyhood. The texture, the range, the very tone and temper of his work would have been different.

From the moment of his mother's murder and the time that he stepped forward to become Mary's legal guardian Lamb knew that he and Mary were "in a manner *marked*." This was bound to be a portion of their fate. There was no hushing their story. It not only pursued them; it ran ahead of them. Sometimes it even forced them to change their lodgings. No shelter could be found from the nudgings, the whisperings, the stares, and the embarrassments it provoked. Charles' determination to care for Mary involved more than living with her. It also meant his living with the knowledge that everyone around them knew her case and their history. If this increased his shyness, it also brought Mary and him closer together. It was only one more of the many bonds, tender and tragic, which united them.

Fortunately, theirs was a relationship based upon more than the perilous stuffs of gratitude or an embittering sense of obligation. Positive as each of them was as a personality, they were united not only by misfortune but by shared tastes and minds which, in spite of dissimilarities, were complementary. When dedicating a volume of his verse, Charles called Mary his best friend. From the dedication of his life she knew she had no better friend than he. Their devotion to each other was genuine and abiding. It shines through their letters. It is unmistakable in every reference to Mary as Bridget in Charles's essays. They were collaborators in life no less than in literature. No brother and sister in history are more inseparably linked. To Lamb their life as old bachelor and maid was "a sort of double singleness."

The glimpses we have of them together are at once heartwarming and heartbreaking. "You would like to see us," wrote Mary to Sarah Stoddart, "as we often sit, writing on one table (but not on one cushion sitting), like Hermia and Helena in the *Midsummer's Night's Dream;* or, rather, like an old literary Darby and Joan: I taking snuff, and he groaning all the while and saying he can make nothing of it, which he always says till he has finished, and then he finds out he has made something of it."

That is a picture of them at their happiest. It belongs with those other pictures we conjure when we imagine them together: playing cards; seeing a play; going to exhibitions; reading books, she doting on narratives— any narratives; he delighting in the reflective passages of the older authors. Visiting friends. Enjoying the adventure of one of their short summer journeys. Presiding over one of their delectable "evenings" at home (held first on Wednesdays, later on Thursdays), which Hazlitt immortalized with his "How often did we cut into the haunch of letters, while we discussed the haunch of mutton on the table!" Or discussing, in the financial comfort of their later years, the greater pleasures they had known when, in their youth, they had been forced to skimp, save, and plan in order to make a purchase or crowd their way into the pit.

Against these brighter moments must be set the darker ones. These are black indeed. By common agreement Mary, in her right mind, was one of the most amiable and admirable of women. But Mary was not always in her right mind. She was "perpetually on the brink of madness." If this was Mary's tragedy, it was also Lamb's.

Their sunniest days together were never cloudless. The threat under which they lived was fearful and incessant. At all times the Furies stalked them. Small wonder this brother and this sister have been likened to a cockney Orestes and Electra.

Mary's was a recurrent illness. There was no telling when it would return. There was only the certainty that return it would, with ever-increasing frequency, with ever-mounting seriousness. Some hints, such as a sudden moroseness or irritability on Mary's part, preceded its coming. For these dreaded signs Charles watched anxiously. Apparently Mary did, too.

"You would laugh, or you would cry, perhaps both," Mary wrote in another letter to Miss Stoddart, "to see us sit together, looking at each other with long and rueful faces, and saying, 'How do you do?' and 'How do *you* do?' and then we fall a-crying and say we will be better on the morrow. Charles says we are like tooth-ache and his friend gum-boil, which though a kind of ease is an uneasy kind of ease."

Their ease at its best was the epitome of uneasiness. Surely few scenes could be more touching than the one several of their friends had witnessed. It was the common sequel to each reappearance of Mary's symptoms. When these had shown themselves, Charles would get ready to take her to the private asylum at Hoxton. She would gather together a few clothes, replace with a bonnet the mobcap she wore indoors, and prepare for the street. He would lead her, unresisting, to the door. Then they would start out hand-in-hand, two figures as somberly dressed as Quakers, walking the whole way, weeping as they walked, and carrying Mary's straitjacket with them.

Even so, Mary, between interruptions, brought Charles a happiness almost as complete as was the unhappiness her madness had brought upon them both. The debt we owe her is at once incalculable and unpayable. If, as readers, we delight in Lamb as he is, we do so because his writing is the product of his life as it was. He never objected to his lot. He faced it squarely, gaily, without whining, and with inexhaustible courage.

The world that knows him as the "gentle Elia" does Lamb an injustice. Gentle he always was with Mary and in most of his writings. It was, however, his strength which enabled him to be gentle and not any softness which forced him into being so. He hated the phrase "gentle-hearted" when applied to him as much as Sir James Barrie abhorred the word "whimsical." "For God's sake (I never was more serious)," wrote Charles to Coleridge, "don't make me ridiculous any more by terming me gentle-hearted in print, or do it in better verse. . . . The meaning of gentle is equivocal at best, and almost always means poor-spirited."

Certainly Lamb was anything but poor-spirited. He had a resilience unknown to noisier men and a toughness unsuspected by those who have read him sparingly, and then only in his fanciful or sentimental moods. Did he look like a clerk? He did not act like one. He was no timid soul. He was fiercely independent. His father may have been a servant, but in a snobbish age Lamb was subservient to no one. He was at all times ready to stammer out his opinions without fear. Everyone who described him noted the sadness of his brown eyes, the thoughtfulness of his expansive brow, the sweetness of his expression, and the smallness of his body. Lamb knew that physically he was "less than the least of the Apostles." A friend thought he looked so fragile that "a breath would overthrow him." But there was iron in his "immaterial legs." His slight body contradicted the largeness of his spirit.

Although Charles knew great sorrow, he was not discontented. If he could refer to Mary and himself, playfully though correctly, as "shorn Lambs," his belief in the tempered wind was nonetheless strong. Living with sorrow was as much a habit with him as climbing up on his high stool each morning to work as a clerk at the East India House. The prospect of any change so staggered him that he convinced himself he would no more reverse the untoward accidents and events of his life than he would alter the incidents of some well-contrived novel. Such was his love of life that he even loved his own. He meant what he said when he confessed, "I am in love with this green earth; the face of town and country; the unspeakable rural solitudes, and the sweet security of streets."

The portion of the earth that Lamb loved best was not green. He preferred cobblestones to grass any day. He was a city man if ever there was one; a cockney in every inch of his small person. The nightingale never released a song so sweet to his ears as the sound of Bow Bells. Had he been compelled to choose between Skiddaw and Soho, Wordsworth's mountain would have had no chance. The pleasure William found in a daffodil, Charles derived from a chimney-sweep.

He did not object to nature—for others. But human nature and the hum of city streets were his delight. Although, with Mary, he liked to venture into the countryside, for a while and as a break, even in the country he was a cockney on vacation. He dared to write to Wordsworth, of all people, "Separate from the pleasure of your company, I don't much care if I never see a mountain in my life." Nature to him was "dead"; London, living. The sun and the moon of the Lake District did not shine for him as brightly as the lamps of London. It was not the beauties of the outdoors which he found "ever fresh and green and warm," but all the inventions and assemblies of men in the congested boroughs by the Thames.

Few writers have described a city more affectionately than Charles his London. Few have outdone him in making strangers, both by the calendar and geography, feel like citizens of vanished times and places. There were scarcely any aspects of the metropolis he did not cherish. He, to whom much of life was denied, often shed tears of joy on his night-walks about London at encountering so much life.

He never tired of the lighted shops of the Strand and Fleet Street; of the innumerable trades, tradesmen, customers, coaches, crowds, wagons, and playhouses; of "all the bustle and wickedness round about Covent Garden, the very women of the Town, the Watchmen, drunken scenes, rattles"; of the city's pungent smells and very dirt and mud; of the sun shining upon houses and pavements; or of the print shops, the old book stalls, and the coffee houses. He rejoiced in the sense they gave him of London being a pantomime and a masquerade where life itself was at last awake. The city for him was at once a stimulant and an escape. Urbanwise, he lived on it no less than in it. He measured his fortune, good or ill, by his distance from the Strand. He was jubilant when, after one of their frequent changes of address, he found that the house in which he and Mary were then stopping was "forty-two inches nearer town."

The city he lived in, though a metropolis, was not for him a capital. Its government was an irrelevance; its politics nonexistent. An historian, hoping to find in Lamb's essays or letters some reflection of the great events of turbulent years, would be hard put to determine whether history had by-passed Lamb or he history. He lived through England's wars as if Europe were at peace. So far as he was concerned, they were undeclared and unwaged. He came to admire Nelson, admitted Wellington's existence, had no love for the early Hanovers, in a mild way championed Queen Caroline's cause, and was curious about Napoleon's height. But the French Revolution left no visible mark upon him, and, though he must have heard of Trafalgar, Austerlitz, and Waterloo, we never hear of them through him.

Did the younger Pitt die in 1806? For Lamb he never seems to have lived. Did "Buoney" threaten England with invasion? Did the Peterloo Massacre spill blood in Manchester? Were trade unions allowed for the first time? Did the Prince Regent's marriage to Mrs. Fitzherbert rock society? Were both the Roman Catholic Emancipation and the First Reform bills passed? Contemporaneous as he was with all of these occurrences, Lamb was apparently the contemporary of none of them.

Unlike such of his intimates as Coleridge, Hazlitt, Leigh Hunt, and Wordsworth, he had no interest in public affairs. Society for him was always a circle of friends and never the collective well-being of a community. "Public affairs—except as they touch upon me, and so turn into private," Lamb wrote to Thomas Manning, "I cannot whip up my mind to feel any interest in." By his own admission, he was deaf to the noises which kept Europe awake. He could not make present times present to him.

He was as insulated against political events as he was susceptible to human, literary, and gastronomic values. In his scheme of things "important people" were unimportant, and for him the "Great World" possessed no fascination. The bearers of titles, more than leaving him unimpressed, left him unamused no less surely than official leaders left him unled. A benevolent eccentric himself, he delighted in the benevolent eccentricities of others. The heads he prized were not those highly placed but those "with some diverting twist in them"; heads lightened by "out of the way humours and opinions."

His absorptions were personal, not public, and small-scaled rather than outsized. Covent Garden was his Buckingham Palace; the art galleries, his House of Commons; the book stalls, his House of Lords. Londoner utter and complete though he was, Lamb never felt, thought, or wrote as a citizen but always as an individual. He took the same pleasure in the "delicious juices of meats and fishes, and society, and the cheerful glass, and candle light and fireside conversations, and innocent vanities and jests, and irony itself," that he did in the passages sublime or melancholy of his favorite old authors. If the oddities of authorship were dear to him, so were the oddities of people and places, and it was these which enchanted him in London.

The London through which Lamb trudged was apt to be two cities—the one he saw as a man, and the other he remembered from his youth. Accordingly, even when solitary, he seldom walked the streets alone. For the author whose attachment to the past was so great that he could exclaim, "Hang the age! I'll write for antiquity," London's past was superimposed upon its present. On his strolls he was attended by the shades of the boys and teachers he had known as a student at Christ's Hospital; by the ghosts of departed players or of journalists with whom he had worked; or by the figures of Old Benchers, long since dead, whom he had watched in his boyhood in the Inner Temple. These rose constantly before his eyes. So double was Lamb's sense of time, so eager his search for reminders of his "joyful" days, that, in spite of his best-known poem, the "old familiar faces" were for him never "all, all . . . gone."

London offered Lamb more than a source of vicarious

life. The city which touched and diverted him also provided him with a release from both his "cold bed of
celibacy" and his long years of confinement at the East
India House. During most of his writing life, Lamb was
a full-time clerk, a part-time author. He contended that
his real "works"—"more MSS. in folio than ever Aquinas
left, and full as useful"—were the great ledgers he had
filled day after day for the thirty-three years of his clerk-
dom, and not the printed volumes to be found at booksellers. There was little of the freelancer in his nature.
There could not be. His being married, as he put it, to
Mary's fortunes meant that he was unable to run risks
with his own. Instead of writing to live, he clerked in
order to be free to write. Generous as he was in his gifts
and loans to others, he could not afford to be without
steady employment himself.

He was horrified when Bernard Barton confided he
was thinking of giving up his job in a Quaker bank to live
by his pen. "Keep to your Bank," he urged Barton, "and
the Bank will keep you. . . . What, is there not from
six to Eleven P.M. 6 days in the week, and is there not
all Sunday?" For Lamb this was writing time enough.
It spared him the insecurities of being a "slave to Booksellers" and "the miseries of subsisting by authorship."
It meant that, when at last he was at liberty to write, his
pen felt its "promotion." His writing was thus kept a release from drudgery, and so avoided being drudgery itself.

He was, of course, fond of seeing himself as a prisoner
at the India House; of claiming that he sat there like
Philomel all day (but not singing) with his "heart
against this thorn of a desk." But he liked his job better
than he guessed, and was lost when he retired from it.
The routine of working at India House from ten to four
at once supported and soothed him. It comforted him in

his loneliness and appealed to what was essentially gregarious in his nature. He missed the friendly eminence of the high stool upon which he had sat for so many years. He missed hanging his hat each day on the same peg. He missed the amiable ease of an office where, though he labored faithfully, he could still find time to write some of his best letters. He missed the companionship of his "old desk fellows"—his "co-brethren of the quill." He missed "the hot huddle of rational creatures." He missed being able to excuse his habitual tardiness by such an explanation as "I m-make up for that by g-going away early."

The truth is he missed his chains. Like many another, he came to realize they had become a necessary part of his apparel. Nothing in his story is more poignant than the sadness which inundated him when, at fifty, his dream of liberty became a reality and he was freed from what he had thought was bondage. During the next nine years, until his death in 1834, he sensed that freedom in itself could be a bondage. He had lived so long "*to* other people" that he could not happily fill his own emancipated hours. Time stood still for him and was empty in its idleness. He lost the "Wednesday feelings" and the "Saturday night sensations" he had once known. To his despair he discovered he walked about, not to and from. Having all holidays, it was as though he had none. No Babbitt and no Dodsworth could have been more rudderless upon retirement than was this man, part Yorick, part Jaques, when he was at last freed by a generous pension.

His Yorick side is known to every reader whose knowledge of him does not stop with the *Tales from Shakspeare*, "A Dissertation upon Roast Pig," or "Dream Children." Lamb turning suddenly to Martin Burney at cards to comment, "Martin, if dirt were t-trumps, what

a hand you would hold!"; Lamb crying out, "Wordsworth says he could have written *H-Hamlet* if he'd had
the m-mind!"; or Lamb answering Coleridge's question
as to whether or not Charles had ever heard him preach
in the days of his Unitarian ministry with, "I never heard
you do anything else"—all these are instances of his
"punch-light" humor which, though familiar, have not
become tired.

As a conversationalist, his stammer was part of his
comic equipment. He relied upon it the way acrobats
rely upon a net. He was a fellow whose jests were infinite, instantaneous, impudent, and deflating. He had
the virtues, and the wisdom, of not being a continuous
conversationalist. His stutter, like his discretion, made
that impossible. His hatred for the "long and much
talkers" was as lusty as theirs for him. He knew the
value of silences, broken suddenly and unexpectedly,
and, one gathers, of deadpanning his way to a joke.
Pomposity he despised, dullness he abhorred, and seers
he loathed when they were "seering."

To be at his best, he had to be among people he knew
and liked. To strangers and incompatibles he was an
enigma, if not an irritant. Carlyle, with his genius for
fermentation, was never sourer than on the subject of
Lamb. "A more pitiful, ricketty, gasping, staggering,
stammering Tomfool I do not know," fumed he. "He is
witty by denying truisms and abjuring good manners."
Yet to Hazlitt, as to many another, Lamb was "the most
delightful, the most provoking, the most witty and sensible of men. . . . No one ever stammered out such
fine, piquant, deep, eloquent things in half a dozen half-
sentences as he does. His jests scald like tears: and he
probes a question with a play upon words."

Among his friends, on the kind of drinking, talking,
smoking evening which he cherished, his relaxation was

to enliven the passing moment as certainly as, when alone, his consolation was to dream of the moments that had been. He had a reply—and an unanswerable one— for those who complained he was always aiming at wit. He said that to do so was at least as good as aiming at dullness.

Macready was shocked to hear Lamb confess at Talfourd's one night that "the last breath he drew in he wished might be through a pipe and exhaled in a pun." Lamb's fondness for puns was notorious. He loved them as much as all people dislike them who cannot make them. There is no such thing as stooping to a pun. There is only the challenge of being able to rise to a good one. Few cadavers could be deader or more emaciated than those occasional puns which, in his letters, Lamb quotes approvingly, pointer in hand, with the subtlety of a window demonstrator. Lamb, however, knew a pun must be heard, not read, and heard at the moment of its birth if it were to live completely or to be fully enjoyed. "A pun," wrote he, "hath a hearty kind of present ear-kissing smack in it; you can no more transmit it in its pristine flavour than you can send a kiss."

That Lamb laughed and could make others laugh, everyone knows. But the nature of his laughter, the keen and enjoying manner in which he detected frailty, the amused details which underwrite his fantasy and are the basis of his reveries, along with the man who could be as realistic in his observation of men as he was in facing the unpleasant realities of his own life—these are what the sentimentalists forget who have made him as sentimental as themselves.

Many authors suffer at the hands of their detractors; just as many (and no less cruelly) at the hands of their admirers. Lamb belongs to this well-nigh smothered brotherhood. He has almost been killed, not so much by his own kindness, which was true and very human, as by the bogus, treacly kindness which others have palmed off as being his. Thornton Wilder once described a modern playwright, addicted to cute and elfin phrases and marshmallow thoughts, as writing in the manner associated with Lamb by people who have not read him. This false notion of Lamb, with its attendant misunderstandings and proper revulsions, is a ghost which, worse than haunting the real Lamb, has all too often obscured him.

In his eagerness to canonize Lamb's palpable and radiant virtues, Thackeray may have dubbed him "Saint Charles." Charles, however, was the more of a saint because he was so much of a man. Although there are those who choose to bury him in lavender, to cushion him on sachets, and to confuse him with old lace, they do Lamb a genuine injustice.

Lamb could be sweet beyond comfortable endurance. He could be whimsical to a disquieting extent. He could dip his pen far too deep in syrup and produce copy, on occasions, which to modern eyes reads like literate valentines from yesteryear. These, however, were the excesses into which his tenderness led him. They were the expressions of his frustration, his regrets, his loneliness, and, in a way, of his period. Though full of sentiment, Lamb was no sentimentalist as a man, and only as an author when he nodded, which he was mortal enough to do at moments. That he was kind and that he was witty, everyone knows. But that he was both kind and witty at one and the same time has so surprised his admirers that some of them have overlooked entirely the sharpness of his mind and tongue.

In his letters, as in his talk, a spade was a spade. It was only in his essays that it became a shovel, a gardener's utensil, or something like Triptolemus's tool. When he

informed Manning that Coleridge's wife was expecting
a baby, did he do so by referring to "a little one," or "an
addition to the family"? He did not. As directly as if he
were a GI in the Army, he wrote, "Coleridge is settled
with his wife (with a child in her guts)."

No one has written about childhood more tenderly
than he. Even so, his was not the bachelor's idealization
of all children. He knew that the young, like their elders,
were either amiable or unamiable. He saw no reason "to
love a whole family, perhaps eight, nine, or ten, indiscriminately—to love all the pretty dears because children are so engaging." His phrase, when a sick child had
at last been removed from his home, after robbing Lamb
of his rest, was, quite simply, "The little bastard is
gone."

He pulled no punches with his friends, and was much
too good a friend to do so. His candor was as great as his
charm. "Cultivate simplicity, Coleridge," wrote he, "or
rather, I should say, banish elaborateness. . . . I allow
no hotbeds in the gardens of Parnassus." No one ever
derived more amusement from a friend's faults than
Lamb did from those of poor, foolish, bumbling George
Dyer. His letters about Dyer, like his references to him
in his essays, are as full of mocking laughter as they are
of love. Few people have played more knowledgeably,
or with greater relish, upon human frailty than Lamb
did when, by "beslabbering" a book Joseph Cottle had
written, he so appealed to its author's vanity that Cottle
forgot all about his dead brother in the next room.

Although by his own confession he could not hate
anyone he knew, Lamb was terrifyingly aware of people's defects. Shelley's voice was to him "the most obnoxious squeak I ever was tormented with, ten thousand
times worse than the Laureat's, whose voice is the worst
part about him except his Laureatcy." Lamb's aversion

to Byron's character was "thorough" and his admiration for his genius "very moderate." "He is great in so little a way" was Lamb's summary of his Lordship.

Once at Godwin's Holcroft and Coleridge were fiercely disputing which was better, *man as he was* or *man as he is to be*. "Give me," said Lamb, "man as he is *not* to be." If, in general, he was willing to take all people as they were, he was taken in by no one. His eye for human absurdity was as keen as his enjoyment of human oddity. Was it a poor relation remembering a birthday so as to drop in just in time for dinner? Was it a liar spinning fabulous yarns on a boat to Margate, or a fact-loving bore on the top of a stagecoach? Lamb saw their failings plain. His gentleness did not prevent his feelings from being strong. "Now, of all God's creatures," wrote he, "I detest letters-affecting, authors-hunting ladies." His loathing for booksellers was equally strong. So was his disrelish for the Scots. Lamb was as "essentially anti-Caledonian" as ever Dr. Johnson was.

The fact—the fine, the beckoning, the all-conquering fact—about Lamb is that he could look "with no indifferent eye upon things or persons." "Whatever is" was to him "a matter of taste or distaste." He knew, as some of his admirers have forgotten, that he was "a bundle of prejudices—made up of likings and dislikings —the veriest thrall to sympathies, apathies, and antipathies." Without these prejudices Lamb would not be Lamb. Nor would he be Lamb if he had not felt and phrased them in a way so unmistakably and beguilingly his own that, though it has won him countless friends, it has removed him from the reach of imitators. An affectionate rather than a passionate man, Lamb's prejudices were his substitutes for passion. It was in them that he lived, and because of them, in part, that he lives for us. They were the proofs of his awareness, his sensibility, his discernment, his humanity. Characteristically enough, he chose to refer to these prejudices as "imperfect sympathies" no less than as prejudices.

One of the major paradoxes of his paradoxical mind was that, as a rule, he could be sympathetic even when he was being witty. His wit was the expression of his love, not his contempt, for men. People who would have irritated others amused him. His knowledge of life was too complete for him to be surprised by human frailty. If he never failed to observe it, he seldom failed to enjoy it. Since he expected it, he was tolerant of it.

His was the laughter of acceptance not protest, of recognition instead of revulsion. His gaiety was as divorced from scorn or cynicism as it was wedded to melancholy. It smiles without being insulting. Unchilled by the arrogance which is the curse of professional wits, it is as warm and human as the "rather smoky, and sometimes rather drinky" little man from whom it emanated. It sprang from a superior mind, unconscious of its superiority; a mind which is the more endearing because its modesty remains unlost in the midst of its most dazzling exhibitions of prowess.

Lamb's mind was the antithesis of neat and office-like. It resembled an antique shop or an old bookstore where, in spite of the clutter, the dust, and the overlay of accumulation, the proprietor can at a moment's notice bring to light whatever treasure is desired. It never judged "system-wise" but always by "fastening on particulars." It was proudly unmethodized, desultory, tangential. If it worked obliquely in ways beyond prediction, it was because it fed upon the tantalizing obliquities of life no less than of literature. Its knowledge was a matter of informed tastes rather than of pursued facts.

Lamb had no desire to keep up with the Joneses. He

had a hard enough time keeping up with the whims of his own interest. The topical left him uncoerced; the popular unpersuaded. When a new book came out, he read an old one. He would have been both amused and amazed by the manuals, digests, and sugarcoated textbooks in which those who mistake facts for learning nowadays stalk culture as if it were a butterfly to be pinioned in a net. Although the most bookish of bookish men, he was no chaser after information for information's sake. Instead, he was a savorer, content to taste and retaste what was best or most flavorsome in the volumes he cherished. If his devotion to what was special, limited, and wayward in his preoccupations was one of his limitations, this did not bother him. Lamb was comfortable in his ignorance of what he did not choose to know.

On all matters relating to science, Elia could boast he was "a whole Encyclopaedia behind the rest of the world." He was equally, and just as proudly, unknowledgeable about geography, modern languages, the shapes and textures of the commonest trees, herbs, or flowers, and tools, engines or mechanical processes. In spite of his attachment to the past, history as a mere sequence of events had so little interest for him that he could brag he had never deliberately sat down to read a chronicle even of his own country. As for astronomy, it did not exist in the orbit of his shining concerns. "If the sun," wrote he, "on some portentous morn were to make his first appearance in the West, I verily believe that, while all the world were gasping in apprehension about me, I alone should stand unterrified, from sheer incuriosity and want of observation."

One of the reasons for Elia's dislike of the Scots was that no excursions could be taken with them, since they always insisted upon keeping to the path. Lamb's thinking, though it could lead to the summits, was nothing if not excursive. The straight highroads dear to historians were not the routes he either elected or was equipped to travel. When he did not spurn the obvious views and inevitable sights, he preferred to reach them by a back door or secret passage. He gave both his mind and heart (the combination, in his case, meaning his attention) to the ignored vistas and overlooked curiosities. Even these he approached by those unblazed trails which, to the personal essayist, are the royal road.

If these footpaths were roads which led to himself, the reason was his modesty, not his egotism. Lamb was one of the most autobiographical of authors. To read him on virtually any subject is to read about him. It is to know him with a sense of daily intimacy with which few writers are known. In his copy Lamb could no more escape from himself than in his living he could leave Mary. Yet self-centered in the ordinary sense he was not. The world, for the conceited man, starts and ends with himself. For Elia, Charles Lamb was merely the point of departure to the world around him. Although with him the first person singular was a favorite pronoun, as he used it, it somehow managed to seem printed with a small "i."

Lamb was too unpretentious to pretend to be omniscient. He was poignantly aware that few people are able to speak for themselves, much less for others. Speaking of and through himself was his way of speaking for all. He knew his own voice contained the echoes of other voices. In this way he chose to write, intertwining with his identity griefs and affections which were not his own, "making himself many, or reducing many unto himself."

Since truth to Lamb was as personal as everything else, facts enjoyed no immunity from his prankishness. It diverted him to distort them when, as Elia, he wrote of his friends, his family, or himself. His love of mystification was one of the abidingly boyish aspects of his character. It pleased him in his essays to mislead his readers by false scents; to write Oxford when he meant Cambridge; to make Bridget his cousin, not his sister; to merge Coleridge's boyhood with his own; or to paint himself as a hopeless drunkard when, as a matter of fact, he was a man who, though he loved to down a drink, was seldom downed by drinking. By deliberate, sometimes mischievous design his familiar essays were but the "shadows of fact." They were "verisimilitudes, not verities." Yet Lamb was present, quintessentially if not factually, in their every phrase and sentence. At least, an important part of him was present, though not by any means the whole man.

Closely related as Elia is to Charles Lamb, they were not—they are not—in any sense of the word identical. When it came to authorship, there were two Charles Lambs. If not that, there was one Lamb who wrote in two styles so different that he could be suspected of employing his left hand for the one, his right hand for the other. As in the case of countless others, inkstained or ink-free, Lamb had a public and a private manner. He did not write to his friends as he wrote for the magazines. Although in either case a natural-born essayist, and a matchless critic of books and men, his style, which was always intimate, altered according to whether his pen or a printer was to be the transmitter of his words.

Hazlitt's portrait of him as a nobleman of another day caught the spirit, not of Lamb the private letter-writer, but of Lamb the public essayist. Certainly, the Lamb who contributed to periodicals was not the Renaissance figure Hazlitt envisaged. Yet Hazlitt was right beyond dispute in dressing this Lamb in the clothes of an age other than his own. When he wrote for publication, Lamb did go into costume as surely as, when he dashed off notes to his friends, he donned a dress so modern that after the passage of more than a century it seems as contemporary to us as it did to them.

The highly, at moments even dangerously, self-conscious artist we cherish as Elia emerged late in Lamb's life as the flowering of his varied career as a professional writer. By that time Lamb had long since mislaid, except for album purposes, the poet of slight endowment he had started out by being. Years before, too, he had discarded the novelist whose all but nonexistent talent for narrative stamped *Rosamund Gray* and his contributions to *Mrs. Leicester's School* as no more than apprentice work. He had also buried the dramatist with "no head for playwriting" whose blank-verse tragedy, *John Woodvil*, was but the feeblest of Elizabethan echoes, and whose little farce, *Mr. H.*, was so disastrous a failure that its author had joined in the hissing.

In the same way Lamb had outgrown those un-Lamb-like *Tales from Shakspeare* upon which he had collaborated with Mary. Although he had predicted such a potboiler would be popular "among the little people," he had never guessed how enduring its popularity would prove among those grownups of little courage who, apparently, are grateful for anything which spares them Shakespeare in the original.

The first volume of the *Elia* essays was published when Lamb was forty-eight; the second, and last, ten years later. In print, and in such memorable papers as his "On the Genius and Character of Hogarth" and "On the Tragedies of Shakspeare," Lamb had already established not only his brilliance as a critic but his unique public manner as an essayist. Yet during all these formative years, in fact from his first preserved letters to Coleridge before and after Mary's murder of her mother, right down to the last note scribbled off to Mrs. Dyer (about a book, appropriately enough) five days before his death thirty-eight years later, Lamb was the possessor of an epistolary style quite at odds with the style we know as Elia's.

In addition to being the best introduction to Lamb, Lamb's are among the world's best letters. In them we almost hear him talk. To be sure, his stutter is gone, and an incredible fluency has replaced it. But, as in all good letters, the illusion of direct communication is maintained. Both the moment and the mood are captured in all the heat of their passing sorrow or amusement. The small details, the great agonies, the first impressions, the play of mind and the play on words, the reflections by means of which a particular instance is lifted into a generality, the tastes of food, the smells of London, the look of friends, the résumé of last night's party, the book just read, the anecdote just heard, this day's sadness, the next day's gaiety—they are all there, caught hot, caught frankly, and transferred without effort by a pen scratching swiftly against stolen time at the office.

Perhaps the speed of their composition was the guarantee of their simplicity. In any case, again and again Charles' letters deny their datelines by remaining undated. They are not so much the products of an age as they are models for all time. Whether they are "thank you" notes for a visit paid or a roast pig sent; apologies for having to be carried home from an overconvivial evening; his proposal of marriage to Fanny Kelly; the gossip of London dispatched across the oceans to Manning in China; religious musings; discussions of death; the account to Coleridge, magnificent in its dignity, of his mother's murder; appraisals of Defoe, Cervantes, Godwin's *Chaucer*, or the second edition of the *Lyrical Ballads*; they are perfect of their kind.

They show the warmth, the originality, the humor, or

the grandeur of the astonishing little man who wrote
them. They are the spontaneous distillations of a writer,
instinctive and superior. They make us companions not
only in Lamb's daily living but in his adult life. Their
every episodic entry fits into a sequence. Without meaning to do so, they form an autobiography from which
Lamb's biographers must quote and to which everyone
who would know him must turn. They give us Lamb
unadorned; Lamb, the writer, without self-consciousness,
hence often at his finest; Lamb, so to speak, at his slip-
pered ease, relaxed, using short sentences, hitting directly; Lamb employing the most vivid and abrupt of
colloquialisms, thus avoiding the calculated, beautiful,
and antique cadences so dear to Elia.

The difference between the letter-writer who signed
himself C.L. and the essayist known as Elia is the difference between a candid camera close-up and a full-length
portrait in oil, appareled for effect and so posed that its
very casualness is studied. It is the difference between
jewels unset and a necklace painstakingly matched. It
is, in short, the everlasting difference between the impromptu and the planned.

When Thackeray's "Saint Charles" wrote for the public prints, he heard voices, Joan-wise. The sonorities of
such favorite prose writers as Sir Thomas Browne, Burton, Marvell, and Fuller, haunted his ears. "I gather myself up into the old things," wrote Lamb. More accu-
rately, he gathered the old authors up into himself. Their
outmoded language was an expression of what was back-
ward-glancing in his spirit. It pleased him by being out
of date. It orchestrated his melancholy. Not only that
When appropriated for his casual personal essays, its
very gravity served as a foil to his humor.

Lamb loved the stately rhythms and obsolete words of
these older writers. While playing chameleon to their

style, he could achieve a style of his own. He imitated in order to create what is inimitable. The borrowed pencil Hazlitt accused him of employing as an essayist was put by Lamb to his own uses. He was aware that, as Elia, his writings were "villainously pranked in an affected arrangement of antique modes and phrases." But he knew these writings would not have been his, had this not been so. "Better it is," said he, "that a writer should be natural in a self-pleasing quaintness, than to affect a naturalness (so called) that should be strange to him."

Quaint, Elia was, and is, and in a manner pleasing not only to himself but to readers everywhere once they have become Elians. This is no hard thing to do, if only, in a more hurried age when prose is thinner and the language employed more often than it is enjoyed, readers are willing to give Elia and themselves a chance. His essays never were *in date*, except for what is dateless in their insight. Stylistically, they were intentional anachronisms when they were published. Their antique flavor was, and remains, a source of their charm.

To modern eyes, accustomed to sentences being the shortest distance between a subject and a predicate (if, indeed, they extend that far), the long, leisurely, and intricate constructions of Lamb the essayist may at first glance appear forbidding. Yet forbidding is the very last word anyone in his right senses, and with the slightest acquaintance with Lamb, would dream of using for those gloriously warm and intimate essays which Lamb wrote as a critic of life, or of art, the theatre, and books. If, at the outset, their subtle and sustained sentences seem difficult, with their "methinks," their "thees" and "thous," their "arts," "werts," "readers," and other pressed flowers from another day, or their addiction to such words as "agnise," "additaments," and "dulcifying," these difficulties soon turn into delights. However truffled, archaic, or self-conscious was Lamb's formal style, it is rich in its rewards. Costume prose it may be, but costume jewelry it never was, because its gems are genuine.

More than taking knowing, Elia survives it. His better essays belong in that class of literature he described as being "perpetually self-reproductive." They bear reading and rereading, and then can be read and reread again. They are habit-forming rather than time-passing. If the style in their case is not the whole man, it is at any rate the essayist. Elia cannot be separated from it. Nor would anyone who has once cultivated a taste for that style be denied its enjoyment. Although, as a word-man, Lamb was deaf to music and could complain about its "measured malice," Elia was able with words to release an incomparable music of his own.

He was the opposite of those writers he dismissed as being "economists only in delight." His prodigality with the pleasures he provides is limitless. The joy he creates from small things is large. The conceits in his phrasing are redeemed by the sincerity of his feeling. If he seldom wrote a bromide, it was because he seldom thought one. The commonest reaction became uncommon in his statement of it. His vocabulary was as much his own as his mind, and both were unpredictable.

As is true of all good essayists, not too much of Elia is to be read at one sitting. He fatigues not by the ardor of his emotions, but by the incessant probing of his perceptions, by the sudden quiet dartings of his mind and the abundance of his allusions. To be enjoyed fully he must be lingered over; read with the same disregard for the present that he showed; savored, as he savored the subjects of his choice. He is a writer who does not raise his voice. He avoids emphasis. His finest phrases spill from his pen without warning. They are tucked away, not paraded. They come jostling, one so close upon the other that they are apt to be overlooked. To miss them is to miss the true satisfactions of Elia, because in his phrases he gives the pleasures other authors give in their paragraphs.

His mood is ruminative, his mind associational. For all the amusement to be had from the felicities of his observations, his was an essentially tragic nature. He was a tragedian who smiled instead of cried. This not only deepens his humor. It insures its humanity.

On the subject of his family, his youth, his London, the places he had visited, or the "characters" he had known, his vision was as detailed and unblinking as it was in his criticism. Yet, uncanny as was his accuracy as a reporter, Lamb was never a journalist. What he wrote as journalism somehow managed to be literature. "In Eternity," pointed out Sir Thomas Browne, "there is no distinction of Tenses." This line in the *Religio Medici* was one which, as both a familiar essayist and a magazine critic, Lamb must have hugged to his heart. For him datelines did not exist. He had no interest in news and less sense of it. News, as he saw it, was whatever happened to interest him, however personal or remote. The measure of his ability is that he made it interesting to his contemporaries, and even now makes us feel contemporaneous with it.

As a critic no less than as a man, Lamb lived in a world where watches had stopped. Yet he creates the illusion that they are still ticking. What he was fond of reviewing was not last night's or last week's play but his memories of twenty or thirty years ago. Although this was all a part of his being unable to make present times present to him, it has never prevented him from making times past present to us.

If Charles Lamb does not belong in the company of the greatest critics, neither do they belong in his. It is not so much that they stride ahead of him as that he elects to amble to one side of them, well off the main thoroughfares. Even in criticism, he is a lonely figure who goes his own way. That the paths of his choice happen to be bypaths is part of the enticement and originality of his approach. He is one of the most satisfying and least pretentious of critics; major in a minor way, though major nonetheless.

Greatness, among other things, is bound to involve scale. Size, spiritual or actual, is part of it. Breadth, width, depth are among its common dimensional attributes. These qualities, in the ordinary heroic sense, were not Lamb's. Perfection, however, is not a matter of size. Although a Borglum may reach the peaks by mutilating them, that he produces bigger works than a Cellini does not mean he is the better artist. It was on the Cellini scale that Lamb worked. In criticism, as in his essays, he was a jeweler, a goblet-fashioner, an unrivaled craftsman in gold and silver. The fact that he was not a titan does not condemn him to being a midget. As a critic, he was an extraordinary artist. His genius as an artist is the reason for his greatness as a critic.

Dryden, Dr. Johnson, Coleridge, Hazlitt, or Shaw, for example, rejoice in a muscularity, a lunge, an intensity, a bigness, or a purpose Lamb does not possess. Yet he possesses charms they cannot claim, perceptions they do not have, and merits which are not theirs. They delve into fundamentals which for him have no interest. They risk complete estimates of a man, a work, or a period which he avoids. They come to their subjects head-on, excelling at large-scale frontal attacks where he excels at minor skirmishes and sudden, fruitful forays at the flanks or behind the lines. Or, convinced that the truth as they have seen it is the whole truth, they can fight lusty battles for causes which leave him unmobilized.

Critically, they and their kind are warriors; male, aggressive, and so magnificent in their energies that they are forces. Lamb is no force. He is only a phenomenon, and a joy. To the embattled realm of opinions he brings his vagaries rather than his convictions, his paradoxes instead of principles. He does not destroy; he re-creates. His critical weapon is a goldminer's sieve, not a battle-axe. He rises to appreciation with the same happy subtle discernment most critics muster for depreciation. He writes less to persuade others than to state for himself what, for the moment, he has been persuaded of. Even his deliberate half-truths are so engagingly advanced by him that, in the reading, they seem preferable to the full truths advanced by others. If Lamb proves little, he almost always proves delightful. In his case, that is enough. Having sought pleasure, he gives it. "It is not in my method," said he, "to inflict pain. I leave that to heaven."

"Criticism," noted Dr. Johnson, "is a study by which men grow important and formidable at very small expense." Lamb had no desire to be either. He disliked "being treated like a grave or respectable character." His sympathy with professional critics was nonexistent. He abhorred all the airs they take on, without the graces, and the way they pride themselves upon being unable to share in the joys of others.

Lamb's attitude toward the theatre was typical of his attitude toward books and paintings. Theatrically he remained in spirit, as in his fondest recollections, a gallery god long after financial ease and his own prominence assured him the best of seats. He could neither understand nor tolerate the "frigid indifference" and "impenetrability" of those who sat in the boxes. Even in the pit he deplored the beginnings of "that accursed critical faculty, which, making a man the judge of his own pleasures, too often constitutes him the executioner of his own and others!"

To Lamb such standoffishness, worse than being incompatible, was downright "vile." Professional critics and reviewers, in his eyes, were "animals." Fastidious, special, and searching as were his tastes, he preferred to identify himself with the *genuine spectators*. By these he had in mind such simple people as a "shopkeeper and his family, whose honest titillations of mirth" could not wait "to take the cue from the sour judging faces about them." In spite of his own inquiring and scholarly spirit, Lamb gave his love to the "uninquiring gratitude" of such spectators. Although he mistakenly identified himself with them, he wrote delectably from an unmistakable capacity for enjoyment which they might well have envied.

Lamb's shortcomings as a critic are self-evident. He does not soar as one of the eagles in a profession more often than not wingless. He hovers like a bee, avid for the taste of honey. Moreover, beelike, he is quick to find it, to linger over it, and to transfer it. He neither intends to be reliable nor pretends to be impartial. He must be read with a caution which comes from understanding him, and from being both able and willing to enter into the game he can play. Since he is truer to his whims than his subject, he is not to be taken literally. He must have foreseen that modern dictionaries would define an opinion as a "judgment based on grounds short of proof." At any rate, he does not bother about being infallible. He writes quite frankly and disarmingly from his prejudices.

He is apt to be fanciful when he seems most dogmatic, or only half in earnest when he appears to be most serious. This aspect of Lamb not only eluded Macaulay but exasperated him. Yet it is the point and pleasure of Elia's defense of that "Utopia of gallantry" which, as he saw it, was the true setting of Restoration comedy and hence lifted it beyond moral judgment "out of Christendom into the land of cuckoldry." It is no less clear in the famous contention of Lamb, the most ardent of theatre-lovers, that Shakespeare is the playwright whose works are "less calculated for performance on a stage than those of almost any other dramatist whatever."

George Saintsbury, a devoted and discerning "Agnist" if ever there was one, had to admit that, notwithstanding his excellences as a critic, Lamb could be guilty of *capriccio* (a word which Elia, no doubt, would have prized every bit as much as did the professor). This is why Saintsbury insisted Lamb, rather than Leigh Hunt, deserves to be known as the "Ariel of Criticism." Beyond dispute, that is better than being the Caliban.

When he described such critics as belong to the *Occult School*, Hazlitt had Lamb in mind. "They discern no beauties but what are concealed from superficial eyes," he wrote, "and overlook all that are obvious to the vulgar part of mankind. . . . If an author is utterly unreadable, they can read him for ever; his intricacies are their delight, his mysteries are their study. . . . They will no more share a book than a mistress with a friend." The charge of occultism, in Lamb's case, is not unfair. It is just, in spite of Lamb's affection for the gallery gods. It is part and parcel of his addiction to oddity. Yet, like the affectations of his public style, it is the natural expression of himself.

Lamb's blindspots were many; his tastes more eccentric than catholic. If he rejoiced in his lack of orthodoxy, so should his readers. Any mediocrity can be orthodox. (Most of them are.) Lamb, however, was nothing if not exceptional. Even the historical persons he once startled a company by naming as the people he would most like to meet were unaverage choices. Heading his list were Pontius Pilate, Sir Thomas Browne, and Dr. Faustus.

In matters literary or artistic he was no less individual. He could discover no merit in *Candide* or *Gil Blas*. As an ardent admirer of Smollett, he was persuaded, and then only with difficulty, by Hazlitt to concede Fielding's superiority. When current authors were being discussed, he talked endlessly of John Donne and Sir Philip Sidney; when others were devouring the Waverley Novels, like as not he was poring over George Wither. If he was allergic to Scott, Byron, and Shelley, he was among the first to recognize Coleridge, Burns, and Wordsworth. His pioneering did not end there. As a critic of painting, his major concern may have been, unfashionably enough by contemporary standards, the story told. Even so, he was among the first to show a proper appreciation for Hogarth and Blake. Moreover, when he writes of their paintings, he so succeeds in using his pen as a brush that he turns painter himself.

Coleridge did not lecture on the early English dramatists, except for Shakespeare, until 1818. Hazlitt's courses were not given until three years later. Yet it was in 1808 that Lamb published his *Specimens of English Dramatic Poets Who Lived about the Time of Shakspeare*. In them, in spite of the spadework already done by specialists, Lamb can be said to have made well-read, though unscholarly, Britishers feel for the first time that Marston, Heywood, Webster, Beaumont and Fletcher, Massinger and Ford were writers they *ought* to know. His notes, fragmentary and informal as they are, are among the most personal and revealing of his critical writings. Shaw, being Shaw, could lament Lamb's fondness for these figures as a "literary aberration." He could say he forgave this addiction of Lamb's "as we forgive him his addiction to gin." But most people, including Shavians, would not deny their debt to Lamb because of the way in which he salvaged the beauties of a body of literature which had come to be almost ignored.

No one has written about the theatre with greater warmth or perception than did Lamb about vanished players or the playhouses of his youth. By common consent, due to common experience, few things are apt to be deader than the review of a forgotten play or a tribute to an actor the reader has neither heard about nor seen. Writing about the stage is usually doomed to be as evanescent as the pleasure or pain which prompted it. Those of us who attempt it professionally know, to our sorrow and chagrin, that what we devote ourselves to doing amounts to tattooing soapbubbles. In spite of its discouragements, this is a process not beyond achievement as is proved by those uncommon, blessed instances when journalism takes on the stature of criticism and criticism that of literature. This happens when the copy read, having lost its immediate or practical usefulness to the reader, somehow survives in time without relying upon news interest, not as a guide to pleasure but as itself a pleasure, self-sustaining and self-contained. It happens when yesterday endures as today and tomorrow.

Lamb joins the proud company of the elect who have been able to pass this test, and to pass it triumphantly. He could put reviewing to his own uses as when, for example, he proposed to Fanny Kelly (with negative results) in a notice of *Rachel*. "What a lass that were to go a gypseying through the world with!" sighed he in the public prints, pretending to quote a mythical neighbor. But, more than putting criticism to his own uses, he could put it to ours.

Bensley, Powel, Munden, Liston, Dodd, and Elliston are truly forgotten men. Except to a stage archivist, their names could not mean less had they been stumbled upon on broken tombstones in an abandoned graveyard. Yet Lamb's writing about them is so lively that not only do they live for us as if we had seen them but we know we are the luckier for having seen them through his eyes. To choose where choice is difficult, Bensley who seizes upon the moment of passion with greatest truth "like a faithful clock never striking before the time—never anticipating, or leading you to anticipate"; Bensley looking, speaking, and moving through the part of Malvolio as an old Castilian nobleman; Bensley keeping back "his intellect as some have had the power to retard their pulsation"; or Bensley allowing "a gleam of understanding" to "appear in a corner of his eye and for lack of fuel go out again" is more than a player described. He is a lesson in comic acting.

The same extension of an assignment, the same complete realization of an opportunity, is shown by Lamb in his notable essays "On the Artificial Comedy of the Last Century" or "On the Tragedies of Shakspeare." In both cases he writes mimetically as a critic should, taking the hint and color from his subject-matter. Wycherley or Congreve did not produce prose wittier, more belaced, or of greater sparkle as verbal marquetry than he did when, in playful earnestness, he rose to the defense of their amoralities.

In "Barbara S——" Lamb could tell sentimentally, with skillful, hot, forced tears, the one backstage story that has come down to us which Woollcott might have written. To read Lamb, however, on the reasons why Shakespeare's greatest tragedies, in the fullness of their tragic statement, were beyond the posturing, grimacing, and gesturing of actors is to realize the extents to which he could carry theatrical writing. As many have pointed out, Lamb, with his admiration for actors, could of course have taken the other side of the argument with equal felicity. But even Lamb the theatre-lover stood no chance against Lamb the bookman, or Lamb the intellectual. As a profound man who doted on the stage, and was more entitled than most to the escapes it offered him, he was too well aware of the theatre's limitations to be limited by them. In a style worthy of his subject he could so enter into Lear's mind that Lear ceased to be a character and became a mortal in agony.

The same Lamb who had abandoned poetry early in his career wrote as a poet when he was at his best as a critic or a correspondent. The stuttering, jesting, smoking, drinking little fellow, valiantly linked to Mary, was little in an abidingly big way. He was big of heart, large of mind, and unique in his endowments. Victim of life though he was, he was never victimized by it. He lived an interior life externally. It was his mind and the abilities out of which he fashioned his style which made his living, on the whole uneventful, eventful for the world no less than for him. Perhaps Pater, another stylist, wrote the best summary of Lamb in these words, "Unoccupied, as he might seem, with great matters, he is in immediate contact with what is real, especially in its caressing littleness, that littleness in which there is much of the whole woeful heart of things, and meets it more than halfway with a perfect understanding of it."

JOHN MASON BROWN

EDITOR'S NOTE

In assembling the following text I have indulged in certain unorthodoxies myself. My hope has been to allow Lamb to paint his own portrait. I have, therefore, put the letters first. They are the easiest, the most direct approach to him, and often the best. As for the essays, even those included in the *Essays of Elia* and the *Last Essays of Elia*, they were written as magazine pieces without continuity or conscious scheme, and were not meant to be gathered together in book form. Accordingly, I have dared to arrange my selections from them into subdivisions, which they constantly defy, representing aspects of the man, his work, or his interests. Furthermore, in order to bring him closer to contemporary readers, I have not hesitated to break up his paragraphs, indeed to reparagraph him throughout, as a necessary concession to altered conventions and increased impatience. The best writing about Lamb has been done by Lamb himself. It is Lamb self-revealed who, I trust, emerges from these pages. Almost every omission, necessitated by space, has cost me anguish.

LAMB CHRONOLOGY

1775. February 10. Charles Lamb was born at No. 2 Crown Office Row, the Temple, London; the youngest of seven children of John and Elizabeth (Field) Lamb. Of these only three lived to grow up: John, born June 5, 1763; Mary Anne, born December 3, 1764; and Charles. The father was servant and assistant to Samuel Salt, a Bencher of the Inner Temple.

1782-89. Charles attended Christ's Hospital, the Blue-coat School. His education was made possible by a scholarship provided through the influence of Mr. Salt. Lamb's lifelong friendship with Samuel Taylor Coleridge began here.

1789-91. Charles worked for Joseph Paice, a city merchant.

1791. September 1. Charles became clerk in Examiner's Office at South-Sea House; employed here until February 8, 1792, at salary of half a guinea a week. An Italian named Elia was one of the clerks.

1792. The death of Samuel Salt, early in February, compelled the Lambs to move out of the Temple. Thereafter Mary supported family as a seamstress.
April 5. Charles began long career as clerk in the Accountants' Office at East India House. Apprentice for three years without pay.
July 31. Grandmother Field died.

1796. September 22. Mary Lamb, in a fit of insanity, stabbed her mother to the heart. At the hearing which followed Charles assumed responsibility for Mary.

1797. February. Aunt Hetty (Sarah Lamb) died.
While visiting the Coleridges at Stowey, Lamb met William Wordsworth and his sister Dorothy.
Charles had four sonnets published in a volume of verse by Coleridge.

1798. *Rosamund Gray* published, Lamb's first prose.

1799. April. Lamb's father died. Mary returned to live with Charles. For the rest of her life Mary suffered recurring attacks of madness.

1800-03. Lamb contributed facetious paragraphs, epigrams, and other trifles to newspapers (*Morning Post, Chronicle, Albion*).

1802. *John Woodvil* published, a five-act drama in blank verse written as early as 1799 with title "Pride's Cure."

1804. Lamb met William Hazlitt through Coleridge.

1806. *Mr. H.*, a farce, completed and accepted by proprietors of Drury Lane Theatre; hissed when produced.

1807. *Tales from Shakspeare* by Charles and Mary Lamb published.

1808. *Adventures of Ulysses* and *Specimens of English Dramatic Poets Who Lived about the Time of Shakspeare* appeared.

1810-11. Contributed essays to Leigh Hunt's *Reflector.*

1818. First publication of *Collected Works,* in two volumes. Included *John Woodvil, Rosamund Gray,* verse, "Recollections of Christ's Hospital," "On the Tragedies of Shakspeare," and "On the Genius and Character of Hogarth."

1819. Lamb proposed to Miss Fanny Kelly, the actress.

1820. The first essay signed "Elia"—"The South-Sea House" —appeared in the August *London Magazine.*
During their autumn holiday at Cambridge, Charles and Mary met Emma Isola, age eleven, the orphan daughter of an Italian family. She lived in the Lamb household as their adopted daughter until her marriage to Edward Moxon, publisher, in 1833.

1821. October 26. John Lamb, Charles's brother, died.

1822. Charles and Mary spent their summer vacation in Paris, Lamb's only trip outside Britain.

1823. *The Essays of Elia* published; mainly from *London Magazine.*

1825. March 29. After thirty-three years Charles retired from India House on a pension of £450 a year, £9 of which was retained to provide for Mary in case she outlived him.

1830. September 18. Hazlitt died.

1833. *The Last Essays of Elia* published by Moxon.

1834. July 25. Coleridge died.
December 22. Lamb fell on the street. Although the injury was not considered serious, erysipelas developed and he died at Enfield on December 27. Buried in Edmonton Churchyard.

1847. May 20. Mary Lamb died, aged eighty-two, having outlived her brother by more than twelve years.

THE PORTABLE

Charles Lamb

PART ONE

Letters

[Postmark[1] 27th May, 1796.]

DEAR C

Make yourself perfectly easy about May. I paid his bill, when I sent your clothes. I was flush of money, and am so still to all the purposes of a single life, so give yourself no further concern about it. The money would be superfluous to me, if I had it.

With regard to Allen,—the woman he has married has some money, I have heard about £200 a year, enough for the maintenance of herself & children, one of whom is a girl nine years old! so Allen has dipt betimes into the cares of a family. I very seldom see him, & do not know whether he has given up the Westminster hospital.

When Southey becomes as modest as his predecessor Milton, and publishes his Epics in duodecimo, I will read 'em,—a Guinea a book is somewhat exorbitant, nor have I the opportunity of borrowing the Work. The extracts from it in the Monthly Review, and the short passages in your Watchman seem to me much superior to any thing in his partnership account with Lovell.

Your poems I shall procure forthwith. There were

[1] Hereafter indicated by "P.M."—J. M. B.

noble lines in what you inserted in one of your Numbers from Religious Musings, but I thought them elaborate. I am somewhat glad you have given up that Paper— it must have been dry, unprofitable, and of "dissonant mood" to your disposition. I wish you success in all your undertakings, and am glad to hear you are employed about the Evidences of Religion. There is need of multiplying such books an hundred fold in this philosophical age to *prevent* converts to Atheism, for they seem too tough disputants to meddle with afterwards. I am sincerely sorry for Allen, as a family man particularly.

Le Grice is gone to make puns in Cornwall. He has got a tutorship to a young boy, living with his Mother, a widow Lady. He will of course initiate him quickly in "whatsoever things are lovely, honorable, and of good report." He has cut Miss Hunt compleatly,—the poor Girl is very ill on the Occasion, but he laughs at it, and justifies himself by saying, "she does not see him laugh."

Coleridge, I know not what suffering scenes you have gone through at Bristol—my life has been somewhat diversified of late. The 6 weeks that finished last year and began this your very humble servant spent very agreeably in a mad house at Hoxton—I am got somewhat rational now, ar I don't bite any one. But mad I was—and many a vagary my imagination played with me, enough to make a volume if all told.

My Sonnets I have extended to the number of nine since I saw you, and will some day communicate to you.

I am beginning a poem in blank verse, which if I finish Ι publish.

White is on the eve of publishing (he took the hint from Vortigern) Original letters of Falstaff, Shallow &c—, a copy you shall have when it comes out. They are without exception the best imitations I ever saw.

Coleridge, it may convince you of my regards for you when I tell you my head ran on you in my madness, as much almost as on another Person, who I am inclined to think was the more immediate cause of my temporary frenzy.

The sonnet I send you has small merit as poetry but you will be curious to read it when I tell you it was written in my prison-house in one of my lucid Intervals.

TO MY SISTER

If from my lips some angry accents fell,
　　Peevish complaint, or harsh reproof unkind,
　'Twas but the error of a sickly mind,
And troubled thoughts, clouding the purer well,
　　And waters clear, of Reason; and for me,
　　Let this my verse the poor atonement be,
My verse, which thou to praise wast ever inclined
　　Too highly, and with a partial eye to see
No blemish: thou to me didst ever shew
　　Fondest affection, and woud'st oftimes lend
An ear to the desponding love sick lay,
　　Weeping my sorrows with me, who repay
But ill the mighty debt of love I owe,
　　Mary, to thee, my sister and my friend.

With these lines, and with that sister's kindest remembrances to C——, I conclude—

Yours sincerely
LAMB.

Your Conciones ad populum are the most eloquent politics that ever came in my way.

Write, when convenient—not as a task, for there is nothing in this letter to answer.

You may inclose under cover to me at the India house what letters you please, for they come post free.

We cannot send our remembrances to Mrs. C—— not having seen her, but believe me our best good wishes attend you both.

My civic and poetic compts to Southey if at Bristol. —Why, he is a very Leviathan of Bards—the small minnow I—

❖

TO S. T. COLERIDGE

Tuesday Night. [*14th June 1796.*]

I have been drinking egg-hot and smoking Oronooko (associated circumstances, which ever forcibly recall to my mind our evenings and nights at Salutation); my eyes and brain are heavy and asleep, but my heart is awake; and if words came as ready as ideas, and ideas as feelings, I could say ten hundred kind things. Coleridge, you know not my supreme happiness at having one on earth (though counties separate us) whom I can call a friend. Remember you those tender lines of Logan?

> Our broken friendships we deplore,
> And loves of youth that are no more;
> No after friendships e'er can raise
> Th' endearments of our early days,
> And ne'er the heart such fondness prove,
> As when we first began to love.

I am writing at random, and half-tipsy, what you may not *equally* understand, as you will be sober when you read it; but *my* sober and *my* half-tipsy hours you are alike a sharer in. Good night.

Then up rose our bard, like a prophet in drink,
Craigdoroch, thou'lt soar when creation shall sink.—BURNS

Thursday [16th *June* 1796].

I am now in high hopes to be able to visit you, if perfectly convenient on your part, by the end of next month —perhaps the last week or fortnight in July. A change of scene and a change of faces would do me good, even if that scene were not to be Bristol, and those faces Coleridge's and his friends. In the words of Terence, a little altered, "Tædet me hujus quotidiani mundi." I am heartily sick of the every-day scenes of life. I shall half wish you unmarried (don't show this to Mrs. C.) for one evening only, to have the pleasure of smoking with you, and drinking egg-hot in some little smoky room in a pothouse, for I know not yet how I shall like you in a decent room, and looking quite happy. My best love and respects to Sara notwithstanding.

Yours sincerely,
CHARLES LAMB.

❖

TO S. T. COLERIDGE

[P.M. 27th *September* 1796.]

My dearest friend—White or some of my friends or the public papers by this time may have informed you of the terrible calamities that have fallen on our family. I will only give you the outlines. My poor dear dearest sister in a fit of insanity has been the death of her own mother. I was at hand only time enough to snatch the knife out of her grasp. She is at present in a mad house, from whence I fear she must be moved to an hospital. God has preserved to me my senses,—I eat and drink and sleep, and have my judgment I believe very sound.

My poor father was slightly wounded, and I am left to take care of him and my aunt.[1] Mr. Norris of the Bluecoat school has been very kind to us, and we have no other friend, but thank God I am very calm and composed and able to do the best that remains to do. Write, —as religious a letter as possible—but no mention of what is gone and done with—with me the former things are passed away, and I have something more to do that [than] to feel——

God almighty

have us all in
his keeping.——

C. LAMB.

mention nothing of poetry. I have destroyed every vestige of past vanities of that kind. Do as you please, but if you publish, publish mine (I give free leave) without name or initial, and never send me a book, I charge you, you [your] own judgment will convince you not to take any notice of this yet to your dear wife.— You look after your family,— I have my reason and strength left to take care of mine. I charge you don't think of coming to see me. Write. I will not see you if you come. God almighty love you and all of us——

❖

TO S. T. COLERIDGE

[P.M. 3rd October 1796.]

My dearest friend, your letter was an inestimable treasure to me. It will be a comfort to you, I know, to know that our prospects are somewhat brighter. My poor dear dearest sister, the unhappy and unconscious

[1] Aunt Hetty, Sarah Lamb.—J. M. B.

instrument of the Almighty's judgments to our house, is restored to her senses; to a dreadful sense and recollection of what has past, awful to her mind, and impressive (as it must be to the end of life) but temper'd with religious resignation, and the reasonings of a sound judgment, which in this early stage knows how to distinguish between a deed committed in a transient fit of frenzy, and the terrible guilt of a Mother's murther.

I have seen her. I found her this morning calm and serene, far very very far from an indecent forgetful serenity; she has a most affectionate and tender concern for what has happened. Indeed from the beginning, frightful and hopeless as her disorder seemed, I had confidence enough in her strength of mind, and religious principle, to look forward to a time when *even she* might recover tranquillity. God be praised, Coleridge, wonderful as it is to tell, I have never once been otherwise than collected, and calm; even on the dreadful day and in the midst of the terrible scene I preserved a tranquillity, which bystanders may have construed into indifference, a tranquillity not of despair; is it folly or sin in me to say that it was a religious principle that *most* supported me? I allow much to other favorable circumstances.

I felt that I had something else to do than to regret; on that first evening my Aunt was lying insensible, to all appearance like one dying,—my father, with his poor forehead plaisterd over from a wound he had received from a daughter dearly loved by him, and who loved him no less dearly,—my mother a dead and murder'd corpse in the next room—yet was I wonderfully supported. I closed not my eyes in sleep that night, but lay without terrors and without despair. I have lost no sleep since. I had been long used not to rest in things of sense, had endeavord after a comprehension of mind, unsatisfied with the "ignorant present time," and this kept me

up. I had the whole weight of the family thrown on me,
for my brother, little disposed (I speak not without tenderness for him) at any time to take care of old age and
infirmities, had now, with his bad leg, an exemption
from such duties, and I was now left alone.

One little incident may serve to make you understand
my way of managing my mind. Within a day or 2 after
the fatal ONE, we drest for dinner a tongue, which we had
had salted for some weeks in the house. As I sat down a
feeling like remorse struck me,—this tongue poor Mary
got for me, and can I partake of it now, when she is far
away—a thought occurrd and relieved me,—if I give in
to this way of feeling, there is not a chair, a room, an
object in our rooms, that will not awaken the keenest
griefs, I must rise above such weaknesses.—I hope this
was not want of true feeling.

I did not let this carry me, tho', too far. On the very
2d day (I date from the day of horrors) as is usual in
such cases there were a matter of 20 people I do think
supping in our room. They prevailed on me to eat *with
them* (for to eat I never refused). They were all making
merry! in the room,—some had come from friendship,
some from busy curiosity, and some from Interest; I was
going to partake with them, when my recollection came
that my poor dead mother was lying in the next room,
the very next room, a mother who thro' life wished nothing but her children's welfare—indignation, the rage of
grief, something like remorse, rushed upon my mind in
an agony of emotion,—I found my way mechanically to
the adjoining room, and fell on my knees by the side of
her coffin, asking forgiveness of heaven, and sometimes
of her, for forgetting her so soon. Tranquillity returned,
and it was the only violent emotion that mastered me,
and I think it did me good.

I mention these things because I hate concealment,

and love to give a faithful journal of what passes within me. Our friends have been very good. Sam Le Grice who was then in town was with me the first 3 or 4 days, and was as a brother to me, gave up every hour of his time, to the very hurting of his health and spirits, in constant attendance and humouring my poor father. Talk'd with him, read to him, play'd at cribbage with him (for so short is the old man's recollection, that he was playing at cards, as tho' nothing had happened, while the Coroner's Inquest was sitting over the way!) Samuel wept tenderly when he went away, for his mother wrote him a very severe letter on his loitering so long in town, and he was forced to go.

Mr. Norris of Christ Hospital has been as a father to me, Mrs. Norris as a mother; tho' we had few claims on them. A Gentleman, brother to my Godmother, from whom we never had right or reason to expect any such assistance, sent my father twenty pounds,—and to crown all these God's blessings to our family at such a time, an old Lady, a cousin of my father and Aunt's, a Gentlewoman of fortune, is to take my Aunt and make her comfortable for the short remainder of her days.

My Aunt is recover'd and as well as ever, and highly pleased at thoughts of going,—and has generously given up the interest of her little money (which was formerly paid my Father for her board) wholely and solely to my Sister's use. Reckoning this we have, Daddy and I, for our two selves and an old maid servant to look after him, when I am out, which will be necessary, £170 or £180 (rather) a year, out of which we can spare 50 or 60 at least for Mary, while she stays at Islington, where she must and shall stay during her father's life for his and her comfort. I know John will make speeches about it, but she shall not go into an hospital. The good Lady of the mad house, and her daughter, an elegant sweet behaved young Lady, love her and are taken with her amazingly, and I know from her own mouth she loves them, and longs to be with them as much.

Poor thing, they say she was but the other morning saying, she knew she must go to Bethlem for life: that one of her brothers would have it so, but the other would wish it not, but be obliged to go with the stream; that she had often as she passed Bedlam thought it likely "here it may be my fate to end my days—" conscious of a certain flightiness in her poor head oftentimes, and mindful of more than one severe illness of that nature before. A Legacy of £100, which my father will have at Xmas, and this 20 I mentioned before, with what is in the house will much more than set us Clear;—if my father, an old servant maid, and I, can't live and live comfortably on £130 or £120 a year we ought to burn by slow fires, and I almost would, that Mary might not go into an hospital. Let me not leave one unfavourable impression on your mind respecting my Brother. Since this has happened he has been very kind and brotherly;. but I fear for his mind,—he has taken his ease in the world, and is not fit himself to struggle with difficulties, nor has much accustomed himself to throw himself into their way,—and I know his language is already, "Charles, you must take care of yourself, you must not abridge yourself of a single pleasure you have been used to," &c &c and in that style of talking. But you, a necessarian, can respect a difference of mind, and love what *is amiable* in a character not perfect. He has been very good, but I fear for his mind. Thank God, I can unconnect myself with him, and shall manage all my father's monies in future myself, if I take charge of Daddy, which poor John has not even hinted a wish, at any future time even, to share with me.

The Lady at this mad house assures me that I may

dismiss immediately both Doctor and apothecary, re-taining occasionally an opening draught or so for a while, and there is a less expensive establishment in her house, where she will only not have a room and nurse to her-self for £50 or guineas a year—the outside would be 60 —You know by œconomy how much more, even, I shall be able to spare for her comforts.

She will, I fancy, if she stays, make one of the family, rather than of the patients, and the old and young ladies I like exceedingly, and she loves dearly, and they, as the saying is, take to her very extraordinarily, if it is extraor-dinary that people who see my sister should love her. Of all the people I ever saw in the world my poor sister was most and thoroughly devoid of the least tincture of selfishness—I will enlarge upon her qualities, poor dear dearest soul, in a future letter for my own comfort, for I understand her throughly; and if I mistake not, in the most trying situation that a human being can be found in, she will be found (I speak not with sufficient humility, I fear, but humanly and foolishly speaking) she will be found, I trust, uniformly great and amiable; God keep her in her present mind, to whom be thanks and praise for all His dispensations to mankind.

LAMB.

Coleridge, continue to write; but do not for ever offend me by talking of sending me cash. Sincerely, and on my soul, we do not want it. God love you both!

I will write again very soon. Do you write directly. These mentioned good fortunes and change of pros-pects had almost brought my mind over to the extreme the very opposite to Despair; I was in danger of making myself too happy; your letter brought me back to a view of things which I had entertained from the beginning; I hope (for Mary I can answer) but I hope that *I* shall thro' life never have less recollection nor a fainter impression of what has happened than I have now; 'tis not a light thing, nor meant by the Almighty to be received lightly. I must be serious, circumspect, and deeply religious thro' life; by such means may *both* of us escape madness in future, if it so please the Almighty.

Send me word, how it fares with Sara. I repeat it, your letter was and will be an inestimable treasure to me; you have a view of what my situation demands of me like my own view; and I trust a just one.

TO S. T. COLERIDGE

Nov. 8th, 1796.

My Brother, my Friend,—I am distrest for you, believe me I am; not so much for your painful, troublesome complaint, which, I trust, is only for a time, as for those anxieties which brought it on, and perhaps even now may be nursing its malignity. Tell me, dearest of my friends, is your mind at peace, or has anything, yet unknown to me, happened to give you fresh disquiet, and steal from you all the pleasant dreams of future rest? Are you still (I fear you are) far from being comfortably settled?

Would to God it were in my power to contribute towards the bringing of you into the haven where you would be! But you are too well skilled in the philosophy of consolation to need my humble tribute of advice; in pain and in sickness, and in all manner of disappointments, I trust you have that within you which shall speak peace to your mind. Make it, I entreat you, one of your puny comforts, that I feel for you, and share all your griefs with you.

I feel as if I were troubling you about *little* things; now I am going to resume the subject of our last two letters, but it may divert us both from unpleasanter feelings to make such matters, in a manner, of importance. Without further apology, then, it was not that I did not relish, that I did not in my heart thank you for, those little pictures of your feelings which you lately sent me, if I neglected to mention them. You may remember you had said much the same things before to me on the same subject in a former letter, and I considered those last verses as only the identical thoughts better clothed; either way (in prose or verse) such poetry must be welcome to me.

I love them as I love the Confessions of Rousseau, and for the same reason: the same frankness, the same openness of heart, the same disclosure of all the most hidden and delicate affections of the mind: they make me proud to be thus esteemed worthy of the place of friend-confessor, brother-confessor, to a man like Coleridge. This last is, I acknowledge, language too high for friendship; but it is also, I declare, too sincere for flattery. Now, to put on stilts, and talk magnificently about trifles—I condescend, then, to your counsel, Coleridge, and allow my first Sonnet (sick to death am I to make mention of my sonnets, and I blush to be so taken up with them, indeed I do)—I allow it to run thus, *"Fairy Land"* &c. &c., as I [? you] last wrote it.

The Fragments I now send you I want printed to get rid of 'em; for, while they stick bur-like to my memory, they tempt me to go on with the idle trade of versifying, which I long—most sincerely I speak it—I long to leave off, for it is unprofitable to my soul; I feel it is; and these questions about words, and debates about alterations, take me off, I am conscious, from the properer business of *my* life.

Take my sonnets once for all, and do not propose any
re-amendments, or mention them again in any shape to
me, I charge you. I blush that my mind can consider
them as things of any worth. And pray admit or reject
these fragments, as you like or dislike them, without
ceremony. Call 'em Sketches, Fragments, or what you
will, but do not entitle any of my *things* Love Sonnets,
as I told you to call 'em; 'twill only make me look little
in my own eyes; for it is a passion of which I retain
nothing; 'twas a weakness, concerning which I may say,
in the words of Petrarch (whose life is now open before
me), "if it drew me out of some vices, it also prevented
the growth of many virtues, filling me with the love of
the creature rather than the Creator, which is the death
of the soul." Thank God, the folly has left me for ever;
not even a review of my love verses renews one wayward wish in me; and if I am at all solicitous to trim
'em out in their best apparel, it is because they are to
make their appearance in good company. Now to my
fragments. Lest you have lost my Grandame, she shall
be one. 'Tis among the few verses I ever wrote (that
to Mary is another) which profit me in the recollection.
God love her,—and may we two never love each other
less!

These, Coleridge, are the few sketches I have thought
worth preserving; how will they relish thus detached?
Will you reject all or any of them? They are thine: do
whatsoever thou listest with them. My eyes ache with
writing long and late, and I wax wondrous sleepy; God
bless you and yours, me and mine! Good night.

C. LAMB.

I will keep my eyes open reluctantly a minute longer
to tell you, that I love you for those simple, tender,

heart-flowing lines with which you conclude your last, and in my eyes best, sonnet (so you call 'em),

> So, for the mother's sake, the child was dear,
> And dearer was the mother for the child.

Cultivate simplicity, Coleridge, or rather, I should say, banish elaborateness; for simplicity springs spontaneous from the heart, and carries into daylight its own modest buds and genuine, sweet, and clear flowers of expression. I allow no hot-beds in the gardens of Parnassus. I am unwilling to go to bed, and leave my sheet unfilled (a good piece of nightwork for an idle body like me), so will finish with begging you to send me the earliest account of your complaint, its progress, or (as I hope to God you will be able to send me) the tale of your recovery, or at least amendment. My tenderest remembrances to your Sara.——

Once more good night.

❖

TO S. T. COLERIDGE

Nov. 14th, 1796.

Coleridge, I love you for dedicating your poetry to Bowles. Genius of the sacred fountain of tears, it was he who led you gently by the hand through all this valley of weeping, showed you the dark green yew trees and the willow shades where, by the fall of waters, you might indulge an uncomplaining melancholy, a delicious regret for the past, or weave fine visions of that awful future,

> When all the vanities of life's brief day
> Oblivion's hurrying hand hath swept away,

And all its sorrows, at the awful blast
Of the archangel's trump, are but as shadows past.

I have another sort of dedication in my head for my few things, which I want to know if you approve of, and can insert. I mean to inscribe them to my sister. It will be unexpected, and it will give her pleasure; or do you think it will look whimsical at all? As I have not spoke to her about it, I can easily reject the idea. But there is a monotony in the affections, which people living together or, as we do now, very frequently seeing each other, are apt to give in to: a sort of indifference in the expression of kindness for each other, which demands that we should sometimes call to our aid the trickery of surprise. Do you publish with Lloyd or without him? in either case my little portion may come last, and after the fashion of orders to a country correspondent I will give directions how I should like to have 'em done. The title-page to stand thus:—

POEMS,
CHIEFLY LOVE SONNETS
BY
CHARLES LAMB, OF THE INDIA HOUSE.

Under this title the following motto, which, for want of room, I put over leaf, and desire you to insert, whether you like it or no. May not a gentleman choose what arms, mottoes, or armorial bearings the herald will give him leave, without consulting his republican friend, who might advise none? May not a publican put up the sign of the Saracen's Head, even though his undiscerning neighbour should prefer, as more genteel, the Cat and Gridiron?

(MOTTO.)

This beauty, in the blossom of my youth,
When my first fire knew no adulterate incense,
Nor I no way to flatter but my fondness,
In the best language my true tongue could tell me,
And all the broken sighs my sick heart lend me,
I sued and served. Long did I love this lady.

MASSINGER.

THE DEDICATION

THE FEW FOLLOWING POEMS,
CREATURES OF THE FANCY AND THE FEELING
IN LIFE'S MORE VACANT HOURS,
PRODUCED, FOR THE MOST PART, BY
LOVE IN IDLENESS,
ARE,
WITH ALL A BROTHER'S FONDNESS,
INSCRIBED TO

MARY ANN LAMB,

THE AUTHOR'S BEST FRIEND AND SISTER.

This is the pomp and paraphernalia of parting, with
which I take my leave of a passion which has reigned
so royally (so long) within me; thus, with its trappings
of laureatship, I fling it off, pleased and satisfied with
myself that the weakness troubles me no longer. I am
wedded, Coleridge, to the fortunes of my sister and my
poor old father. Oh! my friend, I think sometimes, could
I recall the days that are past, which among them
should I choose? not those "merrier days," not the
"pleasant days of hope," not "those wanderings with
a fair hair'd maid," which I have so often and so feelingly regretted, but the days, Coleridge, of a *mother's*
fondness for her *school-boy*.

What would I give to call her back to earth for *one* day, on my knees to ask her pardon for all those little asperities of temper which, from time to time, have given her gentle spirit pain; and the day, my friend, I trust will come; there will be "time enough" for kind offices of love, if "Heaven's eternal year" be ours. Hereafter, her meek spirit shall not reproach me. Oh, my friend, cultivate the filial feelings! and let no man think himself released from the kind "charities" of relationship: these shall give him peace at the last; these are the best foundation for every species of benevolence. I rejoice to hear, by certain channels, that you, my friend, are reconciled with all your relations. 'Tis the most kindly and natural species of love, and we have all the associated train of early feelings to secure its strength and perpetuity. Send me an account of your health; *indeed* I am solicitous about you. God love you and yours.

C. LAMB.

❖

TO S. T. COLERIDGE

[P.M. 10th January 1797.]

. . . My sister, I thank God, is nigh recovered. She was seriously ill. Do, in your next letter, and that right soon, give me some satisfaction respecting your present situation at Stowey. Is it a farm you have got? and what does your worship know about farming? Coleridge, I want you to write an Epic poem. Nothing short of it can satisfy the vast capacity of true poetic genius. Having one great End to direct all your poetical faculties to, and on which to lay out your hopes, your ambition, will shew you to what you are equal. By the sacred energies of Milton, by the dainty sweet and soothing phantasies of honeytongued Spenser, I adjure you to attempt the Epic. Or do something more ample than writing an occasional brief ode or sonnet; something to "make yourself for ever known,—to make the age to come your own." But I prate; doubtless you meditate something.

When you are exalted among the Lords of Epic fame, I shall recall with pleasure, and exultingly, the days of your humility, when you disdained not to put forth in the same volume with mine, your religious musings, and that other poem from the Joan of Arc, those promising first fruits of high renown to come. You have learning, you have fancy, you have enthusiasm—you have strength and amplitude of wing enow for flights like those I recommend. In the vast and unexplored regions of fairyland, there is ground enough unfound and uncultivated; search there, and realize your favourite Susquehana scheme.[1]

In all our comparisons of taste, I do not know whether I have ever heard your opinion of a poet, very dear to me, the now out of fashion Cowley—favor me with your judgment of him, and tell me if his prose essays, in particular, as well as no inconsiderable part of his verse, be not delicious. I prefer the graceful rambling of his essays, even to the courtly elegance and ease of Addison—abstracting from this the latter's exquisite humour. Why is not your poem on Burns in the Monthly Magazine? I was much disappointed. I have a pleasurable but confused remembrance of it. . . .

Priestly, whom I sin in almost adoring, speaks of "such a choice of company, as tends to keep up that right

[1] Pantisocracy, a Utopian plan for communal living, somewhat similar to the later Brook Farm idea. The colony on the Susquehanna River in the United States was never established.—J. M. B.

bent, and firmness of mind, which a necessary intercourse with the world would otherwise warp and relax.
Such fellowship is the true balsam of life, its cement
is infinitely more durable than that of the friendships
of the world, and it looks for its proper fruit, and complete gratification, to the life beyond the Grave." Is
there a possible chance for such an one as me to realize
in this world, such friendships? Where am I to look for
'em? What testimonials shall I bring of my being worthy
of such friendship? Alas! the great and good go together in separate Herds, and leave such as me to lag
far far behind in all intellectual, and far more grievous
to say, in all moral, accomplishments.

Coleridge, I have not one truly elevated character
among my acquaintance: not one Christian: not one
but undervalues Christianity. Singly what am I to do?
Wesley (have you read his life? was *he* not an elevated
character?) Wesley has said, "Religion is not a solitary
thing." Alas! it necessarily is so with me, or next to solitary. 'Tis true, you write to me. But correspondence
by letter, and personal intimacy, are very widely different. Do, do write to me, and do some good to my mind,
already how much "warped and relaxed" by the world!
—'Tis the conclusion of another evening. Good night.
God have us all in his keeping.

If you are sufficiently at leisure, oblige me with an
account of your plan of life at Stowey—your literary occupations and prospects—in short make me acquainted
with every circumstance, which, as relating to you, can
be interesting to me. Are you yet a Berkleyan? Make
me one. I rejoice in being, speculatively, a necessarian.
Would to God, I were habitually a practical one. Confirm me in the faith of that great and glorious doctrine,
and keep me steady in the contemplation of it. You
sometime since exprest an intention you had of finishing

some extensive work on the Evidences of Natural and Revealed Religion. Have you let that intention go? Or are you doing any thing towards it? Make to yourself other ten talents.

My letter is full of nothingness. I talk of nothing. But I must talk. I love to write to you. I take a pride in it. It makes me think less meanly of myself. It makes me think myself not totally disconnected from the better part of Mankind. I know, I am too dissatisfied with the beings around me,—but I cannot help occasionally exclaiming "Woe is me, that I am constrained to dwell with Meshech, and to have my habitation among the tents of Kedar"—I know I am no ways better in practice than my neighbours—but I have a taste for religion, an occasional earnest aspiration after perfection, which they have not. I gain nothing by being with such as myself—we encourage one another in mediocrity—I am always longing to be with men more excellent than myself.

All this must sound odd to you; but these are my predominant feelings, when I sit down to write to you, and I should put force upon my mind, were I to reject them. Yet I rejoyce, and feel my privilege with gratitude, when I have been reading some wise book, such as I have just been reading—Priestley on Philosophical necessity—in the thought that I enjoy a kind of communion, a kind of friendship even, with the great and good. Books are to me instead of friends. I wish they did not resemble the latter in their scarceness.—And how does little David Hartley? "Ecquid in antiquam virtutem?"—does his mighty name work wonders yet upon his little frame, and opening mind? I did not distinctly understand you,—you don't mean to make an actual ploughman of him? Mrs. C—— is no doubt well,—give my kindest respects to her. Is Lloyd with you yet?—are you intimate with Southey? What poems is he about to publish—he hath a most prolific brain, and is indeed a most sweet poet. But how can you answer all the various mass of interrogation I have put to you in the course of this sheet. Write back just what you like, only write something, however brief. I have now nigh finished my page, and got to the end of another evening (Monday evening)—and my eyes are heavy and sleepy, and my brain unsuggestive. I have just heart enough to awake to say good night once more, and God love you my dear friend, God love us all. Mary bears an affectionate remembrance of you.

CHARLES LAMB.

❖

TO S. T. COLERIDGE

Feb. 13th, 1797.

This afternoon I attend the funeral of my poor old aunt, who died on Thursday. I own I am thankful that the good creature has ended all her days of suffering and infirmity. She was to me the "cherisher of infancy," and one must fall on these occasions into reflections which it would be commonplace to enumerate, concerning death, "of chance and change, and fate in human life." Good God, who could have foreseen all this but four months back! I had reckoned, in particular, on my aunt's living many years; she was a very hearty old woman. But she was a mere skeleton before she died, looked more like a corpse that had lain weeks in the grave, than one fresh dead. "Truly the light is sweet, and a pleasant thing it is for the eyes to behold the sun; but let a man live many days and rejoice in them all, yet let him remember the days of darkness, for they shall be many." Coleridge, why are we to live on after all the strength and beauty of existence are gone, when all the life of life is fled, as poor Burns expresses it?

Tell Lloyd, I have had thoughts of turning Quaker, and have been reading, or am rather just beginning to read, a most capital book, good thoughts in good language, William Penn's "No Cross, no Crown"; I like it immensely. Unluckily I went to one of his meetings, tell him, in St. John Street, yesterday, and saw a man under all the agitations and workings of a fanatic, who believed himself under the influence of some "inevitable presence." This cured me of Quakerism; I love it in the books of Penn and Woolman, but I detest the vanity of a man thinking he speaks by the Spirit, when what he says an ordinary man might say without all that quaking and trembling.

In the midst of his inspiration—and the effects of it were most noisy—was handed into the midst of the meeting a most terrible blackguard Wapping sailor; the poor man, I believe, had rather have been in the hottest part of an engagement, for the congregation of broad-brims, together with the ravings of the prophet, were too much for his gravity, though I saw even he had delicacy enough not to laugh out. And the inspired gentleman, though his manner was so supernatural, yet neither talked nor professed to talk anything more than good sober sense, common morality, and with now and then a declaration of not speaking from himself. Among other things, looking back to his childhood and early youth, he told the meeting what a graceless young dog he had been, that in his youth he had a good share of wit: reader, if thou hadst seen the gentleman, thou wouldst have sworn that it must indeed have been many years ago, for his rueful physiognomy would have scared away the playful goddess from the meeting, where he presided, for ever.

A wit! a wit! what could he mean? Lloyd, it minded me of Falkland in the "Rivals," "Am I full of wit and humour? No, indeed you are not. Am I the life and soul of every company I come into? No, it cannot be said you are." That hard-faced gentleman, a wit! Why, Nature wrote on his fanatic forehead fifty years ago, "Wit never comes, that comes to all." I should be as scandalised at a *bon mot* issuing from his oracle-looking mouth, as to see Cato go down a country-dance. God love you all. You are very good to submit to be pleased with reading my nothings. 'Tis the privilege of friendship to talk nonsense, and to have her nonsense respected.—Yours ever,

C. LAMB.

❖

TO THOMAS MANNING[1]

[P.M. *1st March 1800.*]

I hope by this time you are prepared to say the "Falstaff's letters" are a bundle of the sharpest, queerest, profoundest humours, of any these juice-drained latter times have spawned. I should have advertised you, that the meaning is frequently hard to be got at; and so are the future guineas, that now lie ripening and aurifying in the womb of some undiscovered Potosi; but dig, dig, dig, dig, Manning! I set to with an unconquerable propulsion to write, with a lamentable want of what to write.

[1] A mathematics don at Cambridge University to whom Lamb wrote some of his best letters.—J. M. B.

My private goings on are orderly as the movements of the spheres, and stale as their music to angels' ears. Public affairs—except as they touch upon me, and so turn into private, I cannot whip up my mind to feel any interest in. I grieve, indeed, that War and Nature and Mr. Pitt, that hangs up in Lloyd's best parlour, should have conspired to call up three necessaries, simple commoners as our fathers knew them, into the upper house of Luxuries; Bread, and Beer, and Coals, Manning. But as to France and Frenchmen, and the Abbé Sièyes and his constitutions, I cannot make these present times present to me. I read histories of the past, and I live in them; although, to abstract senses, they are far less momentous than the noises which keep Europe awake.

I am reading Burnet's Own Times. Did you ever read that garrulous, pleasant history? He tells his story like an old man past political service, bragging to his sons on winter evenings of the part he took in public transactions, when his "old cap was new." Full of scandal, which all true history is. No palliatives, but all the stark wickedness, that actually gives the *momentum* to national actors. Quite the prattle of age and outlived importance. Truth and sincerity staring out upon you perpetually in *alto relievo*. Himself a party man—he makes you a party man. None of the Damned philosophical Humeian indifference, so cold, and unnatural, and inhuman! None of the damned Gibbonian fine writing, so fine and composite. None of Mr. Robertson's periods with three members. None of Mr. Roscoe's sage remarks, all so apposite, and coming in so clever, lest the reader should have had the trouble of drawing an inference.

Burnet's good old prattle I can bring present to my mind—I can make the revolution present to me; the French Revolution, by a converse perversity in my nature, I fling as far *from* me. To quit this damn'd subject, and to relieve you from two or three dismal yawns, which I hear in spirit, I here conclude my more than commonly obtuse letter; dull up to the dulness of a Dutch commentator on Shakspeare.

My love to Lloyd and Sophia.   C. L.

❖

TO THOMAS MANNING

[P.M. 17th March 1800.]

Dear Manning,

I am living in a continuous feast. Coleridge has been with me now for nigh three weeks, and the more I see of him in the quotidian undress and relaxation of his mind, the more cause I see to love him, and believe him a *very good man*, and all those foolish impressions to the contrary fly off like morning slumbers. He is engaged in translations, which I hope will keep him this month to come. He is uncommonly kind and friendly to me. He ferrets me day and night to *do something*. He tends me, amidst all his own worrying and heart-oppressing occupations, as a gardener tends his young *tulip*. Marry come up! what a pretty similitude, and how like your humble servant! He has lugged me to the brink of engaging to a newspaper, and has suggested to me for a first plan the forgery of a supposed manuscript of Burton the anatomist of melancholy. I have even written the introductory letter; and, if I can pick up a few guineas this way, I feel they will be most *refreshing*, bread being so dear. If I go on with it, I will apprise you of it, as you may like to see my things! and the *tulip*, of all flowers, loves to be admired most.

Pray pardon me, if my letters do not come very thick.

I am so taken up with one thing or other, that I cannot pick out (I will not say time, but) fitting times to write to you.

My dear love to Lloyd and Sophia, and pray split this thin letter into three parts, and present them with the *two biggest* in my name.

They are my oldest friends; but ever the new friend driveth out the old, as the ballad sings!

God bless you all three! I would hear from Lloyd, if I could.

C. L.

Flour has just fallen nine shillings a sack! we shall be all too rich.

Tell Charles I have seen his Mamma, and ham almost fallen in love with *her*, since I mayn't with Olivia. She is so fine and graceful, a complete Matron-Lady-Quaker. She has given me two little books. Olivia grows a charming girl—full of feeling, and *thinner* than she was—

But I have not time to fall in love.

Mary presents her *general compliments*. She keeps in fine health!

Huzza! Boys,
and down with the Atheists.

TO S. T. COLERIDGE

Monday, May 12th, 1800.

MY DEAR COLERIDGE

I don't know why I write, except from the propensity misery has to tell her griefs. Hetty[1] died on Friday

---

[1] Lamb's old servant.—J. M. B.

night, about eleven o'clock, after eight days' illness;
Mary, in consequence of fatigue and anxiety, is fallen
ill again, and I was obliged to remove her yesterday. I
am left alone in a house with nothing but Hetty's dead
body to keep me company. To-morrow I bury her, and
then I shall be quite alone, with nothing but a cat to remind me that the house has been full of living beings
like myself. My heart is quite sunk, and I don't know
where to look for relief. Mary will get better again; but
her constantly being liable to such relapses is dreadful;
nor is it the least of our evils that her case and all our
story is so well known around us. We are in a manner
marked. Excuse my troubling you; but I have nobody
by me to speak to me. I slept out last night, not being
able to endure the change and the stillness. But I did not
sleep well, and I must come back to my own bed. I am
going to try and get a friend to come and be with me to-
morrow. I am completely shipwrecked. My head is quite
bad. I almost wish that Mary were dead.—God bless
you! Love to Sara and Hartley.

C. Lamb.

❖

TO THOMAS MANNING

May 17, 1800.

Dear Manning,

I am quite out of spirits, and feel as if I should never
recover them. But why should not this pass away? I am
foolish, but judge of me by my situation. Our servant is
dead, and my sister is ill—so ill as to make a removal to
a place of confinement absolutely necessary. I have been
left *alone* in a house where but ten days since living beings were, and noises of life were heard. I have made

the experiment and find I cannot bear it any longer. Last night I went to sleep at White's, with whom I am to be until I can find a settlement. I have given up my house, and must look out for lodgings.

I expect Mary will get better before many weeks are gone,—but at present I feel my daily and hourly prop has fallen from me. I totter and stagger with weakness, for nobody can supply her place to me. White has *all kindness*, but not *sympathy*. R. Lloyd, my only correspondent, you except, is a good Being, but a weak one. I know not where to look but to you. If you will suffer me to weary your shoulders with part of my Burthen, I shall write again to let you know how I go on. Meantime a letter from you would be a considerable relief to me.—Believe me, yours most sincerely,

C. L.

❖

TO S. T. COLERIDGE

Aug. 6th, 1800.

DEAR COLERIDGE,

I have taken today, and delivered to Longman and Co., *Imprimis:* your books, viz., three ponderous German dictionaries, one volume (I can find no more) of German and French ditto, sundry other German books unbound, as you left them, Percy's Ancient Poetry, and one volume of Anderson's Poets. I specify them, that you may not lose any. *Secundo:* a dressing-gown (value, fivepence), in which you used to sit and look like a conjuror, when you were translating "Wallenstein." A case of two razors and a shaving-box and strap. This it has cost me a severe struggle to part with. They are in a brown-paper parcel, which also contains sundry papers and poems, sermons, *some few Epic* Poems,—one about Cain and Abel, which came from Poole, &c., &c., and also your tragedy; with one or two small German books, and that drama in which God-fader performs. *Tertio:* a small oblong box containing *all your letters,* collected from all your waste papers, and which fill the said little box. All other waste papers, which I judged worth sending, are in the paper parcel aforesaid. But you will find *all* your letters in the box by themselves.

Thus have I discharged my conscience and my lumber-room of all your property, save and except a folio entitled Tyrrell's Bibliotheca Politica, which you used to learn your politics out of when you wrote for the Post, *mutatis mutandis, i.e.,* applying past inferences to modern *data.* I retain that, because I am sensible I am very deficient in the politics myself; and I have torn up—don't be angry, waste paper has risen forty per cent., and I can't afford to buy it—all Buonaparte's Letters, Arthur Young's Treatise on Corn, and one or two more light-armed infantry, which I thought better suited the flippancy of London discussion than the dignity of Keswick thinking. Mary says you will be in a damned passion about them when you come to miss them; but you must study philosophy. Read Albertus Magnus de Chartis Amissis five times over after phlebotomising,—'tis Burton's recipe—and then be angry with an absent friend if you can.

I have just heard that Mrs. Lloyd is delivered of a fine boy, and mother and boy are doing well. Fie on sluggards, what is thy Sara doing? Sara is obscure. Am I to understand by her letter, that she sends a *kiss* to Eliza Buckingham? Pray tell your wife that a note of interrogation on the superscription of a letter is highly ungrammatical—she proposes writing my name *Lamb?* Lambe is quite enough. I have had the Anthology, and like only one thing in it, *Lewti*; but of that the last stanza is detestable, the rest most exquisite!—the epithet *enviable* would dash the finest poem.

For God's sake (I never was more serious), don't make me ridiculous any more by terming me gentle-hearted in print, or do it in better verses. It did well enough five years ago when I came to see you, and was moral coxcomb enough at the time you wrote the lines, to feed upon such epithets; but, besides that, the meaning of gentle is equivocal at best, and almost always means poor-spirited, the very quality of gentleness is abhorrent to such vile trumpetings. My *sentiment* is long since vanished. I hope my *virtues* have done *sucking*. I can scarce think but you meant it in joke. I hope you did, for I should be ashamed to think that you could think to gratify me by such praise, fit only to be a cordial to some green-sick sonneteer.

I have hit off the following in imitation of old English poetry, which, I imagine, I am a dab at. The measure is unmeasureable; but it most resembles that beautiful ballad of the "Old and Young Courtier"; and in its feature of taking the extremes of two situations for just parallel, it resembles the old poetry certainly. If I could but stretch out the circumstances to twelve more verses, *i.e.*, if I had as much genius as the writer of that old song, I think it would be excellent. It was to follow an imitation of Burton in prose, which you have not seen. But fate "and wisest Stewart" say No.

I can send you 200 pens and six quires of paper *immediately*, if they will answer the carriage by coach. It would be foolish to pack 'em up *cum multis libris et cæteris*,—they would all spoil. I only wait your commands to coach them. I would pay five-and-forty thousand carriages to read W.'s tragedy,[1] of which I have

[1] Wordsworth's *The Borderers.*—J. M. B.

heard so much and seen so little—only what I saw at Stowey. Pray give me an order in writing on Longman for "Lyrical Ballads." I have the first volume, and, truth to tell, six shillings is a broad shot. I cram all I can in, to save a multiplying of letters—those pretty comets with swingeing tails.

I'll just crowd in God bless you!　　　C. LAMB.
Wednesday night.

❖

TO THOMAS MANNING

[P.M. 9th August 1800.]

DEAR MANNING,

I suppose you have heard of Sophia Lloyd's good fortune, and paid the customary compliments to the parents. Heaven keep the new-born infant from star-blasting and moon-blasting, from epilepsy, marasmus, and the devil! May he live to see many days, and they good ones; some friends, and they pretty regular correspondents, with as much wit as [? and] wisdom as will eat their bread and cheese together under a poor roof without quarrelling; as much goodness as will earn heaven if there be such a place and deserve it if there be not, but, rather than go to bed solitary, would truckle with the meanest succubus on her bed of brimstone. Here I must leave off, my benedictory powers failing me. I could *curse* the sheet full; so much stronger is corruption than grace in the Natural Man.

And now, when shall I catch a glimpse of your honest face-to-face countenance again—your fine *dogmatical sceptical* face, by punch-light? O! one glimpse of the human face, and shake of the human hand, is better than whole reams of this cold, thin correspondence—

yea, of more worth than all the letters that have sweated
the fingers of sensibility from Madame Sevigné and
Balzac (observe my Larning!) to Sterne and Shenstone.

Coleridge is settled with his wife (with a child in her
guts) and the young philosopher at Keswick with the
Wordsworths. They have contrived to spawn a new
volume of lyrical ballads, which is to see the light in
about a month, and causes no little excitement in the
literary world. George Dyer too, that good-natured
heathen, is more than nine months gone with his twin
volumes of ode, pastoral, sonnet, elegy, Spenserian,
Horatian, Akensidish, and Masonic verse—Clio pros-
per the birth! it will be twelve shillings out of somebody's pocket. I find he means to exclude "personal
satire," so it appears by his truly original advertisement.
Well, God put it into the hearts of the English gentry
to come in shoals and subscribe to his poems, for He
never put a kinder heart into flesh of man than George
Dyer's!

Now farewell: for dinner is at hand, and yearning
guts do chide.

C. L.

❖

TO THOMAS MANNING

[P.M. 11th August 1800.]

My dear fellow (*N.B.* mighty familiar of late!) for
me to come to Cambridge now is one of G—d Almighty's impossibilities. Metaphysicians tell us, even
He can work nothing which implies a contradiction. I
can explain this by telling you that I am engaged to do
double duty (this hot weather!) for a man who has
taken advantage of this very weather to go and cool himself in "green retreats" all the month of August.

But for you to come to London instead!—muse upon it, revolve it, cast it about in your mind. I have a bed at your command. You shall drink rum, brandy, gin, aquavitæ, usquebaugh, or whiskey a' nights; and for the after-dinner trick I have eight bottles of genuine port, which, if mathematically divided, gives 1⅓ for every day you stay, provided you stay a week. Hear John Milton sing,

> Let Euclid rest and Archimedes pause.
> *Twenty-first Sonnet.*

And elsewhere,

> What neat repast shall feast us, light and choice,
> Of Attic taste, with wine, whence we may rise
> To hear the lute well touch'd, or artful voice
> *Warble immortal notes and Tuscan air?*

Indeed, the poets are full of this pleasing morality—

> Veni cito, Domine Manning!

Think upon it. Excuse the paper: it is all I have.

N.B.—I lives at No. 27 Southampton Buildings, Holborn.

C. LAMB.

❖

TO THOMAS MANNING

[P.M. 21st August 1800.]

DEAR MANNING,

I am going to ask a favour of you, and am at a loss how to do it in the most delicate manner. For this purpose I have been looking into Pliny's Letters, who is noted to have had the best grace in begging of all the ancients (I read him in the elegant translation of Mr.

Melmoth), but not finding any case there exactly similar
with mine, I am constrained to beg in my own barbarian
way. To come to the point then, and hasten into the
middle of things, have you a copy of your Algebra to
give away? I do not ask it for myself; I have too much
reverence for the Black Arts ever to approach thy
circle, illustrious Trismegist! But that worthy man and
excellent Poet, George Dyer, made me a visit yester-
night, on purpose to borrow one, supposing, rationally
enough I must say, that you had made me a present of
one before this; the omission of which I take to have
proceeded only from negligence; but it is a fault. I could
lend him no assistance.

You must know he is just now diverted from the pursuit of BELL LETTERS by a paradox, which he has
heard his friend Frend (that learned mathematician)
maintain, that the negative quantities of mathematicians
were *meræ nugæ*, things scarcely in *rerum naturâ*, and
smacking too much of mystery for gentlemen of Mr.
Frend's clear Unitarian capacity. However, the dispute
once set a-going has seized violently on George's peri-
cranick; and it is necessary for his health that he should
speedily come to a resolution of his doubts. He goes
about teasing his friends with his new mathematics; he
even frantically talks of purchasing Manning's Algebra,
which shows him far gone, for, to my knowledge, he has
not been master of seven shillings a good time. George's
pockets and . . .'s brains are two things in nature which
do not abhor a vacuum. . . .

Now, if you could step in, in this trembling suspense
of his reason, and he should find on Saturday morning,
lying for him at the Porter's Lodge, Clifford's Inn,—
his safest address—Manning's Algebra, with a neat
manuscriptum in the blank leaf, running thus, FROM
THE AUTHOR! it might save his wits and restore the un-

happy author to those studies of poetry and criticism, which are at present suspended, to the infinite regret of the whole literary world.

N.B.—Dirty books [? backs], smeared leaves, and dogs' ears, will be rather a recommendation than otherwise.

N.B.—He must have the book as soon as possible, or nothing can withhold him from madly purchasing the book on tick. . . . Then shall we see him sweetly restored to the chair of Longinus—to dictate in smooth and modest phrase the laws of verse; to prove that Theocritus first introduced the Pastoral, and Virgil and Pope brought it to its perfection; that Gray and Mason (who always hunt in couples in George's brain) have shown a great deal of poetical fire in their lyric poetry; that Aristotle's rules are not to be servilely followed, which George has shown to have imposed great shackles upon modern genius. His poems, I find, are to consist of two vols.—reasonable octavo; and a third book will exclusively contain criticisms, in which he asserts he has gone *pretty deeply* into the laws of blank verse and rhyme—epic poetry, dramatic and pastoral ditto—all which is to come out before Christmas. But above all he has *touched* most *deeply* upon the Drama, comparing the English with the modern German stage, their merits and defects. Apprehending that his *studies* (not to mention his *turn*, which I take to be chiefly towards the lyrical poetry) hardly qualified him for these disquisitions, I modestly inquired what plays he had read? I found by George's reply that he *had* read Shakspeare, but that was a good while since: he calls him a great but irregular genius, which I think to be an original and just remark. (Beaumont and Fletcher, Massinger, Ben Jonson, Shirley, Marlowe, Ford, and the worthies of Dodsley's Collection—he confessed he had read none of them, but professed his *intention* of looking through them all, so as to be able to *touch* upon them in his book.)

So Shakspeare, Otway, and I believe Rowe, to whom he was naturally directed by Johnson's Lives, and these not read lately, are to stand him in stead of a general knowledge of the subject. God bless his dear absurd head!

By the by, did I not write you a letter with something about an invitation in it?—but let that pass; I suppose it is not agreeable.

N.B. It would not be amiss if you were to accompany your *present* with a dissertation on negative quantities.

C. L.

❖

TO THOMAS MANNING

[P.M. 22nd *September* 1800.]

DEAR MANNING,

You needed not imagine any apology necessary. Your fine hare and fine birds (which just now are dangling by our kitchen blaze) discourse most eloquent music in your justification. You just nicked my palate. For, with all due decorum and leave may it be spoken, my worship hath taken physic for his body to-day, and being low and puling, requireth to be pampered. Foh! how beautiful and strong those buttered onions come to my nose! For you must know we extract a divine spirit of gravy from those materials which, duly compounded with a consistence of bread and cream (y'clept bread-sauce), each to each giving double grace, do mutually illustrate and set off (as skilful goldfoils to rare jewels) your partridge, pheasant, woodcock, snipe,

teal, widgeon, and the other lesser daughters of the ark.
My friendship, struggling with my carnal and fleshly
prudence (which suggests that a bird a man is the
proper allotment in such cases), yearneth sometimes to
have thee here to pick a wing or so. I question if your
Norfolk sauces match our London culinaric.

George Dyer has introduced me to the table of an
agreeable old gentleman, Dr. Anderson, who gives hot
legs of mutton and grape pies at his sylvan lodge at
Isleworth, where, in the middle of a street, he has shot
up a wall most preposterously before his small dwelling,
which, with the circumstance of his taking several panes
of glass out of bedroom windows (for air), causeth his
neighbours to speculate strangely on the state of the
good man's pericranicks. Plainly, he lives under the
reputation of being deranged. George does not mind
this circumstances; he rather likes him the better for
it. The Doctor, in his pursuits, joins agricultural to poetical science, and has set George's brains mad about the
old Scotch writers, Barbour, Douglas's Æneid, Blind
Harry, &c.

We returned home in a return postchaise (having
dined with the Doctor), and George kept wondering
and wondering, for eight or nine turnpike miles, what
was the name, and striving to recollect the name, of a
poet anterior to Barbour. I begged to know what was
remaining of his works. "There is nothing *extant* of his
works, Sir, but by all accounts he seems to have been
a fine genius!" This fine genius, without anything to
show for it or any title beyond George's courtesy, without even a name! and Barbour, and Douglas, and Blind
Harry, now are the predominant sounds in George's
pia mater, and their buzzings exclude politics, criticism,
and algebra—the late lords of that illustrious lumber-
room. Mark, he has never read any of these bucks, but

is impatient till he reads them *all* at the Doctor's suggestion. Poor Dyer! his friends should be careful what sparks they let fall into such inflammable matter.

Could I have my will of the heathen, I would lock him up from all access of new ideas; I would exclude all critics that would not swear me first (upon their Virgil) that they would feed him with nothing but the old, safe, familiar notions and sounds (the rightful aborigines of his brain)—Gray, Akenside and Mason. In these sounds, reiterated as often as possible, there could be nothing painful, nothing distracting.

God bless me, here are the birds, smoking hot!
all that is gross and unspiritual in me rises at the sight!
Avaunt friendship! and all memory of absent friends!

C. Lamb.

❖

TO S. T. COLERIDGE

Oct. 9th, 1800.

I suppose you have heard of the death of Amos Cottle. I paid a solemn visit of condolence to his brother, accompanied by George Dyer, of burlesque memory. I went, trembling to see poor Cottle so immediately upon the event. He was in black; and his younger brother was also in black. Every thing wore an aspect suitable to the respect due to the freshly dead.

For some time after our entrance, nobody spake till George modestly put in a question, whether *Alfred* was likely to sell. This was Lethe to Cottle, and his poor face wet with tears, and his kind eye brightened up in a moment. Now I felt it was my cue to speak. I had to thank him for a present of a magnificent copy, and had promised to send him my remarks,—the least thing I could do; so I ventured to suggest, that I perceived a considerable improvement he had made in his first book since the state in which he first read it to me. Joseph, who till now had sat with his knees cowering in by the fire-place, wheeled about, and with great difficulty of body shifted the same round to the corner of a table where I was sitting, and first stationing one thigh over the other, which is his sedentary mood, and placidly fixing his benevolent face right against mine, waited my observations. At that moment it came strongly into my mind, that I had got Uncle Toby before me, he looked so kind and so good. I could not say an unkind thing of *Alfred*. So I set my memory to work to recollect what was the name of Alfred's Queen, and with some adroitness recalled the well-known sound to Cottle's ears of Alswitha.

At that moment I could perceive that Cottle had forgot his brother was so lately become a blessed spirit. In the language of mathematicians the author was as 9, the brother as 1. I felt my cue, and strong pity working at the root, I went to work, and beslabber'd *Alfred* with most unqualified praise, or only qualifying my praise by the occasional politic interposition of an exception taken against trivial faults, slips, and human imperfections, which, by removing the appearance of insincerity, did but in truth heighten the relish. Perhaps I might have spared that refinement, for Joseph was in a humour to hope and believe *all things*.

What I said was beautifully supported, corroborated, and confirmed by the stupidity of his brother on my left hand, and by George on my right, who has an utter incapacity of comprehending that there can be any thing bad in poetry. All poems are *good* poems to George; all men are *fine geniuses*. So what with my actual memory, of which I made the most, and Cottle's own helping me out, for I *really* had forgotten a good deal of *Alfred*, I made shift to discuss the most essential parts entirely to the satisfaction of its author, who repeatedly declared that he loved nothing better than *candid* criticism. Was I a candid greyhound now for all this? or did I do right? I believe I did. The effect was luscious to my conscience.

For all the rest of the evening Amos was no more heard of, till George revived the subject by inquiring whether some account should not be drawn up by the friends of the deceased to be inserted in Phillips's Monthly Obituary; adding, that Amos was estimable both for his head and heart, and would have made a fine poet if he had lived. To the expediency of this measure Cottle fully assented, but could not help adding that he always thought that the qualities of his brother's heart exceeded those of his head. I believe his brother, when living, had formed precisely the same idea of him; and I apprehend the world will assent to both judgments. I rather guess that the Brothers were poetical rivals. I judged so when I saw them together. Poor Cottle, I must leave him, after his short dream, to muse again upon his poor brother, for whom I am sure in secret he will yet shed many a tear. Now send me in return some Greta news.   C. L.

❖

TO THOMAS MANNING

[P.M. *16th October 1800*.]

DEAR MANNING,

Had you written one week before you did, I certainly should have obeyed your injunction; you should have seen me before my letter. I will explain to you my situation. There are six of us in one department. Two of us (within these four days) are confined with severe fevers; and two more, who belong to the Tower Militia, expect to have marching orders on Friday. Now six are absolutely necessary. I have already asked and obtained two young hands to supply the loss of the *Feverites;* and, with the other prospect before me, you may believe I cannot decently ask leave of absence for myself. All I can promise (and I do promise with the sincerity of *Saint* Peter, and the contrition of *Sinner* Peter if I fail) that I will come *the very first spare week,* and go nowhere till I have been at Camb. No matter if you are in a state of pupilage when I come; for I can employ myself in Cambridge very pleasantly in the mornings. Are there not Libraries, Halls, Colleges, Books, Pictures, Statues?

I wish to God you had made London in your way. There is an exhibition quite uncommon in Europe, which would not have escaped *your genius,*—a LIVE RATTLESNAKE, 10 feet in length, and the thickness of a big leg. I went to see it last night by candlelight. We were ushered into a room very little bigger than ours at Pentonville. A man and woman and four boys live in this room, joint tenants with nine snakes, most of them such as no remedy has been discovered for their bite.

We walked into the middle, which is formed by a half-moon of wired boxes, all mansions of *snakes,*— whip-snakes, thunder-snakes, pig-nose-snakes, American vipers, and *this monster.* He lies curled up in folds; and immediately a stranger enters (for he is used to the family, and sees them play at cards,) he set up a rattle like a watchman's in London, or near as loud, and reared up a head, from the midst of these folds, like a toad, and shook his head, and showed every sign a snake

can show of irritation. I had the foolish curiosity to
strike the wires with my finger, and the devil flew at me
with his toad-mouth wide open: the inside of his mouth
is quite white. I had got my finger away, nor could he
well have bit me with his damn'd big mouth, which
would have been certain death in five minutes. But it
frightened me so much, that I did not recover my voice
for a minute's space. I forgot, in my fear, that he was
secured. You would have forgot too, for 'tis incredible
how such a monster can be confined in small gauzy-
looking wires.

I dreamed of snakes in the night. I wish to heaven
you could see it. He absolutely swelled with passion
to the bigness of a large thigh. I could not retreat without infringing on another box, and just behind, a little
devil not an inch from my back, had got his nose out,
with some difficulty and pain, quite through the bars!
He was soon taught better manners. All the snakes
were curious, and objects of terror: but this monster,
like Aaron's serpent, swallowed up the impression of
the rest. He opened his damn'd mouth, when he made
at me, as wide as his head was broad. I hallooed out
quite loud, and felt pains all over my body with the
fright.

I have had the felicity of hearing George Dyer read
out one book of "The Farmer's Boy." I thought it rather
childish. No doubt, there is originality in it, (which, in
your self-taught geniuses, is a most rare quality, they
generally getting hold of some bad models in a scarcity
of books, and forming their taste on them,) but no
selection. All is described.

Mind, I have only heard read one book.

Yours sincerely,
Philo-Snake,   C. L.

❖

TO THOMAS MANNING

[P.M. *28th November 1800.*]

DEAR MANNING,

I have received a very kind invitation from Lloyd and Sophia to go and spend a month with them at the Lakes. Now it fortunately happens (which is so seldom the case!) that I have spare cash by me, enough to answer the expenses of so long a journey; and I am determined to get away from the office by some means. The purpose of this letter is to request of you (my dear friend) that you will not take it unkind if I decline my proposed visit to Cambridge *for the present*. Perhaps I shall be able to take Cambridge *in my way*, going or coming. I need not describe to you the expectations which such an one as myself, pent up all my life in a dirty city, have formed of a tour to the Lakes. Consider Grasmere! Ambleside! Wordsworth! Coleridge! I hope you will. Hills, woods, lakes, and mountains, to the eternal devil. I will eat snipes with thee, Thomas Manning. Only confess, confess, a *bite*.

P.S. I think you name the 16th; but was it not modest of Lloyd to send such an invitation! It shows his knowledge of *money* and *time*. I would be loth to think he meant

> Ironic satire sidelong sklented
> On my poor pursie.—BURNS.

For my part, with reference to my friends northward, I must confess that I am not romance-bit about *Nature*. The earth, and sea, and sky (when all is said) is but as a house to dwell in. If the inmates be courteous, and good liquors flow like the conduits at an old coronation;

if they can talk sensibly and feel properly; I have no need to stand staring upon the gilded looking-glass (that strained my friend's purse-strings in the purchase), nor his five-shilling print over the mantelpiece of old Nabbs the carrier (which only betrays his false taste).

Just as important to me (in a sense) is all the furniture of my world—eye-pampering, but satisfies no heart. Streets, streets, streets, markets, theatres, churches, Covent Gardens, shops sparkling with pretty faces of industrious milliners, neat sempstresses, ladies cheapening, gentlemen behind counters lying, authors in the street with spectacles, George Dyers (you may know them by their gait), lamps lit at night, pastry-cooks' and silversmiths' shops, beautiful Quakers at Pentonville, noise of coaches, drowsy cry of mechanic watchmen at night, with bucks reeling home drunk; if you happen to wake at midnight, cries of Fire and Stop thief; inns of court, with their learned air, and halls, and butteries, just like Cambridge colleges; old book-stalls, Jeremy Taylors, Burtons on Melancholy, and Religio Medicis on every stall. These are thy pleasures, O London with-the-many-sins. O City abounding in whores, for these may Keswick and her giant brood go hang!

C. L.

❖

TO WILLIAM GODWIN

[No date: ? 4th December 1800.]

DEAR SIR,

I send this speedily after the heels of Cooper (O! the dainty expression) to say that Mary is obliged to stay at home on Sunday to receive a female friend, from whom I am equally glad to escape. So that we shall be by ourselves. I write, because it may make *some* difference in your marketing, &c.   **C. L.**

Thursday Morning.

I am sorry to put you to the expense of twopence postage. But I calculate thus: if Mary comes she will

eat Beef 2 plates, . .	4d.
Batter Pudding 1 do. . .	2d.
Beer, a pint, ...	2d.
Wine, 3 glasses, . . .	11d. I drink no wine!
Chesnuts, after dinner, . .	2d.
Tea and supper at moderate calculation, ...	9d.

                              2s. 6d.

From which deduct   2d. postage

                              2s. 4d.

You are a clear gainer by her not coming.

Thursday Morning.

❖

TO WILLIAM WORDSWORTH

[P.M. 30th January 1801.]

Thanks for your Letter and Present. I had already borrowed your second volume. What most please me are, the Song of Lucy. . . . *Simon's sickly daughter* in the Sexton made me *cry*. Next to these are the description of the continuous Echoes in the story of Joanna's laugh, where the mountains and all the scenery absolutely seem alive—and that fine Shakesperian character of the Happy Man, in the Brothers,

> ————that creeps about the fields,
> Following his fancies by the hour, to bring
> Tears down his cheek, or solitary smiles
> Into his face, *until the Setting Sun*
> *Write Fool upon his forehead.*

I will mention one more: the delicate and curious feeling
in the wish for the Cumberland Beggar, that he may
have about him the melody of Birds, altho' he hear
them not. Here the mind knowingly passes a fiction
upon herself, first substituting her own feelings for the
Beggar's, and, in the same breath detecting the fallacy,
will not part with the wish.

The Poet's Epitaph is disfigured, to my taste by the
vulgar satire upon parsons and lawyers in the beginning, and the coarse epithet of pin point in the 6th
stanza. All the rest is eminently good, and your own. I
will just add that it appears to me a fault in the Beggar, that the instructions conveyed in it are too direct
and like a lecture: they don't slide into the mind of the
reader, while he is imagining no such matter. An intelligent reader finds a sort of insult in being told, I
will teach you how to think upon this subject. This
fault, if I am right, is in a ten-thousandth worse degree
to be found in Sterne and many many novelists & modern poets, who continually put a sign post up to shew
where you are to feel. They set out with assuming their
readers to be stupid. Very different from Robinson
Crusoe, the Vicar of Wakefield, Roderick Random, and
other beautiful bare narratives. There is implied an un-
written compact between Author and reader; I will tell
you a story, and I suppose you will understand it. Modern novels "St. Leons" and the like are full of such flowers as these "Let not my reader suppose," "Imagine, *if*
you can"—modest!—&c.—I will here have done with
praise and blame. I have written so much, only that you

may not think I have passed over your book without observation.

I am sorry that Coleridge has christened his Ancient Marinere "a poet's Reverie"—it is as bad as Bottom the Weaver's declaration that he is not a Lion but only the scenical representation of a Lion. What new idea is gained by this Title, but one subversive of all credit, which the tale should force upon us, of its truth? For me, I was never so affected with any human Tale. After first reading it, I was totally possessed with it for many days.

I dislike all the miraculous part of it, but the feelings of the man under the operation of such scenery dragged me along like Tom Piper's magic whistle. I totally differ from your idea that the Marinere should have had a character and profession. This is a Beauty in Gulliver's Travels, where the mind is kept in a placid state of little wonderments; but the Ancient Marinere undergoes such Trials, as overwhelm and bury all individuality or memory of what he was, like the state of a man in a Bad dream, one terrible peculiarity of which is: that all consciousness of personality is gone. Your other observation is I think as well a little unfounded: the Marinere from being conversant in supernatural events *has* acquired a supernatural and strange cast of *phrase*, eye, appearance, &c. which frighten the wedding guest.

You will excuse my remarks, because I am hurt and vexed that you should think it necessary, with a prose apology, to open the eyes of dead men that cannot see. To sum up a general opinion of the second vol.—I do not feel any one poem in it so forcibly as the Ancient Marinere, the Mad Mother, and the Lines at Tintern Abbey in the first.

I could, too, have wished the Critical preface had appeared in a separate treatise. All its dogmas are true and just, and most of them new, *as* criticism. But they associate a *diminishing* idea with the Poems which follow, as having been written for *Experiment* on the public taste, more than having sprung (as they must have done) from living and daily circumstances.

I am prolix, because I am gratifyed in the opportunity of writing to you, and I don't well know when to leave off. I ought before this to have reply'd to your very kind invitation into Cumberland. With you and your Sister I could gang any where. But I am afraid whether I shall ever be able to afford so desperate a Journey. Separate from the pleasure of your company, I don't much care if I never see a mountain in my life.

I have passed all my days in London, until I have formed as many and intense local attachments, as any of you mountaineers can have done with dead nature. The Lighted shops of the Strand and Fleet Street, the innumerable trades, tradesmen and customers, coaches, waggons, playhouses, all the bustle and wickedness round about Covent Garden, the very women of the Town, the Watchmen, drunken scenes, rattles,—life awake, if you awake, at all hours of the night, the impossibility of being dull in Fleet Street, the crowds, the very dirt & mud, the Sun shining upon houses and pavements, the print shops, the old book stalls, parsons cheap'ning books, coffee houses, steams of soups from kitchens, the pantomimes, London itself a pantomime and a masquerade,—all these things work themselves into my mind and feed me, without a power of satiating me. The wonder of these sights impells me into night-walks about her crowded streets, and I often shed tears in the motley Strand from fulness of joy at so much Life.

All these emotions must be strange to you. So are your rural emotions to me. But consider, what must I have been doing all my life, not to have lent great portions of my heart with usury to such scenes?——

My attachments are all local, purely local. I have no passion (or have had none since I was in love, and then it was the spurious engendering of poetry & books) to groves and vallies. The rooms where I was born, the furniture which has been before my eyes all my life, a book case which has followed me about (like a faithful dog, only exceeding him in knowledge) wherever I have moved—old chairs, old tables, streets, squares, where I have sunned myself, my old school,—these are my mistresses. Have I not enough, without your mountains? I do not envy you. I should pity you, did I not know, that the Mind will make friends of anything. Your sun & moon and skys and hills & lakes affect me no more, or scarcely come to me in more venerable characters, than as a gilded room with tapestry and tapers, where I might live with handsome visible objects. I consider the clouds above me but as a roof, beautifully painted but unable to satisfy the mind, and at last, like the pictures of the apartment of a connoisseur, unable to afford him any longer a pleasure. So fading upon me, from disuse, have been the Beauties of Nature, as they have been confinedly called; so ever fresh & green and warm are all the inventions of men and assemblies of men in this great city. I should certainly have laughed with dear Joanna.

Give my kindest love, *and my sister's,* to D. & yourself and a kiss from me to little Barbara Lewthwaite.

C. LAMB.

Thank you for Liking my Play!! [1]

[1] *John Woodvil.*—J. M. B.

❖

TO THOMAS MANNING

[Dated at end: 15th February 1802.]

Not a sentence, not a syllable of Trismegistus, shall be lost through my neglect. I am his word-banker, his storekeeper of puns and syllogisms. You cannot conceive (and if Trismegistus cannot, no man can) the strange joy which I felt at the receipt of a letter from Paris. It seemed to give me a learned importance, which placed me above all who had not Parisian correspondents. Believe that I shall carefully husband every scrap, which will save you the trouble of memory, when you come back.

You cannot write things so trifling, let them only be about Paris, which I shall not treasure. In particular, I must have parallels of actors and actresses. I must be told if any building in Paris is at all comparable to St. Paul's, which, contrary to the usual mode of that part of our nature called admiration, I have looked up to with unfading wonder every morning at ten o'clock, ever since it has lain in my way to business. At noon I casually glance upon it, being hungry; and hunger has not much taste for the fine arts. Is any night-walk comparable to a walk from St. Paul's to Charing Cross, for lighting and paving, crowds going and coming without respite, the rattle of coaches and the cheerfulness of shops? Have you seen a man guillotined yet? is it as good as hanging? are the women *all* painted, and the men *all* monkeys? or are there not a *few* that look like *rational* of *both sexes*? Are you and the First Consul *thick*?

All this expense of ink I may fairly put you to, as

your letters will not be solely for my proper pleasure, but are to serve as memoranda and notices, helps for short memory, a kind of Rumfordising recollection, for yourself on your return. Your letter was just what a letter should be, crammed and very funny. Every part of it pleased me till you came to Paris; and your damn'd philosophical indolence or indifference stung me. You cannot stir from your rooms till you know the language! What the devil!—are men nothing but word-trumpets? are men all tongue and ear? have these creatures, that you and I profess to know *something about*, no faces, gestures, gabble: no folly, no absurdity, no induction of French education upon the abstract idea of men and women, no similitude nor dissimilitude to English! Why! thou damn'd Smell-fungus! your account of your landing and reception, and Bullen (I forget how you spell it—it was spelt my way in Harry the Eighth's time,) was exactly in that minute style which strong impressions INSPIRE (writing to a Frenchman, I write as a Frenchman would).

It appears to me as if I should die with joy at the first landing in a foreign country. It is the nearest pleasure, which a grown man can substitute for that unknown one, which he can never know—the pleasure of the first entrance into life from the womb. I dare say, in a short time, my habits would come back like a "stronger man" armed, and drive out that new pleasure; and I should soon sicken for known objects. Nothing has transpired here that seems to me of sufficient importance to send dry-shod over the water: but I suppose you will want to be told some news. The best and the worst to me is, that I have given up two guineas a week at the "Post," and regained my health and spirits, which were upon the wane. I grew sick, and Stuart unsatisfied. *Ludisti satis, tempus abire est;* I must cut closer, that's all.

In all this time I have done but one thing, which I reckon tolerable, and that I will transcribe, because it may give you pleasure, being a picture of *my* humours. You will find it in my last page. It absurdly is a first Number of a series, thus strangled in its birth.

More news! The Professor's Rib[1] has come out to be a damn'd disagreeable woman, so much so as to drive me and some more old cronies from his house. If a man will keep snakes in his house, he must not wonder if people are shy of coming to see him because of the *snakes*.

Mister Fell—or as you, with your usual facetiousness and drollery, call him, Mr. F+ll has stopped short in the middle of his play. Some *friend* has told him that it has not the least merit in it. Oh! that I had the rectifying of the Litany! I would put in a *libera nos* (*Scriptores videlicet*) *ab amicis!* That's all the news. *A propos* (is it pedantry, writing to a French man, to express myself sometimes by a French word, when an English one would not do as well? methinks, my thoughts fall naturally into it).——

Apropos, I think you wrong about my play. All the omissions are right. And the supplementary scene, in which Sandford narrates the manner in which his master is affected, is the best in the book. It stands where a hodge-podge of German puerilities used to stand. I insist upon it that you like that scene. Love me, love that scene.

I will now transcribe the "Londoner" (No. 1), and wind up all with affection and humble servant at the end. I write small in regard to your good eyesight.[2]

"What is all this about?" said Mrs. Shandy. "A story of a cock and a bull," said Yorick: and so it is; but Man-

---

[1] The second Mrs. Godwin.—J. M. B.
[2] Here the article found on page 316 was inserted.—J. M. B.

ning will take good-naturedly what *God will send him* across the water: only I hope he won't *shut* his *eyes,* and *open* his *mouth,* as the children say, for that is the way to *gape,* and not to *read.* Manning, continue your laudable purpose of making me your register. I will render back all your remarks; and *I, not you,* shall have received usury by having read them. In the mean time, may the great Spirit have you in his keeping, and preserve our Englishmen from the inoculation of frivolity and sin upon French earth.

Allons—or what is it you say, instead of *good-bye?*

Mary sends her kind remembrance, and covets the remarks equally with me.

C. LAMB.

❖

TO THOMAS MANNING

[*23rd April 1802.*]

MY DEAR MANNING,

Although something of the latest, and after two months' waiting, your letter was highly gratifying. Some parts want a little explication; for example, "the godlike face of the First Consul." *What god* does he most resemble? Mars, Bacchus, or Apollo? or the god Serapis who, flying (as Egyptian chronicles deliver) from the fury of the dog Anubis (the hieroglyph of an English mastiff), lighted on Monomotapa (or the land of apes), by some thought to be Old France, and there set up a tyranny, &c. Our London prints of him represent him gloomy and sulky, like an angry Jupiter. I hear that he is very small, even less than me, who am "less than the least of the Apostles," at least than they are painted in the Vatican. I envy you your access to this great man, much more than your séances and conversaziones, which I have a shrewd suspicion must be something dull.

What you assert concerning the actors of Paris, that they exceed our comedians, "bad as ours are," is *impossible*. In one sense it may be true, that their fine gentlemen, in what is called genteel comedy, may possibly be more brisk and *dégagé* than Mr. Caulfield or Mr. Whitfield; but have any of them the power to move *laughter in excess?* or can a Frenchman *laugh?* Can they batter at your judicious ribs till they *shake,* nothing loth to be so shaken? This is John Bull's criterion, and it shall be mine. You are Frenchified. Both your tastes and morals are corrupt and perverted. By-and-by you will come to assert, that Buonaparte is as great a general as the old Duke of Cumberland, and deny that one Englishman can beat three Frenchmen. Read "Henry the Fifth" to restore your orthodoxy.

All things continue at a stay-still in London. I cannot repay your new novelties with my stale reminiscences. Like the prodigal, I have spent my patrimony, and feed upon the superannuated chaff and dry husks of repentance; yet sometimes I remember with pleasure the hounds and horses, which I kept in the days of my prodigality. I find nothing new, nor anything that has so much of the gloss and dazzle of novelty, as may rebound in narrative, and cast a reflective glimmer across the channel.

Something I will say about people that you and I know. Fenwick is still in debt, and the Professor has not done making love to his new spouse. I think he never looks into an almanack, or he would have found by the calendar that the honeymoon was extinct a moon ago. Lloyd has written to me and names you. I think a letter from Maison Magnan (is that a person or a thing?)

would gratify him. G. Dyer is in love with an Ideot who loves a Doctor, who is incapable of loving anything but himself. A puzzling circle of perverse Providences! A maze as un-get-out-again-able as the House which Jack built. Southey is Secretary to the Chancellor of the Irish Exchequer; £400 a year. Stoddart is turned Doctor of Civil Law, and dwells in Doctor's Commons. I fear *his* commons are short, as they say.

Did I send you an epitaph I scribbled upon a poor girl who died at nineteen, a good girl and a pretty girl, and a clever girl, but strangely neglected by all her friends and kin?

> Under this cold marble stone
> Sleep the sad remains of one
> Who, when alive, by few or none
> Was loved, as loved she might have been,
> If she prosperous days had seen,
> Or had thriving been, I ween.
> Only this cold funeral stone
> Tells she was beloved by one,
> Who on the marble graves his moan.

Brief, and pretty, and tender, is it not? I send you this, being the only piece of poetry I have *done*, since the muses all went with T. M. to Paris. I have neither stuff in my brain, nor paper in my drawer, to write you a longer letter. Liquor and company and wicked tobacco a'nights, have quite dispericraniated me, as one may say; but you who spiritualise upon Champagne may continue to write long letters, and stuff 'em with amusement to the end. Too long they cannot be, any more than a codicil to a will which leaves me sundry parks and manors not specified in the deed. But don't be *two months* before you write again. These from merry old England, on the day of her valiant patron St. George.

C. LAMB.

❖

TO THOMAS MANNING

24th Sept., 1802, London.

MY DEAR MANNING,

Since the date of my last letter, I have been a traveller. A strong desire seized me of visiting remote regions. My first impulse was to go and see Paris. It was a trivial objection to my aspiring mind, that I did not understand a word of the language, since I certainly intend some time in my life to see Paris, and equally certainly never intend to learn the language; therefore that could be no objection. However, I am very glad I did not go, because you had left Paris (I see) before I could have set out. I believe, Stoddart promising to go with me another year prevented that plan. My next scheme, (for to my restless, ambitious mind London was become a bed of thorns) was to visit the far-famed Peak in Derbyshire, where the Devil sits, they say, without breeches. *This* my purer mind rejected as indelicate. And my final resolve was a tour to the Lakes.

I set out with Mary to Keswick, without giving Coleridge any notice; for my time being precious did not admit of it. He received us with all the hospitality in the world, and gave up his time to show us all the wonders of the country. He dwells upon a small hill by the side of Keswick, in a comfortable house, quite enveloped on all sides by a net of mountains: great floundering bears and monsters they seemed, all couchant and asleep. We got in in the evening, travelling in a post-chaise from Penrith, in the midst of a gorgeous sunshine, which transmuted all the mountains into colours, purple, &c. &c. We thought we had got into Fairy Land. But that went off (as it never came again—while we stayed we had no more fine sunsets); and we entered Coleridge's comfortable study just in the dusk, when the mountains were all dark with clouds upon their heads. Such an impression I never received from objects of sight before, nor do I suppose I can ever again. Glorious creatures, fine old fellows, Skiddaw, &c. I never shall forget ye, how ye lay about that night, like an intrenchment; gone to bed, as it seemed for the night, but promising that ye were to be seen in the morning.

Coleridge had got a blazing fire in his study; which is a large, antique, ill-shaped room, with an old-fashioned organ, never played upon, big enough for a church, shelves of scattered folios, an Æolian harp, and an old sofa, half-bed, &c. And all looking out upon the last fading view of Skiddaw and his broad-breasted brethren: what a night! Here we stayed three full weeks, in which time I visited Wordsworth's cottage, where we stayed a day or two with the Clarksons (good people and most hospitable, at whose house we tarried one day and night), and saw Lloyd. The Wordsworths were gone to Calais. They have since been in London and past much time with us: he is now gone into Yorkshire to be married to a girl of small fortune, but he is in expectation of augmenting his own in consequence of the death of Lord Lonsdale, who kept him out of his own in conformity with a plan my lord had taken up in early life of making everybody unhappy. So we have seen Keswick, Grasmere, Ambleside, Ulswater (where the Clarksons live), and a place at the other end of Ulswater—I forget the name—to which we travelled on a very sultry day, over the middle of Helvellyn.

We have clambered up to the top of Skiddaw, and I have waded up the bed of Lodore. In fine, I have satisfied myself, that there is such a thing as that which

tourists call *romantic*, which I very much suspected before: they make such a spluttering about it, and toss
their splendid epithets around them, till they give as dim
a light as at four o'clock next morning the lamps do after
an illumination. Mary was excessively tired, when she
got about half-way up Skiddaw, but we came to a cold
rill (than which nothing can be imagined more cold,
running over cold stones), and with the reinforcement
of a draught of cold water she surmounted it most man-
fully. Oh, its fine black head, and the bleak air atop of it,
with a prospect of mountains all about, and about,
making you giddy; and then Scotland afar off, and the
border countries so famous in song and ballad! It was
a day that will stand out, like a mountain, I am sure,
in my life. But I am returned (I have now been come
home near three weeks—I was a month out), and you
cannot conceive the degradation I felt at first, from being accustomed to wander free as air among mountains, and bathe in rivers without being controlled by
any one, to come home and *work*. I felt very *little*. I had
been dreaming I was a very great man.

But that is going off, and I find I shall conform in
time to that state of life to which it has pleased God to
call me. Besides, after all, Fleet-Street and the Strand
are better places to live in for good and all than among
Skiddaw. Still, I turn back to those great places where
I wandered about, participating in their greatness. After
all, I could not *live* in Skiddaw. I could spend a year—
two, three years—among them, but I must have a prospect of seeing Fleet-Street at the end of that time, or I
should mope and pine away, I know. Still, Skiddaw is a
fine creature.

My habits are changing, I think: *i.e.* from drunk to
sober. Whether I shall be happier or not remains to be
proved. I shall certainly be more happy in a morning;

but whether I shall not sacrifice the fat, and the marrow, and the kidneys, *i.e.* the night, the glorious caredrowning night, that heals all our wrongs, pours wine into our mortifications, changes the scene from indifferent and flat to bright and brilliant!—O Manning, if I should have formed a diabolical resolution, by the time you come to England, of not admitting any spirituous liquors into my house, will you be my guest on such shameworthy terms? Is life, with such limitations, worth trying? The truth is, that my liquors bring a nest of friendly harpies about my house, who consume me.

This is a pitiful tale to be read at St. Gothard; but it is just now nearest my heart. Fenwick is a ruined man. He is hiding himself from his creditors, and has sent his wife and children into the country. Fell, my other drunken companion (that has been: nam hic cæstus artemque repono), is turned editor of a "Naval Chronicle." Godwin (with a pitiful artificial wife) continues a steady friend, though the same facility does not remain of visiting him often. That Bitch has detached Marshall from his house, Marshall the man who went to sleep when the "Ancient Mariner" was reading: the old, steady, unalterable friend of the Professor. Holcroft is not yet come to town. I expect to see him, and will deliver your message. How I hate *this part* of a letter. Things come crowding in to say, and no room for 'em. Some things are too little to be told, *i.e.* to have a preference; some are too big and circumstantial. Thanks for yours, which was most delicious. Would I had been with you, benighted &c. I fear my head is turned with wandering. I shall never be the same acquiescent being. Farewell; write again quickly, for I shall not like to hazard a letter, not knowing where the fates have carried you. Farewell, my dear fellow.

C. Lamb.

❖

TO THOMAS MANNING

[Dated at end: *19th February 1803*.]

MY DEAR MANNING,

The general scope of your letter afforded no indications of insanity, but some particular points raised a
scruple. For God's sake don't think any more of "Independent Tartary." What have you to do among such
Ethiopians? Is there no *lineal descendant* of Prester
John?

Is the chair empty? Is the sword unswayed?—de-
pend upon 't they'll never make you their king, as long
as any branch of that great stock is remaining. I tremble
for your Christianity. They'll certainly circumcise you.
Read Sir John Mandevil's travels to cure you, or come
over to England. There is a Tartarman now exhibiting
at Exeter Change. Come and talk with him, and hear
what he says first. Indeed, he is no very favorable speci-
men of his Countrymen! But perhaps the best thing you
can do, is to *try* to get the idea out of your head. For
this purpose repeat to yourself every night, after you
have said your prayers, the words Independent Tartary,
Independent Tartary, two or three times, and associate
with them the *idea of oblivion* ('tis Hartley's method
with obstinate memories), or say, Independent, Independent, have I not already got an *Independence?* That
was a clever way of the old puritans—pun-divinity.

My dear friend, think what a sad pity it would be to
bury such *parts* in heathen countries, among nasty, un-
conversable, horse-belching, Tartar people! Some say,
they are Cannibals; and then conceive a Tartar-fellow
eating my friend, and adding the *cool malignity* of mus-

tard and vinegar! I am afraid 'tis the reading of Chaucer
has misled you; his foolish stories about Cambuscan and
the ring, and the horse of brass. Believe me, there's no
such things, 'tis all the poet's *invention;* but if there were
such *darling* things as old Chaucer sings, I would *up*
behind you on the Horse of Brass, and frisk off for
Prester John's Country. But these are all tales; a Horse
of Brass never flew, and a King's daughter never talked
with Birds! The Tartars, really, are a cold, insipid,
smouchey set. You'll be sadly moped (if you are not
eaten) among them.

Pray *try* and cure yourself. Take Hellebore (the
counsel is Horace's, 'twas none of my thought *originally*). Shave yourself oftener. Eat no saffron, for saf-
fron-eaters contract a terrible Tartar-like yellow. Pray,
to avoid the fiend. Eat nothing that gives the heart-
burn. *Shave the upper lip.* Go about like an European.
Read no books of voyages (they're nothing but lies):
only now and then a Romance, to keep the fancy *under.*
Above all, don't go to any sights of *wild beasts. That has
been your ruin.*

Accustom yourself to write familiar letters on common subjects to your friends in England, such as are
of a moderate understanding. And think about common
things more. There's your friend Holcroft now, has
written a play. You used to be fond of the drama. Nobody went to see it. Notwithstanding this, with an au-
dacity perfectly original, he faces the town down in a
preface, that they *did like* it very much. I have heard
a waspish punster say, "Sir, why did you not laugh at
my jest?" But for a man boldly to face me out with,
"Sir, I maintain it, you did laugh at my jest," is a little
too much. I have seen H. but once. He spoke of you
to me in honorable terms. H. seems to me to be drearily
dull. Godwin is dull, but then he has a dash of affecta-

tion, which smacks of the coxcomb, and your coxcombs
are always agreeable. I supped last night with Rickman,
and met a merry *natural* captain,[1] who pleases himself
vastly with once having made a Pun at Otaheite in the
O. language. 'Tis the same man who said Shakspeare
he liked, because he was so *much of the Gentleman*.
Rickman is a man "absolute in all numbers." I think I
may one day bring you acquainted, if you do not go to
Tartary first; for you'll never come back. Have a care,
my dear friend, of Anthropophagi! their stomachs are
always craving. But if you do go among [them] pray
contrive to *stink* as soon as you can that you may [? not]
hang a [? on] hand at the Butcher's. 'Tis terrible to be
weighed out for 5d. a-pound. To sit at table (the reverse of fishes in Holland), not as a guest, but as a meat.

God bless you: do come to England. Air and exercise
may do great things. Talk with some Minister. Why not
your father?

God dispose all for the best. I have discharged my
duty.

Your sincere fr[d],   C. LAMB.

❖

TO THOMAS MANNING

16 Mitre-court Buildings,
Saturday, 24th [i.e. 23rd] *Feb., 1805.*

DEAR MANNING,

We have executed your commissions. There was
nothing for you at the White Horse. I have been very
unwell since I saw you. A sad depression of spirits, a
most unaccountable nervousness; from which I have
been partially relieved by an odd accident. You knew

---

[1] James Burney (1750-1821), later admiral.—J. M. B.

Dick Hopkins, the swearing scullion of Caius? This fellow, by industry and agility, has thrust himself into the important situations (no sinecures, believe me) of cook to Trinity Hall and Caius College: and the generous creature has contrived with the greatest delicacy imaginable, to send me a present of Cambridge brawn.[1] What makes it the more extraordinary is, that the man never saw me in his life that I know of. I suppose he has *heard* of me. I did not immediately recognise the donor; but one of Richard's cards, which had accidentally fallen into the straw, detected him in a moment. Dick, you know, was always remarkable for flourishing. His card imports, that "orders (to wit, for brawn), from any part of England, Scotland, or Ireland will be duly executed," &c.

At first, I thought of declining the present; but Richard knew my blind side when he pitched upon brawn. 'Tis of all my hobbies the supreme in the eating way. He might have sent sops from the pan, skimmings, crumplets, chips, hog's lard, the tender brown judiciously scalped from a fillet of veal (dexterously replaced by a salamander), the tops of asparagus, fugitive livers, run-away gizzards of fowls, the eyes of martyred pigs, tender effusions of laxative woodcocks, the red spawn of lobsters, leverets' ears, and such pretty filchings common to cooks; but these had been ordinary presents, the everyday courtesies of dishwashers to their sweethearts.

Brawn was a noble thought. It is not every common gullet-fancier that can properly esteem it. It is like a picture of one of the choice old Italian masters. Its gusto

[1] Brawn, says Webster, is "a product made from chopped, edible parts of pig's head, feet, legs, and, sometimes, tongue." —J. M. B.

is of that hidden sort. As Wordsworth sings of a modest poet,—"you must love him, ere to you he will seem worthy of your love"; so brawn, you must taste it, ere to you it will seem to have any taste at all. But 'tis nuts to the adept: those that will send out their tongues and feelers to find it out. It will be wooed, and not unsought be won. Now, ham-essence, lobsters, turtle, such popular minions, absolutely *court you,* lay themselves out to strike you at first smack, like one of David's pictures (they call him *Darveed*), compared with the plain russet-coated wealth of a Titian or a Correggio, as I illustrated above. Such are the obvious glaring heathen virtues of a corporation dinner, compared with the reserved collegiate worth of brawn.

Do me the favour to leave off the business which you may be at present upon, and go immediately to the kitchens of Trinity and Caius, and make my most respectful compliments to Mr. Richard Hopkins, and assure him that his brawn is most excellent; and that I am moreover obliged to him for his innuendo about salt water and bran, which I shall not fail to improve. I leave it to you whether you shall choose to pay him the civility of asking him to dinner while you stay in Cambridge, or in whatever other way you may best like to show your gratitude to *my friend.* Richard Hopkins, considered in many points of view, is a very extraordinary character.

Adieu: I hope to see you to supper in London soon, where we will taste Richard's brawn, and drink his health in a cheerful but moderate cup. We have not many such men in any rank of life as Mr. R. Hopkins. Crisp the barber, of St. Mary's, was just such another. I wonder *he* never sent me any little token, some chesnuts, or a puff, or two pound of hair just to remember him by; gifts are like nails. Præsens ut absens, that is, your *Present* makes amends for your absence.

Yours,   C. Iamb.

❖

TO THOMAS MANNING

[Dated by W. C. Hazlitt: *27th July 1805*.]

DEAR ARCHIMEDES,

Things have gone on badly with thy ungeometrical friend; but they are on the turn. My old housekeeper has shown signs of convalescence, and will shortly resume the power of the keys, so I shan't be cheated of my tea and liquors. Wind in the west, which promotes tranquillity. Have leisure now to anticipate seeing thee again. Have been taking leave of tobacco in a rhyming address. Had thought *that vein* had long since closed up. But the L—d opened Sara's bag after years of unproduction. Find I can rhyme and reason too. Think of studying mathematics, to restrain the fire of my genius, which G. D. recommends. Have frequent bleedings at the nose, which shows plethoric. Maybe shall try the sea myself, that great scene of wonders. Got incredibly sober and regular; shave oftener, and hum a tune, to signify cheerfulness and gallantry.

Suddenly disposed to sleep, having taken a quart of pease with bacon and stout. Will not refuse Nature, who has done such things for me!

Nurse, don't call me unless Mr. Manning comes.—— What, the gentleman in spectacles? Yes.

Dormit.   C. L.

Saturday,
     Hot Noon.

❖

TO THOMAS MANNING

[P.M. 15th November 1805.]

DEAR MANNING,

Certainly you could not have called at all hours from two till ten, for we have been only out of an evening Monday and Tuesday in this week. But if you think you have, your thought shall go for the deed.

We did pray for you on Wednesday night. Oysters unusually luscious—pearls of extraordinary magnitude found in them. I have made bracelets of them—given them in clusters to Ladies. Last night we went out in despite, because you were not come at your hour.

This night we shall be at home, so shall we certainly both Sunday, Monday, Tuesday, and Wednesday. Take your choice, mind I don't say of one, but choose which evening you will not, and come the other four. Doors open at five o'clock. Shells forced about nine. Every gentleman smokes or not as he pleases. O! I forgot, bring the £10, for fear you should lose it.   C. L.

❖

TO WILLIAM HAZLITT

March 15, 1806.

DEAR H.,

I am a little surprised at no letter from you. This day week, to wit, Saturday, the 8th of March, 1806, I booked off by the Wem coach, Bull and Mouth Inn, directed to *you*, at the Rev. Mr. Hazlitt's, Wem, Shropshire, a parcel containing, besides a book, &c., a rare

print, which I take to be a Titian; begging the said
W. H. to acknowledge the receipt thereof; which he not
having done, I conclude the said parcel to be lying at
the inn, and may be lost; for which reason, lest you may
be a Wales-hunting at this instant, I have authorised
any of your family, whosoever first gets this, to open it,
that so precious a parcel may not moulder away for
want of looking after.

What do you in Shropshire when so many fine pictures are a-going, a-going every day in London? Monday I visit the Marquis of Lansdowne's, in Berkeley
Square. Catalogue 2s. 6d. Leonardos in plenty. Some
other day this week I go to see Sir Wm. Young's, in
Stratford Place. Hulse's, of Blackheath, are also to be
sold this month; and in May, the first private collection
in Europe, Wellbore Ellis Agar's. And there are you,
perverting Nature in lying landscapes, filched from old
rusty Titians, such as I can scrape up here to send you,
with an additament from Shropshire Nature thrown in
to make the whole look unnatural.

I am afraid of your mouth watering when I tell you
that Manning and I got into Angerstein's on Wednesday. *Mon Dieu!* such Claudes! Four Claudes bought
for more than £10,000 (those who talk of Wilson being equal to Claude are either mainly ignorant or stupid); one of these was perfectly miraculous. What colours short of *bona fide* sunbeams it could be painted in,
I am not earthly colourman enough to say; but I did
not think it had been in the possibility of things. Then,
a music-piece by Titian—a thousand-pound picture—
five figures standing behind a piano, the sixth playing;
none of the heads, as M. observed, indicating great men,
or affecting it, but so sweetly disposed; all leaning separate ways, but so easy—like a flock of some divine

shepherd; the colouring, like the economy of the picture, so sweet and harmonious—as good as Shakspeare's "Twelfth Night,"—*almost,* that is. It will give you a love of order, and cure you of restless, fidgetty passions for a week after—more musical than the music which it would, but cannot, yet in a manner *does,* show.

I have no room for the rest. Let me say, Angerstein sits in a room—his study (only that and the library are shown)—when he writes a common letter, as I am doing, surrounded with twenty pictures worth £60,000. What a luxury! Apicius and Heliogabalus, hide your diminished heads!

Yours, my dear painter,   C. LAMB.

❖

TO THOMAS MANNING

May 10, 1806.

MY DEAR MANNING,[1]

I didn't know what your going was till I shook a last fist with you, and then 'twas just like having shaken hands with a wretch on the fatal scaffold, and when you are down the ladder, you can never stretch out to him again. Mary says you are dead, and there's nothing to do but to leave it to time to do for us in the end what it always does for those who mourn for people in such a case. But she'll see by your letter you are not quite dead. A little kicking and agony and then——. Martin Burney[2] *took me out* a walking that evening, and we talked of Mister Manning; and then I came home and

[1] Manning had sailed for China; he returned to England in 1817. —J. M. B.
[2] Son of Captain James Burney.—J. M. B.

smoked for you; and at twelve o'Clock came home Mary and Monkey Louisa from the play, and there was more talk and more smoking, and they all seemed first-rate characters, because they knew a certain person. But what's the use of talking about 'em? By the time you'll have made your escape from the Kalmuks, you'll have staid so long I shall never be able to bring to your mind who Mary was, who will have died about a year before, nor who the Holcrofts were! Me perhaps you will mistake for Phillips, or confound me with Mr. Daw, because you saw us together.

Mary (whom you seem to remember yet) is not quite easy that she had not a formal parting from you. I wish it had so happened. But you must bring her a token, a shawl or something, and remember a sprightly little Mandarin for our mantle-piece, as a companion to the Child I am going to purchase at the Museum. She says you saw her writings about the other day, and she wishes you should know what they are. She is doing for Godwin's bookseller twenty of Shakspear's plays, to be made into Children's tales. Six are already done by her, to wit, "The Tempest," "Winter's Tale," "Midsummer Night," "Much Ado," "Two Gentlemen of Verona," and "Cymbeline": "The Merchant of Venice" is in forwardness. I have done "Othello" and "Macbeth," and mean to do all the tragedies. I think it will be popular among the little people. Besides money. It is to bring in 60 guineas. Mary has done them capitally, I think you'd think.

These are the humble amusements we propose, while you are gone to plant the cross of Christ among barbarous Pagan anthropophagi. Quam homo homini præstat! but then, perhaps, you'll get murder'd, and we shall die in our beds with a fair literary reputation. Be sure, if you see any of those people whose heads do grow beneath their shoulders, that you make a draught of them. It will be very curious.

O Manning, I am serious to sinking almost, when I think that all those evenings, which you have made so pleasant, are gone perhaps for ever. Four years you talk of, maybe ten, and you may come back and find such alterations! Some circumstance may grow up to you or to me, that may be a bar to the return of any such intimacy. I daresay all this is Hum, and that all will come back; but indeed we die many deaths before we die, and I am almost sick when I think that such a hold as I had of you is gone. I have friends, but some of 'em are changed. Marriage, or some circumstance, rises up to make them not the same. But I felt sure of you. And that last token you gave me of expressing a wish to have my name joined with yours, you know not how it affected me: like a legacy.

God bless you in every way you can form a wish. May He give you health, and safety, and the accomplishment of all your objects, and return you again to us, to gladden some fireside or other (I suppose we shall be moved from the Temple). I will nurse the remembrance of your steadiness and quiet, which used to infuse something like itself into our nervous minds. Mary called you our ventilator. Farewell, and take her best wishes and mine.

One thing more. When you get to Canton, you will most likely see a young friend of mine, Inspector of Teas, named Ball. He is a very good fellow and I should like to have my name talked of in China. Give my kind remembrances to the same Ball.

Good bye.   C. L.

I have made strict inquiries through my friend Thompson as to your affairs with the Comp^y. If there had been a committee yesterday an order would have been sent to the captain to draw on them for your passage money, but there was no Committee. But in the secretary's orders to receive you on board, it was specified that the Company would defray your passage, all the orders about you to the super-cargoes are certainly in your ship. Here I will manage anything you may want done. What can I add but take care of yourself. We drink tea with the Holcrofts tomorrow.

[Addressed] Mr. Manning, Passenger on Board the *Thames*, East Indiaman, Portsmouth.

❖

TO WILLIAM WORDSWORTH

[P.M. 26th June 1806.]

DEAR WORDSWORTH,

We got the six pounds safe in your sister's letters —are pleased, you may be sure, with the good news of Mrs. W.—hope all is well over by this time. "A fine boy! —have you any more? one more and a girl—poor copies of me," vide Mr. H. a farce which the Proprietors have done me the honor—but I will set down Mr. Wroughton's own words. N.B. the ensuing letter was sent in answer to one which I wrote begging to know if my piece had any chance, as I might make alterations, &c. I writing on the Monday, there comes this letter on the Wednesday. Attend.

(*Copy of a Letter from Mr. R^d. Wroughton*)
Sir, Your Piece of Mr. H— I am desired to say, is accepted at Drury Lane Theatre, by the Proprietors, and, if agreeable to you, will be brought forwards when the proper oppor-

tunity serves—the Piece shall be sent to you for your Alterations in the course of a few days, as the same is not in my
Hands but with the Proprietors.

(dated)   I am Sir,
66 Gower St.,   Your obedient ser*.,
Wednesday   R*. WROUGHTON.
June 11, 1806.

On the following Sunday Mr. Tobin comes. The scent
of a manager's letter brought him. He would have gone
further any day on such a business. I read the letter to
him. He deems it authentic and peremptory. Our conversation naturally fell upon pieces—different sorts of
pieces—what is the best way of offering a piece—how
far the caprice of managers is an obstacle in the way of
a piece—how to judge of the merits of a piece—how
long a piece may remain in the hands of the managers
before it is acted—and my piece—and your piece—
and my poor brother's piece—my poor brother was all
his life endeavouring to get a piece accepted—

I am not sure that when *my poor Brother* bequeathed
the care of his pieces to Mr. James Tobin he did not
therein convey a legacy which in some measure molli-
fied the otherwise first stupefactions of grief. It can't be
expected that the present Earl Nelson passes all this
time in watering the laurels of the Admiral with Right
Reverend Tears. Certainly he steals a fine day now and
then to plot how to lay out the grounds and mansion
at Burnham most suitably to the late Earl's taste, if he
had lived, and how to spend the hundred thousand
pound parliament has given him in erecting some little
neat monument to his memory.

MR. H. I wrote that in mere wantonness of triumph.
Have nothing more to say about it. The Managers I
thank my stars have decided its merits for ever. They

are the best judges of pieces, and it would be insensible
in me to affect a false modesty after the very flattering
letter which I have received and the ample—

I think this will be as good a pattern for Orders as I
can think on. A little thin flowery border round, neat not
gaudy, and the Drury Lane Apollo with the harp at the
top. Or shall I have no Apollo?—simply nothing? Or
perhaps the Comic Muse?

The same form, only I think without the Apollo, will
serve for the pit and galleries. I think it will be best to
write my name at full length; but then if I give away a
great many, that will be tedious. Perhaps *Ch. Lamb* will
do. BOXES now I think on it I'll have in Capitals. The
rest in a neat Italian hand. Or better perhaps, Boxes,
in old English character, like Madoc or Thalaba?

I suppose you know poor Mountague has lost his
wife. That has been the reason for my sending off all we
have got of yours separately. I thought it a bad time to
trouble him. The Tea 25 lb. in 5 5 lb. Papers, two
sheets to each, with the chocolate which we were afraid
Mrs. W. would want, comes in one Box and the Hats in
a small one. I booked them off last night by the Kendal
waggon. There comes with this letter (no, it comes a

day or two earlier) a Letter for you from the Doctor at
Malta, about Coleridge, just received. Nothing of certainty, you see, only that he is not at Malta. We supt
with the Clarksons one night—Mrs. Clarkson pretty well.
Mr. C. somewhat fidgety, but a good man. The Baby
has been on a visit to Mrs. Charlotte Smith, Novelist and
morals-trainer, but is returned. A ludicrous thought
struck me. These two Ladies have both, as you may
have *seen*, great bxttxms. I fancied upon their first meeting and salutation, while the Ladies were bowing and
kissing, the two bxttxms saluting and doing the honour
of a first meeting independently; as I have seen, or fancy
to have seen, when two great Ladies have met on a
country visit, their two housekeepers at the same instant
in the store-room saluting and doing equal courtesies in
separate formality.

Mary is just stuck fast in All's Well that Ends Well.
She complains of having to set forth so many female
characters in boy's clothes. She begins to think Shakspear must have wanted Imagination. I to encourage her,
for she often faints in the prosecution of her great work,
flatter her with telling her how well such a play and
such a play is done. But she is stuck fast and I have been
obliged to promise to assist her. To do this it will be necessary to leave off Tobacco. But I had some thoughts
of doing that before, for I sometimes think it does not
agree with me.

W. Hazlitt is in Town. I took him to see a very pretty
girl professedly, where there were two young girls—the
very head and sum of the Girlery was two young girls
—they neither laughed nor sneered nor giggled nor
whispered—but they were young girls—and he sat and
frowned blacker and blacker, indignant that there should
be such a thing as Youth and Beauty, till he tore me
away before supper in perfect misery and owned he

could not bear young girls. They drove him mad. So I took him home to my old Nurse, where he recover'd perfect tranquillity. Independent of this, and as I am not a young girl myself, he is a great acquisition to us. He is, rather imprudently, I think, printing a political pamphlet on his own account, and will have to pay for the paper, &c. The first duty of an Author, I take it, is never to pay anything. But non cuivis attigit adire Corinthum. The Managers I thank my stars have settled that question for me.

Yours truly,   C. LAMB.

❖

TO THOMAS MANNING

5th Dec., 1806.

Tuthill is at Crabtree's who has married Tuthill's sister.

MANNING,

Your letter dated Hottentots, August the what-was-it? came to hand. I can scarce hope that mine will have the same luck. China—Canton—bless us—how it strains the imagination and makes it ache! I write under another uncertainty, whether it can go tomorrow by a ship which I have just learned is going off direct to your part of the world, or whether the despatches may not be sealed up and this have to wait, for if it is detained here, it will grow staler in a fortnight than in a five months' voyage coming to you. It will be a point of conscience to send you none but bran-new news (the latest edition), which will but grow the better, like oranges, for a sea voyage. Oh, that you should be so many hemispheres off—if I speak incorrectly you can correct me—why, the simplest death or marriage that takes place here must be important to you as news in the old Bastile.

There's your friend Tuthill has got away from France —you remember France? and Tuthill?—ten-to-one but he writes by this post, if he don't get my note in time, apprising him of the vessel sailing. Know then that he has found means to obtain leave from Bonaparte without making use of any *incredible romantic pretences* as some have done, who never meant to fulfil them, to come home; and I have seen him here and at Holcroft's. I have likewise seen his wife, this elegant little French woman whose hair reaches to her heels—by the same token that Tom (Tommy H.) took the comb out of her head, not expecting the issue, and it fell down to the ground to his utter consternation, two ells long.

An't you glad about Tuthill? Now then be sorry for Holcroft, whose new play, called "The Vindictive Man," was damned about a fortnight since. It died in part of its own weakness, and in part for being choked up with bad actors. The two principal parts were destined to Mrs. Jordan and Mr. Bannister, but Mrs. J. has not come to terms with the managers, they have had some squabble, and Bannister shot some of his fingers off by the going off of a gun. So Miss Duncan had her part, and Mr. de Camp, a vulgar brother of Miss De Camp, took his. He is a fellow with the make of a jockey, and the air of a lamplighter. His part, the principal comic hope of the play, was most unluckily Goldfinch, taken out of the "Road to Ruin," not only the same character, but the identical Goldfinch—the same as Falstaff is in two plays of Shakspeare. As the devil of ill-luck would have it, half the audience did not know that H. had written it, but were displeased at his stealing from the "Road to Ruin"; and those who might have borne a gentlemanly coxcomb with his "That's your sort," "Go it"—such as Lewis is—did not relish the intolerable vulgarity and inanity of the idea stript of his manner. De Camp was hooted, more than hist, hooted and bellowed off the stage before the second act was finished, so that the remainder of his part was forced to be, with some violence to the play, omitted.

In addition to this, a whore was another principal character—a most unfortunate choice in this moral day. The audience were as scandalised as if you were to introduce such a personage to their private tea-tables. Besides, her action in the play was gross—wheedling an old man into marriage. But the mortal blunder of the play was that which, oddly enough, H. took pride in, and exultingly told me of the night before it came out, that there were no less than eleven principal characters in it, and I believe he meant of the men only, for the play-bill exprest as much, not reckoning one woman and one whore; and true it was, for Mr. Powell, Mr. Raymond, Mr. Bartlett, Mr. H. Siddons, Mr. Barrymore, &c. &c.,—to the number of eleven, had all parts equally prominent, and there was as much of them in quantity and rank as of the hero and heroine—and most of them gentlemen who seldom appear but as the hero's friend in a farce—for a minute or two—and here they all had their ten-minute speeches, and one of them gave the audience a serious account how he was now a lawyer but had been a poet, and then a long enumeration of the inconveniences of authorship, rascally booksellers, reviewers, &c.; which first set the audience a-gaping; but I have said enough. You will be so sorry, that you will not think the best of me for my detail; but news is news at Canton.

Poor H. I fear will feel the disappointment very seriously in a pecuniary light. From what I can learn he has

saved nothing. You and I were hoping one day that he
had; but I fear he has nothing but his pictures and books,
and a no very flourishing business, and to be obliged to
part with his long-necked Guido that hangs opposite as
you enter, and the game-piece that hangs in the back
drawing-room, and all those Vandykes, &c.! God should
temper the wind to the shorn connoisseur. I hope I need
not say to you, that I feel for the weather-beaten author
and for all his household.

I assure you his fate has soured a good deal the pleasure I should have otherwise taken in my own little farce
being accepted, and I hope about to be acted—it is in
rehearsal actually, and I expect it to come out next
week. It is kept a sort of secret, and the rehearsals have
gone on privately, lest by many folks knowing it, the
story should come out, which would infallibly damn it.
You remember I had sent it before you went. Wroughton read it, and was much pleased with it. I speedily got
an answer. I took it to make alterations, and lazily kept
it some months, then took courage and furbished it up
in a day or two and took it. In less than a fortnight I
heard the principal part was given to Elliston, who
liked it, and only wanted a prologue, which I have since
done and sent; and I had a note the day before yesterday
from the manager, Wroughton (bless his fat face—he
is not a bad actor in some things), to say that I should
be summoned to the rehearsal after the next, which
next was to be yesterday. I had no idea it was so forward. I have had no trouble, attended no reading or
rehearsal, made no interest; what a contrast to the usual
parade of authors! But it is peculiar to modesty to do all
things without noise or pomp! I have some suspicion it
will appear in public on Wednesday next, for W. says
in his note, it is so forward that if wanted it may come
out next week, and a new melo-drama is announced for

every day till then: and "a new farce is in rehearsal,"
is put up in the bills.

Now you'd like to know the subject. The title is "Mr.
H.," no more; how simple, how taking! A great H
sprawling over the play-bill and attracting eyes at every
corner. The story is a coxcomb appearing at Bath, vastly
rich—all the ladies dying for him—all bursting to know
who he is—but he goes by no other name than Mr. H.
—a curiosity like that of the dames of Strasburg about
the man with the great nose. But I won't tell you any
more about it. Yes, I will; but I can't give you an idea
how I have done it. I'll just tell you that after much
vehement admiration, when his true name comes out,
"Hogsflesh," all the women shun him, avoid him, and
not one can be found to change their name for him—
that's the idea—how flat it is here!—but how whimsical
in the farce! and only think how hard upon me it is that
the ship is despatched to-morrow, and my triumph cannot be ascertained till the Wednesday after—but all
China will ring of it by and by.

N.B. (But this is a secret). The Professor has got a
tragedy coming out with the young Roscius in it in
January next, as we say—January last it will be with
you—and though it is a profound secret now, as all his
affairs are, it cannot be much of one by the time you
read this. However, don't let it go any further. I understand there are dramatic exhibitions in China. One
would not like to be forestalled. Do you find in all this
stuff I have written anything like those feelings which
one should send my old adventuring friend, that is gone
to wander among Tartars and may never come again?
I don't—but your going away, and all about you, is a
threadbare topic. I have worn it out with thinking—it
has come to me when I have been dull with anything,
till my sadness has seemed more to have come from it

than to have introduced it. I want you, you don't know how much—but if I had you here in my European garret, we should but talk over such stuff as I have written—so—.

Those "Tales from Shakespear" are near coming out, and Mary has begun a new work. Mr. Dawe is turned author: he has been in such a way lately—Dawe the painter, I mean—he sits and stands about at Holcroft's and says nothing—then sighs and leans his head on his hand. I took him to be in love—but it seems he was only meditating a work,—"The Life of Morland,"—the young man is not used to composition. Rickman and Captain Burney are well; they assemble at my house pretty regularly of a Wednesday—a new institution. Like other great men I have a public day, cribbage and pipes, with Phillips and noisy Martin.

Good Heaven! what a bit only I've got left! How shall I squeeze all I know into this morsel! Coleridge is come home, and is going to turn lecturer on taste at the Royal Institution. I shall get £200 from the theatre if "Mr. H." has a good run, and I hope £100 for the copyright. Nothing if it fails; and there never was a more ticklish thing. The whole depends on the manner in which the name is brought out, which I value myself on, as a chef-d'œuvre. How the paper grows less and less! In less than two minutes I shall cease to talk to you, and you may rave to the Great Wall of China. N.B. Is there such a wall? Is it as big as Old London Wall by Bedlam? Have you met with a friend of mine, named Ball, at Canton?—if you are acquainted, remember me kindly to him. Amongst many queer cattle I have and do meet with at the India Ho. I always liked his behaviour. Tell him his friend Evans &c. are well. Woodruff not dead yet. May-be, you'll think I have not said enough of Tuthill and the Holcrofts. Tuthill is a noble fellow, as far as

I can judge. The Holcrofts bear their disappointment pretty well, but indeed they are sadly mortified. Mrs. H. is cast down. It was well, if it were but on this account, that Tuthill is come home. N.B. If my little thing don't succeed, I shall easily survive, having, as it were, compared to H.'s venture, but a sixteenth in the lottery. Mary and I are to sit next the orchestra in the pit, next the tweedledees. She remembers you. You are more to us than five hundred farces, clappings, &c.

Come back one day.

C. LAMB.

❖

TO WILLIAM WORDSWORTH

[Dated at end: *11th December* (*1806*).]

Mary's Love to all of you—I wouldn't let her write—

DEAR WORDSWORTH,

Mr. H. came out last night and failed. I had many fears; the subject was not susbtantial enough. John Bull must have solider fare than a *Letter*. We are pretty stout about it, have had plenty of condoling friends, but after all, we had rather it should have succeeded. You will see the Prologue in most of the Morning Papers. It was received with such shouts as I never witness'd to a Prologue. It was attempted to be encored. How hard! a thing I did merely as a task, because it was wanted—and set no great store by; and Mr. H—— !!

The quantity of friends we had in the house, my brother and I being in Public Offices, &c. was astonishing —but they yielded at length to a few hisses. A hundred hisses—damn the word, I write it like kisses—how different—a hundred hisses outweigh a 1000 Claps. The former come more directly from the Heart—Well, 'tis withdrawn and there is an end.

Better Luck to us—— C. L.

11 Dec.—(turn over).

P.S. Pray when any of you write to the Clarksons, give our kind Loves, and say we shall not be able to come and see them at Xmas—as I shall have but a day or two,—and tell them we bear our mortification pretty well.

❖

TO THOMAS MANNING

Jan. 2nd, 1810.

Mary sends her love.

DEAR MANNING,

When I last wrote to you, I was in lodgings. I am now in chambers, No. 4, Inner Temple Lane, where I should be happy to see you any evening. Bring any of your friends, the Mandarins, with you. I have two sitting-rooms: I call them so *par excellence*, for you may stand, or loll, or lean, or try any posture in them; but they are best for sitting; not squatting down Japanese fashion, but the more decorous use of the posteriors which European usage has consecrated. I have two of these rooms on the third floor, and five sleeping, cooking, &c., rooms, on the fourth floor. In my best room is a choice collection of the works of Hogarth, an English painter of some humour. In my next best are shelves containing a small but well-chosen library. My best room commands a court, in which there are trees and a pump, the water of which is excellent—cold with brandy, and not very insipid without. Here I hope to set up my rest, and not quit till Mr. Powell, the undertaker, gives me notice that I may have possession of my last lodging. He lets lodgings for single gentlemen.

I sent you a parcel of books by my last, to give you some idea of the state of European literature. There comes with this two volumes, done up as letters, of minor poetry, a sequel to "Mrs. Leicester"; the best you may suppose mine; the next best are my coadjutor's; you may amuse yourself in guessing them out; but I must tell you mine are but one-third in quantity of the whole. So much for a very delicate subject. It is hard to speak of one's self, &c. Holcroft had finished his life when I wrote to you, and Hazlitt has since finished his life— I do not mean his own life, but he has finished a life of Holcroft, which is going to press. Tuthill is Dr. Tuthill. I continue Mr. Lamb. I have published a little book for children on titles of honour: and to give them some idea of the difference of rank and gradual rising, I have made a little scale, supposing myself to receive the following various accessions of dignity from the king, who is the fountain of honour—As at first, 1, Mr. C. Lamb; 2, C. Lamb, Esq.; 3, Sir C Lamb, Bart.; 4, Baron Lamb of Stamford;[1] 5, Viscount Lamb; 6, Earl Lamb; 7, Marquis Lamb; 8, Duke Lamb. It would look like quibbling to carry it on further, and especially as it is not necessary for children to go beyond the ordinary titles of sub-regal dignity in our own country, otherwise I have sometimes in my dreams imagined myself still advancing, as 9th, King Lamb; 10th, Emperor Lamb; 11th, Pope Innocent, higher than which is nothing but the Lamb of God. Puns I have not made many (nor punch much), since the date of my last; one I cannot help relating.

[1] Where my family come from. I have chosen that if ever I should have my choice.—C. L.

A constable in Salisbury Cathedral was telling me that eight people dined at the top of the spire of the cathedral; upon which I remarked, that they must be very sharp-set. But in general I cultivate the reasoning part of my mind more than the imaginative. Do you know Kate *********? I am stuffed out so with eating turkey for dinner, and another turkey for supper yesterday (turkey in Europe and turkey in Asia), that I can't jog on.

It is New-Year here. That is, it was New-Year half a-year back, when I was writing this. Nothing puzzles me more than time and space, and yet nothing puzzles me less, for I never think about them. Miss Knap is turned midwife. Never having had a child herself, she can't draw any wrong analogies from her own case. Dr. Stoddart has had Twins. There was five shillings to pay the Nurse. Mrs. Godwin was impannelled on a jury of Matrons last Sessions. She saved a criminal's life by giving it as her opinion that ————. The Judge listened to her with the greatest deference. The Persian ambassador is the principal thing talked of now. I sent some people to see him worship the sun on Primrose Hill at half past six in the morning, 28th November; but he did not come, which makes me think the old fire-worshippers are a sect almost extinct in Persia. Have you trampled on the Cross yet? The Persian ambassador's name is Shaw Ali Mirza. The common people call him Shaw Nonsense.

While I think of it, I have put three letters besides my own three into the India post for you, from your brother, sister, and some gentleman whose name I forget. Will they, have they, did they, come safe? The distance you are at, cuts up tenses by the root. I think you said you did not know Kate *********. I express her by nine stars, though she is but one, but if ever one star

differed from another in glory——. You must have seen
her at her father's. Try and remember her.

Coleridge is bringing out a paper in weekly numbers,
called the "Friend," which I would send, if I could; but
the difficulty I had in getting the packets of books out
to you before deters me; and you'll want something new
to read when you come home. It is chiefly intended to
puff off Wordsworth's poetry; but there are some noble
things in it by the by. Except Kate, I have had no vision
of excellence this year, and she passed by like the queen
on her coronation day; you don't know whether you
saw her or not. Kate is fifteen: I go about moping, and
sing the old pathetic ballad I used to like in my youth—

> She's sweet Fifteen,
> I'm *one year more*.

Mrs. Bland sung it in boy's clothes the first time I
heard it. I sometimes think the lower notes in my voice
are like Mrs. Bland's. That glorious singer Braham, one
of my lights, is fled. He was for a season. He was a rare
composition of the Jew, the gentleman, and the angel,
yet all these elements mixed up so kindly in him, that
you could not tell which predominated; but he is gone,
and one Phillips is engaged instead. Kate is vanished,
but Miss B ****** is always to be met with!

> Queens drop away, while blue-legg'd Maukin thrives;
> And courtly Mildred dies while country Madge survives.

That is not my poetry, but Quarles's; but haven't you
observed that the rarest things are the least obvious?
Don't show anybody the names in this letter. I write
confidentially, and wish this letter to be considered as
private. Hazlitt has written a *grammar* for Godwin;
Godwin sells it bound up with a treatise of his own on
language, but the *grey mare is the better horse*. I don't

allude to Mrs. Godwin, but to the word *grammar*, which comes near to *grey mare*, if you observe, in sound. That figure is called paranomasia in Greek. I am sometimes happy in it. An old woman begged of me for charity. "Ah! sir," said she, "I have seen better days;" "So have I, good woman," I replied; but I meant literally, days not so rainy and overcast as that on which she begged: she meant more prosperous days. Mr. Dawe is made associate of the Royal Academy. By what law of association I can't guess. Mrs. Holcroft, Miss Holcroft, Mr. and Mrs. Godwin, Mr. and Mrs. Hazlitt, Mrs. Martin and Louisa, Mrs. Lum, Capt. Burney, Mrs. Burney, Martin Burney, Mr. Rickman, Mrs. Rickman, Dr. Stoddart, William Dollin, Mr. Thompson, Mr. and Mrs. Norris, Mr. Fenwick, Mrs. Fenwick, Miss Fenwick, a man that saw you at our house one day, and a lady that heard me speak of you; Mrs. Buffam that heard Hazlitt mention you, Dr. Tuthill, Mrs. Tuthill, Colonel Harwood, Mrs. Harwood, Mr. Collier, Mrs. Collier, Mr. Sutton, Nurse, Mr. Fell, Mrs. Fell, Mr. Marshall, are very well, and occasionally inquire after you. Mary sends her love

[*Rest cut away.*]

❖

TO DOROTHY WORDSWORTH

13 Nov. 1810.

Mary has left a little space for me to fill up with nonsense, as the Geographers used to cram monsters in the voids of their maps & call it Terra Incognita. She has told you how she has taken to water, like a hungry otter. I too limp after her in lame imitation, but it goes against me a little *at first*. I have been *aquavorous* now for full four days, and it seems a moon. I am full of cramps &

rheumatisms, and cold internally so that fire won't warm me, yet I bear all for virtues sake. Must I then leave you, Gin, Rum, Brandy, Aqua Vitæ—pleasant jolly fellows —Damn Temperance and them that first invented it, some Anti Noahite.

Coleridge has powdered his head, and looks like Bacchus, Bacchus ever sleek and young. He is going to turn sober, but his Clock has not struck yet, meantime he pours down goblet after goblet, the 2d to see where the 1st is gone, the 3d to see no harm happens to the second, a fourth to say there's another coming, and a 5th to say he's not sure he's the last. William Henshaw is dead. He died yesterday, aged 56. It was but a twelve-month or so back that his Father, an ancient Gunsmith & my Godfather, sounded me as to my willingness to be guardian to this William in case of his (the old man's) death. William had three times broke in business, twice in England, once in t'other Hemisphere. He returned from America a sot & hath liquidated all debts. What a hopeful ward I am rid of. Ætatis 56. I must have taken care of his morals, seen that he did not form imprudent connections, given my consent before he could have married &c. From all which the stroke of death hath relieved me.

Mrs. Reynolds is the name of the Lady to whom I will remember you to-morrow. Farewell. Wish me strength to continue. I've been eating jugg'd Hare. The toast & water makes me quite sick.

C. LAMB.

❖

TO WILLIAM HAZLITT

2 Oct. 1811.

DEAR HAZLITT,

I cannot help accompanying my sister's congratulations to Sarah with some of my own to you on this happy occasion of a man child being born—

Delighted Fancy already sees him some future rich alderman or opulent merchant; painting perhaps a little in his leisure hours for amusement like the late H. Bunbury, Esq.

Pray, are the Winterslow Estates entailed? I am afraid lest the young dog when he grows up should cut down the woods, and leave no groves for widows to take their lonesome solace in. The Wem Estate of course can only devolve on him, in case of your brother leaving no male issue.

Well, my blessing and heaven's be upon him, and make him like his father, with something a better temper and a smoother head of hair, and then all the men and women must love him.

Martin and the Card-boys join in congratulations. Love to Sarah. Sorry we are not within Caudle-shot.

C. LAMB.

If the widow be assistant on this notable occasion, give our due respects and kind remembrances to her.

❖

TO ROBERT SOUTHEY

Aug. 9th, 1815.

DEAR SOUTHEY,

Robinson is not on the circuit, as I erroneously stated
in a letter to W. W., which travels with this, but is gone
to Brussels, Ostend, Ghent, &c. But his friends the Col-
liers, whom I consulted respecting your friend's fate,
remember to have heard him say, that Father Pardo had
effected his escape (the cunning greasy rogue), and to
the best of their belief is at present in Paris. To my thinking, it is a small matter whether there be one fat friar
more or less in the world. I have rather a taste for clerical executions, imbibed from early recollections of the
fate of the excellent Dodd. I hear Bonaparte has sued
his habeas corpus, and the twelve judges are now sitting
upon it at the Rolls.

Your boute-feu (bonfire) must be excellent of its
kind. Poet Settle presided at the last great thing of the
kind in London, when the pope was burnt in form. Do
you provide any verses on this occasion? Your fear for
Hartley's intellectuals is just and rational. Could not the
Chancellor be petitioned to remove him? His lordship
took Mr. Betty[1] from under the paternal wing. I think
at least he should go through a course of matter-of-fact
with some sober man after the mysteries. Could not he
spend a week at Poole's before he goes back to Oxford?
Tobin is dead. But there is a man in my office, a Mr.
Hedges, who proses it away from morning to night, and
never gets beyond corporal and material verities. He'd

[1] William Henry West Betty (1791-1874), famous as a child
actor in Shakespearean roles.—J. M. B.

get these crack-brain metaphysics out of the young gentleman's head as soon as any one I know.

When I can't sleep o' nights, I imagine a dialogue with Mr. H. upon any given subject, and go prosing on in fancy with him, till I either laugh or fall asleep. I have literally found it answer. I am going to stand godfather; I don't like the business; I cannot muster up decorum for these occasions; I shall certainly disgrace the font. I was at Hazlitt's marriage, and had like to have been turned out several times during the ceremony. Any thing awful makes me laugh. I misbehaved once at a funeral. Yet I can read about these ceremonies with pious and proper feelings. The realities of life only seem the mockeries. I fear I must get cured along with Hartley, if not too inveterate. Don't you think Louis the Desirable is in a sort of quandary?

After all, Bonaparte is a fine fellow, as my barber says, and I should not mind standing bareheaded at his table to do him service in his fall. They should have given him Hampton Court or Kensington, with a tether extending forty miles round London. Qu. Would not the people have ejected the Brunswicks some day in his favour? Well, we shall see.

C. LAMB.

❖

TO SARAH HUTCHINSON[1]

Thursday 19 Oct. 1815.

My brother is gone to Paris.

DEAR MISS H.,

I am forced to be the replier to your Letter, for Mary

---

[1] The sister of Mrs. William Wordsworth.—J. M. B.

has been ill and gone from home these five weeks yesterday. She has left me very lonely and very miserable.
I stroll about, but there is no rest but at one's own fireside, and there is no rest for me there now. I look forward to the worse half being past, and keep up as well
as I can. She has begun to show some favorable symptoms. The return of her disorder has been frightfully
soon this time, with scarce a six month's interval. I am
almost afraid my worry of spirits about the E. I. House
was partly the cause of her illness, but one always imputes it to the cause next at hand; more probably it
comes from some cause we have no control over or conjecture of. It cuts sad great slices out of the time, the
little time we shall have to live together.

I don't know but the recurrence of these illnesses
might help me to sustain her death better than if we
had had no partial separations. But I won't talk of death.
I will imagine us immortal, or forget that we are otherwise; by God's blessing in a few weeks we may be making our meal together, or sitting in the front row of the
Pit at Drury Lane, or taking our evening walk past the
theatres, to look at the outside of them at least, if not
to be tempted in. Then we forget we are assailable, we
are strong for the time as rocks, the wind is tempered to
the shorn Lambs. Poor C. Lloyd, and poor Priscilla, I
feel I hardly feel enough for him, my own calamities
press about me and involve me in a thick integument
not to be reached at by other folks' misfortunes. But
I feel all I can, and all the kindness I can towards you
all. God bless you. I hear nothing from Coleridge.

Yours truly   C. LAMB.

❖

Dec. 25th, 1815.

DEAR OLD FRIEND AND ABSENTEE,

This is Christmas-day 1815 with us; what it may be
with you I don't know, the 12th of June next year perhaps; and if it should be the consecrated season with
you, I don't see how you can keep it. You have no tur-
keys; you would not desecrate the festival by offering up
a withered Chinese bantam, instead of the savoury
grand Norfolcian holocaust, that smokes all around my
nostrils at this moment from a thousand firesides. Then
what puddings have you? Where will you get holly to
stick in your churches, or churches to stick your dried
tea-leaves (that must be the substitute) in? What me-
morials you can have of the holy time, I see not. A
chopped missionary or two may keep up the thin idea of
Lent and the wilderness; but what standing evidence
have you of the Nativity?—'tis our rosy-cheeked, home-
stalled divines, whose faces shine to the tune of *unto us
a child;* faces fragrant with the mince-pies of half a
century, that alone can authenticate the cheerful mystery—I feel.

I feel my bowels refreshed with the holy tide—my
zeal is great against the unedified heathen. Down with
the Pagodas—down with the idols—Ching-chong-fo
and his foolish priesthood! Come out of Babylon, O my
friend! for her time is come, and the child that is native, and the Proselyte of her gates, shall kindle and
smoke together! And in sober sense what makes you so
long from among us, Manning? You must not expect to
see the same England again which you left.

Empires have been overturned, crowns trodden into dust, the face of the western world quite changed: your friends have all got old—those you left blooming —myself (who am one of the few that remember you) those golden hairs which you recollect my taking a pride in, turned to silvery and grey. Mary has been dead and buried many years—she desired to be buried in the silk gown you sent her. Rickman, that you remember active and strong, now walks out supported by a servant-maid and a stick.

Martin Burney is a very old man. The other day an aged woman knocked at my door, and pretended to my acquaintance; it was long before I had the most distant cognition of her; but at last together we made her out to be Louisa, the daughter of Mrs. Topham, formerly Mrs. Morton, who had been Mrs. Reynolds, formerly Mrs. Kenney, whose first husand was Holcroft, the dramatic writer of the last century. St. Paul's Church is a heap of ruins; the Monument isn't half so high as you knew it, divers parts being successively taken down which the ravages of time had rendered dangerous; the horse at Charing Cross is gone, no one knows whither, —and all this has taken place while you have been settling whether Ho-hing-tong should be spelt with a —— or a ——.

For aught I see you had almost as well remain where you are, and not come like a Struldbug into a world where few were born when you went away. Scarce here and there one will be able to make out your face; all your opinions will be out of date, your jokes obsolete, your puns rejected with fastidiousness as wit of the last age. Your way of mathematics has already given way to a new method, which after all is I believe the old doctrine of Maclaurin, new-vamped up with what he borrowed of the negative quantity of fluxions from Euler.

Poor Godwin! I was passing his tomb the other day in Cripplegate churchyard. There are some verses upon it written by Miss Hayes, which if I thought good enough I would send you. He was one of those who would have hailed your return, not with boisterous shouts and clamours, but with the complacent gratulations of a philosopher anxious to promote knowledge as leading to happiness—but his systems and his theories are ten feet deep in Cripplegate mould. Coleridge is just dead, having lived just long enough to close the eyes of Wordsworth, who paid the debt to nature but a week or two before. Poor Col., but two days before he died he wrote to a bookseller proposing an epic poem on the "Wanderings of Cain," in twenty-four books. It is said he has left behind him more than forty thousand treatises in criticism and metaphysics, but few of them in a state of completion. They are now destined, perhaps, to wrap up spices. You see what mutations the busy hand of Time has produced, while you have consumed in foolish voluntary exile that time which might have gladdened your friends—benefited your country; but reproaches are useless. Gather up the wretched reliques, my friend, as fast as you can, and come to your old home. I will rub my eyes and try to recognise you. We will shake withered hands together, and talk of old things—of St. Mary's Church and the barber's opposite, where the young students in mathematics used to assemble. Poor Crisp, that kept it afterwards, set up a fruiterer's shop in Trumpington-street, and for aught I know, resides there still, for I saw the name up in the last journey I took there with my sister just before she died. I suppose you heard that I had left the India House, and gone into the Fishmongers' Almshouses over the bridge. I have a little cabin there, small and homely; but you shall be welcome to it. You like oysters, and to open them yourself; I'll get you some if you come in oyster time. Marshall, Godwin's old friend, is still alive, and talks of the faces you used to make.

Come as soon as you can. C. LAMB.

❖

TO THOMAS MANNING

Dec. 26th, 1815.

DEAR MANNING,

Following your brother's example, I have just ventured one letter to Canton, and am now hazarding another (not exactly a duplicate) to St. Helena. The first was full of unprobable romantic fictions, fitting the remoteness of the mission it goes upon; in the present I mean to confine myself nearer to truth as you come nearer home. A correspondence with the uttermost parts of the earth necessarily involves in it some heat of fancy; it sets the brain agoing; but I can think on the half-way house tranquilly. Your friends, then, are not all dead or grown forgetful of you through old age, as that lying letter asserted, anticipating rather what must happen if you kept tarrying on for ever on the skirts of creation, as there seemed a danger of your doing— but they are all tolerably well and in full and perfect comprehension of what is meant by Manning's coming home again.

Mrs. Kenney (ci-devant Holcroft) never let her tongue run riot more than in remembrances of you. Fanny expends herself in phrases that can only be justified by her romantic nature. Mary reserves a portion of your silk, not to be buried in (as the false nuncio asserts), but to make up spick and span into a bran new gown to wear when you come.

I am the same as when you knew me, almost to a surfeiting identity. This very night I am going to *leave off
tobacco!* Surely there must be some other world in which
this unconquerable purpose shall be realized. The soul
hath not her generous aspirings implanted in her in
vain. One that you knew, and I think the only one of
those friends we knew much of in common, has died
in earnest. Poor Priscilla, wife of Kit Wordsworth! Her
brother Robert is also dead, and several of the grown-up
brothers and sisters, in the compass of a very few years.
Death has not otherwise meddled much in families that
I know. Not but he has his damn'd eye upon us, and is
w[h]etting his infernal feathered dart every instant, as
you see him truly pictured in that impressive moral picture, "The good man at the hour of death."

I have in trust to put in the post four letters from
Diss, and one from Lynn, to St. Helena, which I hope
will accompany this safe, and one from Lynn, and the
one before spoken of from me, to Canton. But we all
hope that these latter may be waste paper. I don't
know why I have forborne writing so long. But it is
such a forlorn hope to send a scrap of paper straggling
over wide oceans. And yet I know when you come
home, I shall have you sitting before me at our fireside
just as if you had never been away. In such an instant
does the return of a person dissipate all the weight of
imaginary perplexity from distance of time and space!
I'll promise you good oysters.

Cory is dead, that kept the shop opposite St. Dunstan's, but the tougher materials of the shop survive the
perishing frame of its keeper. Oysters continue to flourish there under as good auspices. Poor Cory! But if you
will absent yourself twenty years together, you must
not expect numerically the same population to congratulate your return which wetted the sea-beach with their

tears when you went away. Have you recovered the breathless stone-staring astonishment into which you must have been thrown upon learning at landing that an Emperor of France was living in St. Helena? What an event in the solitude of the seas! like finding a fish's bone at the top of Plinlimmon; but these things are nothing in our western world. Novelties cease to affect. Come and try what your presence can.

God bless you.—Your old friend,   C. LAMB.

❖

TO DOROTHY WORDSWORTH

[P.M. 21st November 1817.]

DEAR MISS WORDSWORTH,

Here we are, transplanted from our native soil. I thought we never could have been torn up from the Temple. Indeed it was an ugly wrench, but like a tooth, now 'tis out and I am easy. We never can strike root so deep in any other ground. This, where we are, is a light bit of gardener's mold, and if they take us up from it, it will cost no blood and groans like mandrakes pull'd up. We are in the individual spot I like best in all this great city. The theatres with all [*a few words cut away: Talfourd has "their noises. Covent Garden"*] dearer to me than any gardens of Alcinous, where we are morally sure of the earliest peas and 'sparagus. Bow Street, where the thieves are examined, within a few yards of us.

Mary had not been here four and twenty hours before she saw a Thief. She sits at the window working, and casually throwing out her eyes, she sees a concourse of people coming this way, with a constable to conduct the solemnity. These little incidents agreeably diversify

a female life. It is a delicate subject, but is Mr.
* * * really married? and has he found a gargle
to his mind? O how funny he did talk to me about
her in terms of such mild quiet whispering speculative profligacy. But did the animalcule and she crawl
over the rubric together, or did they not? Mary has
brought her part of this letter to an orthodox and loving
conclusion, which is very well, for I have no room for
pansies and remembrances. What a nice holyday I got
on Wednesday by favor of a princess dying.

[*A line and signature cut away.*]

❖

TO MRS. WILLIAM WORDSWORTH

18 feb. 1818. East India House.

(Mary shall send you all the *news*, which I find I
have left out.)

MY DEAR MRS. WORDSWORTH,

I have repeatedly taken pen in hand to answer your
kind letter. My sister should more properly have done
it, but she having failed, I consider myself answerable
for her debts. I am now trying to do it in the midst of
Commercial noises, and with a quill which seems more
ready to glide into arithmetical figures and names of
Goods, Cassia, Cardemoms, Aloes, Ginger, Tea, than
into kindly responses and friendly recollections.

The reason why I cannot write letters at home is, that
I am never alone. Plato's (I write to *W. W.* now) Plato's
double animal parted never longed [? more] to be reciprocally reunited in the system of its first creation,
than I sometimes do to be but for a moment single and
separate. Except my morning's walk to the office, which

is like treading on sands of gold for that reason, I am never so.

I cannot walk home from office but some officious friend offers his damn'd unwelcome courtesies to accompany me. All the morning I am pestered. I could sit and gravely cast up sums in great Books, or compare sum with sum, and write PAID against this and UNP'D against t'other, and yet reserve in some "corner of my mind" some darling thoughts all my own—faint memory of some passage in a Book—or the tone of an absent friend's Voice—a snatch of Miss Burrell's singing—a gleam of Fanny Kelly's divine plain face—The two operations might be going on at the same time without thwarting, as the sun's two motions (earth's I mean), or as I sometimes turn round till I am giddy, in my back parlour, while my sister is walking longitudinally in the front— or as the shoulder of veal twists round with the spit, while the smoke wreathes up the chimney—but there are a set of amateurs of the Belle Lettres—the gay science—who come to me as a sort of rendezvous, putting questions of criticism, of British Institutions, Lalla Rooks &c., what Coleridge said at the Lecture last night—who have the form of reading men, but, for any possible use Reading can be to them but to talk of, might as well have been Ante-Cadmeans born, or have lain sucking out the sense of an Egypt^n. hieroglyph as long as the Pyramids will last before they should find it.

These pests worrit me at business and in all its intervals, perplexing my accounts, poisoning my little salutary warming-time at the fire, puzzling my paragraphs if I take a newspaper, cramming in between my own free thoughts and a column of figures which had come to an amicable compromise but for them. Their noise ended, one of them, as I said, accompanys me home lest I should be solitary for a moment; he at length takes his

welcome leave at the door, up I go, mutton on table,
hungry as hunter, hope to forget my cares and bury
them in the agreeable abstraction of mastication, knock
at the door, in comes Mrs. Hazlitt, or M. Burney, or
Morgan, or Demogorgon, or my brother, or somebody,
to prevent my eating alone, a Process absolutely necessary to my poor wretched digestion.

O the pleasure of eating alone!—eating my dinner
alone! let me think of it. But in they come, and make it
absolutely necessary that I should open a bottle of
orange—for my meat turns into stone when any one
dines with me, if I have not wine—wine can mollify
stones. Then *that* wine turns into acidity, acerbity, mis-
anthropy, a hatred of my interrupters (God bless 'em!
I love some of 'em dearly), and with the hatred a still
greater aversion to their going away. Bad is the dead
sea they bring upon me, choaking and death-doing, but
worse is the deader dry sand they leave me on if they go
before bed time. Come never, I would say to these
spoilers of my dinner, but if you come, never go.

The fact is, this interruption does not happen very
often, but every time it comes by surprise that present
bane of my life, orange wine, with all its dreary stifling
consequences, follows. Evening Company I should always like had I any mornings, but I am saturated with
human faces (*divine* forsooth) and voices all the golden
morning, and five evenings in a week would be as much
as I should covet to be in company, but I assure you
that is a wonderful week in which I can get two, or one,
to myself. I am never C. L. but always C. L. and Co.

He, who thought it not good for man to be alone,
preserve me from the more prodigious monstrosity of
being never by myself. I forget bed time, but even
there these social frogs clamber up to annoy me. Once
a week, generally some singular evening that, being

alone, I go to bed at the hour I ought always to be abed, just close to my bedroom window, is the club room of a public house, where a set of singers, I take them to be chorus-singers of the two theatres (it must be *both of them*), begin their orgies. They are a set of fellows (as I conceive) who being limited by their talents to the burthen of the song at the play houses, in revenge have got the common popular airs by Bishop or some cheap composer arranged for choruses, that is, to be sung all in chorus. At least I never can catch any of the text of the plain song, nothing but the Babylonish choral howl at the tail on't. "That fury being quenchd" —the howl I mean—a curseder burden succeeds, of shouts and clapping and knocking of the table. At length over tasked nature drops under it and escapes for a few hours into the society of the sweet silent creatures of Dreams, which go away with mocks and mows at cockcrow. And then I think of the words Christobel's father used (bless me, I have dipt in the wrong ink) to say every morning by way of variety when he awoke— "Every knell, the Baron saith, Wakes us up to a world of death," or something like it.

All I mean by this senseless interrupted tale is that by my central situation I am a little over companied. Not that I have any animosity against the good creatures that are so anxious to drive away the Harpy solitude from me. I like 'em, and cards, and a chearful glass, but I mean merely to give you an idea between office confinement and after office society, how little time I can call my own. I mean only to draw a picture, not to make an inference. I would not that I know of have it otherwise. I only wish sometimes I could exchange some of my faces and voices for the faces and voices which a late visitation brought most welcome and carried away leaving regret, but more pleasure, even a kind of grati-

tude at being so often favored with that kind northern
visitation. My London faces and noises don't hear me—
I mean no disrespect—or I should explain myself that
instead of their return 220 times a year and the return of W. W. &c. 7 times in 104 weeks, some more
equal distribution might be found. I have scarce room
to put in Mary's kind love and my poor name.

Ch. Lamb.

This to be read last.

W. H. goes on lecturing against W. W. and making
copious use of quotations from said W. W. to give a
zest to said lectures. S. T. C. is lecturing with success.
I have not heard either him or H. but I dined with
S. T. C. at Gilman's a Sunday or two since and he was
well and in good spirits. I mean to hear some of the
course, but lectures are not much to my taste, whatever
the lecturer may be. If *read,* they are dismal flat, and
you can't think why you are brought together to hear
a man read his works which you could read so much
better at leisure yourself; if delivered extempore, I am
always in pain lest the gift of utterance should suddenly
fail the orator in the middle, as it did me at the dinner
given in honour of me at the London Tavern. "Gentlemen," said I, and there I stoppt,—the rest my feelings
were under the necessity of supplying.

Mrs. Wordsworth *will* go on, kindly haunting us with
visions of seeing the lakes once more which never can
be realized. Between us there is a great gulf—not of
inexplicable moral antipathies and distances, I hope
(as there seemd to be between me and that Gentleman
concern'd in the Stamp office that I so strangely coiled
up from at Haydons). I think I had an instinct that he
was the head of an office. I hate all such people—Ac-

countants, Deputy Accountants. The dear abstract notion of the East India Company, as long as she is unseen,
is pretty, rather Poetical; but as SHE makes herself manifest by the persons of such Beasts, I loathe and detest
her as the Scarlet what-do-you-call-her of Babylon. I
thought, after abridging us of all our red letter days,
they had done their worst, but I was deceived in the
length to which Heads of offices, those true Liberty haters, can go. They are the tyrants, not Ferdinand, nor
Nero—by a decree past this week, they have abridged
us of the immemorially-observed custom of going at one
o'clock of a Saturday, the little shadow of a holiday left
us. Blast them. I speak it soberly. Dear W. W., be
thankful for your Liberty.

We have spent two very pleasant Evenings lately with
Mr. Monkhouse.

❖

TO FANNY KELLY[1]

[Dated at end: 9th July 1819.]

DEAR MISS KELLY,

If your Bones[2] are not engaged on Monday night, will
you favor us with the use of them? I know, if you can
oblige us, you will make no bones of it; if you cannot, it
shall break none betwixt us. We might ask somebody
else, but we do not like the bones of any strange animal. We should be welcome to dear Mrs. Liston's, but
then she is so plump, there is no getting at them. I should
prefer Miss Iver's—they must be ivory I take it for

---

[1] The three letters to Fanny Kelly were first printed in E. V. Lucas'
Life of Charles Lamb (London: Methuen, 1921), and are included
by courtesy of J. M. Dent & Sons, Ltd., publishers jointly with
Methuen of Lamb's letters.—J. M. B.

[2] Free passes to the theatre, made of bone or ivory.—J. M. B.

granted—but she is married to Mr. xxx, and become bone of his bone, consequently can have none of her own to dispose of. Well, it all comes to this,—if you can let us have them, you will, I dare say; if you cannot, God rest your bones. I am almost at the end of my bon-mots. C. LAMB.

❖

TO FANNY KELLY

20 July, 1819.

DEAR MISS KELLY,

We had the pleasure, *pain* I might better call it, of seeing you last night in the new Play. It was a most consummate piece of Acting, but what a task for you to undergo! at a time when your heart is sore from real sorrow! it has given rise to a train of thinking, which I cannot suppress.

Would to God you were released from this way of life; that you could bring your mind to consent to take your lot with us, and throw off for ever the whole burden of your Profession. I neither expect or wish you to take notice of this which I am writing, in your present over occupied & hurried state.—But to think of it at your leisure. I have quite income enough, if that were all, to justify for me making such a proposal, with what I may call even a handsome provision for my survivor. What you possess of your own would naturally be appropriated to those, for whose sakes chiefly you have made so many hard sacrifices.

I am not so foolish as not to know that I am a most unworthy match for such a one as you, but you have for years been a principal object in my mind. In many a sweet assumed character I have learned to love you,

but simply as F. M. Kelly I love you better than them
all. Can you quit these shadows of existence, & come
& be a reality to us? can you leave off harassing yourself
to please a thankless multitude, who know nothing of
you, & begin at last to live to yourself & your friends?

As plainly & frankly as I have seen you give or refuse assent in some feigned scene, so frankly do me the
justice to answer me. It is impossible I should feel in-
jured or aggrieved by your telling me at once, that the
proposal does not suit you. It is impossible that I should
ever think of molesting you with idle importunity and
persecution after your mind [was] once firmly spoken
—but happier, far happier, could I have leave to hope
a time might come, when our friends might be your
friends; our interests yours; our book-knowledge, if in
that inconsiderable particular we have any little advantage, might impart something to you, which you would
every day have it in your power ten thousand fold to
repay by the added cheerfulness and joy which you
could not fail to bring as a dowry into whatever family
should have the honor and happiness of receiving *you*,
the most welcome accession that could be made to it.

In haste, but with entire respect & deepest affection,
I subscribe myself, C. LAMB.

❖

TO FANNY KELLY

July 20th, 1819.

DEAR MISS KELLY,

Your injunctions shall be obeyed to a tittle. I feel myself in a lackadaisacal no-how-ish kind of a humour. I
believe it is the rain, or something. I had thought to
have written seriously, but I fancy I succeed best in

epistles of mere fun; puns & *that* nonsense. You will be
good friends with us, will you not? let what has past
"break no bones" between us. You will not refuse us
them next time we send for them?

Yours very truly,   C. L.

Do you observe the delicacy of not signing my full
name? N.B. Do not paste that last letter of mine into
your Book.

❖

TO DOROTHY WORDSWORTH

[P.M. *25th November 1819.*]

DEAR MISS WORDSWORTH,

You will think me negligent, but I wanted to see
more of Willy,[1] before I ventured to express a prediction. Till yesterday I had barely seen him—Virgilium
Tantum Vidi—but yesterday he gave us his small company to a bullock's heart—and I can pronounce him a
lad of promise. He is no pedant nor bookworm, so far
I can answer. Perhaps he has hitherto paid too little attention to other men's inventions, preferring, like Lord
Foppington, the "natural sprouts of his own." But he
has observation, and seems thoroughly awake.

I am ill at remembering other people's bon mots, but
the following are a few. Being taken over Waterloo
Bridge, he remarked that if we had no mountains, we
had a fine river at least, which was a Touch of the Comparative, but then he added, in a strain which augured
less for his future abilities as a Political Economist, that
he supposed they must take at least a pound a week
Toll. Like a curious naturalist he inquired if the tide did

---

[1] William Wordsworth, Jr., age nine.—J. M. B.

not come up a little salty. This being satisfactorily answered, he put another question as to the flux and reflux, which being rather cunningly evaded than artfully solved by that she-Aristotle Mary, who muttered something about its getting up an hour sooner and sooner every day, he sagely replied, "Then it must come to the same thing at last," which was a speech worthy of an infant Halley!

The Lion in the 'Change by no means came up to his ideal standard. So impossible it is for Nature in any of her works to come up to the standard of a child's imagination. The whelps (Lionets) he was sorry to find were dead, and on particular enquiry his old friend the Ouran Outang had gone the way of all flesh also. The grand Tiger was also sick, and expected in no short time to exchange this transitory world for another—or none. But again, there was a Golden Eagle (I do not mean that of Charing) which did much arride and console him.

William's genius, I take it, leans a little to the figurative, for being at play at Tricktrack (a kind of minor Billiard-table which we keep for smaller wights, and sometimes refresh our own mature fatigues with taking a hand at), not being able to hit a ball he had iterate aimed at, he cried out, "I cannot hit that beast." Now the balls are usually called men, but he felicitously hit upon a middle term, a term of approximation and imaginative reconciliation, a something where the two ends, of the brute matter (ivory) and their human and rather violent personification into *men,* might meet, as I take it, illustrative of that Excellent remark in a certain Preface about Imagination, explaining "like a sea-beast that had crawled forth to sun himself." Not that I accuse William Minor of hereditary plagiary, or conceive the image to have come ex traduce. Rather he seemeth to keep aloof from any source of imitation, and purposely to remain ignorant of what mighty poets have done in this kind before him. For being asked if his father had ever been on Westminster Bridge, he answer'd that he did not know.

It is hard to discern the Oak in the Acorn, or a Temple like St. Paul's in the first stone which is laid, nor can I quite prefigure what destination the genius of William Minor hath to take. Some few hints I have set down, to guide my future observations. He hath the power of calculation in no ordinary degree for a chit. He combineth figures, after the first boggle, rapidly. As in the Tricktrack board, where the hits are figured, at first he did not perceive that 15 and 7 made 22, but by a little use he could combine 8 with 25—and 33 again with 16, which approacheth something in kind (far let me be from flattering him by saying in degree) to that of the famous American boy. I am sometimes inclined to think I perceive the future satirist in him, for he hath a subsardonic smile which bursteth out upon occasion, as when he was asked if London were as big as Ambleside, and indeed no other answer was given, or proper to be given, to so ensnaring and provoking a question. In the contour of scull certainly I discern something paternal. But whether in all respects the future man shall transcend his father's fame, Time the trier of geniuses must decide. Be it pronounced peremptorily at present, that Willy is a well-mannered child, and though no great student, hath yet a lively eye for things that lie before him. Given in haste from my desk at Leadenhall. Your's and yours' most sincerely

C. LAMB.

❖

TO JOHN TAYLOR

June 30, 1821.

DEAR SIR,

You will do me injustice if you do not convey to the writer of the beautiful lines, which I now return you, my sense of the extreme kindness which dictated them. Poor Elia (call him *Ellia*) does not pretend to so very clear revelations of a future state of being as Olen seems gifted with. He stumbles about dark mountains at best; but he knows at least how to be thankful for this life, and is too thankful indeed for certain relationships lent him here, not to tremble for a possible resumption of the gift. He is too apt to express himself lightly, and cannot be sorry for the present occasion, as it has called forth a reproof so Christian-like. His *animus* at least (whatever become of it in the female termination) hath always been *cum Christianis.*

Pray make my gratefullest respects to the Poet, (do I flatter myself when I hope it may be M——y?) and say how happy I should feel myself in an acquaintance with him. I will just mention that in the middle of the second column, where I have affixed a cross, the line

One in a skeleton's ribb'd hollow cooped,

is undoubtedly wrong. Should it not be—

A skeleton's rib or ribs?

or,

In a skeleton ribb'd, hollow-coop'd?

I perfectly remember the plate in Quarles. In the first page exoteric is pronounced exòteric. It should be (if that is the word) exotèric. The false accent may be corrected by omitting the word *old*. Pray, for certain reasons, give me to the 18th *at furthest extremity* for my next.

Poor ELIA, the real, (for I am but a counterfeit,) is dead. The fact is, a person of that name, an Italian, was a fellow clerk of mine at the South Sea House, thirty (not forty) years ago, when the characters I described there existed, but had left it like myself many years; and I having a brother now there, and doubting how he might relish certain descriptions in it, I clapt down the name of Elia to it, which passed off pretty well, for Elia himself added the function of an author to that of a scrivener, like myself.

I went the other day (not having seen him for a year) to laugh over with him at my usurpation of his name, and found him, alas! no more than a name, for he died of consumption eleven months ago, and I knew not of it.

So the name has fairly devolved to me, I think; and 'tis all he has left me.

Dear sir, yours truly,

C. LAMB.

❖

TO S. T. COLERIDGE

March 9th, 1822.

DEAR C.,

It gives me great satisfaction to hear that the pig turned out so well—they are interesting creatures at a certain age—what a pity such buds should blow out into the maturity of rank bacon! You had all some of the crackling—and brain sauce—did you remember to rub it with butter, and gently dredge it a little, just before the crisis? Did the eyes come away kindly with no Œdipean avulsion? Was the crackling the colour of the ripe pomegranate? Had you no complement of boiled neck of mutton before it, to blunt the edge of delicate desire? Did you flesh maiden teeth in it? Not that I sent the pig, or can form the remotest guess what part Owen could play in the business. I never knew him give anything away in my life. He would not begin with strangers. I suspect the pig, after all, was meant for me; but at the unlucky juncture of time being absent, the present somehow went round to Highgate.

To confess an honest truth, a pig is one of those things I could never think of sending away. Teals, wigeons, snipes, barn-door fowl, ducks, geese—your tame villatic things—Welsh mutton, collars of brawn, sturgeon, fresh or pickled, your potted char, Swiss cheeses, French pies, early grapes, muscadines, I impart as freely unto my friends as to myself. They are but self-extended; but pardon me if I stop somewhere—where the fine feeling of benevolence giveth a higher smack than the sensual rarity—there my friends (or any good man) may command me; but pigs are pigs, and I myself therein am nearest to myself. Nay, I should think it an affront, an undervaluing done to Nature who bestowed such a boon upon me, if in a churlish mood I parted with the precious gift.

One of the bitterest pangs of remorse I ever felt was when a child—when my kind old aunt had strained her pocket-strings to bestow a sixpenny whole plum-cake upon me. In my way home through the Borough, I met a venerable old man, not mendicant, but thereabouts —a look-beggar, not a verbal petitionist; and in the coxcombry of taught-charity I gave away the cake to him. I walked on a little in all the pride of an Evangelical peacock, when of a sudden my old aunt's kindness crossed me—the sum it was to her—the pleasure she had a right to expect that I—not the old impostor—should take in eating her cake—the cursed ingratitude by which, under the colour of a Christian virtue, I had frustrated her cherished purpose. I sobbed, wept, and took it to heart so grievously, that I think I never suffered the like—and I was right. It was a piece of unfeeling hypocrisy, and proved a lesson to me ever after. The cake has long been masticated, consigned to the dunghill with the ashes of that unseasonable pauper.

But when Providence, who is better to us all than our aunts, gives me a pig, remembering my temptation and my fall, I shall endeavour to act towards it more in the spirit of the donor's purpose.

Yours (short of pig) to command in everything,

C. L.

❖

TO WILLIAM WORDSWORTH

20th March, 1822.

MY DEAR WORDSWORTH,

A letter from you is very grateful, I have not seen a Kendal postmark so long! We are pretty well save colds and rheumatics, and a certain deadness to every thing, which I think I may date from poor John's Loss, and another accident·or two at the same time, that has made me almost bury myself at Dalston, where yet I see more faces than I could wish. Deaths over-set one and put one out long after the recent grief. Two or three have died within this last two twelvem^ths., and so many parts of me

have been numbed. One sees a picture, reads an anecdote, starts a casual fancy, and thinks to tell of it to this
person in preference to every other—the person is gone
whom it would have peculiarly suited. It won't do for
another. Every departure destroys a class of sympathies.

There's Capt. Burney gone!—what fun has whist
now? what matters it what you lead, if you can no
longer fancy him looking over you? One never hears any
thing, but the image of the particular person occurs
with whom alone almost you would care to share the
intelligence. Thus one distributes oneself about—and
now for so many parts of me I have lost the market.
Common natures do not suffice me. Good people, as
they are called, won't serve. I want individuals. I am
made up of queer points and I want so many answering
needles. The going away of friends does not make the
remainder more precious. It takes so much from them
as there was a common link. A. B. and C. make a party.
A. dies. B. not only loses A. but all A.'s part in C. C.
loses A.'s part in B., and so the alphabet sickens by sub-
traction of interchangeables. I express myself muddily,
capite dolente. I have a dulling cold.

My theory is to enjoy life, but the practice is against
it. I grow ominously tired of official confinement. Thirty
years have I served the Philistines, and my neck is not
subdued to the yoke. You don't know how wearisome
it is to breathe the air of four pent walls without relief
day after day, all the golden hours of the day between
10 and 4 without ease or interposition. Tædet me harum
quotidianarum formarum, these pestilential clerk faces
always in one's dish. O for a few years between the
grave and the desk! they are the same, save that at
the latter you are outside the machine. The foul enchanter—letters four do form his name—Busirane is his

name in hell—that has curtailed you of some domestic comforts, hath laid a heavier hand on me, not in present infliction, but in taking away the hope of enfranchisement.

I dare not whisper to myself a Pension on this side of absolute incapacitation and infirmity, till years have sucked me dry. Otium cum indignitate. I had thought in a green old age (O green thought!) to have retired to Ponder's End—emblematic name how beautifull in the Ware road, there to have made up my accounts with Heaven and the Company, toddling about between it and Cheshunt, anon stretching on some fine Izaac Walton morning to Hoddesdon or Amwell, careless as a Beggar, but walking, walking ever, till I fairly walkd myself off my legs, dying walking!

The hope is gone. I sit like Philomel all day (but not singing) with my breast against this thorn of a Desk, with the only hope that some Pulmonary affliction may relieve me. Vide Lord Palmerston's report of the Clerks in the war office (Debates, this morning's Times) by which it appears in 20 years, as many Clerks have been coughd and catarrhd out of it into their freer graves.

Thank you for asking about the Pictures. Milton hangs over my fire side in Covt. Gard. (when I am there), the rest have been sold for an old song, wanting the eloquent tongue that should have set them off!

You have gratifyd me with liking my meeting with Dodd. For the Malvolio story—the thing is become in verity a sad task and I eke it out with any thing. If I could slip out of it I sh^d be happy, but our chief reputed assistants have forsaken us. The opium eater crossed us once with a dazzling path, and hath as suddenly left us darkling; and in short I shall go on from dull to worse,

because I cannot resist the Bookseller's importunity—
the old plea you know of authors, but I believe on my
part sincere.

Hartley I do not so often see, but I never see him in
unwelcome hour. I thoroughly love and honor him.

I send you a frozen Epistle, but it is winter and dead
time of the year with me. May heaven keep something
like spring and summer up with you, strengthen your
eyes and make mine a little lighter to encounter with
them, as I hope they shall yet and again, before all are
closed.

Yours, with every kind rem^{be}.　　　C. L.

I had almost forgot to say, I think you thoroughly
right about presentation copies. I should like to see you
print a book I should grudge to purchase for its size.
D——n me, but I would have it though!

❖

TO BARRON FIELD

Sept. 22, 1822.

MY DEAR F.,

I scribble hastily at office. Frank wants my letter
presently. I & sister are just returned from Paris!! We
have eaten frogs. It has been such a treat! You know
our monotonous general Tenor. Frogs are the nicest
little delicate things—rabbity-flavoured. Imagine a Lil-
liputian rabbit! They fricassee them; but in my mind,
drest seethed, plain, with parsley and butter, would have
been the decision of Apicius.

Shelley the great Atheist has gone down by water to
eternal fire! Hunt and his young fry are left stranded at
Pisa, to be adopted by the remaining duumvir, Lord

Byron—his wife and 6 children & their maid. What a cargo of Jonases, if they had foundered too! The only use I can find of friends, is that they do to borrow money of you. Henceforth I will consort with none but rich rogues.

Paris is a glorious picturesque old City. London looks mean and New to it, as the town of Washington would, seen after *it*. But they have no St. Paul's or Westminster Abbey. The Seine, so much despised by Cockneys, is exactly the size to run thro' a magnificent street; palaces a mile long on one side, lofty Edinbro' stone (O the glorious antiques!): houses on the other. The Thames disunites London & Southwark.

I had Talma to supper with me. He has picked up, as I believe, an authentic portrait of Shakspere. He paid a broker about £40 English for it. It is painted on the one half of a pair of bellows—a lovely picture, corresponding with the Folio head. The bellows has old carved *wings* round it, and round the visnomy is inscribed, near as I remember, not divided into rhyme— I found out the rhyme—

> Whom have we here,
> Stuck on this bellows,
> But the Prince of good fellows,
> Willy Shakspere?

At top—

> O base and coward luck!
> To be here stuck.—Poins.

At bottom—

Nay! rather a glorious lot is to him assign'd,
Who, like the Almighty, rides upon the *wind*.—Pistol.

This is all in old carved wooden letters. The countenance smiling, sweet, and intellectual beyond measure,

even as He was immeasurable. It may be a forgery.
They laugh at me and tell me Ireland is in Paris, and has
been putting off a portrait of the Black Prince. How far
old wood may be imitated I cannot say. Ireland was not
found out by his parchments, but by his poetry. I am
confident no painter on either side the Channel could
have painted any thing near like the face I saw. Again,
would such a painter and forger have expected £40 for
a thing, if authentic, worth £4000? Talma is not in the
secret, for he had not even found out the rhymes in the
first inscription. He is coming over with it, and, my life
to Southey's Thalaba, it will gain universal faith.

The letter is wanted, and I am wanted. Imagine the
blank filled up with all kind things.

Our joint hearty remembrances to both of you. Yours
as ever.

C. LAMB.

❖

TO WALTER WILSON

E. I. H. *16 dec. 22.*

DEAR WILSON

Lightening I was going to call you—

You must have thought me negligent in not answering your letter sooner. But I have a habit of never writing letters, but at the office—'tis so much time cribbed
out of the Company—and I am but just got out of the
thick of a Tea Sale, in which most of the Entry of Notes,
deposits &c. usually falls to my share. Dodwell is willing,
but alas! slow. To compare a pile of my notes with his
little hillock (which has been as long a building), what
is it but to compare Olympus with a mole-hill. Then
Wadd is a sad shuffler.—

I have nothing of Defoe's but two or three Novels, and the Plague History. I can give you no information about him. As a slight general character of what I remember of them (for I have not look'd into them latterly) I would say that "in the appearance of *truth* in all the incidents and conversations that occur in them they exceed any works of fiction I am acquainted with. It is perfect illusion.

"The *Author* never appears in these self-narratives (for so they ought to be called or rather Autobiographies) but the *narrator* chains us down to an implicit belief in every thing he says. There is all the minute detail of a log-book in it. Dates are painfully pressed upon the memory. Facts are repeated over and over in varying phrases, till you cannot chuse but believe them. It is like reading Evidence given in a Court of Justice. So anxious the story-teller seems, that the truth should be clearly comprehended, that when he has told us a matter of fact, or a motive, in a line or two farther down he *repeats* it with his favorite figure of speech, 'I say,' so and so,—though he had made it abundantly plain before. This is in imitation of the common people's way of speaking, or rather of the way in which they are addressed by a master or mistress, who wishes to impress something upon their memories; and has a wonderful effect upon matter-of-fact readers. Indeed it is to such principally that he writes. His style is elsewhere beautiful, but plain & *homely*.

"Robinson Crusoe is delightful to all ranks and classes, but it is easy to see that it is written in phraseology peculiarly adapted to the lower conditions of readers: hence it is an especial favorite with seafaring men, poor boys, servant maids &c. His novels are capital kitchen-reading, while they are worthy from their deep interest to find a shelf in the Libraries of the wealthiest, and the most learned. His passion for *matter of fact narrative* sometimes betrayed him into a long relation of common incidents which might happen to any man, and have no interest but the intense appearance of truth in them, to recommend them.

"The whole latter half, or two thirds, of Colonel Jack is of this description. The beginning of Colonel Jack is the most affecting natural picture of a young thief that was ever drawn. His losing the stolen money in the hollow of a tree, and finding it again when he was in despair, and then being in equal distress at not knowing how to dispose of it, and several similar touches in the early history of the Colonel, evince a deep knowledge of human nature; and, putting out of question the superior *romantic* interest of the latter, in my mind very much exceed Crusoe. Roxana (1st Edition) is the next in Interest, though he left out the best part of it [in] subsequent Editions from a foolish hypercriticism of his friend, Southerne. But Moll Flanders, the account of the Plague &c. &c. are all of one family, and have the same stamp of character."—

[*At the top of the first page is added:*]
Omitted at the end . . . believe me with friendly recollections, *Brother* (as I used to call you) Yours
C. LAMB.

[*Below the "Dear Wilson" is added in smaller writing:*]
The review was not mine, nor have I seen it.

❖

TO BERNARD BARTON

[Dated at end: 23rd December 1822.]

Dear Sir,

I have been so distracted with business and one thing or other, I have not had a quiet quarter of an hour for epistolary purposes. Christmas too is come, which always puts a rattle into my morning scull. It is a visiting unquiet un-Quakerish season. I get more and more in love with solitude, and proportionately hampered with company. I hope you have some holydays at this period. I have one day, Christmas day, alas! too few to commemorate the season. All work and no play dulls me. Company is not play, but many times hard work. To play, is for a man to do what he please, or to do nothing —to go about soothing his particular fancies. I have lived at a time of life, to have outlived the good hours, the nine o'Clock suppers, with a bright hour or two to clear up in afterw^{ds}.—Now you cannot get tea before that hour, and then sit gaping, music-bother'd perhaps, till half-past 12 brings up the tray, and what you steal of convivial enjoym^t after, is heavily paid for in the disquiet of to-morrow's head.

I am pleased with your liking John Woodvil, and amused with your knowledge of our drama being confined to Shakspeare and Miss Bailly. What a world of fine territory between Land's End and Johnny Grots have you missed traversing. I almost envy you to have so much to read. I feel as if I had read all the Books I want to read. O to forget Fielding, Steele, &c., and read 'em new.

Can you tell me a likely place where I could pick up

cheap Fox's Journal?—There are no Quaker Circulating Libraries?—Ellwood, too, I must have.—I rather grudge that S[outhe]y has taken up the History of your People. I am afraid he will put in some Levity. I am afraid I am not quite exempt from that fault in certain magazine Articles where I have introduced mention of them. Were they to do again, I would reform them.

Why should not you write a poetical Account of your old Worthies, deducing them from Fox to Woolman?—but I remember you did talk of something in that kind, as a counterpart to the Ecclesiastical Sketches. But would not a Poem be more consecutive than a string of Sonnets? You have no Martyrs *quite to the Fire,* I think, among you. But plenty of Heroic Confessors, Spirit-Martyrs—Lamb-Lions—Think of it—

It would be better than a series of Sonnets on "Eminent Bankers."—I like a hit at our way of life, tho' it does well for me, better than anything short of *all one's time to one's self,* for which alone I rankle with envy at the rich. Books are good, and Pictures are good, and Money to buy them therefore good, but to buy *TIME!* in other words, LIFE—

The "compliments of the time to you" should end my letter, to a Friend I suppose I must say the "sincerity of the season"; I hope they both mean the same. With excuses for this hastily penn'd note, believe me with great respect—

C. LAMB.

❖

TO MR. AND MRS. J. D. COLLIER

Twelfth Day [6th January], 1823.

The pig was above my feeble praise. It was a dear pigmy. There was some contention as to who should have the ears, but in spite of his obstinacy (deaf as these little creatures are to advice) I contrived to get at one of them.

It came in boots too, which I took as a favor. Generally those petty toes, pretty toes! are missing. But I suppose he wore them, to look taller.

He must have been the least of his race. His little foots would have gone into the silver slipper. I take him to have been Chinese, and a female.—

If Evelyn could have seen him, he would never have farrowed two such prodigious volumes, seeing how much good can be contained in—how small a compass!

He crackled delicately.

John Collier Junʳ has sent me a Poem which (without the smallest bias from the aforesaid present, believe me) I pronounce *sterling*.

I set about Evelyn, and finished the first volume in the course of a natural day. To-day I attack the second. —Parts are very interesting.—

I left a blank at top of my letter, not being determined *which* to address it to, so Farmer and Farmer's wife will please to divide our thanks. May your granaries be full, and your rats empty, and your chickens plump, and your envious neighbors lean, and your labourers busy, and you as idle and as happy as the day is long!

Vive l'Agriculture!

Frank Field's marriage of course you have seen in the papers, and that his brother Barron is expected home.

> How do you make your pigs so little?
> They are vastly engaging at that age.
>   I was so myself.
> Now I am a disagreeable old hog—
>   A middle-aged-gentleman-and-a-half.

My faculties, thank God, are not much impaired. I have my sight, hearing, taste, pretty perfect; and can read the Lord's Prayer in the common type, by the help of a candle, without making many mistakes.

Believe me, while my faculties last, a proper appreciator of your many kindnesses in this way; and that the last lingering relish of past flavors upon my dying memory will be the smack of that little Ear. It was the left ear, which is lucky. Many happy returns (not of the Pig) but of the New Year to both.—

Mary for her share of the Pig and the memoirs desires to send the same—

D^r. M^r. C. and M^{rs}. C.—

Yours truly

C. LAMB.

❖

TO BERNARD BARTON

9 Jan., 1823.

"Throw yourself on the world without any rational plan of support, beyond what the chance employ of Booksellers would afford you"!!!

Throw yourself rather, my dear Sir, from the steep Tarpeian rock, slap-dash headlong upon iron spikes. If you had but five consolatory minutes between the desk and the bed, make much of them, and live a century in them, rather than turn slave to the Booksellers. They are Turks and Tartars, when they have poor Authors at their beck. Hitherto you have been at arm's length from them. Come not within their grasp. I have known many authors for bread, some repining, others envying the blessed security of a Counting House, all agreeing they had rather have been Taylors, Weavers, what not? rather than the things they were. I have known some starved, some to go mad, one dear friend literally dying in a workhouse. You know not what a rapacious, dishonest set these booksellers are. Ask even Southey who (a single case almost) has made a fortune by book drudgery, what he has found them.

O you know not, may you never know! the miseries of subsisting by authorship. 'Tis a pretty appendage to a situation like yours or mine, but a slavery worse than all slavery to be a bookseller's dependent, to drudge your brains for pots of ale and breasts of mutton, to change your free thoughts and voluntary numbers for ungracious TASK-WORK. Those fellows hate *us*. The reason I take to be, that, contrary to other trades, in which the Master gets all the credit (a Jeweller or Silversmith for instance), and the Journeyman, who really does the fine work, is in the background: in *our* work the world gives all the credit to Us, whom *they* consider as *their* Journeymen, and therefore do they hate us, and cheat us, and oppress us, and would wring the blood of us out, to put another sixpence in their mechanic pouches.

I contend, that a Bookseller has a *relative honesty* towards Authors, not like his honesty to the rest of the world. B[aldwin], who first engag'd me as Elia, has not paid me up yet (nor any of us without repeated mortifying applials), yet how the Knave fawned while I was of service to him! Yet I dare say the fellow is punctual in settling his milk-score, &c.

Keep to your Bank, and the Bank will keep you. Trust not to the Public, you may hang, starve, drown yourself, for anything that worthy *Personage* cares. I bless every star, that Providence, not seeing good to make me independent, has seen it next good to settle me upon the stable foundation of Leadenhall. Sit down, good B. B., in the Banking Office; what, is there not from six to Eleven P.M. 6 days in the week, and is there not all Sunday? Fie, what a superfluity of man's time if you could think so! Enough for relaxation, mirth, converse, poetry, good thoughts, quiet thoughts. O the corroding torturing tormenting thoughts, that disturb the Brain of the unlucky wight, who must draw upon it for daily sustenance. Henceforth I retract all my fond complaints of mercantile employment, look upon them as Lovers' quarrels. I was but half in earnest. Welcome, dead timber of a desk, that makes me live. A little grumbling is a wholesome medicine for the spleen, but in my inner heart do I approve and embrace this our close but unharassing way of life. I am quite serious.

If you can send me Fox, I will not keep it six *weeks*, and will return it, with warm thanks to yourself and friend, without blot or dog's ear. You much oblige me by this kindness.

Yours truly,   C. LAMB.

Please to direct to me at India Ho. in future. [? I am] not always at Russell St.

❖

TO BERNARD BARTON

[P.M. 5th April 1823.]

DEAR SIR,

You must think me ill mannered not to have replied to your first letter sooner, but I have an ugly habit of aversion from letter writing, which makes me an unworthy correspondent. I have had no spring, or cordial call to the occupation of late. I have been not well lately, which must be my lame excuse.

Your poem, which I consider very affecting, found

me engaged about a humorous Paper for the London,
which I had called a "Letter to an *Old Gentleman* whose
Education had been neglected"—and when it was done
Taylor and Hessey would not print it, and it discouraged
me from doing any thing else, so I took up Scott, where
I had scribbled some petulant remarks, and for a make
shift father'd them on Ritson. It is obvious I could not
make your Poem a part of them, and as I did not know
whether I should ever be able to do to my mind what
you suggested, I thought it not fair to keep back the
verses for the chance.

Mr. Mitford's sonnet I like very well; but as I also have
my reasons against interfering at all with the Editorial
arrangement of the London, I transmitted it (not in my
own handwriting) to them, who I doubt not will be
glad to insert it. What eventual benefit it can be to you
(otherwise than that a kind man's wish is a benefit)
I cannot conjecture. Your Society are eminently men of
Business, and will probably regard you as an idle fellow,
possibly disown you, that is to say, if you had put your
own name to a sonnet of that sort, but they cannot ex-
communicate Mr. Mitford, therefore I thoroughly approve of printing the said verses. When I see any Quaker
names to the Concert of Antient Music, or as Directors
of the British Institution, or bequeathing medals to
Oxford for the best classical themes, etc.—then I shall
begin to hope they will emancipate you. But what as a
Society can they do for you? you would not accept a
Commission in the Army, nor they be likely to procure
it; Posts in Church or State have they none in their giving; and then if they disown you—think—you must
live "a man forbid."

I wishd for you yesterday. I dined in Parnassus, with
Wordsworth, Coleridge, Rogers, and Tom Moore—half
the Poetry of England constellated and clustered in

Gloster Place! It was a delightful Even^g. Coleridge was in his finest vein of talk, had all the talk, and let 'em talk as evilly as they do of the envy of Poets, I am sure not one there but was content to be nothing but a listener. The Muses were dumb, while Apollo lectured on his and their fine Art. It is a lie that Poets are envious, I have known the best of them, and can speak to it, that they give each other their merits, and are the kindest critics as well as best authors. I am scribbling a muddy epistle with an aking head, for we did not quaff Hippocrene last night. Marry, it was Hippocras rather. Pray accept this as a letter in the mean time, and do me the favor to mention my respects to Mr. Mitford, who is so good as to entertain good thoughts of Elia, but don't show this almost impertinent scrawl. I will write more respectfully next time, for believe me, if not in words, in feelings, yours most so.

❖

TO BERNARD BARTON

May 15, 1824.

Dear B. B.,

I am oppressed with business all day, and Company all night. But I will snatch a quarter of an hour. Your recent acquisitions of the Picture and the Letter are greatly to be congratulated. I too have a picture of my father and the copy of his first love verses; but they have been mine long.

Blake is a real name, I assure you, and a most extraordinary man, if he be still living. He is the Robert [William] Blake, whose wild designs accompany a splendid folio edition of the "Night Thoughts," which you may have seen, in one of which he pictures the parting of soul and body by a solid mass of human form floating off, God knows how, from a lumpish mass (fac Simile to itself) left behind on the dying bed. He paints in water colours marvellous strange pictures, visions of his brain, which he asserts that he has seen. They have great merit. He has *seen* the old Welsh bards on Snowdon—he has seen the Beautifullest, the strongest, and the Ugliest Man, left alone from the Massacre of the Britons by the Romans, and has painted them from memory (I have seen his paintings), and asserts them to be as good as the figures of Raphael and Angelo, but not better, as they had precisely the same retro-visions and prophetic visions with themself [himself].

The painters in oil (which he will have it that neither of them practised) he affirms to have been the ruin of art, and affirms that all the while he was engaged in his Water paintings, Titian was disturbing him, Titian the Ill Genius of Oil Painting. His Pictures—one in particular, the Canterbury Pilgrims (far above Stothard's)— have great merit, but hard, dry, yet with grace. He has written a Catalogue of them with a most spirited criticism on Chaucer, but mystical and full of Vision. His poems have been sold hitherto only in Manuscript. I never read them; but a friend at my desire procured the "Sweep Song." There is one to a tiger, which I have heard recited, beginning:

> Tiger, Tiger, burning bright,
> Thro' the desarts of the night,

which is glorious, but, alas! I have not the book; for the man is flown, whither I know not—to Hades or a Mad House. But I must look on him as one of the most extraordinary persons of the age.

Montgomery's book I have not much hope from. The Society, with the affected name, has been labouring at it for these 20 years, and made few converts. I think it was injudicious to mix stories avowedly colour'd by fiction with the sad true statements from the parliamentary records, etc. but I wish the little Negroes all the good that can come from it. I batter'd my brains (not butter'd them—but it is a bad *a*) for a few verses for them, but I could make nothing of it. You have been luckier. But Blake's are the flower of the set, you will, I am sure, agree, tho' some of Montgomery's at the end are pretty; but the Dream awkwardly paraphras'd from B.

With the exception of an Epilogue for a Private Theatrical, I have written nothing now for near 6 months. It is in vain to spur me on. I must wait. I cannot write without a genial impulse, and I have none. 'Tis barren all and dearth. No matter; life is something without scribbling. I have got rid of my bad spirits, and hold up pretty well this rain-damn'd May.

So we have lost another Poet. I never much relished his Lordship's mind, and shall be sorry if the Greeks have cause to miss him. He was to me offensive, and I never can make out his great *power*, which his admirers talk of. Why, a line of Wordsworth's is a lever to lift the immortal spirit! Byron can only move the Spleen. He was at best a Satyrist,—in any other way he was mean enough. I dare say I do him injustice; but I cannot love him, nor squeeze a tear to his memory. He did not like the world, and he has left it, as Alderman Curtis advised the Radicals, "If they don't like their country, damn 'em, let 'em leave it," they possessing no rood of ground in England, and he 10,000 acres. Byron was better than many Curtises.

Farewell, and accept this apology for a letter from one who owes you so much in that kind.

Yours ever truly,   C. L.

❖

TO HENRY CRABB ROBINSON

[*29th March*} *1825*.

I have left the d——d India House for Ever!
Give me great Joy.   C. LAMB.

❖

TO WILLIAM WORDSWORTH

Colebrook Cottage,
6 April, 1825.

DEAR WORDSWORTH,

I have been several times meditating a letter to you
concerning the good thing which has befallen me, but
the thought of poor Monkhouse came across me. He was
one that I had exulted in the prospect of congratulating
me. He and you were to have been the first participators,
for indeed it has been ten weeks since the first motion of
it.

Here I am then after 33 years slavery, sitting in my
own room at 11 o'Clock this finest of all April mornings
a freed man, with £441 a year for the remainder of my
life, live I as long as John Dennis, who outlived his
annuity and starved at 90. £441, i.e. £450, with a de-
duction of £9 for a provision secured to my sister, she
being survivor, the Pension guaranteed by Act Georgii
Tertii, &c.

I came home for ever on Tuesday in last week. The
incomprehensibleness of my condition overwhelm'd me.
It was like passing from life into Eternity. Every year

to be as long as three, i.e. to have three times as much real time, time that is my own, in it! I wandered about thinking I was happy, but feeling I was not. But that tumultuousness is passing off, and I begin to understand the nature of the gift. Holy-days, even the annual month, were always uneasy joys: their conscious fugitiveness— the craving after making the most of them. Now, when all is holyday, there are no holydays. I can sit at home in rain or shine without a restless impulse for walkings. I am daily steadying, and shall soon find it as natural to me to be my own master, as it has been irksome to have had a master. Mary wakes every morning with an obscure feeling that some good has happened to us.

Leigh Hunt and Montgomery after their releasements describe the shock of their emancipation much as I feel mine. But it hurt their frames. I eat, drink, and sleep sound as ever. I lay no anxious schemes for going hither and thither, but take things as they occur. Yesterday I excursioned 20 miles, to day I write a few letters. Pleasuring was for fugitive play days, mine are fugitive only in the sense that life is fugitive. Freedom and life coexistent.

At the foot of such a call upon you for gratulation, I am ashamed to advert to that melancholy event. Monkhouse was a character I learnd to love slowly, but it grew upon me, yearly, monthly, daily. What a chasm has it made in our pleasant parties! His noble friendly face was always coming before me, till this hurrying event in my life came, and for the time has absorpt all interests. In fact it has shaken me a little. My old desk companions with whom I have had such merry hours seem to reproach me for removing my lot from among them. They were pleasant creatures, but to the anxieties of business, and a weight of possible worse ever impending, I was not equal. Tuthill and Gilman gave me my certificates. I laughed at the friendly lie implied in them, but my sister shook her head and said it was all true. Indeed this last winter I was jaded out, winters were always worse than other parts of the year, because the spirits are worse, and I had no daylight. In summer I had daylight evenings. The relief was hinted to me from a superior power, when I poor slave had not a hope but that I must wait another 7 years with Jacob—and lo! the Rachel which I coveted is bro^t. to me—

Have you read the noble dedication of Irving's "Missionary Orations" to S. T. C. Who shall call this man a Quack hereafter? What the Kirk will think of it neither I nor Irving care. When somebody suggested to him that it would not be likely to do him good, videlicet among his own people, "That is a reason for doing it" was his noble answer.

That Irving thinks he has profited mainly by S. T. C., I have no doubt. The very style of the Ded. shows it.

Communicate my news to Southey, and beg his pardon for my being so long acknowledging his kind present of the "Church," which circumstances I do not wish to explain, but having no reference to himself, prevented at the time. Assure him of my deep respect and friendliest feelings.

Divide the same, or rather each take the whole to you, I mean you and all yours. To Miss Hutchinson I must write separate. What's her address? I want to know about Mrs. M.

Farewell! and end at last, long selfish Letter!

C. LAMB.

❖

TO JOHN BATES DIBDIN

Friday, some day in June, 1826. [P.M. *30th June 1826.*]

DEAR D.,

My first impulse upon opening your letter was pleasure at seeing your old neat hand, nine parts gentlemanly, with a modest dash of the clerical: my second a Thought, natural enough this hot weather, Am I to answer all this? why 'tis as long as those to the Ephesians and Galatians put together—I have counted the words for curiosity. But then Paul has nothing like the fun which is ebullient all over yours.

I don't remember a good thing (good like yours) from the 1st Romans to the last of the Hebrews. I remember but one Pun in all the Evangely, and that was made by his and our master: Thou art Peter (that is Doctor Rock) and upon this rock will I build &c.; which sanctifies Punning with me against all gainsayers. I never knew an enemy to puns, who was not an ill-natured man. Your fair critic in the coach reminds me of a Scotchman who assured me that he did not see much in Shakspeare. I replied, I dare say *not.* He felt the equivoke, lookd awkward, and reddish, but soon returnd to the attack, by saying that he thought Burns was as good as Shakspeare: I said that I had no doubt he was—to a *Scotchman.* We exchangd no more words that day.—

Your account of the fierce faces in the Hanging, with the presumed interlocution of the Eagle and the Tyger, amused us greatly. You cannot be so very bad, while you can pick mirth off from rotten walls. But let me hear you have escaped out of your oven. May the

Form of the Fourth Person who clapt invisible wet blankets about the shoulders of Shadrach Meshach and Abednego, be with you in the fiery Trial. But get out of the frying pan. Your business, I take it, is bathing, not baking.

Let me hear that you have clamber'd up to Lover's Seat; it is as fine in that neighbourhood as Juan Fernandez, as lonely too, when the Fishing boats are not out; I have sat for hours, staring upon a shipless sea. The salt is never so grand as when it is left to itself. One cockboat spoils it. A sea-mew or two improves it. And go to the little church, which is a very protestant Loretto, and seems dropt by some angel for the use of a hermit, who was at once parishioner and a whole parish. It is not too big. Go in the night, bring it away in your portmanteau, and I will plant it in my garden. It must have been erected in the very infancy of British Christianity, for the two or three first converts; yet hath it all the appertenances of a church of the first magnitude, its pulpit, its pews, its baptismal font; a cathedral in a nutshell. Seven people would crowd it like a Caledonian Chapel.

The minister that divides the word there, must give lumping pennyworths. It is built to the text of two or three assembled in my name. It reminds me of the grain of mustard seed. If the glebe land is proportionate, it may yield two potatoes. Tythes out of it could be no more split than a hair. Its First fruits must be its Last, for 'twould never produce a couple. It is truly the strait and narrow way, and few there be (of London visitants) that find it. The still small voice is surely to be found there, if any where. A sounding board is merely there for ceremony. It is secure from earthquakes, not more from sanctity than size, for 'twould feel a mountain thrown upon it no more than a taper-worm would. Go and see, but not without your spectacles. By the way, there's a capital farm house two thirds of the way to the Lover's Seat, with incomparable plum cake, ginger beer, etc.

Mary bids me warn you not to read the Anatomy of Melancholy in your present *low way*. You'll fancy yourself a pipkin, or a headless bear, as Burton speaks of. You'll be lost in a maze of remedies for a labyrinth of diseasements, a plethora of cures. Read Fletcher; above all the Spanish Curate, the Thief or Little Nightwalker, the Wit Without Money, and the Lover's Pilgrimage. Laugh and come home fat. Neither do we think Sir T. Browne quite the thing for you just at present. Fletcher is as light as Soda water. Browne and Burton are too strong potions for an Invalid. And don't thumb or dirt the books. Take care of the bindings. Lay a leaf of silver paper under 'em, as you read them. And don't smoke tobacco over 'em, the leaves will fall in and burn or dirty their namesakes.

If you find any dusty atoms of the Indian Weed crumbled up in the Beaum^t and Fletcher, they are *mine*. But then, you know, so is the Folio also. A pipe and a comedy of Fletcher's the last thing of a night is the best recipe for light dreams and to scatter away Nightmares. Probatum est. But do as you like about the former. Only cut the Baker's. You will come home else all crust; Rankings must chip you before you can appear in his counting house. And my dear Peter Fin Junr., do contrive to see the sea at least once before you return. You'll be ask'd about it in the Old Jewry. It will appear singular not to have seen it. And rub up your Muse, the family Muse, and send us a rhyme or so. Don't waste your wit upon that damn'd Dry Salter. I never knew but one Dry Salter, who could relish those mellow effusions, and he broke. You knew Tommy Hill, the wettest of dry

salters. Dry Salters, what a word for this thirsty weather!
I must drink after it. Here's to thee, my dear Dibdin,
and to our having you again snug and well at Colebrooke. But our nearest hopes are to hear again from you
shortly. An epistle only a quarter as agreeable as your
last, would be a treat.

Yours most truly   C. LAMB.

Timothy B. Dibdin, Esq. No. 9, Blucher Row, Priory,
Hastings.

❖

TO HENRY CRABB ROBINSON

Colebrooke Row, Islington,
Saturday, 20th Jan., 1827.

DEAR ROBINSON,

I called upon you this morning, and found that you
were gone to visit a dying friend. I had been upon a like
errand. Poor Norris has been lying dying for now almost
a week, such is the penalty we pay for having enjoyed
a strong constitution! Whether he knew me or not, I
know not, or whether he saw me through his poor glazed
eyes; but the group I saw about him I shall not forget.
Upon the bed, or about it, were assembled his wife and
two daughters, and poor deaf Richard, his son, looking
doubly stupified. There they were, and seemed to have
been sitting all the week. I could only reach out a hand
to Mrs. Norris. Speaking was impossible in that mute
chamber. By this time I hope it is all over with him.
In him I have a loss the world cannot make up.

He was my friend and my father's friend all the life
I can remember. I seem to have made foolish friendships
since. Those are the friendships which outlive a second

generation. Old as I am waxing, in his eyes I was still
the child he knew me. To the last he called me Charley.
I have none to call me Charley now. He was the last
link that bound me to the Temple. You are but of yesterday. In him seem to have died the old plainness of
manners and singleness of heart. Letters he knew nothing
of, nor did his reading extend beyond the pages of the
"Gentleman's Magazine." Yet there was a pride of literature about him from being amongst books (he was
librarian), and from some scraps of doubtful Latin which
he had picked up in his office of entering students, that
gave him very diverting airs of pedantry.

Can I forget the erudite look with which, when he
had been in vain trying to make out a black-letter text
of Chaucer in the Temple Library, he laid it down and
told me that—"in those old books, Charley, there is
sometimes a deal of very indifferent spelling"; and
seemed to console himself in the reflection! His jokes, for
he had his jokes, are now ended, but they were old
trusty perennials, staple, hearty, that pleased after *decies
repetita*, and were always as good as new. One song he
had, which was reserved for the night of Christmas-day,
which we always spent in the Temple. It was an old
thing, and spoke of the flat bottoms of our foes and the
possibility of their coming over in darkness, and alluded
to threats of an invasion many years blown over; and
when he came to the part

> We'll still make 'em run, and we'll still make 'em sweat,
> In spite of the devil and Brussels Gazette!

his eyes would sparkle as with the freshness of an impending event. And what is the "Brussels Gazette"
now? I cry while I enumerate these trifles. "How shall
we tell them in a stranger's ear?" His poor good girls
will now have to receive their afflicted mother in an

unsuccessful home in an obscure village in Herts, where
they have been long struggling to make a school without
effect; and poor deaf Richard—and the more helpless
for being so—is thrown on the wide world. They are
almost provisionless. Some insurance there was, but I
think not exceeding £660.

My first motive in writing, and, indeed, in calling on
you, was to ask if you were enough acquainted with any
of the Benchers, to lay a plain statement before them of
the circumstances of the family. I almost fear not, for
you are of another Hall. But if you can oblige me and
my poor friend, who is now insensible to any favours,
pray exert yourself. You cannot say too much good of
poor Norris and his poor wife.

Yours ever,   CHAS. LAMB.

TO PETER GEORGE PATMORE

Mrs. Leishman's, Chace, Enfield,
[No date: June 1827.]

DEAR PATMORE,

Excuse my anxiety—buc how is Dash? (I should have
asked if Mrs. Patmore kept her rules, and was improving
—but Dash came uppermost. The order of our thoughts
should be the order of our writing.) Goes he muzzled,
or *aperto ore?* Are his intellects sound, or does he wander
a little in *his* conversation? You cannot be too careful to
watch the first symptoms of incoherence. The first illog-
ical snarl he makes, to St. Luke's with him! All the dogs
here are going mad, if you believe the overseers; but I
protest they seem to me very rational and collected. But
nothing is so deceitful as mad people to those who are
not used to them.

Try him with hot water. If he won't lick it up, it is a sign he does not like it. Does his tail wag horizontally or perpendicularly? That has decided the fate of many dogs in Enfield. Is his general deportment cheerful? I mean when he is pleased—for otherwise there is no judging. You can't be too careful. Has he bit any of the children yet? If he has, have them shot, and keep *him* for curiosity, to see if it was the hydrophobia. They say all our army in India had it at one time—but that was in *Hyder*-Ally's time. Do you get paunch for him? Take care the sheep was sane. You might pull out his teeth (if he would let you), and then you need not mind if he were as mad as a Bedlamite. It would be rather fun to see his odd ways. It might amuse Mrs. Patmore and the children. They'd have more sense than he! He'd be like a Fool kept in the family, to keep the household in good humour with their own understanding. You might teach him the mad dance set to the mad howl. *Madge Owl-et* be nothing to him. "My, how he capers!"

[*In the margin:*] One of the children speaks this. . . .

What I scratch out is a German quotation from Lessing on the bite of rabid animals; but, I remember, you don't read German. But Mrs. Patmore may, so I wish I had let it stand. The meaning in English is—"Avoid to approach an animal suspected of madness, as you would avoid fire or a precipice:"—which I think is a sensible observation. The Germans are certainly profounder than we.

If the slightest suspicion arises in your breast, that all is not right with him (Dash), muzzle him, and lead him in a string (common pack-thread will do; he don't care for twist) to Hood's, his quondam master, and he'll take him in at any time. You may mention your suspicion or not, as you like, or as you think it may wound or not Mr. H.'s feelings. Hood, I know, will wink at a few follies

in Dash, in consideration of his former sense. Besides,
Hood is deaf, and if you hinted anything, ten to one he
would not hear you. Besides, you will have discharged
your conscience, and laid the child at the right door, as
they say.

We are dawdling our time away very idly and pleasantly, at a Mrs. Leishman's, Chace, Enfield, where, if
you come a-hunting, we can give you cold meat and a
tankard. Her husband is a tailor; but that, you know,
does not make her one. I knew a jailor (which rhymes),
but his wife was a fine lady.

Let us hear from you respecting Mrs. Patmore's regi-
men. I send my love in a —— to Dash.

C. LAMB.

[On the outside of the letter was written:]

Seriously, I wish you would call upon Hood when you
are that way. He's a capital fellow. I sent him a couple
of poems—one ordered by his wife, and written to order;
and 'tis a week since, and I've not heard from him. I
fear something is the matter.

Omitted within

Our kindest remembrance to Mrs. P.

TO BERNARD BARTON

Enfield Chase Side
Saturday 25 July A.D. 1829.—11 A.M.

There—a fuller plumper juiceier date never dropt
from Idumean palm. Am I in the dateive case now? if
not, a fig for dates, which is more than a date is worth.

I never stood much affected to these limitary specialities.
Least of all since the date of my superannuation.

What have I with Time to do? Slaves of desks, twas meant for you.	Dear B. B.—Your hand writing has conveyed much pleasure to me

in the report of Lucy's restoration. Would I could send
you as good news of my poor Lucy. But some wearisome
weeks I must remain lonely yet. I have had the loneliest
time near 10 weeks, broken by a short apparition of
Emma[1] for her holydays, whose departure only deepend
the returning solitude, and by 10 days I have past in
Town.

But Town, with all my native hankering after it, is
not what it was. The streets, the shops are left, but all
old friends are gone. And in London I was frightfully
convinced of this as I past houses and places—empty
caskets now. I have ceased to care almost about any
body. The bodies I cared for are in graves, or dispersed.
My old Clubs, that lived so long and flourish'd so stead-
ily, are crumbled away. When I took leave of our
adopted young friend at Charing Cross, 'twas heavy unfeeling rain, and I had no where to go. Home have I
none—and not a sympathising house to turn to in the
great city. Never did the waters of the heaven pour
down on a forlorner head. Yet I tried 10 days at a sort
of a friend's house, but it was large and straggling—one
of the individuals of my old long knot of friends, card
players, pleasant companions—that have tumbled to
pieces into dust and other things—and I got home on
Thursday, convinced that I was better to get home to
my hole at Enfield, and hide like a sick cat in my corner.
  Less than a month I hope will bring home Mary. She

[1] Emma Isola, the Lambs' foster-daughter; married Edward Moxon
in 1833.—J. M. B.

is at Fulham, looking better in her health than ever, but sadly rambling, and scarce showing any pleasure in seeing me, or curiosity when I should come again. But the old feelings will come back again, and we shall drown old sorrows over a game at Picquet again. But 'tis a tedious cut out of a life of sixty four, to lose twelve or thirteen weeks every year or two. And to make me more alone, our illtemperd maid is gone, who with all her airs, was yet a home piece of furniture, a record of better days; the young thing that has succeeded her is good and attentive, but she is nothing—and I have no one here to talk over old matters with. Scolding and quarreling have something of familiarity and a community of interest—they imply acquaintance—they are of resentment, which is of the family of dearness. I can neither scold nor quarrel at this insignificant implement of household services; she is less than a cat, and just better than a deal Dresser. What I can do, and do over-do, is to walk, but deadly long are the days—these summer all-day days, with but a half hour's candlelight and no firelight. I do not write, tell your kind inquisitive Eliza, and can hardly read.

In the ensuing Blackwood will be an old rejected farce of mine, which may be new to you, if you see that same dull Medley. What things are all the Magazines now! I contrive studiously not to see them. The popular New Monthly is perfect trash. Poor Hessey, I suppose you see, has failed. Hunt and Clarke too. Your "Vulgar truths" will be a good name—and I think your prose must please—me at least—but 'tis useless to write poetry with no purchasers. 'Tis cold work Authorship without something to puff one into fashion. Could you not write something on Quakerism—for Quakers to read—but nominally addrest to Non Quakers? explaining your dogmas—waiting on the Spirit—by the analogy

of human calmness and patient waiting on the judgment?
I scarcely know what I mean, but to make Non Quakers
reconciled to your doctrines, by shewing something
like them in mere human operations—but I hardly understand myself, so let it pass for nothing.

I pity you for over-work, but I assure you no-work is
worse. The mind preys on itself, the most unwholesome
food. I brag'd formerly that I could not have too much
time. I have a surfeit. With few years to come, the days
are wearisome. But weariness is not eternal. Something
will shine out to take the load off, that flags me, which
is at present intolerable. I have killed an hour or two
in this poor scrawl. I am a sanguinary murderer of time,
and would kill him inchmeal just now. But the snake is
vital. Well, I shall write merrier anon.—'Tis the present
copy of my countenance I send—and to complain is a
little to alleviate.—May you enjoy yourself as far as the
wicked wood will let you—and think that you are not
quite alone, as I am. Health to Lucia and to Anna and
kind rememb^{ces}.

Yours forlorn.   C. L.

❖

TO WILLIAM WORDSWORTH

[P.M. 22nd January 1830.]

And is it a year since we parted from you at the steps
of Edmonton Stage? There are not now the years that
there used to be. The tale of the dwindled age of men,
reported of successional mankind, is true of the same
man only. We do not live a year in a year now. 'Tis a
punctum stans. The seasons pass us with indifference.
Spring cheers not, nor winter heightens our gloom,

Autumn hath foregone its moralities, they are hey-pass
re-pass [as] in a show-box. Yet as far as last year occurs
back, for they scarce shew a reflex now, they make no
memory as heretofore—'twas sufficiently gloomy. Let
the sullen nothing pass.

Suffice it that after sad spirits prolonged thro' many
of its months, as it called them, we have cast our skins,
have taken a farewell of the pompous troublesome trifle
calld housekeeping, and are settled down into poor
boarders and lodgers at next door with an old couple,
the Baucis and Baucida of dull Enfield. Here we have
nothing to do with our victuals but to eat them, with
the garden but to see it grow, with the tax gatherer but
to hear him knock, with the maid but to hear her
scolded. Scot and lot, butcher, baker, are things unknown to us save as spectators of the pageant. We are
fed we know not how, quietists, confiding ravens. We
have the otium pro dignitate, a respectable insignificance. Yet in the self condemned obliviousness, in the
stagnation, some molesting yearnings of life, not quite
kill'd, rise, prompting me that there was a London, and
that I was of that old Jerusalem.

In dreams I am in Fleetmarket, but I wake and cry
to sleep again. I die hard, a stubborn Eloisa in this detestable Paraclete. What have I gained by health? intolerable dulness. What by early hours and moderate meals?
—a total blank. O never let the lying poets be believed,
who 'tice men from the chearful haunts of streets—or
think they mean it not of a country village. In the ruins
of Palmyra I could gird myself up to solitude, or use
to the snorings of the Seven Sleepers, but to have a
little teazing image of a town about one, country folks
that do not look like country folks, shops two yards
square, half a dozen apples and two penn'orth of over-
lookd gingerbread for the lofty fruiterers of Oxford

Street—and, for the immortal book and print stalls, a circulating library that stands still, where the shew-picture is a last year's Valentine, and whither the fame of the last ten Scotch novels has not yet travel'd (marry, they just begin to be conscious of the Red Gauntlet), to have a new plasterd flat church, and to be wishing that it was but a Cathedral.

The very blackguards here are degenerate. The top-ping gentry, stock brokers. The passengers too many to ensure your quiet, or let you go about whistling, or gaping—too few to be the fine indifferent pageants of Fleet Street. Confining, room-keeping, thickest winter is yet more bearable here than the gaudy months. Among one's books at one's fire by candle one is soothed into an oblivion that one is not in the country, but with the light the green fields return, till I gaze, and in a calen-ture can plunge myself into Saint Giles's. O let no native Londoner imagine that health, and rest, and innocent occupation, interchange of converse sweet and recreative study, can make the country any thing better than al-together odious and detestable. A garden was the primi-tive prison till man with promethean felicity and bold-ness luckily sinn'd himself out of it. Thence followd Babylon, Nineveh, Venice, London, haberdashers, gold-smiths, taverns, playhouses, satires, epigrams, puns—these all came in on the town part, and the thither side of innocence. Man found out inventions.

From my den I return you condolence for your decay-ing sight, not for any thing there is to see in the country, but for the miss of the pleasure of reading a London newspaper. The poets are as well to listen to, any thing high may, nay must, be read out—you read it to your-self with an imaginary auditor—but the light paragraphs must be glid over by the proper eye, mouthing mumbles their gossamery substance. 'Tis these trifles I should mourn in fading sight. A newspaper is the single gleam of comfort I receive here, it comes from rich Cathay with tidings of mankind. Yet I could not attend to it read out by the most beloved voice. But your eyes do not get worse, I gather. O for the collyrium of Tobias inclosed in a whiting's liver to send you with no apocryphal good wishes! The last long time I heard from you, you had knock'd your head against something. Do not do so. For your head (I do not flatter) is not a nob, or the top of a brass nail, or the end of a nine pin—unless a Vulcanian hammer could fairly batter a Recluse out of it, then would I bid the smirch'd god knock and knock lustily, the two-handed skinker.

What a nice long letter Dorothy has written! Mary must squeeze out a line propriâ manu, but indeed her fingers have been incorrigibly nervous to letter writing for a long interval. 'Twill please you all to hear that, tho' I fret like a lion in a net, her present health and spirits are better than they have been for some time past: she is absolutely three years and half younger, as I tell her, since we have adopted this boarding plan.

Our providers are an honest pair, dame Westwood and her husband—he, when the light of prosperity shined on them, a moderately thriving haberdasher within Bow Bells, retired since with something under a competence, writes himself parcel gentleman, hath borne parish offices, sings fine old sea songs at threescore and ten, sighs only now and then when he thinks that he has a son on his hands about 15, whom he finds a difficulty in getting out into the world, and then checks a sigh with muttering, as I once heard him prettily, not meaning to be heard, "I have married my daughter however," —takes the weather as it comes, outsides it to town in severest season, and a' winter nights tells old stories not tending to literature, how comfortable to author-rid folks! and has *one anecdote,* upon which and about forty pounds a year he seems to have retired in green old age. It was how he was a *rider* in his youth, travelling for shops, and once (not to baulk his employer's bargain) on a sweltering day in August, rode foaming into Dunstable upon a *mad horse* to the dismay and expostulary wonderment of innkeepers, hostlers &c. who declared they would not have bestrid the beast to win the Darby. Understand the creature gall'd to death and desperation by gad flies, cormorants winged, worse than beset Inachus' daughter.

This he tells, this he brindles and burnishes on a' winter's eves, 'tis his star of set glory, his rejuvenescence to descant upon. Far from me be it (dii avertant) to look a gift story in the mouth, or cruelly to surmise (as those who doubt the plunge of Curtius) that the inseparate conjuncture of man and beast, the centaur-phenomenon that staggered all Dunstable, might have been the effect of unromantic necessity, that the horse-part carried the reasoning, willy nilly, that needs must when such a devil drove, that certain spiral configurations in the frame of Thomas Westwood unfriendly to alighting, made the alliance more forcible than voluntary. Let him enjoy his fame for me, nor let me hint a whisper that shall dismount Bellerophon. Put case he was an involuntary martyr, yet if in the fiery conflict he buckled the soul of a constant haberdasher to him, and adopted his flames, let Accident and He share the glory! You would all like Thomas Westwood.

How weak is painting to describe a man! Say that he stands four feet and a nail high by his own yard measure, which like the Sceptre of Agamemnon shall never sprout again, still you have no adequate idea, nor when I tell you that his dear hump, which I have favord in the picture, seems to me of the buffalo—indicative and repository of mild qualities, a budget of kindnesses, still you have not the man. Knew you old Norris of the Temple, 60 years ours and our father's friend, he was not more natural to us than this old W. the acquaintance of scarce more weeks. Under his roof now ought I to take my rest, but that back-looking ambition tells me I might yet be a Londoner.

Well, if we ever do move, we have encumbrances the less to impede us: all our furniture has faded under the auctioneer's hammer, going for nothing like the tarnishd frippery of the prodigal, and we have only a spoon or two left to bless us. Clothed we came into Enfield, and naked we must go out of it. I would live in London shirtless, bookless.

Henry Crabb is at Rome, advices to that effect have reach'd Bury. But by solemn legacy he bequeath'd at parting (whether he should live or die) a Turkey of Suffolk to be sent every succeeding Xmas to us and divers other friends. What a genuine old Bachelor's action! I fear he will find the air of Italy too classic. His station is in the Hartz forest, his soul is *Begoethed*. Miss Kelly we never see; Talfourd not this half-year; the latter flourishes, but the exact number of his children, God forgive me, I have utterly forgotten, we single people are often out in our count there. Shall I say two? One darling I know they have lost within a twelvemonth, but scarce known to me by sight, and that was a second child lost.

We see scarce anybody. We have just now Emma with

us for her holydays; you remember her playing at brag
with Mr. Quillinan at poor Monkhouse's! She is grown
an agreeable young woman; she sees what I write, so
you may understand me with limitations. She was our
inmate for a twelvemonth, grew natural to us, and then
they told us it was best for her to go out as a Governess,
and so she went out, and we were only two of us, and
our pleasant house-mate is changed to an occasional
visitor. If they want my sister to go out (as they call it)
there will be only one of us. Heaven keep us all from this
acceding to Unity!

Can I cram loves enough to you all in this little O?
Excuse particularizing.   C. L.

❖

TO DR. J. VALE ASBURY

[*April, 1830?*]

DEAR SIR,

It is an observation of a wise man that "moderation is
best in all things." I cannot agree with him "in liquor."
There is a smoothness and oiliness in wine that makes it
go down by a natural channel, which I am positive was
made for that descending. Else, why does not wine choke
us? could Nature have made that sloping lane, not to
facilitate the down-going? She does nothing in vain. You
know that better than I. You know how often she has
helped you at a dead lift, and how much better entitled
she is to a fee than yourself sometimes, when you carry
off the credit. Still there is something due to manners and
customs, and I should apologise to you and Mrs. Asbury
for being absolutely carried home upon a man's shoulder
thro' Silver Street, up Parson's Lane, by the Chapels
(which might have taught me better), and then to be

deposited like a dead log at Gaffar Westwood's, who it
seems does not "insure" against intoxication. Not that
the mode of conveyance is objectionable. On the contrary, it is more easy than a one-horse chaise. Ariel in the
"Tempest" says

> On a Bat's back do I fly,
> After sunset merrily.

Now I take it that Ariel must sometimes have stayed out
late of nights. Indeed, he pretends that "where the bee
sucks, there lurks he," as much as to say that his suction
is as innocent as that little innocent (but damnably sting-
ing when he is provok'd) winged creature. But I take it,
that Ariel was fond of metheglin, of which the Bees are
notorious Brewers.

But then you will say: What a shocking sight to see a
middle-aged gentleman-and-a-half riding a Gentleman's
back up Parson's Lane at midnight. Exactly the time for
that sort of conveyance, when nobody can see him, nobody but Heaven and his own conscience; now Heaven
makes fools, and don't expect much from her own creation; and as for conscience, She and I have long since
come to a compromise. I have given up false modesty,
and she allows me to abate a little of the true. I like to
be liked, but I don't care about being respected. I don't
respect myself. But, as I was saying, I thought he would
have let me down just as we got to Lieutenant Barker's
Coalshed (or emporium) but by a cunning jerk I eased
myself, and righted my posture.

I protest, I thought myself in a palanquin, and never
felt myself so grandly carried. It was a slave under me.
There was I, all but my reason. And what is reason? and
what is the loss of it? and how often in a day do we do
without it, just as well? Reason is only counting, two and
two makes four. And if on my passage home, I thought

it made five, what matter? Two and two will just make four, as it always did, before I took the finishing glass that did my business.

My sister has begged me to write an apology to Mrs. A. and you for disgracing your party; now it does seem to me, that I rather honoured your party, for every one that was not drunk (and one or two of the ladies, I am sure, were not) must have been set off greatly in the contrast to me. I was the scapegoat. The soberer they seemed. By the way is magnesia good on these occasions? *iii* pol: [? pil:] med: sum: ante noct: in rub: can:. I am no licentiate, but know enough of simples to beg you to send me a draught after this model. But still you'll say (or the men and maids at your house will say) that it is not a seemly sight for an old gentleman to go home pick-a-back. Well, may be it is not. But I have never studied grace. I take it to be a mere superficial accomplishment. I regard more the internal acquisitions. The great object after supper is to get home, and whether that is obtained in a horizontal posture or perpendicular (as foolish men and apes affect for dignity) I think is little to the purpose. The end is always greater than the means. Here I am, able to compose a sensible rational apology, and what signifies how I got here? I have just sense enough to remember I was very happy last night, and to thank our kind host and hostess, and that's sense enough, I hope.

CHARLES LAMB.

N.B.—What is good for a desperate head-ache? Why, Patience, and a determination not to mind being miserable all day long. And that I have made my mind up to.

So, here goes. It is better than not being alive at all, which I might have been, had your man toppled me

down at Lieut. Barker's Coalshed. My sister sends her
sober compliments to Mrs. A. She is not much the worse.

Yours truly,

C. LAMB.

❖

TO GEORGE DYER

Feb. 22nd, 1831.

DEAR DYER,

Mr. Rogers, and Mr. Rogers's friends, are perfectly assured, that you never intended any harm by an innocent
couplet, and that in the revivification of it by blundering
Barker you had no hand whatever. To imagine that, at
this time of day, Rogers broods over a fantastic expression of more than thirty years' standing, would be to
suppose him indulging his pleasures of memory with a
vengeance. You never penn'd a line which for its own
sake you need, dying, wish to blot. You mistake your
heart if you think you *can* write a lampoon. Your whips
are rods of roses. Your spleen has ever had for its objects
vices, not the vitious; abstract offences, not the concrete
sinner. But you are sensitive; and wince as much at the
consciousness of having committed a compliment, as
another man would at the perpetration of an affront. But
do not lug me into the same soreness of conscience with
yourself.

I maintain, and will to the last hour, that I never writ
of you but *con amore*. That if any allusion was made to
your near sightedness, it was not for the purpose of mocking an infirmity, but of connecting it with scholar-like
habits; for is it not erudite and scholarly to be somewhat
near of sight, before age naturally brings on the malady?

You could not *then* plead the *obrepens senectus*. Did I not moreover make it an apology for a certain *absence*, which some of your friends may have experienced, when you have not on a sudden made recognition of them in a casual street-meeting? and did I not strengthen your excuse for this slowness of recognition by further accounting morally for the present engagement of your mind in worthy objects? Did I not, in your person, make the handsomest apology for absent-of-mind people that was ever made? If these things be not so, I never knew what I wrote, or meant by my writing, and have been penning libels all my life without being aware of it. Does it follow that I should have exprest myself exactly in the same way of those dear old eyes of yours *now*, now that Father Time has conspired with a hard task-master to put a last extinguisher upon them? I should as soon have insulted the Answerer of Salmasius, when he awoke up from his ended task, and saw no more with mortal vision.

But you are many films removed yet from Milton's calamity. You write perfectly intelligibly. Marry, the Letters are not all of the same size or tallness; but that only shows your proficiency in the *hands*, text, german hand, court-hand, sometimes Law hand, and affords variety. You pen better than you did a twelvemonth ago, and if you continue to improve, you bid fair to win the golden pen which is the prize of your young Gentlemen's academy. But you must beware of Valpy, and his printing house, that hazy cave of Trophonius, out of which it was a mercy that you escaped with a glimmer. Beware of M.S.S.—and Variæ Lectiones. Settle the text for once in your mind, and stick to it. You have some years' good sight in you yet, if you do not tamper with it. It is not for you (for *us* I should say) to go poring into Greek contractions, and star-gazing upon slim Hebrew points. We have yet the sight

—of sun, and moon, and star, throughout the year,
And man and woman—

you have vision enough to discern Mrs. Dyer from the
other comely Gentlewoman who lives up at staircase No.
5; or if you should make a blunder in the twilight, Mrs.
Dyer has too much good sense to be jealous for a mere
effect of imperfect optics. But don't try to write the
Lord's Prayer, Creed, and Ten Commandments, in the
compass of a half-penny; nor run after a midge, or a
mote, to catch it, and leave off hunting for needles in
bushels of hay—for all these things strain the eyes.

By the way, Mrs. Dyer seems to have misled you respecting the price of bread and flour. Perhaps she may
have her family reasons for it. So this is all entrè nous.
She may not always make her accounts right at the end
of the week, and then she says *things are dearer.* They
tell me, loaves have *not* risen; and there is moreover a
considerable reduction in starch and powder blue. As
Agamemnon counsels Ulysses in the Odysee, Penelope
was a good housewife in the main, but she might be
trusted too far. It is as well to look into these things
yourself. But then again, those baker's bills are in such
a *small hand.* I believe you must go on trusting her.

The snow is six feet deep in some parts here. I must
put on jack boots to get at the post office with this. It is
not good for weak eyes to pore upon snow too much. It
lies in drifts. I wonder what its drift is, only that it makes
good pancakes, remind Mrs. Dyer. It turns a pretty green
world into a white one. It glares too much for an innocent colour, methinks.

I wonder why you think I dislike gilt edges. They set
off a Letter marvellously. Yours for instance looks for
all the world like a tablet of curious *hieroglyphics* in a
gold frame. But d'ont go and lay this to your eyes. You

always wrote hieroglyphically, yet not to come up to the mystical notations and conjuring characters of Dr. Parr. You never wrote what I call a schoolmaster's hand, like Clarke; nor a woman's hand, like Southey; nor a Missal hand, like Porson: nor an all-of-the-wrong-side-sloping hand, like Miss Hayes; nor a dogmatic Mede-and-Persian, peremptory hand, like Rickman; but you ever wrote what I call a Grecian's hand—what the Grecians write (or used) at Christs Hospital; such as Whalley would have admired, and Boyer have applauded, but Smith or Atwood (writing master) would have horsed you for. Your boy-of-genius hand and your mercantile hand are various. By your flourishes, I should think you never learn'd to make eagles or corkscrews, or flourish the governors' names in the writing school; and by the tenor and cut of your Letters I suspect you were never in it at all.

By the length of this scrawl you will think I have a design upon your optics; but I have writ as large as I could, out of respect to them, too large, indeed, for beauty. Mine is a sort of deputy Grecians hand, a little better, and more of a worldly hand than a Grecian's, but still remote from the mercantile. I d'ont know how it is, but I keep my rank in fancy still since school-days. I can never forget I was a deputy Grecian! And writing to you, or to Coleridge, besides affection, I feel a reverential deference as to Grecians still—I keep my soaring way above the Great Erasmians yet far beneath the other: Alas! what am I now? what is a Leadenhall clerk, or India pensioner, to a deputy Grecian? How art thou fallen, O Lucifer! Just room for our loves to Mrs. D., Miss Mather &c. and don't let the former see this.

C. LAMB.

❖

TO S. T. COLERIDGE

April 14th, 1832.

MY DEAR COLERIDGE,

Not an unkind thought has passed in my brain about you. But I have been wofully neglectful of you, so that I do not deserve to announce to you, that if I do not hear from you before then, I will set out on Wednesday morning to take you by the hand. I would do it this moment, but an unexpected visit might flurry you. I shall take silence for acquiescence, and come. I am glad you could write so long a letter. Old loves to, and hope of kind looks from, the Gilman's, when I come.

Yours *semper idem*   C. L.

If you ever thought an offence, much more wrote it, against me, it must have been in the times of Noah; and the great waters swept it away. Mary's most kind love, and maybe a wrong prophet of your bodings!—here she is crying for mere love over your letter. I wring out less, but not sincerer, showers.

My direction is simply, Enfield.

❖

TO EDWARD MOXON

[P.M. *27th April 1833.*]

DEAR M.,

Mary and I are very poorly. Asbury says tis nothing but influenza. Mr. W. appears all but dying, he is delirious. Mrs. W. was taken so last night, that Mary was obliged at midnight to knock up Mrs. Waller to come and sit up with her. We have had a sick child, who sleeping, or not sleeping, next me with a pasteboard partition between, killed my sleep. The little bastard is gone. My bedfellows are Cough and cramp, we slccp 3 in a bed. Domestic arrangem^ts (Blue Butcher and all) devolve on Mary. Don't come yet to this house of pest and age. We propose when E. and you agree on the time, to come up and meet her at the Buffams', say a week hence, but do you make the appointm^t. The Lachlans send her their love.

I do sadly want those 2 last Hogarths—and an't I to have the Play?

Mind our spirits are good and we are happy in your happinesses.

C. L.

Our old and ever loves to dear Em.

❖

TO WILLIAM WORDSWORTH

End of May nearly, [1833].

DEAR WORDSWORTH,

Your letter, save in what respects your dear Sister's health, chear'd me in my new solitude. Mary is ill again. Her illnesses encroach yearly. The last was three months, followed by two of depression most dreadful. I look back upon her earlier attacks with longing. Nice little durations of six weeks or so, followed by complete restoration—shocking as they were to me then. In short, half her life she is dead to me, and the other half is made anxious with fears and lookings forward to the next shock. With such prospects, it seem'd to me necessary

that she should no longer live with me, and be fluttered
with continual removals, so I am come to live with her,
at a Mr. Walden's and his wife, who take in patients, and
have arranged to lodge and board us only. They have
had the care of her before. I see little of her; alas! I too
often hear her. Sunt lachrymæ rerum—and you and I
must bear it—

To lay a little more load on it, a circumstance has
happen'd, *cujus pars magna fui,* and which at another
crisis I should have more rejoiced in. I am about to lose
my old and only walk-companion, whose mirthful spirits
were the "youth of our house," Emma Isola. I have her
here now for a little while, but she is too nervous properly to be under such a roof, so she will make short visits,
be no more an inmate. With my perfect approval, and
more than concurrence, she is to be wedded to Moxon at
the end of Augst. So "perish the roses and the flowers"—
how is it?

Now to the brighter side, I am emancipated from most
hated and *detestable* people, the Westwoods. I am with
attentive people, and younger—I am 3 or 4 miles nearer
the Great City, Coaches half-price less, and going always of which I will avail myself. I have few friends
left there, one or two tho' most beloved. But London
Streets and faces cheer me inexpressibly, tho' of the
latter not one known one were remaining.

Thank you for your cordial reception of Elia. Inter nos
the Ariadne is not a darling with me, several incongruous
things are in it, but in the composition it served me as
illustrative.

I want you in the popular fallacies to like the "Home
that is no home" and "rising with the lark."

I am feeble, but chearful in this my genial hot
weather,—walk'd 16 miles yesterd^y. I can't read much
in Summer time.

With very kindest love to all and prayers for dear Dorothy,

> I remain
>
>> most attachedly yours   C. LAMB.

at mr. walden's, church street, *edmonton,* middlesex.

Moxon has introduced Emma to Rogers, and he smiles upon the project. I have given E. my MILTON—will you pardon me?—in part of a *portion.* It hangs famously in his Murray-like shop.

[*On the wrapper is written:*]
D^r M[oxon], inclose this in a better-looking paper, and get it frank'd, and good by'e till Sund^y. Come early—

>> C. L.

❖

TO LOUISA BADAMS

[P.M. *20th August 1833.*]

DEAR MRS. BADAMS,
I was at church, as the grave Father, and behaved tolerably well, except at first entrance, when Emma in a whisper repressed a nascent giggle. I am not fit for weddings or burials. Both incite a chuckle. Emma look'd as pretty as Pamela, and made her responses delicately and firmly. I tripped a little at the altar, was engaged in admiring the altar-piece; but, recalled seasonably by a Parsonic rebuke, "Who gives this woman?" was in time resolutely to reply, "I do." Upon the whole the thing went off decently & devoutly.—Your dodging post is excellent; I take it, it was at Wilsdon—.
We shall this week or next dine at Islington,—I am

writing to know the day—& in that case see you the next
day, & talk of beds. *My* lodging may be on the cold floor.
I long for a *hard fought game* with Badams. With haste
& thanks for your *unusually* entertaining letter,

Yours truly,

Chas. & Mary Lamb.

I will write to Miss Ja*ª*. soon, was meditating it.

❖

TO MARIA FRYER

Feb. 14, 1834.

Dear Miss Fryer,

Your letter found me just returned from keeping my
birthday (pretty innocent!) at Dover-street. I see them
pretty often. I have since had letters of business to write,
or should have replied earlier. In one word, be less uneasy about me; I bear my privations very well; I am not
in the depths of desolation, as heretofore. Your admonitions are not lost upon me. Your kindness has sunk into
my heart. Have faith in me! It is no new thing for me to
be left to my sister. When she is not violent her rambling chat is better to me than the sense and sanity of
this world. Her heart is obscured, not buried; it breaks
out occasionally; and one can discern a strong mind
struggling with the billows that have gone over it. I
could be nowhere happier than under the same roof
with her. Her memory is unnaturally strong; and from
ages past, if we may so call the earliest records of our
poor life, she fetches thousands of names and things
that never would have dawned upon me again, and
thousands from the ten years she lived before me.

What took place from early girlhood to her coming of
age principally lives again (every important thing and

every trifle) in her brain with the vividness of real presence. For twelve hours incessantly she will pour out
without intermission all her past life, forgetting nothing,
pouring out name after name to the Waldens as a dream;
sense and nonsense; truths and errors huddled together;
a medley between inspiration and possession. What
things we are! I know you will bear with me, talking of
these things. It seems to ease me; for I have nobody to
tell these things to now. Emma, I see, has got a harp!
and is learning to play. She has framed her three Walton
pictures, and pretty they look. That is a book you should
read; such sweet religion in it—next to Woolman's!
though the subject be baits and hooks, and worms, and
fishes. She has my copy at present to do two more from.

Very, very tired, I began this epistle, having been
epistolising all the morning, and very kindly would I end
it, could I find adequate expressions to your kindness.
We did set our minds on seeing you in spring. One of us
will indubitably. But I am not skilled in almanac learning, to know when spring precisely begins and ends.
Pardon my blots; I am glad you like your book. I wish it
had been half as worthy of your acceptance as "John
Woolman." But 'tis a good-natured book.

❖

TO THOMAS MANNING

[P.M. 10th May 1834.]

You made me feel so funny, so happy-like, it was as if
I was reading one of your old letters taken out of hazard
any time between the last twenty years, twas so the
same. The Unity of place, a Garden! the old Dramatis
personæ, a Landlady and Daughter. The puns the same
in mold. Will nothing change you? Tis but a short week

since honest Ryle & I were lamenting the gone by days
of Manning and Whist. How savourily did he remember
them! Might some Great Year but bring them back
again. This was my exclaim, and R. did not ask for an
explanation.

I have had a scurvy nine years of it, and am now in
the sorry fifth act. Twenty weeks nigh has she been now
violent, with but a few sound months before, and those
in such dejection that her fever might seem a relief to it.
I tried to bring her down in the winter once or twice, but
it failed. Tuthill led me to expect that this illness would
lengthen with her years, & it has cruelly, with that new
feature of despondency after. I am with her alone now
in a proper house. She is I hope recovering.

We play picquet, and it is like the old times a while,
then goes off—I struggle up town rarely, and then to see
London with little other motive, for what is left there
hardly! The streets and shops entertaining ever, else I
feel as in a desert, & get me home to my cave. Save that
once a month I pass a day, a gleam in my life, with Cary
at the Museum. (He is the flower of Clergymen) &
breakfast next morn with Robinson. I look to this as a
treat. It sustains me. C is a dear fellow, with but two
vices, which in any less good than himself would be
crimes, past redemption. He has no relish for Parson
Adams—hints that he might not be a very great Greek
Scholar after all, (does Fielding hint that he was a
Porson?) and prefers "Ye Shepherds so cheerful & gay"
& "my banks they are furnished with bees" to the
"Schoolmistress." I have not seen Wright's—but the
faithfulness of C—Mary & I can attest.

For last year in a good interval, I giving some lessons
to Emma, now Mrs. Moxon, in the sense part of her
Italian (I knew no words) Mary pertinaciously under-
took, being 69, to read the Inferno all thro' with the help

of his translation, and we got thro' it with Dictionaries &
Grammars of course to our satisfaction. Her perseverance
was gigantic, almost painful. Her head was over her task
like a sticking bee, morn to night. We were beginning
the Purgatory, but got on less rapidly, our great authority for Grammar, Emma, being fled, but should have
proceeded but for this misfortune. Do not come to town
without apprising me. We must all 3 meet somehow, &
"drink a cup."   Yours ever C. L.

Mary strives & struggles to be content, when she *is*
well. Last year when we talk'd of being dull (we had
just lost our 7 years nearly inmate) & Carys invitation
came, she said "Did not I say something or other would
turn up?" In her first walk *out* of the house, she would
read every Auction Advertisement along the road, and
when I would stop her, she said "These are *my* play-
bills." She felt glad to get into the world again, but
then follows lowness.—

She is getting about tho' I very much hope. She is
rising, & will claim her morning picquet. I go to put this
in the post first—
I walk 9 or 10 miles a day alway up the road, dear
Londonwards. Fields, flowers, birds, & green lanes I have
no heart for. The Ware road is chearful, & almost good
as a street. I saunter to the Red Lion duly, as you used
to the Peacock!

❖

TO MRS. GEORGE DYER

Dec. 22nd, 1834.[1]

DEAR MRS. DYER,

I am very uneasy about a *Book* which I either have lost or left at your house on Thursday. It was the book I went out to fetch from Miss Buffam's, while the tripe was frying. It is called Phillip's Theatrum Poetarum; but it is an English book. I think I left it in the parlour. It is Mr. Cary's book, and I would not lose it for the world. Pray, if you find it, book it at the Swan, Snow Hill, by an Edmonton stage immediately, directed to Mr. Lamb, Church-street, Edmonton, or write to say you cannot find it. I am quite anxious about it. If it is lost, I shall never like tripe again.

With kindest love to Mr. Dyer and all.

Yours truly,

C. LAMB

[1] Lamb's last letter. On this day he fell in the street, developed erysipelas, and died December 27, 1834.—J. M. B.

PART TWO

Himself, His Youth, and His Family

CHARLES LAMB'S AUTOBIOGRAPHY

CHARLES LAMB, born in the Inner Temple, 10th February, 1775; educated in Christ's Hospital; afterwards a clerk in the Accountants' Office, East India House; pensioned off from that service, 1825, after thirty-three years' service; is now a gentleman at large; can remember few specialities in his life worth noting, except that he once caught a swallow flying (*teste suâ manu*). Below the middle stature; cast of face slightly Jewish, with no Judaic tinge in his complexional religion; stammers abominably, and is therefore more apt to discharge his occasional conversation in a quaint aphorism, or a poor quibble, than in set and edifying speeches; has consequently been libelled as a person always aiming at wit; which, as 1e told a dull fellow that charged him with it, is at least as good as aiming at dullness. A small eater, but not drinker; confesses a partiality for the production of the juniper-berry; was a fierce smoker of tobacco, but may be resembled to a volcano burnt out, emitting only now and then a casual puff.

Has been guilty of obtruding upon the public a tale, in prose, called *Rosamund Gray*; a dramatic sketch, named *John Woodvil*; a "Farewell Ode to Tobacco," with sundry other poems, and light prose matter, collected in two slight crown octavos, and pompously christened his "works," though in fact they were his recreations. His true works may be found on the shelves of Leadenhall Street, filling some hundred folios. He is also the true Elia, whose Essays are extant in a little volume, published a year or two since, and rather better known from that name without a meaning than from anything he has done, or can hope to do, in his own name.

He was also the first to draw the public attention to the old English dramatists, in a work called *Specimens of English Dramatic Writers Who Lived about the Time of Shakspeare*, published about fifteen years since. In short, all his merits and demerits to set forth would take to the end of Mr. Upcott's book, and then not be told truly.

He died   18   , much lamented.[1]

          Witness his hand.

                    CHARLES LAMB.

18th April, 1827

    Published posthumously in *New Monthly Magazine*, April 1835.

A CHARACTER OF THE LATE ELIA

BY A FRIEND

THIS gentleman, who for some months past had been in a declining way, hath at length paid his final tribute to

[1] To anybody—please to fill up these blanks.—C. L.

Nature. He just lived long enough (it was what he wished) to see his papers collected into a volume. The pages of the *London Magazine* will henceforth know him no more.

Exactly at twelve, last night, his queer spirit departed; and the bells of Saint Bride's rang him out with the old year. The mournful vibrations were caught in the dining-room of his friends T. and H.[1]; and the company, assembled there to welcome in another 1st of January, checked their carousals in mid-earth, and were silent. Janus wept. The gentle P——r,[2] in a whisper, signified his intention of devoting an elegy; and Allan C.,[3] nobly forgetful of his countrymen's wrongs, vowed a memoir to his *manes*, full and friendly, as a *Tale of Lyddalcross*.

To say truth, it is time he were gone. The humour of the thing, if there was ever much in it, was pretty well exhausted; and a two years and a half's existence has been a tolerable duration for a phantom.

I am now at liberty to confess, that much which I have heard objected to my late friend's writings was well founded. Crude they are, I grant you—a sort of unlicked, incondite things—villainously pranked in an affected array of antique modes and phrases. They had not been *his* if they had been other than such; and better it is that a writer should be natural in a self-pleasing quaintness, than to affect a naturalness (so called) that should be strange to him.

Egotistical they have been pronounced by some who did not know that what he tells us as of himself was often true only (historically) of another; as in his Third Essay[4] (to save many instances), where, under the *first person*

---

[1] Taylor and Hessey, the publishers of the *London Magazine*.—J. M. B.

[2] Proctor, better known as Barry Cornwall.—J. M. B.

[3] Cunningham.—J. M. B.

[4] See "Christ's Hospital Five-and-thirty Years Ago."—J. M. B.

(his favourite figure), he shadows forth the forlorn estate of a country boy placed at a London school, far from his friends and connections—in direct opposition to his own early history. If it be egotism to imply and twine with his own identity the griefs and affections of another —making himself many, or reducing many unto himself —then is the skilful novelist, who all along brings in his hero or heroine, speaking of themselves, the greatest egotist of all; who yet has never, therefore, been accused of that narrowness. And how shall the intenser dramatist escape being faulty, who doubtless, under cover of passion uttered by another, oftentimes gives blameless vent to his most inward feelings, and expresses his own story modestly?

My late friend was in many respects a singular character. Those who did not like him hated him; and some, who once liked him, afterwards became his bitterest haters. The truth is, he gave himself too little concern about what he uttered, and in whose presence. He observed neither time nor place, and would ever out with what came uppermost. With the severe religionist he would pass for a free-thinker; while the other faction set him down for a bigot, or persuaded themselves that he belied his sentiments. Few understood him; and I am not certain that at all times he quite understood himself. He too much affected that dangerous figure—irony. He sowed doubtful speeches, and reaped plain, unequivocal hatred. He would interrupt the gravest discussion with some light jest; and yet, perhaps, not quite irrelevant in ears that could understand it. Your long and much talkers hated him. The informal habit of his mind, joined to an inveterate impediment of speech, forbade him to be an orator; and he seemed determined that no one else should play that part when he was present.

He was *petit* and ordinary in his person and appear-

ance. I have seen him sometimes in what is called good
company, but, where he has been a stranger, sit silent,
and be suspected for an odd fellow, till (some unlucky
occasion provoking it) he would stutter out some senseless pun (not altogether senseless perhaps, if rightly
taken), which has stamped his character for the evening.
It was hit or miss with him; but, nine times out of ten,
he contrived by this device to send away a whole company his enemies. His conceptions rose kindlier than his
utterance, and his happiest impromptus had the appearance of effort. He has been accused of trying to be witty,
when in truth he was but struggling to give his poor
thoughts articulation.

He chose his companions for some individuality of
character which they manifested. Hence not many persons of science, and few professed *literati*, were of his
councils. They were, for the most part, persons of an uncertain fortune; and as to such people, commonly, nothing is more obnoxious than a gentleman of settled
(though moderate) income, he passed with most of them
for a great miser. To my knowledge, this was a mistake.
His *intimados*, to confess a truth, were, in the world's
eye, a ragged regiment. He found them floating on the
surface of society; and the colour, or something else, in
the weed, pleased him. The burs stuck to him; but they
were good and loving burs for all that.

He never greatly cared for the society of what are
called good people. If any of these were scandalised
(and offences were sure to arise), he could not help it.
When he has been remonstrated with for not making
more concessions to the feelings of good people, he
would retort by asking, What one point did these good
people ever concede to him?

He was temperate in his meals and diversions, but
always kept a little on this side of abstemiousness. Only

in the use of the Indian weed he might be thought a little excessive. He took it, he would say, as a solvent of speech. Marry—as the friendly vapour ascended, how his prattle would curl up sometimes with it! the ligaments, which tongue-tied him, were loosened, and the stammerer proceeded a statist!

I do not know whether I ought to bemoan or rejoice that my old friend is departed. His jests were beginning to grow obsolete, and his stories to be found out. He felt the approaches of age; and, while he pretended to cling to life, you saw how slender were the ties left to bind him. Discoursing with him latterly on this subject, he expressed himself with a pettishness which I thought unworthy of him. In our walks about his suburban retreat (as he called it) at Shacklewell, some children belonging to a School of Industry met us, and bowed and courtesied, as he thought, in an especial manner to *him*. "They take me for a visiting governor," he muttered earnestly. He had a horror, which he carried to a foible, of looking like anything important and parochial. He thought that he approached nearer to that stamp daily. He had a general aversion from being treated like a grave or respectable character, and kept a wary eye upon the advances of age that should so entitle him.

He herded always, while it was possible, with people younger than himself. He did not conform to the march of time, but was dragged along in the procession. His manners lagged behind his years. He was too much of the boy-man. The *toga virilis* never sat gracefully on his shoulders. The impressions of infancy had burnt into him, and he resented the impertinence of manhood. These were weaknesses; but such as they were, they are a key to explicate some of his writings.

He left little property behind him. Of course, the little that is left (chiefly in India bonds) devolves upon his cousin Bridget.[1] A few critical dissertations were found in his *escritoire*, which have been handed over to the editor of this magazine, in which it is to be hoped they will shortly appear, retaining his accustomed signature.

He has himself not obscurely hinted that his employment lay in a public office. The gentlemen in the export department of the East India House will forgive me if I acknowledge the readiness with which they assisted me in the retrieval of his few manuscripts. They pointed out in a most obliging manner the desk at which he had been planted for forty years; showed me ponderous tomes of figures, in his own remarkably neat hand, which, more properly than his few printed tracts, might be called his "Works." They seemed affectionate to his memory, and universally commended his expertness in book-keeping. It seems he was the inventor of some ledger which should combine the precision and certainty of the Italian double entry (I think they called it) with the brevity and facility of some newer German system; but I am not able to appreciate the worth of the discovery.

I have often heard him express a warm regard for his associates in office, and how fortunate he considered himself in having his lot thrown in amongst them. There is more sense, more discourse, more shrewdness, and even talent, among these clerks (he would say), than in twice the number of authors by profession that I have conversed with. He would brighten up sometimes upon the "old days of the India House," when he consorted with Woodroffe and Wissett, and Peter Corbet (a descendant and worthy representative, bating the point of sanctity, of old facetious Bishop Corbet); and Hoole, who translated Tasso; and Bartlemy Brown, whose father (God assoil him therefore!) modernized Walton: and sly, warm hearted old Jack Cole (King Cole they

---

[1] Lamb's name for his sister Mary.—J. M. B.

called him in those days), and Campe and Fombelle, and a world of choice spirits, more than I can remember to name, who associated in those days with Jack Burrell (the *bon vivant* of the South-Sea House); and little Eyton (said to be a *facsimile* of Pope—he was a miniature of a gentleman), that was cashier under him; and Dan Voight of the Custom House, that left the famous library.

Well, Elia is gone—for aught I know, to be reunited with them—and these poor traces of his pen are all we have to show for it. How little survives of the wordiest authors! Of all they said or did in their lifetime, a few glittering words only! His Essays found some favourers, as they appeared separately. They shuffled their way in the crowd well enough singly: how they will *read*, now they are brought together, is a question for the publishers, who have thus ventured to draw out into one piece his "weaved-up follies."   PHIL-ELIA

London Magazine, 1823.

MY RELATIONS

I AM arrived at that point of life at which a man may account it a blessing, as it is a singularity, if he have either of his parents surviving. I have not that felicity— and sometimes think feelingly of a passage in Browne's Christian Morals, where he speaks of a man that hath lived sixty or seventy years in the world. "In such a compass of time," he says, " a man may have a close apprehension what it is to be forgotten, when he hath lived to find none who could remember his father, or scarcely the friends of his youth, and may sensibly see with what a face in no long time OBLIVION will look upon him-self."

I had an aunt,[1] a dear and good one. She was one whom single blessedness had soured to the world. She often used to say, that I was the only thing in it which she loved; and, when she thought I was quitting it, she grieved over me with mother's tears. A partiality quite so exclusive my reason cannot altogether approve. She was from morning till night poring over good books, and devotional exercises. Her favourite volumes were, Thomas à Kempis, in Stanhope's translation; and a Roman Catholic Prayer Book, with the *matins and complines* regularly set down—terms which I was at that time too young to understand. She persisted in reading them, although admonished daily concerning their Papistical tendency; and went to church every Sabbath as a good Protestant should do. These were the only books she studied; though, I think at one period of her life, she told me, she had read with great satisfaction the "Adventures of an Unfortunate Young Nobleman."

Finding the door of the chapel in Essex Street open one day—it was in the infancy of that heresy—she went in, liked the sermon, and the manner of worship, and frequented it at intervals for some time after. She came not for doctrinal points, and never missed them. With some little asperities in her constitution, which I have above hinted at, she was a steadfast, friendly being, and a fine *old Christian*. She was a woman of strong sense, and a shrewd mind—extraordinary at a *repartee*; one of the few occasions of her breaking silence—else she did not much value wit. The only secular employ-ment I remember to have seen her engaged in, was, the splitting of French beans, and dropping them into a china basin of fair water. The odour of those tender

[1] Aunt Hetty, Sarah Lamb, his father's sister.—J. M. B.

vegetables to this day comes back upon my sense, redolent of soothing recollections. Certainly it is the most
delicate of culinary operations.

Male aunts, as somebody calls them, I had none—to
remember. By the uncle's side I may be said to have been
born an orphan. Brother, or sister, I never had any—to
know them. A sister, I think, that should have been
Elizabeth, died in both our infancies. What a comfort,
or what a care, may I not have missed in her!—But I
have cousins sprinkled about in Hertfordshire—besides
two, with whom I have been all my life in habits of the
closest intimacy, and whom I may term cousins *par
excellence*. These are James and Bridget Elia.[1] They are
older than myself by twelve, and ten, years; and neither
of them seems disposed, in matters of advice and guidance, to waive any of the prerogatives which primogeni-
ture confers. May they continue still in the same mind;
and when they shall be seventy-five, and seventy-
three, years old (I cannot spare them sooner), persist
in treating me in my grand climacteric precisely as a
stripling, or younger brother!

James is an inexplicable cousin. Nature hath her
unities, which not every critic can penetrate: or, if we
feel, we cannot explain them. The pen of Yorick, and of
none since his, could have drawn J. E. entire—those fine
Shandean lights and shades, which make up his story. I
must limp after in my poor antithetical manner, as the
fates have given me grace and talent. J. E. then—to the
eye of a common observer at least—seemeth made up of
contradictory principles. The genuine child of impulse,
the frigid philosopher of prudence—the phlegm of my
cousin's doctrine is invariably at war with his temperament, which is high sanguine. With always some fire-new

[1] Lamb's older brother John and, of course, his sister Mary.—
J. M. B.

project in his brain, J. E. is the systematic opponent of innovation, and crier down of everything that has not stood the test of age and experiment. With a hundred fine notions chasing one another hourly in his fancy, he is startled at the least approach to the romantic in others: and, determined by his own sense in everything, commends *you* to the guidance of common sense on all occasions.

With a touch of the eccentric in all which he does, or says, he is only anxious that *you* should not commit yourself by doing anything absurd or singular. On my once letting slip at table, that I was not fond of a certain popular dish, he begged me at any rate not to *say* so—for the world would think me mad. He disguises a passionate fondness for works of high art (whereof he hath amassed a choice collection), under the pretext of buying only to sell again—that his enthusiasm may give no encouragement to yours. Yet, if it were so, why does that piece of tender, pastoral Domenichino hang still by his wall?—is the ball of his sight much more dear to him?—or what picture-dealer can talk like him?

Whereas mankind in general are observed to warp their speculative conclusions to the bent of their individual humours, *his* theories are sure to be in diametrical opposition to his conclusions. He is courageous as Charles of Sweden, upon instinct; chary of his person upon principle, as a travelling Quaker. He has been preaching up to me, all my life, the doctrine of bowing to the great—the necessity of forms, and manner, to a man's getting on in the world. He himself never aims at either, that I can discover—and has a spirit that would stand upright in the presence of the Cham of Tartary.

It is pleasant to hear him discourse of patience—extolling it as the truest wisdom—and to see him during the last seven minutes that his dinner is getting ready.

Nature never ran up in her haste a more restless piece of workmanship than when she moulded this impetuous cousin—and Art never turned out a more elaborate orator than he can display himself to be, upon his favourite topic of the advantages of quiet and contentedness in the state, whatever it be, that we are placed in.

He is triumphant on this theme, when he has you safe in one of those short stages that ply for the western road, in a very obstructing manner, at the foot of John Murray's Street—where you get in when it is empty, and are expected to wait till the vehicle hath completed her just freight—a trying three-quarters of an hour to some people. He wonders at your fidgetiness—"where could we be better than we are, *thus sitting, thus consulting?*" —"prefers, for his part, a state of rest to locomotion"— with an eye all the while upon the coachman—till at length, waxing out of all patience, at *your want of it*, he breaks out into a pathetic remonstrance at the fellow for detaining us so long over the time which he had professed, and declares peremptorily, that "the gentleman in the coach is determined to get out, if he does not drive on that instant."

Very quick at inventing an argument, or detecting a sophistry, he is incapable of attending *you* in any chain of arguing. Indeed, he makes wild work with logic; and seems to jump at most admirable conclusions by some process, not at all akin to it. Consonantly enough to this, he hath been heard to deny, upon certain occasions, that there exists such a faculty at all in man as *reason;* and wondereth how man came first to have a conceit of it— enforcing his negation with all the might of *reasoning* he is master of.

He has some speculative notions against laughter, and will maintain that laughing is not natural to *him*—when peradventure the next moment his lungs shall crow like

Chanticleer. He says some of the best things in the world
—and declareth that wit is his aversion. It was he who
said, upon seeing the Eton boys at play in their grounds
—*What a pity to think, that these fine ingenuous lads in
a few years will all be changed into frivolous Members
of Parliament!*

His youth was fiery, glowing, tempestuous—and in
age he discovereth no symptom of cooling. This is that
which I admire in him. I hate people who meet Time
half-way. I am for no compromise with that inevitable
spoiler. While he lives, J. E. will take his swing. It does
me good, as I walk towards the street of my daily avo-
cation, on some fine May morning, to meet him marching
in a quite opposite direction, with a jolly handsome
presence, and shining sanguine face, that indicate some
purchase in his eye—a Claude—or a Hobbima—for
much of his enviable leisure is consumed at Christie's
and Phillips's—or where not, to pick up pictures, and
such gauds. On these occasions he mostly stoppeth me,
to read a short lecture on the advantage a person like me
possesses above himself, in having his time occupied
with business which he *must* do—assureth me that he
often feels it hang heavy on his hands—wishes he had
fewer holidays—and goes off—Westward Ho!—chanting a tune, to Pall Mall—perfectly convinced that he
has convinced me—while I proceed in my opposite
direction tuneless.

It is pleasant, again, to see this Professor of Indifference doing the honours of his new purchase, when he
has fairly housed it. You must view it in every light, till
he has found the best—placing it at this distance, and at
that, but always suiting the focus of your sight to his
own. You must spy at it through your fingers, to catch
the aërial perspective—though you assure him that to
you the landscape shows much more agreeable without

that artifice. Woe be to the luckless wight who does not only not respond to his rapture, but who should drop an unseasonable intimation of preferring one of his anterior bargains to the present!

The last is always his best hit—his "Cynthia of the minute."—Alas! how many a mild Madonna have I known to *come in*—a Raphael!—keep its ascendancy for a few brief moons—then, after certain intermedial degradations, from the front drawing-room to the back gallery, thence to the dark parlour—adopted in turn by each of the Carracci, under successive lowering ascriptions of filiation, mildly breaking its fall—consigned to the oblivious lumber-room, *go out* at last a Lucca Giordano, or plain Carlo Maratti!—which things when I beheld—musing upon the chances and mutabilities of fate below, hath made me to reflect upon the altered condition of great personages, or that woeful Queen of Richard the Second—

> ———set forth in pomp,
> She came adornèd hither like sweet May.
> Sent back like Hallowmass or shortest day.

With great love for *you*, J. E. hath but a limited sympathy with what you feel or do. He lives in a world of his own, and makes slender guesses at what passes in your mind. He never pierces the marrow of your habits. He will tell an old-established play-goer, that Mr. Such-a-one, of So-and-so (naming one of the theatres), is a very lively comedian—as a piece of news! He advertised me but the other day of some pleasant green lanes which he had found out for me, *knowing me to be a great walker,* in my own immediate vicinity—who have haunted the identical spot any time these twenty years!

He has not much respect for that class of feelings which goes by the name of sentimental. He applies the

definition of real evil to bodily sufferings exclusively—
and rejecteth all others as imaginary. He is affected by
the sight, or the bare supposition, of a creature in pain,
to a degree which I have never witnessed out of woman-
kind. A constitutional acuteness to this class of sufferings may in part account for this. The animal tribe in
particular he taketh under his especial protection. A
broken-winded or spur-galled horse is sure to find an
advocate in him. An overloaded ass is his client for ever.
He is the apostle to the brute kind—the never-failing
friend of those who have none to care for them. The
contemplation of a lobster boiled, or eels skinned *alive*,
will wring him so, that "all for pity he could die." It
will take the savour from his palate, and the rest from
his pillow, for days and nights.

With the intense feeling of Thomas Clarkson, he
wanted only the steadiness of pursuit, and unity of purpose, of that "true yoke-fellow with Time," to have
effected as much for the *Animal* as *he* hath done for the
Negro Creation. But my uncontrollable cousin is but
imperfectly formed for purposes which demand co-op-
eration. He cannot wait. His amelioration plans must be
ripened in a day. For this reason he has cut but an equivocal figure in benevolent societies, and combinations
for the alleviation of human sufferings. His zeal constantly makes him to outrun, and put out, his coadjutors.
He thinks of relieving,—while they think of debating.
He was black-balled out of a society for the Relief of
——, because the fervour of his humanity toiled beyond
the formal apprehension, and creeping processes, of his
associates. I shall always consider this distinction as a
patent of nobility in the Elia family!

Do I mention these seeming inconsistencies to smile
at, or upbraid, my unique cousin? Marry, heaven, and
all good manners, and the understanding that should be

between kinsfolk, forbid!—With all the strangenesses of this *strangest of the Elias*—I would not have him in one jot or tittle other than he is; neither would I barter or exchange my wild kinsman for the most exact, regular, and every way consistent kinsman breathing.

In my next, reader, I may perhaps give you some account of my cousin Bridget—if you are not already surfeited with cousins—and take you by the hand, if you are willing to go with us, on an excursion which we made a summer or two since, in search of *more cousins*—

Through the green plains of pleasant Hertfordshire.

London Magazine, June 1821; Elia.

MACKERY END, IN HERTFORDSHIRE

BRIDGET ELIA[1] has been my housekeeper for many a long year. I have obligations to Bridget, extending beyond the period of memory. We house together, old bachelor and maid, in a sort of double singleness; with such tolerable comfort, upon the whole, that I, for one, find in myself no sort of disposition to go out upon the mountains, with the rash king's offspring, to bewail my celibacy. We agree pretty well in our tastes and habits —yet so, as "with a difference." We are generally in harmony, with occasional bickerings—as it should be among near relations. Our sympathies are rather understood than expressed; and once, upon my dissembling a tone in my voice more kind than ordinary, my cousin burst into tears, and complained that I was altered.

We are both great readers in different directions.

[1] Mary Lamb.—J. M. B.

While I am hanging over (for the thousandth time)
some passage in old Burton, or one of his strange contemporaries, she is abstracted in some modern tale, or
adventure, whereof our common reading-table is daily
fed with assiduously fresh supplies. Narrative teases me.
I have little concern in the progress of events. She must
have a story—well, ill, or indifferently told—so there be
life stirring in it, and plenty of good or evil accidents.
The fluctuations of fortune in fiction—and almost in real
life—have ceased to interest, or operate but dully upon
me. Out-of-the-way humours and opinions—heads with
some diverting twist in them—the oddities of authorship, please me most.

My cousin has a native disrelish of anything that
sounds odd or bizarre. Nothing goes down with her that
is quaint, irregular, or out of the road of common sympathy. She "holds Nature more clever." I can pardon
her blindness to the beautiful obliquities of the *Religio
Medici*; but she must apologize to me for certain dis-
respectful insinuations, which she has been pleased to
throw out latterly, touching the intellectuals of a dear
favourite of mine, of the last century but one—the thrice
noble, chaste, and virtuous, but again somewhat fantastical and original-brained, generous Margaret Newcastle.

It has been the lot of my cousin, oftener perhaps than
I could have wished, to have had for her associates and
mine, free thinkers—leaders, and disciples, of novel
philosophies and systems; but she neither wrangles with,
nor accepts, their opinions. That which was good and
venerable to her, when a child, retains its authority over
her mind still. She never juggles or plays tricks with her
understanding.

We are both of us inclined to be a little too positive;
and I have observed the result of our disputes to be
almost uniformly this—that in matters of fact, dates,

and circumstances, it turns out, that I was in the right,
and my cousin in the wrong. But where we have differed
upon moral points; upon something proper to be done,
or let alone; whatever heat of opposition, or steadiness
of conviction, I set out with, I am sure always, in the
long-run, to be brought over to her way of thinking.

I must touch upon the foibles of my kinswoman with
a gentle hand, for Bridget does not like to be told of her
faults. She hath an awkward trick (to say no worse of it)
of reading in company: at which times she will answer
yes or no to a question, without fully understanding its
purport—which is provoking, and derogatory in the
highest degree to the dignity of the putter of the said
question. Her presence of mind is equal to the most
pressing trials of life, but will sometimes desert her upon
trifling occasions. When the purpose requires it, and is a
thing of moment, she can speak to it greatly; but in matters which are not stuff of the conscience, she hath been
known sometimes to let slip a word less seasonably.

Her education in youth was not much attended to;
and she happily missed all that train of female garniture
which passeth by the name of accomplishments. She was
tumbled early, by accident or design, into a spacious
closet of good old English reading, without much selection or prohibition, and browsed at will upon that fair
and wholesome pasturage. Had I twenty girls, they
should be brought up exactly in this fashion. I know not
whether their chance in wedlock might not be diminished by it; but I can answer for it, that it makes (if the
worst come to the worst) most incomparable old maids.

In a season of distress, she is the truest comforter; but
in the teasing accidents, and minor perplexities, which
do not call out the *will* to meet them, she sometimes
maketh matters worse by an excess of participation. If
she does not always divide your trouble, upon the pleas-

anter occasions of life she is sure always to treble your satisfaction. She is excellent to be at a play with, or upon a visit; but best, when she goes a journey with you.

We made an excursion together a few summers since, into Hertfordshire, to beat up the quarters of some of our less-known relations in that fine corn country.

The oldest thing I remember is Mackery End; or Mackarel End, as it is spelt, perhaps more properly, in some old maps of Hertfordshire; a farm-house—delightfully situated within a gentle walk from Wheathampstead. I can just remember having been there, on a visit to a great-aunt, when I was a child, under the care of Bridget; who, as I have said, is older than myself by some ten years. I wish that I could throw into a heap the remainder of our joint existences; that we might share them in equal division. But that is impossible. The house was at that time in the occupation of a substantial yeoman, who had married my grandmother's sister. His name was Gladman. My grandmother was Bruton, married to a Field. The Gladmans and the Brutons are still flourishing in that part of the county, but the Fields are almost extinct. More than forty years had elapsed since the visit I speak of; and, for the greater portion of that period, we had lost sight of the other two branches also. Who or what sort of persons inherited Mackery End—kindred or strange folk—we were afraid almost to conjecture, but determined some day to explore.

By somewhat a circuitous route, taking the noble park at Luton in our way from St. Albans, we arrived at the spot of our anxious curiosity about noon. The sight of the old farm-house, though every trace of it was effaced from my recollection, affected me with a pleasure which I had not experienced for many a year. For though I had forgotten it, *we* had never forgotten being there together, and we had been talking about Mackery End all our lives, till memory on my part became mocked with a phantom of itself, and I thought I knew the aspect of a place, which, when present, O how unlike it was to *that*, which I had conjured up so many times instead of it!

Still the air breathed balmily about it; the season was in "the heart of June," and I could say with the poet,

> But thou, that didst appear so fair
> To fond imagination,
> Dost rival in the light of day
> Her delicate creation!

Bridget's was more a waking bliss than mine, for she easily remembered her old acquaintance again—some altered features, of course, a little grudged at. At first, indeed, she was ready to disbelieve for joy; but the scene soon reconfirmed itself in her affections—and she traversed every outpost of the old mansion, to the wood-house, the orchard, the place where the pigeon-house had stood (house and birds were alike flown)—with a breathless impatience of recognition, which was more pardonable perhaps than decorous at the age of fifty odd. But Bridget in some things is behind her years.

The only thing left was to get into the house—and that was a difficulty which to me singly would have been insurmountable; for I am terribly shy in making myself known to strangers and out-of-date kinsfolk. Love, stronger than scruple, winged my cousin in without me; but she soon returned with a creature that might have sat to a sculptor for the image of Welcome. It was the youngest of the Gladmans; who, by marriage with a Bruton, had become mistress of the old mansion. A comely brood are the Brutons. Six of them, females, were noted as the handsomest young women in the

county. But this adopted Bruton, in my mind, was better
than they all—more comely. She was born too late to
have remembered me. She just recollected in early life to
have had her cousin Bridget once pointed out to her,
climbing a stile. But the name of kindred, and of cousin-
ship, was enough.

Those slender ties, that prove slight as gossamer in
the rending atmosphere of a metropolis, bind faster, as
we found it, in hearty, homely, loving Hertfordshire. In
five minutes we were as thoroughly acquainted as if we
had been born and bred up together; were familiar, even
to the calling each other by our Christian names. So
Christians should call one another. To have seen Bridget,
and her—it was like the meeting of the two scriptural
cousins!

There was a grace and dignity, an amplitude of form
and stature, answering to her mind, in this farmer's wife,
which would have shined in a palace—or so we thought
it. We were made welcome by husband and wife equally
—we, and our friend that was with us. I had almost forgotten him—but B. F.[1] will not so soon forget that meeting, if peradventure he shall read this on the far distant
shores where the kangaroo haunts. The fatted calf was
made ready, or rather was already so, as if in anticipation of our coming; and, after an appropriate glass of
native wine, never let me forget with what honest pride
this hospitable cousin made us proceed to Wheathampstead, to introduce us (as some newfound rarity) to her
mother and sister Gladmans, who did indeed know
something more of us, at a time when she almost knew
nothing.

With what corresponding kindness we were received
by them also—how Bridget's memory, exalted by the
occasion, warmed into a thousand half-obliterated rec-

[1] Barron Field, a friend.—J. M. B.

ollections of things and persons, to my utter astonishment, and her own—and to the astoundment of B. F., who sat by, almost the only thing that was not a cousin there—old effaced images of more than half-forgotten names and circumstances still crowding back upon her, as words written in lemon come out upon exposure to a friendly warmth—when I forget all this, then may my country cousins forget me; and Bridget no more remember, that in the days of weakling infancy I was her tender charge—as I have been her care in foolish manhood since—in those pretty pastoral walks, long ago, about Mackery End, in Hertfordshire.

London Magazine, July 1821; Elia.

BLAKESMOOR IN H——SHIRE

I DO not know a pleasure more affecting than to range at will over the deserted apartments of some fine old family mansion. The traces of extinct grandeur admit of a better passion than envy: and contemplations on the great and good, whom we fancy in succession to have been its inhabitants, weave for us illusions, incompatible with the bustle of modern occupancy, and vanities of foolish present aristocracy.

The same difference of feeling, I think, attends us between entering an empty and a crowded church. In the latter it is chance but some present human frailty—an act of inattention on the part of some of the auditory—or a trait of affectation, or worse, vainglory on that of the preacher—puts us by our best thoughts, disharmonizing the place and the occasion. But wouldst thou know the beauty of holiness?—go alone on some weekday, borrowing the keys of good Master Sexton, traverse the cool aisles of some country church: think of the piety that has kneeled there—the congregations, old and young, that have found consolation there—the meek pastor—the docile parishioner. With no disturbing emotions, no cross conflicting comparisons, drink in the tranquillity of the place, till thou thyself become as fixed and motionless as the marble effigies that kneel and weep around thee.

Journeying northward lately, I could not resist going some few miles out of my road to look upon the remains of an old great house with which I had been impressed in this way in infancy. I was apprised that the owner of it had lately pulled it down; still I had a vague notion that it could not all have perished, that so much solidity with magnificence could not have been crushed all at once into the mere dust and rubbish which I found it.

The work of ruin had proceeded with a swift hand indeed, and the demolition of a few weeks had reduced it to—an antiquity.

I was astonished at the indistinction of everything. Where had stood the great gates? What bounded the court-yard? Whereabout did the outhouses commence? A few bricks only lay as representatives of that which was so stately and so spacious.

Death does not shrink up his human victim at this rate. The burnt ashes of a man weigh more in their proportion.

Had I seen these brick-and-mortar knaves at their process of destruction, at the plucking of every panel I should have felt the varlets at my heart. I should have cried out to them to spare a plank at least out of the cheerful store-room, in whose hot window-seat I used to sit and read Cowley, with the grass-plot before, and the hum and flappings of that one solitary wasp that ever haunted it about me—it is in mine ears now, as oft as summer returns; or a panel of the yellow-room.

Why, every plank and panel of that house for me had magic in it. The tapestried bedrooms—tapestry so much better than painting—not adorning merely, but peopling the wainscots—at which childhood ever and anon would steal a look, shifting its coverlid (replaced as quickly) to exercise its tender courage in a momentary eye-encounter with those stern bright visages, staring reciprocally—all Ovid on the walls, in colours vivider than his descriptions. Actæon in mid sprout, with the unappeasable prudery of Diana; and the still more provoking, and almost culinary coolness of Dan Phœbus, eel-fashion, deliberately divesting of Marsyas.

Then, that haunted room—in which old Mrs. Battle died—whereinto I have crept, but always in the daytime, with a passion of fear; and a sneaking curiosity, terror-tainted, to hold communication with the past.—*How shall they build it up again?*

It was an old deserted place, yet not so long deserted but that traces of the splendour of past inmates were everywhere apparent. Its furniture was still standing—even to the tarnished gilt leather battledores, and crumbling feathers of shuttlecocks in the nursery, which told that children had once played there. But I was a lonely child, and had the range at will of every apartment, knew every nook and corner, wondered and worshipped everywhere.

The solitude of childhood is not so much the mother of thought, as it is the feeder of love, and silence, and admiration. So strange a passion for the place possessed me in those years, that, though there lay—I shame to say how few roods distant from the mansion—half hid by trees what I judged some romantic lake, such was the spell which bound me to the house, and such my care-

fulness not to pass its strict and proper precincts, that
the idle waters lay unexplored for me; and not till late in
life, curiosity prevailing over elder devotion, I found, to
my astonishment, a pretty brawling brook had been the
Lacus Incognitus of my infancy.

Variegated views, extensive prospects—and those at
no great distance from the house—I was told of such
—what were they to me, being out of the boundaries of
my Eden?—So far from a wish to roam, I would have
drawn, methought, still closer the fences of my chosen
prison; and have been hemmed in by a yet securer cinc-
ture of those excluding garden walls. I could have exclaimed with that garden-loving poet [1]—

> Bind me, ye woodbines, in your twines;
> Curl me about, ye gadding vines;
> And oh so close your circles lace,
> That I may never leave this place;
> But, lest your fetters prove too weak,
> Ere I your silken bondage break,
> Do you, O brambles, chain me too,
> And, courteous briars, nail me through.

I was here as in a lonely temple. Snug firesides—the
low-built roof—parlours ten feet by ten—frugal boards,
and all the homeliness of home—these were the condition of my birth—the wholesome soil which I was
planted in. Yet, without impeachment to their tenderest lessons, I am not sorry to have had glances at something beyond; and to have taken, if but a peep, in childhood, at the contrasting accidents of a great fortune.

To have the feeling of gentility, it is not necessary to
have been born gentle. The pride of ancestry may be
had on cheaper terms than to be obliged to an importu-

[1] Andrew Marvell (1621-78).—J. M. B.

nate race of ancestors; and the coatless antiquary in his unemblazoned cell, revolving the long line of a Mowbray's or De Clifford's pedigree, at those sounding names may warm himself into as gay a vanity as these who do inherit them. The claims of birth are ideal merely, and what herald shall go about to strip me of an idea? Is it trenchant to their swords? can it be hacked off as a spur can? or torn away like a tarnished garter?

What else were the families of the great to us? what pleasure should we take in their tedious genealogies, or their capitulatory brass monuments? What to us the uninterrupted current of their bloods, if our own did not answer within us to a cognate and correspondent elevation.

Or wherefore else, O tattered and diminished 'Scutcheon that hung upon the time-worn walls of thy princely stairs, Blakesmoor! have I in childhood so oft stood poring upon the mystic characters—thy emblematic supporters, with their prophetic "Resurgam"—till, every dreg of peasantry purging off, I received into myself Very Gentility? Thou wert first in my morning eyes; and of nights hast detained my steps from bedward, till it was but a step from gazing at thee to dreaming on thee.

This is the only true gentry by adoption; the veritable change of blood, and not, as empirics have fabled, by transfusion.

Who it was by dying that had earned the splendid trophy, I know not, I inquired not; but its fading rags, and colours cobweb-stained, told that its subject was of two centuries back.

And what if my ancestor at that date was some Damœtas—feeding flocks—not his own, upon the hills of Lincoln—did I in less earnest vindicate to myself the family trappings of this once proud Ægon? repaying by a backward triumph the insults he might possibly have heaped in his lifetime upon my poor pastoral progenitor.

If it were presumption so to speculate, the present owners of the mansion had least reason to complain. They had long forsaken the old house of their fathers for a newer trifle; and I was left to appropriate to myself what images I could pick up, to raise my fancy, or to soothe my vanity.

I was the true descendant of those old W——s; and not the present family of that name, who had fled the old waste places.

Mine was that gallery of good old family portraits, which as I have gone over, giving them in fancy my own family name, one—and then another—would seem to smile, reaching forward from the canvas, to recognize the new relationship; while the rest looked grave, as it seemed, at the vacancy in their dwelling, and thoughts of fled posterity.

The Beauty with the cool blue pastoral drapery, and a lamb—that hung next the great bay window—with the bright yellow H——shire hair, and eye of watchet hue—so like my Alice!—I am persuaded she was a true Elia—Mildred Elia, I take it.

Mine, too, Blakesmoor, was thy noble Marble Hall, with its mosaic pavements, and its Twelve Cæsars—stately busts in marble—ranged round; of whose countenances, young reader of faces as I was, the frowning beauty of Nero, I remember, had most of my wonder: but the mild Galba had my love. There they stood in the coldness of death, yet freshness of immortality.

Mine, too, thy lofty Justice Hall, with its one chair of authority, high-backed and wickered, once the terror of luckless poacher, or self-forgetful maiden—so common since, that bats have roosted in it.

Mine, too—whose else?—thy costly fruit-garden, with its sunbaked southern wall; the ampler pleasure-garden, rising backwards from the house in triple terraces, with flower-pots now of palest lead, save that a speck here and there, saved from the elements, bespake their pristine state to have been gilt and glittering; the verdant quarters backwarder still; and, stretching still beyond, in old formality, thy firry wilderness, the haunt of the squirrel, and the day-long murmuring wood-pigeon, with that antique image in the centre, God or Goddess I wist not; but child of Athens or old Rome paid never a sincerer worship to Pan or to Sylvanus in their native groves, than I to that fragmental mystery.

Was it for this, that I kissed my childish hands too fervently in your idol-worship, walks and windings of Blakesmoor! for this, or what sin of mine, has the plough passed over your pleasant places? I sometimes think that as men, when they die, do not die all, so of their extinguished habitations there may be a hope—a germ to be revivified.

London Magazine, September 1824; Last Essays of Elia.

CHRIST'S HOSPITAL
FIVE-AND-THIRTY YEARS AGO

IN MR. LAMB's "Works," published a year or two since, I find a magnificent eulogy on my old school,[1] such as it was, or now appears to him to have been, between the years 1782 and 1789. It happens very oddly that my own standing at Christ's was nearly corresponding with his; and, with all gratitude to him for his enthusiasm for

[1] "Recollections of Christ's Hospital."—J. M. B.

the cloisters, I think he has contrived to bring together whatever can be said in praise of them, dropping all the other side of the argument most ingeniously.

I remember L. at school, and can well recollect that he had some peculiar advantages, which I and others of his schoolfellows had not. His friends lived in town, and were near at hand; and he had the privilege of going to see them almost as often as he wished, through some invidious distinction, which was denied to us. The present worthy subtreasurer to the Inner Temple can explain how that happened. He had his tea and hot rolls in a morning, while we were battening upon our quarter of a penny loaf—our *crug*—moistened with attenuated small beer, in wooden piggins, smacking of the pitched leathern jack it was poured from. Our Monday's milk porritch, blue and tasteless, and the pease soup of Saturday, coarse and choking, were enriched for him with a slice of "extraordinary bread and butter," from the hot loaf of the Temple.

The Wednesday's mess of millet, somewhat less repugnant—(we had three banyan to four meat days in the week)—was endeared to his palate with a lump of double-refined, and a smack of ginger (to make it go down the more glibly) or the fragrant cinnamon. In lieu of our *half-pickled* Sundays, or *quite fresh* boiled beef on Thursdays (strong as *caro equina*), with detestable marigolds floating in the pail to poison the broth—our scanty mutton scrags on Friday—and rather more savoury, but grudging, portions of the same flesh, rotten-roasted or rare, on the Tuesdays (the only dish which excited our appetites, and disappointed our stomachs, in almost equal proportion)—he had his hot plate of roast veal, or the more tempting griskin (exotics unknown to our palates), cooked in the paternal kitchen (a great thing), and brought him daily by his maid or aunt!

I remember the good old relative (in whom love forbade pride) squatting down upon some odd stone in a bynook of the cloisters, disclosing the viands (of higher regale than those cates which the ravens ministered to the Tishbite); and the contending passions of L. at the unfolding. There was love for the bringer; shame for the thing brought, and the manner of its bringing; sympathy for those who were too many to share in it; and, at top of all, hunger (eldest, strongest of the passions!) predominant, breaking down the stony fences of shame, and awkwardness, and a troubling over-consciousness.

I was a poor friendless boy.[1] My parents, and those who should care for me, were far away. Those few acquaintances of theirs, which they could reckon upon being kind to me in the great city, after a little forced notice, which they had the grace to take of me on my first arrival in town, soon grew tired of my holiday visits. They seemed to them to recur too often, though I thought them few enough; and, one after another, they all failed me, and I felt myself alone among six hundred playmates.

O the cruelty of separating a poor lad from his early homestead! The yearnings which I used to have towards it in those unfledged years! How, in my dreams, would my native town (far in the west) come back, with its church, and trees, and faces! How I would wake weeping, and in the anguish of my heart exclaim upon sweet Calne in Wiltshire!

To this late hour of my life, I trace impressions left

[1] Written by Lamb in the character of his fellow Christ's Hospitaller, Samuel Taylor Coleridge.—J. M. B.

by the recollections of those friendless holidays. The long warm days of summer never return but they bring with them a gloom from the haunting memory of those *whole-day leaves,* when, by some strange arrangement, we were turned out for the live-long day, upon our own hands, whether we had friends to go to or none.

I remember those bathing excursions to the New River which L. recalls with such relish, better, I think, than he can—for he was a home-seeking lad, and did not much care for such water pastimes: How merrily we would sally forth into the fields; and strip under the first warmth of the sun; and wanton like young dace in the streams; getting us appetites for noon, which those of us that were penniless (our scanty morning crust long since exhausted) had not the means of allaying—while the cattle, and the birds, and the fishes were at feed about us and we had nothing to satisfy our cravings—the very beauty of the day, and the exercise of the pastime, and the sense of liberty, setting a keener edge upon them! How faint and languid, finally, we would return, towards nightfall, to our desired morsel, half-rejoicing, half-reluctant, that the hours of our uneasy liberty had expired!

It was worse in the days of winter, to go prowling about the streets objectless—shivering at cold windows of print-shops, to extract a little amusement; or haply, as a last resort in the hopes of a little novelty, to pay a fifty-times repeated visit (where our individual faces should be as well known to the warden as those of his own charges) to the Lions in the Tower—to whose levee, by courtesy immemorial, we had a prescriptive title to admission.

L.'s governor (so we called the patron who presented us to the foundation) lived in a manner under his paternal roof. Any complaint which he had to make was sure of being attended to. This was understood at Christ's, and was an effectual screen to him against the severity of masters, or worse tyranny of the monitors. The oppressions of these young brutes are heart-sickening to call to recollection. I have been called out of my bed, and *waked for the purpose,* in the coldest winter nights— and this not once, but night after night—in my shirt, to receive the discipline of a leathern thong, with eleven other sufferers, because it pleased my callow overseer, when there has been any talking heard after we were gone to bed, to make the six last beds in the dormitory, where the youngest children of us slept, answerable for an offence they neither dared to commit nor had the power to hinder. The same execrable tyranny drove the younger part of us from the fires, when our feet were perishing with snow; and, under the cruellest penalties, forbade the indulgence of a drink of water when we lay in sleepless summer nights fevered with the season and the day's sports.

There was one H., who, I learned, in after days was seen expiating some maturer offence in the hulks. (Do I flatter myself in fancying that this might be the planter of that name, who suffered—at Nevis, I think, or St. Kitts—some few years since? My friend Tobin was the benevolent instrument of bringing him to the gallows.) This petty Nero actually branded a boy who had offended him with a red-hot iron; and nearly starved forty of us with exacting contributions, to the one half of our bread, to pamper a young ass, which, incredible as it may seem, with the connivance of the nurse's daughter (a young flame of his) he had contrived to smuggle in, and keep upon the leads of the *ward,* as they called our dormitories.

This game went on for better than a week, till the foolish beast, not able to fare well but he must cry roast meat—happier than Caligula's minion, could he have kept his own counsel—but, foolisher, alas! than any of his species in the fables—waxing fat, and kicking, in the fullness of bread, one unlucky minute would needs proclaim his good fortune to the world below; and, laying out his simple throat, blew such a ram's-horn blast, as (toppling down the walls of his own Jericho) set concealment any longer at defiance. The client was dismissed, with certain attentions, to Smithfield; but I never understood that the patron underwent any censure on the occasion. This was in the stewardship of L.'s admired Perry.

Under the same *facile* administration, can L. have forgotten the cool impunity with which the nurses used to carry away openly, in open platters, for their own tables, one out of two of every hot joint, which the careful matron had been seeing scrupulously weighed out for our dinners? These things were daily practised in that magnificent apartment which L. (grown connoisseur since, we presume) praises so highly for the grand paintings "by Verrio, and others," with which it is "hung round and adorned." But the sight of sleek, well-fed blue-coat boys in pictures was, at that time, I believe, little consolatory to him, or us, the living ones, who saw the better part of our provisions carried away before our faces by harpies; and ourselves reduced (with the Trojan in the hall of Dido)

To feed our mind with idle portraiture.

L. has recorded the repugnance of the school to *gags,* or the fat of fresh beef boiled; and sets it down to some superstition. But these unctuous morsels are never grateful to young palates (children are universally fat-haters), and in strong, coarse, boiled meats, *unsalted,* are detestable. A *gag-eater* in our time was equivalent to a *goule*, and held in equal detestation. —— suffered under the imputation:

> . . . . 'Twas said
> He ate strange flesh.

He was observed, after dinner, carefully to gather up the remnants left at his table (not many nor very choice fragments, you may credit me)—and, in an especial manner, these disreputable morsels, which he would convey away and secretly stow in the settle that stood at his bedside. None saw when he ate them. It was rumoured that he privately devoured them in the night. He was watched, but no traces of such midnight practices were discoverable. Some reported that on leave-days he had been seen to carry out of the bounds a large blue check handkerchief, full of something. This then must be the accursed thing.

Conjecture next was at work to imagine how he could dispose of it. Some said he sold it to the beggars. This belief generally prevailed. He went about moping. None spake to him. No one would play with him. He was excommunicated; put out of the pale of the school. He was too powerful a boy to be beaten, but he underwent every mode of that negative punishment which is more grievous than many stripes. Still he persevered.

At length he was observed by two of his schoolfellows, who were determined to get at the secret, and had traced him one leave-day for the purpose, to enter a large worn-out building, such as there exist specimens of in Chancery Lane, which are let out to various scales of pauperism, with open door and a common staircase. After him they silently slunk in, and followed by stealth up four flights, and saw him tap at a poor wicket, which was opened by an aged woman, meanly clad. Suspicion was now ripened into certainty. The informers had se-

cured their victim. They had him in their toils. Accusa-
tion was formally preferred, and retribution most signal
was looked for.

Mr. Hathaway, the then steward (for this happened
a little after my time), with that patient sagacity which
tempered all his conduct, determined to investigate the
matter before he proceeded to sentence. The result was
that the supposed mendicants, the receivers or purchasers of the mysterious scraps, turned out to be the parents
of ——, an honest couple come to decay—whom this
seasonable supply had, in all probability, saved from
mendicancy; and that this young stork, at the expense
of his own good name, had all this while been only feeding the old birds!

The governors on this occasion, much to their honour,
voted a present relief to the family of ——, and presented him with a silver medal. The lesson which the
steward read upon RASH JUDGMENT, on the occasion of
publicly delivering the medal to ——, I believe would
not be lost upon his auditory. I had left school then, but
I well remember ——. He was a tall, shambling youth,
with a cast in his eye, not at all calculated to conciliate
hostile prejudices. I have since seen him carrying a baker's basket. I think I heard he did not do quite so
well by himself as he had done by the old folks.

I was a hypochondriac lad; and the sight of a boy in
fetters, upon the day of my first putting on the blue
clothes, was not exactly fitted to assuage the natural
terrors of initiation. I was of tender years, barely turned
of seven; and had only read of such things in books, or
seen them but in dreams. I was told he had *run away*.
This was the punishment for the first offence. As a novice
I was soon after taken to see the dungeons. These were
little, square, Bedlam cells, where a boy could just lie at
his length upon straw and a blanket—a mattress, I think,

was afterwards substituted—with a peep of light, let in askance, from a prison-orifice at top, barely enough to read by.

Here the poor boy was locked in by himself all day, without sight of any but the porter who brought him his bread and water—who *might not speak to him*—or of the beadle, who came twice a week to call him out to receive his periodical chastisement, which was almost welcome, because it separated him for a brief interval from solitude: and here he was shut up by himself *of nights* out of the reach of any sound, to suffer whatever horrors the weak nerves, and superstition incident to his time of life, might subject him to.[1] This was the penalty for the second offence. Wouldst thou like, reader, to see what became of him in the next degree?

The culprit, who had been a third time an offender, and whose expulsion was at this time deemed irreversible, was brought forth, as at some solemn *auto da fé*, arrayed in uncouth and most appalling attire—all trace of his late "watchet weeds" carefully effaced, he was exposed in a jacket resembling those which London lamplighters formerly delighted in, with a cap of the same. The effect of this divestiture was such as the ingenious devisers of it could have anticipated. With his pale and frighted features, it was as if some of those disfigurements in Dante had seized upon him.

In this disguisement he was brought into the hall (*L.'s favourite stateroom*), where awaited him the whole number of his schoolfellows, whose joint lessons and sports he was thenceforth to share no more; the awful

---

[1] One or two instances of lunacy, or attempted suicide, accordingly, at length convinced the governors of the impolicy of this part of the sentence, and the midnight torture to the spirits was dispensed with. This fancy of dungeons for children was a sprout of Howard's brain; for which (saving the reverence due to Holy Paul) methinks I could willingly spit upon his statue.—C. L.

presence of the steward, to be seen for the last time; of the executioner beadle, clad in his state robe for the occasion; and of two faces more, of direr import, because never but in these extremities visible. These were governors; two of whom by choice, or charter, were always accustomed to officiate at these *Ultima Supplicia;* not to mitigate (so at least we understood it), but to enforce the uttermost stripe.

Old Bamber Gascoigne, and Peter Aubert, I remember, were colleagues on one occasion, when the beadle turning rather pale, a glass of brandy was ordered to prepare him for the mysteries. The scourging was, after the old Roman fashion, long and stately. The lictor accompanied the criminal quite round the hall. We were generally too faint, with attending to the previous disgusting circumstances, to make accurate report with our eyes of the degree of corporal suffering inflicted. Report, of course, gave out the back knotty and livid. After scourging, he was made over, in his *San Benito,* to his friends, if he had any (but commonly such poor runagates were friendless), or to his parish officer, who, to enhance the effect of the scene, had his station allotted to him on the outside of the hall gate.

These solemn pageantries were not played off so often as to spoil the general mirth of the community. We had plenty of exercise and recreation *after* school hours; and, for myself, I must confess, that I was never happier than *in* them. The Upper and the Lower Grammar Schools were held in the same room; and an imaginary line only divided their bounds. Their character was as different as that of the inhabitants on the two sides of the Pyrenees.

The Rev. James Boyer was the Upper Master; but the Rev. Matthew Field presided over that portion of the apartment of which I had the good fortune to be a member. We lived a life as careless as birds. We talked lad, roar out, "Od's my life, sirrah" (his favourite adjuration), "I have a great mind to whip you"—then, with as sudden a retracting impulse, fling back into his lair—and, after a cooling lapse of some minutes (during which all but the culprit had totally forgotten the context) drive headlong out again, piecing out his imperfect sense, as if it had been some Devil's Litany, with the expletory yell—"*and I* WILL, *too.*"

In his gentler moods, when the *rabidus furor* was assuaged, he had resort to an ingenious method, peculiar, for what I have heard, to himself, of whipping the boy, and reading the Debates, at the same time; a paragraph, and a lash between; which in those times, when parliamentory oratory was most at a height and flourishing in these realms, was not calculated to impress the patient with a veneration for the diffuser graces of rhetoric.

Once, and but once, the uplifted rod was known to fall ineffectual from his hand—when droll squinting W. having been caught putting the inside of the master's desk to a use for which the architect had clearly not designed it, to justify himself, with great simplicity averred, that *he did not know that the thing had been forewarned.* This exquisite irrecognition of any law antecedent to the *oral* or *declaratory*, struck so irresistibly upon the fancy of all who heard it (the pedagogue himself not excepted)—that remission was unavoidable.

L. has given credit to B.'s great merits as an instructor. Coleridge, in his literary life, has pronounced a more intelligible and ample encomium on them. The author of the *Country Spectator* doubts not to compare him with the ablest teachers of antiquity. Perhaps we cannot dismiss him better than with the pious ejaculation of C. when he heard that his old master was on his deathbed: "Poor J. B.!—may all his faults be forgiven;

and did just what we pleased, and nobody molested us. We carried an accidence, or a grammar, for form; but, for any trouble it gave us, we might take two years in getting through the verbs deponent, and another two in forgetting all that we had learned about them. There was now and then the formality of saying a lesson, but if you had not learned it, a brush across the shoulders (just enough to disturb a fly) was the sole remonstrance.

Field never used the rod; and in truth he wielded the cane with no great goodwill—holding it "like a dancer." It looked in his hands rather like an emblem than an instrument of authority; and an emblem, too, he was ashamed of. He was a good, easy man, that did not care to ruffle his own peace, nor perhaps set any great consideration upon the value of juvenile time. He came among us, now and then, but often stayed away whole days from us; and when he came it made no difference to us—he had his private room to retire to, the short time he stayed, to be out of the sound of our noise.

Our mirth and uproar went on. We had classics of our own, without being beholden to "insolent Greece or haughty Rome," that passed current among us—Peter Wilkins—the Adventures of the Hon. Captain Robert Boyle—the Fortunate Bluecoat Boy—and the like. Or we cultivated a turn for mechanic and scientific operations; making little sundials of paper; or weaving those ingenious parentheses called cat-cradles; or making dry peas to dance upon the end of a tin pipe; or studying the art military over that laudable game "French and English," and a hundred other such devices to pass away the time—mixing the useful with the agreeable—as would have made the souls of Rousseau and John Locke chuckle to have seen us.

Matthew Field belonged to that class of modest divines who affect to mix in equal proportion the gentle-

man, the scholar, and the Christian; but, I know not
how, the first ingredient is generally found to be the
predominating dose in the composition. He was engaged
in gay parties, or with his courtly bow at some episcopal
levee, when he should have been attending upon us.
He had for many years the classical charge of a hundred
children, during the four or five first years of their education, and his very highest form seldom proceeded
further than two or three of the introductory fables of
Phædrus. How things were suffered to go on thus, I cannot guess.

Boyer, who was the proper person to have remedied
these abuses, always affected, perhaps felt, a delicacy
in interfering in a province not strictly his own. I have
not been without my suspicions, that he was not altogether displeased at the contrast we presented to his
end of the school. We were a sort of Helots to his young
Spartans. He would sometimes, with ironic deference,
send to borrow a rod of the Under Master, and then,
with Sardonic grin, observe to one of his upper boys,
"how neat and fresh the twigs looked." While his pale
students were battering their brains over Xenophon
and Plato, with a silence as deep as that enjoyed by the
Samite, we were enjoying ourselves at our ease in our
little Goshen.

We saw a little into the secrets of his discipline, and
the prospect did but the more reconcile us to our lot.
His thunders rolled innocuous for us: his storms came
near, but never touched us; contrary to Gideon's mir-
acle, while all around were drenched, our fleece was
dry.[1] His boys turned out the better scholars; we, I
suspect, have the advantage in temper. His pupils cannot speak of him without something of terror allaying
their gratitude; the remembrance of Field comes back

[1] Cowley.—J. M. B.

with all the soothing images of indolence, and summer slumbers, and work like play, and innocent idleness, and Elysian exemptions, and life itself a "playing holiday."

Though sufficiently removed from the jurisdiction of Boyer, we were near enough (as I have said) to understand a little of his system. We occasionally heard sounds of the *Ululantes*, and caught glances of Tartarus. B. was a rabid pedant. His English style was crampt to barbarism. His Easter anthems (for his duty obliged him to those periodical flights) were grating as scrannel pipes.[1] He would laugh, ay, and heartily, but then it must be at Flaccus's quibble about *Rex* —— or at the *tristis serveritas in vultu*, or *inspicere in patinas*, of Terence—thin jests, which at their first broaching could hardly have had *vis* enough to move a Roman muscle.

He had two wigs, both pedantic, but of different omen. The one serene, smiling, fresh powdered, betokening a mild day. The other, an old, discoloured, unkempt, angry caxon, denoting frequent and bloody execution. Woe to the school, when he made his morning appearance in his *passy*, or *passionate wig*. No comet expounded surer. J. B. had a heavy hand. I have known him double his knotty fist at a poor trembling child (the maternal milk hardly dry upon its lips) with a "Sirrah, do you presume to set your wits at me?" Nothing was more common than to see him make a headlong entry into the schoolroom, from his inner recess, or library, and, with turbulent eye, singling out a

[1] In this and everything B. was the antipodes of his coadjutor. While the former was digging his brains for crude anthems, worth a pig-nut, F. would be recreating his gentlemanly fancy in the more flowery walks of the Muses. A little dramatic effusion of his, under the name of Vertumnus and Pomona, is not yet forgotten by the chroniclers of that sort of literature. It was accepted by Garrick, but the town did not give it their sanction.—B. used to say of it, in a way of half-compliment, half-irony, that it was "too classical for representation."—C. L.

lad, roar out, "Od's my life, sirrah" (his favourite adjuration), "I have a great mind to whip you"—then, with as sudden a retracting impulse, fling back into his lair—and, after a cooling lapse of some minutes (during which all but the culprit had totally forgotten the context) drive headlong out again, piecing out his imperfect sense, as if it had been some Devil's Litany, with the expletory yell—"*and I* WILL, *too.*"

In his gentler moods, when the *rabidus furor* was assuaged, he had resort to an ingenious method, peculiar, for what I have heard, to himself, of whipping the boy, and reading the Debates, at the same time; a paragraph, and a lash between; which in those times, when parliamentory oratory was most at a height and flourishing in these realms, was not calculated to impress the patient with a veneration for the diffuser graces of rhetoric.

Once, and but once, the uplifted rod was known to fall ineffectual from his hand—when droll squinting W. having been caught putting the inside of the master's desk to a use for which the architect had clearly not designed it, to justify himself, with great simplicity averred, that *he did not know that the thing had been forewarned.* This exquisite irrecognition of any law antecedent to the *oral* or *declaratory*, struck so irresistibly upon the fancy of all who heard it (the pedagogue himself not excepted)—that remission was unavoidable.

L. has given credit to B.'s great merits as an instructor. Coleridge, in his literary life, has pronounced a more intelligible and ample encomium on them. The author of the *Country Spectator* doubts not to compare him with the ablest teachers of antiquity. Perhaps we cannot dismiss him better than with the pious ejaculation of C. when he heard that his old master was on his deathbed: "Poor J. B.!—may all his faults be forgiven;

and may he be wafted to bliss by little cherub boys all
head and wings, with no *bottoms* to reproach his sub-
lunary infirmities."

Under him were many good and sound scholars bred.
First Grecian of my time was Lancelot Pepys Stevens,
kindest of boys and men, since Co-grammar-master
(and inseparable companion) with Dr. T——e. What
an edifying spectacle did this brace of friends present
to those who remembered the anti-socialities of their
predecessors! You never met the one by chance in the
street without a wonder, which was quickly dissipated by the almost immediate sub-appearance of the
other. Generally arm-in-arm, these kindly coadjutors
lightened for each other the toilsome duties of their
profession, and when, in advanced age, one found it
convenient to retire, the other was not long in discover-
ing that it suited him to lay down the fasces also.

Oh, it is pleasant, as it is rare, to find the same arm
linked in yours at forty, which at thirteen helped it to
turn over the *Cicero de Amicitiâ,* or some tale of Antique Friendship, which the young heart even then was
burning to anticipate! Co-Grecian with S. was Th——,
who has since executed with ability various diplomatic
functions at the Northern courts. Th—— was a tall,
dark, saturnine youth, sparing of speech, with raven
locks.

Thomas Fanshaw Middleton followed him (now
Bishop of Calcutta), a scholar and a gentleman in his
teens. He has the reputation of an excellent critic; and
is author (besides the *Country Spectator*) of a "Treatise
on the Greek Article," against Sharpe. M. is said to bear
his mitre high in India, where the *regni novitas* (I dare
say) sufficiently justifies the bearing. A humility quite
as primitive as that of Jewel or Hooker might not be
exactly fitted to impress the minds of those Anglo-

Asiatic diocesans with a reverence for home institutions, and the church which those fathers watered. The manners of M. at school, though firm, were mild and unassuming.

Next to M. (if not senior to him) was Richards, author of the "Aboriginal Britons," the most spirited of the Oxford Prize Poems; a pale, studious Grecian. Then followed poor S., ill-fated M.! of these the Muse is silent.

Finding some of Edward's race
Unhappy, pass their annals by.

Come back into memory, like as thou wert in the dayspring of thy fancies, with hope like a fiery column before thee—the dark pillar not yet turned—Samuel Taylor Coleridge—Logician, Metaphysician, Bard! How have I seen the casual passer through the Cloisters stand still, entranced with admiration (while he weighed the disproportion between the *speech* and the *garb* of the young Mirandula), to hear thee unfold, in thy deep and sweet intonations, the mysteries of Jamblichus, or Plotinus (for even in those years thou waxedst not pale at such philosophic draughts), or reciting Homer in his Greek, or Pindar—while the walls of the old Grey Friars re-echoed to the accents of the *inspired charity-boy!* Many were the "wit-combats" (to dally awhile with the words of old Fuller) between him and C. V. Le G., "which two I behold like a Spanish great galleon, and an English man-of-war; Master Coleridge, like the former, was built far higher in learning, solid, but slow in his performances. C. V. L., with the English man-of-war, lesser in bulk, but lighter in sailing, could turn with all tides, tack about, and take advantage of all winds, by the quickness of his wit and invention."

Nor shalt thou, their compeer, be quickly forgotten,

Allen, with the cordial smile, and still more cordial laugh, with which thou wert wont to make the old Cloisters shake, in thy cognition of some poignant jest of theirs; or the anticipation of some more material, and, peradventure practical one, of thine own. Extinct are those smiles, with that beautiful countenance, with which (for thou wert the *Nireus formosus* of the school), in the days of thy maturer waggery, thou didst disarm the wrath of infuriated town-damsel, who, incensed by provoking pinch, turning tigress-like round, suddenly converted by thy angel-look, exchanged the half-formed terrible "bl——," for a gentler greeting— "bless thy handsome face!"

Next follow two, who ought to be now alive, and the friends of Elia—the junior Le G. and F.; who, impelled, the former by a roving temper, the latter by too quick a sense of neglect—ill capable of enduring the slights poor Sizars are sometimes subject to in our seats of learning—exchanged their Alma Mater for the camp; perishing, one by climate, and one on the plains of Salamanca: —Le G., sanguine, volatile, sweet-natured; F., dogged faithful, anticipative of insult, warm-hearted, with something of the old Roman height about him.

Fine, frank-hearted Fr., the present master of Hertford, with Marmaduke T., mildest of Missionaries—and both my good friends still—close the catalogue of Grecians in my time.

London Magazine, November 1820; *Elia.*

THE OLD AND THE NEW SCHOOLMASTER

MY READING has been lamentably desultory and im-methodical. Odd, out of the way, old English plays, and treatises, have supplied me with most of my notions, and ways of feeling. In everything that relates to *science*, I am a whole Encyclopædia behind the rest of the world. I should have scarcely cut a figure among the franklins, or country gentlemen, in King John's days. I know less geography than a schoolboy of six weeks' standing. To me a map of old Ortelius is as authentic as Arrowsmith. I do not know whereabout Africa merges into Asia; whether Ethiopia lie in one or other of these great divisions; nor can form the remotest conjecture of the position of New South Wales, or Van Diemen's Land. Yet do I hold a correspondence with a very dear friend in the first-named of these two Terræ Incognitæ.

I have no astronomy. I do not know where to look for the Bear, or Charles's Wain; the place of any star; or the name of any of them at sight. I guess at Venus only by her brightness—and if the sun on some portentous morn were to make his first appearance in the West, I verily believe, that, while all the world were gasping in apprehension about me, I alone should stand unterrified, from sheer incuriosity and want of observation.

Of history and chronology I possess some vague points, such as one cannot help picking up in the course of mis-cellaneous study; but I never deliberately sat down to a chronicle, even of my own country. I have most dim apprehensions of the four great monarchies; and sometimes the Assyrian, sometimes the Persian, floats as *first,* in my fancy. I make the widest conjectures concerning Egypt and her shepherd kings. My friend M., with great painstaking, got me to think I understood the first proposition in Euclid, but gave me over in despair at the second.

I am entirely unacquainted with the modern languages; and, like a better man than myself, have "small Latin and less Greek." I am a stranger to the shapes and texture of the commonest trees, herbs, flowers— not from the circumstance of my being town-born—for I should have brought the same inobservant spirit into the world with me, had I first seen it "on Devon's leafy shores"—and am no less at a loss among purely town-objects, tools, engines, mechanic processes. Not that I affect ignorance—but my head has not many mansions, nor spacious; and I have been obliged to fill it with such cabinet curiosities as it can hold without aching.

I sometimes wonder, how I have passed my probation with so little discredit in the world, as I have done, upon so meagre a stock. But the fact is, a man may do very well with a very little knowledge, and scarce be found out, in mixed company; everybody is so much more ready to produce his own, than to call for a display of your acquisitions. But in a *tête-à-tête* there is no shuffling. The truth will out. There is nothing which I dread so much, as the being left alone for a quarter of an hour with a sensible, well-informed man, that does not know me. I lately got into a dilemma of this sort.

In one of my daily jaunts between Bishopsgate and Shacklewell, the coach stopped to take up a staid-looking gentleman, about the wrong side of thirty, who was giving his parting directions (while the steps were adjusting), in a tone of mild authority, to a tall youth, who seemed to be neither his clerk, his son, nor his servant, but something partaking of all three. The youth was dismissed, and we drove on.

As we were the sole passengers, he naturally enough addressed his conversation to me; and we discussed the merits of the fare, the civility and punctuality of the driver; the circumstance of an opposition coach having been lately set up, with the probabilities of its success—to all which I was enabled to return pretty satisfactory answers, having been drilled into this kind of etiquette by some years' daily practice of riding to and fro in the stage aforesaid—when he suddenly alarmed me by a startling question, whether I had seen the show of prize cattle that morning in Smithfield? Now, as I had not seen it, and do not greatly care for such sort of exhibitions, I was obliged to return a cold negative. He seemed a little mortified, as well as astonished, at my declaration, as (it appeared) he was just come fresh from the sight, and doubtless had hoped to compare notes on the subject. However, he assured me that I had lost a fine treat, as it far exceeded the show of last year.

We were now approaching Norton Folgate, when the sight of some shop-goods *ticketed* freshened him up into a dissertation upon the cheapness of cottons this spring. I was now a little in heart, as the nature of my morning avocations had brought me into some sort of familiarity with the raw material; and I was surprised to find how eloquent I was becoming on the state of the India market—when, presently, he dashed my incipient vanity to the earth at once, by inquiring whether I had ever made any calculations as to the value of the rental of all the retail shops in London. Had he asked of me, what song the Syrens sang, or what name Achilles assumed when he hid himself among women, I might, with Sir Thomas Browne, have hazarded a "wide solution." [1]

My companion saw my embarrassment, and, the almhouses beyond Shoreditch just coming in view, with great good-nature and dexterity shifted his conversation to the subject of public charities; which led to the comparative merits of provisions for the poor in past and present times, with observations on the old monastic institutions, and charitable orders; but, finding me rather dimly impressed with some glimmering notions from old poetic associations, than strongly fortified with any speculations reducible to calculation on the subject, he gave the matter up; and, the country beginning to open more and more upon us, as we approached the turnpike at Kingsland (the destined termination of his journey), he put a home thrust upon me, in the most unfortunate position he could have chosen, by advancing some queries relative to the North Pole Expedition.

While I was muttering out something about the Panorama of those strange regions (which I had actually seen), by way of parrying the question, the coach stopping relieved me from any further apprehensions. My companion getting out, left me in the comfortable possession of my ignorance; and I heard him, as he went off, putting questions to an outside passenger, who had alighted with him, regarding an epidemic disorder, that had been rife about Dalston, and which my friend assured him had gone through five or six schools in that neighbourhood. The truth now flashed upon me, that my companion was a schoolmaster; and that the youth, whom he had parted from at our first acquaintance, must have been one of the bigger boys, or the usher.

He was evidently a kind-hearted man, who did not

[1] *Urn Burial.*—J. M. B.

seem so much desirous of provoking discussion by the
questions which he put, as of obtaining information at
any rate. It did not appear that he took any interest,
either, in such kind of inquiries, for their own sake; but
that he was in some way bound to seek for knowledge.
A greenish-coloured coat, which he had on, forbade
me to surmise that he was a clergyman. The adventure
gave birth to some reflections on the difference between
persons of his profession in past and present times.

Rest to the souls of those fine old Pedagogues; the
breed, long since extinct, of the Lilys, and the Linacres:
who believing that all learning was contained in the languages which they taught, and despising every other
acquirement as superficial and useless, came to their
task as to a sport! Passing from infancy to age, they
dreamed away all their days as in a grammar-school. Revolving in a perpetual cycle of declensions, conjuga-
tions, syntaxes, and prosodies; renewing constantly the
occupations which had charmed their studious childhood; rehearsing continually the part of the past; life
must have slipped from them at last like one day. They
were always in their first garden, reaping harvests of
their golden time, among their *Flori* and their *Spici-
legia;* in Arcadia still, but kings; the ferule of their
sway not much harsher, but of like dignity with that
mild sceptre attributed to king Basileus; the Greek and
Latin, their stately Pamela and their Philoclea; with the
occasional duncery of some untoward tyro, serving for
a refreshing interlude of a Mopsa, or a clown Damœtas!

With what a savour doth the Preface to Colet's, or
(as it is sometimes called) Paul's Accidence, set forth!
"To exhort every man to the learning of grammar, that
intendeth to attain the understanding of the tongues,
wherein is contained a great treasury of wisdom and
knowledge, it would seem but vain and lost labour;

for so much as it is known, that nothing can surely be ended, whose beginning is either feeble or faulty; and no building be perfect whereas the foundation and groundwork is ready to fall, and unable to uphold the burden of the frame."

How well doth this stately preamble (comparable to those which Milton commendeth as "having been the usage to prefix to some solemn law, then first promulgated by Solon or Lycurgus") correspond with and illustrate that pious zeal for conformity, expressed in a succeeding clause, which would fence about grammar-rules with the severity of faith-articles!—"as for the diversity of grammars, it is well profitably taken away by the king majesties wisdom, who foreseeing the inconvenience, and favourably providing the remedie, caused one kind of grammar by sundry learned men to be diligently drawn, and so to be set out, only everywhere to be taught for the use of learners, and for the hurt in changing of schoolmaisters." What a *gusto* in that which follows: "wherein it is profitable that he [the pupil] can orderly decline his noun and his verb." *His* noun!

The fine dream is fading away fast; and the least concern of a teacher in the present day is to inculcate grammar-rules.

The modern schoolmaster is expected to know a little of everything, because his pupil is required not to be entirely ignorant of anything. He must be superficially, if I may so say, omniscient. He is to know something of pneumatics; of chemistry; of whatever is curious or proper to excite the attention of the youthful mind; an insight into mechanics is desirable, with a touch of statistics; the quality of soils, etc., botany, the constitution of his country, *cum multis aliis*. You may get a notion of some part of his expected duties by con-

sulting the famous Tractate on Education, addressed
to Mr. Hartlib.

All these things—these, or the desire of them—he
is expected to instil, not by set lessons from professors,
which he may charge in the bill, but at school intervals,
as he walks the streets, or saunters through green fields
(those natural instructors), with his pupils. The least
part of what is expected from him is to be done in school-
hours. He must insinuate knowledge at the *mollia tem-
pora fandi*. He must seize every occasion—the season
of the year—the time of the day—a passing cloud—a
rainbow—a wagon of hay—a regiment of soldiers going
by—to inculcate something useful. He can receive no
pleasure from a casual glimpse of Nature, but must catch
at it as an object of instruction. He must interpret
beauty into the picturesque. He cannot relish a beggar-
man, or a gipsy, for thinking of the suitable improvement. Nothing comes to him, not spoiled by the sophis-
ticating medium of moral uses.

The Universe—that Great Book, as it has been called
—is to him, indeed, to all intents and purposes, a book
out of which he is doomed to read tedious homilies to
distasting schoolboys. Vacations themselves are none to
him, he is only rather worse off than before; for commonly he has some intrusive upper-boy fastened upon
him at such times; some cadet of a great family; some
neglected lump of nobility, or gentry; that he must drag
after him to the play, to the Panorama, to Mr. Bartley's
Orrery, to the Panopticon, or into the country, to a
friend's house, or his favourite watering-place. Wherever he goes this uneasy shadow attends him. A boy is
at his board, and in his path, and in all his movements.
He is boy-rid, sick of perpetual boy.

Boys are capital fellows in their own way, among
their mates; but they are unwholesome companions

for grown people. The restraint is felt no less on the one side than on the other. Even a child, that "plaything for an hour," tires *always*. The noises of children, playing their own fancies—as I now hearken to them, by fits, sporting on the green before my window, while I am engaged in these grave speculations at my neat suburban retreat at Shacklewell—by distance made more sweet—inexpressibly take from the labour of my task. It is like writing to music. They seem to modulate my periods. They ought at least to do so—for in the voice of that tender age there is a kind of poetry, far unlike the harsh prose-accents of man's conversation. I should but spoil their sport, and diminish my own sympathy for them, by mingling in their pastime.

I would not be domesticated all my days with a person of very superior capacity to my own—not, if I know myself at all, from any considerations of jealousy or self-comparison, for the occasional communion with such minds has constituted the fortune and felicity of my life—but the habit of too constant intercourse with spirits above you, instead of raising you, keeps you down. Too frequent doses of original thinking from others, restrain what lesser portion of that faculty you may possess of your own. You get entangled in another man's mind, even as you lose yourself in another man's grounds. You are walking with a tall varlet, whose strides outpace yours to lassitude. The constant operation of such potent agency would reduce me, I am convinced, to imbecility. You may derive thoughts from others; your way of thinking, the mould in which your thoughts are cast, must be your own. Intellect may be imparted, but not each man's intellectual frame.

As little as I should wish to be always thus dragged upward, as little (or rather still less) is it desirable to be stunted downwards by your associates. The trumpet does not more stun you by its loudness, than a whisper teases you by its provoking inaudibility.

Why are we never quite at our ease in the presence of a schoolmaster?—because we are conscious that he is not quite at his ease in ours. He is awkward, and out of place, in the society of his equals. He comes like Gulliver from among his little people, and he cannot fit the stature of his understanding to yours. He cannot meet you on the square. He wants a point given him, like an indifferent whist-player. He is so used to teaching, that he wants to be teaching *you*. One of these professors, upon my complaining that these little sketches of mine were anything but methodical, and that I was unable to make them otherwise, kindly offered to instruct me in the method by which young gentlemen in *his* seminary were taught to compose English themes. The jests of a schoolmaster are coarse, or thin. They do not *tell* out of school. He is under the restraint of a formal or didactive hypocrisy in company, as a clergyman is under a moral one. He can no more let his intellect loose in society than the other can his inclinations. He is forlorn among his coevals; his juniors cannot be his friends.

"I take blame to myself," said a sensible man of this profession, writing to a friend respecting a youth who had quitted his school abruptly, "that your nephew was not more attached to me. But persons in my situation are more to be pitied than can well be imagined. We are surrounded by young, and, consequently, ardently affectionate hearts, but *we* can never hope to share an atom of their affections. The relation of master and scholar forbids this. 'How pleasing this must be to you, how I envy your feelings!' my friends will sometimes say to me, when they see young men whom I have educated return after some years' absence from school, their eyes shining with pleasure, while they shake hands with their old master, bringing a present of game to me, or a toy to my wife, and thanking me in the warmest terms for my care of their education. A holiday is begged for the boys; the house is a scene of happiness; I, only, am sad at heart.

"This fine-spirited and warm-hearted youth, who fancies he repays his master with gratitude for the care of his boyish years—this young man—in the eight long years I watched over him with a parent's anxiety, never could repay me with one look of genuine feeling. He was proud, when I praised; he was submissive, when I reproved him; but he did never *love* me—and what he now mistakes for gratitude and kindness for me, is but the pleasant sensation which all persons feel at revisiting the scenes of their boyish hopes and fears; and the seeing on equal terms the man they were accustomed to look upon with reverence.

"My wife, too," this interesting correspondent goes on to say, "my once darling Anna, is the wife of a schoolmaster. When I married her—knowing that the wife of a schoolmaster ought to be a busy notable creature, and fearing that my gentle Anna would ill supply the loss of my dear bustling mother, just then dead, who never sat still, was in every part of the house in a moment, and whom I was obliged sometimes to threaten to fasten down in a chair, to save her from fatiguing herself to death—I expressed my fears that I was bringing her into a way of life unsuitable to her; and she, who loved me tenderly, promised for my sake to exert herself to perform the duties of her new situation. She promised, and she has kept her word.

"What wonders will not woman's love perform? My house is managed with a propriety and decorum unknown in other schools; my boys are well fed, look healthy, and have every proper accommodation; and all this performed with a careful economy, that never descends to meanness. But I have lost my gentle *helpless* Anna! When we sit down to enjoy an hour of repose after the fatigue of the day, I am compelled to listen to what have been her useful (and they are really useful) employments through the day, and what she proposes for her tomorrow's task. Her heart and her features are changed by the duties of her situation. To the boys, she never appears other than the *master's wife,* and she looks up to me as the *boys' master;* to whom all show of love and affection would be highly improper, and unbecoming the dignity of her situation and mine. Yet *this* my gratitude forbids me to hint to her. For my sake she submitted to be this altered creature, and can I reproach her for it?"

For the communication of this letter I am indebted to my cousin Bridget.

London Magazine, May 1821; *Elia.*

POOR RELATIONS

A POOR RELATION—is the most irrelevant thing in nature—a piece of impertinent correspondency—an odious approximation—a haunting conscience—a preposterous shadow, lengthening in the noon-tide of our prosperity—an unwelcome remembrancer—a perpetually recurring mortification—a drain on your purse, a more intolerable dun upon your pride—a drawback upon success—a rebuke to your rising—a stain in your blood —a blot on your 'scutcheon—a rent in your garment— a death's-head at your banquet—Agathocles' pot—a

Mordecai in your gate, a Lazarus at your door—a lion
in your path—a frog in your chamber—a fly in your
ointment—a mote in your eye—a triumph to your
enemy, an apology to your friends—the one thing not
needful—the hail in harvest—the ounce of sour in a
pound of sweet.

He is known by his knock. Your heart telleth you
"That is Mr. ——." A rap, between familiarity and respect; that demands, and at the same time seems to
despair of, entertainment. He entereth smiling and—
embarrassed. He holdeth out his hand to you to shake,
and—draweth it back again. He casually looketh in
about dinner-time—when the table is full. He offereth
to go away, seeing you have company—but is induced
to stay. He filleth a chair, and your visitor's two children
are accommodated at a side-table.

He never cometh upon open days, when your wife
says, with some complacency, "My dear, perhaps Mr.
—— will drop in to-day." He remembereth birthdays—
and professeth he is fortunate to have stumbled upon
one. He declareth against fish, the turbot being small—
yet suffereth himself to be importuned into a slice,
against his first resolution. He sticketh by the port—yet
will be prevailed upon to empty the remainder glass of
claret, if a stranger press it upon him. He is a puzzle to
the servants, who are fearful of being too obsequious, or
not civil enough, to him. The guests think "they have
seen him before." Every one speculateth upon his
condition; and the most part take him to be—a tide-
waiter.

He calleth you by your Christian name, to imply
that his other is the same with your own. He is too
familiar by half, yet you wish he had less diffidence.
With half the familiarity, he might pass for a casual
dependant; with more boldness, he would be in no

danger of being taken for what he is. He is too humble for a friend; yet taketh on him more state than befits a client. He is a worse guest than a country tenant, inasmuch as he bringeth up no rent—yet 'tis odds, from his garb and demeanour, that your guests take him for one. He is asked to make one at the whist table; refuseth on the score of poverty, and—resents being left out. When the company break up, he proffereth to go for a coach—and lets the servant go.

He recollects your grandfather; and will thrust in some mean and quite unimportant anecdote of the family. He knew it when it was not quite so flourishing as "he is blest in seeing it now." He reviveth past situations, to institute what he calleth—favourable comparisons. With a reflecting sort of congratulation, he will inquire the price of your furniture; and insults you with a special commendation of your window-curtains. He is of opinion that the urn is the more elegant shape, but, after all, there was something more comfortable about the old teakettle—which you must remember.

He dare say you must find a great convenience in having a carriage of your own, and appealeth to your lady if it is not so. Inquireth if you have had your arms done on vellum yet; and did not know, till lately, that such-and-such had been the crest of the family. His memory is unseasonable; his compliments perverse; his talk a trouble; his stay pertinacious; and when he goeth away, you dismiss his chair into a corner, as precipitately as possible, and feel fairly rid of two nuisances.

There is a worse evil under the sun, and that is—a female Poor Relation. You may do something with the other; you may pass him off tolerably well; but your indigent she-relative is hopeless. "He is an old humourist," you may say, "and affects to go threadbare. His circumstances are better than folks would take them to be. You are fond of having a Character at your table, and truly he is one." But in the indications of female poverty there can be no disguise. No woman dresses below herself from caprice. The truth must out without shuffling. "She is plainly related to the L.'s; or what does she at their house?" She is, in all probability, your wife's cousin. Nine times out of ten, at least, this is the case. Her garb is something between a gentlewoman and a beggar, yet the former evidently predominates. She is most provokingly humble, and ostentatiously sensible to her inferiority.

He may require to be repressed sometimes—*aliquando sufflaminandus erat*—but there is no raising her. You send her soup at dinner, and she begs to be helped—after the gentlemen. Mr. —— requests the honour of taking wine with her; she hesitates between Port and Madeira, and chooses the former—because he does. She calls the servant *Sir;* and insists on not troubling him to hold her plate. The housekeeper patronizes her. The children's governess takes upon her to correct her, when she has mistaken the piano for harpsichord.

Richard Amlet, Esq. in the play, is a notable instance of the disadvantages to which this chimerical notion of *affinity constituting a claim to acquaintance,* may subject the spirit of a gentleman. A little foolish blood is all that is betwixt him and a lady with a great estate. His stars are perpetually crossed by the malignant maternity of an old woman, who persists in calling him "her son Dick." But she has wherewithal in the end to recompense his indignities, and float him again upon the brilliant surface, under which it has been her seeming business and pleasure all along to sink him. All men, besides, are not of Dick's temperament.

I knew an Amlet in real life, who, wanting Dick's buoyancy, sank indeed. Poor W.[1] was of my own standing at Christ's, a fine classic, and a youth of promise. If he had a blemish, it was too much pride; but its quality was inoffensive; it was not of that sort which hardens the heart, and serves to keep inferiors at a distance; it only sought to ward off derogation from itself. It was the principle of self-respect carried as far as it could go, without infringing upon that respect, which he would have every one else equally maintain for himself. He would have you to think alike with him on this topic. Many a quarrel have I had with him, when we were rather older boys, and our tallness made us more obnoxious to observation in the blue clothes, because I would not thread the alleys and blind ways of the town with him to elude notice, when we have been out together on a holiday in the streets of this sneering and prying metropolis.

W. went, sore with these notions, to Oxford, where the dignity and sweetness of a scholar's life, meeting with the alloy of a humble introduction, wrought in him a passionate devotion to the place, with a profound aversion from the society. The servitor's gown (worse than his school array) clung to him with Nessian venom. He thought himself ridiculous in a garb, under which Latimer must have walked erect, and in which Hooker, in his young days, possibly flaunted in a vein of no discommendable vanity. In the depth of college shades, or in his lonely chamber, the poor student shrunk from observation. He found shelter among books, which insult not; and studies, that ask no questions of a youth's finances. He was lord of his library, and seldom cared for looking out beyond his domains. The healing in-

[1] The F. (Favell) of "Christ's Hospital Five-and-thirty Years Ago."—J. M. B.

fluence of studious pursuits was upon him, to soothe and to abstract. He was almost a healthy man; when the waywardness of his fate broke out against him with a second and worse malignity.

The father of W. had hitherto exercised the humble profession of house-painter at N., near Oxford. A supposed interest with some of the heads of colleges had now induced him to take up his abode in that city, with the hope of being employed upon some public works which were talked of. From that moment I read in the countenance of the young man the determination which at length tore him from academical pursuits for ever.

To a person unacquainted with our universities, the distance between the gownsmen and the townsmen, as they are called—the trading part of the latter especially—is carried to an excess that would appear harsh and incredible. The temperament of W.'s father was diametrically the reverse of his own. Old W. was a little, busy, cringing tradesman, who, with his son upon his arm, would stand bowing and scraping, cap in hand, to any thing that wore the semblance of a gown— insensible to the winks and opener remonstrances of the young man, to whose chamber-fellow, or equal in standing, perhaps, he was thus obsequiously and gratuitously ducking.

Such a state of things could not last. W. must change the air of Oxford, or be suffocated. He chose the former; and let the sturdy moralist, who strains the point of the filial duties as high as they can bear, censure the dereliction; he cannot estimate the struggle. I stood with W., the last afternoon I ever saw him, under the eaves of his paternal dwelling. It was in the fine lane leading from the High Street to the back of —— college, where W. kept his rooms. He seemed thoughtful and more reconciled. I ventured to rally him—finding him in a better mood—upon a representation of the Artist Evangelist, which the old man, whose affairs were beginning to flourish, had caused to be set up in a splendid sort of frame over his really handsome shop, either as a token of prosperity or badge of gratitude to his saint.

W. looked up at the Luke, and, like Satan, "knew his mounted sign—and fled." A letter on his father's table, the next morning, announced that he had accepted a commission in a regiment about to embark for Portugal. He was among the first who perished before the walls of St. Sebastian.

I do not know how, upon a subject which I began with treating half seriously, I should have fallen upon a recital so eminently painful; but this theme of poor relationship is replete with so much matter for tragic as well as comic associations, that it is difficult to keep the account distinct without blending. The earliest impressions which I received on this matter, are certainly not attended with anything painful, or very humiliating, in the recalling. At my father's table (no very splendid one) was to be found, every Saturday, the mysterious figure of an aged gentleman, clothed in neat black, of a sad yet comely appearance. His deportment was of the essence of gravity; his words few or none; and I was not to make a noise in his presence. I had little inclination to have done so—for my cue was to admire in silence. A particular elbow-chair was appropriated to him, which was in no case to be violated. A peculiar sort of sweet pudding, which appeared on no other occasion, distinguished the days of his coming.

I used to think him a prodigiously rich man. All I could make out of him was, that he and my father had been schoolfellows, a world ago, at Lincoln, and that he came from the Mint. The Mint I knew to be a place

where all the money was coined—and I thought he
was the owner of all that money. Awful ideas of the
Tower twined themselves about his presence. He seemed
above human infirmities and passions. A sort of melancholy grandeur invested him. From some inexplicable
doom I fancied him obliged to go about in an eternal
suit of mourning; a captive—a stately being let out of
the Tower on Saturdays. Often have I wondered at the
temerity of my father, who, in spite of an habitual
general respect which we all in common manifested towards him, would venture now and then to stand up
against him in some argument, touching their youthful
days.

The houses of the ancient city of Lincoln are divided
(as most of my readers know) between the dwellers
on the hill and in the valley. This marked distinction
formed an obvious division between the boys who lived
above (however brought together in a common school)
and the boys whose paternal residence was on the plain;
a sufficient cause of hostility in the code of these young
Grotiuses.

My father had been a leading Mountaineer; and
would still maintain the general superiority, in skill
and hardihood, of the *Above Boys* (his own faction)
over the *Below Boys* (so were they called), of which
party his contemporary had been a chieftain. Many
and hot were the skirmishes on this topic—the only one
upon which the old gentleman was ever brought out—
and bad blood bred; even sometimes almost to the re-
commencement (so I expected) of actual hostilities.
But my father, who scorned to insist upon advantages,
generally contrived to turn the conversation upon some
adroit by-commendation of the old Minster; in the
general preference of which, before all other cathedrals

in the island, the dweller on the hill, and the plain-born, could meet on a conciliating level, and lay down their less important differences.

Once only I saw the old gentleman really ruffled, and I remembered with anguish the thought that came over me: "Perhaps he will never come here again." He had been pressed to take another plate of the viand, which I have already mentioned as the indispensable concomitant of his visits. He had refused with a resistance amounting to rigour, when my aunt, an old Lincolnian, but who had something of this, in common with my cousin Bridget, that she would sometimes press civility out of season—uttered the following memorable application—"Do take another slice, Mr. Billet, for you do not get pudding every day." The old gentleman said nothing at the time—but he took occasion in the course of the evening, when some argument had intervened between them, to utter with an emphasis which chilled the company, and which chills me now as I write it— "Woman, you are superannuated!"

John Billet did not survive long after the digesting of this affront; but he survived long enough to assure me that peace was actually restored! and, if I remember aright, another pudding was discreetly substituted in the place of that which had occasioned the offence. He died at the Mint (anno 1781), where he had long held, what he accounted, a comfortable independence; and with five pounds, fourteen shillings, and a penny, which were found in his escritoire after his decease, left the world, blessing God that he had enough to bury him, and that he had never been obliged to any man for a sixpence. This was—a Poor Relation.

London Magazine, May 1823; Last Essays of Elia.

A CHAPTER ON EARS

I HAVE no ear.

Mistake me not, reader—nor imagine that I am by nature destitute of those exterior twin appendages, hanging ornaments, and (architecturally speaking) handsome volutes to the human capital. Better my mother had never borne me. I am, I think, rather delicately than copiously provided with those conduits; and I feel no disposition to envy the mule for his plenty, or the mole for her exactness, in those ingenious labyrinthine inlets—those indispensable side-intelligencers.

Neither have I incurred, or done anything to incur, with Defoe, that hideous disfigurement, which constrained him to draw upon assurance—to feel "quite unabashed," and at ease upon that article. I was never, I thank my stars, in the pillory; nor, if I read them aright, is it within the compass of my destiny, that I ever should be.

When therefore I say that I have no ear, you will understand me to mean—*for music.* To say that this heart never melted at the concord of sweet sounds, would be a foul self-libel. "Water parted from the sea" never fails to move it strangely. So does "In infancy." But they were used to be sung at her harpsichord (the old-fashioned instrument in vogue in those days) by a gentlewoman—the gentlest, sure, that ever merited the appellation—the sweetest—why should I hesitate to name Mrs. S., once the blooming Fanny Weatheral of the Temple—who had power to thrill the soul of Elia, small imp as he was, even in his long coats; and to

make him glow, tremble, and blush with a passion, that
not faintly indicated the dayspring of that absorbing
sentiment which was afterwards destined to overwhelm
and subdue his nature quite for Alice W——n.

I even think that *sentimentally* I am disposed to
harmony. But *organically* I am incapable of a tune. I
have been practising "God save the King" all my life;
whistling and humming of it over to myself in solitary
corners; and am not yet arrived, they tell me, within
many quavers of it. Yet hath the loyalty of Elia never
been impeached.

I am not without suspicion, that I have an unde-
veloped faculty of music within me. For thrumming,
in my wild way, on my friend A.'s[1] piano, the other
morning, while he was engaged in an adjoining parlour,
—on his return he was pleased to say, "he thought it
could not be the maid!" On his first surprise at hearing
the keys touched in somewhat an airy and masterful
way, not dreaming of me, his suspicions had lighted on
Jenny. But a grace, snatched from a superior refinement,
soon convinced him that some being—technically perhaps deficient, but higher informed from a principle
common to all the fine arts—had swayed the keys to a
mood which Jenny, with all her (less cultivated) enthusiasm, could never have elicited from them. I mention
this as a proof of my friend's penetration, and not with
any view of disparaging Jenny.

Scientifically I could never be made to understand
(yet have I taken some pains) what a note in music
is; or how one note should differ from another. Much
less in voices can I distinguish a soprano from a tenor.
Only sometimes the thorough-bass I contrive to guess
at, from its being supereminently harsh and disagreeable. I tremble, however, for my misapplication of the

[1] William Ayrton, a musical critic.—J. M. B.

simplest terms of *that* which I disclaim. While I profess my ignorance, I scarce know what to *say* I am ignorant of. I hate, perhaps, by misnomers. *Sostenuto* and *adagio* stand in the like relation of obscurity to me; and *Sol, Fa, Mi, Re,* is as conjuring as *Baralipton.*

It is hard to stand alone in an age like this—(constituted to the quick and critical perception of all harmonious combinations, I verily believe, beyond all preceding ages, since Jubal stumbled upon the gamut) to remain, as it were, singly unimpressible to the magic influences of an art, which is said to have such an especial stroke at soothing, elevating, and refining the passions. Yet, rather than break the candid current of my confessions, I must avow to you, that I have received a great deal more pain than pleasure from this so cried-up faculty.

I am constitutionally susceptible of noises. A carpenter's hammer, in a warm summer noon, will fret me into more than midsummer madness. But those unconnected, unset sounds are nothing to the measured malice of music. The ear is passive to those single strokes; willingly enduring stripes while it hath no task to con. To music it cannot be passive. It will strive—mine at least will—spite of its inaptitude, to thrid the maze; like an unskilled eye painfully poring upon hieroglyphics.

I have sat through an Italian Opera, till, for sheer pain, and inexplicable anguish, I have rushed out into the noisiest places of the crowded streets, to solace myself with sounds, which I was not obliged to follow, and get rid of the distracting torment of endless, fruitless, barren attention! I take refuge in the unpretending assemblage of honest common-life sounds; and the purgatory of the Enraged Musician becomes my paradise.

I have sat at an Oratorio (that profanation of the pur-

poses of the cheerful play-house) watching the faces
of the auditory in the pit (what a contrast to Hogarth's
"Laughing Audience!") immovable, or affecting some
faint emotion—till (as some have said, that our occupations in the next world will be but a shadow of what
delighted us in this) I have imagined myself in some
cold Theatre in Hades, where some of the *forms* of the
earthly one should be kept up, with none of the *enjoyment;* or like that

> ——Party in a parlour
> All silent, and all DAMNED.

Above all, those insufferable concertos, and pieces
of music, as they are called, do plague and embitter my
apprehension.

Words are something; but to be exposed to an endless battery of mere sounds; to be long a dying; to lie
stretched upon a rack of roses; to keep up languor by
unintermitted effort; to pile honey upon sugar, and
sugar upon honey, to an interminable tedious sweetness; to fill up sound with feeling, and strain ideas to
keep pace with it; to gaze on empty frames, and be
forced to make the pictures for yourself; to read a book,
all stops, and be obliged to supply the verbal matter;
to invent extempore tragedies to answer to the vague
gestures of an inexplicable rambling mime—these are
faint shadows of what I have undergone from a series
of the ablest-executed pieces of this empty *instrumental
music.*

I deny not, that in the opening of a concert, I have
experienced something vastly lulling and agreeable:
afterwards followeth the languor and the oppression.
Like that disappointing book in Patmos; or, like the
comings on of melancholy, described by Burton, doth

music make her first insinuating approaches: "Most pleasant it is to such as are melancholy given to walk alone in some solitary grove, betwixt wood and water, by some brook side, and to meditate upon some delightsome and pleasant subject, which shall affect him most, *amabilis insania,* and *mentis gratissimus error.* A most incomparable delight to build castles in the air, to go smiling to themselves, acting an infinite variety of parts, which they suppose, and strongly imagine, they act, or that they see done.

"So delightsome these toys at first, they could spend whole days and nights without sleep, even whole years, in such contemplations, and fantastical meditations, which are like so many dreams, and will hardly be drawn from them—winding and unwinding themselves as so many clocks, and still pleasing their humours, until at the last the SCENE TURNS UPON A SUDDEN, and they being now habitated to such meditations and solitary places, can endure no company, can think of nothing but harsh and distasteful subjects.

"Fear, sorrow, suspicion, *subrusticus pudor,* discontent, cares, and weariness of life, surprise them on a sudden and they can think of nothing else; continually suspecting, no sooner are their eyes open, but this infernal plague of melancholy seizeth on them, and terrifies their souls, representing some dismal object to their minds; which now, by no means, no labour, no persuasions, they can avoid, they cannot be rid of, they cannot resist."

Something like this "SCENE TURNING" I have experienced at the evening parties, at the house of my good Catholic friend Nov——[1]; who, by the aid of a capital organ, himself the most finished of players, converts

[1] Vincent Novello, organist and composer.—J. M. B.

his drawing-room into a chapel, his week days into
Sundays, and these latter into minor heavens.[1]

When my friend commences upon one of those
solemn anthems, which peradventure struck upon my
heedless ear, rambling in the side aisles of the dim
Abbey, some five-and-thirty years since, waking a new
sense, and putting a soul of old religion into my young
apprehension—(whether it be *that*, in which the Psalm-
ist, weary of the persecutions of bad men, wisheth to
himself dove's wings—or *that other*, which, with a
like measure of sobriety and pathos, inquireth by what
means the young man shall best cleanse his mind)—
a holy calm pervadeth me. I am for the time

——rapt above earth,
And possess joys not promised at my birth.

But when this master of the spell, not content to have
laid a soul prostrate, goes on, in his power, to inflict
more bliss than lies in her capacity to receive—impatient
to overcome her "earthly" with his "heavenly"—still
pouring in, for protracted hours, fresh waves and fresh
from the sea of sound, or from that inexhausted *German*
ocean, above which, in triumphant progress, dolphin-
seated, ride those Arions Haydn and Mozart, with their
attendant Tritons, Bach, Beethoven, and a countless
tribe, whom to attempt to reckon up would but plunge
me again in the deeps—I stagger under the weight of
harmony, reeling to and fro at my wits' end; clouds,
as of frankincense, oppress me—priests, altars, censers,
dazzle before me—the genius of *his* religion hath me
in her toils—a shadowy triple tiara invests the brow of
my friend, late so naked, so ingenuous—he is Pope—

[1] I have been there, and still would go;
'Tis like a little heaven below.—Dr. Watts.
—C. L.

and by him sits, like as in the anomaly of dreams, a she-Pope too—tri-coroneted like himself!

I am converted, and yet a Protestant; at once *malleus hereticorum,* and myself grand heresiarch: or three heresies centre in my person: I am Marcion, Ebion, and Cerinthus—Gog and Magog—what not?—till the coming in of the friendly supper-tray dissipates the figment, and a draught of true Lutheran beer (in which chiefly my friend shows himself no bigot) at once reconciles me to the rationalities of a purer faith; and restores to me the genuine unterrifying aspects of my pleasant-countenanced host and hostess.

London Magazine, March 1821; *Elia.*

IMPERFECT SYMPATHIES

I am of a constitution so general, that it consorts and sympathizeth with all things; I have no antipathy, or rather idiosyncrasy in anything. Those natural repugnancies do not touch me, nor do I behold with prejudice the French, Italian, Spaniard, or Dutch.—*Religio Medici.*

THAT the author of the *Religio Medici,* mounted upon the airy stilts of abstraction, conversant about notional and conjectural essences; in whose categories of Being the possible took the upper hand of the actual; should have overlooked the impertinent individualities of such poor concretions as mankind, is not much to be admired. It is rather to be wondered at, that in the genus of animals he should have condescended to distinguish that species at all. For myself—earth-bound and fettered to the scene of my activities,

Standing on earth, not rapt above the sky,

I confess that I do feel the differences of mankind, national or individual, to an unhealthy excess. I can look with no indifferent eye upon things or persons. Whatever is, is to me a matter of taste or distaste; or when once it becomes indifferent, it begins to be dis-relishing. I am, in plainer words, a bundle of prejudices —made up of likings and dislikings—the variest thrall to sympathies, apathies, antipathies. In a certain sense, I hope it may be said of me that I am a lover of my species. I can feel for all indifferently, but I cannot feel towards all equally. The more purely-English word that expresses sympathy, will better explain my mean-ing. I can be a friend to a worthy man, who upon another account cannot be my mate or *fellow*. I cannot *like* all people alike.[1]

---

[1] I would be understood as confining myself to the subject of *im-perfect sympathies*. To nations or classes of men there can be no direct antipathy. There may be individuals born and constellated so opposite to another individual nature, that the same sphere cannot hold them. I have met with my moral antipodes, and can believe the story of two persons meeting (who never saw one another before in their lives) and instantly fighting.

> ————We by proof find there should be
> 'Twixt man and man such an antipathy,
> That though he can show no just reason why
> For any former wrong or injury,
> Can neither find a blemish in his fame,
> Nor aught in face or feature justly blame,
> Can challenge or accuse him of no evil,
> Yet notwithstanding hates him as a devil.

The lines are from old Heywood's "Hierarchie of Angels," and he subjoins a curious story in confirmation, of a Spaniard who attempted to assassinate a King Ferdinand of Spain, and being put to the rack could give no other reason for the deed but an inveterate antipathy which he had taken to the first sight of the King.

> ————The cause which to that act compell'd him
> Was, he ne'er loved him since he first beheld him.

—C. L.

I have been trying all my life to like Scotchmen, and am obliged to desist from the experiment in despair. They cannot like me—and in truth, I never knew one of that nation who attempted to do it. There is something more plain and ingenuous in their mode of proceeding. We know one another at first sight. There is an order of imperfect intellects (under which mine must be content to rank) which in its constitution is essentially anti-Caledonian.

The owners of the sort of faculties I allude to, have minds rather suggestive than comprehensive. They have no pretences to much clearness or precision in their ideas, or in their manner of expressing them. Their intellectual wardrobe (to confess fairly) has few whole pieces in it. They are content with fragments and scattered pieces of Truth. She presents no full front to them—a feature or sideface at the most.

Hints and glimpses, germs and crude essays at a system, is the utmost they pretend to. They beat up a little game peradventure—and leave it to knottier heads, more robust constitutions, to run it down. The light that lights them is not steady and polar, but mutable and shifting: waxing, and again waning. Their conversation is accordingly. They will throw out a random word in or out of season, and be content to let it pass for what it is worth. They cannot speak always as if they were upon their oath—but must be understood, speaking or writing, with some abatement. They seldom wait to mature a proposition, but e'en bring it to market in the green ear. They delight to impart their defective discoveries as they arise, without waiting for their full development. They are no systematizers, and would but err more by attempting it. Their minds, as I said before, are suggestive merely.

The brain of a true Caledonian (if I am not mistaken)

is constituted upon quite a different plan. His Minerva is born in panoply. You are never admitted to see his ideas in their growth—if, indeed, they do grow, and are not rather put together upon principles of clock-work. You never catch his mind in an undress. He never hints or suggests anything, but unlades his stock of ideas in perfect order and completeness. He brings his total wealth into company, and gravely unpacks it. His riches are always about him. He never stoops to catch a glittering something in your presence to share it with you, before he quite knows whether it be true touch or not. You cannot cry *halves* to anything that he finds, He does not find, but bring. You never witness his first apprehension of a thing. His understanding is always at its meridian—you never see the first dawn, the early streaks.

He has no falterings of self-suspicion. Surmises, guesses, misgivings, half-intuitions, semi-consciousnesses, partial illuminations, dim instincts, embryo conceptions, have no place in his brain, or vocabulary. The twi-light of dubiety never falls upon him. Is he orthodox—he has no doubts. Is he an infidel—he has none either. Between the affirmative and the negative there is no borderland with him. You cannot hover with him upon the confines of truth, or wander in the maze of a prob-able argument. He always keeps the path. You cannot make excursions with him—for he sets you right. His taste never fluctuates. His morality never abates. He cannot compromise, or understand middle actions. There can be but a right and a wrong.

His conversation is as a book. His affirmations have the sanctity of an oath. You must speak upon the square with him. He stops a metaphor like a suspected person in an enemy's country. "A healthy book!"—said one of his countrymen to me, who had ventured to give

that appellation to *John Buncle*—"Did I catch rightly what you said? I have heard of a man in health, and of a healthy state of body, but I do not see how that epithet can be properly applied to a book." Above all, you must beware of indirect expressions before a Caledonian. Clap an extinguisher upon your irony, if you are unhappily blest with a vein of it. Remember you are upon your oath.

I have a print of a graceful female after Leonardo da Vinci, which I was showing off to Mr. ——. After he had examined it minutely, I ventured to ask him how he liked MY BEAUTY (a foolish name it goes by among my friends)—when he very gravely assured me, that "he had considerable respect for my character and talents" (so he was pleased to say), "but had not given himself much thought about the degree of my personal pretensions." The misconception staggered me, but did not seem much to disconcert him.

Persons of this nation are particularly fond of affirming a truth—which nobody doubts. They do not so properly affirm, as annunciate it. They do indeed appear to have such a love of truth (as if, like virtue, it were valuable for itself) that all truth becomes equally valuable, whether the proposition that contains it be new or old, disputed, or such as is impossible to become a subject of disputation.

I was present not long since at a party of North Britons, where a son of Burns was expected; and happened to drop a silly expression (in my South British way), that I wished it were the father instead of the son—when four of them started up at once to inform me, that "that was impossible, because he was dead." An impracticable wish, it seems, was more than they could conceive. Swift has hit off this part of their character, namely their love of truth, in his biting way, but

with an illiberality that necessarily confines the passage
to the margin.[1] The tediousness of these people is certainly provoking. I wonder if they ever tire one another!

In my early life I had a passionate fondness for the
poetry of Burns. I have sometimes foolishly hoped to
ingratiate myself with his countrymen by expressing
it. But I have always found that a true Scot resents your
admiration of his compatriot, even more than he would
your contempt of him. The latter he imputes to your
"imperfect acquaintance with many of the words which
he uses"; and the same objection makes it a presumption
in you to suppose that you can admire him.

Thomson they seem to have forgotten. Smollett they
have neither forgotten nor forgiven, for his delinea-
tion of Rory and his companion, upon their first introduction to our metropolis. Speak of Smollett as a great
genius, and they will retort upon you Hume's History
compared with *his* Continuation of it. What if the historian had continued *Humphrey Clinker?*

I have, in the abstract, no disrespect for Jews. They
are a piece of stubborn antiquity, compared with which
Stonehenge is in its nonage. They date beyond the pyramids. But I should not care to be in habits of familiar
intercourse with any of that nation. I confess that I
have not the nerves to enter their synagogues.

Old prejudices cling about me. I cannot shake off the
story of Hugh of Lincoln. Centuries of injury, contempt,

[1] There are some people who think they sufficiently acquit themselves, and entertain their company, with relating facts of no
consequence, not at all out of the road of such common incidents
as happen every day; and this I have observed more frequently
among the Scots than any other nation, who are very careful not to
omit the minutest circumstances of time or place; which kind of
discourse, if it were not a little relieved by the uncouth terms and
phrases, as well as accent and gesture, peculiar to that country,
would be hardly tolerable.—*Hints towards an Essay on Conversation.*—C. L.

and hate, on the one side—of cloaked revenge, dissimulation, and hate, on the other, between our and their fathers, must and ought to affect the blood of the children. I cannot believe it can run clear and kindly yet; or that a few fine words, such as candour, liberality, the light of a nineteenth century, can close up the breaches of so deadly a disunion.

A Hebrew is nowhere congenial to me. He is least distasteful on 'Change—for the mercantile spirit levels all distinctions, as all are beauties in the dark. I boldly confess that I do not relish the approximation of Jew and Christian, which has become so fashionable. The reciprocal endearments have, to me, something hypocritical and unnatural in them. I do not like to see the Church and Synagogue kissing and congeeing in awkward postures of an affected civility. If *they* are converted, why do they not come over to us altogether? Why keep up a form of separation, when the life of it is fled? If they can sit with us at table, why do they keck at our cookery? I do not understand these half convertites.

Jews christianizing—Christians judaizing—puzzle me. I like fish or flesh. A moderate Jew is a more confounding piece of anomaly than a wet Quaker. The spirit of the synagogue is essentially *separative*. B.[1] would have been more in keeping if he had abided by the faith of his forefathers. There is a fine scorn in his face, which nature meant to be of—Christians. The Hebrew spirit is strong in him, in spite of his proselytism. He cannot conquer the Shibboleth. How it breaks out, when he sings, "The Children of Israel pass through the Red Sea!" The auditors, for the moment, are as Egyptians to him, and he rides over our necks in triumph. There is no mistaking him.

[1] John Braham, a tenor singer.—J. M. B.

B. has a strong expression of sense in his countenance, and it is confirmed by his singing. The foundation of his vocal excellence is sense. He sings with
understanding, as Kemble delivered dialogue. He would
sing the Commandments, and give an appropriate character to each prohibition. His nation, in general, have
not oversensible countenances. How should they?—but
you seldom see a silly expression among them. Gain, and
the pursuit of gain, sharpen a man's visage. I never
heard of an idiot being born among them. Some admire
the Jewish female-physiognomy. I admire it—but with
trembling. Jael had those full dark inscrutable eyes.

In the Negro countenance you will often meet with
strong traits of benignity. I have felt yearnings of tenderness towards some of these faces—or rather masks—
that have looked out kindly upon one in casual en-
counters in the streets and highways. I love what Fuller
beautifully calls—these "images of God cut in ebony."
But I should not like to associate with them, to share
my meals and my good-nights with them—because
they are black.

I love Quaker ways, and Quaker worship. I venerate
the Quaker principles. It does me good for the rest
of the day when I meet any of their people in my path.
When I am ruffled or disturbed by any occurrence,
the sight, or quiet voice of a Quaker, acts upon me as
a ventilator, lightening the air, and taking off a load
from the bosom. But I cannot like the Quakers (as
Desdemona would say) "to live with them."

I am all over sophisticated—with humours, fancies,
craving hourly sympathy. I must have books, pictures,
theatres, chit-chat, scandal, jokes, ambiguities, and a
thousand whim-whams, which their simpler taste can do
without. I should starve at their primitive banquet. My
appetites are too high for the salads which (according

to Evelyn) Eve dressed for the angel, my gusto too excited

To sit a guest with Daniel at his pulse.

The indirect answers which Quakers are often found
to return to a question put to them may be explained,
I think, without the vulgar assumption, that they are
more given to evasion and equivocating than other people. They naturally look to their words more carefully,
and are more cautious of committing themselves. They
have a peculiar character to keep up on his head. They
stand in a manner upon their veracity.

A Quaker is by law exempted from taking an oath.
The custom of resorting to an oath in extreme cases,
sanctified as it is by all religious antiquity, is apt (it must
be confessed) to introduce into the laxer sort of minds
the notion of two kinds of truth—the one applicable to
the solemn affairs of justice, and the other to the common proceedings of daily intercourse. As truth bound
upon the conscience by an oath can be but truth, so in
the common affirmations of the shop and the market-
place a latitude is expected, and conceded upon questions wanting this solemn covenant. Something less than
truth satisfies.

It is common to hear a person say, "You do not expect
me to speak as if I were upon my oath." Hence a great
deal of incorrectness and inadvertancy, short of falsehood, creeps into ordinary conversation; and a kind of
secondary or laic-truth is tolerated, where clergy-truth
—oath-truth, by the nature of the circumstances, is not
required.

A Quaker knows none of this distinction. His simple
affirmation being received, upon the most sacred occasions, without any further test, stamps a value upon the
words which he is to use upon the most indifferent topics of life. He looks to them, naturally, with more se-

verity. You can have of him no more than his word. He knows, if he is caught tripping in a casual expression, he forfeits, for himself at least, his claim to the invidious exemption. He knows that his syllables are weighed— and how far a consciousness of this particular watchfulness, exerted against a person, has a tendency to produce indirect answers, and a diverting of the question by honest means, might be illustrated, and the practice justified, by a more sacred example than is proper to be adduced upon this occasion.

The admirable presence of mind, which is notorious in Quakers upon all contingencies, might be traced to this imposed self-watchfulness—if it did not seem rather an humble and secular scion of that old stock of religious constancy, which never bent or faltered, in the Primitive Friends, or gave way to the winds of persecution, to the violence of judge or accuser, under trials and racking examinations.

"You will never be the wiser, if I sit here answering your questions till midnight," said one of those upright Justicers to Penn, who had been putting law-cases with a puzzling subtlety. "Thereafter as the answers may be," retorted the Quaker. The astonishing composure of this people is sometimes ludicrously displayed in lighter instances.

I was travelling in a stage-coach with three male Quakers, buttoned up in the straitest nonconformity of their sect. We stopped to bait at Andover, where a meal, partly tea apparatus, partly supper, was set before us. My friends confined themselves to the tea-table. I in my way took supper. When the landlady brought in the bill, the eldest of my companions discovered that she had charged for both meals. This was resisted. Mine hostess was very clamorous and positive. Some mild arguments were used on the part of the Quakers, for which the heated mind of the good lady seemed by no means a fit recipient.

The guard came in with his usual peremptory notice. The Quakers pulled out their money and formally tendered it—so much for tea—I, in humble imitation, tendering mine—for the supper which I had taken. She would not relax in her demand. So they all three quietly put up their silver, as did myself, and marched out of the room, the eldest and gravest going first, with myself closing up the rear, who thought I could not do better than follow the example of such grave and warrantable personages. We got in. The steps went up. The coach drove off.

The murmurs of mine hostess, not very indistinctly or ambiguously pronounced, became after a time inaudible—and now my conscience, which the whimsical scene had for a while suspended, beginning to give some twitches, I waited, in the hope that some justification would be offered by these serious persons for the seeming injustice of their conduct. To my great surprise not a syllable was dropped on the subject. They sat as mute as at a meeting. At length the eldest of them broke silence, by inquiring of his next neighbour, "Hath thee heard how indigos go at the India House?" and the question operated as a soporific on my moral feeling as far as Exeter.

London Magazine, August 1821; Elia.

MANY FRIENDS

UNFORTUNATE is the lot of that man, who can look round about the wide world, and exclaim with truth, *I*

have no friend! Do you know any such lonely sufferer?
For mercy sake send him to me. I can afford him plenty.
He shall have them good, cheap. I have enough and to
spare. Truly society is the balm of human life. But you
may take a surfeit from sweetest odours administered to
satiety. Hear my case, dear VARIORUM, and pity me.

I am an elderly gentleman—not old—a sort of middle-
aged-gentleman-and-a-half—with a tolerable larder,
cellar, etc.; and a most unfortunately easy temper for
the callous front of impertinence to try conclusions on.
My day times are entirely engrossed by the business of
a public office, where I am anything but alone from nine
till five. I have forty fellow-clerks about me during those
hours; and, though the human face be divine, I protest
that so many human faces seen every day do very much
diminish the homage I am willing to pay to that divinity.

It fares with these divine resemblances as with a
Polytheism. Multiply the object and you infallibly en-
feeble the adoration. "What a piece of work is Man! how
excellent in faculty," etc. But a great many men together
—a hot huddle of rational creatures—Hamlet himself
would have lowered his contemplation a peg or two in
my situation. *Tædet me harum quotidianarum formarum.* I go home every day to my late dinner, absolutely
famished and face-sick.

I am sometimes fortunate enough to go off unaccompanied. The relief is restorative like sleep; but far oftener, alas! some one of my fellows, who lives *my way*
(as they call it) does me the sociality of walking with
me. He sees me to the door; and now I figure to myself
a snug fireside—comfortable meal—a respiration from
the burthen of society—and the blessedness of a single
knife and fork.

I sit down to my solitary mutton, happy as Adam
when a bachelor. I have not swallowed a mouthful,

before a startling ring announces the visit of *a friend*.
O! for an everlasting muffle upon that appalling instrument of torture! A knock makes me nervous; but a ring
is a positive fillip to all the sour passions of my nature—
and yet such is my effeminacy of temperament, I neither tie up the one nor dumbfound the other. But
these accursed friends, or fiends, that torture me thus!
They come in with a full consciousness of their being unwelcome—with a sort of grin of triumph over your weakness. My soul sickens within when they enter. I can
scarcely articulate a "how d'ye." My digestive powers
fail. I have enough to do to maintain them in any health-
iness when alone.

Eating is a solitary function; you may drink in company. Accordingly the bottle soon succeeds; and such
is my infirmity, that the reluctance soon subsides before
it. The visitor becomes agreeable. I find a great deal
that is good in him; wonder I should have felt such aversion on his first entrance; we get chatty, conversible;
insensibly comes midnight; and I am dismissed to the
cold bed of celibacy (the only place, alas! where I am
suffered to be alone) with the reflection that another
day has gone over my head without the possibility of
enjoying my own free thoughts in solitude even for a
solitary moment. O! for a Lodge in some vast wilderness! the den of those Seven Sleepers (conditionally the
other six were away)! a *Crusoe* solitude!

What most disturbs me is, that my chief annoyers
are mostly young men. Young men, let them think as
they please, are no company *singly* for a gentleman of
my years. They do mighty well in a mixed society, and
where there are females to take them off, as it were. But
to have the load of one of them to one's own self for
successive hours conversation is unendurable.

There was my old friend Captain Beacham—he died

some six years since, bequeathing to my friendship three stout young men, his sons, and seven girls, the tallest in the land. Pleasant, excellent young women they were, and for their sakes I did, and could endure much. But they were too tall. I am superstitious in that respect, and think that to a just friendship, something like proportion in stature as well as mind is desirable. Now I am five feet and a trifle more. Each of these young women rose to six, and one exceeded by two inches. The brothers are proportionably taller. I have sometimes taken the altitude of this friendship; and on a modest computation I may be said to have known at one time a whole furlong of Beachams. But the young women are married off, and dispersed among the provinces. The brothers are left.

Nothing is more distasteful than these relics and parings of past fr˙   ˙nips—unmeaning records of agreeable hours flown. There are three of them. If they hunted in triples, or even couples, it were something; but by a refinement of persecution, they contrive to come singly; and so spread themselves out into three evenings molestation in a week. Nothing is so distasteful as the sight of their long legs, couched for continuance upon my fender.

They have been mates of Indiamen; and one of them in particular has a story of a shark swallowing a boy in the bay of Calcutta. I wish the shark had swallowed *him*. Nothing can be more useless than their conversation to me, unless it is mine to them. We have no ideas (save of eating and drinking) in common. The shark story has been told till it cannot elicit a spark of attention; but it goes on just as usual. When I try to introduce a point of literature, or common life, the mates gape at me. When I fill a glass, they fill one too. Here is sympathy. And for this poor correspondency

of having a gift of swallowing and retaining liquor
in common with my fellow-creatures, I am to be tied
up to an ungenial intimacy, abhorrent from every sentiment, and every sympathy besides. But I cannot break
the bond. They are sons of my old friend.

LEPUS

The New Times, January 8, 1825.

OLD CHINA

I HAVE an almost feminine partiality for old china.
When I go to see any great house, I inquire for the
china-closet, and next for the picture gallery. I cannot
defend the order of preference, but by saying, that we
have all some taste or other, of too ancient a date to admit of our remembering distinctly that it was an acquired one. I can call to mind the first play, and the first
exhibition, that I was taken to; but I am not conscious
of a time when china jars and saucers were introduced
into my imagination.

I had no repugnance then—why should I now have?
—to those little, lawless, azure-tinctured grotesques,
that under the notion of men and women, float about,
uncircumscribed by any element, in that world before
perspective—a china teacup.

I like to see my old friends—whom distance cannot
diminish—figuring up in the air (so they appear to our
optics), yet on *terra firma* still—for so we must in courtesy interpret that speck of deeper blue, which the
decorous artist, to prevent absurdity, had made to
spring up beneath their sandals.

I love the men with women's faces, and the women, if possible, with still more womanish expressions.

Here is a young and courtly Mandarin, handing tea to a lady from a salver—two miles off. See how distance seems to set off respect! And here the same lady, or another—for likeness is identity on teacups—is stepping into a little fairy boat, moored on the hither side of this calm garden river, with a dainty mincing foot, which in a right angle of incidence (as angles go in our world) must infallibly land her in the midst of a flowery mead—a furlong off on the other side of the same strange stream!

Farther on—if far or near can be predicated of their world—see horses, trees, pagodas, dancing the hays.

Here—a cow and rabbit couchant, and coextensive —so objects show, seen through the lucid atmosphere of fine Cathay.

I was pointing out to my cousin last evening, over our Hyson (which we are old-fashioned enough to drink unmixed still of an afternoon), some of these *speciosa miracula* upon a set of extraordinary old blue china (a recent purchase) which we were now for the first time using; and could not help remarking, how favourable circumstances had been to us of late years, that we could afford to please the eye sometimes with trifles of this sort—when a passing sentiment seemed to overshade the brows of my companion. I am quick at detecting these summer clouds in Bridget.

"I wish the good old times would come again," she said, "when we were not quite so rich. I do not mean, that I want to be poor; but there was a middle state" —so she was pleased to ramble on—"in which I am sure we were a great deal happier. A purchase is but a purchase, now that you have money enough and to spare. Formerly it used to be a triumph. When we coveted a

cheap luxury (and, O! how much ado I had to get you
to consent in those times!)—we were used to have a
debate two or three days before, and to weigh the *for*
and *against,* and think what we might spare it out of,
and what saving we could hit upon, that should be
an equivalent. A thing was worth buying then, when
we felt the money that we paid for it.

"Do you remember the brown suit, which you made
to hang upon you, till all your friends cried shame upon
you, it grew so threadbare—and all because of that folio Beaumont and Fletcher, which you dragged home
late at night from Barker's in Covent Garden? Do
you remember how we eyed it for weeks before we
could make up our minds to the purchase, and had not
come to a determination till it was near ten o'clock of
the Saturday night, when you set off from Islington,
fearing you should be too late—and when the old bookseller with some grumbling opened his shop, and by the
twinkling taper (for he was setting bedwards) lighted
out the relic from his dusty treasures—and when you
lugged it home, wishing it were twice as cumbersome
—and when you presented it to me—and when we
were exploring the perfectness of it (*collating,* you
called it)—and while I was repairing some of the
loose leaves with paste, which your impatience would
not suffer to be left till daybreak— Was there no pleasure in being a poor man? or can those neat black clothes
which you wear now, and are so careful to keep
brushed, since we have become rich and finical, give
you half the honest vanity with which you flaunted it
about in that overworn suit—your old corbeau—for
four or five weeks longer than you should have done, to
pacify your conscience for the mighty sum of fifteen—
or sixteen shillings was it?—a great affair we thought
it then—which you had lavished on the old folio. Now

you can afford to buy any book that pleases you, but I do not see that you ever bring me home any nice old purchases now.

"When you came home with twenty apologies for laying out a less number of shillings upon that print after Lionardo, which we christened the 'Lady Blanch'; when you looked at the purchase, and thought of the money—and thought of the money, and looked again at the picture—was there no pleasure in being a poor man? Now, you have nothing to do but to walk into Colnaghi's, and buy a wilderness of Lionardos. Yet do you?

"Then, do you remember our pleasant walks to Enfield, and Potter's Bar, and Waltham, when we had a holyday—holydays, and all other fun, are gone now we are rich—and the little hand-basket in which I used to deposit our day's fare of savoury cold lamb and salad—and how you would pry about at noontide for some decent house, where we might go in and produce our store—only paying for the ale that you must call for —and speculate upon the looks of the landlady, and whether she was likely to allow us a table-cloth—and wish for such another honest hostess as Izaak Walton has described many a one on the pleasant banks of the Lea, when he went a-fishing—and sometimes they would prove obliging enough, and sometimes they would look grudgingly upon us—but we had cheerful looks still for one another, and would eat our plain food savourily, scarcely grudging Piscator his Trout Hall? Now—when we go out a day's pleasuring, which is seldom, moreover, we *ride* part of the way—and go into a fine inn, and order the best of dinners, never debating the expense—which, after all, never has half the relish of those chance country snaps, when we were at the mercy of uncertain usage, and a precarious welcome.

"You are too proud to see a play anywhere now but in the pit. Do you remember where it was we used to sit, when we saw the *Battle of Hexham*, and the *Surrender of Calais*, and Bannister and Mrs. Bland in the *Children in the Wood*—when we squeezed out our shillings apiece to sit three or four times in a season in the one-shilling gallery—where you felt all the time that you ought not to have brought me—and more strongly I felt obligation to you for having brought me—and the pleasure was the better for a little shame—and when the curtain drew up, what cared we for our place in the house, or what mattered it where we were sitting, when our thoughts were with Rosalind in Arden, or with Viola at the Court of Illyria.

"You used to say that the Gallery was the best place of all for enjoying a play socially—that the relish of such exhibitions must be in proportion to the infrequency of going—that the company we met there, not being in general readers of plays, were obliged to attend the more, and did attend, to what was going on, on the stage—because a word lost would have been a chasm, which it was impossible for them to fill up. With such reflections we consoled our pride then—and I appeal to you whether, as a woman, I met generally with less attention and accommodation than I have done since in more expensive situations in the house? The getting in indeed, and the crowding up those inconvenient staircases, was bad enough—but there was still a law of civility to woman recognized to quite as great an extent as we ever found in the other passages—and how a little difficulty overcome heightened the snug seat and the play, afterwards! Now we can only pay our money and walk in. You cannot see, you say, in the galleries now. I am sure we saw, and heard too, well enough then— but sight, and all, I think, is gone with our poverty.

"There was pleasure in eating strawberries, before they became quite common—in the first dish of peas, while they were yet dear—to have them for a nice supper, a treat. What treat can we have now? If we were to treat ourselves now—that is, to have dainties a little above our means, it would be selfish and wicked. It is the very little more that we allow ourselves beyond what the actual poor can get at, that makes what I call a treat—when two people living together, as we have done, now and then indulge themselves in a cheap luxury, which both like; while each apologizes, and is willing to take both halves of the blame to his single share. I see no harm in people making much of themselves, in that sense of the word. It may give them a hint how to make much of others. But now—what I mean by the word—we never *do* make much of ourselves. None but the poor can do it. I do not mean the veriest poor of all, but persons as we were, just above poverty.

"I know what you were going to say, that it is mighty pleasant at the end of the year to make all meet—and much ado we used to have every Thirty-first Night of December to account for our exceedings—many a long face did you make over your puzzled accounts, and in contriving to make it out how we had spent so much— or that we had not spent so much—or that it was impossible we should spend so much next year—and still we found our slender capital decreasing—but then, betwixt ways, and projects, and compromises of one sort or another, and talk of curtailing this charge, and doing without that for the future—and the hope that youth brings, and laughing spirits (in which you were never poor till now), we pocketed up our loss, and in conclusion, with 'lusty brimmers' (as you used to quote it out of 'hearty cheerful Mr. Cotton,' as you called him), we used to welcome in 'the coming guest.' Now we have no reckoning at all at the end of the old year—no flattering promises about the new year doing better for us."

Bridget is so sparing of her speech on most occasions, that when she gets into a rhetorical vein, I am careful how I interrupt it. I could not help, however, smiling at the phantom of wealth which her dear imagination had conjured up out of a clear income of poor —— hundred pounds a year.

"It is true we were happier when we were poor but we were also younger, my cousin. I am afraid we must put up with the excess, for if we were to shake the superflux into the sea, we should not much mend ourselves. That we had much to struggle with, as we grew up together, we have reason to be most thankful. It strengthened and knit our compact closer. We could never have been what we have been to each other, if we had always had the sufficiency which you now complain of.

"The resisting power—those natural dilations of the youthful spirit, which circumstances cannot straiten—with us are long since passed away. Competence to age is supplementary youth, a sorry supplement indeed, but I fear the best that is to be had. We must ride where we formerly walked: live better and lie softer—and shall be wise to do so—than we had means to do in those good old days you speak of.

"Yet could those days return—could you and I once more walk our thirty miles a day—could Bannister and Mrs. Bland again be young, and you and I be young to see them—could the good old one-shilling gallery days return—they are dreams, my cousin, now—but could you and I at this moment, instead of this quiet argument, by our well-carpeted fireside, sitting on this luxurious sofa—be once more struggling up those inconvenient staircases, pushed about, and squeezed, and elbowed by the poorest rabble of poor gallery scramblers—could I once more hear those anxious shrieks of yours—and the delicious 'Thank God, we are safe,' which always followed when the topmost stair, conquered, let in the first light of the whole cheerful theatre down beneath us—I know not the fathom line that ever touched a descent so deep as I would be willing to bury more wealth in than Crœsus had, or the great Jew R. is supposed to have, to purchase it. And now do just look at that merry little Chinese waiter holding an umbrella, big enough for a bed-tester, over the head of that pretty insipid half Madonna-ish chit of a lady in that very blue summer-house."

London Magazine, March 1823; *Last Essays of Elia.*

NEW YEAR'S EVE

EVERY man hath two birthdays: two days, at least, in every year, which set him upon revolving the lapse of time, as it affects his mortal duration. The one is that which in an especial manner he termeth *his.* In the gradual desuetude of old observances, this custom of solemnizing our proper birthday hath nearly passed away, or is left to children, who reflect nothing at all about the matter, nor understand anything in it beyond cake and orange. But the birth of a New Year is of an interest too wide to be pretermitted by king or cobbler. No one ever regarded the first of January with indifference. It is that from which all date their time, and count

upon what is left. It is the nativity of our common
Adam.

Of all sound of all bells—(bells, the music nighest
bordering upon heaven)—most solemn and touching is
the peal which rings out the Old Year. I never hear it
without a gathering-up of my mind to a concentration of
all the images that have been diffused over the past
twelve-month; all I have done or suffered, performed or
neglected—in that regretted time. I begin to know its
worth, as when a person dies. It takes a personal colour;
nor was it a poetical flight in a contemporary, when he
exclaimed,

> I saw the skirts of the departing Year.

It is no more than what in sober sadness every one
of us seems to be conscious of, in that awful leave-taking.
I am sure I felt it, and all felt it with me, last night;
though some of my companions affected rather to manifest an exhilaration at the birth of the coming year, than
any very tender regrets for the decease of its predecessor. But I am none of those who

> Welcome the coming, speed the parting guest.

I am naturally, beforehand, shy of novelties; new
books, new faces, new years—from some mental twist
which makes it difficult in me to face the prospective.
I have almost ceased to hope; and am sanguine only in
the prospects of other (former) years. I plunge into
foregone visions and conclusions. I encounter pell-mell
with past disappointments. I am armour-proof against
old discouragements. I forgive, or overcome in fancy,
old adversaries. I play over again *for love,* as the gamesters phrase it, games, for which I once paid so dear. I
would scarce now have any of those untoward accidents
and events of my life reversed. I would no more alter

them than the incidents of some well-contrived novel. Methinks it is better that I should have pined away seven of my goldenest years, when I was thrall to the fair hair, and fairer eyes of Alice W——n, than that so passionate a love-adventure should be lost. It was better that our family should have missed that legacy, which old Dorrell cheated us of, than that I should have at this moment two thousand pounds *in banco*, and be without the idea of that specious old rogue.

In a degree beneath manhood, it is my infirmity to look back upon those early days. Do I advance a paradox, when I say, that, skipping over the intervention of forty years, a man may have leave to love *himself*, without the imputation of self-love?

If I know aught of myself, no one whose mind is introspective—and mine is painfully so—can have a less respect for his present identity than I have for the man Elia. I know him to be light, and vain, and humoursome; a notorious ——; addicted to ——; averse from counsel, neither taking it nor offering it;—— besides; a stammering buffoon; what you will; lay it on, and spare not: I subscribe to it all, and much more than thou canst be willing to lay at his door; but for the child Elia, that "other me," there, in the background—I must take leave to cherish the remembrance of that young master—with as little reference, I protest, to this stupid changeling of five-and-forty, as if it had been a child of some other house, and not of my parents. I can cry over its patient smallpox at five, and rougher medicaments. I can lay its poor fevered head upon the sick pillow at Christ's, and wake with it in surprise at the gentle posture of maternal tenderness hanging over it, that unknown had watched its sleep. I know how it shrank from any the least colour of falsehood. God help thee, Elia, how art thou changed!—Thou art sophisticated. I know how honest, how courageous (for a weakling) it was—how religious, how imaginative, how hopeful! From what have I not fallen, if the child I remember was indeed myself,—and not some dissembling guardian, presenting a false identity, to give the rule to my unpractised steps, and regulate the tone of my moral being!

That I am fond of indulging, beyond a hope of sympathy, in such retrospection, may be the symptom of some sickly idiosyncrasy. Or is it owing to another cause: simply, that being without wife or family, I have not learned to project myself enough out of myself; and having no offspring of my own to dally with, I turn back upon memory, and adopt my own early idea, as my heir and favourite? If these speculations seem fantastical to thee, reader (a busy man perchance), if I tread out of the way of thy sympathy, and am singularly conceited only, I retire, impenetrable to ridicule, under the phantom cloud of Elia.

The elders, with whom I was brought up, were of a character not likely to let slip the sacred observance of any old institution; and the ringing out of the Old Year was kept by them with circumstances of peculiar ceremony. In those days the sound of those midnight chimes, though it seemed to raise hilarity in all around me, never failed to bring a train of pensive imagery into my fancy. Yet I then scarce conceived what it meant, or thought of it as a reckoning that concerned me.

Not childhood alone, but the young man till thirty, never feels practically that he is mortal. He knows it indeed, and, if need were, he could preach a homily on the fragility of life; but he brings it not home to himself, any more than in a hot June we can appropriate to our imagination the freezing days of December. But now, shall I confess a truth?—I feel these audits but too powerfully.

I begin to count the probabilities of my duration, and to grudge at the expenditure of moments and shortest periods, like misers' farthings. In proportion as the years both lessen and shorten, I set more count upon their periods, and would fain lay my ineffectual finger upon the spoke of the great wheel. I am not content to pass away "like a weaver's shuttle." Those metaphors solace me not, nor sweeten the unpalatable draught of mortality. I care not to be carried with the tide, that smoothly bears human life to eternity; and reluct at the inevitable course of destiny. I am in love with this green earth; the face of town and country; the unspeakable rural solitudes, and the sweet security of streets. I would set up my tabernacle here. I am content to stand still at the age to which I am arrived; I, and my friends: to be no younger, no richer, no handsomer. I do not want to be weaned by age; or drop, like mellow fruit, as they say, into the grave.

Any alteration, on this earth of mine, in diet or in lodging, puzzles and discomposes me. My household-gods plant a terrible fixed foot, and are not rooted up without blood. They do not willingly seek Lavinian shores. A new state of being staggers me.

Sun, and sky, and breeze, and solitary walks, and summer holidays, and the greenness of fields, and the delicious juices of meats and fishes, and society, and the cheerful glass, and candlelight, and fireside conversations, and innocent vanities, and jests, and *irony itself*— do these things go out with life?

Can a ghost laugh, or shake his gaunt sides, when you are pleasant with him?

And you, my midnight darlings, my Folios! must I

part with the intense delight of having you (huge arm-
fuls) in my embraces? Must knowledge come to me,
if it come at all, by some awkward experiment of intuition, and no longer by this familiar process of reading?

Shall I enjoy friendships there, wanting the smiling
indications which point me to them here—the recog-
nizable face—the "sweet assurance of a look"?

In winter this intolerable disinclination to dying—to
give it its mildest name—does more especially haunt
and beset me. In a genial August noon, beneath a
sweltering sky, death is almost problematic. At those
times do such poor snakes as myself enjoy an immortality. Then we expand and burgeon. Then we are as
strong again, as valiant again, as wise again, and a great
deal taller. The blast that nips and shrinks me, puts me
in thoughts of death. All things allied to the insubstantial, wait upon that master feeling; cold, numbness,
dreams, perplexity; moonlight itself, with its shadowy
and spectral appearances—that cold ghost of the sun,
or Phœbus' sickly sister, like that innutritious one de-
nounced in the Canticles: I am none of her minions—
I hold with the Persian.

Whatsoever thwarts, or puts me out of my way,
brings death into my mind. All partial evils, like humours, run into that capital plague-sore.—I have heard
some profess an indifference to life. Such hail the end
of their existence as a port of refuge; and speak of the
grave as of some soft arms, in which they may slumber
as on a pillow. Some have wooed death—but out upon
thee, I say, thou foul, ugly phantom! I detest, abhor,
execrate, and (with Friar John) give thee to six score
thousand devils, as in no instance to be excused or tolerated, but shunned as an universal viper; to be branded,
proscribed, and spoken evil of! In no way can I be

brought to digest thee, thou thin, melancholy *Privation,* or more frightful and confounding *Positive!*

Those antidotes, prescribed against the fear of thee, are altogether frigid and insulting, like thyself. For what satisfaction hath a man, that he shall "lie down with kings and emperors in death," who in his lifetime never greatly coveted the society of such bedfellows?—or, forsooth, that "so shall the fairest face appear"?—why, to comfort me, must Alice W——n be a goblin? More than all, I conceive disgust at those impertinent and misbecoming familiarities inscribed upon your ordinary tombstones. Every dead man must take upon himself to be lecturing me with his odious truism, that "Such as he now is I must shortly be." Not so shortly, friend, perhaps as thou imaginest. In the meantime I am alive. I move about. I am worth twenty of thee. Know thy betters! Thy New Years' days are past. I survive, a jolly candidate for 1821. Another cup of wine—and while that turncoat bell, that just now mournfully chanted the obsequies of 1820 departed, with changed notes lustily rings in a successor, let us attune to its peal the song made on a like occasion, by hearty, cheerful Mr. Cotton.

THE NEW YEAR

Hark, the cock crows, and yon bright star
Tells us, the day himself's not far;
And see where, breaking from the night,
He gilds the western hills with light.
With him old Janus doth appear,
Peeping into the future year,
With such a look as seems to say,
The prospect is not good that way.
Thus do we rise ill sights to see,
And 'gainst ourselves to prophesy;
When the prophetic fear of things

A more tormenting mischief brings,
More full of soul-tormenting gall
Than direst mischiefs can befall.
But stay! but stay! methinks my sight,
Better inform'd by clearer light,
Discerns sereneness in that brow,
That all contracted seem'd but now.
His revers'd face may show distaste,
And frown upon the ills are past;
But that which this way looks is clear,
And smiles upon the New-born Year.
He looks too from a place so high,
The year lies open to his eye;
And all the moments open are
To the exact discoverer.
Yet more and more he smiles upon
The happy revolution.
Why should we then suspect or fear
The influences of a year,
So smiles upon us the first morn,
And speaks us good so soon as born?
Plague on't! the last was ill enough,
This cannot but make better proof;
Or, at the worst, as we brush'd through
The last, why so we may this too;
And then the next in reason shou'd
Be superexcellently good:
For the worst ills (we daily see)
Have no more perpetuity
Than the best fortunes that do fall;
Which also bring us wherewithal
Longer their being to support,
Than those do of the other sort:
And who has one good year in three,
And yet repines a destiny,
Appears ungrateful in the case,
And merits not the good he has.
Then let us welcome the New Guest

With lusty brimmers of the best:
Mirth always should Good Fortune meet,
And renders e'en Disaster sweet:
And though the Princess turn her back,
Let us but line ourselves with sack,
We better shall by far hold out,
Till the next Year she face about.

How say you, reader—do not these verses smack of
the rough magnanimity of the old English vein? Do
they not fortify like a cordial; enlarging the heart, and
productive of sweet blood, and generous spirits, in the
concoction? Where be those puling fears of death, just
now expressed or affected? Passed like a cloud—absorbed in the purging sunlight of clear poetry—clean
washed away by a wave of genuine Helicon, your only
Spa for these hypochondries. And now another cup of
the generous! and a merry New Year, and many of them
to you all, my masters!

London Magazine, January 1821; *Elia.*

THE SUPERANNUATED MAN

Sera tamen respexit
Libertas.   VIRGIL.

A Clerk I was in London gay.—O'KEEFE.

IF PERADVENTURE, Reader, it has been thy lot to
waste the golden years of thy life—thy shining youth
—in the irksome confinement of an office; to have thy
prison days prolonged through middle age down to
decrepitude and silver hairs, without hope of release

or respite; to have lived to forget that there are such things as holidays, or to remember them but as the prerogatives of childhood; then, and then only, will you be able to appreciate my deliverance.

It is now six-and-thirty years since I took my seat at the desk in Mincing Lane. Melancholy was the transition at fourteen from the abundant playtime, and the frequently-intervening vacations of school days, to the eight, nine, and sometimes ten hours' a day attendance at the counting-house. But time partially reconciles us to anything. I gradually became content—doggedly contented, as wild animals in cages.

It is true I had my Sundays to myself; but Sundays, admirable as the institution of them is for purposes of worship, are for that very reason the very worst adapted for days of unbending and recreation. In particular, there is a gloom for me attendant upon a city Sunday, a weight in the air. I miss the cheerful cries of London, the music, and the ballad-singers—the buzz and stirring murmur of the streets.

Those eternal bells depress me. The closed shops repel me. Prints, pictures, all the glittering and endless succession of knacks and gewgaws, and ostentatiously displayed wares of tradesmen, which make a weekday saunter through the less busy parts of the metropolis so delightful—are shut out. No book-stalls deliciously to idle over—no busy faces to recreate the idle man who contemplates them ever passing by—the very face of business a charm by contrast to his temporary relaxation from it. Nothing to be seen but unhappy countenances —or half-happy at best—of emancipated 'prentices and little tradesfolks, with here and there a servant-maid that has got leave to go out, who, slaving all the week, with the habit has lost almost the capacity of enjoying a free hour; and livelily expressing the hollowness of a day's pleasuring. The very strollers in the fields on that day look anything but comfortable.

But besides Sundays, I had a day at Easter, and a day at Christmas, with a full week in the summer to go and air myself in my native fields of Hertfordshire. This last was a great indulgence; and the prospect of its recurrence, I believe, alone kept me up through the year, and made my durance tolerable. But when the week came round, did the glittering phantom of the distance keep touch with me? or rather was it not a series of seven uneasy days, spent in restless pursuit of pleasure, and a wearisome anxiety to find out how to make the most of them? Where was the quiet, where the promised rest? Before I had a taste of it, it was vanished. I was at the desk again, counting upon the fifty-one tedious weeks that must intervene before such another snatch would come. Still the prospect of its coming threw something of an illumination upon the darker side of my captivity. Without it, as I have said, I could scarcely have sustained my thraldom.

Independently of the rigours of attendance, I have ever been haunted with a sense (perhaps a mere caprice) of incapacity for business. This, during my latter years, had increased to such a degree, that it was visible in all the lines of my countenance. My health and my good spirits flagged. I had perpetually a dread of some crisis, to which I should be found unequal. Besides my daylight servitude, I served over again all night in my sleep, and would awake with terrors of imaginary false entries, errors in my accounts, and the like. I was fifty years of age, and no prospect of emancipation presented itself. I had grown to my desk, as it were; and the wood had entered into my soul.

My fellows in the office would sometimes rally me

upon the trouble legible in my countenance; but I did not know that it had raised the suspicions of any of my employers, when, on the fifth of last month, a day ever to be remembered by me, L., the junior partner in the firm, calling me on one side, directly taxed me with my bad looks, and frankly inquired the cause of them. So taxed, I honestly made confession of my infirmity, and added that I was afraid I should eventually be obliged to resign his service. He spoke some words of course to hearten me, and there the matter rested.

A whole week I remained labouring under the impression that I had acted imprudently in my disclosure; that I had foolishly given a handle against myself, and had been anticipating my own dismissal. A week passed in this manner, the most anxious one, I verily believe, in my whole life, when on the evening of the 12th of April, just as I was about quitting my desk to go home (it might be about eight o'clock) I received an awful summons to attend the presence of the whole assembled firm in the formidable back parlour.

I thought now my time is surely come, I have done for myself, I am going to be told that they have no longer occasion for me. L., I could see, smiled at the terror I was in, which was a little relief to me, when to my utter astonishment B., the eldest partner, began a formal harangue to me on the length of my services, my very meritorious conduct during the whole of the time (the deuce, thought I, how did he find out that? I protest I never had the confidence to think as much). He went on to descant on the expediency of retiring at a certain time of life (how my heart panted!), and asking me a few questions as to the amount of my own property, of which I have a little, ended with a proposal, to which his three partners nodded a grave assent, that

I should accept from the house, which I had served so well, a pension for life to the amount of two-thirds of my accustomed salary—a magnificent offer!

I do not know what I answered between surprise and gratitude, but it was understood that I accepted their proposal, and I was told that I was free from that hour to leave their service. I stammered out a bow, and at just ten minutes after eight I went home—for ever. This noble benefit—gratitude forbids me to conceal their names—I owe to the kindness of the most munificent firm in the world—the house of Boldero, Merryweather, Bosanquet, and Lacy.

Esto perpetua!

For the first day or two I felt stunned, overwhelmed. I could only apprehend my felicity; I was too confused to taste it sincerely. I wandered about, thinking I was happy, and knowing that I was not. I was in the condition of a prisoner in the old Bastille, suddenly let loose after a forty years' confinement. I could scarce trust myself with myself. It was like passing out of Time into Eternity—for it is a sort of Eternity for a man to have his Time all to himself. It seemed to me that I had more time on my hands than I could ever manage.

From a poor man, poor in Time, I was suddenly lifted up into a vast revenue; I could see no end of my possessions; I wanted some steward, or judicious bailiff, to manage my estates in Time for me. And here let me caution persons grown old in active business, not lightly, nor without weighing their own resources, to forego their customary employment all at once, for there may be danger in it. I feel it by myself, but I know that my resources are sufficient; and now that those first giddy raptures have subsided, I have a quiet home-feeling of the blessedness of my condition.

I am in no hurry. Having all holidays, I am as though I had none. If Time hung heavy upon me, I could walk it away; but I do *not* walk all day long, as I used to do in those old transient holidays, thirty miles a day, to make the most of them. If Time were troublesome, I could read it away; but I do *not* read in that violent measure, with which, having no Time in my own but candlelight Time, I used to weary out my head and eyesight in bygone winters. I walk, read, or scribble (as now), just when the fit seizes me. I no longer hunt after pleasure; I let it come to me. I am like the man

———— that's born, and has his years come to him,
In some green desert.

"Years!" you will say; "what is this superannuated simpleton calculating upon? He has already told us he is past fifty."

I have indeed lived nominally fifty years, but deduct out of them the hours which I have lived to other people, and not to myself, and you will find me still a young fellow. For *that* is the only true Time, which a man can properly call his own, that which he has all to himself; the rest, though in some sense he may be said to live it, is other people's Time, not his. The remnant of my poor days, long or short, is at least multiplied for me threefold. My ten next years, if I stretch so far, will be as long as any preceding thirty. 'Tis a fair rule-of-three sum.

Among the strange fantasies which beset me at the commencement of my freedom, and of which all traces are not yet gone, one was, that a vast tract of time had intervened since I quitted the Counting House. I could not conceive of it as an affair of yesterday. The partners, and the clerks with whom I had for so many years, and for so many hours in each day of the year, been closely associated—being suddenly removed from them—they seemed as dead to me. There is a fine passage, which may serve to illustrate this fancy, in a Tragedy by Sir Robert Howard, speaking of a friend's death:

> ———— 'Twas but just now he went away;
> I have not since had time to shed a tear;
> And yet the distance does the same appear
> As if he had been a thousand years from me.
> Time takes no measure in Eternity.

To dissipate this awkward feeling, I have been fain to go among them once or twice since; to visit my old desk-fellows—my co-brethren of the quill—that I had left below in the state militant. Not all the kindness with which they received me could quite restore to me that pleasant familiarity, which I had heretofore enjoyed among them.

We cracked some of our old jokes, but methought they went off but faintly. My old desk; the peg where I hung my hat, were appropriated to another. I knew it must be, but I could not take it kindly. D——l take me, if I did not feel some remorse—beast, if I had not—at quitting my old compeers, the faithful partners of my toils for six-and-thirty years, that smoothed for me with their jokes and conundrums the ruggedness of my professional road. Had it been so rugged then, after all? or was I a coward simply? Well, it is too late to repent; and I also know that these suggestions are a common fallacy of the mind on such occasions. But my heart smote me. I had violently broken the bands betwixt us. It was at least not courteous. I shall be some time before I get quite reconciled to the separation.

Farewell, old cronies, yet not for long, for again and again I will come among ye, if I shall have your leave. Farewell, Ch——, dry, sarcastic, and friendly! Do——,

mild, slow to move, and gentlemanly! Pl——, officious
to do, and to volunteer, good services!—and thou, thou
dreary pile, fit mansion for a Gresham or a Whittington
of old, stately house of Merchants; with thy labyrinthine
passages, and light-excluding, pent-up offices, where
candles for one-half the year supplied the place of the
sun's light; unhealthy contributor to my weal, stern
fosterer of my living, farewell! In thee remain, and not
in the obscure collection of some wandering bookseller,
my "works"! There let them rest, as I do from my labours, piled on thy massy shelves, more MSS. in folio
than ever Aquinas left, and full as useful! My mantle I
bequeath among ye.

A fortnight has passed since the date of my first communication. At that period I was approaching to tranquillity, but had not reached it. I boasted of a calm indeed, but it was comparative only. Something of the
first flutter was left; an unsettling sense of novelty; the
dazzle to weak eyes of unaccustomed light. I missed my
old chains, forsooth, as if they had been some necessary
part of my apparel. I was a poor Carthusian, from strict
cellular discipline suddenly by some revolution returned
upon the world.

I am now as if I had never been other than my own
master. It is natural to me to go where I please, to do
what I please. I find myself at eleven o'clock in the day
in Bond Street, and it seems to me that I have been
sauntering there at that very hour for years past. I digress into Soho, to explore a book-stall. Methinks I have
been thirty years a collector. There is nothing strange
nor new in it. I find myself before a fine picture in the
morning. Was it ever otherwise? What is become of
Fish Street Hill? Where is Fenchurch Street? Stones
of old Mincing Lane, which I have worn with my daily
pilgrimage for six-and-thirty years, to the footsteps of

what toil-worn clerk are your everlasting flints now vocal? I indent the gayer flags of Pall Mall. It is 'Change time, and I am strangely among the Elgin marbles.

It was no hyperbole when I ventured to compare the change in my condition to a passing into another world. Time stands still in a manner to me. I have lost all distinction of season. I do not know the day of the week or of the month. Each day used to be individually felt by me in its reference to the foreign post days; in its distance from, or propinquity to, the next Sunday.

I had my Wednesday feelings, my Saturday nights' sensations. The genius of each day was upon me distinctly during the whole of it, affecting my appetite, spirits, etc. The phantom of the next day, with the dreary five to follow, sate as a load upon my poor Sabbath recreations. What charm has washed that Ethiop white? What is gone of Black Monday? All days are the same. Sunday itself—that unfortunate failure of a holiday, as it too often proved, what with my sense of its fugitiveness, and over-care to get the greatest quantity of pleasure out of it—is melted down into a weekday. I can spare to go to church now, without grudging the huge cantle which it used to seem to cut out of the holiday.

I have Time for everything. I can visit a sick friend. I can interrupt the man of much occupation when he is busiest. I can insult over him with an invitation to take a day's pleasure with me to Windsor this fine Maymorning. It is Lucretian pleasure to behold the poor drudges, whom I have left behind in the world, carking and caring; like horses in a mill, drudging on in the same eternal round—and what is it all for?

A man can never have too much Time to himself, nor too little to do. Had I a little son, I would christen him NOTHING-TO-DO; he should do nothing. Man, I

verily believe, is out of his element as long as he is opera-
tive. I am altogether for the life contemplative. Will no
kindly earthquake come and swallow up those accursed
cotton mills? Take me that lumber of a desk there, and
bowl it down

> As low as to the fiends.

I am no longer ———, clerk to the Firm of, etc. I am
Retired Leisure. I am to be met with in trim gardens. I
am already come to be known by my vacant face and
careless gesture, perambulating at no fixed pace, nor
with any settled purpose. I walk about; not to and from.
They tell me, a certain *cum dignitate* air, that has been
buried so long with my other good parts, has begun to
shoot forth in my person. I grow into gentility percep-
tibly. When I take up a newspaper, it is to read the
state of the opera. *Opus operatum est.* I have done all
that I came into this world to do. I have worked task-
work, and have the rest of the day to myself.

London Magazine, May 1825; Last Essays of Elia.

PART THREE

London

THE LONDONER

IN COMPLIANCE with my own particular humour, no less than with thy laudable curiosity, Reader, I proceed to give thee some account of my history and habits. I was born under the nose of St. Dunstan's steeple, just where the conflux of the eastern and western inhabitants of this twofold city meet and justle in friendly opposition at Temple-bar. The same day which gave me to the world saw London happy in the celebration of her great annual feast. This I cannot help looking upon as a lively type or omen of the future great goodwill which I was destined to bear toward the City, resembling in kind that solicitude which every Chief Magistrate is supposed to feel for whatever concerns her interests and well-being. Indeed, I consider myself in some sort a speculative Lord Mayor of London: for, though circumstances unhappily preclude me from the hope of ever arriving at the dignity of a gold chain and spital sermon, yet thus much will I say of myself, in truth, that Whittington himself with his Cat (just emblem of *vigilance* and a *furred gown*), never went beyond me in affection, which I bear to the citizens. Shut out from

316

serving them in the most honourable mode, I aspire to
do them benefit in another, scarcely less honourable;
and if I cannot, by virtue of office, commit vice and
irregularity to the *material Counter*, I will, at least,
erect a *spiritual one*, where they shall be *laid fast by
the heels*. In plain words, I will do my best endeavour
to *write them down*.

To return to *myself* (from whence my zeal for the
Public good is perpetually causing me to digress), I will
let thee, Reader, into certain more of my peculiarities.
I was born (as you have heard), bred, and have passed
most of my time, in a *crowd*. This has begot in me an
entire affection for that way of life, amounting to an almost insurmountable aversion from solitude and rural
scenes. This aversion was never interrupted or suspended, except for a few years in the younger part of
my life, during a period in which I had fixed my affections upon a charming young woman. Every man, while
the *passion* is upon him, is for a time at least addicted
to groves and meadows and purling streams. During this
short period of my existence, I contracted just enough
familiarity with rural objects to understand tolerably
well ever after the Poets, when they declaim in such
passionate terms in favour of a country life.

For my own part, now the *fit* is long past, I have no
hesitation in declaring, that a mob of happy faces crowding up at the pit door of Drury-Lane Theatre just
at the hour of five, give me ten thousand finer pleasures,
than I ever received from all the flocks of *silly sheep*,
that have whitened the plains of Arcadia or Epsom
Downs.

This passion for crowds is no where feasted so full as
in London. The man must have a rare *recipe* for melancholy, who can be dull in Fleet-street. I am naturally
inclined to *hypochondria*, but in London it vanishes, like

all other ills. Often when I have felt a weariness or distaste at home, have I rushed out into her crowded Strand, and fed my humour, till tears have wetted my cheek for inutterable sympathies with the multitudinous moving picture, which she never fails to present at all hours, like the shifting scenes of a skilful Pantomime.

The very deformities of London, which give distaste to others, from habit do not displease me. The endless succession of shops, where Fancy (miscalled Folly) is supplied with perpetual new gauds and toys, excite in me no puritanical aversion. I gladly behold every appetite supplied with its proper food. The obliging customer, and the obliged tradesmen—things which live by bowing, and things which exist but for homage, do not affect me with disgust; from habit I perceive nothing but urbanity, where other men, more refined, discover meanness. I love the very smoke of London, because it has been the medium most familiar to my vision. I see grand principles of honour at work in the dirty ring which encompasses two combatants with fists, and principles of no less eternal justice in the tumultuous detectors of a pickpocket. The salutary astonishment with which an execution is surveyed, convinces me more forcibly than an hundred volumes of abstract polity, that the universal instinct of man, in all ages, has leaned to order and good government. Thus an art of extracting morality, from the commonest incidents of a town life, is attained by the same well-natured alchemy, with which the *Foresters* of *Arden* in a beautiful country

Found tongues in trees, books in the running brooks,
Sermons in stones, and good in every thing—

Where has spleen her food but in London—humour, interest, curiosity, suck at her measureless breasts without a possibility of being satiated. Nursed amid her noise,

her crowds, her beloved smoke—what have I been doing all my life, if I have not lent out my heart with usury
to such scenes?

Reader, in the course of my peregrinations about the
great city, it is hard, if I have not picked up matter,
which may serve to amuse thee, as it has done me, a
winter evening long. When next we meet, I purpose
opening my budget—Till when, farewell.

Morning Post, February 1, 1802.

THE SOUTH-SEA HOUSE

READER, in thy passage from the Bank—where thou
hast been receiving thy half-yearly dividends (supposing thou art a lean annuitant like myself)—to the Flower
Pot, to secure a place for Dalston, or Shacklewell, or
some other thy suburban retreat northerly—didst thou
never observe a melancholy-looking, handsome brick
and stone edifice, to the left—where Threadneedle
Street abuts upon Bishopsgate? I dare say thou hast
often admired its magnificent portals ever gaping wide,
and disclosing to view a grave court, with cloisters,
and pillars, with few or no traces of goers-in or comers-
out—a desolation something like Balclutha's.[1]

This was once a house of trade—a centre of busy interests. The throng of merchants was here—the quick
pulse of gain—and here some forms of business are still
kept up, though the soul be long since fled. Here are
still to be seen stately porticos; imposing staircases; offices roomy as the state apartments in palaces—deserted,

[1] I passed by the walls of Balclutha, and they were desolate.
—OSSIAN.—C. L.

or thinly peopled with a few straggling clerks; the still more sacred interiors of court and committee-rooms, with venerable faces of beadles, doorkeepers—directors seated in form on solemn days (to proclaim a dead dividend), at long worm-eaten tables, that have been mahogany, with tarnished gilt-leather coverings, supporting massy silver inkstands long since dry; the oaken wainscots hung with pictures of deceased governors and sub-governors, of Queen Anne, and the two first monarchs of the Brunswick dynasty; huge charts, which subsequent discoveries have antiquated; dusty maps of Mexico, dim as dreams—and soundings of the Bay of Panama! The long passages hung with buckets, appended, in idle row, to walls, whose substance might defy any, short of the last, conflagration; with vast ranges of cellarage under all, where dollars and pieces-of-eight once lay, an "unsunned heap," for Mammon to have solaced his solitary heart withal, long since dissipated, or scattered into air at the blast of the breaking of that famous Bubble.

Such is the South-Sea House. At least, such it was forty years ago, when I knew it—a magnificent relic! What alterations may have been made in it since, I have had no opportunities of verifying. Time, I take for granted, has not freshened it. No wind has resuscitated the face of the sleeping waters. A thicker crust by this time stagnates upon it.

The moths, that were then battering upon its obsolete ledgers and daybooks, have rested from their depredations, but other light generations have succeeded, making fine fretwork among their single and double entries. Layers of dust have accumulated (a superfœtation of dirt!) upon the old layers, that seldom used to be disturbed, save by some curious finger, now and then, inquisitive to explore the mode of book-keeping in

Queen Anne's reign; or, with less hallowed curiosity, seeking to unveil some of the mysteries of that tremendous HOAX whose extent the petty peculators of our day look back upon with the same expression of incredulous admiration, and hopeless ambition of rivalry, as would become the puny face of modern conspiracy contemplating the Titan size of Vaux's superhuman plot.

Peace to the manes of the Bubble! Silence and destitution are upon thy walls, proud house, for a memorial!

Situated as thou art, in the very heart of stirring and living commerce—amid the fret and fever of speculation—with the Bank, and the 'Change, and the India House about thee, in the hey-day of present prosperity, with their important faces, as it were, insulting thee, their *poor neighbour out of business*—to the idle and merely contemplative—to such as me, old house! there is a charm in thy quiet: a cessation—a coolness from business—an indolence almost cloistral—which is delightful! With what reverence have I paced thy great bare rooms and courts at eventide! They spoke of the past: the shade of some dead accountant, with visionary pen in ear, would flit by me, stiff as in life.

Living accounts and accountants puzzle me. I have no skill in figuring. But thy great dead tomes, which scarce three degenerate clerks of the present day could lift from their enshrining shelves—with their old fantastic flourishes, and decorative rubric interlacings—their sums in triple columniations, set down with formal superfluity of ciphers—with pious sentences at the beginning, without which our religious ancestors never ventured to open a book of business, or bill of lading—the costly vellum covers of some of them almost persuading us that we are got into some *better library*—are very agreeable and edifying spectacles. I can look upon these defunct dragons with complacency. Thy heavy odd-shaped ivory-handled penknives (our ancestors had everything on a larger scale than we have hearts for) are as good as anything from Herculaneum. The pounce-boxes of our days have gone retrograde.

The very clerks which I remember in the South-Sea House—I speak of forty years back—had an air very different from those in the public offices that I have had to do with since. They partook of the genius of the place!

They were mostly (for the establishment did not admit of superfluous salaries) bachelors. Generally (for they had not much to do) persons of a curious and speculative turn of mind. Old-fashioned, for a reason mentioned before. Humourists, for they were of all descriptions; and, not having been brought together in early life (which has a tendency to assimilate the members of corporate bodies to each other), but, for the most part, placed in this house in ripe or middle age, they necessarily carried into it their separate habits and oddities, unqualified, if I may so speak, as into a common stock. Hence they formed a sort of Noah's ark. Odd fishes. A lay monastery. Domestic retainers in a great house, kept more for show than used. Yet pleasant fellows, full of chat—and not a few among them had arrived at considerable proficiency on the German flute.

The cashier at that time was one Evans, a Cambro-Briton. He had something of the choleric complexion of his countrymen stamped on his visage, but was a worthy sensible man at bottom. He wore his hair, to the last, powdered and frizzed out, in the fashion which I remember to have seen in caricatures of what were termed, in my young days, *Maccaronies*. He was the last of that race of beaux. Melancholy as a gib-cat over his counter all the forenoon, I think I see him, making up his cash (as they call it) with tremulous fingers, as if he feared every one about him was a de-

faulter; in his hypochondry ready to imagine himself
one; haunted, at least, with the idea of the possibility
of his becoming one; his tristful visage clearing up a
little over his roast neck of veal at Anderton's at two
(where his picture still hangs, taken a little before his
death by desire of the master of the coffee-house, which
he had frequented for the last five-and-twenty years),
but not attaining the meridian of its animation till evening brought on the hour of tea and visiting.

The simultaneous sound of his well-known rap at
the door with the stroke of the clock announcing six,
was a topic of never-failing mirth in the families which
this dear old bachelor gladdened with his presence.
Then was his *forte,* his glorified hour! How would he
chirp, and expand, over a muffin! How would he dilate
into secret history! His countryman, Pennant himself,
in particular, could not be more eloquent than he in relation to old and new London—the site of old theatres,
churches, streets gone to decay—where Rosamond's
Pond stood—the Mulberry gardens—and the Conduit
in Cheap—with many a pleasant anecdote, derived from
paternal tradition, of those grotesque figures which Hogarth has immortalized in his picture of "Noon"—the
worthy descendants of those heroic confessors, who,
flying to this country, from the wrath of Louis the Fourteenth and his dragoons, kept alive the flame of pure religion in the sheltering obscurities of Hog Lane, and the
vicinity of the Seven Dials!

Deputy, under Evans, was Thomas Tame. He had
the air and stoop of a nobleman. You would have taken
him for one, had you met him in one of the passages
leading to Westminster Hall. By stoop, I mean that
gentle bending of the body forwards, which, in great
men, must be supposed to be the effect of an habitual
condescending attention to the applications of their

inferiors. While he held you in converse, you felt strained to the height in the colloquy. The conference over, you were at leisure to smile at the comparative insignificance of the pretensions which had just awed you. His intellect was of the shallowest order. It did not reach to a saw or a proverb. His mind was in its original state of white paper. A sucking-babe might have posed him. What was it then? Was he rich?

Alas, no! Thomas Tame was very poor. Both he and his wife looked outwardly gentlefolks, when I fear all was not well at all times within. She had a neat meagre person, which it was evident she had not sinned in over-pampering; but in its veins was noble blood. She traced her descent, by some labyrinth of relationship, which I never thoroughly understood—much less can explain with any heraldic certainty at this time of day—to the illustrious, but unfortunate house of Derwentwater. This was the secret of Thomas's stoop. This was the thought—the sentiment—the bright solitary star of your lives—ye mild and happy pair—which cheered you in the night of intellect, and in the obscurity of your station! This was to you instead of riches, instead of rank, instead of glittering attainments: and it was worth them all together. You insulted none with it; but while you wore it as a piece of defensive armour only, no insult likewise could reach you through it. *Decus et solamen.*

Of quite another stamp was the then accountant, John Tipp. He neither pretended to high blood, nor, in good truth, cared one fig about the matter. He "thought an accountant the greatest character in the world, and himself the greatest accountant in it." Yet John was not without his hobby. The fiddle relieved his vacant hours. He sang, certainly, with other notes than to the Orphean lyre. He did, indeed, scream and scrape most abominably.

His fine suite of official rooms in Threadneedle Street, which, without anything very substantial appended to them, were enough to enlarge a man's notions of himself that lived in them (I know not who is the occupier of them now), resounded fortnightly to the notes of a concert of "sweet breasts," as our ancestors would have called them, culled from clubrooms and orchestras —chorus-singers—first and second violoncellos—double-basses—and clarionets—who ate his cold mutton, and drank his punch, and praised his ear. He sate like Lord Midas among them. But at the desk Tipp was quite another sort of creature. Thence all ideas, that were purely ornamental, were banished. You could not speak of anything romantic without rebuke. Politics were excluded. A newspaper was thought too refined and abstracted. The whole duty of man consisted in writing off dividend warrants. The striking of the annual balance in the company's books (which, perhaps, differed from the balance of last year in the sum of £25:1:6) occupied his days and nights for a month previous.

Not that Tipp was blind to the deadness of *things* (as they call them in the city) in his beloved house, or did not sigh for a return of the old stirring days when South-Sea hopes were young—(he was indeed equal to the wielding of any of the most intricate accounts of the most flourishing company in these or those days) —but to a genuine accountant the difference of proceeds is as nothing. The fractional farthing is as dear to his heart as the thousands which stand before it. He is the true actor, who, whether his part be a prince or a peasant, must act it with like intensity.

With Tipp form was everything. His life was formal. His actions seemed ruled with a ruler. His pen was not less erring than his heart. He made the best executor in the world; he was plagued with incessant executorships accordingly, which excited his spleen and soothed his vanity in equal ratios. He would swear (for Tipp swore) at the little orphans, whose rights he would guard with a tenacity like the grasp of the dying hand that commended their interests to his protection. With all this there was about him a sort of timidity—(his few enemies used to give it a worse name)—a something which in reverence to the dead, we will place, if you please, a little on this side of the heroic.

Nature certainly had been pleased to endow John Tipp with a sufficient measure of the principle of self-preservation. There is a cowardice which we do not despise, because it has nothing base or treacherous in its elements; it betrays itself, not you: it is mere temperament; the absence of the romantic and the enterprising; it sees a lion in the way, and will not, with Fortinbras, "greatly find quarrel in a straw," when some supposed honour is at stake. Tipp never mounted the box of a stage-coach in his life; or leaned against the rails of a balcony; or walked upon the ridge of a parapet; or looked down a precipice; or let off a gun; or went upon a water-party; or would willingly let you go, if he could have helped it: neither was it recorded of him, that for lucre, or for intimidation, he ever forsook friend or principle.

Whom next shall we summon from the dusty dead, in whom common qualities become uncommon? Can I forget thee, Henry Man, the wit, the polished man of letters, the *author*, of the South-Sea House? who never enteredst thy office in a morning, or quittedst it in midday—(what didst *thou* in an office?)—without some quirk that left a sting! Thy gibes and thy jokes are now extinct, or survive but in two forgotten volumes, which I had the good fortune to rescue from a stall in Barbican, not three days ago, and found thee terse, fresh, epigrammatic, as alive. Thy wit is a little gone by in these fastidious days—thy topics are staled by the "new-born gauds" of the time—but great thou used to be in Public Ledgers, and in Chronicles, upon Chatham, and Shelburne, and Rockingham, and Howe, and Burgoyne, and Clinton, and the war which ended in the tearing from Great Britain her rebellious colonies —and Keppel, and Wilkes, and Sawbridge, and Bull, and Dunning, and Pratt, and Richmond—and such small politics.

A little less facetious, and a great deal more obstreperous, was fine rattling, rattle-headed Plumer. He was descended—not in a right line, reader (for his lineal pretensions, like his personal, favoured a little of the sinister bend)—from the Plumers of Hertfordshire. So tradition gave him out; and certain family features not a little sanctioned the opinion. Certainly old Walter Plumer (his reputed author) had been a rake in his days, and visited much in Italy, and had seen the world. He was uncle, bachelor-uncle, to the fine old whig still living, who has represented the county in so many successive parliaments, and has a fine old mansion near Ware. Walter flourished in George the Second's days, and was the same who was summoned before the House of Commons about a business of franks, with the old Duchess of Marlborough. You may read of it in Johnson's *Life of Cave*. Cave came off cleverly in that business. It is certain our Plumer did nothing to discountenance the rumour. He rather seemed pleased whenever it was, with all gentleness, insinuated. But, besides his family pretensions, Plumer was an engaging fellow, and sang gloriously.

Not so sweetly sang Plumer as thou sangest, mild, childlike, pastoral M.; a flute's breathing less divinely whispering than thy Arcadian melodies, when, in tones worthy of Arden, thou didst chant that song sung by Amiens to the banished Duke, which proclaims the winter wind more lenient than for a man to be ungrateful. Thy sire was old surly M., the unapproachable churchwarden of Bishopsgate. He knew not what he did, when he begat thee, like spring, gentle offspring of blustering winter: only unfortunate in thy ending, which should have been mild, conciliatory, swanlike.

Much remains to sing. Many fantastic shapes rise up, but they must be mine in private: already I have fooled the reader to the top of his bent; else could I omit that strange creature Woollett, who existed in trying the question, and *bought litigations?*—and still stranger, inimitable, solemn Hepworth, from whose gravity Newton might have deduced the law of gravitation. How profoundly would he nib a pen—with what deliberation would he wet a wafer!

But it is time to close—night's wheels are rattling fast over me—it is proper to have done with this solemn mockery.

Reader, what if I have been playing with thee all this while?—peradventure the very *names,* which I have summoned up before thee, are fantastic—insubstantial—like Henry Pimpernel, and old John Naps of Greece. . . .

Be satisfied that something answering to them has had a being. Their importance is from the past.

London Magazine, August 1820; Elia.

THE OLD BENCHERS OF THE INNER TEMPLE

I WAS born, and passed the first seven years of my life, in the Temple. Its church, its halls, its gardens, its fountain, its river, I had almost said—for in those young years, what was this king of rivers to me but a stream that watered our pleasant places?—these are of my oldest recollections. I repeat, to this day, no verses to myself more frequently, or with kindlier emotion, than those of Spenser, where he speaks of this spot.

> There when they came, whereas those bricky towers,
> The which on Themmes brode aged back doth ride,
> Where now the studios lawyers have their bowers,
> There whylome wont the Templer knights to bide,
> Till they decayed through pride.

Indeed, it is the most elegant spot in the metropolis. What a transition for a countryman visiting London for the first time—the passing from the crowded Strand or Fleet Street, by unexpected avenues, into its magnificent ample squares, its classic green recesses! What a cheerful, liberal look hath that portion of it, which, from three sides, overlooks the greater garden; that goodly pile

> Of building strong, albeit of Paper hight,

confronting with massy contrast, the lighter, older, more fantastically shrouded one, named of Harcourt, with the cheerful Crown Office Row (place of my kindly engendure), right opposite the stately stream, which washes the garden-foot with her yet scarcely trade-polluted waters, and seems but just weaned from her Twickenham Naïades! a man would give something to have been born in such places.

What a collegiate aspect has that fine Elizabethan hall, where the fountain plays, which I have made to rise and fall, how many times! to the astoundment of the young urchins, my contemporaries, who, not being able to guess at its recondite machinery, were almost tempted to hail the wondrous work as magic! What an antique air had the now almost effaced sundials, with their moral inscriptions, seeming coevals with that Time which they measured, and to take their revelations of its flight immediately from heaven, holding correspondence with the fountain of light! How would the dark line steal imperceptibly on, watched by the eye of childhood, eager to detect its movement, never catched, nice as an evanescent cloud, or the first arrests of sleep!

> Ah! yet doth beauty like a dial hand
> Steal from his figure, and no pace perceived!

What a dead thing is a clock, with its ponderous embowelments of lead and brass, its pert or solemn dullness of communication, compared with the simple altar-like structure, and silent heart-language of the old dial! It stood as the garden god of Christian gardens. Why is it almost everywhere vanished? If its business-use be superseded by more elaborate inventions, its moral uses, its beauty, might have pleaded for its continuance. It spoke of moderate labours, of pleasures not protracted after sunset, of temperance, and good hours. It was the primitive clock, the horologe of the first world. Adam could scarce have missed it in Paradise. It was the measure appropriate for sweet plants and flowers to spring by, for the birds to apportion

their silver warblings by, for flocks to pasture and be
led to fold by. The shepherd "carved it out quaintly
in the sun"; and, turning philosopher by the very occupation, provided it with mottoes more touching than
tombstones. It was a pretty device of the gardener,
recorded by Marvell, who, in the days of artificial
gardening, made a dial out of herbs and flowers. I must
quote his verses a little higher up, for they are full, as
all his serious poetry was, of a witty delicacy. They
will not come in awkwardly, I hope, in a talk of fountains and sundials. He is speaking of sweet garden
scenes:

> What wondrous life is this I lead!
> Ripe apples drop about my head.
> The luscious clusters of the vine
> Upon my mouth do crush their wine.
> The nectarine, and curious peach,
> Into my hands themselves do reach.
> Stumbling on melons, as I pass,
> Insnared with flowers, I fall on grass.
> Meanwhile the mind from pleasure less
> Withdraws into its happiness.
> The mind, that ocean, where each kind
> Does straight its own resemblance find;
> Yet it creates, transcending these,
> Far other worlds and other seas;
> Annihilating all that's made
> To a green thought in a green shade.
> Here at the fountain's sliding foot,
> Or at some fruit-tree's mossy root,
> Casting the body's vest aside,
> My soul into the boughs does glide;
> There, like a bird, it sits and sings,
> Then wets and claps its silver wings,
> And, till prepared for longer flight,
> Waves in its plumes the various light.
> How well the skilful gardener drew,

Of flowers and herbs, this dial new!
Where, from above, the milder sun
Does through a fragrant zodiac run:
And, as it works, the industrious bee
Computes its time as well as we.
How could such sweet and wholesome hours
Be reckon'd, but with herbs and flowers? [1]

The artificial fountains of the metropolis are, in like manner, fast vanishing. Most of them are dried up or bricked over. Yet, where one is left, as in that little green nook behind the South-Sea House, what a freshness it gives to the dreary pile! Four little winged marble boys used to play their virgin fancies, spouting out ever fresh streams from their innocent-wanton lips in the square of Lincoln's Inn, when I was no bigger than they were figured. They are gone, and the spring choked up. The fashion, they tell me, is gone by, and these things are esteemed childish. Why not, then, gratify children, by letting them stand? Lawyers, I suppose, were children once. They are awakening images to them at least. Why must everything smack of man and mannish? Is the world all grown up? Is childhood dead? Or is there not in the bosoms of the wisest and the best some of the child's heart left, to respond to its earliest enchantments? The figures were grotesque. Are the stiff-wigged living figures, that still flitter and chatter about that area, less Gothic in appearance? or is the splutter of their hot rhetoric one-half so refreshing and innocent as the little cool playful streams those exploded cherubs uttered?

They have lately gothicized the entrance to the Inner Temple, and the library front; to assimilate them, I suppose, to the body of the hall, which they do not at all resemble. What is become of the winged horse that

[1] From a copy of verses entitled "The Garden."—C. L.

stood over the former? a stately arms! and who has removed those frescoes of the Virtues, which Italianized the end of the Paper Buildings?—my first hint of allegory! They must account to me for these things, which I miss so greatly.

The terrace is, indeed, left, which we used to call the parade; but the traces are passed away of the footsteps which made its pavement awful! It is become common and profane. The old benchers had it almost sacred to themselves, in the forepart of the day at least. They might not be sided or jostled. Their air and dress asserted the parade. You left wide spaces betwixt you when you passed them. We walk on even terms with their successors.

The roguish eye of J——ll, ever ready to be delivered of a jest, almost invites a stranger to vie a repartee with it. But what insolent familiar durst have mated Thomas Coventry?—whose person was a quadrate, his step massy and elephantine, his face square as the lion's, his gait peremptory and path-keeping, indivertible from his way as a moving column, the scarecrow of his inferiors, the browbeater of equals and superiors, who made a solitude of children wherever he came, for they fled his insufferable presence, as they would have shunned an Elisha bear. His growl was as thunder in their ears, whether he spake to them in mirth or in rebuke; his invitatory notes being, indeed, of all, the most repulsive and horrid. Clouds of snuff, aggravating the natural terrors of his speech, broke from each majestic nostril, darkening the air. He took it, not by pinches, but a palmful at once, diving for it under the mighty flaps of his old-fashioned waistcoat pocket; his waistcoat red and angry, his coat dark rappee, tinctured by dye original, and by adjuncts, with buttons of obsolete gold. And so he paced the terrace.

By his side a milder form was sometimes to be seen; the pensive gentility of Samuel Salt. They were coevals, and had nothing but that and their benchership in common. In politics Salt was a whig, and Coventry a staunch tory. Many a sarcastic growl did the latter cast out—for Coventry had a rough spinous humour— at the political confederates of his associate, which rebounded from the gentle bosom of the latter like cannon-balls from wool. You could not ruffle Samuel Salt.

S. had the reputation of being a very clever man, and of excellent discernment in the chamber practice of the law. I suspect his knowledge did not amount to much. When a case of difficult disposition of money, testamentary or otherwise, came before him, he ordinarily handed it over, with a few instructions, to his man Lovel,[1] who was a quick little fellow, and would despatch it out of hand by the light of natural understanding, of which he had an uncommon share. It was incredible what repute for talents S. enjoyed by the mere trick of gravity. He was a shy man; a child might pose him in a minute—indolent and procrastinating to the last degree. Yet men would give him credit for vast application, in spite of himself. He was not to be trusted with himself with impunity. He never dressed for a dinner party but he forgot his sword—they wore swords then—or some other necessary part of his equipage.

Lovel had his eye upon him on all these occasions, and ordinarily gave him his cue. If there was anything which he could speak unseasonably, he was sure to do it. He was to dine at a relative's of the unfortunate Miss Blandy on the day of her execution; and L., who had

[1] In the character of Lovel, Lamb is describing his father, John Lamb, Sr.—J. M. B.

a wary foresight of his probable hallucinations, before he set out schooled him, with great anxiety, not in any possible manner to allude to her story that day. S. promised faithfully to observe the injunction. He had not been seated in the parlour, where the company was expecting the dinner summons, four minutes, when, a pause in the conversation ensuing, he got up, looked out of window, and pulling down his ruffles—an ordinary motion with him—observed, "it was a gloomy day," and added, "Miss Blandy must be hanged by this time, I suppose."

Instances of this sort were perpetual. Yet S. was thought by some of the greatest men of his time a fit person to be consulted, not alone in matters pertaining to the law, but in the ordinary niceties and embarrassments of conduct—from force of manner entirely. He never laughed. He had the same good fortune among the female world—was a known toast with the ladies, and one or two are said to have died for love of him—I suppose, because he never trifled or talked gallantry with them, or paid them, indeed, hardly common attentions. He had a fine face and person, but wanted, methought, the spirit that should have shown them off with advantage to the women. His eye lacked lustre.

Not so, thought Susan P., who, at the advanced age of sixty, was seen, in the cold evening time, unaccompanied, wetting the pavement of B——d Row, with tears that fell in drops which might be heard, because her friend had died that day—he, whom she had pursued with a hopeless passion for the last forty years—a passion which years could not extinguish or abate; nor the long-resolved, yet gently-enforced, puttings-off of unrelenting bachelorhood dissuade from its cherished purpose. Mild Susan P., thou hast now thy friend in heaven!

Thomas Coventry was a cadet of the noble family of that name. He passed his youth in contracted circumstances, which gave him early those parsimonious habits which in after life never forsook him, so that with one windfall or another, about the time I knew him he was master of four or five hundred thousand pounds; nor did he look or walk worth a moidore less. He lived in a gloomy house opposite the pump in Serjeant's Inn, Fleet Street. J., the counsel, is doing self-imposed penance in it, for what reason I divine not, at this day.

C. had an agreeable seat at North Cray, where he seldom spent above a day or two at a time in the summer; but preferred, during the hot months, standing at his window in this damp, close, well-like mansion, to watch, as he said, "the maids drawing water all day long." I suspect he had his within-door reasons for the preference. *Hic currus et arma fuere.* He might think his treasures more safe. His house had the aspect of a strong-box.

C. was a close hunks—a hoarder rather than a miser —or, if a miser, none of the mad Elwes breed, who have brought discredit upon a character which cannot exist without certain admirable points of steadiness and unity of purpose. One may hate a true miser, but cannot, I suspect, so easily despise him. By taking care of the pence he is often enabled to part with the pounds, upon a scale that leaves us careless generous fellows halting at an immeasurable distance behind. C. gave away £30,000 at once in his lifetime to a blind charity. His housekeeping was severely looked after, but he kept the table of a gentleman. He would know who came in and who went out of his house, but his kitchen chimney was never suffered to freeze.

Salt was his opposite in this, as in all—never knew

what he was worth in the world; and having but a competency for his rank, which his indolent habits were little calculated to improve, might have suffered severely if he had not had honest people about him. Lovel took care of everything. He was at once his clerk, his good servant, his dresser, his friend, his "flapper," his guide, stopwatch, auditor, treasurer. He did nothing without consulting Lovel, or failed in anything without expecting and fearing his admonishing. He put himself almost too much in his hands, had they not been the purest in the world. He resigned his title almost to respect as a master, if L. could ever have forgotten for a moment that he was a servant.

I knew this Lovel. He was a man of an incorrigible and losing honesty. A good fellow withal, and "would strike." In the cause of the oppressed he never considered inequalities, or calculated the number of his opponents. He once wrested a sword out of the hand of a man of quality that had drawn upon him, and pommelled him severely with the hilt of it. The swordsman had offered insult to a female—an occasion upon which no odds against him could have prevented the interference of Lovel. He would stand next day bareheaded to the same person modestly to excuse his interference—for L. never forgot rank where something better was not concerned.

L. was the liveliest little fellow breathing, had a face as gay as Garrick's, whom he was said greatly to resemble (I have a portrait of him which confirms it), possessed a fine turn for humorous poetry—next to Swift and Prior—moulded heads in clay or plaster of Paris to admiration, by the dint of natural genius merely; turned cribbage boards, and such small cabinet toys, to perfection; took a hand at quadrille or bowls with equal facility; made punch better than any man of his degree in England; had the merriest quips and conceits; and was altogether as brimful of rogueries and inventions as you could desire.

He was a brother of the angle, moreover, and just such a free, hearty, honest companion as Mr. Izaak Walton would have chosen to go a-fishing with. I saw him in his old age and the decay of his faculties, palsy-smitten, in the last sad stage of human weakness—"a remnant most forlorn of what he was"—yet even then his eye would light up upon the mention of his favourite Garrick. He was greatest, he would say, in Bayes—"was upon the stage nearly throughout the whole performance, and as busy as a bee."

At intervals, too, he would speak of his former life, and how he came up a little boy from Lincoln, to go to service, and how his mother cried at parting with him, and how he returned, after some years' absence, in his smart new livery, to see her, and she blessed herself at the change, and could hardly be brought to believe that it was "her own bairn." And then, the excitement subsiding, he would weep, till I have wished that sad second-childhood might have a mother still to lay its head upon her lap. But the common mother of us all in no long time after received him .gently into hers.

With Coventry, and with Salt, in their walks upon the terrace, most commonly Peter Pierson would join to make up a third. They did not walk linked arm-in-arm in those days—"as now our stout triumvirs sweep the streets"—but generally with both hands folded behind them for state, or with one at least behind, the other carrying a cane. P. was a benevolent, but not a prepossessing man. He had that in his face which you could not term unhappiness; it rather implied an incapacity of being happy. His cheeks were colourless, even to whiteness. His look was uninviting, resembling (but without his sourness) that of our great philanthropist. I know that he *did* good acts, but I could never make out what he *was*.

Contemporary with these, but subordinate, was Daines Barrington—another oddity—he walked burly and square—in imitation, I think, of Coventry—howbeit he attained not to the dignity of his prototype. Nevertheless, he did pretty well, upon the strength of being a tolerable antiquarian, and having a brother a bishop. When the account of his year's treasurership came to be audited the following singular charge was unanimously disallowed by the bench: "Item, disbursed Mr. Allen, the gardener, twenty shillings for stuff to poison the sparrows, by my orders."

Next to him was old Barton—a jolly negation, who took upon him the ordering of the bills of fare for the parliament chamber, where the benchers dine—answering to the combination rooms at College—much to the easement of his less epicurean brethren. I know nothing more of him. Then Read, and Twopeny—Read, good-humoured and personable—Twopeny, good-humoured, but thin, and felicitous in jests upon his own figure.

If T. was thin, Wharry was attenuated and fleeting. Many must remember him (for he was rather of later date) and his singular gait, which was performed by three steps and a jump regularly succeeding. The steps were little efforts, like that of a child beginning to walk; the jump comparatively vigorous, as a foot to an inch. Where he learned this figure, or what occasioned it, I could never discover. It was neither graceful in itself, nor seemed to answer the purpose any better than common walking. The extreme tenuity of his frame, I suspect, set him upon it. It was a trial of poising. Twopeny would often rally him upon his leanness, and hail him as Brother Lusty; but W. had no relish of a joke. His features were spiteful. I have heard that he would pinch his cat's ears extremely when anything had offended him.

Jackson—the omniscient Jackson he was called—was of this period. He had the reputation of possessing more multifarious knowledge than any man of his time. He was the Friar Bacon of the less literate portion of the Temple. I remember a pleasant passage of the cook applying to him, with much formality of apology, for instructions how to write down *edge* bone of beef in his bill of commons. He was supposed to know, if any man in the world did. He decided the orthography to be—as I have given it—fortifying his authority with such anatomical reasons as dismissed the manciple (for the time) learned and happy. Some do spell it yet, perversely, *aitch* bone, from a fanciful resemblance between its shape and that of the aspirate so denominated.

I had almost forgotten Mingay with the iron hand—but he was somewhat later. He had lost his right hand by some accident, and supplied it with a grappling-hook, which he wielded with a tolerable adroitness. I detected the substitute before I was old enough to reason whether it were artificial or not. I remember the astonishment it raised in me. He was a blustering, loud-talking person; and I reconciled the phenomenon to my ideas as an emblem of power—somewhat like the horns in the forehead of Michelangelo's Moses. Baron Maseres, who walks (or did till very lately) in the costume of the reign of George the Second, closes my imperfect recollections of the old benchers of the Inner Temple.

Fantastic forms, whither are ye fled? Or, if the like of you exist, why exist they no more for me? Ye in-

explicable, half-understood appearances, why comes
in reason to tear away the preternatural mist, bright
or gloomy, that enshrouded you? Why make ye so
sorry a figure in my relation, who made up to me—to
my childish eyes—the mythology of the Temple? In
those days I saw Gods, as "old men covered with a
mantle" walking upon the earth.

Let the dreams of classic idolatry perish—extinct be
the fairies and fairy trumpery of legendary fabling,
in the heart of childhood there will, for ever, spring
up a well of innocent or wholesome superstition—the
seeds of exaggeration will be busy there, and vital—
from everyday forms educing the unknown and the
uncommon. In that little Goshen there will be light
when the grown world flounders about in the darkness
of sense and materiality. While childhood, and while
dreams, reducing childhood, shall be left, imagination
shall not have spread her holy wings totally to fly the
earth.

P.S.—I have done injustice to the soft shade of
Samuel Salt. See what it is to trust to imperfect memory, and the erring notices of childhood! Yet I protest
I always thought that he had been a bachelor! This
gentleman, R. N. informs me, married young, and
losing his lady in childbed, within the first year of their
union, fell into a deep melancholy, from the effects of
which, probably, he never thoroughly recovered.

In what a new light does this place his rejection
(O call it by a gentler name!) of mild Susan P., un-
ravelling into beauty certain peculiarities of this very
shy and retiring character! Henceforth let no one receive the narratives of Elia for true records! They are,
in truth, but shadows of fact—verisimilitudes, not verities—or sitting but upon the remote edges and out-

skirts of history. He is no such honest chronicler as R. N., and would have done better perhaps to have consulted that gentleman before he sent these incondite reminiscences to press. But the worthy sub-treasurer— who respects his old and his new masters—would but have been puzzled at the indecorous liberties of Elia. The good man wots not, peradventure, of the licence which *Magazines* have arrived at in this plain-speaking age, or hardly dreams of their existence beyond the *Gentleman's*—his furthest monthly excursions in this nature having been long confined to the holy ground of honest *Urban's* obituary. May it be long before his own name shall help to swell those columns of un-envied flattery!

Meantime, O ye New Benchers of the Inner Temple, cherish him kindly, for he is himself the kindliest of human creatures. Should infirmities overtake him— he is yet in green and vigorous senility—make allowances for them, remembering that "ye yourselves are old." So may the Winged Horse, your ancient badge and cognizance, still flourish! so may future Hookers and Seldens illustrate your church and chambers! so may the sparrows, in default of more melodious quiristers, un-poisoned hop about your walks; so may the fresh-col-oured and cleanly nursery-maid, who, by leave, airs her playful charge in your stately gardens, drop her prettiest blushing curtsy as ye pass, reductive of juvenescent emotion! so may the younkers of this generation eye you, pacing your stately terrace, with the same superstitious veneration with which the child Elia gazed on the Old Worthies that solemnized the parade before ye!

London Magazine, September 1821; *Elia.*

THE PRAISE OF CHIMNEY-SWEEPERS

I LIKE to meet a sweep—understand me—not a grown sweeper—old chimney-sweepers are by no means attractive—but one of those tender novices, blooming through their first nigritude, the maternal washings not quite effaced from the cheek—such as come forth with the dawn, or somewhat earlier, with their little professional notes sounding like the *peep-peep* of a young sparrow; or liker to the matin lark should I pronounce them, in their aërial ascents not seldom anticipating the sunrise?

I have a kindly yearning toward these dim specks —poor blots—innocent blacknesses—

I reverence these young Africans of our own growth —these almost clergy imps, who sport their cloth without assumption; and from their little pulpits (the tops of chimneys), in the nipping air of a December morning, preach a lesson of patience to mankind.

When a child, what a mysterious pleasure it was to witness their operation! to see a chit no bigger than one's-self, enter, one knew not by what process, into what seemed the *fauces Averni*—to pursue him in imagination, as he went sounding on through so many dark stifling caverns, horrid shades! to shudder with the idea that "now, surely, he must be lost for ever!" —to revive at hearing his feeble shout of discovered daylight—and then (O fullness of delight!) running out of doors, to come just in time to see the sable phenomenon emerge in safety, the brandished weapon of his art victorious like some flag waved over a conquered citadel! I seem to remember having been told, that a bad sweep was once left in a stack with his brush, to indicate which way the wind blew. It was an awful spectacle certainly; not much unlike the old stage direction in *Macbeth,* where the "Apparition of a child crowned, with a tree in his hand, rises."

Reader, if thou meetest one of these small gentry in thy early rambles, it is good to give him a penny. It is better to give him twopence. If it be starving weather, and to the proper troubles of his hard occupation, a pair of kibed heels (no unusual accompaniment) be superadded, the demand on thy humanity will surely rise to a tester.

There is a composition, the groundwork of which I have understood to be the sweet wood yclept sassafras. This wood boiled down to a kind of tea, and tempered with an infusion of milk and sugar, hath to some tastes a delicacy beyond the China luxury. I know not how thy palate may relish it; for myself, with every deference to the judicious Mr. Read, who hath time out of mind kept open a shop (the only one he avers in London) for the vending of this "wholesome and pleasant beverage," on the south side of Fleet Street, as thou approachest Bridge Street—*the only Salopian house*— I have never yet adventured to dip my own particular lip in a basin of his commended ingredients—a cautious premonition to the olfactories constantly whispering to me, that my stomach must infallibly, with all due courtesy, decline it. Yet I have seen palates, otherwise not uninstructed in dietetical elegancies, sup it up with avidity.

I know not by what particular conformation of the organ it happens, but I have always found that this composition is surprisingly gratifying to the palate of a young chimney-sweeper—whether the oily particles (sassafras is slightly oleaginous) do attenuate and soften the fuliginous concretions, which are sometimes found (in dissections) to adhere to the roof of the mouth in these unfledged practitioners; or whether Nature, sensible that she had mingled too much of bitter wood in the lot of these raw victims, caused to grow out of the earth her sassafras for a sweet lenitive —but so it is, that no possible taste or odour to the senses of a young chimney-sweeper can convey a delicate excitement comparable to this mixture. Being penniless, they will yet hang their black heads over the ascending steam, to gratify one sense if possible, seemingly no less pleased than those domestic animals —cats—when they purr over a new-found sprig of valerian. There is something more in these sympathies than philosophy can inculcate.

Now albeit Mr. Read boasteth, not without reason, that his is the *only Salopian house;* yet be it known to thee, reader—if thou art one who keepest what are called good hours, thou art haply ignorant of the fact —he hath a race of industrious imitators, who from stalls, and under open sky, dispense the same savoury mess to humbler customers, at that dead time of the dawn, when (as extremes meet) the rake, reeling home from his midnight cups, and the hard-handed artisan leaving his bed to resume the premature labours of the day, jostle, not unfrequently to the manifest disconcerting of the former, for the honours of the pavement. It is the time when, in summer, between the expired and the not yet relumined kitchen-fires, the kennels of our fair metropolis give forth their least satisfactory odours. The rake, who wisheth to dissipate his o'ernight vapours in more grateful coffee, curses the ungenial fume, as he passeth; but the artisan stops to taste, and blesses the fragrant breakfast.

This is *saloop*—the precocious herb-woman's darling
—the delight of the early gardener, who transports
his smoking cabbages by break of day from Hammer-
smith to Covent Garden's famed piazzas—the delight,
and oh! I fear, too often the envy, of the unpennied
sweep. Him shouldst thou haply encounter, with his
dim visage pendent over the grateful steam, regale
him with a sumptuous basin (it will cost thee but
three-halfpennies) and a slice of delicate bread and
butter (an added half-penny)—so may thy culinary
fires, eased of the o'ercharged secretions from thy
worse-placed hospitalities, curl up a lighter volume
to the welkin—so may the descending soot never taint
thy costly well-ingredienced soups—nor the odious
cry, quick-reaching from street to street, of the *fired
chimney*, invite the rattling engines from ten adjacent
parishes, to disturb for a casual scintillation thy peace
and pocket!

I am by nature extremely susceptible of street af-
fronts; the jeers and taunts of the populace; the low-
bred triumph they display over the casual trip, or
splashed stocking, of a gentleman. Yet can I endure the
jocularity of a young sweep with something more than
forgiveness.

In the last winter but one, pacing along Cheapside
with my accustomed precipitation when I walk westward, a treacherous slide brought me upon my back in
an instant. I scrambled up with pain and shame enough
—yet outwardly trying to face it down, as if nothing
had happened—when the roguish grin of one of these
young wits encountered me.

There he stood, pointing me out with his dusky
finger to the mob, and to a poor woman (I suppose
his mother) in particular, till the tears for the exquisite-
ness of the fun (so he thought it) worked themselves

out at the corners of his poor red eyes, red from many
a previous weeping, and soot-inflamed, yet twinkling
through all with such a joy, snatched out of desolation,
that Hogarth—but Hogarth has got him already (how
could he miss him?) in the "March to Finchley,"
grinning at the pieman—there he stood, as he stands
in the picture, irremovable, as if the jest was to last
for ever—with such a maximum of glee, and minimum
of mischief, in his mirth—for the grin of a genuine
sweep hath absolutely no malice in it—that I could
have been content, if the honour of a gentleman might
endure it, to have remained his butt and his mockery
till midnight.

I am by theory obdurate to the seductiveness of
what are called a fine set of teeth. Every pair of rosy
lips (the ladies must pardon me) is a casket presumably
holding such jewels; but, methinks, they should take
leave to "air" them as frugally as possible. The fine lady,
or fine gentleman, who show me their teeth, show me
bones. Yet must I confess, that from the mouth of a
true sweep a display (even to ostentation) of those
white and shining ossifications, strikes me as an agreeable anomaly in manners, and an. allowable piece of
foppery. It is, as when

A sable cloud
Turns forth her silver lining on the night.

It is like some remnant of gentry not quite extinct; a
badge of better days; a hint of nobility—and, doubtless, under the obscuring darkness and double night
of their forlorn disguisement, oftentimes lurketh good
blood, and gentle conditions, derived from lost ancestry, and a lapsed pedigree. The premature appren-
ticements of these tender victims give but too much
encouragement, I fear, to clandestine and almost in-

fantile abductions; the seeds of civility and true courtesy, so often discernible in these young grafts (not
otherwise to be accounted for) plainly hint at some
forced adoptions; many noble Rachels mourning for
their children, even in our days, countenance the fact;
the tales of fairy-spiriting may shadow a lamentable
verity, and the recovery of the young Montagu be but
a solitary instance of good fortune out of many irrepa-
rable and hopeless *defiliations*.

In one of the state-beds at Arundel Castle, a few
years since—under a ducal canopy—(that seat of the
Howards is an object of curiosity to visitors, chiefly
for its beds, in which the late duke was especially
a connoisseur)—encircled with curtains of delicate
crimson, with starry coronets inwoven—folded between a pair of sheets whiter and softer than the lap
where Venus lulled Ascanius—was discovered by chance,
after all methods of search had failed, at noonday,
fast asleep, a lost chimney-sweeper. The little creature,
having somehow confounded his passage among the
intricacies of those lordly chimneys, by some unknown
aperture had alighted upon this magnificent chamber;
and, tired with his tedious explorations, was unable
to resist the delicious invitement to repose, which he
there saw exhibited; so creeping between the sheets
very quietly, laid his black head upon the pillow, and
slept like a young Howard.

Such is the account given to the visitors at the
Castle. But I cannot help seeming to perceive a confirmation of what I had just hinted at in this story. A
high instinct was at work in the case, or I am mistaken.
Is it probable that a poor child of that description, with
whatever weariness he might be visited, would have
ventured, under such a penalty as he would be taught
to expect, to uncover the sheets of a duke's bed, and

deliberately to lay himself down between them, when
the rug, or the carpet, presented an obvious couch,
still far above his pretensions—is this probable, I would
ask, if the great power of nature, which I contend for,
had not been manifested within him, prompting to the
adventure?

Doubtless this young nobleman (for such my mind
misgives me that he must be) was allured by some
memory, not amounting to full consciousness, of his
condition in infancy, when he was used to be lapped
by his mother, or his nurse, in just such sheets as he
there found, into which he was now but creeping back
as into his proper *incunabula,* and resting-place. By
no other theory than by this sentiment of a pre-existent
state (as I may call it), can I explain a deed so ventur-
ous, and, indeed, upon any other system, so indecorous,
in this tender, but unseasonable, sleeper.

My pleasant friend Jem White was so impressed
with a belief of metamorphoses like this frequently
taking place, that in some sort to reverse the wrongs
of fortune in these poor changelings, he instituted an
annual feast of chimney-sweepers, at which it was his
pleasure to officiate as host and waiter. It was a solemn
supper held in Smithfield, upon the yearly return
of the fair of St. Bartholomew. Cards were issued a
week before to the master-sweeps in and about the
metropolis, confining the invitation to their younger fry.

Now and then an elderly stripling would get in
among us, and be good-naturedly winked at; but our
main body were infantry. One unfortunate wight,
indeed, who, relying upon his dusky suit, had intruded
himself into our party, but by tokens was providentially
discovered in time to be no chimney-sweeper (all is
not soot which look so), was quoited out of the presence
with universal indignation, as not having on the wed-

ding garment; but in general the greatest harmony
prevailed.

The place chosen was a convenient spot among the
pens, at the north side of the fair, not so far distant
as to be impervious to the agreeable hubbub of that
vanity; but remote enough not to be obvious to the
interruption of every gaping spectator in it. The guests
assembled about seven. In those little temporary parlours three tables were spread with napery, not so fine
as substantial, and at every board a comely hostess
presided with her pan of hissing sausages. The nostrils
of the young rogues dilated at the savour.

James White, as head waiter, had charge of the first
table; and myself, with our trusty companion Bigod,
ordinarily ministered to the other two. There was
clambering and jostling, you may be sure, who should
get at the first table—for Rochester in his maddest days
could not have done the humours of the scene with
more spirit than my friend. After some general expression of thanks for the honour the company had done
him, his inaugural ceremony was to clasp the greasy
waist of old dame Ursula (the fattest of the three),
that stood frying and fretting, half-blessing, half-
cursing "the gentleman," and imprint upon her chaste
lips a tender salute, whereat the universal host would
set up a shout that tore the concave, while hundreds
of grinning teeth startled the night with their brightness.

O it was a pleasure to see the sable younkers lick
in the unctuous meat, with *his* more unctuous sayings
—how he would fit the titbits to the puny mouths,
reserving the lengthier links for the seniors—how he
would intercept a morsel even in the jaws of some
young desperado, declaring it "must to the pan again
to be browned, for it was not fit for a gentleman's eat-

ing"—how he would recommend this slice of white bread, or that piece of kissing-crust, to a tender juvenile, advising them all to have a care of cracking their teeth, which were their best patrimony—how genteelly he would deal about the small ale, as if it were wine, naming the brewer, and protesting, if it were not good, he should lose their custom; with a special recommendation to wipe the lip before drinking. Then we had our toasts—"The King"—"the Cloth"—which, whether they understood or not, was equally diverting and flattering—and for a crowning sentiment, which never failed, "May the Brush supersede the Laurel!"

All these, and fifty other fancies, which were rather felt than comprehended by his guests, would he utter, standing upon tables, and prefacing every sentiment with a "Gentlemen, give me leave to propose so and so," which was a prodigious comfort to those young orphans; every now and then stuffing into his mouth (for it did not do to be squeamish on these occasions) indiscriminate pieces of those reeking sausages, which pleased them mightily, and was the savouriest part, you may believe, of the entertainment.

> Golden lads and lasses must,
> As chimney-sweepers, come to dust—

James White is extinct, and with him these suppers have long ceased. He carried away with him half the fun of the world when he died—of my world at least. His old clients look for him among the pens; and, missing him, reproach the altered feast of St. Bartholomew, and the glory of Smithfield departed for ever.

London Magazine, May 1822; Elia

NEWSPAPERS THIRTY-FIVE YEARS AGO

DAN STUART once told us, that he did not remember that he ever deliberately walked into the Exhibition at Somerset House in his life. He might occasionally have escorted a party of ladies across the way that were going in; but he never went in of his own head. Yet the office of the *Morning Post* newspaper stood then just where it does now—we are carrying you back, Reader, some thirty years or more—with its gilt-globe-topt front facing that emporium of our artists' grand Annual Exposure. We sometimes wish that we had observed the same abstinence with Daniel.

A word or two of D. S. He ever appeared to us one of the finest-tempered of Editors. Perry, of the *Morning Chronicle*, was equally pleasant, with a dash, no slight one either, of the courtier. S. was frank, plain, and English all over. We have worked for both these gentlemen.

It is soothing to contemplate the head of the Ganges; to trace the first little bubblings of a mighty river,

With holy reverence to approach the rocks,
Whence glide the streams renowned in ancient song.

Fired with a perusal of the Abyssinian Pilgrim's exploratory ramblings after the cradle of the infant Nilus, we well remember on one fine summer holyday (a "whole day's leave" we called it at Christ's Hospital) sallying forth at rise of sun, not very well provisioned either for such an undertaking, to trace the current of the New River—Myddeltonian stream!—to its scaturient source, as we had read, in meadows by fair Amwell.

Gallantly did we commence our solitary quest—for it was essential to the dignity of a Discovery, that no eye of schoolboy, save our own, should beam on the detection. By flowery spots, and verdant lanes skirting Hornsey, Hope trained us on in many a baffling turn; endless, hopeless meanders, as it seemed; or as if the jealous waters had *dodged* us, reluctant to have the humble spot of their nativity revealed; till spent, and nigh famished, before set of the same sun, we sate down somewhere by Bowes Farm near Tottenham, with a tithe of our proposed labours only yet accomplished; sorely convinced in spirit, that that Brucian enterprise was as yet too arduous for our young shoulders.

Not more refreshing to the thirsty curiosity of the traveller is the tracing of some mighty waters up to their shallow fontlet, than it is to a pleased and candid reader to go back to the inexperienced essays, the first callow flights in authorship, of some established name in literature; from the Gnat which preluded to the Æneid, to the Duck which Samuel Johnson trod on.

In those days every Morning Paper, as an essential retainer to its establishment, kept an author, who was bound to furnish daily a quantum of witty paragraphs. Sixpence a joke—and it was thought pretty high too—was Dan Stuart's settled remuneration in these cases. The chat of the day, scandal, but, above all, *dress*, furnished the material. The length of no paragraph was to exceed seven lines. Shorter they might be, but they must be poignant.

A fashion of *flesh*, or rather *pink*-coloured hose for the ladies, luckily coming up at the juncture when we were on our probation for the place of Chief Jester to S.'s Paper, established our reputation in that line.

We were pronounced a "capital hand." O the conceits which we varied upon *red* in all its prismatic differences! from the trite and obvious flower of Cytherea, to the flaming costume of the lady that has her sitting upon "many waters."

Then there was the collateral topic of ankles. What an occasion to a truly chaste writer, like ourself, of touching that nice brink, and yet never tumbling over it, of a seemingly ever approximating something "not quite proper"; while, like a skilful posture-master, balancing betwixt decorums and their opposites, he keeps the line, from which a hair's-breadth deviation is destruction; hovering in the confines of light and darkness, or where "both seem either"; a hazy uncertain delicacy; Autolycus-like in the Play, still putting off his expectant auditory with "Whoop, do me no harm, good man!" But, above all, that conceit arrided us most at that time, and still tickles our midriff to remember, where, allusively to the flight of Astræa—*ultima Cælestûm terras reliquist*—we pronounced—in reference to the stockings still—that Modesty, TAKING HER FINAL LEAVE OF MORTALS, HER LAST BLUSH WAS VISIBLE IN HER ASCENT TO THE HEAVENS BY THE TRACT OF THE GLOWING INSTEP. This might be called the crowning conceit: and was esteemed tolerable writing in those days.

But the fashion of jokes, with all other things, passes away; as did the transient mode which had so favoured us. The ankles of our fair friends in a few weeks began to reassume their whiteness, and left us scarce a leg to stand upon. Other female whims followed, but none methought so pregnant, so invitatory of shrewd conceits, and more than single meanings.

Somebody has said, that to swallow six cross-buns daily, consecutively for a fortnight, would surfeit the stoutest digestion. But to have to furnish as many jokes daily, and that not for a fortnight, but for a long twelvemonth, as we were constrained to do, was a little harder exaction. "Man goeth forth to his work until the evening"—from a reasonable hour in the morning, we presume it was meant. Now, as our main occupation took us up from eight till five every day in the City; and as our evening hours, at that time of life, had generally to do with anything rather than business, it follows, that the only time we could spare for this manufactory of jokes—our supplementary livelihood, that supplied us in every want beyond mere bread and cheese—was exactly that part of the day which (as we have heard of No Man's Land) may be fitly denominated No Man's Time; that is, no time in which a man ought to be up, and awake, in. To speak more plainly, it is that time of an hour, or an hour and a half's duration, in which a man, whose occasions call him up so preposterously, has to wait for his breakfast.

O those headaches at dawn of day, when at five, or half-past five in summer, and not much later in the dark seasons, we were compelled to rise, having been perhaps not above four hours in bed—(for we were no go-to-beds with the lamb, though we anticipated the lark ofttimes in her rising—we like a parting cup at midnight, as all young men did before these effeminate times, and to have our friends about us—we were not constellated under Aquarius, that watery sign, and therefore incapable of Bacchus, cold, washy, bloodless— we were none of your Basilian water-sponges, nor had taken our degrees at Mount Ague—we were right toping Capulets, jolly companions, we and they)—but to have to get up, as we said before, curtailed of half our fair sleep, fasting, with only a dim vista of refreshing bohea, in the distance—to be necessitated to rouse ourselves at the detestable rap of an old hag of a domestic, who seemed to take a diabolical pleasure in her announcement that it was "time to rise"; and whose chappy knuckles we have often yearned to amputate, and string them up at our chamber door, to be a terror to all such unseasonable rest-breakers in future——

"Facil" and sweet, as Virgil sings, had been the "descending" of the overnight, balmy the first sinking of the heavy head upon the pillow; but to get up, as he goes on to say,

—*revocare gradus, superasque evadere ad auras*—

and to get up, moreover, to make jokes with malice prepended—there was the "labour," there the "work."

No Egyptian taskmaster ever devised a slavery like to that, our slavery. No fractious operants ever turned out for half the tyranny which this necessity exercised upon us. Half a dozen jests in a day (bating Sundays too), why, it seems nothing! We make twice the number every day in our lives as a matter of course, and claim no Sabbatical exemptions. But then they come into our head. But when the head has to go out to them —when the mountain must go to Mahomet—

Reader, try it for once, only for one short twelvemonth.

It was not every week tnat a fashion of pink stockings came up; but mostly, instead of it, some rugged untractable subject; some topic impossible to be contorted into the risible; some feature, upon which no smile could play; some flint, from which no process of ingenuity could procure a scintillation. There they lay; there your appointed tale of brick-making was set before you, which you must finish, with or without straw, as it happened. The craving Dragon—*the Public*

—like him in Bel's temple—must be fed; it expected its daily rations; and Daniel, and ourselves, to do us justice, did the best we could on this side bursting him.

While we were wringing out coy sprightlinesses for the *Post*, and writhing under the toil of what is called "easy writing," Bob Allen, our *quondam* schoolfellow, was tapping his impracticable brains in a like service for the *Oracle*. Not that Robert troubled himself much about wit. If his paragraphs had a sprightly air about them, it was sufficient. He carried this nonchalance so far at last, that a matter of intelligence, and that no very important one, was not seldom palmed upon his employers for a good jest; for example sake—"Walking yesterday morning casually down Snow Hill, who should we meet but Mr. Deputy Humphreys! we rejoice to add, that the worthy Deputy appeared to enjoy a good state of health. We do not remember ever to have seen him look better."

This gentleman so surprisingly met upon Snow Hill, from some peculiarities in gait or gesture, was a constant butt for mirth to the small paragraphmongers of the day; and our friend thought that he might have his fling at him with the rest. We met A. in Holborn shortly after this extraordinary rencounter, which he told with tears of satisfaction in his eyes, and chuckling at the anticipated effects of its announcement next day in the paper. We did not quite comprehend where the wit of it lay at the time; nor was it easy to be detected, when the thing came out advantaged by type and letter-press. He had better have met anything that morning than a Common Council Man. His services were shortly after dispensed with, on the plea that his paragraphs of late had been deficient in point. The one in question, it must be owned, had an air, in the opening especially, proper to awaken curiosity; and the sentiment, or moral, wears the aspect of humanity and good neighbourly feeling. But somehow the conclusion was not judged altogether to answer to the magnificent promise of the premises.

We traced our friend's pen afterwards in the *True Briton,* the *Star,* the *Traveller*—from all which he was successively dismissed, the Proprietors having "no further occasion for his services." Nothing was easier than to detect him. When wit failed, or topics ran low, there constantly appeared the following: "It is not generally known that the three Blue Balls at the Pawnbrokers' shops are the ancient arms of Lombardy. The Lombards were the first money-brokers in Europe." Bob has done more to set the public right on this important point of blazonry, than the whole College of Heralds.

The appointment of a regular wit has long ceased to be a part of the economy of a Morning Paper. Editors find their own jokes, or do as well without them. Parson Este, and Topham, brought up the set custom of "witty paragraphs" first in the *World.* Boaden was a reigning paragraphist in his day, and succeeded poor Allen in the *Oracle.* But, as we said, the fashion of jokes passes away; and it would be difficult to discover in the biographer of Mrs. Siddons, any traces of that vivacity and fancy which charmed the whole town at the commencement of the present century. Even the prelusive delicacies of the present writer—the curt "Astræan allusion"—would be thought pedantic and out of date, in these days.

From the office of the *Morning Post* (for we may as well exhaust our Newspaper Reminiscences at once) by change of property in the paper, we were transferred, mortifying exchange! to the office of the *Albion* Newspaper, late Rackstrow's Museum, in Fleet Street.

What a transition—from a handsome apartment, from rosewood desks, and silver inkstands, to an office—no office, but a *den* rather, but just redeemed from the occupation of dead monsters, of which it seemed redolent—from the centre of loyalty and fashion, to a focus of vulgarity and sedition! Here in murky closet, inadequate from its square contents to the receipt of the two bodies of Editor and humble paragraph-maker, together at one time, sat in the discharge of his new editorial functions (the "Bigod" of Elia) the redoubted John Fenwick.

F., without a guinea in his pocket, and having left not many in the pockets of his friends whom he might command, had purchased (on tick doubtless) the whole and sole Editorship, Proprietorship, with all the rights and titles (such as they were worth) of the *Albion* from one Lovell; of whom we know nothing, save that he had stood in the pillory for a libel on the Prince of Wales. With this hopeless concern—for it had been sinking ever since its commencement, and could now reckon upon not more than a hundred subscribers— F. resolutely determined upon pulling down the Government in the first instance, and making both our fortunes by way of corollary. For seven weeks and more did this infatuated democrat go about borrowing seven-shilling pieces, and lesser coin, to meet the daily demands of the Stamp office, which allowed no credit to publications of that side in politics. An outcast from politer bread, we attached our small talents to the forlorn fortunes of our friend. Our occupation now was to write treason.

Recollections of feelings—which were all that now remained from our first boyish heats kindled by the French Revolution, when, if we were misled, we erred in the company of some who are accounted very good

men now—rather than any tendency at this time to
Republican doctrines—assisted us in assuming a style
of writing, while the paper lasted, consonant in no
very under tone to the right earnest fanaticism of F.
Our cue was now to insinuate, rather than recommend,
possible abdications. Blocks, axes, Whitehall tribunals,
were covered with flowers of so cunning a periphrasis
—as Mr. Bayes says, never naming the *thing* directly—
that the keen eye of an Attorney General was insufficient
to detect the lurking snake among them. There were
times, indeed, when we sighed for our more gentlemanlike occupation under Stuart. But with change of masters it is ever change of service.

Already one paragraph, and another, as we learned
afterwards from a gentleman at the Treasury, had
begun to be marked at that office, with a view of its
being submitted at least to the attention of the proper
Law Officers—when an unlucky, or rather lucky epi-
gram from our pen, aimed at Sir J——s M——h, who
was on the eve of departing for India to reap the fruits
of his apostasy, as F. pronounced it (it is hardly worth
particularizing), happening to offend the nice sense of
Lord, or, as he then delighted to be called, Citizen
Stanhope, deprived F. at once of the last hopes of a
guinea from the last patron that had stuck by us; and
breaking up our establishment, left us to the safe, but
somewhat mortifying, neglect of the Crown Lawyers.
It was about this time, or a little earlier, that Dan Stuart made that curious confession to us, that he had
"never deliberately walked into an Exhibition at Somerset House in his life."

Englishman's Magazine, October 1831; *Last Essays of Elia.*

PART FOUR

Fantasies and Tales

DREAM CHILDREN: A REVERIE

CHILDREN love to listen to stories about their elders, when *they* were children; to stretch their imagination to the conception of a traditionary great-uncle, or grandame, whom they never saw. It was in this spirit that my little ones crept about me the other evening to hear about their great-grandmother Field, who lived in a great house in Norfolk (a hundred times bigger than that in which they and papa lived) which had been the scene—so at least it was generally believed in that part of the country—of the tragic incidents which they had lately become familiar with from the ballad of the "Children in the Wood." Certain it is that the whole story of the children and their cruel uncle was to be seen fairly carved out in wood upon the chimney-piece of the great hall, the whole story down to the Robin Redbreasts; till a foolish rich person pulled it down to set up a marble one of modern invention in its stead, with no story upon it.

Here Alice put out one of dear mother's looks, too tender to be called upbraiding. Then I went on to say, how religious and how good their great-grandmother

Field was, how beloved and respected by everybody, though she was not indeed the mistress of this great house, but had only the charge of it (and yet in some respects she might be said to be the mistress of it too) committed to her by the owner, who preferred living in a newer and more fashionable mansion which he had purchased somewhere in the adjoining county; but still she lived in it in a manner as if it had been her own, and kept up the dignity of the great house in a sort while she lived, which afterwards came to decay, and was nearly pulled down, and all its old ornaments stripped and carried away to the owner's other house, where they were set up, and looked as awkward as if some one were to carry away the old tombs they had seen lately at the Abbey, and stick them up in Lady C.'s tawdry gilt drawing-room.

Here John smiled, as much as to say, "that would be foolish indeed." And then I told how, when she came to die, her funeral was attended by a concourse of all the poor, and some of the gentry too, of the neighbourhood for many miles round, to show their respect for her memory, because she had been such a good and religious woman; so good indeed that she knew all the Psaltery by heart, ay, and a great part of the Testament besides. Here little Alice spread her hands.

Then I told what a tall, upright, graceful person their great-grandmother Field once was; and how in her youth she was esteemed the best dancer—here Alice's little right foot played an involuntary movement, till, upon my looking grave, it desisted—the best dancer, I was saying, in the county, till a cruel disease, called a cancer, came, and bowed her down with pain; but it could never bend her good spirits, or make them stoop, but they were still upright, because she was so good and religious. Then I told how she was used to

sleep by herself in a lone chamber of the great lone
house; and how she believed that an apparition of two
infants was to be seen at midnight gliding up and down
the great staircase near where she slept, but she said
"those innocents would do her no harm"; and how
frightened I used to be, though in those days I had
my maid to sleep with me, because I was never half
so good or religious as she—and yet I never saw the
infants. Here John expanded all his eyebrows and tried
to look courageous.

Then I told how good she was to all her grandchildren, having us to the great house in the holydays,
where I in particular used to spend many hours by
myself, in gazing upon the old busts of the twelve
Cæsars, that had been Emperors of Rome, till the old
marble heads would seem to live again, or I to be turned
into marble with them; how I never could be tired
with roaming about that huge mansion, with its vast
empty rooms, with their worn-out hangings, fluttering
tapestry, and carved oaken panels, with the gilding
almost rubbed out—sometimes in the spacious old-
fashioned gardens, which I had almost to myself, unless
when now and then a solitary gardening man would
cross me—and how the nectarines and peaches hung
upon the walls, without my ever offering to pluck
them, because they were forbidden fruit, unless now
and then—and because I had more pleasure in strolling about among the old melancholy-looking yew-trees,
or the firs, and picking up the red berries, and the fir-
apples, which were good for nothing but to look at—
or in lying about upon the fresh grass with all the fine
garden smells around me—or basking in the orangery,
till I could almost fancy myself ripening too along with
the oranges and the limes in that grateful warmth—
or in watching the dace that darted to and fro in the

fish-pond, at the bottom of the garden, with here and there a great sulky pike hanging midway down the water in silent state, as if it mocked at their impertinent friskings—I had more pleasure in these busy-idle diversions than in all the sweet flavours of peaches, nectarines, oranges, and such-like common baits of children.

Here John slyly deposited back upon the plate a bunch of grapes, which, not unobserved by Alice, he had meditated dividing with her, and both seemed willing to relinquish them for the present as irrelevant.

Then, in somewhat a more heightened tone, I told how, though their great-grandmother Field loved all her grandchildren, yet in an especial manner she might be said to love their uncle, John L., because he was so handsome and spirited a youth, and a king to the rest of us; and, instead of moping about in solitary corners, like some of us, he would mount the most mettlesome horse he could get, when but an imp no bigger than themselves, and make it carry him half over the county in a morning, and join the hunters when there were any out—and yet he loved the old great house and gardens too, but had too much spirit to be always pent up within their boundaries—and how their uncle grew up to man's estate as brave as he was handsome, to the admiration of everybody, but of their great-grandmother Field most especially; and how he used to carry me upon his back when I was a lame-footed boy—for he was a good bit older than me—many a mile when I could not walk for pain—and how in after life he became lame-footed too, and I did not always (I fear) make allowances enough for him when he was impatient, and in pain, nor remember sufficiently how considerate he had been to me when I was lame-footed; and how when he died, though he had not been dead an hour, it seemed as if he had died a great while ago, such a distance there is betwixt life and death; and how I bore his death as I thought pretty well at first, but afterwards it haunted and haunted me; and though I did not cry or take it to heart as some do, and as I think he would have done if I had died, yet I missed him all day long, and knew not till then how much I had loved him. I missed his kindness, and I missed his crossness, and wished him to be alive again, to be quarrelling with him (for we quarrelled sometimes), rather than not have him again, and was as uneasy without him, as he their poor uncle must have been when the doctor took off his limb.

Here the children fell a-crying, and asked if their little mourning which they had on was not for uncle John, and they looked up, and prayed me not to go on about their uncle, but to tell them some stories about their pretty dead mother. Then I told how for seven long years, in hope sometimes, sometimes in despair, yet persisting ever, I courted the fair Alice W——n; and, as much as children could understand, I explained to them what coyness, and difficulty, and denial, meant in maidens—when suddenly, turning to Alice, the soul of the first Alice looked out at her eyes with such a reality of re-presentment, that I became in doubt which of them stood there before me, or whose that bright hair was; and while I stood gazing, both the children gradually grew fainter to my view, receding, and still receding, till nothing at last but two mournful features were seen in the uttermost distance, which, without speech, strangely impressed upon me the effects of speech: "We are not of Alice, nor of thee, nor are we children at all. The children of Alice call Bartrum father. We are nothing; less than nothing, and dreams. We are only what might have been, and must wait upon the te-

dious shores of Lethe millions of ages before we have
existence, and a name"—and immediately awaking, I
found myself quietly seated in my bachelor arm-chair,
where I had fallen asleep, with the faithful Bridget un-
changed by my side—but John L. (or James Elia) was
gone for ever.

London Magazine, January 1822; Elia.

A DISSERTATION UPON ROAST PIG

MANKIND, says a Chinese manuscript, which my friend
M.[1] was obliging enough to read and explain to me,
for the first seventy thousand ages ate their meat raw,
clawing or biting it from the living animal, just as they
do in Abyssinia to this day. This period is not obscurely
hinted at by their great Confucius in the second chap-
ter of his Mundane Mutations, where he designates
a kind of golden age by the term Chofang, literally
the Cooks' Holiday.

The manuscript goes on to say, that the art of roasting, or rather broiling (which I take to be the elder
brother) was accidentally discovered in the manner
following. The swineherd, Ho-ti, having gone out into
the woods one morning, as his manner was, to collect
mast for his hogs, left his cottage in the care of his
eldest son Bo-bo, a great lubberly boy, who being fond
of playing with fire, as younkers of his age commonly
are, let some sparks escape into a bundle of straw,
which kindling quickly, spread the conflagration over
every part of their poor mansion, till it was reduced
to ashes.

[1] Thomas Manning.—J. M. B.

Together with the cottage (a sorry antediluvian makeshift of a building, you may think it), what was of much more importance, a fine litter of new-farrowed pigs, no less than nine in number, perished. China pigs have been esteemed a luxury all over the East, from the remotest periods that we read of. Bo-bo was in the utmost consternation, as you may think, not so much for the sake of the tenement, which his father and he could easily build up again with a few dry branches, and the labour of an hour or two, at any time, as for the loss of the pigs.

While he was thinking what he should say to his father, and wringing his hands over the smoking remnants of one of those untimely sufferers, an odour assailed his nostrils, unlike any scent which he had before experienced. What could it proceed from?—not from the burnt cottage—he had smelt that smell before —indeed this was by no means the first accident of the kind which had occurred through the negligence of this unlucky young fire-brand. Much less did it resemble that of any known herb, weed, or flower. A premonitory moistening at the same time overflowed his nether lip. He knew not what to think.

He next stooped down to feel the pig, if there were any signs of life in it. He burnt his fingers, and to cool them he applied them in his booby fashion to his mouth. Some of the crumbs of the scorched skin had come away with his fingers, and for the first time in his life (in the world's life indeed, for before him no man had known it) he tasted—*crackling!* Again he felt and fumbled at the pig. It did not burn him so much now, still he licked his fingers from a sort of habit.

The truth at length broke into his slow understanding, that it was the pig that smelt so, and the pig that tasted so delicious; and surrendering himself up to the newborn pleasure, he fell to tearing up whole handfuls of the scorched skin with the flesh next it, and was cramming it down his throat in his beastly fashion, when his sire entered amid the smoking rafters, armed with retributory cudgel, and finding how affairs stood, began to rain blows upon the young rogue's shoulders, as thick as hailstones, which Bo-bo heeded not any more than if they had been flies. The tickling pleasure, which he experienced in his lower regions, had rendered him quite callous to any inconveniences he might feel in those remote quarters. His father might lay on, but he could not beat him from his pig, till he had fairly made an end of it, when, becoming a little more sensible of his situation, something like the following dialogue ensued.

"You graceless whelp, what have you got there devouring? Is it not enough that you have burnt me down three houses with your dog's tricks, and be hanged to you! but you must be eating fire, and I know not what—what have you got there, I say?"

"O father, the pig, the pig! do come and taste how nice the burnt pig eats."

The ears of Ho-ti tingled with horror. He cursed his son, and he cursed himself that ever he should beget a son that should eat burnt pig.

Bo-bo, whose scent was wonderfully sharpened since morning, soon raked out another pig, and fairly rending it asunder, thrust the lesser half by main force into the fists of Ho-ti, still shouting out, "Eat, eat, eat the burnt pig, father, only taste—O Lord!"—with such-like barbarous ejaculations, cramming all the while as if he would choke.

Ho-ti trembled every joint while he grasped the abominable thing, wavering whether he should not put his son to death for an unnatural young monster, when the crackling scorching his fingers, as it had done his son's, and applying the same remedy to them, he in his turn tasted some of its flavour, which, make what sour mouths he would for a pretense, proved not altogether displeasing to him. In conclusion (for the manuscript here is a little tedious), both father and son fairly set down to the mess, and never left off till they had despatched all that remained of the litter.

Bo-bo was strictly enjoined not to let the secret escape, for the neighbours would certainly have stoned them for a couple of abominable wretches, who could think of improving upon the good meat which God had sent them. Nevertheless, strange stories got about. It was observed that Ho-ti's cottage was burnt down now more frequently than ever. Nothing but fires from this time forward. Some would break out in broad day, others in the night-time. As often as the sow farrowed, so sure was the house of Ho-ti to be in a blaze; and Ho-ti himself, which was the more remarkable, instead of chastizing his son, seemed to grow more indulgent to him than ever.

At length they were watched, the terrible mystery discovered, and father and son summoned to take their trial at Pekin, then an inconsiderable assize town. Evidence was given, the obnoxious food itself produced in court, and verdict about to be pronounced, when the foreman of the jury begged that some of the burnt pig, of which the culprits stood accused, might be handed into the box. He handled it, and they all handled it; and burning their fingers, as Bo-bo and his father had done before them, and nature prompting to each of them the same remedy, against the face of all the facts, and the clearest charge which judge had ever given—to the surprise of the whole court, townsfolk,

strangers, reporters, and all present—without leaving
the box, or any manner of consultation whatever, they
brought in a simultaneous verdict of Not Guilty.

The judge, who was a shrewd fellow, winked at the
manifest iniquity of the decision: and when the court
was dismissed, went privily and bought up all the pigs
that could be had for love or money. In a few days
his lordship's town-house was observed to be on fire.
The thing took wing, and now there was nothing to
be seen but fire in every direction. Fuel and pigs grew
enormously dear all over the district. The insurance-
offices one and all shut up shop. People built slighter
and slighter every day, until it was feared that the
very science of architecture would in no long time be
lost to the world.

Thus this custom of firing houses continued, till in
process of time, says my manuscript, a sage arose, like
our Locke, who made a discovery that the flesh of
swine, or indeed of any other animal, might be cooked
(*burnt,* as they called it) without the necessity of con-
suming a whole house to dress it. Then first began the
rude form of a gridiron. Roasting by the string or
spit came in a century or two later, I forget in whose
dynasty. By such slow degrees, concludes the manuscript, do the most useful, and seemingly the most obvious, arts make their way among mankind. . . .

Without placing too implicit faith in the account
above given, it must be agreed that if a worthy pretext for so dangerous an experiment as setting houses
on fire (especially in these days) could be assigned in
favour of any culinary object, that pretext and excuse
might be found in ROAST PIG.

Of all the delicacies in the whole *mundus edibilis,*
I will maintain it to be the most delicate—*princeps
obsoniorum.*

I speak not of your grown porkers—things between pig and pork—those hobbydehoys—but a young and tender suckling—under a moon old—guiltless as yet of the sty—with no original speck of the *amor immunditæ*, the hereditary failing of the first parent, yet manifest—his voice as yet not broken, but something between a childish treble and a grumble—the mild forerunner or *præludium* of a grunt.

He must be roasted. I am not ignorant that our ancestors ate them seethed, or boiled—but what a sacrifice to the exterior tegument!

There is no flavour comparable, I will contend, to that of the crisp, tawny, well-watched, not over-roasted, *crackling*, as it is well called—the very teeth are invited to their share of the pleasure at this banquet in overcoming the coy, brittle resistance—with the adhesive oleaginous—O call it not fat! but an indefinable sweetness growing up to it—the tender blossoming of fat—fat cropped in the bud—taken in the shoot—in the first innocence—the cream and quintessence of the child-pig's yet pure food—the lean, no lean, but a kind of animal manna—or, rather, fat and lean (if it must be so) so blended and running into each other, that both together make but one ambrosian result or common substance.

Behold him, while he is "doing"—it seemeth rather a refreshing warmth, than a scorching heat, that he is so passive to. How equably he twirleth round the string! Now he is just done. To see the extreme sensibility of that tender age! he hath wept out his pretty eyes—radiant jellies—shooting stars.

See him in the dish, his second cradle, how meek he lieth!—wouldst thou have had this innocent grow up to the grossness and indocility which too often accompany maturer swinehood? Ten to one he would have proved a glutton, a sloven, an obstinate, disagreeable animal—wallowing in all manner of filthy conversation —from these sins he is happily snatched away—

> Ere sin could blight or sorrow fade,
> Death came with timely care—

his memory is odoriferous—no clown curseth, while his stomach half rejecteth, the rank bacon—no coal-heaver bolteth him in reeking sausages—he hath a fair sepulchre in the grateful stomach of the judicious epi-cure—and for such a tomb might be content to die.

He is the best of sapors. Pineapple is great. She is indeed almost too transcendent—a delight, if not sinful, yet so like to sinning that really a tender-conscienced person would do well to pause—too ravishing for mortal taste, she woundeth and excoriateth the lips that approach her—like lovers' kisses, she biteth—she is a pleasure bordering on pain from the fierceness and insanity of her relish—but she stoppeth at the palate—she meddleth not with the appetite—and the coarsest hunger might barter her consistently for a mutton-chop.

Pig—let me speak his praise—is no less provocative of the appetite, than he is satisfactory to the criticalness of the censorious palate. The strong man may batten on him, and the weakling refuseth not his mild juices.

Unlike to mankind's mixed characters, a bundle of virtues and vices, inexplicably intertwisted, and not to be unravelled without hazard, he is—good throughout. No part of him is better or worse than another. He helpeth, as far as his little means extend, all around. He is the least envious of banquets. He is all neighbours' fare.

I am one of those, who freely and ungrudgingly impart a share of the good things of this life which fall to their lot (few as mine are in this kind) to a friend.

I protest I take as great an interest in my friend's pleasures, his relishes, and proper satisfactions, as in mine
own. "Presents," I often say, "endear Absents." Hares,
pheasants, partridges, snipes, barndoor chickens (those
"tame villatic fowl"), capons, plovers, brawn, barrels of
oysters, I dispense as freely as I receive them. I love to
taste them, as it were, upon the tongue of my friend.
But a stop must be put somewhere. One would not,
like Lear, "give everything." I make my stand upon
pig. Methinks it is an ingratitude to the Giver of all good
flavours to extra-domiciliate, or send out of the house
slightingly (under pretext of friendship, or I know not
what) a blessing so particularly adapted, predestined,
I may say, to my individual palate. It argues an insensibility.

I remember a touch of conscience in this kind at
school. My good old aunt, who never parted from me
at the end of a holiday without stuffing a sweetmeat, or
some nice thing into my pocket, had dismissed me one
evening with a smoking plum-cake, fresh from the oven.
In my way to school (it was over London Bridge) a
grey-headed old beggar saluted me (I have no doubt,
at this time of day, that he was a counterfeit). I had no
pence to console him with, and in the vanity of self-
denial and the very coxcombry of charity, schoolboy-
like, I made him a present of—the whole cake!

I walked on a little, buoyed up, as one is on such
occasions, with a sweet soothing of self-satisfaction; but
before I had got to the end of the bridge, my better feelings returned, and I burst into tears, thinking how ungrateful I had been to my good aunt, to go and give
her good gift away to a stranger that I had never seen
before, and who might be a bad man for aught I knew;
and then I thought of the pleasure my aunt would be
taking in thinking that I—I myself, and not another—

would eat her nice cake—and what should I say to her
the next time I saw her—how naughty I was to part
with her pretty present!—and the odour of that spicy
cake came back upon my recollection, and the pleasure
and the curiosity I had taken in seeing her make it, and
her joy when she sent it to the oven, and how disappointed she would feel that I had never had a bit of it in
my mouth at last—and I blamed my impertinent spirit
of alms-giving, and out-of-place hypocrisy of goodness;
and above all I wished never to see the face again of
that insidious, good-for-nothing, old grey impostor.

Our ancestors were nice in their method of sacrificing
these tender victims. We read of pigs whipt to death
with something of a shock, as we hear of any other obsolete custom. The age of discipline is gone by, or it
would be curious to inquire (in a philosophical light
merely) what effect this process might have towards
intenerating and dulcifying a substance, naturally so
mild and dulcet as the flesh of young pigs. It looks like
refining a violet. Yet we should be cautious, while we
condemn the inhumanity, how we censure the wisdom
of the practice. It might impart a gusto.

I remember an hypothesis, argued upon by the
young students, when I was at St. Omer's, and maintained with much learning and pleasantry on both sides,
"Whether, supposing that the flavour of a pig who obtained his death by whipping (*per flagellationem ex-
tremam*) superadded a pleasure upon the palate of a
man more intense than any possible suffering we can
conceive in the animal, is man justified in using that
method of putting the animal to death?" I forget the
decision.

His sauce should be considered. Decidedly, a few
bread crumbs, done up with his liver and brains, and
a dash of mild sage. But banish, dear Mrs. Cook, I

beseech you, the whole onion tribe. Barbecue your
whole hogs to your palate, steep them in shalots, stuff
them out with plantations of the rank and guilty garlic;
you cannot poison them, or make them stronger than
they are—but consider, he is a weakling—a flower.

London Magazine, September 1822; *Elia.*

BARBARA S——

ON THE noon of the 14th of November, 1743 or 4, I
forget which it was, just as the clock had struck one,
Barbara S——, with her accustomed punctuality, ascended the long rambling staircase, with awkward inter-
posed landing-places, which led to the office, or rather a
sort of box with a desk in it, whereat sat the then Treasurer of (what few of our readers may remember) the
Old Bath Theatre. All over the island it was the custom,
and remains so I believe to this day, for the players to
receive their weekly stipend on the Saturday. It was
not much that Barbara had to claim.

This little maid had just entered her eleventh year;
but her important station at the theatre, as it seemed
to her, with the benefits which she felt to accrue from
her pious application of her small earnings, had given
an air of womanhood to her steps and to her behaviour.
You would have taken her to have been at least five
years older.

Till latterly she had merely been employed in choruses, or where children were wanted to fill up the scene.
But the manager, observing a diligence and adroitness
in her above her age, had for some few months past
intrusted to her the performance of whole parts. You

may guess the self-consequence of the promoted Barbara. She had already drawn tears in young Arthur; had rallied Richard with infantine petulance in the Duke of York; and in her turn had rebuked that petulance when she was Prince of Wales. She would have done the elder child in Morton's pathetic afterpiece to the life; but as yet the *Children in the Wood* was not.

Long after this little girl was grown an aged woman, I have seen some of these small parts, each making two or three pages at most, copied out in the rudest hand of the then prompter, who doubtless transcribed a little more carefully and fairly for the grown-up tragedy ladies of the establishment. But such as they were, blotted and scrawled, as for a child's use, she kept them all; and in the zenith of her after reputation it was a delightful sight to behold them bound up in costliest morocco, each single—each small part making a *book* —with fine clasps, gilt-splashed, etc.

She had conscientiously kept them as they had been delivered to her; not a blot had been effaced or tampered with. They were precious to her for their affecting remembrancings. They were her principia, her rudiments; the elementary atoms; the little steps by which she pressed forward to perfection. "What," she would say, "could India-rubber, or a pumice-stone, have done for these darlings?"

I am in no hurry to begin my story—indeed I have little or none to tell—so I will just mention an observation of hers connected with that interesting time.

Not long before she died I had been discoursing with her on the quantity of real present emotion which a great tragic performer experiences during acting. I ventured to think, that though in the first instance such players must have possessed the feelings which they so powerfully called up in others, yet by frequent repe-

tition those feelings must become deadened in great
measure, and the performer trust to the memory of past
emotion, rather than express a present one.

She indignantly repelled the notion, that with a truly
great tragedian the operation, by which such effects
were produced upon an audience, could ever degrade
itself into what was purely mechanical. With much
delicacy, avoiding to instance in her *self*-experience,
she told me, that so long ago as when she used to play
the part of the Little Son to Mrs. Porter's Isabella (I
think it was), when that impressive actress has been
bending over her in some heart-rending colloquy, she
has felt real hot tears come trickling from her, which (to
use her powerful expression) have perfectly scalded her
back.

I am not quite so sure that it was Mrs. Porter; but it
was some great actress of that day. The name is indifferent; but the fact of the scalding tears I most distinctly remember.

I was always fond of the society of players, and
am not sure that an impediment in my speech (which
certainly kept me out of the pulpit) even more than
certain personal disqualifications, which are often got
over in that profession, did not prevent me at one time
of life from adopting it. I have had the honour (I
must ever call it) once to have been admitted to the
tea-table of Miss Kelly. I have played at serious whist
with Mr. Liston. I have chattered with ever good-
humoured Mrs. Charles Kemble. I have conversed as
friend to friend with her accomplished husband. I have
been indulged with a classical conference with Macready; and with a sight of the Player-picture gallery, at
Mr. Mathews's, when the kind owner, to remunerate me
for my love of the old actors (whom he loves so much),
went over it with me, supplying to his capital collection,

what alone the artist could not give them—voice; and
their living motion. Old tones, half-faded, of Dodd, and
Parsons, and Baddeley, have lived again for me at his
bidding. Only Edwin he could not restore to me. I have
supped with ——; but I am growing a coxcomb.

As I was about to say—at the desk of the then treasurer of the Old Bath Theatre—not Diamond's—presented herself the little Barbara S——.

The parents of Barbara had been in reputable circumstances. The father had practised, I believe, as an
apothecary in the town. But his practice, from causes
which I feel my own infirmity too sensibly that way
to arraign—or perhaps from that pure infelicity which
accompanies some people in their walk through life, and
which it is impossible to lay at the door of imprudence
—was now reduced to nothing. They were in fact in the
very teeth of starvation, when the manager, who knew
and respected them in better days, took the little Barbara into his company.

At the period I commenced with, her slender earnings were the sole support of the family, including two
younger sisters. I must throw a veil over some mortifying circumstances. Enough to say, that her Saturday's
pittance was the only chance of a Sunday's (generally
their only) meal of meat.

One thing I will only mention, that in some child's
part, where in her theatrical character she was to sup
off a roast fowl (O joy to Barbara!) some comic actor,
who was for the night caterer for this dainty—in the
misguided humour of his part, threw over the dish such
a quantity of salt (O grief and pain of heart to Barbara!) that when she crammed a portion of it into her
mouth, she was obliged sputteringly to reject it; and
what with shame of her ill-acted part, and pain of real
appetite at missing such a dainty, her little heart

sobbed almost to breaking, till a flood of tears, which the well-fed spectators were totally unable to comprehend, mercifully relieved her.

This was the little starved, meritorious maid, who stood before old Ravenscroft, the treasurer, for her Saturday's payment.

Ravenscroft was a man, I have heard many old theatrical people besides herself say, of all men least calculated for a treasurer. He had no head for accounts, paid away at random, kept scarce any books, and summing up at the week's end, if he found himself a pound or so deficient, blest himself that it was no worse.

Now Barbara's weekly stipend was a bare half guinea. By mistake he popped into her hand—a whole one.

Barbara tripped away.

She was entirely unconscious at first of the mistake: God knows, Ravenscroft would never have discovered it.

But when she had got down to the first of those uncouth landing-places, she became sensible of an unusual weight of metal pressing her little hand.

Now mark the dilemma.

She was by nature a good child. From her parents and those about her she had imbibed no contrary influence. But then they had taught her nothing. Poor men's smoky cabins are not always porticoes of moral philosophy. This little maid had no instinct to evil, but then she might be said to have no fixed principle. She had heard honesty commended, but never dreamed of its application to herself. She thought of it as something which concerned grown-up people, men and women. She had never known temptation, or thought of preparing resistance against it.

Her first impulse was to go back to the old treasurer, and explain to him his blunder. He was already so confused with age, besides a natural want of punctuality, that she would have had some difficulty in making him understand it. She saw *that* in an instant. And then it was such a bit of money! and then the image of a larger allowance of butcher's-meat on their table next day came across her, till her little eyes glistened, and her mouth moistened. But then Mr. Ravenscroft had always been so good-natured, had stood her friend behind the scenes, and even recommended her promotion to some of her little parts.

But again the old man was reputed to be worth a world of money. He was supposed to have fifty pounds a year clear of the theatre. And then came staring upon her the figures of her little stockingless and shoeless sisters. And when she looked at her own neat white cotton stockings, which her situation at the theatre had made it indispensable for her mother to provide for her, with hard straining and pinching from the family stock, and thought how glad she should be to cover their poor feet with the same—and how then they could accompany her to rehearsals, which they had hitherto been precluded from doing, by reason of their unfashionable attire—in these thoughts she reached the second landing-place—the second, I mean, from the top—for there was still another left to traverse.

Now virtue support Barbara!

And that never-failing friend *did* step in—for at that moment a strength not her own, I have heard her say, was revealed to her—a reason above reasoning—and without her own agency, as it seemed (for she never felt her feet to move), she found herself transported back to the individual desk she had just quitted, and her hand in the old hand of Ravenscroft, who in silence took back the refunded treasure, and who had been sitting (good man) insensible to the lapse of minutes, which to her were anxious ages, and from that moment a deep peace fell upon her heart, and she knew the quality of honesty.

A year or two's unrepining application to her profession brightened up the feet and the prospects of her little sisters, set the whole family upon their legs again, and released her from the difficulty of discussing moral dogmas upon a landing-place.

I have heard her say that it was a surprise, not much short of mortification to her, to see the coolness with which the old man pocketed the difference, which had caused her such mortal throes.

This anecdote of herself I had in the year 1800, from the mouth of the late Mrs. Crawford,[1] then sixty-seven years of age (she died soon after); and to her struggles upon this childish occasion I have sometimes ventured to think her indebted for that power of rending the heart in the representation of conflicting emotions, for which in after years she was considered as little inferior (if at all so in the part of Lady Randolph) even to Mrs. Siddons.

London Magazine, April 1825; Last Essays of Elia.

---

[1] The maiden name of this lady was Street, which she changed, by successive marriages, for those of Dancer, Barry, and Crawford. She was Mrs. Crawford, a third time a widow, when I knew her. —C. L.

PART FIVE

Men, "Characters," and Places

WILLIAM HAZLITT

FROM the *other gentleman* I neither expect nor desire
(as he is well assured) any such concessions as L [eigh]
H[unt] made to C[oleridge]. What hath soured him, and
made him to suspect his friends of infidelity towards
him, when there was no such matter, I know not. I stood
well with him for fifteen years (the proudest of my life),
and have ever spoken my full mind of him to some, to
whom his panegyric must naturally be least tasteful. I
never in thought swerved from him, I never betrayed
him, I never slackened in my admiration of him; I was
the same to him (neither better nor worse), though he
could not see it, as in the days when he thought fit to
trust me. At this instant he may be preparing for me
some compliment, above my deserts, as he has sprinkled
many such among his admirable books, for which I rest
his debtor; or, for anything I know, or can guess to the
contrary, he may be about to read a lecture on my weaknesses. He is welcome to them (as he was to my humble
hearth), if they can divert a spleen, or ventilate a fit of
sullenness.

I wish he would not quarrel with the world at the

rate he does; but the reconciliation must be effected by
himself, and I despair of living to see that day. But protesting against much that he has written, and some
things which he chooses to do; judging him by his
conversation which I enjoyed so long, and relished so
deeply; or by his books, in those places where no clouding passion intervenes—I should belie my own conscience, if I said less, than that I think W[illiam] H[az-
litt] to be, in his natural and healthy state, one of the
wisest and finest spirits breathing. So far from being
ashamed of that intimacy, which was betwixt us, it is my
boast that I was able for so many years to have preserved
it entire; and I think I shall go to my grave without finding, or expecting to find, such another companion.

From "Letter to Robert Southey, Esq.,"
London Magazine, October 1823.

ON THE DEATH OF COLERIDGE

WHEN I heard of the death of Coleridge, it was without grief. It seemed to me that he long had been on the
confines of the next world—that he had a hunger for
eternity. I grieved then that I could not grieve. But,
since, I feel how great a part he was of me. His great
and dear spirit haunts me. I cannot think a thought, I
cannot make a criticism on men and books, without an
ineffectual turning and reference to him. He was the
proof and touchstone of all my cogitations. He was
a Grecian (or in the first form) at Christ's Hospital,
where I was Deputy-Grecian; and the same subordina-
tion and deference to him I have preserved through a
lifelong acquaintance.

Great in his writings, he was greatest in his conversation. In him was disproved that old maxim, that we should allow every one his share of talk. He would talk from morn to dewy eve, nor cease till far midnight; yet who ever would interrupt him? who would obstruct that continuous flow of converse, fetched from Helicon or Zion? He had the tact of making the unintelligible seem plain. Many who read the abstruser parts of his "Friend" would complain that his words did not answer to his spoken wisdom. They were identical. But he had a tone in oral delivery which seemed to convey sense to those who were otherwise imperfect recipients. He was my fifty-years-old friend without a dissension. Never saw I his likeness, nor probably the world can see again. I seem to love the house he died at more passionately than when he lived. I love the faithful Gillmans more than while they exercised their virtues towards him living. What was his mansion is consecrated to me a chapel.

Edmonton, Nov. 21, 1834.

THE TWO RACES OF MEN

THE human species, according to the best theory I can form of it, is composed of two distinct races, the men who borrow, and the men who lend. To these two original diversities may be reduced all those impertinent classifications of Gothic and Celtic tribes, white men, black men, red men. All the dwellers upon earth, "Parthians, and Medes, and Elamites," flock hither, and do naturally fall in with one or other of these primary distinctions. The infinite superiority of the former, which

I choose to designate as the *great race,* is discernible in their figure, port, and a certain instinctive sovereignty. The latter are born degraded. "He shall serve his brethren." There is something in the air of one of this cast, lean and suspicious; contrasting with the open, trusting, generous manners of the other.

Observe who have been the greatest borrowers of all ages—Alcibiades—Falstaff—Sir Richard Steele—our late incomparable Brinsley—what a family likeness in all four!

What a careless, even deportment hath your borrower! what rosy gills! what a beautiful reliance on Providence doth he manifest—taking no more thought than lilies! What contempt for money—accounting it (yours and mine especially) no better than dross! What a liberal confounding of those pedantic distinctions of *meum* and *tuum!* or rather, what a noble simplification of language (beyond Tooke), resolving these supposed opposites into one clear, intelligible pronoun adjective!— What near approaches doth he make to the primitive *community*—to the extent of one half of the principle at least.

He is the true taxer who "calleth all the world up to be taxed"; and the distance is as vast between him and *one of us,* as subsisted between the Augustan Majesty and the poorest obolary Jew that paid it tribute-pittance at Jerusalem!—His exactions, too, have such a cheerful, voluntary air! So far removed from your sour parochial or state-gatherers—those inkhorn varlets, who carry their want of welcome in their faces! He cometh to you with a smile, and troubleth you with no receipt; confining himself to no set season. Every day is his Candlemas, or his Feast of Holy Michael.

He applieth the *lene tormentum* of a pleasant look to your purse—which to that gentle warmth expands her silken leaves, as naturally as the cloak of the traveller, for which sun and wind contended! He is the true Propontic which never ebbeth! The sea which taketh handsomely at each man's hand. In vain the victim, whom he delighteth to honour, struggles with destiny; he is in the net. Lend therefore cheerfully, O man ordained to lend—that thou lose not in the end, with thy worldly penny, the reversion promised. Combine not preposterously in thine own person the penalties of Lazarus and of Dives!—but, when thou seest the proper authority coming, meet it smilingly, as it were halfway. Come, a handsome sacrifice! See how light *he* makes of it! Strain not courtesies with a noble enemy.

Reflections like the foregoing were forced upon my mind by the death of my old friend, Ralph Bigod, Esq., who parted this life, on Wednesday evening; dying, as he had lived, without much trouble. He boasted himself a descendant from mighty ancestors of that name, who heretofore held ducal dignities in this realm. In his actions and sentiments he belied not the stock to which he pretended. Early in life he found himself invested with ample revenues; which, with that noble disinterestedness which I have noticed as inherent in men of the *great race,* he took almost immediate measures entirely to dissipate and bring to nothing: for there is something revolting in the idea of a king holding a private purse; and the thoughts of Bigod were all regal. Thus furnished by the very act of disfurnishment; getting rid of the cumbersome luggage of riches, more apt (as one sings)

> To slacken virtue, and abate her edge,
> Than prompt her to do aught may merit praise—

he set forth, like some Alexander, upon his great enterprise, "borrowing and to borrow!"

In his periegesis, or triumphant progress throughout this island, it has been calculated that he laid a tythe part of the inhabitants under contribution. I reject this estimate as greatly exaggerated—but having had the honour of accompanying my friend divers times, in his perambulations about this vast city, I own I was greatly struck at first with the prodigious number of faces we met who claimed a sort of respectful acquaintance with us. He was one day so obliging as to explain the phenomenon. It seems, these were his tributaries; feeders of his exchequer; gentlemen, his good friends (as he was pleased to express himself), to whom he had occasionally been beholden for a loan. Their multitudes did no way disconcert him. He rather took a pride in numbering them; and, with Comus, seemed pleased to be "stocked with so fair a herd."

With such sources, it was a wonder how he contrived to keep his treasury always empty. He did it by force of an aphorism, which he had often in his mouth, that "money kept longer than three days stinks." So he made use of it while it was fresh. A good part he drank away (for he was an excellent toss-pot); some he gave away, the rest he threw away, literally tossing and hurling it violently from him—as boys do burrs, or as if it had been infectious—into ponds, or ditches, or deep holes, inscrutable cavities of the earth; or he would bury it (where he would never seek it again) by a river's side under some bank, which (he would facetiously observe) paid no interest—but out away from him it must go peremptorily, as Hagar's offspring into the wilderness, while it was sweet. He never missed it. The streams were perennial which fed his fisc.

When new supplies became necessary, the first person that had the felicity to fall in with him, friend or stranger, was sure to contribute to the deficiency. For

Bigod had an *undeniable* way with him. He had a cheerful, open exterior, a quick jovial eye, a bald forehead,
just touched with grey (*cana fides*). He anticipated no
excuse, and found none. And, waiving for a while my
theory as to the *great race*, I would put it to the most
untheorizing reader, who may at times have disposable
coin in his pockets, whether it is not more repugnant
to the kindliness of his nature to refuse such a one as I
am describing, than to say *no* to a poor petitionary rogue
(your bastard borrower), who, by his mumping visnomy, tells you, that he expects nothing better; and,
therefore, whose preconceived notions and expectations
you do in reality so much less shock in the refusal.

When I think of this man; his fiery glow of heart;
his swell of feeling; how magnificent, how *ideal* he was;
how great at the midnight hour; and when I compare
with him the companions with whom I have associated
since, I grudge the saving of a few idle ducats, and
think that I am fallen into the society of *lenders*, and
little men.

To one like Elia, whose treasures are rather cased
in leather covers than closed in iron coffers, there is a
class of alienators more formidable than that which I
have touched upon; I mean your *borrowers of books*—
those mutilators of collections, spoilers of the symmetry
of shelves, and creators of odd volumes. There is Comberbatch, matchless in his depredations!

That foul gap in the bottom shelf facing you, like a
great eyetooth knocked out—(you are now with me in
my little back study in Bloomsbury, reader!)—with the
huge Switzer-like tomes on each side (like the Guildhall
giants, in their reformed posture, guardant of nothing),
once held the tallest of my folios, *Opera Bonaventuræ,*
choice and massy divinity, to which its two supporters
(school divinity also, but of a lesser calibre—Bellar-

mine, and Holy Thomas), showed but as dwarfs—itself an Ascapart!—*that* Comberbatch abstracted upon
the faith of a theory he holds, which is more easy, I
confess, for me to suffer by than to refute, namely, that
"the title to property in a book (my Bonaventure, for
instance), is in exact ratio to the claimant's powers of
understanding and appreciating the same." Should he
go on acting upon this theory, which of our shelves is
safe?

The slight vacuum in the left-hand case—two shelves
from the ceiling—scarcely distinguishable but by the
quick eye of a loser—was whilom the commodious resting-place of Browne on *Urn Burial*. C. will hardly allege
that he knows more about that treatise than I do, who
introduced it to him, and was indeed the first (of
the moderns) to discover its beauties—but so have I
known a foolish lover to praise his mistress in the presence of a rival more qualified to carry her off than himself. Just below, Dodsley's dramas want their fourth
volume, where Vittoria Corombona is! The remainder
nine are as distasteful as Priam's refuse sons when
Fates *borrowed* Hector. Here stood the *Anatomy of
Melancholy*, in sober state. There loitered the *Compleat
Angler;* quiet as in life, by some stream side. In yon-
der nook, *John Buncle*, a widower-volume, with "eyes
closed," mourns his ravished mate.

One justice I must do my friend, that if he sometimes,
like the sea, sweeps away a treasure, at another time,
sea-like, he throws up as rich an equivalent to match
it. I have a small under-collection of this nature (my
friend's gatherings in his various calls), picked up, he
has forgotten at what odd places, and deposited with as
little memory at mine. I take in these orphans, the twice-
deserted. These proselytes of the gate are welcome as
the true Hebrews. There they stand in conjunction; na-

tives, and naturalized. The latter seem as little disposed
to inquire out their true lineage as I am. I charge no
warehouse-room for these deodands, nor shall ever put
myself to the ungentlemanly trouble of advertising a
sale of them to pay expenses.

To lose a volume to C. carries some sense and meaning in it. You are sure that he will make one hearty meal
on your viands, if he can give no account of the platter after it. But what moved thee, wayward, spiteful
K., to be so importunate to carry off with thee, in spite
of tears and adjurations to thee to forbear, the *Letters*
of that princely woman, the thrice noble Margaret Newcastle?—knowing at the time, and knowing that I
knew also, thou most assuredly wouldst never turn over
one leaf of the illustrious folio—what but the mere
spirit of contradiction, and childish love of getting the
better of thy friend?—Then, worst cut of all! to transport
it with thee to the Gallican land—

> Unworthy land to harbour such a sweetness,
> A virtue in which all ennobling thoughts dwelt,
> Pure thoughts, kind thoughts, high thoughts, her
>   sex's wonder!

—hadst thou not thy play-books, and books of jests and
fancies, about thee, to keep thee merry, even as thou
keepest all companies with thy quips and mirthful tales?
Child of the Green-room, it was unkindly done of thee.
Thy wife, too, that part-French, better-part English-
woman!—that *she* could fix upon no other treatise to
bear away, in kindly token of remembering us, than
the works of Fulke Greville, Lord Brooke—of which no
Frenchman, nor woman of France, Italy, or England,
was ever by nature constituted to comprehend a tittle!
—*Was there not Zimmerman on Solitude?*

Reader, if haply thou art blest with a moderate collection, be shy of showing it; or if thy heart overfloweth to lend them, lend thy books; but let it be to such a one as S. T. C.—he will return them (generally anticipating the time appointed) with usury; enriched with annotations tripling their value. I have had experience. Many are these precious MSS. of his—(in *matter* oftentimes, and almost in *quantity* not unfrequently, vying with the originals) in no very clerky hand—legible in my Daniel; in old Burton; in Sir Thomas Browne; and those abstruser cogitations of the Greville, now, alas! wandering in Pagan lands. I counsel thee, shut not thy heart, nor thy library, against S. T. C.

London Magazine, December 1820; Elia.

MRS. BATTLE'S OPINIONS ON WHIST

"A CLEAR fire, a clean hearth, and the rigour of the game." This was the celebrated *wish* of old Sarah Battle[1] (now with God), who, next to her devotions, loved a good game of whist. She was none of your lukewarm gamesters, your half-and-half players, who have no objection to take a hand, if you want one to make up a rubber; who affirm that they have no pleasure in winning; that they like to win one game and lose another; that they can while away an hour very agreeably at a card-table, but are indifferent whether they play or no; and will desire an adversary, who has slipped a wrong card, to take it up and play another. These insufferable

---

[1] Said to be Mrs. Burney, wife of Captain Burney and mother of Martin.—J. M. B.

triflers are the curse of a table. One of these flies will spoil a whole pot. Of such it may be said that they do not play at cards, but only play at playing at them.

Sarah Battle was none of that breed. She detested them, as I do, from her heart and soul, and would not, save upon a striking emergency, willingly seat herself at the same table with them. She loved a thorough-paced partner, a determined enemy. She took, and gave, no concessions. She hated favours. She never made a revoke, nor ever passed it over in her adversary without exacting the utmost forfeiture. She fought a good fight: cut and thrust. She held not her good sword (her cards) "like a dancer." She sate bolt upright; and neither showed you her cards, nor desired to see yours. All people have their blind side—their superstitions; and I have heard her declare, under the rose, that hearts was her favourite suit.

I never in my life—and I knew Sarah Battle many of the best years of it—saw her take out her snuffbox when it was her turn to play; or snuff a candle in the middle of a game; or ring for a servant, till it was fairly over. She never introduced, or connived at, miscellaneous conversation during its process. As she emphatically observed, cards were cards; and if I ever saw unmingled distaste in her fine last-century countenance, it was at the airs of a young gentleman of a literary turn, who had been with difficulty persuaded to take a hand; and who, in his excess of candour, declared, that he thought there was no harm in unbending the mind now and then, after serious studies, in recreations of that kind! She could not bear to have her noble occupation, to which she wound up her faculties, considered in that light. It was her business, her duty, the thing she came into the world to do—and she did it. She unbent her mind afterwards over a book.

Pope was her favourite author: his *Rape of the Lock* her favourite work. She once did me the favour to play over with me (with the cards) his celebrated game of Ombre in that poem; and to explain to me how far it agreed with, and in what points it would be found to differ from, tradrille. Her illustrations were apposite and poignant; and I had the pleasure of sending the substance of them to Mr. Bowles; but I suppose they came too late to be inserted among his ingenious notes upon that author.

Quadrille, she has often told me, was her first love; but whist had engaged her maturer esteem. The former, she said, was showy and specious, and likely to allure young persons. The uncertainty and quick shifting of partners—a thing which the constancy of whist abhors; the dazzling supremacy and regal investiture of Spadille —absurd, as she justly observed, in the pure aristocracy of whist, where his crown and garter gave him no proper power above his brother-nobility of the Aces; the giddy vanity, so taking to the inexperienced, of playing alone; above all, the overpowering attractions of a *Sans Prendre Vole,* to the triumph of which there is certainly nothing parallel or approaching, in the contingencies of whist—all these, she would say, make quadrille a game of captivation to the young and enthusiastic. But whist was the *solider* game: that was her word. It was a long meal; not, like quadrille, a feast of snatches.

One or two rubbers might co-extend in duration with an evening. They gave time to form rooted friendships, to cultivate steady enmities. She despised the chance-started, capricious, and ever-fluctuating alliances of the other. The skirmishes of quadrille, she would say, reminded her of the petty ephemeral embroilments of the little Italian states, depicted by Machiavel: per-

petually changing postures and connexions; bitter foes
today, sugared darlings tomorrow; kissing and scratching in a breath—but the wars of whist were comparable
to the long, steady, deep-rooted, rational antipathies of
the great French and English nations.

A grave simplicity was what she chiefly admired in
her favourite game. There was nothing silly in it, like the
nob in cribbage—nothing superfluous. No *flushes*—that
most irrational of all pleas that a reasonable being can
set up:—that any one should claim four by virtue of
holding cards of the same mark and colour, without
reference to the playing of the game, or the individual
worth or pretensions of the cards themselves! She held
this to be a solecism; as pitiful an ambition at cards as
alliteration is in authorship. She despised superficiality,
and looked deeper than the colours of things.

Suits were soldiers, she would say, and must have an
uniformity of array to distinguish them: but what should
we say to a foolish squire, who should claim a merit
from dressing up his tenantry in red jackets, that never
were to be marshalled—never to take the field?—She
even wished that whist were more simple than it is; and,
in my mind, would have stripped it of some appendages, which, in the state of human frailty, may be veni-
ally, and even commendably, allowed of. She saw no
reason for the deciding of the trump by the turn of the
card. Why not one suit always trumps? Why two colours, when the mark of the suits would have sufficiently
distinguished them without it?

"But the eye, my dear Madam, is agreeably refreshed
with the variety. Man is not the creature of pure reason
—he must have his senses delightfully appealed to. We
see it in Roman Catholic countries, where the music and
the paintings draw in many to worship, whom your
Quaker spirit of unsensualizing would have kept out.

You yourself have a pretty collection of paintings—but confess to me, whether, walking in your gallery at Sandham, among those clear Vandykes, or among the Paul Potters in the ante-room, you ever felt your bosom glow with an elegant delight, at all comparable to *that* you have it in your power to experience most evenings over a well-arranged assortment of the court-cards?—the pretty antic habits, like heralds in a procession—the gay triumph-assuring scarlets—the contrasting deadly-killing sables—the 'hoary majesty of spades'—Pam in all his glory!

"All these might be dispensed with; and with their naked names upon the drab pasteboard, the game might go on very well pictureless. But the *beauty* of cards would be extinguished for ever. Stripped of all that is imaginative in them, they must degenerate into mere gambling. Imagine a dull deal board, or drum head, to spread them on, instead of that nice verdant carpet (next to nature's), fittest arena for those courtly combatants to play their gallant jousts and tourneys in! Exchange those delicately-turned ivory markers—(work of Chinese artist, unconscious of their symbol—or as profanely slighting their true application as the arrantest Ephesian journeyman that turned out those little shrines for the goddess)—exchange them for little bits of leather (our ancestors' money) or chalk and a slate!"

The old lady, with a smile, confessed the soundness of my logic; and to her approbation of my arguments on her favourite topic that evening, I have always fancied myself indebted for the legacy of a curious cribbage-board, made of the finest Sienna marble, which her maternal uncle (old Walter Plumer, whom I have elsewhere celebrated) brought with him from Florence: this, and a trifle of five hundred pounds, came to me at her death.

The former bequest (which I do not least value) I have kept with religious care; though she herself, to confess a truth, was never greatly taken with cribbage. It was an essentially vulgar game, I have heard her say, disputing with her uncle, who was very partial to it. She could never heartily bring her mouth to pronounce "Go"—or "That's a go." She called it an ungrammatical game. The pegging teased her. I once knew her to forfeit a rubber (a five-dollar stake) because she would not take advantage of the turn-up knave, which would have given it her, but which she must have claimed by the disgraceful tenure of declaring "two for his heels." There is something extremely genteel in this sort of self-denial. Sarah Battle was a gentlewoman born.

Piquet she held the best game at the cards for two persons, though she would ridicule the pedantry of the terms—such as pique—repique—the capot—they savoured (she thought) of affectation. But games for two, or even three, she never greatly cared for. She loved the quadrate, or square. She would argue thus: Cards are warfare: the ends are gain with glory. But cards are war, in disguise of a sport: when single adversaries encounter, the ends proposed are too palpable. By themselves it is too close a fight; with spectators it is not much bettered. No looker-on can be interested, except for a bet, and then it is a mere affair of money; he cares not for your luck *sympathetically*, or for your play.

Three are still worse; a mere naked war of every man against every man, as in cribbage, without league or alliance; or a rotation of petty and contradictory interests, a succession of heartless leagues, and not much more hearty infractions of them, as in tradrille. But in square games (*she meant whist*), all that is possible to be attained in card-playing is accomplished. There are

the incentives of profit with honour, common to every
species—though the *latter* can be but very imperfectly
enjoyed in those other games, where the spectator is
only feebly a participator. But the parties in whist
are spectators and principals too. They are a theatre to
themselves, and a looker-on is not wanted. He is rather
worse than nothing, and an impertinence.

Whist abhors neutrality, or interests beyond its
sphere. You glory in some surprising stroke of skill or
fortune, not because a cold—or even an interested—
bystander witnesses it, but because your *partner* sym-
pathizes in the contingency. You win for two. You triumph for two. Two are exalted. Two again are mortified; which divides their disgrace, as the conjunction
doubles (by taking off the invidiousness) your glories.
Two losing to two are better reconciled, than one to one
in that close butchery. The hostile feeling is weakened
by multiplying the channels. War becomes a civil game.
By such reasonings as these the old lady was accustomed to defend her favourite pastime.

No inducement could ever prevail upon her to play at
any game, where chance entered into the composition,
for nothing. Chance, she would argue—and here again,
admire the subtlety of her conclusion—chance is nothing, but where something else depends upon it. It is
obvious that cannot be *glory*. What rational cause of
exultation could it give to a man to turn up size ace a
hundred times together by himself? or before spectators,
where no stake was depending. Make a lottery of a hundred thousand tickets with but one fortunate number—
and what possible principle of our nature, except stupid
wonderment, could it gratify to gain that number as
many times successively, without a prize?

Therefore she disliked the mixture of chance in back-
gammon, where it was not played for money. She called

it foolish, and those people idiots, who were taken with
a lucky hit under such circumstances. Games of pure
skill were as little to her fancy. Played for a stake, they
were a mere system of overreaching. Played for glory,
they were a mere setting of one man's wit—his memory, or combination-faculty rather—against another's;
like a mock-engagement at a review, bloodless and prof-
itless.

She could not conceive a *game* wanting the spritely
infusion of chance, the handsome excuses of good fortune. Two people playing at chess in a corner of a room,
while whist was stirring in the centre, would inspire her
with insufferable horror and ennui. Those well-cut si-
militudes of Castles, and Knights, the *imagery* of the
board, she would argue (and I think in this case justly),
were entirely misplaced and senseless. Those hard head-
contests can in no instance ally with the fancy. They
reject form and colour. A pencil and dry slate (she used
to say) were the proper arena for such combatants.

To those puny objectors against cards, as nurturing
the bad passions, she would retort, that man is a gam-
ing animal. He must be always trying to get the better
in something or other: that this passion can scarcely be
more safely expended than upon a game at cards: that
cards are a temporary illusion; in truth, a mere drama;
for we do but *play* at being mightily concerned, where
a few idle shillings are at stake, yet, during the illusion,
we *are* as mightily concerned as those whose stake is
crowns and kingdoms. They are a sort of dream-fighting;
much ado; great battling, and little bloodshed; mighty
means for disproportioned ends; quite as diverting, and
a great deal more innoxious, than many of those more
serious *games* of life, which men play, without esteem-
ing them to be such.

With great deference to the old lady's judgment in

these matters, I think I have experienced some moments in my life, when playing at cards *for nothing* has even been agreeable. When I am in sickness, or not in the best spirits, I sometimes call for the cards, and play a game at piquet *for love* with my cousin Bridget—Bridget Elia.

I grant there is something sneaking in it; but with a toothache, or a sprained ankle—when you are subdued and humble—you are glad to put up with an inferior spring of action.

There is such a thing in nature, I am convinced, as *sick whist*.

I grant it is not the highest style of man—I deprecate the manes of Sarah Battle—she lives not, alas! to whom I should apologize.

At such times, those *terms* which my old friend objected to, come in as something admissible. I love to get a tierce or a quatorze, though they mean nothing. I am subdued to an inferior interest. Those shadows of winning amuse me.

That last game I had with my sweet cousin (I capotted her)—(dare I tell thee, how foolish I am?)—I wished it might have lasted for ever, though we gained nothing, and lost nothing, though it was a mere shade of play: I would be content to go on in that idle folly for ever. The pipkin should be ever boiling, that was to prepare the gentle lenitive to my foot, which Bridget was doomed to apply after the game was over: and, as I do not much relish appliances, there it should ever bubble. Bridget and I should be ever playing.

THE GENTLE GIANTESS

THE Widow Blacket, of Oxford, is the largest female I ever had the pleasure of beholding. There may be her parallel upon the earth; but surely I never saw it. I take her to be lineally descended from the maid's aunt of Brainford, who caused Master Ford such uneasiness. She hath Atlantean shoulders; and, as she stoopeth in her gait—with as few offences to answer for in her own particular as any of Eve's daughters—her back seems broad enough to bear the blame of all the peccadilloes that have been committed since Adam.

She girdeth her waist—or what she is pleased to esteem as such—nearly up to her shoulders; from beneath which, that huge dorsal expanse, in mountainous declivity, emergeth. Respect for her alone preventeth the idle boys, who follow her about in shoals, whenever she cometh abroad, from getting up, and riding. But her presence infallibly commands a reverence. She is indeed, as the Americans would express it, something awful. Her person is a burthen to herself no less than to the ground which bears her. To her mighty bone, she hath a pinguitude withal, which makes the depth of winter to her the most desirable season.

Her distress in the warmer solstice is pitiable. During the months of July and August she usually renteth a cool cellar, where ices are kept, whereinto she descendeth when Sirius rageth. She dates from a hot Thursday—some twenty-five years ago. Her apartment in summer is pervious to the four winds. Two doors, in north and south direction, and two windows, fronting

the rising and the setting sun, never closed, from every
cardinal point, catch the contributory breezes. She loves
to enjoy what she calls a quadruple draught. That must
be a shrew zephyr that can escape her. I owe a painful
face-ache, which oppresses me at this moment, to a
cold caught, sitting by her, one day in last July, at this
receipt of coolness. Her fan, in ordinary, resembles a
banner spread, which she keepeth continually on the
alert to detect the least breeze.

She possesseth an active and gadding mind, totally
incommensurate with her person. No one delighteth
more than herself in country exercises and pastimes. I
have passed many an agreeable holyday with her in her
favourite park at Woodstock. She performs her part in
these delightful ambulatory excursions by the aid of a
portable garden chair. She setteth out with you at a
fair foot-gallop, which she keepeth up till you are both
well breathed, and then she reposeth for a few seconds.
Then she is up again for a hundred paces or so, and
again resteth; her movement, on these sprightly occasions, being something between walking and flying. Her
great weight seemeth to propel her forward, ostrich-
fashion. In this kind of relieved marching I have traversed with her many scores of acres on those well-
wooded and well-watered domains.

Her delight at Oxford is in the public walks and gardens, where, when the weather is not too oppressive, she
passeth much of her valuable time. There is a bench
at Maudlin, or rather situated between the frontiers of
that and ——'s College (some litigation, latterly, about
repairs, has vested the property of it finally in ——'s),
where, at the hour of noon, she is ordinarily to be found
sitting—so she calls it by courtesy—but, in fact, pressing and breaking of it down with her enormous settlement, as both those foundations, who, however, are

good-natured enough to wink at it, have found, I believe, to their cost. Here she taketh the fresh air, principally at vacation times, when the walks are freest from interruption of the younger fry of students. Here she passeth her idle hours, not idly, but generally accompanied with a book—blessed if she can but intercept some resident Fellow (as usually there are some of that brood left behind at these periods) or stray Master of Arts (to most of whom she is better known than their dinner-bell), with whom she may confer upon any curious topic of literature.

I have seen these shy gownsmen, who truly set but a very slight value upon female conversation, cast a hawk's eye upon her from the length of Maudlin Grove, and warily glide off into another walk—true monks as they are, and ungently neglecting the delicacies of her polished converse for their own perverse and uncommunicating solitariness!

Within doors her principal diversion is music, vocal and instrumental; in both which she is no mean professor. Her voice is wonderfully fine; but, till I got used to it, I confess it staggered me. It is, for all the world, like that of a piping bullfinch; while, from her size and stature, you would expect notes to drown the deep organ. The shake, which most fine singers reserve for the close or cadence, by some unaccountable flexibility, or tremulousness of pipe, she carrieth quite through the composition; so that her time, to a common air or ballad, keeps double motion, like the earth—running the primary circuit of the tune, and still revolving upon its own axis. The effect, as I said before, when you are used to it, is as agreeable as it is altogether new and surprising.

The spacious apartment of her outward frame lodgeth a soul in all respects disproportionate. Of more than mortal make, she evinceth withal a trembling sensibility, a yielding infirmity of purpose, a quick susceptibility to reproach, and all the train of diffident and blushing vir- tues, which for their habitation usually seek out a feeble frame, an attenuated and meagre constitution. With more than man's bulk, her humours and occupations are eminently feminine. She sighs—being six foot high. She languisheth—being two feet wide. She worketh slender sprigs upon the delicate muslin, her fingers be- ing capable of moulding a Colossus. She sippeth her wine out of her glass daintily—her capacity being that of a tun of Heidelberg. She goeth mincingly with those feet of hers, whose solidity need not fear the black ox's pressure.

Softest and largest of thy sex, adieu! By what parting attribute may I salute thee, last and best of the Titan- esses—Ogress, fed with milk instead of blood; not least, or least handsome, among Oxford's stately structures— Oxford, who, in its deadest time of vacation, can never properly be said to be empty, having thee to fill it.

London Magazine, December 1822.

AMICUS REDIVIVUS

> Where were ye, Nymphs, when the remorseless deep
> Closed o'er the head of your loved Lycidas?

I DO not know when I have experienced a stranger sen- sation, than on seeing my old friend, G. D.,[1] who had been paying me a morning visit, a few Sundays back, at my cottage at Islington, upon taking leave, instead of

---

[1] George Dyer, a lifelong friend of Charles Lamb.—J. M. B.

turning down the right-hand path by which he had entered—with staff in hand, and at noonday, deliberately march right forwards into the midst of the stream that runs by us, and totally disappear.

A spectacle like this at dusk would have been appalling enough; but in the broad, open daylight, to witness such an unreserved motion towards self-destruction in a valued friend, took from me all power of speculation.

How I found my feet I know not. Consciousness was quite gone. Some spirit, not my own, whirled me to the spot. I remember nothing but the silvery apparition of a good white head emerging; nigh which a staff (the hand unseen that wielded it) pointed upwards, as feeling for the skies. In a moment (if time was in that time) he was on my shoulders; and I—freighted with a load more precious than his who bore Anchises.

And here I cannot but do justice to the officious zeal of sundry passers-by, who, albeit arriving a little too late to participate in the honours of the rescue, in philanthropic shoals came thronging to communicate their advice as to the recovery; prescribing variously the application, or nonapplication, of salt, etc., to the person of the patient. Life, meantime, was ebbing fast away, amidst the stifle of conflicting judgments, when one, more sagacious than the rest, by a bright thought, proposed sending for the Doctor. Trite as the counsel was, and impossible, as one should think, to be missed on—shall I confess?—in this emergency it was to me as if an Angel had spoken. Great previous exertions—and mine had not been inconsiderable—are commonly followed by a debility of purpose. This was a moment of irresolution.

Monoculus—for so, in default of catching his true name, I choose to designate the medical gentleman who now appeared—is a grave, middle-aged person, who, without having studied at the college, or truckled to the pedantry of a diploma, hath employed a great portion of his valuable time in experimental processes upon the bodies of unfortunate fellow-creatures, in whom the vital spark, to mere vulgar thinking, would seem extinct and lost for ever.

He omitteth no occasion of obtruding his services, from a case of common surfeit suffocation to the ignobler obstructions, sometimes induced by a too-wilful application of the plant *cannabis* outwardly. But though he declineth not altogether these drier extinctions, his occupation tendeth, for the most part, to water-practice; for the convenience of which, he hath judiciously fixed his quarters near the grand repository of the stream mentioned, where day and night, from his little watchtower, at the Myddelton Head, he listeneth to detect the wrecks of drowned mortality—partly, as he saith, to be upon the spot—and partly, because the liquids which he useth to prescribe to himself and his patients, on these distressing occasions, are ordinarily more conveniently to be found at these common hostelries than in the shops and phials of the apothecaries.

His ear hath arrived to such finesse by practice, that it is reported he can distinguish a plunge, at half a furlong distance; and can tell if it be casual or deliberate. He weareth a medal, suspended over a suit, originally of a sad brown, but which, by time and frequency of nightly divings, has been dinged into a true professional sable. He passeth by the name of Doctor, and is remarkable for wanting his left eye. His remedy—after a sufficient application of warm blankets, friction, etc., is a simple tumbler or more, of the purest Cognac, with water, made as hot as the convalescent can bear it. Where he findeth, as in the case of my friend, a squeamish subject, he condescendeth to be the taster; and showeth, by his own example, the innocuous nature of the prescription.

Nothing can be more kind or encouraging than this procedure. It addeth confidence to the patient, to see his medical adviser go hand in hand with himself in the remedy. When the doctor swalloweth his own draught, what peevish invalid can refuse to pledge him in the potion? In fine, Monoculus is a humane, sensible man, who, for a slender pittance, scarce enough to sustain life, is content to wear it out in the endeavour to save the lives of others—his pretensions so moderate that with difficulty I could press a crown upon him, for the price of restoring the existence of such an invaluable creature to society as G. D.

It was pleasant to observe the effect of the subsiding alarm upon the nerves of the dear absentee. It seemed to have given a shake to memory, calling up notice after notice, of all the providential deliverances he had experienced in the course of his long and innocent life. Sitting up in my couch—my couch which, naked and void of furniture hitherto, for the salutary repose which it administered, shall be honoured with costly valance, at some price, and henceforth be a state-bed at Colebrook—he discoursed of marvellous escapes —by carelessness of nurses—by pails of gelid, and kettles of the boiling element, in infancy—by orchard pranks, and snapping twigs, in schoolboy frolics—by descent of tiles at Trumpington, and of heavier tomes at Pembroke—by studious watchings, inducing frightful vigilance—by want, and the fear of want, and all the sore throbbings of the learned head.

Anon, he would burst out into little fragments of chanting—of songs long ago—ends of deliverance hymns, not remembered before since childhood, but coming up now, when his heart was made tender as a

child's—for the *tremor cordis,* in the retrospect of a
recent deliverance, as in the case of impending danger,
acting upon an innocent heart, will produce a self-ten-
derness, which we should do ill to christen cowardice;
and Shakspeare, in the latter crisis, has made his good
Sir Hugh to remember the sitting by Babylon, and to
mutter of shallow rivers.

Waters of Sir Hugh Myddelton—what a spark you
were like to have extinguished for ever! Your salubrious
streams to this City, for now near two centuries, would
hardly have atoned for what you were in a moment
washing away. Mockery of a river—liquid artifice—
wretched conduit! henceforth rank with canals and
sluggish aqueducts. Was it for this that, smit in boyhood with the explorations of that Abyssinian traveller,
I paced the vales of Amwell to explore your tributary
springs, to trace your salutary waters, sparkling through
green Hertfordshire, and cultured Enfield parks?—Ye
have no swans—no Naiads—no river God—or did the
benevolent hoary aspect of my friend tempt ye to suck
him in, that ye also might have the tutelary genius of
your waters?

Had he been drowned in Cam, there would have
been some consonancy in it; but what willows had ye
to wave and rustle over his moist sepulture?—or, having no *name,* besides that unmeaning assumption of
eternal novity, did ye think to get one by the noble
prize, and henceforth to be termed the Stream Dyerian?

> And could such spacious virtue find a grave
> Beneath the imposthumed bubble of a wave?

I protest, George, you shall not venture out again—
no, not by daylight—without a sufficient pair of spectacles—in your musing moods especially. Your absence of mind we have borne, till your presence of body

came to be called in question by it. You shall not go wandering into Euripus with Aristotle, if we can help it. Fie, man, to turn dipper at your years, after your many tracts in favour of sprinkling only!

I have nothing but water in my head o'nights since this frightful accident. Sometimes I am with Clarence in his dream. At others, I behold Christian beginning to sink, and crying out to his good brother Hopeful (that is, to me), "I sink in deep waters; the billows go over my head, all the waves go over me. Selah."

Then I have before me Palinurus, just letting go the steerage. I cry out too late to save. Next follow— a mournful procession—*suicidal faces*, saved against their will from drowning; dolefully trailing a length of reluctant gratefulness, with ropy weeds pendent from locks of watchet hue—constrained Lazari—Pluto's half-subjects—stolen fees from the grave—bilking Charon of his fare. At their head Arion—or is it G. D.? —in his singing garments marcheth singly, with harp in hand, and votive garland, which Machaon (or Dr. Hawes) snatcheth straight, intending to suspend it to the stern God of Sea. Then follow dismal streams of Lethe, in which the half-drenched on earth are constrained to drown downright, by wharfs where Ophelia twice acts her muddy death.

And, doubtless, there is some notice in that invisible world when one of us approacheth (as my friend did so lately) to their inexorable precincts. When a soul knocks once, twice, at Death's door, the sensation aroused within the palace must be considerable; and the grim Feature, by modern science so often dispossessed of his prey, must have learned by this time to pity Tantalus.

A pulse assuredly was felt along the line of the Elysian shades, when the near arrival of G. D. was announced by no equivocal indications. From their seats of Asphodel arose the gentler and the graver ghosts—poet, or historian—of Grecian or of Roman lore—to crown with unfading chaplets the half-finished love-labours of their unwearied scholiast. Him Markland expected—him Tyrwhitt hoped to encounter—him the sweet lyrist of Peter House, whom he had barely seen upon earth,[1] with newest airs prepared to greet—; and patron of the gentle Christ's boy—who should have been his patron through life—the mild Askew, with longing aspirations leaned foremost from his venerable Æsculapian chair, to welcome into that happy company the matured virtues of the man, whose tender scions in the boy he himself upon earth had so prophetically fed and watered.

London Magazine, December 1823; Last Essays of Elia.

MODERN GALLANTRY

IN COMPARING modern with ancient manners, we are pleased to compliment ourselves upon the point of gallantry; a certain obsequiousness, or deferential respect, which we are supposed to pay to females, as females.

I shall believe that this principle actuates our conduct, when I can forget, that in the nineteenth century of the era from which we date our civility, we are but just beginning to leave off the very frequent practice of whipping females in public, in common with the coarsest male offenders.

I shall believe it to be influential, when I can shut my

---

[1] GRAIUM *tantum vidit.*—C. L.

eyes to the fact, that in England women are still occasionally—hanged.

I shall believe in it, when actresses are no longer subject to be hissed off a stage by gentlemen.

I shall believe in it, when Dorimant hands a fishwife
across the kennel; or assists the apple-woman to pick up
her wandering fruit, which some unlucky dray has just
dissipated.

I shall believe in it, when the Dorimants in humbler
life, who would be thought in their way notable adepts
in this refinement, shall act upon it in places where they
are not known, or think themselves not observed—when
I shall see the traveller for some rich tradesman part
with his admired boxcoat, to spread it over the defence-
less shoulders of the poor woman, who is passing to her
parish on the roof of the same stage-coach with him,
drenched in the rain—when I shall no longer see a
woman standing up in the pit of a London theatre, till
she is sick and faint with the exertion, with men about
her, seated at their ease, and jeering at her distress; till
one, that seems to have more manners or conscience
than the rest, significantly declares "she should be welcome to his seat, if she were a little younger and handsomer." Place this dapper warehouseman, or that rider,
in a circle of their own female acquaintance, and you
shall confess you have not seen a politer-bred man in
Lothbury.

Lastly, I shall begin to believe that there is some such
principle influencing our conduct, when more than
one-half of the drudgery and coarse servitude of the
world shall cease to be performed by women.

Until that day comes, I shall never believe this boasted
point to be anything more than a conventional fiction;
a pageant got up between the sexes, in a certain rank,

and at a certain time of life, in which both find their account equally.

I shall be even disposed to rank it among the salutary fictions of life, when in polite circles I shall see the same attentions paid to age as to youth, to homely features as to handsome, to coarse complexions as to clear —to the woman, as she is a woman, not as she is a beauty, a fortune, or a title.

I shall believe it to be something more than a name, when a well-dressed gentleman in a well-dressed company can advert to the topic of *female old age* without exciting, and intending to excite, a sneer—when the phrases "antiquated virginity," and such a one has "overstood her market," pronounced in good company, shall raise immediate offence in man, or woman, that shall hear them spoken.

Joseph Paice, of Bread Street Hill, merchant, and one of the Directors of the South-Sea Company—the same to whom Edwards, the Shakspeare commentator, has addressed a fine sonnet—was the only pattern of consistent gallantry I have met with. He took me under his shelter at an early age, and bestowed some pains upon me. I owe to his precepts and example whatever there is of the man of business (and that is not much) in my composition. It was not his fault that I did not profit more.

Though bred a Presbyterian, and brought up a merchant, he was the finest gentleman of his time. He had not *one* system of attention to females in the drawing-room, and *another* in the shop, or at the stall. I do not mean that he made no distinction. But he never lost sight of sex, or overlooked it in the casualties of a disadvantageous situation. I have seen him stand bareheaded—smile if you please—to a poor servant-girl, while she has been inquiring of him the way to some street—in such a posture of unforced civility, as neither to embarrass her in the acceptance, nor himself in the offer, of it. He was no dangler, in the common acceptation of the word, after women: but he reverenced and upheld, in every form in which it came before him, *womanhood*.

I have seen him—nay, smile not—tenderly escorting a market-woman, whom he had encountered in a shower, exalting his umbrella over her poor basket of fruit, that it might receive no damage, with as much carefulness as if she had been a Countess. To the reverend form of Female Eld he would yield the wall (though it were to an ancient beggar-woman) with more ceremony than he can afford to show our grandams. He was the Preux Chevalier of Age; the Sir Calidore, or Sir Tristan, to those who have no Calidores or Tristans to defend them. The roses, that had long faded thence, still bloomed for him in those withered and yellow cheeks.

He was never married, but in his youth he paid his addresses to the beautiful Susan Winstanley—old Winstanley's daughter of Clapton—who dying in the early days of their courtship, confirmed in him the resolution of perpetual bachelorship. It was during their short courtship, he told me, that he had been one day treating his mistress with a profusion of civil speeches—the common gallantries—to which kind of thing she had hitherto manifested no repugnance—but in this instance with no effect. He could not obtain from her a decent acknowledgment in return. She rather seemed to resent his compliments. He could not set it down to caprice, for the lady had always shown herself above that littleness.

When he ventured on the following day, finding her a little better humoured, to expostulate with her on her

coldness of yesterday, she confessed, with her usual
frankness, that she had no sort of dislike to his attentions;
that she could even endure some high-flown compliments; that a young woman placed in her situation had
a right to expect all sort of civil things said to her; that
she hoped she could digest a dose of adulation, short of
insincerity, with as little injury to her humility as most
young women; but that—a little before he had commenced his compliments—she had overheard him by
accident, in rather rough language, rating a young
woman, who had not brought home his cravats quite to
the appointed time, and she thought to herself, "As I
am Miss Susan Winstanley, and a young lady—a reputed beauty, and known to be a fortune—I can have
my choice of the finest speeches from the mouth of
this very fine gentleman who is courting me—but if I
had been poor Mary Such-a-one"—naming the milliner
—"and had failed of bringing home the cravats to the
appointed hour—though perhaps I had sat up half the
night to forward them—what sort of compliments should
I have received then? And my woman's pride came to
my assistance; and I thought, that if it were only to do
me honour, a female, like myself, might have received
handsomer usage: and I was determined not to accept
any fine speeches, to the compromise of that sex, the
belonging to which was after all my strongest claim and
title to them."

I think the lady discovered both generosity, and a just
way of thinking, in this rebuke which she gave her
lover; and I have sometimes imagined, that the uncommon strain of courtesy, which through life regulated the
actions and behaviour of my friend towards all of wom-
ankind indiscriminately, owed its happy origin to this
seasonable lesson from the lips of his lamented mistress.

I wish the whole female world would entertain the

same notion of these things that Miss Winstanley showed. Then we should see something of the spirit of consistent gallantry; and no longer witness the anomaly of the same man—a pattern of true politeness to a wife —of cold contempt, or rudeness, to a sister—the idolater of his female mistress—the disparager and despiser of his no less female aunt, or unfortunate—still female— maiden cousin.

Just so much respect as a woman derogates from her own sex, in whatever condition placed—her hand-maid, or dependant—she deserves to have diminished from herself on that score; and probably will feel the diminution, when youth, and beauty, and advantages, not inseparable from sex, shall lose of their attraction. What a woman should demand of a man in courtship, or after it, is first—respect for her as she is a woman; and next to that—to be respected by him above all other women. But let her stand upon her female character as upon a foundation; and let the attentions, incident to individual preference, to so many pretty additaments and ornaments—as many, and as fanciful, as you please —to that main structure. Let her first lesson be with sweet Susan Winstanley—to *reverence her sex*.

London Magazine, November 1822; *Elia*.

CAPTAIN JACKSON

AMONG the deaths in our obituary for this month, I observe with concern "At his cottage on the Bath road, Captain Jackson." The name and attribution are common enough; but a feeling like reproach persuades me, that this could have been no other in fact than my dear old friend, who some five-and-twenty years ago rented a tenement, which he was pleased to dignify with the appellation here used, about a mile from Westbourn Green. Alack, how good men, and the good turns they do us, slide out of memory, and are recalled but by the surprise of some such sad memento as that which now lies before us!

He whom I mean was a retired half-pay officer, with a wife and two grown-up daughters, whom he maintained with the port and notions of gentlewomen upon that slender professional allowance. Comely girls they were too.

And was I in danger of forgetting this man?—his cheerful suppers—the noble tone of hospitality, when first you set your foot in *the cottage*—the anxious ministerings about you, where little or nothing (God knows) was to be ministered. Althea's horn in a poor platter—the power of self-enchantment, by which, in his magnificent wishes to entertain you, he multiplied his means to bounties.

You saw with your bodily eyes indeed what seemed a bare scrag, cold savings from the foregone meal—remnant hardly sufficient to send a mendicant from the door contented. But in the copious will—the revelling imagination of your host—the "mind, the mind, Master Shallow," whole beeves were spread before you—hecatombs—no end appeared to the profusion.

It was the widow's cruse—the loaves and fishes; carving could not lessen, nor helping diminish it—the stamina were left—the elemental bone still flourished, divested of its accidents.

"Let us live while we can," methinks I hear the open-handed creature exclaim; "while we have, let us not want," "here is plenty left"; "want for nothing"—with many more such hospitable sayings, the spurs of appetite, and old concomitants of smoking boards, and feast-oppressed chargers. Then sliding a slender ratio of Single Gloucester upon his wife's plate, or the daughters', he would convey the remanent rind into his own, with a merry quirk of "the nearer the bone," etc., and declaring that he universally preferred the outside. For we had our table distinctions, you are to know, and some of us in a manner sate above the salt. None but his guest or guests dreamed of tasting flesh luxuries at night, the fragments were *verè hospitibus sacra*. But of one thing or another there was always enough, and leavings: only he would sometimes finish the remainder crust, to show that he wished no savings.

Wine we had none; nor, except on very rare occasions, spirits; but the sensation of wine was there. Some thin kind of ale I remember—"British beverage," he would say! "Push about, my boys"; "Drink to your sweethearts, girls." At every meagre draught a toast must ensue, or a song. All the forms of good liquor were there, with none of the effects wanting. Shut your eyes, and you would swear a capacious bowl of punch was foaming in the centre, with beams of generous Port or Madeira radiating to it from each of the table corners. You got flustered, without knowing whence; tipsy upon words; and reeled under the potency of his unperforming Bacchanalian encouragements.

We had our songs—"Why, Soldiers, Why"—and the "British Grenadiers"—in which last we were all obliged to bear chorus. Both the daughters sang. Their proficiency was a nightly theme—the masters he had given them—the "no-expense" which he spared to accomplish them in a science "so necessary to young women." But then—they could not sing "without the instrument."

Sacred, and, by me, never-to-be-violated, secrets of

Poverty! Should I disclose your honest aims at grandeur, your makeshift efforts of magnificence? Sleep, sleep, with all thy broken keys, if one of the bunch be extant; thrummed by a thousand ancestral thumbs; dear, cracked spinnet of dearer Louisa! Without mention of mine, be dumb, thou thin accompanier of her thinner warble! A veil be spread over the dear delighted face of the well-deluded father, who now haply listening to cherubic notes, scarce feels sincerer pleasure than when she awakened thy time shaken chords responsive to the twitterings of that slender image of a voice.

We were not without our literary talk either. It did not extend far, but as far as it went, it was good. It was bottomed well; had good grounds to go upon. In *the cottage* was a room, which tradition authenticated to have been the same in which Glover, in his occasional retirements, had penned the greater part of his Leonidas. This circumstance was nightly quoted, though none of the present inmates, that I could discover, appeared ever to have met with the poem in question. But that was no matter. Glover had written there, and the anecdote was pressed into the account of the family importance. It diffused a learned air through the apartment, the little side casement of which (the poet's study window), opening upon a superb view as far as the pretty spire of Harrow, over domains and patrimonial acres, not a rood nor square yard whereof our host could call his own, yet gave occasion to an immoderate expansion of—vanity shall I call it?—in his bosom, as he showed them in a glowing summer evening. It was all his, he took it all in, and communicated rich portions of it to his guests. It was a part of his largess, his hospitality; it was going over his grounds; he was lord for the time of showing them, and you the implicit lookers-up to his magnificence.

He was a juggler, who threw mists before your eyes—you had no time to detect his fallacies. He would say, "Hand me the *silver* sugar tongs"; and before you could discover it was a single spoon, and that *plated,* he would disturb and captivate your imagination by a misnomer of "the urn" for a tea-kettle; or by calling a homely bench a sofa. Rich men direct you to their furniture, poor ones divert you from it; he neither did one nor the other, but by simply assuming that everything was handsome about him, you were positively at a demur what you did, or did not see, at *the cottage.* With nothing to live on, he seemed to live on everything. He had a stock of wealth in his mind; not that which is properly termed *Content,* for in truth he was not to be *contained* at all, but overflowed all bounds by the force of a magnificent self-delusion.

Enthusiasm is catching; and even his wife, a sober native of North Britain, who generally saw things more as they were, was not proof against the continual collision of his credulity. Her daughters were rational and discreet young women; in the main, perhaps, not insensible to their true circumstances. I have seen them assume a thoughtful air at times. But such was the preponderating opulence of his fancy, that I am persuaded, not for any half-hour together did they ever look their own prospects fairly in the face. There was no resisting the vortex of his temperament. His riotous imagination conjured up handsome settlements before their eyes, which kept them up in the eye of the world too, and seem at last to have realized themselves; for they both have married since, I am told, more than respectably.

It is long since, and my memory waxes dim on some subjects, or I should wish to convey some notion of the manner in which the pleasant creature described the circumstances of his own wedding-day. I faintly remember something of a chaise-and-four, in which he made his entry into Glasgow on that morning to fetch the bride home, or carry her thither, I forget which. It so completely made out the stanza of the old ballad—

> When we came down through Glasgow town,
>   We were a comely sight to see;
> My love was clad in black velvet,
>   And I myself in cramasie.

I suppose it was the only occasion upon which his own actual splendour at all corresponded with the world's notions on that subject. In homely cart, or travelling caravan, by whatever humble vehicle they chanced to be transported in less prosperous days, the ride through Glasgow came back upon his fancy, not as a humiliating contrast, but as a fair occasion for reverting to that one day's state. It seemed an "equipage-etern" from which no power of fate or fortune, once mounted, had power thereafter to dislodge him.

There is some merit in putting a handsome face upon indigent circumstances. To bully and swagger away the sense of them before strangers, may not be always discommendable. Tibbs, and Bobadil, even when detected, have more of our admiration than contempt. But for a man to put the cheat upon himself; to play the Bobadil at home; and, steeped in poverty up to the lips, to fancy himself all the while chin-deep in riches, is a strain of constitutional philosophy, and a mastery over fortune, which was reserved for my old friend Captain Jackson.

London Magazine, November 1824; *Last Essays of Elia*.

OXFORD IN THE VACATION

CASTING a preparatory glance at the bottom of this article—as the wary connoisseur in prints, with cursory eye (which, while it reads, seems as though it read not), never fails to consult the *quis sculpsit* in the corner, before he pronounces some rare piece to be a Vivares, or a Woollet—methinks I hear you exclaim, reader, *Who is Elia?*

Because in my last I tried to divert thee with some half-forgotten humours of some old clerks defunct, in an old house of business, long since gone to decay, doubtless you have already set me down in your mind as one of the self-same college—a votary of the desk—a notched and cropt scrivener—one that sucks his sustenance, as certain sick people are said to do, through a quill.

Well, I do agnize something of the sort. I confess that it is my humour, my fancy—in the forepart of the day, when the mind of your man of letters requires some relaxation—(and none better than such as at first sight seems most abhorrent from his beloved studies)—to while away some good hours of my time in the contemplation of indigos, cottons, raw silks, piece-goods, flowered or otherwise. In the first place . . . and then it sends you home with such increased appetite to your books . . . not to say, that your outside sheets, and waste wrappers of foolscap, do receive into them, most kindly and naturally, the impression of sonnets, epigrams, *essays*—so that the very parings of a counting-house are, in some sort, the settings up of an author.

The enfranchised quill, that has plodded all the morning among the cart-rucks of figures and ciphers, frisks and curvets so at its ease over the flowery carpet-ground of a midnight dissertation. It feels its promotion. . . . So that you see, upon the whole, the literary dignity of *Elia* is very little, if at all, compromised in the condescension.

Not that, in my anxious detail of the many commodities incidental to the life of a public office, I would be thought blind to certain flaws, which a cunning carper might be able to pick in this Joseph's vest. And here I must have leave, in the fullness of my soul, to regret the abolition, and doing away-with altogether, of those consolatory interstices and sprinklings of freedom, through the four seasons—the *red-letter days*, now become, to all intents and purposes, *dead-letter days*. There was Paul, and Stephen, and Barnabas—

> Andrew and John, men famous in old times

—we were used to keep all their days holy as long back as I was at school at Christ's.

I remember their effigies, by the same token, in the old Baskett Prayer-Book. There hung Peter in his uneasy posture—holy Bartlemy in the troublesome act of flaying, after the famous Marsyas by Spagnoletti. I honoured them all, and could almost have wept the defalcation of Iscariot—so much did we love to keep holy memories sacred: only methought I a little grudged at the coalition of the *better Jude* with Simon—clubbing (as it were) their sanctities together to make up one poor gaudy-day between them—as an economy unworthy of the dispensation.

These were bright visitations in a scholar's and a clerk's life—"far off their coming shone." I was as good as an almanac in those days. I could have told you such a saint's day falls out next week, or the week after. Peradventure the Epiphany, by some periodical infelicity, would, once in six years, merge in a Sabbath. Now am I little better than one of the profane. Let me not be thought to arraign the wisdom of my civil superiors, who have judged the further observation of these holy tides to be papistical, superstitious. Only in a custom of such long standing, methinks, if their Holinesses the Bishops had, in decency, been first sounded—but I am wading out of my depths. I am not the man to decide the limits of civil and ecclesiastical authority—I am plain Elia—no Selden, nor Archbishop Usher—though at present in the thick of their books, here in the heart of learning, under the shadow of the mighty Bodley.

I can here play the gentleman, enact the student. To such a one as myself, who has been defrauded in his young years of the sweet food of academic institution, nowhere is so pleasant, to while away a few idle weeks at, as one or other of the Universities. Their vacation, too, at this time of the year, falls in so pat with *ours.* Here I can take my walks unmolested, and fancy myself of what degree or standing I please. I seem admitted *ad eundem.* I fetch up past opportunities. I can rise at the chapel-bell, and dream that it rings for *me.* In moods of humility I can be a Sizar, or a Servitor. When the peacock vein rises, I strut a Gentleman Commoner. In graver moments I proceed Master of Arts. Indeed I do not think I am much unlike that respectable character. I have seen your dim-eyed vergers, and bedmakers in spectacles, drop a bow or a curtsy, as I pass, wisely mistaking me for something of the sort. I go about in black, which favours the notion. Only in Christ Church reverend quadrangle, I can be content to pass for nothing short of a Seraphic Doctor.

The walks at these times are so much one's own—the

tall trees of Christ's, the groves of Magdalen! The halls
deserted, and with open doors inviting one to slip in
unperceived, and pay a devoir to some Founder, or noble or royal Benefactress (that should have been ours),
whose portrait seems to smile upon their overlooked
beadsman, and to adopt me for their own. Then, to take
a peep in by the way at the butteries, and sculleries,
redolent of antique hospitality: the immense caves of
kitchens, kitchen fireplaces, cordial recesses; ovens
whose first pies were baked four centuries ago; and spits
which have cooked for Chaucer! Not the meanest minister among the dishes but is hallowed to me through his
imagination, and the Cook goes forth a Manciple.

Antiquity! thou wondrous charm, what art thou? that,
being nothing, art everything! When thou *wert,* thou
wert not antiquity—then thou wert nothing, but hadst
a remoter *antiquity,* as thou calledst it, to look back to
with blind veneration; thou thyself being to thyself flat,
jejune, *modern!* What mystery lurks in this retrover-
sion? or what half Januses[1] are we, that cannot look forward with the same idolatry with which we for ever
revert! The mighty future is as nothing, being everything! the past is everything, being nothing!

What were thy *dark ages?* Surely the sun rose as
brightly then as now, and man got him to his work in
the morning. Why is it we can never hear mention of
them without an accompanying feeling as though a
palpable obscure had dimmed the face of things, and
that our ancestors wandered to and fro groping!

Above all thy rarities, old Oxenford, what do most
arride and solace me, are thy repositories of mouldering
learning, thy shelves. . . .

What a place to be in is an old library! It seems as
though all the souls of all the writers, that have be-

[1] Januses of one face.—SIR THOMAS BROWNE.—C. L.

queathed their labours to these Bodleians, were repos-
ing here, as in some dormitory, or middle state. I do
not want to handle, to profane the leaves, their winding-
sheets. I could as soon dislodge a shade. I seem to inhale
learning, walking amid their foliage; and the odour of
their old moth-scented coverings is fragrant as the first
bloom of those sciential apples which grew amid the
happy orchard.

Still less have I curiosity to disturb the elder repose
of MSS. Those *variæ lectiones*, so tempting to the more
erudite palates, do but disturb and unsettle my faith.
I am no Herculanean raker. The credit of the three witnesses might have slept unimpeached for me. I leave
these curiosities to Porson, and to G. D.[1]—whom, by
the way, I found busy as a moth over some rotten ar-
chive, rummaged out of some seldom-explored press,
in a nook at Oriel. With long poring he is grown almost into a book. He stood as passive as one by the side
of the old shelves. I longed to new-coat him in russia,
and assign him his place. He might have mustered for a
tall Scapula.

D. is assiduous in his visits to these seats of learning.
No inconsiderable portion of his moderate fortune, I
apprehend, is consumed in journeys between them and
Clifford's Inn—where, like a dove on the asp's nest, he
has long taken up his unconscious abode, amid an incongruous assembly of attorneys, attorneys' clerks, ap-
paritors, promoters, vermin of the law, among whom he
sits "in calm and sinless peace." The fangs of the law
pierce him not—the winds of litigation blow over his
humble chambers—the hard sheriff's officer moves his
hat as he passes—legal nor illegal discourtesy touches
him—none thinks of offering violence or injustice to him
—you would as soon "strike an abstract idea."

[1] George Dyer.—J. M. B.

D. has been engaged, he tells me, through a course of laborious years, in an investigation into all curious matter connected with the two Universities; and has lately lit upon a MS. collection of charters, relative to C., by which he hopes to settle some disputed points—particularly that long controversy between them as to priority of foundation.

The ardour with which he engages in these liberal pursuits, I am afraid, has not met with all the encouragement it deserved, either here, or at C. Your caputs, and heads of colleges, care less than anybody else about these questions. Contented to suck the milky fountains of their Alma Maters, without inquiring into the venerable gentlewomen's years, they rather hold such curiosities to be impertinent—unreverend. They have their good glebe lands *in manu,* and care not much to rake into the title-deeds. I gather at least so much from other sources, for D. is not a man to complain.

D. started like an unbroke heifer when I interrupted him. *A priori* it was not very probable that we should have met in Oriel. But D. would have done the same, had I accosted him on the sudden in his own walks in Clifford's Inn, or in the Temple. In addition to a provoking short-sightedness (the effect of late studies and watchings at the midnight oil) D. is the most absent of men. He made a call the other morning at our friend M.'s in Bedford Square; and, finding nobody at home, was ushered into the hall, where, asking for pen and ink, with great exactitude of purpose he enters me his name in the book—which ordinarily lies about in such places, to record the failures of the untimely or unfortunate visitor—and takes his leave with many ceremonies and professions of regret.

Some two or three hours after, his walking destinies returned him into the same neighbourhood again, and again the quiet image of the fireside circle at M.'s—Mrs. M. presiding at it like a Queen Lar, with pretty A. S. at her side—striking irresistibly on his fancy, he makes another call (forgetting that they were "certainly not to return from the country before that day week"), and disappointed a second time, inquires for pen and paper as before: again the book is brought, and in the line just above that in which he is about to print his second name (his re-script)—his first name (scarce dry) looks out upon him like another Sosia, or as if a man should suddenly encounter his own duplicate! The effect may be conceived. D. made many a good resolution against any such lapses in future. I hope he will not keep them too rigorously.

For with G. D.—to be absent from the body is sometimes (not to speak it profanely) to be present with the Lord. At the very time when, personally encountering thee, he passes on with no recognition—or, being stopped, starts like a thing surprised—at that moment, reader, he is on Mount Tabor—or Parnassus—or co-sphered with Plato—or, with Harrington, framing "immortal commonwealths"—devising some plan of amelioration to thy country, or thy species—peradventure meditating some individual kindness or courtesy, to be done to *thee thyself*, the returning consciousness of which made him to start so guiltily at thy obtruded personal presence.

D. is delightful anywhere, but he is at the best in such places as these. He cares not much for Bath. He is out of his element at Buxton, at Scarborough, or Harrowgate. The Cam and the Isis are to him "better than all the waters of Damascus." On the Muses' hill he is happy, and good, as one of the Shepherds on the Delectable Mountains; and when he goes about with you

to show you the halls and colleges, you think you have
with you the Interpreter at the House Beautiful.

London Magazine, October 1820; *Elia*.

THE OLD MARGATE HOY

I AM fond of passing my vacations (I believe I have
said so before) at one or other of the Universities. Next
to these my choice would fix me at some woody spot,
such as the neighbourhood of Henley affords in abundance, on the banks of my beloved Thames. But somehow or other my cousin contrives to wheedle me, once
in three or four seasons, to a watering-place.

Old attachments cling to her in spite of experience.
We have been dull at Worthing one summer, duller at
Brighton another, dullest at Eastbourn a third, and are
at this moment doing dreary penance at—Hastings!—
and all because we were happy many years ago for a
brief week at Margate. That was our first seaside experiment, and many circumstances combined to make it the
most agreeable holiday of my life. We had neither of us
seen the sea, and we had never been from home so long
together in company.

Can I forget thee, thou old Margate Hoy, with thy
weatherbeaten, sunburnt captain, and his rough accom-
modations—ill exchanged for the foppery and fresh-
water niceness of the modern steam-packet? To the
winds and waves thou committedst thy goodly freight-
age, and didst ask no aid of magic fumes, and spells, and
boiling caldrons. With the gales of heaven thou wentest
swimmingly; or, when it was their pleasure, stoodest

still with sailor-like patience. Thy course was natural, not forced, as in a hot-bed; nor didst thou go poisoning the breath of ocean with sulphureous smoke—a great sea chimera, chimneying and furnacing the deep; or liker to that fire-god parching up Scamander.

Can I forget thy honest, yet slender crew, with their coy reluctant responses (yet to the suppression of anything like contempt) to the raw questions, which we of the great city would be ever and anon putting to them, as to the uses of this or that strange naval implement? 'Specially can I forget thee, thou happy medium, thou shade of refuge between us and them, conciliating interpreter of their skill to our simplicity, comfortable ambassador between sea and land!—whose sailor-trousers did not more convincingly assure thee to be an adopted denizen of the former, than thy white cap, and whiter apron over them, with thy neat-fingered practice in thy culinary vocation, bespoke thee to have been of inland nurture heretofore—a master cook of Eastcheap?

How busily didst thou ply thy multifarious occupation, cook, mariner, attendant, chamberlain: here, there, like another Ariel, flaming at once about all parts of the deck, yet with kindlier ministrations—not to assist the tempest, but, as if touched with a kindred sense of our infirmities, to soothe the qualms which that untried motion might haply raise in our crude land-fancies. And when the o'erwashing billows drove us below deck (for it was far gone in October, and we had stiff and blowing weather), how did thy officious ministerings, still catering for our comfort, with cards, and cordials, and thy more cordial conversation, alleviate the closeness and the confinement of thy else (truth to say) not very savoury, nor very inviting, little cabin!

With these additaments to boot, we had on board a fellow-passenger, whose discourse in verity might have beguiled a longer voyage than we meditated, and have made mirth and wonder abound as far as the Azores. He was a dark, Spanish-complexioned young man, remarkably handsome, with an officer-like assurance and an insuppressible volubility of assertion. He was, in fact, the greatest liar I had met with then, or since.

He was none of your hesitating, half-story-tellers (a most painful description of mortals) who go on sounding your belief, and only giving you as much as they see you can swallow at a time—the nibbling pickpockets of your patience—but one who committed downright, daylight depredations upon his neighbour's faith. He did not stand shivering upon the brink, but was a hearty, thorough-paced liar, and plunged at once into the depths of your credulity. I partly believe, he made pretty sure of his company.

Not many rich, not many wise, or learned, composed at that time the common stowage of a Margate packet. We were, I am afraid, a set of as unseasoned Londoners (let our enemies give it a worse name) as Aldermanbury, or Watling Street, at that time of day could have supplied. There might be an exception or two among us, but I scorn to make any invidious distinctions among such a jolly, companionable ship's company, as those were whom I sailed with.

Something too must be conceded to the *Genius Loci.* Had the confident fellow told us half the legends on land which he favoured us with on the other element, I flatter myself the good sense of most of us would have revolted. But we were in a new world, with everything unfamiliar about us, and the time and place disposed us to the reception of any prodigious marvel whatsoever.

Time has obliterated from my memory much of his wild fablings; and the rest would appear but dull, as written, and to be read on shore. He had been Aide-de-

camp (among other rare accidents and fortunes) to a
Persian Prince, and at one blow had stricken off the
head of the King of Carimania on horseback. He, of
course, married the Prince's daughter. I forget what unlucky turn in the politics of that court, combining with
the loss of his consort, was the reason of his quitting
Persia; but, with the rapidity of a magician, he transported himself, along with his hearers, back to England,
where we still found him in the confidence of great ladies.

There was some story of a princess—Elizabeth, if I
remember—having intrusted to his care an extraordinary casket of jewels, upon some extraordinary occasion
—but, as I am not certain of the name or circumstance
at this distance of time, I must leave it to the Royal
daughters of England to settle the honour among themselves in private. I cannot call to mind half his pleasant
wonders; but I perfectly remember, that in the course
of his travels he had seen a phœnix; and he obligingly
undeceived us of the vulgar error, that there is but one
of that species at a time, assuring us that they were not
uncommon in some parts of Upper Egypt.

Hitherto he had found the most implicit listeners. His
dreaming fancies had transported us beyond the "ignorant present." But when (still hardying more and
more in his triumphs over our simplicity) he went on to
affirm that he had actually sailed through the legs of
the Colossus at Rhodes, it really became necessary to
make a stand. And here I must do justice to the good
sense and intrepidity of one of our party, a youth,
that had hitherto been one of his most deferential auditors, who, from his recent reading, made bold to assure
the gentleman, that there must be some mistake, as "the
Colossus in question had been destroyed long since";
to whose opinion, delivered with all modesty, our hero

was obliging enough to concede thus much, that "the figure was indeed a little damaged."

This was the only opposition he met with, and it did not at all seem to stagger him, for he proceeded with his fables, which the same youth appeared to swallow with still more complacency than ever—confirmed, as it were, by the extreme candour of that concession. With these prodigies he wheedled us on till we came in sight of the Reculvers, which one of our own company (having been the voyage before) immediately recognizing, and pointing out to us, was considered by us as no ordinary seaman.

All this time sat upon the edge of the deck quite a different character. It was a lad, apparently very poor, very infirm, and very patient. His eye was ever on the sea, with a smile; and, if he caught now and then some snatches of these wild legends, it was by accident, and they seemed not to concern him. The waves to him whispered more pleasant stories. He was as one, being with us, but not of us. He heard the bell of dinner ring without stirring; and when some of us pulled out our private stores—our cold meat and our salads—he produced none, and seemed to want none. Only a solitary biscuit he had laid in; provision for the one or two days and nights, to which these vessels then were oftentimes obliged to prolong their voyage.

Upon a nearer acquaintance with him, which he seemed neither to court nor decline, we learned that he was going to Margate, with the hope of being admitted into the Infirmary there for sea-bathing. His disease was a scrofula, which appeared to have eaten all over him. He expressed great hopes of a cure; and when we asked him, whether he had any friends where he was going, he replied "he *had* no friends."

These pleasant, and some mournful passages, with the

first sight of the sea, co-operating with youth, and a sense of holidays, and out-of-door adventure, to me that had been pent up in populous cities for many months before—have left upon my mind the fragrance as of summer days gone by, bequeathing nothing but their remembrance for cold and wintry hours to chew upon.

Will it be thought a digression (it may spare some unwelcome comparisons), if I endeavour to account for the *dissatisfaction* which I have heard so many persons confess to have felt (as I did myself feel in part on this occasion), *at the sight of the sea for the first time?*

I think the reason usually given—referring to the incapacity of actual objects for satisfying our preconceptions of them—scarcely goes deep enough into the question. Let the same person see a lion, an elephant, a mountain for the first time in his life, and he shall perhaps feel himself a little mortified. The things do not fill up that space which the idea of them seemed to take up in his mind. But they have still a correspondency to his first notion, and in time grow up to it, so as to produce a very similar impression: enlarging themselves (if I may say so) upon familiarity. But the sea remains a disappointment.

Is it not, that in *the latter* we had expected to behold (absurdly, I grant, but, I am afraid, by the law of imagination, unavoidably) not a definite object, as those wild beasts, or that mountain compassable by the eye, but *all the sea at once*, THE COMMENSURATE ANTAGONIST OF THE EARTH? I do not say we tell ourselves so much, but the craving of the mind is to be satisfied with nothing less. I will suppose the case of a young person of fifteen (as I then was) knowing nothing of the sea, but from description. He comes to it for the first time— all that he has been reading of it all his life, and *that* the most enthusiastic part of life—all he has gathered from narratives of wandering seamen—what he has gained from true voyages, and what he cherishes as credulously from romance and poetry—crowding their images, and exacting strange tributes from expectation.

He thinks of the great deep, and of those who go down unto it; of its thousand isles, and of the vast continents it washes; of its receiving the mighty Plata, or Orellana, into its bosom, without disturbance, or sense of augmentation; of Biscay swells, and the mariner

> For many a day, and many a dreadful night,
> Incessant labouring round the stormy Cape;

of fatal rocks, and the "still-vexed Bermoothes"; of great whirlpools, and the water-spout; of sunken ships, and sumless treasures swallowed up in the unrestoring depths; of fishes and quaint monsters, to which all that is terrible on earth—

> Be but as buggs to frighten babes withal,
> Compared with the creatures in the sea's entral;

of naked savages, and Juan Fernandez; of pearls, and shells; of coral beds, and of enchanted isles; of mermaids' grots—

I do not assert that in sober earnest he expects to be shown all these wonders at once, but he is under the tyranny of a mighty faculty, which haunts him with confused hints and shadows of all these; and when the actual object opens first upon him, seen (in tame weather, too, most likely) from our unromantic coasts— a speck, a slip of sea-water, as it shows to him—what can it prove but a very unsatisfying and even diminutive entertainment? Or if he has come to it from the mouth of a river, was it much more than the river widening? and, even out of sight of land, what had he but a flat watery horizon about him, nothing comparable to the vast o'er-curtaining sky, his familiar object, seen daily without dread or amazement?

Who, in similar circumstances, has not been tempted to exclaim with Charoba, in the poem of Gebir,

Is this the mighty ocean? is this *all*?

I love town or country; but this detestable Cinque Port is neither. I hate these scrubbed shoots, thrusting out their starved foliage from between the horrid fissures of dusty innutritious rocks; which the amateur calls "verdure to the edge of the sea." I require woods, and they show me stunted coppices. I cry out for the water-brooks, and pant for fresh streams, and inland murmurs. I cannot stand all day on the naked beach, watching the capricious hues of the sea, shifting like the colours of a dying mullet. I am tired of looking out at the windows of this island-prison. I would fain retire into the interior of my cage.

While I gaze upon the sea, I want to be on it, over it, across it. It binds me in with chains, as of iron. My thoughts are abroad. I should not so feel in Staffordshire. There is no home for me here. There is no sense of home at Hastings. It is a place of fugitive resort, an heterogeneous assemblage of sea-mews and stock-brokers, Amphitrites of the town, and misses that coquet with the Ocean.

If it were what it was in its primitive shape, and what it ought to have remained, a fair, honest fishing-town, and no more, it were something—with a few straggling fishermen's huts scattered about, artless as its cliffs, and with their materials filched from them, it were something. I could abide to dwell with Meshech; to assort with fisher-swains, and smugglers.

There are, or I dream there are, many of this latter

occupation here. Their faces become the place. I like a
smuggler. He is the only honest thief. He robs nothing
but the revenue—an abstraction I never greatly cared
about. I could go out with them in their mackerel boats,
or about their less ostensible business, with some satisfaction.

I can even tolerate those poor victims to monotony,
who from day to day pace along the beach, in endless
progress and recurrence, to watch their illicit countrymen—townsfolk or brethren perchance—whistling to
the sheathing and unsheathing of their cutlasses (their
only solace), who, under the mild name of preventive
service, keep up a legitimated civil warfare in the de-
plorable absence of a foreign one, to show their detestation of run hollands, and zeal for Old England.

But it is the visitants from town, that come here to
say that they have been here, with no more relish of the
sea than a pond-perch or a dace might be supposed to
have, that are my aversion. I feel like a foolish dace in
these regions, and have as little toleration for myself
here as for them. What can they want here? if they had
a true relish of the ocean, why have they brought all
this land luggage with them? or why pitch their civilized
tents in the desert? What mean these scanty book-rooms
—marine libraries as they entitle them—if the sea were,
as they would have us believe, a book "to read strange
matter in"? what are their foolish concert-rooms, if
they come, as they would fain be thought to do, to listen
to the music of the waves? All is false and hollow pre-
tension.

They come, because it is the fashion, and to spoil the
nature of the place. They are, mostly, as I have said,
stock-brokers; but I have watched the better sort of
them—now and then, an honest citizen (of the old
stamp), in the simplicity of his heart, shall bring down

his wife and daughters, to taste the sea breezes. I always know the date of their arrival. It is easy to see it in their countenance. A day or two they go wandering on the shingles, picking up cockle-shells, and thinking them great things; but, in a poor week, imagination slackens: they begin to discover that cockles produce no pearls, and then—O then!—if I could interpret for the pretty creatures (I know they have not the courage to confess it themselves) how gladly would they exchange their seaside rambles for a Sunday walk on the green-sward of their accustomed Twickenham meadows!

I would ask of one of these sea-charmed emigrants, who think they truly love the sea, with its wild usages, what would their feelings be, if some of the unsophisticated aborigines of this place, encouraged by their courteous questionings here, should venture, on the faith of such assured sympathy between them, to return the visit, and come up to see—London. I must imagine them with their fishing-tackle on their back, as we carry our town necessaries. What a sensation would it cause in Lothbury? What vehement laughter would it not excite among

The daughters of Cheapside, and wives of Lombard Street!

I am sure that no town-bred or inland-born subjects can feel their true and natural nourishment at these sea-places. Nature, where she does not mean us for mariners and vagabonds, bids us stay at home. The salt foam seems to nourish a spleen. I am not half so good-natured as by the milder waters of my natural river. I would exchange these sea-gulls for swans, and scud a swallow for ever about the banks of Thamesis.

London Magazine, July 1823; Last Essays of Elia.

PART SIX

Books and Paintings

❖

DETACHED THOUGHTS
ON BOOKS AND READING

To mind the inside of a book is to entertain one's self with the forced product of another man's brain. Now I think a man of quality and breeding may be much amused with the natural sprouts of his own.

Lord Foppington, in *The Relapse*.

AN INGENIOUS acquaintance of my own was so much struck with this bright sally of his Lordship, that he has left off reading altogether, to the great improvement of his originality. At the hazard of losing some credit on this head, I must confess that I dedicate no inconsiderable portion of my time to other people's thoughts. I dream away my life in others' speculations. I love to lose myself in other men's minds. When I am not walking, I am reading; I cannot sit and think. Books think for me.

I have no repugnances. Shaftesbury is not too genteel for me, nor Jonathan Wild too low. I can read anything which I call *a book*. There are things in that shape which I cannot allow for such.

In this catalogue of *books which are no books—bib-*

lia a-biblia—I reckon Court Calendars, Directories, Pocket Books, Draught Boards, bound and lettered on the back, Scientific Treatises, Almanacs, Statutes at Large: the works of Hume, Gibbon, Robertson, Beattie, Soame Jenyns, and generally, all those volumes which "no gentleman's library should be without": the Histories of Flavius Josephus (that learned Jew), and Paley's Moral Philosophy. With these exceptions, I can read almost anything. I bless my stars for a taste so catholic, so unexcluding.

I confess that it moves my spleen to see these *things in books' clothing* perched upon shelves, like false saints, usurpers of true shrines, intruders into the sanctuary, thrusting out the legitimate occupants. To reach down a well-bound semblance of a volume, and hope it some kind-hearted play-book, then, opening what "seem its leaves," to come bolt upon a withering Population Essay. To expect a Steele or a Farquhar, and find—Adam Smith. To view a well-arranged assortment of block-headed Encyclopædias (Anglicanas or Metropolitanas) set out in an array of russia, or morocco, when a tithe of that good leather would comfortably reclothe my shivering folios—would renovate Paracelsus himself, and enable old Raymund Lully to look like himself again in the world. I never see these impostors, but I long to strip them, to warm my ragged veterans in their spoils.

To be strong-backed and neat-bound is the desideratum of a volume. Magnificence comes after. This, when it can be afforded, is not to be lavished upon all kinds of books indiscriminately. I would not dress a set of Magazines, for instance, in full suit. The dishabille, or half-binding (with russia backs ever) is *our* costume. A Shakspeare or a Milton (unless the first editions), it were mere foppery to trick out in gay apparel. The possession of them confers no distinction. The exterior of them (the things themselves being so common), strange to say, raises no sweet emotions, no tickling sense of property in the owner. Thomson's *Seasons,* again, looks best (I maintain it) a little torn and dog's-eared.

How beautiful to a genuine lover of reading are the sullied leaves, and worn-out appearance, nay, the very odour (beyond russia), if we would not forget kind feelings in fastidiousness, of an old "Circulating Library" *Tom Jones,* or *Vicar of Wakefield!* How they speak of the thousand thumbs that have turned over their pages with delight!—of the lone sempstress, whom they may have cheered (milliner, or harder-working mantua-maker) after her long day's needle-toil, running far into midnight, when she has snatched an hour, ill spared from sleep, to steep her cares, as in some Lethean cup, in spelling out their enchanting contents! Who would have them a whit less soiled? What better condition could we desire to see them in?

In some respects the better a book is, the less it demands from binding. Fielding, Smollett, Sterne, and all that class of perpetually self-reproductive volumes— Great Nature's Stereotypes—we see them individually perish with less regret, because we know the copies of them to be "eterne." But where a book is at once both good and rare—where the individual is almost the species, and when *that* perishes,

> We know not where is that Promethean torch
> That can its light relumine,

such a book, for instance, as the *Life of the Duke of Newcastle,* by his Duchess—no casket is rich enough, no casing sufficiently durable, to honour and keep safe such a jewel.

Not only rare volumes of this description, which

seem hopeless ever to be reprinted, but old editions of
writers, such as Sir Philip Sydney, Bishop Taylor, Milton in his prose works, Fuller—of whom we *have* reprints, yet the books themselves, though they go about,
and are talked of here and there, we know have not endenizened themselves (nor possibly ever will) in the
national heart, so as to become stock books—it is good
to possess these in durable and costly covers.

I do not care for a First Folio of Shakspeare. You cannot make a *pet* book of an author whom everybody
reads. I rather prefer the common editions of Rowe and
Tonson, without notes, and with *plates*, which, being so
execrably bad, serve as maps or modest remembrances,
to the text; and without pretending to any supposable
emulation with it, are so much better than the Shakspeare gallery *engravings*, which *did*. I have a community of feeling with my countrymen about his Plays, and
I like those editions of him best which have been oftenest tumbled about and handled.

On the contrary, I cannot read Beaumont and Fletcher
but in Folio. The Octavo editions are painful to look
at. I have no sympathy with them. If they were as much
read as the current editions of the other poet, I should
prefer them in that shape to the older one. I do not know
a more heartless sight than the reprint of the *Anatomy
of Melancholy*. What need was there of unearthing the
bones of that fantastic old great man, to expose them in
a winding-sheet of the newest fashion to modern censure? what hapless stationer could dream of Burton ever
becoming popular?

The wretched Malone could not do worse, when he
bribed the sexton of Stratford church to let him whitewash the painted effigy of old Shakspeare, which stood
there, in rude but lively fashion depicted, to the very
colour of the cheek, the eye, the eyebrow, hair, the

very dress he used to wear—the only authentic testi-
mony we had, however imperfect, of these curious parts
and parcels of him. They covered him over with a coat
of white paint. By ——, if I had been a justice of peace
for Warwickshire, I would have clapt both commentator and sexton fast in the stocks, for a pair of meddling
sacrilegious varlets.

I think I see them at their work—these sapient
trouble-tombs.

Shall I be thought fantastical if I confess that the
names of some of our poets sound sweeter, and have a
finer relish to the ear—to mine, at least—than that of
Milton or of Shakspeare? It may be that the latter are
more staled and rung upon in common discourse. The
sweetest names, and which carry a perfume in the mention, are, Kit Marlowe, Drayton, Drummond of Haw-
thornden, and Cowley.

Much depends upon *when* and *where* you read a
book. In the five or six impatient minutes, before the
dinner is quite ready, who would think of taking up *The
Faerie Queen* for a stop-gap, or a volume of Bishop An-
drewes' sermons?

Milton almost requires a solemn service of music to
be played before you enter upon him. But he brings
his music, to which, who listens, had need bring docile
thoughts, and purged ears.

Winter evenings—the world shut out—with less of
ceremony the gentle Shakspeare enters. At such a season
The Tempest, or his own *Winter's Tale*—

These two poets you cannot avoid reading aloud—to
yourself, or (as it chances) to some single person listening. More than one—and it degenerates into an audience.

Books of quick interest, that hurry on for incidents,
are for the eye to glide over only. It will not do to read

them out. I could never listen to even the better kind of modern novels without extreme irksomeness.

A newspaper, read out, is intolerable. In some of the Bank offices it is the custom (to save so much individual time) for one of the clerks—who is the best scholar —to commence upon the *Times* or the *Chronicle* and recite its entire contents aloud, *pro bono publico*. With every advantage of lungs and elocution, the effect is singularly vapid. In barbers' shops and public-houses a fellow will get up and spell out a paragraph, which he communicates as some discovery. Another follows with *his* selection. So the entire journal transpires at length by piecemeal. Seldom-readers are slow readers, and, without this expedient, no one in the company would probably ever travel through the contents of a whole paper.

Newspapers always excite curiosity. No one ever lays one down without a feeling of disappointment.

What an eternal time that gentleman in black, at Nando's, keeps the paper! I am sick of hearing the waiter bawling out incessantly, "The *Chronicle* is in hand, Sir."

Coming into an inn at night—having ordered your supper—what can be more delightful than to find lying in the window-seat, left there time out of mind by the carelessness of some former guest—two or three numbers of the old *Town and Country Magazine,* with its amusing *tête-à-tête* pictures—"The Royal Lover and Lady G——"; "The Melting Platonic and the Old Beau" —and such-like antiquated scandal? Would you exchange it—at that time, and in that place—for a better book?

Poor Tobin, who latterly fell blind, did not regret it so much for the weightier kinds of reading—the *Paradise Lost,* or *Comus,* he could have *read* to him—but he missed the pleasure of skimming over with his own eye a magazine, or a light pamphlet.

I should not care to be caught in the serious avenues of some cathedral alone, and reading *Candide*.

I do not remember a more whimsical surprise than having been once detected—by a familiar damsel—reclined at my ease upon the grass, on Primrose Hill (her Cythera), reading—*Pamela*. There was nothing in the book to make a man seriously ashamed at the exposure; but as she seated herself down by me, and seemed determined to read in company, I could have wished it had been—any other book. We read on very sociably for a few pages; and, not finding the author much to her taste, she got up, and—went away. Gentle casuist, I leave it to thee to conjecture, whether the blush (for there was one between us) was the property of the nymph or the swain in this dilemma. From me you shall never get the secret.

I am not much a friend to out-of-doors reading. I cannot settle my spirits to it. I knew a Unitarian minister, who was generally to be seen upon Snow Hill (as yet Skinner's Street *was not*), between the hours of ten and eleven in the morning, studying a volume of Lardner. I own this to have been a strain of abstraction beyond my reach. I used to admire how he sidled along, keeping clear of secular contacts. An illiterate encounter with a porter's knot, or a bread-basket, would have quickly put to flight all the theology I am master of, and have left me worse than indifferent to the five points.

There is a class of street-readers, whom I can never contemplate without affection—the poor gentry, who, not having wherewithal to buy or hire a book, filch a little learning at the open stalls—the owner, with his hard eye, casting envious looks at them all the while, and thinking when they will have done. Venturing tenderly, page after page, expecting every moment when he shall interpose his interdict, and yet unable to deny themselves the gratification, they "snatch a fearful joy."

Martin B., in this way, by daily fragments, got through two volumes of *Clarissa*, when the stall-keeper damped his laudable ambition, by asking him (it was in his younger days) whether he meant to purchase the work. M. declares, that under no circumstances in his life did he ever peruse a book with half the satisfaction which he took in those uneasy snatches. A quaint poetess of our day[1] has moralized upon this subject in two very touching but homely stanzas.

I saw a boy with eager eye
Open a book upon a stall,
And read, as he'd devour it all;
Which, when the stall-man did espy,
Soon to the boy I heard him call,
"You Sir, you never buy a book,
Therefore in one you shall not look."
The boy pass'd slowly on, and with a sigh
He wish'd he never had been taught to read,
Then of the old churl's books he should have had no need.

Of sufferings the poor have many,
Which never can the rich annoy:
I soon perceived another boy,
Who look'd as if he had not any
Food, for that day at least—enjoy
The sight of cold meat in a tavern larder.
This boy's case, then thought I, is surely harder,
Thus hungry, longing, thus without a penny,
Beholding choice of dainty-dressèd meat:
No wonder if he wish he ne'er had learn'd to eat.

London Magazine, July 1822; Last Essays of Elia.

[1] Mary Lamb, in *Poetry for Children.*—J. M. B.

READERS AGAINST THE GRAIN

NO ONE can pass through the streets, alleys, and blindest thoroughfares of this Metropolis, without surprise at the number of shops opened everywhere for the sale of cheap publications—not blasphemy and sedition—nor altogether flimsy periodicals, though the latter abound to a surfeit—but I mean fair reprints of good old books. Fielding, Smollett, the Poets, Historians, are daily becoming accessible to the purses of poor people.

I cannot behold this result from the enlargement of the reading public without congratulations to my country. But as every blessing has its wrong side, it is with aversion I behold springing up with this phenomenon a race of *Readers against the grain.* Young men who thirty years ago would have been play-goers, punch-drinkers, cricketers, etc. with one accord are now—readers!—a change in some respects, perhaps, salutary; but I liked the old way best.

Then people read because they liked reading. He must have been indigent indeed, and, as times went then, probably unable to enjoy a book, who from one little circulating library or another (those slandered benefactions to the public) could not pick out an odd volume to satisfy the intervals of the workshop and the desk. Then if a man told you that he "loved reading mightily, but had no books," you might be sure that in the first assertion at least he was mistaken. Neither had he, perhaps, the materials that should enliven a punch-bowl in his own cellar; but if the rogue loved his liquor, he would quickly find out where the arrack, the lemons, and the sugar dwelt—he would speedily find out the circulating shop for them.

I will illustrate this from my own observation. It may detract a little from the gentility of your columns when I tell your readers that I am—what I hinted at in my last —a Bank Clerk. Three and thirty years ago, when I took my first station at the desk, out of as many fellows in office one or two there were that had read a little. One could give a pretty good account of the *Spectator*. A second knew *Tom Jones*. A third recommended *Telemachus*. One went so far as to quote *Hudibras*, and was looked on as a phenomenon. But the far greater number neither cared for books, nor affected to care. They were, as I said, in their leisure hours, cricketers, punch-drinkers, playgoers, and the rest.

Times are altered now. We are all readers; our young men are split up into so many book-clubs, knots of literati; we criticize; we read the *Quarterly* and *Edinburgh*, I assure you; and instead of the old, honest, unpretending illiterature so becoming to our profession—we read and *judge* of every thing.

I have something to do in these book-clubs, and know the trick and mystery of it. Every new publication that is likely to make a noise, must be had at any rate. By some they are devoured with avidity. These would have been readers in the old time I speak of. The only loss is, that for the good old reading of Addison or Fielding's days is substituted that never-ending flow of thin novelties which are kept up like a ball, leaving no possible time for better things, and threatening in the issue to bury or sweep away from the earth the memory of their nobler predecessors.

We read to say that we have read. No reading can keep pace with the writing of this age, but we pant and toil after it as fast as we can. I smile to see an honest lad, who ought to be at trap-ball, laboring up hill against this giant load, taking his toil for a pleasure, and with that utter incapacity for reading which *betrays itself by a certain silent movement of the lips when the reader reads to himself,* undertaking the infinite contents of fugitive poetry, or travels, what not—to see them with their snail pace undertaking so vast a journey as might make faint a giant's speed; keeping a volume, which a real reader would get through in an hour, three, four, five, six days, and returning it with the last leaf but one folded down.

These are your readers against the grain, who yet *must* read or be thought nothing of—who, crawling through a book with tortoise-pace, go creeping to the next Review to learn what they shall say of it. Upon my soul, I pity the honest fellows mightily. The self-denials of virtue are nothing to the patience of these self tormentors.

If I hate one day before another, it is the accursed first day of the month, when a load of periodicals is ushered in and distributed to feed the reluctant monster. How it gapes and takes in its prescribed diet, as little savoury as that which Daniel ministered to that Apocryphal dragon, and not more wholesome! Is there no stopping the eternal wheels of the Press for a half century or two, till the nation recover its senses? Must we *magazine* it and *review* it at this sickening rate for ever? Shall we never again read to be *amused?* but to judge, to criticize, to talk about it and about it? Farewell, old honest delight taken in books not quite contemporary, before this plague-token of modern endless novelties broke out upon us—farewell to reading for its own sake!

Rather than follow in the train of this insatiable monster of modern reading, I would forswear my spectacles, play at put, mend pens, kill fleas, stand on one leg, shell peas, or do whatsoever ignoble diversion you shall put me to. Alas! I am hurried on in the vortex. I die of new books, or the everlasting talk about them. I faint of Longman's, I sicken of the Constables. Blackwood and Cadell have me by the throat.

I will go and relieve myself with a page of honest John Bunyan, or Tom Brown. Tom anybody will do, so long as they are not of this whiffling century.

Your Old-fashioned Correspondent,
LEPUS

The New Times, Jan. 13, 1825.

ON THE GENIUS AND CHARACTER
OF HOGARTH

WITH SOME REMARKS ON A PASSAGE
IN THE WRITINGS OF THE LATE MR. BARRY

ONE OF the earliest and noblest enjoyments I had when a boy, was in the contemplation of those capital prints by Hogarth, the Harlot's and Rake's Progresses, which, along with some others, hung upon the walls of a great hall in an old-fashioned house in ——shire, and seemed the solitary tenants (with myself) of that antiquated and life-deserted apartment.

Recollection of the manner in which those prints used to affect me has often made me wonder, when I have heard Hogarth described as a mere comic painter, as one of those whose chief ambition was to *raise a laugh*. To deny that there are throughout the prints which I have mentioned circumstances introduced of a laughable tendency, would be to run counter to the common notions of mankind; but to suppose that in their *ruling character* they appeal chiefly to the risible faculty, and not first and foremost to the very heart of man, its best and most serious feelings, would be to mistake no less grossly their aim and purpose. A set of severer Satires (for they are not so much Comedies, which they have been likened to, as they are strong and masculine Satires) less mingled with anything of mere fun, were never written upon paper, or graven upon copper. They resemble Juvenal, or the satiric touches in *Timon of Athens*.

I was pleased with the reply of a gentleman, who being asked which book he esteemed most in his library, answered—"Shakspeare": being asked which he esteemed next best, replied, "Hogarth." His graphic representations are indeed books: they have the teeming, fruitful, suggestive meaning of *words*. Other pictures we look at—his prints we read.

In pursuance of this parallel, I have sometimes entertained myself with comparing the *Timon of Athens* of Shakspeare (which I have just mentioned) and Hogarth's "Rake's Progress" together. The story, the moral, in both is nearly the same. The wild course of riot and extravagance, ending in the one with driving the Prodigal from the society of men into the solitude of the deserts, and in the other with conducting the Rake through his several stages of dissipation into the still more complete desolations of the madhouse, in the play and in the picture, are described with almost equal force and nature. The levee of the Rake, which forms the subject of the second plate in the series, is almost a transcript of Timon's levee in the opening scene of that play. We find a dedicating poet, and other similar characters, in both.

The concluding scene in the "Rake's Progress" is perhaps superior to the last scenes of *Timon*. If we seek for something of kindred excellence in poetry, it must be in

the scenes of Lear's beginning madness, where the King
and the Fool and the Tom-o'-Bedlam conspire to produce
such a medley of mirth checked by misery, and misery
rebuked by mirth; where the society of those "strange
bedfellows" which misfortunes have brought Lear acquainted with, so finely sets forth the destitute state of
the monarch; while the lunatic bans of the one, and the
disjointed sayings and wild but pregnant allusions of the
other, so wonderfully sympathize with that confusion,
which they seem to assist in the production of, in the
senses of that "child-changed father."

In the scene in Bedlam, which terminates the "Rake's
Progress," we find the same assortment of the ludicrous
with the terrible. Here is desperate madness, the over-
turning of originally strong thinking faculties, at which
we shudder, as we contemplate the duration and pressure of affliction which it must have asked to destroy
such a building; and here is the gradual hurtless lapse
into idiocy, of faculties, which at their best of times
never having been strong, we look upon the consummation of their decay with no more of pity than is consistent with a smile. The mad tailor, the poor driveller that
has gone out of his wits (and truly he appears to have
had no great journey to go to get past their confines) for
the love of Charming Betty Careless—these half-laugh-
able, scarce-pitiable objects, take off from the horror
which the principal figure would of itself raise, at the
same time that they assist the feeling of the scene by
contributing to the general notion of its subject:

> Madness, thou chaos of the brain,
> What art, that pleasure giv'st and pain?
> Tyranny of Fancy's reign!
> Mechanic Fancy, that can build
> Vast labyrinths and mazes wild,
> With rule disjointed, shapeless measure,

Fill'd with horror, fill'd with pleasure!
Shapes of horror, that would even
Cast doubts of mercy upon heaven;
Shapes of pleasure, that but seen,
Would split the shaking sides of Spleen.[1]

Is it carrying the spirit of comparison to excess to remark, that in the poor kneeling weeping female who accompanies her seducer in his sad decay, there is something analogous to Kent, or Caius, as he delights rather
to be called, in Lear—the noblest pattern of virtue
which even Shakspeare has conceived—who follows his
royal master in banishment, that had pronounced *his*
banishment, and, forgetful at once of his wrongs and
dignities, taking on himself the disguise of a menial, retains his fidelity to the figure, his loyalty to the carcass,
the shadow, the shell and empty husk of Lear?

In the perusal of a book, or of a picture, much of the
impression which we receive depends upon the habit of
mind which we bring with us to such perusal. The same
circumstance may make one person laugh, which shall
render another very serious; or in the same person the
first impression may be corrected by after-thought. The
misemployed incongruous characters at the "Harlot's
Funeral," on a superficial inspection, provoke to laughter; but when we have sacrificed the first emotion to
levity a very different frame of mind succeeds, or the
painter has lost half his purpose. I never look at that
wonderful assemblage of depraved beings, who, without
a grain of reverence or pity in their perverted minds, are
performing the sacred exteriors of duty to the relics of
their departed partner in folly, but I am as much moved
to sympathy from the very want of it in them, as I
should be by the finest representation of a virtuous
death-bed surrounded by real mourners, pious children,

[1] Lines inscribed under the plate.—C. L.

weeping friends—perhaps more by the very contrast. What reflections does it not awake, of the dreadful heartless state in which the creature (a female too) must have lived, who in death wants the accompaniment of one genuine tear. That wretch who is removing the lid of the coffin to gaze upon the corpse with a face which indicates a perfect negation of all goodness or womanhood —the hypocrite parson and his demure partner—all the fiendish group—to a thoughtful mind present a moral emblem more affecting than if the poor friendless carcass had been depicted as thrown out to the woods, where wolves had assisted at its obsequies, itself furnishing forth its own funeral banquet.

It is easy to laugh at such incongruities as are met together in this picture—incongruous objects being of the very essence of laughter—but surely the laugh is far different in its kind from that thoughtless species to which we are moved by mere farce and grotesque. We laugh when Ferdinand Count Fathom, at the first sight of the white cliffs of Britain, feels his heart yearn with filial fondness towards the land of his progenitors, which he is coming to fleece and plunder—we smile at the exquisite irony of the passage—but if we are not led on by such passages to some more salutary feeling than laughter, we are very negligent perusers of them in book or picture.

It is the fashion with those who cry up the great Historical School in this country, at the head of which Sir Joshua Reynolds is placed, to exclude Hogarth from that school, as an artist of an inferior and vulgar class. Those persons seem to me to confound the painting of subjects in common or vulgar life with the being a vulgar artist. The quantity of thought which Hogarth crowds into every picture would alone *unvulgarize* every subject which he might choose. Let us take the lowest of his

subjects, the print called "Gin Lane." Here is plenty of
poverty and low stuff to disgust upon a superficial view;
and accordingly a cold spectator feels himself immediately disgusted and repelled. I have seen many turn
away from it, not being able to bear it. The same persons
would perhaps have looked with great complacency
upon Poussin's celebrated picture of the "Plague at
Athens." [1]

Disease and Death and bewildering Terror, in *Athe-
nian garments,* are endurable, and come, as the delicate critics express it, within the "limits of pleasurable
sensation." But the scenes of their own St. Giles's, delin-
eated by their own countryman, are too shocking to
think of. Yet if we could abstract our minds from the
fascinating colours of the picture, and forget the coarse
execution (in some respects) of the print, intended as it
was to be a cheap plate, accessible to the poorer sort of
people, for whose instruction it was done, I think we
could have no hesitation in conferring the palm of superior genius upon Hogarth, comparing this work of his
with Poussin's picture. There is more of imagination in it
—that power which draws all things to one—which
makes things animate and inanimate, beings with their
attributes, subjects, and their accessories, take one colour and serve to one effect. Everything in the print, to
use a vulgar expression, *tells.* Every part is full of
"strange images of death." It is perfectly amazing and as-
tounding to look at.

Not only the two prominent figures, the woman and
the half-dead man, which are as terrible as anything
which Michelangelo ever drew, but everything else in
the print, contributes to bewilder and stupefy—the very
houses, as I heard a friend of mine express it, tumbling

[1] At the late Mr. Hope's in Cavendish Square.—C. L.

all about in various directions, seem drunk—seem absolutely reeling from the effect of that diabolical spirit of frenzy which goes forth over the whole composition. To show the poetical and almost prophetical conception in the artist, one little circumstance may serve. Not content with the dying and dead figures, which he has strewed in profusion over the proper scene of the action, he shows you what (of a kindred nature) is passing beyond it.

Close by the shell, in which, by direction of the parish beadle, a man is depositing his wife, is an old wall, which, partaking of the universal decay around it, is tumbling to pieces. Through a gap in this wall are seen three figures, which appear to make a part in some funeral procession which is passing by on the other side of the wall, out of the sphere of the composition. This extending of the interest beyond the bounds of the subject could only have been conceived by a great genius. Shakspeare, in his description of the painting of the Trojan War, in his "Tarquin and Lucrece," has introduced a similar device, where the painter made a part stand for the whole:

> For much imaginary work was there,
> Conceit deceitful, so compact, so kind,
> That for Achilles' image stood his spear,
> Grip'd in an armed hand; himself behind
> Was left unseen, save to the eye of mind:
> A hand, a foot, a face, a leg, a head,
> Stood for the whole to be imagined.

This he well calls *imaginary work,* where the spectator must meet the artist in his conceptions halfway; and it is peculiar to the confidence of high genius alone to trust so much to spectators or readers. Lesser artists show everything distinct and full, as they require an object to

be made out to themselves before they can comprehend it.

When I think of the power displayed in this (I will not hesitate to say) sublime print, it seems to me the extreme narrowness of system alone, and of that rage for classification, by which, in matters of taste at least, we are perpetually perplexing, instead of arranging, our ideas, that would make us concede to the work of Poussin above mentioned, and deny to this of Hogarth, the name of a grand serious composition.

We are for ever deceiving ourselves with names and theories. We call one man a great historical painter, because he has taken for his subjects kings or great men, or transactions over which time has thrown a grandeur. We term another the painter of common life, and set him down in our minds for an artist of an inferior class, without reflecting whether the quantity of thought shown by the latter may not much more than level the distinction which their mere choice of subjects may seem to place between them; or whether, in fact, from that very common life a great artist may not extract as deep an interest as another man from that which we are pleased to call history.

I entertain the highest respect for the talents and virtues of Reynolds, but I do not like that his reputation should overshadow and stifle the merits of such a man as Hogarth, nor that to mere names and classifications we should be content to sacrifice one of the greatest ornaments of England.

I would ask the most enthusiastic admirer of Reynolds, whether in the countenances of his "Staring and Grinning Despair," which he has given us for the faces of Ugolino and dying Beaufort, there be anything comparable to the expression which Hogarth has put into the

face of his broken-down rake in the last plate but one of the "Rake's Progress," [1] where a letter from the manager is brought to him to say that his play "will not do"? Here all is easy, natural, undistorted, but withal what a mass of woe is here accumulated!—the long history of a mis-spent life is compressed into the countenance as plainly as the series of plates before had told it; here is no at-tempt at Gorgonian looks, which are to freeze the be-holder—no grinning at the antique bedposts—no face-making, or consciousness of the presence of spectators in or out of the picture, but grief kept to a man's self, a face retiring from notice with the shame which great an-guish sometimes brings with it—a final leave taken of hope—the coming on of vacancy and stupefaction—a beginning alienation of mind looking like tranquillity. Here is matter for the mind of the beholder to feed on for the hour together—matter to feed and fertilize the mind. It is too real to admit one thought about the power of the artist who did it.

When we compare the expression in subjects which so fairly admit of comparison, and find the superiority so clearly to remain with Hogarth, shall the mere contempt-ible difference of the scene of it being laid, in the one case, in our Fleet or King's Bench Prison, and, in the other, in the State Prison of Pisa, or the bedroom of a cardinal—or that the subject of the one has never been authenticated, and the other is matter of history—so weigh down the real points of the comparison, as to induce us to rank the artist who has chosen the one scene or subject (though confessedly inferior in that which constitutes the soul of his art) in a class from which we

[1] The first perhaps in all Hogarth for serious expression. That which comes next to it, I think, is the jaded morning countenance of the debauchee in the second plate of the "Marriage Alamode." which lectures on the vanity of pleasure as audibly as anything in Ecclesiastes.—C. L.

exclude the better genius (who has happened to make choice of the other) with something like disgrace?[1]

"The Boys under Demoniacal Possession" of Raphael and Domenichino, by what law of classification are we bound to assign them to belong to the great style in painting, and to degrade into an inferior class the Rake of Hogarth when he is the Madman in the Bedlam scene? I am sure he is far more impressive than either. It is a face which no one that has seen can easily forget. There is the stretch of human suffering to the utmost endurance, severe bodily pain brought on by strong mental agony, the frightful obstinate laugh of madness—yet all so unforced and natural, that those who never were witness to madness in real life, think they see nothing but what is familiar ˎ ˎhem in this face. Here are no tricks of distortion, nothinˎ ˎt the natural face of agony. This is high tragic painting, ˎ d we might as well deny to Shakspeare the honours oˎ ˎeat tragedian, because he has interwoven scenes of mirth with the serious business of his plays, as refuse to Hogarth the same praise for

---

[1] Sir Joshua Reynolds, somewhere in his Lectures, speaks of the presumption of Hogarth in attempting the grand style in painting, by which he means his choice of certain Scripture subjects. Hogarth's excursions into Holy Land were not very numerous, but what he has left us in this kind have at least this merit, that they have expression of some sort or other in them—the "Child Moses before Pharaoh's Daughter," for instance: which is more than can be said of Sir Joshua Reynolds's "Repose in Egypt," painted for Macklin's Bible, where for a Madonna he has substituted a sleepy, insensible, unmotherly girl, one so little worthy to have been selected as the Mother of the Saviour, that she seems to have neither heart nor feeling to entitle her to become a mother at all. But indeed the race of Virgin Mary painters seems to have been cut up, root and branch, at the Reformation. Our artists are too good Protestants to give life to that admirable commixture of maternal tenderness with reverential awe and wonder approaching to worship, with which the Virgin Mothers of L. da Vinci and Raphael (themselves by their divine countenances inviting men to worship) contemplate the union of the two natures in the person of their Heaven-born Infant.—C. L.

the two concluding scenes of the "Rake's Progress," be-cause of the Comic Lunatics[1] which he has thrown into the one, or the Alchymist that he has introduced in the other, who is paddling in the coals of his furnace, keep-ing alive the flames of vain hope within the very walls of the prison to which the vanity has conducted him, which have taught the darker lesson of extinguished hope to the desponding figure who is the principal per-son of the scene.

It is the force of these kindly admixtures which as-similates the scenes of Hogarth and of Shakspeare to the drama of real life, where no such thing as pure tragedy is to be found; but merriment and infelicity, ponderous crime and feather-light vanity, like twi-formed births, disagreeing complexions of one intertexture, perpetually unite to show forth motley spectacles to the world. Then it is that the poet or painter shows his art, when in the selection of these comic adjuncts he chooses such cir-cumstances as shall relieve, contrast with, or fall into, without forming a violent opposition to his principal ob-ject. Who sees not that the Grave-digger in *Hamlet*, the Fool in *Lear*, have a kind of correspondency to, and fall in with, the subjects which they seem to interrupt: while the comic stuff in *Venice Preserved*, and the dog-gerel nonsense of the Cook and his poisoning associates in the *Rollo* of Beaumont and Fletcher, are pure, irrele-vant, impertinent discords—as bad as the quarrelling

---

[1] There are of madmen, as there are of tame,
All humour'd not alike. We have here some
So apish and fantastic, play with a feather;
And though 'twould grieve a soul to see God's image
So blemish'd and defac'd, yet do they act
Such antick and such pretty lunacies,
That, spite of sorrow, they will make you smile.
Others again we have, like angry lions,
Fierce as wild bulls, untameable as flies.
—*Honest Whore.*—C. L.

dog and cat under the table of the "Lord and the Disciples at Emmaus" of Titian?

Not to tire the reader with perpetual reference to prints which he may not be fortunate enough to possess, it may be sufficient to remark, that the same tragic cast of expression and incident, blended in some instances with a greater alloy of comedy, characterizes his other great work, the "Marriage Alamode," as well as those less elaborate exertions of his genius, the prints called "Industry and Idleness," the "Distrest Poet," etc., forming, with the Harlot's and Rake's Progresses, the most considerable if not the largest class of his productions— enough surely to rescue Hogarth from the imputation of being a mere buffoon, or one whose general aim was only to *shake the sides*.

There remains a very numerous class of his performances, the object of which must be confessed to be principally comic. But in all of them will be found something to distinguish them from the droll productions of Bunbury and others. They have this difference, that we do not merely laugh at, we are led into long trains of reflection by them. In this respect they resemble the characters of Chaucer's Pilgrims, which have strokes of humour in them enough to designate them for the most part as comic, but our strongest feeling still is wonder at the comprehensiveness of genius which could crowd, as poet and painter have done, into one small canvas so many diverse yet co-operating materials.

The faces of Hogarth have not a mere momentary interest, as in caricatures, or those grotesque physiognomies which we sometimes catch a glance of in the street, and, struck with their whimsicality, wish for a pencil and the power to sketch them down; and forget them again as rapidly—but they are permanent abiding ideas. Not the sports of nature, but her necessary eternal classes.

We feel that we cannot part with any of them, lest a link should be broken.

It is worthy of observation, that he has seldom drawn a mean or insignificant countenance.[1] Hogarth's mind was eminently reflective; and, as it has been well observed of Shakspeare, that he has transfused his own poetical character into the persons of his drama (they are all more or less *poets*) Hogarth has impressed a *thinking character* upon the persons of his canvas. This remark must not be taken universally. The exquisite idiotism of the little gentleman in the bag and sword beating his drum in the print of the "Enraged Musician," would of itself rise up against so sweeping an assertion. But I think it will be found to be true of the generality of his countenances. The knife-grinder and Jew flute-player in the plate just mentioned, may serve as instances instead of a thousand. They have intense thinking faces, though the purpose to which they are subservient by no means required it; but indeed it seems as if it was painful to Hogarth to contemplate mere vacancy or insignificance.

This reflection of the artist's own intellect from the faces of his characters, is one reason why the works of Hogarth, so much more than those of any other artist, are objects of meditation. Our intellectual natures love the mirror which gives them back their own likenesses. The mental eye will not bend long with delight upon vacancy.

Another line of eternal separation between Hogarth and the common painters of droll or burlesque subjects,

---

[1] If there are any of that description, they are in his "Strolling Players," a print which has been cried up by Lord Orford as the richest of his productions, and it may be, for what I know, in the mere lumber, the properties, and dead furniture of the scene, but in living character and expression it is (for Hogarth) lamentably poor and wanting; it is perhaps the only one of his performances at which we have a right to feel disgusted.—C. L.

with whom he is often confounded, is the sense of beauty, which in the most unpromising subjects seems never wholly to have deserted him. "Hogarth himself," says Mr. Coleridge,[1] from whom I have borrowed this observation, speaking of a scene which took place at Ratzeburg, "never drew a more ludicrous distortion, both of attitude and physiognomy, than this effect occasioned: nor was there wanting beside it one of those beautiful female faces which the same Hogarth, *in whom the satirist never extinguished that love of beauty which belonged to him as a poet,* so often and so gladly introduces as the central figure in a crowd of humorous deformities, which figure (such is the power of true genius) neither acts nor is meant to act as a contrast; but diffuses through all and over each of the group a spirit of reconciliation and human kindness; and even when the attention is no longer consciously directed to the cause of this feeling, still blends its tenderness with our laughter: and *thus prevents the instructive merriment at the whims of nature, or the foibles or humours of our fellow-men, from degenerating into the heart-poison of contempt or hatred.*"

To the beautiful females in Hogarth, which Mr. C. has pointed out, might be added, the frequent introduction of children (which Hogarth seems to have taken a particular delight in) into his pieces. They have a singular effect in giving tranquillity and a portion of their own innocence to the subject. The baby riding in its mother's lap in the "March to Finchley" (its careless innocent face placed directly behind the intriguing time-furrowed countenance of the treason-plotting French priest), perfectly sobers the whole of that tumultuous scene. The boy mourner winding up his top with so much unpretending insensibility in the plate of the "Harlot's Fu-

[1] *The Friend,* No. XVI.—C. L.

neral" (the only thing in that assembly that is not a hypocrite), quiets and soothes the mind that has been disturbed at the sight of so much depraved man and woman kind.

I had written thus far, when I met with a passage in the writings of the late Mr. Barry, which, as it falls in with the *vulgar notion* respecting Hogarth, which this Essay has been employed in combating, I shall take the liberty to transcribe, with such remarks as may suggest themselves to me in the transcription; referring the reader for a full answer to that which has gone before.

"Notwithstanding Hogarth's merit does undoubtedly entitle him to an honourable place among the artists, and that his little compositions, considered as so many dramatic representations, abounding with humour, character, and extensive observations on the various incidents of low, faulty, and vicious life, are very ingeniously brought together, and frequently tell their own story with more facility than is often found in many of the elevated and more noble inventions of Raphael and other great men; yet it must be honestly confessed, that in what is called knowledge of the figure, foreigners have justly observed, that Hogarth is often so raw and unformed, as hardly to deserve the name of an artist. But this capital defect is not often perceivable, as examples of the naked and of elevated nature but rarely occur in his subjects, which are for the most part filled with characters that in their nature tend to deformity; besides his figures are small, and the jonctures, and other difficulties of drawing that might occur in their limbs, are artfully concealed with their clothes, rags, etc. But what would atone for all his defects, even if they were twice told, is his admirable fund of invention, ever inexhaustible in its resources; and his satire. which is always sharp and pertinent, and often highly moral, was (except in a few instances, where he weakly and meanly suffered his integrity to give way to his envy) seldom or never employed in a dishonest or unmanly way. Hogarth has been often imitated in his satirical vein, sometimes in his humorous: but very few have attempted to rival him in his moral walk.

"The line of art pursued by my very ingenious predecessor and brother Academician, Mr. Penny, is quite distinct from that of Hogarth, and is of a much more delicate and superior relish; he attempts the heart, and reaches it, whilst Hogarth's general aim is only to shake the sides; in other respects no comparison can be thought of, as Mr. Penny has all that knowledge of the figure and academical skill which the other wanted. As to Mr. Bunbury, who had so happily succeeded in the vein of humour and caricatura, he has for some time past altogether relinquished it, for the more amiable pursuit of beautiful nature: this, indeed, is not to be wondered at, when we recollect that he has, in Mrs. Bunbury, so admirable an exemplar of the most finished grace and beauty continually at his elbow. But (to say all that occurs to me on this subject) perhaps it may be reasonably doubted, whether the being much conversant with Hogarth's method of exposing meanness, deformity, and vice, in many of his works, is not rather a dangerous, or, at least, a worthless pursuit; which, if it does not find a false relish and a love of and search after satire and buffoonery in the spectator, is at least not unlikely to give him one. Life is short; and the little leisure of it is much better laid out upon that species of art which is employed about the amiable and the admirable, as it is more likely to be attended with better and nobler consequences to ourselves. These two pursuits in art may be compared with two sets of people with whom we might associate:

if we give ourselves up to the Footes, the Kenricks, etc., we shall be continually busied and paddling in whatever is ridiculous, faulty, and vicious in life; whereas there are those to be found with whom we should be in the constant pursuit and study of all that gives a value and a dignity to human nature." [1]

". . . it must be honestly confessed, that in what is called knowledge of the figure, foreigners have justly observed," etc.

It is a secret well known to the professors of the art and mystery of criticism, to insist upon what they do not find in a man's works, and to pass over in silence what they do. That Hogarth did not draw the naked figure so well as Michael Angelo might be allowed, especially as "examples of the naked," as Mr. Barry acknowledges, "rarely"—he might almost have said never—"occur in his subjects"; and that his figures under their draperies do not discover all the fine graces of an Antinoüs or an Apollo, may be conceded likewise; perhaps it was more suitable to his purpose to represent the average forms of mankind in the mediocrity (as Mr. Burke expresses it) of the age in which he lived: but that his figures in general, and in his best subjects, are so glaringly incorrect as is here insinuated, I dare trust my own eye so far as positively to deny the fact. And there is one part of the figure in which Hogarth is allowed to have excelled, which these foreigners seem to have overlooked, or perhaps calculating from its proportion to the whole (a seventh or an eighth, I forget which), deemed it of trifling importance; I mean the human face; a small part,

[1] Account of a Series of Pictures in the Great Room of the Society of Arts, Manufactures, and Commerce, at the Adelphi, by James Barry, R.A., Professor of Painting to the Royal Academy; reprinted in the last quarto edition of his works.—C. L.

reckoning by geographical inches, in the map of man's body, but here it is that the painter of expression must condense the wonders of his skill, even at the expense of neglecting the "jonctures and other difficulties of drawing in the limbs," which it must be a cold eye that, in the interest so strongly demanded by Hogarth's countenances, has leisure to survey and censure.

"The line of art pursued by my very ingenious predecessor and brother Academician, Mr. Penny."

The first impression caused in me by reading this passage was an eager desire to know who this Mr. Penny was. This great surpasser of Hogarth in the "delicacy of his relish," and the "line which he pursued," where is he, what are his works, what has he to show? In vain I tried to recollect, till by happily putting the question to a friend who is more conversant in the works of the illustrious obscure than myself, I learnt that he was the painter of a "Death of Wolfe" which missed the prize the year that the celebrated picture of West on the same subject obtained it; that he also made a picture of the "Marquis of Granby relieving a Sick Soldier"; moreover, that he was the inventor of two pictures of "Suspended and Restored Animation," which I now remember to have seen in the Exhibition some years since, and the prints from which are still extant in good men's houses. This then, I suppose, is the line of subjects in which Mr. Penny was so much superior to Hogarth. I confess I am not of that opinion. The relieving of poverty by the purse, and the restoring a young man to his parents by using the methods prescribed by the Humane Society, are doubtless very amiable subjects, pretty things to teach the first rudiments of humanity; they amount to about as much instruction as the stories of good boys that give away their custards to poor beggar-boys in

children's books. But, good God! is this *milk for babes*
to be set up in opposition to Hogarth's moral scenes, his
strong meat for men? As well might we prefer the ful-
some verses upon their own goodness to which the gentlemen of the Literary Fund annually sit still with such
shameless patience to listen, to the satires of Juvenal and
Persius; because the former are full of tender images of
Worth relieved by Charity, and Charity stretching out
her hand to rescue sinking Genius, and the theme of the
latter is men's crimes and follies with their black consequences—forgetful meanwhile of those strains of moral
pathos, those sublime heart-touches, which these poets
(in *them* chiefly showing themselves poets) are perpetually darting across the otherwise appalling gloom of their
subject—consolatory remembrancers, when their pictures of guilty mankind have made us even to despair for
our species, that there is such a thing as virtue and moral
dignity in the world, that her unquenchable spark is not
utterly out—refreshing admonitions, to which we turn
for shelter from the too great heat and asperity of the
general satire.

And is there nothing analogous to this in Hogarth?
nothing which "attempts and reaches the heart"?—no
aim beyond that of "shaking the sides"? If the kneeling
ministering female in the last scene of the "Rake's Progress," the Bedlam scene, of which I have spoken before, and have dared almost to parallel it with the most
absolute idea of Virtue which Shakspeare has left us, be
not enough to disprove the assertion; if the sad endings
of the Harlot and the Rake, the passionate heart-bleed-
ing entreaties for forgiveness which the adulterous wife
is pouring forth to her assassinated and dying lord in the
last scene but one of the "Marriage Alamode"—if these
be not things to touch the heart, and dispose the mind
to a meditative tenderness: is there nothing sweetly

conciliatory in the mild patient face and gesture with which the wife seems to allay and ventilate the feverish irritated feelings of her poor poverty-distracted mate (the true copy of the *genus irritabile*) in the print of the "Distrest Poet"? or if an image of maternal love be required, where shall we find a sublimer view of it than in that aged woman in "Industry and Idleness" (Plate V) who is clinging with the fondness of hope not quite extinguished to her brutal vice-hardened child, whom she is accompanying to the ship which is to bear him away from his native soil, of which he has been adjudged unworthy: in whose shocking face every trace of the human countenance seems obliterated, and a brute beast's to be left instead, shocking and repulsive to all but her who watched over it in its cradle before it was so sadly altered, and feels it must belong to her while a pulse by the vindictive laws of his country shall be suffered to continue to beat in it. Compared with such things, what is Mr. Penny's "knowledge of the figure and academical skill which Hogarth wanted"?

With respect to what follows concerning another gentleman, with the congratulations to him on his escape out of the regions of "humour and caricatura," in which it appears he was in danger of travelling side by side with Hogarth, I can only congratulate my country, that Mrs. Hogarth knew *her* province better than, by disturbing her husband at his palette, to divert him from that universality of subject, which has stamped him perhaps, next to Shakspeare, the most inventive genius which this island has produced, into the "amiable pursuit of beautiful nature," *i.e.*, copying *ad infinitum* the individual charms and graces of Mrs. H.

"Hogarth's method of exposing meanness, deformity, and vice, paddling in whatever is ridiculous, faulty, and vicious."

A person unacquainted with the works thus stigmatized would be apt to imagine that in Hogarth there was
nothing else to be found but subjects of the coarsest
and most repulsive nature. That his imagination was
naturally unsweet, and that he delighted in raking into
every species of moral filth. That he preyed upon sore
places only, and took a pleasure in exposing the unsound
and rotten parts of human nature: whereas, with the
exception of some of the plates of the "Harlot's Progress," which are harder in their character than any of
the rest of his productions (the "Stages of Cruelty" I
omit as mere worthless caricaturas, foreign to his general
habits, the offspring of his fancy in some wayward humour), there is scarce one of his pieces where vice is
most strongly satirized, in which some figure is not introduced upon which the moral eye may rest satisfied;
a face that indicates goodness, or perhaps mere good-
humouredness and carelessness of mind (negation of
evil) only, yet enough to give a relaxation to the frowning brow of satire, and keep the general air from taint-
ing.

Take the mild, supplicating posture of patient Poverty
in the poor woman that is persuading the pawnbroker
to accept her clothes in pledge, in the plate of "Gin
Lane," for an instance. A little does it, a little of the
good nature overpowers a world of *bad*. One cordial
honest laugh of a Tom Jones absolutely clears the atmosphere that was reeking with the black putrefying
breathings of a hypocrite Blifil. One homely expostulating shrug from Strap warms the whole air which the
suggestions of a gentlemanly ingratitude from his friend
Random had begun to freeze. One "Lord bless us!" of
Parson Adams upon the wickedness of the time, exor-
cises and purges off the mass of iniquity which the
world-knowledge of even a Fielding could cull out and

rake together. But of the severer class of Hogarth's
performances, enough, I trust, has been said to show
that they do not merely shock and repulse; that there
is in them the "scorn of vice" and the "pity" too; something to touch the heart, and keep alive the sense of
moral beauty; the "*lacrymæ rerum*," and the sorrowing
by which the heart is made better. If they be bad things,
then is satire and tragedy a bad thing; let us proclaim at
once an age of gold, and sink the existence of vice and
misery in our speculations: let us

> —— wink, and shut our apprehensions up
> From common sense of what men were and are:

let us *make believe* with the children, that everybody
is good and happy; and, with Dr. Swift, write panegyrics
upon the world.

But that larger half of Hogarth's works, which were
painted more for entertainment than instruction (though
such was the suggestiveness of his mind that there is
always something to be learnt from them), his humorous scenes—are they such as merely to disgust and
set us against our species?

The confident assertions of such a man as I consider
the late Mr. Barry to have been, have that weight of
authority in them which staggers at first hearing, even
a long preconceived opinion. When I read his pathetic
admonition concerning the shortness of life, and how
much better the little leisure of it were laid out upon
"that species of art which is employed about the amiable and the admirable"; and Hogarth's "method," proscribed as a "dangerous or worthless pursuit," I began to
think there was something in it; that I might have been
indulging all my life a passion for the works of this artist,
to the utter prejudice of my taste and moral sense; but
my first convictions gradually returned, a world of good-

natured English faces came up one by one to my recollection, and a glance at the matchless "Election Entertainment," which I have the happiness to have hanging up in my parlour, subverted Mr. Barry's whole
theory in an instant.

In that inimitable print (which in my judgment as
far exceeds the more known and celebrated "March to
Finchley," as the best comedy exceeds the best farce
that ever was written), let a person look till he be
saturated, and when he has done wondering at the in-
ventiveness of genius which could bring so many characters (more than thirty distinct classes of face) into a
room and set them down at table together, or otherwise
dispose them about, in so natural a manner, engage
them in so many easy sets and occupations, yet all partaking of the spirit of the occasion which brought them
together, so that we feel that nothing but an election
time could have assembled them; having no central
figure or principal group (for the hero of the piece, the
Candidate, is properly set aside in the levelling indistinction of the day, one must look for him to find him),
nothing to detain the eye from passing from part to part,
where every part is alike instinct with life—for here are
no furniture-faces, no figures brought in to fill up the
scene like stage choruses, but all *dramatis personæ:*
when he shall have done wondering at all these faces so
strongly charactered, yet finished with the accuracy of
the finest miniature; when he shall have done admiring
the numberless appendages of the scene, those gratui-
tous doles which rich genius flings into the heap when
it has already done enough, the over-measure which it
delights in giving, as if it felt its stores were exhaustless;
the dumb rhetoric of the scenery—for tables, and chairs,
and joint-stools in Hogarth are living and significant
things: the witticisms that are expressed by words (all

artists but Hogarth have failed when they have endeav-
oured to combine two mediums of expression, and have
introduced words into their pictures), and the unwrit-
ten numberless little allusive pleasantries that are scattered about; the work that is going on in the scene, and
beyond it, as is made visible to the "eye of mind," by
the mob which chokes up the doorway, and the sword
that has forced an entrance before its master; when he
shall have sufficiently admired this wealth of genius,
let him fairly say what is the *result* left on his mind.

Is it an impression of the vileness and worthlessness
of his species? or is it not the general feeling which remains, after the individual faces have ceased to act sensibly on his mind, a *kindly one in favour of his species?*
was not the general air of the scene wholesome? did it
do the heart hurt to be among it? Something of a riotous
spirit to be sure is there, some worldly-mindedness in
some of the faces, a Doddingtonian smoothness which
does not promise any superfluous degree of sincerity in
the fine gentleman who has been the occasion of calling
so much good company together; but is not the general
cast of expression in the faces of the good sort? do they
not seem cut out of the *good old rock,* substantial English honesty? would one fear treachery among characters of their expression? or shall we call their honest
mirth and seldom-returning relaxation by the hard names
of vice and profligacy?

That poor country fellow, that is grasping his staff
(which, from that difficulty of feeling themselves at
home which poor men experience at a feast, he has
never parted with since he came into the room), and is
enjoying with a relish that seems to fit all the capacities
of his soul the slender joke, which that facetious wag
his neighbour is practising upon the gouty gentleman,
whose eyes the effort to suppress pain has made as

round as rings—does it shock the "dignity of human nature" to look at that man, and to sympathize with him
in the seldom-heard joke which has unbent his care-
worn, hard-working visage, and drawn iron smiles from
it? or with that full-hearted cobbler, who is honouring
with the grasp of an honest fist the unused palm of that
annoyed patrician, whom the licence of the time has
seated next him?

I can see nothing "dangerous" in the contemplation
of such scenes as this, or the "Enraged Musician," or the
"Southwark Fair," or twenty other pleasant prints which
come crowding in upon my recollection, in which the
restless activities, the diversified bents and humours, the
blameless peculiarities of men, as they deserve to be
called, rather than their "vices and follies," are held up
in a laughable point of view. All laughter is not of a
dangerous or soul-hardening tendency. There is the pet-
rifying sneer of a demon which excludes and kills Love,
and there is the cordial laughter of a man which implies
and cherishes it. What heart was ever made the worse
by joining in a hearty laugh at the simplicities of Sir
Hugh Evans or Parson Adams, where a sense of the ridiculous mutually kindles and is kindled by a perception
of the amiable? That tumultuous harmony of singers
that are roaring out the words, "The world shall bow to
the Assyrian throne," from the opera of *Judith*, in the
third plate of the series called the "Four Groups of
Heads," which the quick eye of Hogarth must have
struck off in the very infancy of the rage for sacred ora-
torios in this country, while "Music yet was young";
when we have done smiling at the deafening distortions,
which these tearers of devotion to rags and tatters, these
takers of heaven by storm, in their boisterous mimicry
of the occupation of angels, are making—what unkindly
impression is left behind, or what more of harsh or con-

temptuous feeling, than when we quietly leave Uncle
Toby and Mr. Shandy riding their hobby-horses about
the room? The conceited, long-backed Sign-painter, that
with all the self-applause of a Raphael or Correggio (the
twist of body which his conceit has thrown him into has
something of the Correggiesque in it), is contemplating
the picture of a bottle, which he is drawing from an
actual bottle that hangs beside him, in the print of "Beer
Street"—while we smile at the enormity of the self-
delusion, can we help loving the good-humour and self-
complacency of the fellow? would we willingly wake
him from his dream?

I say not that all the ridiculous subjects of Hogarth
have, necessarily, something in them to make us like
them; some are indifferent to us, some in their natures
repulsive, and only made interesting by the wonderful
skill and truth to nature in the painter; but I contend
that there is in most of them that sprinkling of the better
nature, which, like holy water, chases away and dis-
perses the contagion of the bad. They have this in them,
besides, that they bring us acquainted with the everyday human face—they give us skill to detect those gra-
dations of sense and virtue (which escape the careless or
fastidious observer) in the countenances of the world
about us; and prevent that disgust at common life, that
tædium quotidianarum formarum, which an unrestricted
passion for ideal forms and beauties is in danger of pro-
ducing. In this, as in many other things, they are analogous to the best novels of Smollett or Fielding.

The Reflector, 1811.

PART SEVEN

In General

A BACHELOR'S COMPLAINT
OF THE BEHAVIOUR OF MARRIED PEOPLE

AS A SINGLE man, I have spent a good deal of my time in noting down the infirmities of Married People, to console myself for those superior pleasures, which they tell me I have lost by remaining as I am.

I cannot say that the quarrels of men and their wives ever made any great impression upon me, or had much tendency to strengthen in those anti-social resolutions, which I took up long ago upon more substantial considerations. What oftenest offends me at the houses of married persons where I visit, is an error of quite a different description; it is that they are too loving.

Not too loving neither: that does not explain my meaning. Besides, why should that offend me? The very act of separating themselves from the rest of the world, to have the fuller enjoyment of each other's society, implies that they prefer one another to all the world.

But what I complain of is, that they carry this preference so undisguisedly, they perk it up in the faces of us single people so shamelessly, you cannot be in their company a moment without being made to feel, by some indirect hint or open avowal, that *you* are not the object of this preference. Now there are some things which give no offence, while implied or taken for granted merely; but expressed, there is much offence in them.

If a man were to accost the first homely-featured or plain-dressed young woman of his acquaintance, and tell her bluntly, that she was not handsome or rich enough for him, and he could not marry her, he would deserve to be kicked for his ill manners; yet no less is implied in the fact, that having access and opportunity of putting the question to her, he has never yet thought fit to do it. The young woman understands this as clearly as if it were put into words; but no reasonable young woman would think of making this the ground of a quarrel. Just as little right have a married couple to tell me by speeches, and looks that are scarce less plain than speeches, that I am not the happy man—the lady's choice. It is enough that I know I am not: I do not want this perpetual reminding.

The display of superior knowledge or riches may be made sufficiently mortifying; but these admit of a palliative. The knowledge which is brought out to insult me, may accidentally improve me; and in the rich man's houses and pictures—his parks and gardens. I have a temporary usufruct at least. But the display of married happiness has none of these palliatives: it is throughout pure, unrecompensed, unqualified insult.

Marriage by its best title is a monopoly, and not of the least invidious sort. It is the cunning of most possessors of any exclusive privilege to keep their advantage as much out of sight as possible, that their less favoured neighbours, seeing little of the benefit, may the less be disposed to question the right. But these married monopolists thrust the most obnoxious part of their patent into our faces.

Nothing is to me more distasteful than that entire complacency and satisfaction which beam in the countenances of a new-married couple—in that of the lady particularly: it tells you, that her lot is disposed of in this world: that *you* can have no hopes of her. It is true, I have none: nor wishes either, perhaps; but this is one of those truths which ought, as I said before, to be taken for granted, not expressed.

The excessive airs which those people give themselves, founded on the ignorance of us unmarried people, would be more offensive if they were less irrational. We will allow them to understand the mysteries belonging to their own craft better than we, who have not had the happiness to be made free of the company: but their arrogance is not content within these limits. If a single person presume to offer his opinion in their presence, though upon the most indifferent subject, he is immediately silenced as an incompetent person. Nay, a young married lady of my acquaintance, who, the best of the jest was, had not changed her condition above a fortnight before, in a question on which I had the misfortune to differ from her, respecting the properest mode of breeding oysters for the London market, had the assurance to ask with a sneer, how such an old Bachelor as I could pretend to know anything about such matters!

But what I have spoken of hitherto is nothing to the airs these creatures give themselves when they come, as they generally do, to have children. When I consider how little of a rarity children are—that every street and blind alley swarms with them—that the poorest people commonly have them in most abundance—that there are few marriages that are not blest with at least one of these bargains—how often they turn out ill, and defeat the fond hopes of their parents, taking to vicious courses, which end in poverty, disgrace, the gallows, etc.—I cannot for my life tell what cause for pride there can possibly be in having them. If they were young phœnixes, indeed, that were born but one in a year, there might be a pretext. But when they are so common. . . .

I do not advert to the insolent merit which they assume with their husbands on these occasions. Let *them* look to that. But why *we*, who are not their natural-born subjects, should be expected to bring our spices, myrrh, and incense—our tribute and homage of admiration— I do not see.

"Like as the arrows in the hand of the giant, even so are the young children": so says the excellent office in our Prayer-book appointed for the churching of women. "Happy is the man that hath his quiver full of them." So say I; but then don't let him discharge his quiver upon us that are weaponless; let them be arrows, but not to gall and stick us. I have generally observed that these arrows are double-headed: they have two forks, to be sure to hit with one or the other. As for instance, where you come into a house which is full of children, if you happen to take no notice of them (you are thinking of something else, perhaps, and turn a deaf ear to their innocent caresses), you are set down as untractable, morose, a hater of children. On the other hand, if you find them more than usually engaging—if you are taken with their pretty manners, and set about in earnest to romp and play with them, some pretext or other is sure to be found for sending them out of the room; they are too noisy or boisterous, or Mr. —— does not like children. With one or other of these folks the arrow is sure to hit you.

I could forgive their jealousy, and dispense with toying with their brats, if it gives them any pain; but I think it unreasonable to be called upon to *love* them,

where I see no occasion—to love a whole family, perhaps eight, nine, or ten, indiscriminately—to love all
the pretty dears, because children are so engaging!

I know there is a proverb, "Love me, love my dog":
that is not always so very practicable, particularly if
the dog be set upon you to tease you or snap at you in
sport. But a dog, or a lesser thing—any inanimate substance, as a keepsake, a watch or a ring, a tree, or the
place where we last parted when my friend went away
upon a long absence, I can make shift to love, because
I love him, and anything that reminds me of him; provided it be in its nature indifferent, and apt to receive
whatever hue fancy can give it. But children have a real
character, and an essential being of themselves: they
are amiable or unamiable *per se;* I must love or hate
them as I see cause for either in their qualities.

A child's nature is too serious a thing to admit of its
being regarded as a mere appendage to another being,
and to be loved or hated accordingly: they stand with
me upon their own stock, as much as men and women
do. Oh! but you will say, sure it is an attractive age—
there is something in the tender years of infancy that of
itself charms us? This is the very reason why I am more
nice about them. I know that a sweet child is the sweetest thing in nature, not even excepting the delicate
creatures which bear them; but the prettier the kind of
a thing is, the more desirable it is that it should be pretty
of its kind. One daisy differs not much from another in
glory; but a violet should look and smell the daintiest.
I was always rather squeamish in my women and children.

But this is not the worst: one must be admitted into
their familiarity at least, before they can complain of
inattention. It implies visits, and some kind of inter-

course. But if the husband be a man with whom you have lived on a friendly footing before marriage—if you did not come in on the wife's side—if you did not sneak into the house in her train, but were an old friend in fast habits of intimacy before their courtship was so much as thought on—look about you—your tenure is precarious—before a twelvemonth shall roll over your head, you shall find your old friend gradually grow cool and altered towards you, and at last seek opportunities of breaking with you.

I have scarce a married friend of my acquaintance, upon whose firm faith I can rely, whose friendship did not commence *after the period of his marriage.* With some limitations, they can endure that; but that the good man should have dared to enter into a solemn league of friendship in which they were not consulted, though it happened before they knew him—before they that are now man and wife ever met—this is intolerable to them. Every long friendship, every old authentic intimacy, must be brought into their office to be new stamped with their currency, as a sovereign prince calls in the good old money that was coined in some reign before he was born or thought of, to be new marked and minted with the stamp of his authority, before he will let it pass current in the world. You may guess what luck generally befalls such a rusty piece of metal as I am in these *new mintings.*

Innumerable are the ways which they take to insult and worm you out of their husband's confidence. Laughing at all you say with a kind of wonder, as if you were a queer kind of fellow that said good things, *but an oddity,* is one of the ways—they have a particular kind of stare for the purpose—till at last the husband, who used to defer to your judgment, and would pass over some excrescences of understanding and manner for the sake of a general vein of observation (not quite vulgar) which he perceived in you, begins to suspect whether you are not altogether a humourist—a fellow well enough to have consorted with in his bachelor days, but not quite so proper to be introduced to ladies. This may be called the staring way; and is that which has oftenest been put in practice against me.

Then there is the exaggerating way, or the way of irony; that is, where they find you an object of especial regard with their husband, who is not so easily to be shaken from the lasting attachment founded on esteem which he has conceived towards you, by never qualified exaggerations to cry up all that you say or do, till the good man, who understands well enough that it is all done in compliment to him, grows weary of the debt of gratitude which is due to so much candour, and by relaxing a little on his part, and taking down a peg or two in his enthusiasm, sinks at length to the kindly level of moderate esteem—that "decent affection and complacent kindness" towards you, where she herself can join in sympathy with him without much stretch and violence to her sincerity.

Another way (for the ways they have to accomplish so desirable a purpose are infinite) is, with a kind of innocent simplicity, continually to mistake what it was which first made their husband fond of you. If an esteem for something excellent in your moral character was that which riveted the chain which she is to break, upon any imaginary discovery of a want of poignancy in your conversation, she will cry, "I thought, my dear, you described your friend, Mr. ——, as a great wit?" If, on the other hand, it was for some supposed charm in your conversation that he first grew to like you, and was content for this to overlook some trifling irregularities in your moral deportment, upon the first notice of any of these she as readily exclaims, "This, my dear, is your good Mr. ——!"

One good lady whom I took the liberty of expostulating with for not showing me quite so much respect as I thought due to her husband's old friend, had the candour to confess to me that she had often heard Mr. —— speak of me before marriage, and that she had conceived a great desire to be acquainted with me, but that the sight of me had very much disappointed her expectations; for from her husband's representations of me, she had formed a notion that she was to see a fine, tall, officer-like-looking man (I use her very words), the very reverse of which proved to be the truth.

This was candid; and I had the civility not to ask her in return, how she came to pitch upon a standard of personal accomplishments for her husband's friends which differed so much from his own; for my friend's dimensions as near as possible approximate to mine; he standing five feet five in his shoes, in which I have the advantage of him by about half an inch; and he no more than myself exhibiting any indications of a martial character in his air or countenance.

These are some of the mortifications which I have encountered in the absurd attempt to visit at their houses. To enumerate them all would be a vain endeavour; I shall therefore just glance at the very common impropriety of which married ladies are guilty—of treating us as if we were their husbands, and vice versa. I mean, when they use us with familiarity, and their husbands with ceremony. *Testacea*, for instance, kept me the other night two or three hours beyond my usual time of supping, while she was fretting because Mr.

—— did not come home, till the oysters were all spoiled, rather than she would be guilty of the impoliteness of touching one in his absence.

This was reversing the point of good manners: for ceremony is an invention to take off the uneasy feeling which we derive from knowing ourselves to be less the object of love and esteem with a fellow-creature than some other person is. It endeavours to make up, by superior attentions in little points, for that invidious preference which it is forced to deny in the greater. Had *Testacea* kept the oysters back for me, and withstood her husband's importunities to go to supper, she would have acted according to the strict rules of propriety.

I know no ceremony that ladies are bound to observe to their husbands, beyond the point of a modest behaviour and decorum: therefore I must protest against the vicarious gluttony of *Cerasia,* who at her own table sent away a dish of Morellas, which I was applying to with great goodwill, to her husband at the other end of the table, and recommended a plate of less extraordinary gooseberries to my unwedded palate in their stead. Neither can I excuse the wanton affront of ——

But I am weary of stringing up all my married acquaintances by Roman denominations. Let them amend and change their manners, or I promise to record the full-length English of their names, to the terror of all such desperate offenders in future.

Leigh Hunt's Reflector, 1811;
London Magazine, September 1822; Elia.

GRACE BEFORE MEAT

THE custom of saying grace at meals had, probably, its origin in the early times of the world, and the hunter-state of man, when dinners were precarious things, and a full meal was something more than a common blessing! when a bellyfull was a windfall, and looked like a special providence. In the shouts and triumphal songs with which, after a season of sharp abstinence, a lucky booty of deer's or goat's flesh would naturally be ushered home, existed, perhaps, the germ of the modern grace. It is not otherwise easy to be understood, why the blessing of food—the act of eating—should have had a particular expression of thanksgiving annexed to it, distinct from that implied and silent gratitude with which we are expected to enter upon the enjoyment of the many other various gifts and good things of existence.

I own that I am disposed to say grace upon twenty other occasions in the course of the day besides my dinner. I want a form for setting out upon a pleasant walk, for a moonlight ramble, for a friendly meeting, or a solved problem. Why have we none for books, those spiritual repasts—a grace before Milton—a grace before Shakspeare—a devotional exercise proper to be said before reading *The Faerie Queen?*—but the received ritual having prescribed these forms to the solitary ceremony of manducation, I shall confine my observations to the experience which I have had of the grace, properly so called; commending my new scheme for extension to a niche in the grand philosophical, poetical, and perchance in part heretical, liturgy, now compiling by my friend Homo Humanus, for the use of a certain snug congregation of Utopian Rabelaisian Christians, no matter where assembled.

The form, then, of the benediction before eating has its beauty at a poor man's table, or at the simple and unprovocative repast of children. It is here that the grace becomes exceedingly graceful. The indigent man, who hardly knows whether he shall have a meal the next day or not, sits down to his fare with a present sense of the blessing, which can be but feebly acted by the rich, into whose minds the conception of wanting a dinner could never, but by some extreme theory, have entered. The proper end of food—the animal sustenance—is barely contemplated by them. The poor man's bread is his daily bread, literally his bread for the day. Their courses are perennial.

Again, the plainest diet seems the fittest to be preceded by the grace. That which is least stimulative to appetite, leaves the mind most free for foreign considerations. A man may feel thankful, heartily thankful, over a dish of plain mutton with turnips, and have leisure to reflect upon the ordinance and institution of eating; when he shall confess a perturbation of mind, inconsistent with the purposes of the grace, at the presence of venison or turtle.

When I have sate (a *rarus hospes*) at rich men's tables, with the savoury soup and messes steaming up the nostrils, and moistening the lips of the guests with desire and a distracted choice, I have felt the introduction of that ceremony to be unseasonable. With the ravenous orgasm upon you, it seems impertinent to interpose a religious sentiment. It is a confusion of purpose to mutter out praises from a mouth that waters. The heats of epicurism put out the gentle flame of devotion. The incense which rises round is pagan, and the belly-god intercepts it for his own. The very excess of the provision beyond the needs, takes away all sense of proportion between the end and means. The giver is veiled by his gifts. You are startled at the injustice of returning thanks —for what?—for having too much, while so many starve. It is to praise the Gods amiss.

I have observed this awkwardness felt, scarce consciously perhaps, by the good man who says the grace. I have seen it in clergymen and others—a sort of shame —a sense of the co-presence of circumstances which unhallow the blessing. After a devotional tone put on for a few seconds, how rapidly the speaker will fall into his common voice! helping himself or his neighbour, as if to get rid of some uneasy sensation of hypocrisy. Not that the good man was a hypocrite, or was not most conscientious in the discharge of the duty; but he felt in his inmost mind the incompatibility of the scene and the viands before him with the exercise of a calm and rational gratitude.

I hear somebody exclaim—Would you have Christians sit down at table, like hogs to their troughs, without remembering the Giver?—no—I would have them sit down as Christians, remembering the Giver, and less like hogs. Or if their appetites must run riot, and they must pamper themselves with delicacies for which east and west are ransacked, I would have them postpone their benediction to a fitter season, when appetite is laid; when the still small voice can be heard, and the reason of the grace returns—with temperate diet and restricted dishes.

Gluttony and surfeiting are no proper occasions for thanksgiving. When Jeshurun waxed fat, we read that he kicked. Virgil knew the harpy-nature better, when he put into the mouth of Celæno anything but a blessing. We may be greatly sensible of the deliciousness of some kinds of food beyond others, though that is a meaner and inferior gratitude: but the proper object of the grace is sustenance, not relishes; daily bread, not delicacies; the means of life, and not the means of pampering the carcass.

With what frame or composure, I wonder, can a city chaplain pronounce his benediction at some great Hall-feast, when he knows that his last concluding pious word—and that, in all probability, the sacred name which he preaches—is but the signal for so many impatient harpies to commence their foul orgies, with as little sense of true thankfulness (which is temperance) as those Virgilian fowl! It is well if the good man himself does not feel his devotions a little clouded, those foggy sensuous steams mingling with and polluting the pure altar sacrifice.

The severest satire upon full tables and surfeits is the banquet which Satan, in the *Paradise Regained*, provides for a temptation in the wilderness:

> A table richly spread in regal mode
> With dishes piled, and meats of noblest sort
> And savour; beasts of chase, or fowl of game,
> In pastry built, or from the spit, or boiled,
> Gris-amber-steamed; all fish from sea or shore,
> Freshet or purling brook, for which was drained
> Pontus, and Lucrine bay, and Afric coast.

The Tempter, I warrant you, thought these cates would go down without the recommendatory preface of a benediction. They are like to be short graces where the devil plays the host. I am afraid the poet wants his usual decorum in this place. Was he thinking of the old Roman luxury, or of a gaudy day at Cambridge? This was a temptation fitter for a Heliogabalus. The whole banquet is too civic and culinary, and the accompaniments altogether a profanation of that deep, abstracted holy scene. The mighty artillery of sauces, which the cook-fiend conjures up, is out of proportion to the simple wants and plain hunger of the guest. He that disturbed him in his dreams, from his dreams might have been taught better. To the temperate fantasies of the famished Son of God, what sort of feasts presented themselves? He dreamed indeed,

> ——As appetite is wont to dream,
> Of meats and drinks, nature's refreshment sweet.

But what meats?

> Him thought, he by the brook of Cherith stood,
> And saw the ravens with their horny beaks
> Food to Elijah bringing even and morn;
> Though ravenous, taught to abstain from what they brought;
> He saw the prophet also how he fled
> Into the desert and how there he slept
> Under a juniper; then how awaked
> He found his supper on the coals prepared,
> And by the angel was bid rise and eat,
> And ate the second time after repose,
> The strength whereof sufficed him forty days:
> Sometimes, that with Elijah he partook,
> Or as a guest with Daniel at his pulse.

Nothing in Milton is finelier fancied than these temperate dreams of the divine Hungerer. To which of these two visionary banquets, think you, would the introduction of what is called the grace have been the most fitting and pertinent?

Theoretically I am no enemy to graces; but practically I own that (before meat especially) they seem to involve something awkward and unseasonable. Our appetites, of one or another kind, are excellent spurs to our reason, which might otherwise but feebly set about

the great ends of preserving and continuing the species.
They are fit blessings to be contemplated at a distance
with a becoming gratitude; but the moment of appetite
(the judicious reader will apprehend me) is, perhaps,
the least fit season for that exercise.

The Quakers, who go about their business of every
description with more calmness than we, have more title
to the use of these benedictory prefaces. I have always
admired their silent grace, and the more because I have
observed their applications to the meat and drink following to be less passionate and sensual than ours.
They are neither gluttons nor wine-bibbers as a people.
They eat, as a horse bolts his chopped hay, with indifference, calmness, and cleanly circumstances. They
neither grease nor slop themselves. When I see a citizen
in his bib and tucker, I cannot imagine it a surplice.

I am no Quaker at my food. I confess I am not indifferent to the kinds of it. Those unctuous morsels of deer's
flesh were not made to be received with dispassionate
services. I hate a man who swallows it, affecting not to
know what he is eating. I suspect his taste in higher
matters. I shrink instinctively from one who professes
to like minced veal. There is a physiognomical character
in the tastes for food. C. holds that a man cannot have
a pure mind who refuses apple-dumplings. I am not certain but he is right. With the decay of my first innocence, I confess a less and less relish daily for those innocuous cates. The whole vegetable tribe have lost their
gust with me. Only I stick to asparagus, which still
seems to inspire gentle thoughts. I am impatient and
querulous under culinary disappointments, as to come
home at the dinner-hour, for instance, expecting some
savoury mess, and to find one quite tasteless and sapid-
less. Butter ill melted—that commonest of kitchen failures—puts me beside my tenor.

The author of *The Rambler* used to make inarticulate animal noises over a favourite food. Was this the music quite proper to be preceded by the grace? or would the pious man have done better to postpone his devotions to a season when the blessing might be contemplated with less perturbation? I quarrel with no man's tastes, nor would set my thin face against those excellent things, in their way, jollity and feasting. But as these exercises, however laudable, have little in them of grace or gracefulness, a man should be sure, before he ventures so to grace them, that while he is pretending his devotions otherwhere, he is not secretly kissing his hand to some great fish—his Dagon—with a special consecration of no ark but the fat tureen before him.

Graces are the sweet preluding strains to the banquets of angels and children; to the roots and severer repasts of the Chartreuse; to the slender, but not slenderly acknowledged, refection of the poor and humble man: but at the heaped-up boards of the pampered and the luxurious they become of dissonant mood, less timed and tuned to the occasion, methinks, than the noise of those better befitting organs would be which children hear tales of, at Hog's Norton. We sit too long at our meals, or are too curious in the study of them, or too disordered in our application to them, or engross too great a portion of those good things (which should be common) to our share, to be able with any grace to say grace.

To be thankful for what we grasp exceeding our proportion, is to add hypocrisy to injustice. A lurking sense of this truth is what makes the performance of this duty so cold and spiritless a service at most tables. In houses where the grace is as indispensable as the napkin, who has not seen that never-settled question arise, as to *who shall say it?* while the good man of the house and the visitor clergyman, or some other guest belike of next authority, from years or gravity, shall be bandying about the office between them as a matter of compliment, each of them not unwilling to shift the awkward burthen of an equivocal duty from his own shoulders?

I once drank tea in company with two Methodist divines of different persuasions, whom it was my fortune to introduce to each other for the first time that evening. Before the first cup was handed round, one of these reverend gentlemen put it to the other, with all due solemnity, whether he chose to *say anything*. It seems it is the custom with some sectaries to put up a short prayer before this meal also. His reverend brother did not at first quite apprehend him, but upon an explanation, with little less importance he made answer that it was not a custom known in his church: in which courteous evasion the other acquiescing for good manners' sake, or in compliance with a weak brother, the supplementary or tea-grace was waived altogether.

With what spirit might not Lucian have painted two priests, of *his* religion, playing into each other's hands the compliment of performing or omitting a sacrifice— the hungry God meantime, doubtful of his incense, with expectant nostrils hovering over the two flamens, and (as between two stools) going away in the end without his supper.

A short form upon these occasions is felt to want reverence; a long one, I am afraid, cannot escape the charge of impertinence. I do not quite approve of the epigrammatic conciseness with which that equivocal wag (but my pleasant schoolfellow) C. V. L, when importuned for a grace, used to inquire, first slyly leering down the table, "Is there no clergyman here?"—significantly adding, "Thank G——."

Nor do I think our old form at school quite pertinent,

where we were used to preface our bald bread-and-cheese-suppers with a preamble, connecting with that humble blessing a recognition of benefits the most awful and overwhelming to the imagination which religion has to offer. *Non tunc illis erat locus.* I remember we were put to it to reconcile the phrase "good creatures," upon which the blessing rested, with the fare set before us, wilfully understanding that expression in a low and animal sense—till some one recalled a legend, which told how, in the golden days of Christ's, the young Hospitallers were wont to have smoking joints of roast meat upon their nightly boards, till some pious bene-factor, commiserating the decencies, rather than the palates, of the children, commuted our flesh for gar-ments, and gave us—*horresco referens*—trousers instead of mutton.

London Magazine, November 1821; Elia.

DISTANT CORRESPONDENTS

In a letter to B. F., Esq., at Sydney, New South Wales

MY DEAR F.—When I think how welcome the sight of a letter from the world where you were born must be to you in that strange one to which you have been trans-planted, I feel some compunctious visitings at my long silence. But, indeed, it is no easy effort to set about a correspondence at our distance. The weary world of waters between us oppresses the imagination. It is dif-ficult to conceive how a scrawl of mine should ever stretch across it. It is a sort of presumption to expect that one's thoughts should live so far. It is like writing for posterity; and reminds me of one of Mrs. Rowe's superscriptions, "Alcander to Strephon in the shades."

Cowley's Post-Angel is no more than would be expedient in such an intercourse. One drops a packet at Lombard Street, and in twenty-four hours a friend in Cumberland gets it as fresh as if it came in ice. It is only like whispering through a long trumpet. But suppose a tube let down from the moon, with yourself at one end and *the man* at the other; it would be some balk to the spirit of conversation, if you knew that the dialogue exchanged with that interesting theosophist would take two or three revolutions of a higher luminary in its passage. Yet, for aught I know, you may be some parasangs nigher that primitive idea—Plato's man—than we in England here have the honour to reckon ourselves.

Epistolary matter usually compriseth three topics; news, sentiment, and puns. In the latter, I include all non-serious subjects; or subjects serious in themselves, but treated after my fashion, non-seriously. And first, for news. In them the most desirable circumstance, I suppose, is that they shall be true. But what security can I have that what I now send you for truth shall not, before you get it, unaccountably turn into a lie?

For instance, our mutual friend P. is at this present writing—*my Now*—in good health, and enjoys a fair share of worldly reputation. You are glad to hear it. This is natural and friendly. But at this present reading —*your Now*—he may possibly be in the Bench, or going to be hanged, which in reason ought to abate something of your transport (*i.e.* at hearing he was well, etc.), or at least considerably to modify it.

I am going to the play this evening, to have a laugh with Munden. You have no theatre, I think you told me, in your land of d——d realities. You naturally lick your lips, and envy me my felicity. Think but a moment, and you will correct the hateful emotion. Why, it is Sunday morning with you, and 1823. This confusion of tenses, this grand solecism of *two presents,* is in a degree common to all postage. But if I sent you word to Bath or Devizes, that I was expecting the aforesaid treat this evening, though at the moment you received the intelligence my full feast of fun would be over, yet there would be for a day or two after, as you would well know, a smack, a relish left upon my mental palate, which would give rational encouragment for you to foster a portion, at least, of the disagreeable passion, which it was in part my intention to produce. But ten months hence, your envy or your sympathy would be as useless as a passion spent upon the dead. Not only does truth, in these long intervals, un-essence herself, but (what is harder) one cannot venture a crude fiction, for the fear that it may ripen into a truth upon the voyage.

What a wild improbable banter I put upon you, some three years since—of Will Weatherall having married a servant-maid! I remember gravely consulting you how we were to receive her—for Will's wife was in no case to be rejected; and your no less serious replication in the matter; how tenderly you advised an abstemious introduction of literary topics before the lady, with a caution not to be too forward in bringing on the carpet matters more within the sphere of her intelligence; your deliberate judgment, or rather wise suspension of sentence, how far jacks, and spits, and mops, could, with propriety, be introduced as subjects; whether the conscious avoiding of all such matters in discourse would not have a worse look than the taking of them casually in our way; in what manner we should carry ourselves to our maid Becky, Mrs. William Weatherall being by; whether we should show more delicacy, and a truer sense of respect for Will's wife, by treating Becky with our customary chiding before her, or by an unusual deferential civility paid to Becky, as to a person of great worth, but thrown by the caprice of fate into a humble station.

There were difficulties, I remember, on both sides, which you did me the favour to state with the precision of a lawyer, united to the tenderness of a friend. I laughed in my sleeve at your solemn pleadings, when lo! while I was valuing myself upon this flam put upon you in New South Wales, the devil in England, jealous possibly of any lie-children not his own, or working after my copy, has actually instigated our friend (not three days since) to the commission of a matrimony, which I had only conjured up for your diversion. William Weatherall has married Mrs. Cotterel's maid. But to take it in its truest sense, you will see, my dear F., that news from me must become history to you; which I neither profess to write, nor indeed care much for reading. No person, under a diviner, can, with any prospect of veracity, conduct a correspondence at such an arm's length. Two prophets, indeed, might thus interchange intelligence with effect; the epoch of the writer (Habakkuk) falling in with the true present time of the receiver (Daniel); but then we are no prophets.

Then as to sentiment. It fares little better with that. This kind of dish, above all, requires to be served up hot, or sent off in water-plates, that your friend may have it almost as warm as yourself. If it have time to cool, it is the most tasteless of all cold meats.

I have often smiled at a conceit of the late Lord C. It seems that travelling somewhere about Geneva, he came to some pretty green spot, or nook, where a willow, or something, hung so fantastically and invitingly over a stream—was it?—or a rock?—no matter—but the stillness and the repose, after a weary journey, 'tis likely, in a languid moment of his Lordship's hot, restless life, so took his fancy that he could imagine no place so proper, in the event of his death, to lay his bones in.

This was all very natural and excusable as a sentiment, and shows his character in a very pleasing light. But when from a passing sentiment it came to be an act; and when, by a positive testamentary disposal, his remains were actually carried all that way from England; who was there, some desperate sentimentalists excepted, that did not ask the question, Why could not his Lordship have found a spot as solitary, a nook as romantic, a tree as green and pendent, with a stream as emblematic to his purpose, in Surrey, in Dorset, or in Devon?

Conceive the sentiment boarded up, freighted, entered at the Custom House (startling the tide-waiters with the novelty), hoisted into a ship. Conceive it pawed about and handled between the rude jests of tarpaulin ruffians—a thing of its delicate texture—the salt bilge wetting it till it became as vapid as a damaged lustring. Suppose it in material danger (mariners have some superstition about sentiments) of being tossed over in a fresh gale to some propitiatory shark (spirit of Saint Gothard, save us from a quietus so foreign to the deviser's purpose!), but it has happily evaded a fishy consummation. Trace it then to its lucky landing—at Lyons shall we say?—I have not the map before me—jostled upon four men's shoulders—baiting at this town—stopping to refresh at t'other village—waiting a passport here, a license there; the sanction of the magistracy in this district, the concurrence of the ecclesiastics in that canton; till at length it arrives at its destination, tired out and jaded, from a brisk sentiment into a feature of silly

pride or tawdry senseless affectation. How few sentiments, my dear F., I am afraid we can set down, in the
sailor's phrase, as quite seaworthy.

Lastly, as to the agreeable levities, which, though contemptible in bulk, are the twinkling corpuscula which
should irradiate a right friendly epistle—your puns and
small jests are, I apprehend, extremely circumscribed in
their sphere of action. They are so far from a capacity of
being packed up and sent beyond sea, they will scarce
endure to be transported by hand from this room to the
next. Their vigour is as the instant of their birth. Their
nutriment for their brief existence is the intellectual atmosphere of the bystanders: or this last is the fine slime
of Nilus—the *melior lutus*—whose maternal recipiency
is as necessary as the *sol pater* to their equivocal generation. A pun hath a hearty kind of present ear-kissing
smack with it; you can no more transmit it in its pristine
flavour than you can send a kiss.

Have you not tried in some instances to palm off a yesterday's pun upon a gentleman, and has it answered?
Not but it was new to his hearing, but it did not seem to
come new from you. It did not hitch in. It was like picking up at a village ale-house a two-days'-old newspaper.
You have not seen it before, but you resent the stale
thing as an affront. This sort of merchandise above all requires a quick return. A pun, and its recognitory laugh,
must be co-instantaneous. The one is the brisk lightning,
the other the fierce thunder. A moment's interval, and
the link is snapped. A pun is reflected from a friend's
face as from a mirror. Who would consult his sweet visnomy, if the polished surface were two or three minutes
(not to speak of twelve months, my dear F.) in giving
back its copy?

I cannot image to myself whereabout you are. When
I try to fix it, Peter Wilkins's island comes across me.

Sometimes you seem to be in the *Hades* of *Thieves*. I see
Diogenes prying among you with his perpetual fruitless
lantern. What must you be willing by this time to give
for the sight of an honest man! You must almost have
forgotten how *we* look. And tell me what your Sydney-
ites do? are they th——v—ng all day long? Merciful
heaven! what property can stand against such a depre-
dation! The kangaroos—your Aborigines—do they keep
their primitive simplicity un-Europe-tainted, with those
little short fore pads, looking like a lesson framed by nature to the pickpocket! Marry, for diving into fobs they
are rather lamely provided *a priori;* but if the hue and
cry were once up, they would show as fair a pair of
hind-shifters as the expertest loco-motor in the colony.

We hear the most improbable tales at this distance.
Pray is it true that the young Spartans among you are
born with six fingers, which spoils their scanning? It
must look very odd, but use reconciles. For their scan-
sion, it is less to be regretted; for if they take it into
their heads to be poets, it is odds but they turn out, the
greater part of them, vile plagiarists. Is there much difference to see, too, between the son of a th——f and the
grandson? or where does the taint stop? Do you bleach
in three or in four generations? I have many questions
to put, but ten Delphic voyages can be made in a shorter
time than it will take to satisfy my scruples. Do you grow
your own hemp? What is your staple trade—exclusive of
the national profession, I mean? Your locksmiths, I take
it, are some of your great capitalists.

I am insensibly chatting to you as familiarly as when
we used to exchange good-morrows out of our old con-
tiguous windows, in pump-famed Hare Court in the
Temple. Why did you ever leave that quiet corner?—
why did I?—with its complement of four poor elms,
from whose smoke-dyed barks, the theme of jesting ru-

ralists, I picked my first lady-birds! My heart is as dry as
that spring sometimes proves in a thirsty August, when
I revert to the space that is between us; a length of passage enough to render obsolete the phrases of our English letters before they can reach you. But while I talk
I think you hear me—thoughts dallying with vain surmise—

> Aye me! while thee the seas and sounding shores
> Hold far away.

Come back, before I am grown into a very old man, so
as you shall hardly know me. Come, before Bridget
walks on crutches. Girls whom you left children have
become sage matrons while you are tarrying there. The
blooming Miss W——r (you remember Sally W——r)
called upon us yesterday, an aged crone. Folks whom
you knew die off every year. Formerly, I thought that
death was wearing out—I stood ramparted about with
so many healthy friends. The departure of J. W., two
springs back, corrected my delusion. Since then the old
divorcer has been busy. If you do not make haste to return, there will be little left to greet you, of me, or mine.

London Magazine, March 1822; Elia.

THE CONVALESCENT

A PRETTY severe fit of indisposition which, under the
name of a nervous fever, has made a prisoner of me for
some weeks past, and is but slowly leaving me, has reduced me to an incapacity of reflecting upon any topic
foreign to itself. Expect no healthy conclusions from

me this month, reader; I can offer you only sick men's dreams.

And truly the whole state of sickness is such; for what else is it but a magnificent dream for a man to lie a-bed, and draw daylight curtains about him; and, shutting out the sun, to induce a total oblivion of all the works which are going on under it? To become insensible to all the operations of life, except the beatings of one feeble pulse?

If there be a regal solitude, it is a sick bed. How the patient lords it there; what caprices he acts without control! how kinglike he sways his pillow—tumbling, and tossing, and shifting, and lowering, and thumping, and flatting, and moulding it, to the ever-varying requisitions of his throbbing temples.

He changes sides oftener than a politician. Now he lies full length, then half-length, obliquely, transversely, head and feet quite across the bed; and none accuses him of tergiversation. Within the four curtains he is absolute. They are his Mare Clausum.

How sickness enlarges the dimensions of a man's self to himself! he is his own exclusive object. Supreme selfishness is inculcated upon him as his only duty. 'Tis the Two Tables of the Law to him. He has nothing to think of but how to get well. What passes out-of-doors, or within them, so he hear not the jarring of them, affects him not.

A little while ago he was greatly concerned in the event of a lawsuit, which was to be the making or the marring of his dearest friend. He was to be seen trudging about upon this man's errand to fifty quarters of the town at once, jogging this witness, refreshing that solicitor. The cause was to come on yesterday. He is absolutely as indifferent to the decision as if it were a question to be tried at Pekin. Peradventure from some whispering, going on about the house, not intended for his hearing, he picks up enough to make him understand that things went cross-grained in the court yesterday, and his friend is ruined. But the word "friend," and the word "ruin," disturb him no more than so much jargon. He is not to think of anything but how to get better.

What a world of foreign cares are merged in that absorbing consideration!

He has put on the strong armour of sickness; he is wrapped in the callous hide of suffering; he keeps his sympathy, like some curious vintage, under trusty lock and key, for his own use only.

He lies pitying himself, honing and moaning to himself; he yearneth over himself; his bowels are even melted within him, to think what he suffers; he is not ashamed to weep over himself.

He is for ever plotting how to do some good to himself; studying little stratagems and artificial alleviations.

He makes the most of himself; dividing himself, by an allowable fiction, into as many distinct individuals, as he hath sore and sorrowing members. Sometimes he meditates—as of a thing apart from him—upon his poor aching head, and that dull pain which, dozing or waking, lay in it all the past night like a log, or palpable substance of pain, not to be removed without opening the very skull, as it seemed, to take it thence. Or he pities his long, clammy, attenuated fingers. He compassionates himself all over; and his bed is a very discipline of humanity, and tender heart.

He is his own sympathizer; and instinctively feels that none can so well perform that office for him. He cares for few spectators to his tragedy. Only that punctual face of the old nurse pleases him, that announces his broths and his cordials. He likes it because it is so unmoved, and because he can pour forth his feverish ejaculations before it as unreservedly as to his bedpost.

To the world's business he is dead. He understands not what the callings and occupations of mortals are; only he has a glimmering conceit of some such thing, when the doctor makes his daily call: and even in the lines on that busy face he reads no multiplicity of patients, but solely conceives of himself as *the sick man.* To what other uneasy couch the good man is hastening, when he slips out of his chamber, folding up his thin douceur so carefully, for fear of rustling—is no speculation which he can at present entertain. He thinks only of the regular return of the same phenomenon at the same hour tomorrow.

Household rumours touch him not. Some faint murmur, indicative of life going on within the house, soothes him, while he knows not distinctly what it is. He is not to know anything, not to think of anything. Servants gliding up or down the distant staircase, treading as upon velvet, gently keep his ear awake, so long as he troubles not himself further than with some feeble guess at their errands. Exacter knowledge would be a burthen to him: he can just endure the pressure of conjecture. He opens his eye faintly at the dull stroke of the muffled knocker, and closes it again without asking "Who was it?" He is flattered by a general notion that inquiries are making after him, but he cares not to know the name of the inquirer. In the general stillness, and awful hush of the house, he lies in state, and feels his sovereignty.

To be sick is to enjoy monarchal prerogatives. Compare the silent tread, and quiet ministry, almost by the eye only, with which he is served—with the careless demeanour, the unceremonious goings in and out (slapping of doors, or leaving them open) of the very same attendants, when he is getting a little better—and you will confess, that from the bed of sickness (throne let me rather call it) to the elbow-chair of convalescence, is a fall from dignity, amounting to a deposition.

How convalescence shrinks a man back to his pristine stature! where is now the space, which he occupied so lately, in his own, in the family's eye?

The scene of his regalities, his sick-room, which was his presence chamber, where he lay and acted his despotic fancies—how is it reduced to a common bedroom! The trimness of the very bed has something petty and unmeaning about it. It is *made* every day. How unlike to that wavy, many-furrowed, oceanic surface, which it presented so short a time since, when to *make* it was a service not to be thought of at oftener than three or four day revolutions, when the patient was with pain and grief to be lifted for a little while out of it, to submit to the encroachments of unwelcome neatness, and decencies which his shaken frame deprecated; then to be lifted into it again, for another three or four days' respite, to flounder it out of shape again, while every fresh furrow was an historical record of some shifting posture, some uneasy turning, some seeking for a little ease; and the shrunken skin scarce told a truer story than the crumpled coverlid.

Hushed are those mysterious sighs—those groans—so much more awful, while we knew not from what caverns of vast hidden suffering they proceeded. The Lernean pangs are quenched. The riddle of sickness is solved; and Philoctetes is become an ordinary personage.

Perhaps some relic of the sick man's dream of greatness survives in the still lingering visitations of the medical attendant. But how is he, too, changed with everything else! Can this be he—this man of news—of chat —of anecdote—of everything but physic—can this be he, who so lately came between the patient and his cruel

enemy, as on some solemn embassy from Nature, erecting herself into a high mediating party?—Pshaw! 'tis
some old woman.

Farewell with him all that made sickness pompous—
the spell that hushed the household—the desertlike stillness, felt throughout its inmost chambers—the mute
attendance—the inquiry by looks—the still softer delicacies of self-attention—the sole and single eye of distem-
per alonely fixed upon itself—world-thoughts excluded
—the man a world unto himself—his own theatre—

What a speck is he dwindled into!

In this flat swamp of convalescence, left by the ebb of
sickness, yet far enough from the terra firma of established health, your note, dear Editor, reached me, re-
questing—an article. In Articulo Mortis, thought I; but
it is something hard—and the quibble, wretched as it
was, relieved me. The summons, unseasonable as it appeared, seemed to link me on again to the petty busi-
nesses of life, which I had lost sight of; a gentle call to
activity, however trivial; a wholesome meaning from
that preposterous dream of self-absorption—the puffy
state of sickness—in which I confess to have lain so long,
insensible to the magazines and monarchies of the world
alike; to its laws, and to its literature. The hypochondriac flatus is subsiding; the acres, which in imagination
I had spread over—for the sick man swells in the sole
contemplation of his single sufferings, till he becomes a
Tityus to himself—are wasting to a span; and for the
giant of self-importance, which I was so lately, you
have me once again in my natural pretensions—the lean
and meagre figure of your insignificant Essayist.

London Magazine, July 1825; Last Essays of Elia.

A QUAKERS' MEETING

Still-born Silence! thou that art
Flood-gate of the deeper heart!
Offspring of a heavenly kind!
Frost o' the mouth, and thaw o' the mind!
Secrecy's confidant, and he
Who makes religion mystery!
Admiration's speaking'st tongue!
Leave, thy desert shades among,
Reverend hermits' hallow'd cells,
Where retired devotion dwells!
With thy enthusiasms come,
Seize our tongues, and strike us dumb! [1]

READER, would'st thou know what true peace and quiet mean; would'st thou find a refuge from the noises and clamours of the multitude; would'st thou enjoy at once solitude and society; would'st thou possess the depth of thine own spirit in stillness, without being shut out from the consolatory faces of thy species; would'st thou be alone and yet accompanied; solitary, yet not desolate; singular, yet not without some to keep thee in countenance; a unit in aggregate; a simple in composite—come with me into a Quakers' Meeting.

Dost thou love silence deep as that "before the winds were made"? go not out into the wilderness, descend not into the profundities of the earth; shut not up thy casements; nor pour wax into the little cells of thy ears, with little-faith'd self-mistrusting Ulysses. Retire with me into a Quakers' Meeting.

[1] From *Poems of All Sorts*, by Richard Flecknoe, 1653.—C. L.

For a man to refrain even from good words, and to hold his peace, it is commendable; but for a multitude it is great mastery.

What is the stillness of the desert compared with this place? what the uncommunicating muteness of fishes?— here the goddess reigns and revels. "Boreas, and Cesias, and Argestes loud," do not with their interconfounding uproars more augment the brawl—nor the waves of the blown Baltic with their clubbed sounds—than their opposite (Silence her sacred self) is multiplied and rendered more intense by numbers, and by sympathy. She too hath her deeps, that call unto deeps. Negation itself hath a positive more and less; and closed eyes would seem to obscure the great obscurity of midnight.

There are wounds which an imperfect solitude cannot heal. By imperfect I mean that which a man enjoyeth by himself. The perfect is that which he can sometimes attain in crowds, but nowhere so absolutely as in a Quakers' Meeting. Those first hermits did certainly understand this principle, when they retired into Egyptian solitudes, not singly, but in shoals, to enjoy one another's want of conversation. The Carthusian is bound to his brethren by this agreeing spirit of incommunicativeness.

In secular occasions, what so pleasant as to be reading a book through a long winter evening, with a friend sitting by—say, a wife—he, or she, too (if that be probable), reading another, without interruption, or oral communication?—can there be no sympathy without the gabble of words?—away with this inhuman, shy, single, shade-and-cavern-haunting solitariness. Give me, Master Zimmermann, a sympathetic solitude.

To pace alone in the cloisters or side aisles of some cathedral, time-stricken;

> Or under hanging mountains,
> Or by the fall of fountains;

is but a vulgar luxury compared with that which those enjoy who come together for the purposes of more complete, abstracted solitude. This is the loneliness "to be felt." The Abbey Church of Westminster hath nothing so solemn, so spirit-soothing, as the naked walls and benches of a Quakers' Meeting. Here are no tombs, no inscriptions.

> ——Sands, ignoble things,
> Dropt from the ruined sides of kings—

but here is something which throws Antiquity herself into the foreground—SILENCE—eldest of things—language of old Night—primitive discourser—to which the insolent decays of mouldering grandeur have but arrived by a violent, and, as we may say, unnatural progression.

> How reverend is the view of these hushed heads,
> Looking tranquillity!

Nothing-plotting, nought-caballing, unmischievous synod! convocation without intrigue! parliament without debate! what a lesson dost thou read to council, and to consistory!—if my pen treat of you lightly—as haply it will wander—yet my spirit hath gravely felt the wisdom of your custom, when sitting among you in deepest peace, which some outwelling tears would rather confirm than disturb, I have reverted to the times of your beginnings, and the sowings of the seed by Fox and Dewesbury.

I have witnessed that which brought before my eyes your heroic tranquillity, inflexible to the rude jests and serious violence of the insolent soldiery, republican or royalist, sent to molest you—for ye sate betwixt the fires of two persecutions, the outcast and offscouring

of church and presbytery. I have seen the reeling sea-
ruffian, who had wandered into your receptacle with the
avowed intention of disturbing your quiet, from the very
spirit of the place receive in a moment a new heart, and
presently sit among ye as a lamb amidst lambs. And I
remember Penn before his accusers, and Fox in the bail-
dock, where he was lifted up in spirit, as he tells us, and
"the Judge and the Jury became as dead men under his
feet."

Reader, if you are not acquainted with it, I would
recommend to you, above all church-narratives, to read
Sewel's *History of the Quakers*. It is in folio, and is the
abstract of the journals of Fox and the primitive Friends.
It is far more edifying and affecting than anything you
will read of Wesley and his colleagues. Here is nothing
to stagger you, nothing to make you mistrust, no suspicion of alloy, no drop or dreg of the worldly or ambitious
spirit.

You will here read the true story of that much-injured,
ridiculed man (who perhaps hath been a byword in
your mouth)—James Naylor: what dreadful sufferings,
with what patience, he endured, even to the boring
through of his tongue with red-hot irons, without a murmur; and with what strength of mind, when the delusion
he had fallen into, which they stigmatized for blasphemy, had given way to clearer thoughts, he could re-
nounce his error, in a strain of the beautifullest humility,
yet keep his first grounds, and be a Quaker still!—so different from the practice of your common converts from
enthusiasm, who, when they apostatize, *apostatize all*,
and think they can never get far enough from the society of their former errors, even to the renunciation of
some saving truths, with which they had been mingled,
not implicated.

Get the writings of John Woolman by heart; and love the early Quakers.

How far the followers of these good men in our days have kept to the primitive spirit, or in what proportion they have substituted formality for it, the Judge of Spirits can alone determine. I have seen faces in their assemblies upon which the dove sate visibly brooding. Others, again, I have watched, when my thoughts should have been better engaged, in which I could possibly detect nothing but a blank inanity. But quiet was in all, and the disposition to unanimity, and the absence of the fierce controversial workings.

If the spiritual pretensions of the Quakers have abated, at least they make few pretences. Hypocrites they certainly are not, in their preaching. It is seldom, indeed, that you shall see one get up amongst them to hold forth. Only now and then a trembling, female, generally *ancient*, voice is heard—you cannot guess from what part of the meeting it proceeds—with a low, buzzing, musical sound, laying out a few words which "she thought might suit the condition of some present," with a quaking diffidence, which leaves no possibility of supposing that anything of female vanity was mixed up, where the tones were so full of tenderness, and a restraining modesty. The men, for what I have observed, speak seldomer.

Once only, and it was some years ago, I witnessed a sample of the old Foxian orgasm. It was a man of giant stature, who, as Wordsworth phrases it, might have danced "from head to foot equipt in iron mail." His frame was of iron, too. But *he* was malleable. I saw him shake all over with the spirit—I dare not say of delusion. The strivings of the outer man were unutterable—he seemed not to speak, but to be spoken from. I saw the

strong man bowed down, and his knees to fail—his
joints all seemed loosening—it was a figure to set off
against Paul preaching—the words he uttered were few,
and sound—he was evidently resisting his will—keeping down his own word-wisdom with more mighty effort
than the world's orators strain for theirs.

"He had been a WIT in his youth," he told us, with
expressions of a sober remorse. And it was not till long
after the impression had begun to wear away that I was
enabled, with something like a smile, to recall the striking incongruity of the confession—understanding the
term in its worldly acceptation—with the frame and
physiognomy of the person before me. His brow would
have scared away the Levities—the Jocos Risus-que—
faster than the Loves fled the face of Dis at Enna. By
wit, even in his youth, I will be sworn he understood
something far within the limits of an allowable liberty.

More frequently the Meeting is broken up without a
word having been spoken. But the mind has been fed.
You go away with a sermon not made with hands.
You have been in the milder caverns of Trophonius; or
as in some den, where that fiercest and savagest of all
wild creatures, the TONGUE, that unruly member, has
strangely lain tied up and captive. You have bathed with
stillness. O, when the spirit is sore fretted, even tired
to sickness of the janglings and nonsense-noises of the
world, what a balm and a solace it is to go and seat yourself for a quiet half-hour upon some undisputed corner
of a bench, among the gentle Quakers!

Their garb and stillness conjoined, present a uniformity, tranquil and herdlike—as in the pasture—"forty
feeding like one."

The very garments of a Quaker seem incapable of receiving a soil; and cleanliness in them to be something

more than the absence of its contrary. Every Quakeress is a lily; and when they come up in bands to their Whitsun-conferences, whitening the easterly streets of the metropolis, from all parts of the United Kingdom, they show like troops of the Shining Ones.

London Magazine, April 1821; Elia.

PART EIGHT

Poems

THE OLD FAMILIAR FACES

Where are they gone, the old familiar faces?

I had a mother, but she died, and left me,
Died prematurely in a day of horrors—
All, all are gone, the old familiar faces.[1]

I have had playmates, I have had companions,
In my days of childhood, in my joyful school-days—
All, all are gone, the old familiar faces.

I have been laughing, I have been carousing,
Drinking late, sitting late, with my bosom cronies—
All, all are gone, the old familiar faces.

I loved a love once, fairest among women;
Closed are her doors on me, I must not see her—
All, all are gone, the old familiar faces.

[1] This verse is omitted in *The Oxford Book of English Verse* and in *The Golden Treasury.*—J. M. B.

I have a friend, a kinder friend has no man;
Like an ingrate, I left my friend abruptly;
Left him, to muse on the old familiar faces.

Ghostlike I paced round the haunts of my childhood.
Earth seem'd a desert I was bound to traverse,
Seeking to find the old familiar faces.

Friend of my bosom, thou more than a brother,
Why wert not thou born in my father's dwelling?
So might we talk of the old familiar faces—

How some they have died, and some they have left me,
And some are taken from me; all are departed;
All, all are gone, the old familiar faces.

[Jan. 1798.]

HESTER

When maidens such as Hester die,
Their place ye may not well supply,
Though ye among a thousand try,
    With vain endeavour.

A month or more hath she been dead,
Yet cannot I by force be led
To think upon the wormy bed,
    And her together.

A springy motion in her gait,
A rising step, did indicate

Of pride and joy no common rate,
    That flush'd her spirit.

I know not by what name beside
I shall it call:—if 'twas not pride,
It was a joy to that allied,
    She did inherit.

Her parents held the Quaker rule,
Which doth the human feeling cool,
But she was train'd in Nature's school,
    Nature had blest her.

A waking eye, a prying mind,
A heart that stirs, is hard to bind,
A hawk's keen sight ye cannot blind,
    Ye could not Hester.

My sprightly neighbour! gone before
To that unknown and silent shore,
Shall we not meet, as heretofore,
    Some summer morning,

When from thy cheerful eyes a ray
Hath struck a bliss upon the day,
A bliss that would not go away,
    A sweet forewarning?

[1803.]

TO MISS KELLY

You are not, Kelly, of the common strain,
That stoop their pride and female honour down

To please that many-headed beast *the town,*
And vend their lavish smiles and tricks for gain;
By fortune thrown amid the actors' train,
You keep your native dignity of thought;
The plaudits that attend you come unsought,
As tributes due unto your natural vein.
Your tears have passion in them, and a grace
Of genuine freshness, which our hearts avow;
Your smiles are winds whose ways we cannot trace,
That vanish and return we know not how—
And please the better from a pensive face,
A thoughtful eye, and a reflecting brow.

[1818.]

PART NINE

Playgoing and the Drama

MY FIRST PLAY

AT THE north end of Cross Court there yet stands a portal, of some architectural pretensions, though reduced to humble use, serving at present for an entrance to a printing-office. This old doorway, if you are young, reader, you may not know was the identical pit entrance to old Drury—Garrick's Drury—all of it that is left. I never pass it without shaking some forty years from off my shoulders, recurring to the evening when I passed through it to see *my first play*. The afternoon had been wet, and the condition of our going (the elder folks and myself) was, that the rain should cease. With what a beating heart did I watch from the window the puddles, from the stillness of which I was taught to prognosticate the desired cessation! I seem to remember the last spurt, and the glee with which I ran to announce it.

We went with orders, which my godfather F. had sent us. He kept the oil shop (now Davies's) at the corner of Featherstone Buildings, in Holborn. F. was a tall grave person, lofty in speech, and had pretensions above his rank. He associated in those days with John Palmer, the comedian, whose gait and bearing he seemed to

515

copy; if John (which is quite as likely) did not rather
borrow somewhat of his manner from my godfather. He
was also known to, and visited by, Sheridan. It was to
his house in Holborn that young Brinsley brought his
first wife on her elopement with him from a boarding-
school at Bath—the beautiful Maria Linley. My parents
were present (over a quadrille table) when he arrived in
the evening with his harmonious charge.

From either of these connexions it may be inferred
that my godfather could command an order for the then
Drury Lane Theatre at pleasure—and, indeed, a pretty
liberal issue of those cheap billets, in Brinsley's easy au-
tograph, I have heard him say was the sole remuneration
which he had received for many years' nightly illumination of the orchestra and various avenues of that theatre
—and he was content it should be so. The honour of
Sheridan's familiarity—or supposed familiarity—was
better to my godfather than money.

F. was the most gentlemanly of oilmen; grandilo-
quent, yet courteous. His delivery of the commonest
matters of fact was Ciceronian. He had two Latin words
almost constantly in his mouth (how odd sounds Latin
from an oilman's lips!), which my better knowledge
since has enabled me to correct. In strict pronunciation
they should have been sounded *vice versa*—but in those
young years they impressed me with more awe than they
would now do, read aright from Seneca or Varro—in his
own peculiar pronunciation, monosyllabically elabo-
rated, or Anglicized, into something like *verse verse*. By
an imposing manner, and the help of these distorted syllables, he climbed (but that was little) to the highest
parochial honours which St. Andrew's has to bestow.

He is dead—and thus much I thought due to his
memory, both for my first orders (little wondrous talis-
mans!—slight keys, and insignificant to outward sight,

but opening to me more than Arabian paradises!) and moreover that by his testamentary beneficence I came into possession of the only landed property which I could ever call my own—situate near the roadway village of pleasant Puckeridge, in Hertfordshire. When I journeyed down to take possession, and planted foot on my own ground, the stately habits of the donor descended upon me, and I strode (shall I confess the vanity?) with larger paces over my allotment of three-quarters of an acre, with its commodious mansion in the midst, with the feeling of an English freeholder that all betwixt sky and centre was my own. The estate has passed into more prudent hands, and nothing but an agrarian can restore it.

In those days were pit-orders. Beshrew the uncomfortable manager who abolished them!—with one of these we went. I remember the waiting at the door—not that which is left—but between that and an inner door in shelter—O when shall I be such an expectant again!—with the cry of nonpareils, an indispensable play-house accompaniment in those days. As near as I can recollect, the fashionable pronunciation of the theatrical fruiteresses then was, "Chase some oranges, chase some numparels, chase a bill of the play"—chase *pro* chuse. But when we got in, and I beheld the green curtain that veiled a heaven to my imagination, which was soon to be disclosed—the breathless anticipations I endured! I had seen something like it in the plate prefixed to *Troilus and Cressida*, in Rowe's Shakspeare—the tent scene with Diomede—and a sight of that plate can always bring back in a measure the feeling of that evening.

The boxes at that time, full of well-dressed women of quality, projected over the pit: and the pilasters reaching down were adorned with a glistering substance (I know not what) under glass (as it seemed), resembling

—a homely fancy—but I judged it to be sugar-candy—
yet, to my raised imagination, divested of its homelier
qualities, it appeared a glorified candy! The orchestra
lights at length arose, those "fair Auroras"! Once the
bell sounded. It was to ring out yet once again—and,
incapable of the anticipation, I reposed my shut eyes in
a sort of resignation upon the maternal lap. It rang the
second time. The curtain drew up—I was not past six
years old, and the play was *Artaxerxes!*

I had dabbled a little in the Universal History—the
ancient part of it—and here was the court of Persia. It
was being admitted to a sight of the past. I took no
proper interest in the action going on, for I understood
not its import—but I heard the word Darius, and I
was in the midst of Daniel. All feeling was absorbed
in vision. Gorgeous vests, gardens, palaces, princesses,
passed before me. I knew not players. I was in Persepolis
for the time, and the burning idol of their devotion almost converted me into a worshipper. I was awestruck,
and believed those significations to be something more
than elemental fires. It was all enchantment and a dream.
No such pleasure has since visited me but in dreams.

Harlequin's invasion followed; where, I remember,
the transformation of the magistrates into reverend bel-
dams seemed to me a piece of grave historic justice, and
the tailor carrying his own head to be as sober a verity
as the legend of St. Denys.

The next play to which I was taken was *The Lady of
the Manor,* of which, with the exception of some scenery, very faint traces are left in my memory. It was followed by a pantomime, called *Lun's Ghost*—a satiric
touch, I apprehend, upon Rich, not long since dead—
but to my apprehension (too sincere for satire), Lun
was as remote a piece of antiquity as Lud—the father of
a line of Harlequins—transmitting his dagger of lath

(the wooden sceptre) through countless ages. I saw the primeval Motley come from his silent tomb in a ghastly vest of white patchwork, like the apparition of a dead rainbow. So Harlequins (thought I) look when they are dead.

My third play followed in quick succession. It was *The Way of the World*. I think I must have sat at it as grave as a judge; for, I remember, the hysteric affectations of good Lady Wishfort affected me like some solemn tragic passion. *Robinson Crusoe* followed; in which Crusoe, man Friday, and the parrot were as good and authentic as in the story. The clownery and pantaloonery of these pantomimes have clean passed out of my head. I believe, I no more laughed at them, than at the same age I should have been disposed to laugh at the grotesque Gothic heads (seeming to me then replete with devout meaning) that gape, and grin, in stone around the inside of the old Round Church (my church) of the Templars.

I saw these plays in the season 1781-2, when I was from six to seven years old. After the intervention of six or seven other years (for at school all playgoing was inhibited) I again entered the doors of a theatre. That old *Artaxerxes* evening had never done ringing in my fancy. I expected the same feelings to come again with the same occasion. But we differ from ourselves less at sixty and sixteen, than the latter does from six. In that interval what had I not lost! At the first period I knew nothing, understood nothing, discriminated nothing. I felt all, loved all, wondered all—

Was nourished, I could not tell how—

I had left the temple a devotee, and was returned a rationalist. The same things were there materially; but the emblem, the reference, was gone!

The green curtain was no longer a veil, drawn between two worlds, the unfolding of which was to bring
back past ages to present a "royal ghost"—but a certain
quantity of green baize, which was to separate the audience for a given time from certain of their fellowmen
who were to come forward and pretend those parts. The
lights—the orchestra lights—came up a clumsy machinery. The first ring, and the second ring, was now but a
trick of the prompter's bell—which had been, like the
note of the cuckoo, a phantom of a voice, no hand seen
or guessed at which ministered to its warning. The actors were men and women painted. I thought the fault
was in them; but it was in myself, and the alteration
which those many centuries—of six short twelvemonths
—had wrought in me.

Perhaps it was fortunate for me that the play of the
evening was but an indifferent comedy, as it gave me
time to crop some unreasonable expectations, which
might have interfered with the genuine emotions with
which I was soon after enabled to enter upon the first
appearance to me of Mrs. Siddons in *Isabella*. Comparison and retrospection soon yielded to the present attraction of the scene; and the theatre became to me, upon a
new stock, the most delightful of recreations.

London Magazine, December 1821; *Elia.*

PLAY-HOUSE MEMORANDA

I ONCE sat in the Pit of Drury Lane Theatre next to a
blind man, who, I afterwards learned, was a street musician, well known about London. The play was *Richard
the Third*, and it was curious to observe the interest

which he took in every successive scene, so far more
lively than could be perceived in any of the company
around him. At those pathetic interviews between the
Queen and Duchess of York, after the murder of the
children, his eyes (or rather the places where eyes
should have been) gushed out tears in torrents, and he
sat intranced in attention, while every one about him
was tittering, partly at him, and partly at the grotesque
figures and wretched action of the women, who had
been selected by managerial taste to personate those
royal mourners. Having no drawback of sight to impair
his sensibilities, he simply attended to the scene, and received its unsophisticated impression. *So much the
rather her celestial light shone inward.* I was pleased
with an observation which he made, when I asked him
how he liked Kemble, who played Richard. I should
have thought (said he) that that man had been reading
something out of a book, if I had not known that I was
in a play-house.

I was once amused in a different way by a knot of
country people who had come to see a play at that same
Theatre. They seemed perfectly inattentive to all the
best performers for the first act or two, though the piece
was admirably played, but kept poring in the play-bill,
and were evidently watching for the appearance of one,
who was to be the source of supreme delight to them
that night. At length the expected actor arrived, who
happened to be in possession of a very insignificant part,
not much above a mute. I saw their faint attempt at raising a clap on his appearance, and their disappointment
at not being seconded by the audience in general. I saw
them try to admire and to find out something very wonderful in him, and wondering all the while at the moderate sensation he produced. I saw their pleasure and their
interest subside at last into flat mortification, when the

riddle was at once unfolded by my recollecting that this performer bore the same name with an actor, then in the acme of his celebrity, at Covent-Garden, but who lately finished his theatrical and mortal career on the other side of the Atlantic. They had come to see Mr. C., but had come to the wrong house.

Is it a stale remark to say, that I have constantly found the interest excited at a play-house to bear an exact inverse proportion to the price paid for admission? Formerly, when my sight and hearing were more perfect, and my purse a little less so, I was a frequenter of the upper gallery in the old theatres. The eager attention, the breathless listening, the anxiety not to lose a word, the quick anticipation of the significance of the scene (every sense kept as it were upon a sharp lookout), which are exhibited by the occupiers of those higher and now almost out-of-sight regions (who, going seldom to a play, cannot afford to lose anything by inattention), suffer some little diminution, as you descend to the lower or two-shilling ranks; but still the joy is lively and unallayed, save that by some little *incursion* of *manners,* the expression of it is expected to abate somewhat of its natural liveliness. The oaken plaudits of the trunk-maker would *here* be considered as going a little beyond the line.

In the Pit first begins that accursed critical faculty, which, making a man the judge of his own pleasures, too often constitutes him the executioner of his own and others! You may see the *jealousy of being unduly pleased,* the *suspicion of being taken in to admire;* in short, the vile critical spirit, creeping and diffusing itself, and spreading from the wrinkled brows and cloudy eyes of the front row sages and newspaper reporters (its proper residence), till it infects and clouds over the thoughtless, vacant countenance, of John Bull tradesmen, and clerks of counting-houses, who, but for that approximation, would have been contented to have grinned without rule, and to have been pleased without asking why.

The sitting next a critic is contagious. Still now and then, a *genuine spectator* is to be found among them, a shopkeeper and his family, whose honest titillations of mirth, and generous chucklings of applause, cannot wait or be at leisure to take the cue from the sour judging faces about them. Haply they never dreamed that there were such animals in nature as critics or reviewers; even the idea of an author may be a speculation they never entered into; but they take the mirth they find as a pure effusion of the actor-folks, set there on purpose to make them fun. I love the unenquiring gratitude of such spectators.

As for the Boxes, I never can understand what brings the people there. I see such frigid indifference, such unconcerned spectatorship, such impenetrability to pleasure or its contrary, such being *in the house* and yet not *of it,* certainly they come far nearer the nature of *the Gods,* upon the system of Lucretius at least, than those honest, hearty, well-pleased, unindifferent mortals above, who, from time immemorial, have had that name, upon no other ground than situation, assigned them.

Take the play-house altogether, there is a less sum of enjoyment than used to be. Formerly you might see something like the effect of a novelty upon a citizen, his wife and daughters, in the Pit; their curiosity upon every new face that entered upon the stage. The talk of how they got in at the door, and how they were crowded upon some former occasion, made a topic till the curtain drew up. People go too often now-a-days to make their ingress or egress of consequence. Children of seven years of age will talk as familiarly of the performers, aye and as knowingly (according to the received opinion) as grown persons; more than the grown persons in my time.

Oh when shall I forget first seeing a play, at the age of five or six? It was *Artaxerxes*. Who played, or who sang in it, I know not. Such low ideas as actors' names, or actors' merits, never entered my head. The mystery of delight was not cut open and dissipated for me by those who took me there. It was Artaxerxes and Arbaces and Mandane that I saw, not Mr. Beard, or Mr. Leoni, or Mrs. Kennedy. It was all enchantment and a dream. No such pleasure has since visited me but in dreams. I was in Persia for the time, and the burning idol of their devotion in the Temple almost converted me into a worshipper. I was awestruck, and believed those significations to be something more than elemental fires. I was, with Uriel, in the body of the sun.

What should I have gained by knowing (as I should have done, had I been born thirty years later) that that solar representation was a mere painted scene, that had neither fire nor light in itself, and that the royal phantoms, which passed in review before me, were but such common mortals as I could see every day out of my father's window? We crush the faculty of delight and wonder in children, by explaining every thing. We take them to the source of the Nile, and show them the scanty runnings, instead of letting the beginnings of that sevenfold stream remain in impenetrable darkness, a mysterious question of wonderment and delight to ages.

The Examiner, Dec. 19, 1813.

ON SOME OF THE OLD ACTORS

THE casual sight of an old play-bill, which I picked up
the other day—I know not by what chance it was preserved so long—tempts me to call to mind a few of the
players, who make the principal figure in it. It presents
the cast of parts in the *Twelfth Night*, at the old Drury
Lane Theatre two-and-thirty years ago. There is something very touching in these old remembrances. They
make us think how we *once* used to read a play-bill—
not, as now peradventure, singling out a favourite performer, and casting a negligent eye over the rest; but
spelling out every name, down to the very mutes and
servants of the scene; when it was a matter of no small
moment to us whether Whitfield, or Packer, took the
part of Fabian; when Benson, and Burton, and Philli-
more—names of small account—had an importance, beyond what we can be content to attribute now to the
time's best actors. "Orsino, by Mr. Barrymore." What a
full Shakspearian sound it carries! how fresh to memory
arise the image and the manner of the gentle actor!

Those who have only seen Mrs. Jordan[1] within the
last ten or fifteen years, can have no adequate notion of
her performance of such parts as Ophelia; Helena, in
All's Well That Ends Well; and Viola in this play. Her
voice had latterly acquired a coarseness, which suited
well enough with her Nells and Hoydens, but in those
days it sank, with her steady, melting eye, into the heart.
Her joyous parts—in which her memory now chiefly
lives—in her youth were outdone by her plaintive ones.

[1] Stage name of Dorothy Bland (1762-1816).—J. M. B.

There is no giving an account how she delivered the disguised story of her love for Orsino. It was no set speech, that she had foreseen, so as to weave it into an harmonious period, line necessarily following line, to make up the music—yet I have heard it so spoken, or rather *read,* not without its grace and beauty—but, when she had declared her sister's history to be a "blank," and that she "never told her love," there was a pause, as if the story had ended—and then the image of the "worm in the bud," came up as a new suggestion —and the heightened image of "Patience" still followed after that, as by some growing (and not mechanical) process, thought springing up after thought, I would almost say, as they were watered by her tears. So in those fine lines—

> Write loyal cantons of contemned love—
> Halloa your name to the reverberate hills—

there was no preparation made in the foregoing image for that which was to follow. She used no rhetoric in her passion; or it was nature's own rhetoric, most legitimate then, when it seemed altogether without rule or law.

Mrs. Powel (now Mrs. Renard), then in the pride of her beauty, made an admirable Olivia. She was particularly excellent in her unbending scenes in conversation with the Clown. I have seen some Olivias—and those very sensible actresses too—who in these interlocutions have seemed to set their wits at the jester, and to vie conceits with him in downright emulation. But she used him for her sport, like what he was, to trifle a leisure sentence or two with, and then to be dismissed, and she to be the Great Lady still. She touched the imperious fantastic humour of the character with nicety. Her fine spacious person filled the scene.

The part of Malvolio has, in my judgment, been so often misunderstood, and the *general merits* of the actor, who then played it, so unduly appreciated, that I shall hope for pardon, if I am a little prolix upon these points.

Of all the actors who flourished in my time—a melancholy phrase if taken aright, reader—Bensley[1] had most of the swell of soul, was greatest in the delivery of heroic conceptions, the emotions consequent upon the presentment of a great idea to the fancy. He had the true poetical enthusiasm—the rarest faculty among players. None that I remember possessed even a portion of that fine madness which he threw out in Hotspur's famous rant about glory, or the transports of the Venetian incendiary at the vision of the fired city. His voice had the dissonance, and at times the inspiriting effect, of the trumpet. His gait was uncouth and stiff, but no way embarrassed by affectation; and the thorough-bred gentleman was uppermost in every movement.

He seized the moment of passion with greatest truth; like a faithful clock, never striking before the time; never anticipating or leading you to anticipate. He was totally destitute of trick and artifice. He seemed come upon the stage to do the poet's message simply, and he did it with as genuine fidelity as the nuncios in Homer deliver the errands of the gods. He let the passion or the sentiment do its own work without prop or bolstering. He would have scorned to mountebank it; and betrayed none of that *cleverness* which is the bane of serious acting.

For this reason, his Iago was the only endurable one which I remember to have seen. No spectator, from his action, could divine more of his artifice than Othello was supposed to do. His confessions in soliloquy alone

[1] Robert Bensley [1786(?)-1817(?)].—J. M. B.

put you in possession of the mystery. There were no
by-intimations to make the audience fancy their own
discernment so much greater than that of the Moor—
who commonly stands like a great helpless mark, set up
for mine Ancient, and a quantity of barren spectators,
to shoot their bolts at. The Iago of Bensley did not go
to work so grossly. There was a triumphant tone about
the character, natural to a general consciousness of
power; but none of that petty vanity which chuckles
and cannot contain itself upon any little successful
stroke of its knavery—as is common with your small
villains, and green probationers in mischief. It did not
clap or crow before its time. It was not a man setting his
wits at a child, and winking all the while at other children, who are mightily pleased at being let into the
secret; but a consummate villain entrapping a noble nature into toils, against which no discernment was available, where the manner was as fathomless as the purpose seemed dark, and without motive.

The part of Malvolio, in the *Twelfth Night*, was performed by Bensley, with a richness and a dignity, of
which (to judge from some recent castings of that
character) the very tradition must be worn out from
the stage. No manager in those days would have
dreamed of giving it to Mr. Baddeley,[1] or Mr. Parsons[2];
when Bensley was occasionally absent from the theatre,
John Kemble[3] thought it no derogation to succeed to the
part.

Malvolio is not essentially ludicrous. He becomes
comic but by accident. He is cold, austere, repelling;
but dignified, consistent, and, for what appears, rather
of an overstretched morality. Maria describes him as

[1] Robert Baddeley (1733-94).—J. M. B.
[2] William Parsons (d. 1795).—J. M. B.
[3] John Philip Kemble (1757-1823).—J. M. B.

a sort of Puritan; and he might have worn his gold chain with honour in one of our old roundhead families, in the service of a Lambert, or a Lady Fairfax. But his morality and his manners are misplaced in Illyria. He is opposed to the proper *levities* of the piece, and falls in the unequal contest. Still his pride, or his gravity (call it which you will), is inherent, and native to the man, not mock or affected, which latter only are the fit objects to excite laughter. His quality is at the best unlovely, but neither buffoon nor contemptible. His bearing is lofty, a little above his station, but probably not much above his deserts. We see no reason why he should not have been brave, honourable, accomplished. His careless committal of the ring to the ground (which he was commissioned to restore to Cesario), bespeaks a generosity of birth and feeling. His dialect on all occasions is that of a gentleman, and a man of education.

We must not confound him with the eternal old, low steward of comedy. He is master of the household to a great princess; a dignity probably conferred upon him for other respects than age or length of service. Olivia, at the first indication of his supposed madness, declares that she "would not have him miscarry for half of her dowry." Does this look as if the character was meant to appear little or insignificant? Once, indeed, she accuses him to his face—of what?—of being "sick of self-love"—but with a gentleness and considerateness, which could not have been, if she had not thought that this particular infirmity shaded some virtues.

His rebuke to the knight, and his sottish revellers, is sensible and spirited; and when we take into consideration the unprotected condition of his mistress, and the strict regard with which her state of real or dissembled mourning would draw the eyes of the world upon her house-affairs, Malvolio might feel the honour of the family in some sort in his keeping; as it appears not that Olivia had any more brothers, or kinsmen, to look to it—for Sir Toby had dropped all such nice respects at the buttery-hatch. That Malvolio was meant to be represented as possessing estimable qualities, the expression of the Duke, in his anxiety to have him reconciled, almost infers: "Pursue him, and entreat him to a peace."

Even in his abused state of chains and darkness, a sort of greatness seems never to desert him. He argues highly and well with the supposed Sir Topas, and philosophizes gallantly upon his straw.[1] There must have been some shadow of worth about the man; he must have been something more than a mere vapour—a thing of straw, or Jack in office—before Fabian and Maria could have ventured sending him upon a courting-errand to Olivia. There was some consonancy (as he would say) in the undertaking, or the jest would have been too bold even for that house of misrule.

Bensley, accordingly, threw over the part an air of Spanish loftiness. He looked, spake, and moved like an old Castilian. He was starch, spruce, opinionated, but his superstructure of pride seemed bottomed upon a sense of worth. There was something in it beyond the coxcomb. It was big and swelling, but you could not be sure that it was hollow. You might wish to see it taken down, but you felt that it was upon an elevation. He was magnificent from the outset; but when the decent sobrieties of the character began to give way, and the poison of self-love, in his conceit of the Countess's affection, gradually to work, you would have thought that the hero of La Mancha in person stood before you.

---

[1] CLOWN. What is the opinion of Pythagoras concerning wild fowl?
MAL. That the soul of our grandam might haply inhabit a bird.
CLOWN. What thinkest thou of his opinion?
MAL. I think nobly of the soul, and no way approve of his opinion.
—C. L.

How he went smiling to himself! with what ineffable
carelessness would he twirl his gold chain! what a dream
it was! you were infected with the illusion, and did not
wish that it should be removed! you had no room for
laughter! if an unseasonable reflection of morality obtruded itself, it was a deep sense of the pitiable infirmity
of man's nature, that can lay him open to such frenzies
—but, in truth, you rather admired than pitied the
lunacy while it lasted—you felt that an hour of such
mistake was worth an age with the eyes open.

Who would not wish to live but for a day in the conceit of such a lady's love as Olivia? Why, the Duke
would have given his principality but for a quarter of
a minute, sleeping or waking, to have been so deluded.
The man seemed to tread upon air, to taste manna, to
walk with his head in the clouds, to mate Hyperion. O!
shake not the castles of his pride—endure yet for a season bright moments of confidence—"stand still, ye
watches of the element," that Malvolio may be still in
fancy fair Olivia's lord!—but fate and retribution say
no—I hear the mischievous titter of Maria—the witty
taunts of Sir Toby—the still more insupportable triumph
of the foolish knight—the counterfeit Sir Topas is un-
masked—and "thus the whirligig of time," as the true
clown hath it, "brings in his revenges." I confess that I
never saw the catastrophe of this character, while Bensley played it, without a kind of tragic interest. There
was good foolery too.

Few now remember Dodd.[1] What an Aguecheek the
stage lost in him! Lovegrove, who came nearest to the
old actors, revived the character some few seasons
ago, and made it sufficiently grotesque; but Dodd was
it, as it came out of nature's hands. It might be said to
remain *in puris naturalibus.* In expressing slowness of

[1] James William Dodd (1740-96).—J. M. B.

apprehension, this actor surpassed all others. You could see the first dawn of an idea stealing slowly over his countenance, climbing up by little and little, with a painful process, till it cleared up at last to the fullness of a twilight conception—its highest meridian. He seemed to keep back his intellect, as some have had the power to retard their pulsation. The balloon takes less time in filling than it took to cover the expansion of his broad moony face over all its quarters with expression. A glimmer of understanding would appear in a corner of his eye, and for lack of fuel go out again. A part of his forehead would catch a little intelligence, and be a long time in communicating it to the remainder.

I am ill at dates, but I think it is now better than five-and-twenty years ago, that walking in the gardens of Gray's Inn—they were then far finer than they are now —the accursed Verulam Buildings had not encroached upon all the east side of them, cutting out delicate green crankles, and shouldering away one of two of the stately alcoves of the terrace—the survivor stands gaping and relationless as if it remembered its brother— they are still the best gardens of any of the Inns of Court, my beloved Temple not forgotten—have the gravest character; their aspect being altogether reverend and law-breathing—Bacon has left the impress of his foot upon their gravel walks. Taking my afternoon solace on a summer day upon the aforesaid terrace, a comely sad personage came towards me, whom, from his grave air and deportment, I judged to be one of the old Benchers of the Inn. He had a serious, thoughtful forehead, and seemed to be in meditations of mortality.

As I have an instinctive awe of old Benchers, I was passing him with that sort of subindicative token of respect which one is apt to demonstrate towards a venerable stranger, and which rather denotes an inclination to greet him, than any positive motion of the body to that effect—a species of humility and will-worship which I observe, nine times out of ten, rather puzzles than pleases the person it is offered to—when the face turning full upon me, strangely identified itself with that of Dodd. Upon close inspection I was not mistaken. But could this sad thoughtful countenance be the same vacant face of folly which I had hailed so often under circumstances of gaiety; which I had never seen without a smile, or recognized but as the usher of mirth; that looked out so formally flat in Foppington, so frothily pert in Tattle, so impotently busy in Backbite; so blankly divested of all meaning, or resolutely expressive of none, in Acres, in Fribble, and a thousand agreeable impertinences? Was this the face—full of thought and carefulness—that had so often divested itself at will of every trace of either to give me diversion, to clear my cloudy face for two or three hours at least of its furrows? Was this the face—manly, sober, intelligent—which I had so often despised, made mocks at, made merry with?

The remembrance of the freedoms which I had taken with it came upon me with a reproach of insult. I could have asked it pardon. I thought it looked upon me with a sense of injury. There is something strange as well as sad in seeing actors—your pleasant fellows particularly—subjected to and suffering the common lot; their fortunes, their casualties, their deaths, seem to belong to the scene, their actions to be amenable to poetic justice only. We can hardly connect them with more awful responsibilities. The death of this fine actor took place shortly after this meeting. He had quitted the stage some months; and, as I learned afterwards, had been in the habit of resorting daily to these gardens, almost to the day of his decease. In these serious walks, probably, he was divesting himself of many scenic and some real vanities—weaning himself from the frivolities of the lesser and the greater theatre—doing gentle penance for a life of no very reprehensible fooleries—taking off by degrees the buffoon mask, which he might feel he had worn too long—and rehearsing for a more solemn cast of part. Dying, he "put on the weeds of Dominic." [1]

If few can remember Dodd, many yet living will not easily forget the pleasant creature who in those days enacted the part of the Clown to Dodd's Sir Andrew. Richard, or rather Dicky Suett [2]—for so in his lifetime he delighted to be called, and time hath ratified the appellation—lieth buried on the north side of the cemetery of Holy Paul, to whose service his nonage and tender years were dedicated. There are who do yet remember him at that period—his pipe clear and harmonious. He would often speak of his chorister days, when he was "cherub Dicky."

What clipped his wings, or made it expedient that he should exchange the holy for the profane state; whether he had lost his good voice (his best recommendation to that office), like Sir John, "with hallooing and singing of anthems"; or whether he was adjudged to lack something, even in those early years, of the gravity indispensable to an occupation which professeth to "commerce with the skies"—I could never rightly learn; but we find

[1] Dodd was a man of reading, and left at his death a choice collection of old English literature. I should judge him to have been a man of wit. I know one instance of an impromptu which no length of study could have bettered. My merry friend, Jem White, had seen him one evening in Aguecheek, and recognizing Dodd the next day in Fleet Street, was irresistibly impelled to take off his hat and salute him as the identical Knight of the preceding evening with a "Save you, Sir Andrew." Dodd, not at all disconcerted at his unusual address from a stranger, with a courteous half-rebuking wave of the hand, put him off with an "Away, Fool."—C. L.

[2] Richard Suett (1758-1805).—J. M. B.

him, after the probation of a twelvemonth or so, reverting to a secular condition, and become one of us.

I think he was not altogether of that timber out of which cathedral seats and sounding-boards are hewed. But if a glad heart—kind, and therefore glad—be any part of sanctity, then might the robe of Motley, with which he invested himself with so much humility after his deprivation, and which he wore so long with so much blameless satisfaction to himself and to the public, be accepted for a surplice—his white stole, and *albe*.

The first fruits of his secularization was an engagement upon the boards of Old Drury, at which theatre he commenced, as I have been told, with adopting the manner of Parsons in old men's characters. At the period in which most of us knew him, he was no more an imitator than he was in any true sense himself imitable.

He was the Robin Goodfellow of the stage. He came in to trouble all things with a welcome perplexity, himself no whit troubled for the matter. He was known, like Puck, by his note—*Ha! Ha! Ha!*—sometimes deepening to *Ho! Ho! Ho!* with an irresistible accession, derived, perhaps, remotely from his ecclesiastical education, foreign to his prototype of—*O La!* Thousands of hearts yet respond to the chuckling *O La!* of Dicky Suett, brought back to their remembrance by the faithful transcript of his friend Mathews's mimicry. The "force of nature could no further go." He drolled upon the stock of these two syllables richer than the cuckoo.

Care, that troubles all the world, was forgotten in his composition. Had he had but two grains (nay, half a grain) of it, he could never have supported himself upon those two spider's strings, which served him (in the latter part of his unmixed existence) as legs. A doubt or a scruple must have made him totter, a sigh have puffed him down; the weight of a frown had staggered him, a wrinkle made him lose his balance. But on he went, scrambling upon those airy stilts of his, with Robin Goodfellow, "thorough brake, thorough briar," reckless of a scratched face or a torn doublet.

Shakspeare foresaw him, when he framed his fools and jesters. They have all the true Suett stamp, a loose and shambling gait, a slippery tongue, this last the ready midwife to a without-pain-delivered jest; in words, light as air, venting truths deep as the centre; with idlest rhymes tagging conceit when busiest, singing with Lear in the tempest, or Sir Toby at the buttery-hatch.

Jack Bannister[1] and he had the fortune to be more of personal favourites with the town than any actors before or after. The difference, I take it, was this: Jack was more *beloved* for his sweet, good-natured moral pretensions. Dicky was more *liked* for his sweet, good-natured, no pretensions at all. Your whole conscience stirred with Bannister's performance of Walter in the *Children in the Wood*—but Dicky seemed like a thing, as Shakspeare says of Love, too young to know what conscience is. He put us into Vesta's days. Evil fled before him—not as from Jack, as from an antagonist— but because it could not touch him, any more than a cannon-ball a fly. He was delivered from the burthen of that death; and, when Death came himself, not in metaphor, to fetch Dicky, it is recorded of him by Robert Palmer, who kindly watched his exit, that he received the last stroke, neither varying his accustomed tranquillity, nor tune, with the simple exclamation, worthy to have been recorded in his epitaph—*O La! O La! Bobby!*

The elder Palmer[2] (of stage-treading celebrity) commonly played Sir Toby in those days; but there is a

---

[1] John Bannister (1760-1836).—J. M. B.
[2] John Palmer (1747-98).—J. M. B.

solidity of wit in the jests of that half-Falstaff which he did not quite fill out. He was as much too showy as Moody[1] (who sometimes took the part) was dry and sottish. In sock or buskin there was an air of swaggering gentility about Jack Palmer. He was a *gentleman* with a slight infusion of *the footman*. His brother Bob (of recenter memory), who was his shadow in everything while he lived, and dwindled into less than a shadow afterwards—was a *gentleman* with a little stronger infusion of the *latter ingredient;* that was all. It is amazing how a little of the more or less makes a difference in these things. When you saw Bobby in the Duke's Servant,[2] you said "What a pity such a pretty fellow was only a servant!" When you saw Jack figuring as Captain Absolute, you thought you could trace his promotion to some lady of quality who fancied the handsome fellow in his topknot, and had bought him a commission. Therefore Jack in Dick Amlet was insuperable.

Jack had two voices, both plausible, hypocritical, and insinuating; but his secondary or supplemental voice still more decisively histrionic than his common one. It was reserved for the spectator; and the *dramatis personæ* were supposed to know nothing at all about it. The *lies* of Young Wilding, and the *sentiments* in Joseph Surface, were thus marked out in a sort of italics to the audience. This secret correspondence with the company before the curtain (which is the bane and death of tragedy) has an extremely happy effect in some kinds of comedy, in the more highly artificial comedy of Congreve or of Sheridan especially, where the absolute sense of reality (so indispensable to scenes of interest) is not required, or would rather interfere to diminish your pleasure. The fact is, you do not believe in such

[1] John Moody (retired 1796).—J. M. B.
- *High Life below Stairs.*—C. L.

characters as Surface—the villain of artificial comedy
—even while you read or see them. If you did, they
would shock and not divert you. When Ben, in *Love for
Love*, returns from sea, the following exquisite dialogue occurs at his first meeting with his father:

SIR SAMPSON. Thou has been many a weary league, Ben,
since I saw thee.

BEN. Ey, ey, been. Been far enough, an that be all. Well,
father how do all at home? how does brother Dick, and
brother Val?

SIR SAMPSON. Dick! body o' me, Dick has been dead these
two years. I writ you word when you were at Leghorn.

BEN. Mess, that's true; Marry, I had forgot. Dick's dead, as
you say—well, and how?—I have a many questions to ask
you—

Here is an instance of insensibility which in real life
would be revolting, or rather in real life could not have
co-existed with the warm-hearted temperament of
the character. But when you read it in the spirit with
which such playful selections and specious combinations rather than strict *metaphrases* of nature should be
taken, or when you saw Bannister play it, it neither did,
nor does, wound the moral sense at all. For what is Ben
—the pleasant sailor which Bannister gives us—but a
piece of satire—a creation of Congreve's fancy—a
dreamy combination of all the accidents of a sailor's
character—his contempt of money—his credulity to
women—with that necessary estrangement from home
which it is just within the verge of credibility to suppose
might produce such an hallucination as is here described.
We never think the worse of Ben for it, or feel it as a
strain upon his character. But when an actor comes,
and instead of the delightful phantom—the creature
dear to half-belief—which Bannister exhibited—displays before our eyes a downright concretion of a Wap-

ping sailor—a jolly warm-hearted Jack Tar—and nothing else—when instead of investing it with a delicious confusedness of the head, and a veering undirected goodness of purpose—he gives to it a downright daylight understanding, and a full consciousness of its actions; thrusting forward the sensibilities of the character with a pretence as if it stood upon nothing else, and was to be judged by them alone—we feel the discord of the thing; the scene is disturbed; a real man has got in among the *dramatis personæ,* and puts them out. We want the sailor turned out. We feel that his true place is not behind the curtain, but in the first or second gallery.

London Magazine, February 1822; *Elia.*

ON THE ACTING OF MUNDEN [1]

NOT many nights ago I had come home from seeing this extraordinary performer in Cockletop; and when I retired to my pillow, his whimsical image still stuck by me, in a manner as to threaten sleep. In vain I tried to divest myself of it, by conjuring up the most opposite associations. I resolved to be serious. I raised up the gravest topics of life; private misery, public calamity. All would not do:

> ———There the antic sate
> Mocking our state———

his queer visnomy—his bewildering costume—all the strange things which he had raked together—his serpentine rod, swagging about in his pocket—Cleopatra's

---

[1] Joseph Shepherd Munden (1758-1832).—J. M. B.

tear, and the rest of his relics—O'Keefe's wild farce, and *his* wilder commentary—till the passion of laughter, like grief in excess, relieved itself by its own weight, inviting the sleep which in the first instance it had driven away.

But I was not to escape so easily. No sooner did I fall into slumbers, than the same image, only more perplexing, assailed me in the shape of dreams. Not one Munden, but five hundred, were dancing before me, like the faces which, whether you will or no, come when you have been taking opium—all the strange combinations, which this strangest of all strange mortals ever shot his proper countenance into, from the day he came commissioned to dry up the tears of the town for the loss of the now almost forgotten Edwin. O for the power of the pencil to have fixed them when I awoke! A season or two since, there was exhibited a Hogarth gallery. I do not see why there should not be a Munden gallery. In richness and variety, the latter would not fall far short of the former.

There is one face of Farley,[1] one face of Knight,[2] one (but what a one it is!) of Liston[3]; but Munden has none that you can properly pin down, and call *his*. When you think he has exhausted his battery of looks, in unaccountable warfare with your gravity, suddenly he sprouts out an entirely new set of features, like Hydra. He is not one, but legion; not so much a comedian, as a company. If his name could be multiplied like his countenance, it might fill a play-bill. He, and he alone, literally *makes faces*: applied to any other person, the phrase is a mere figure, denoting certain modifications of the human countenance. Out of some invisible wardrobe he

[1] Charles Farley (1771-1859).—J. M. B.
[2] Thomas Knight (d. 1804).—J. M. B.
[3] John Liston (1776-1846).—J. M. B.

dips for faces, as his friend Suett used for wigs, and
fetches them out as easily. I should not be surprised to
see him some day put out the head of a river-horse; or
come forth a pewitt, or lap-wing, some feathered meta-
morphosis.

I have seen this gifted actor in Sir Christopher Curry
—in old Dornton—diffuse a glow of sentiment which
has made the pulse of a crowded theatre beat like that
of one man; when he has come in aid of the pulpit, doing good to the moral heart of a people. I have seen
some faint approaches to this sort of excellence in other
players. But in the grand grotesque of farce, Munden
stands out as single and unaccompanied as Hogarth.
Hogarth, strange to tell, had no followers. The school of
Munden began, and must end, with himself.

Can any man *wonder*, like him? can any man *see
ghosts*, like him? or *fight with his own shadow*—"SESSA"
—as he does in that strangely-neglected thing, the *Cobbler of Preston*—where his alternations from the Cobbler
to the Magnifico, and from the Magnifico to the Cobbler,
keep the brain of the spectator in as wild a ferment, as if
some Arabian Night were being acted before him. Who
like him can throw, or ever attempted to throw, a preternatural interest over the commonest daily-life objects?
A table or a joint-stool, in his conception, rises into a dignity equivalent to Cassiopeia's chair. It is invested with
constellatory importance. You could not speak of it with
more deference, if it were mounted into the firmament.

A beggar in the hands of Michael Angelo, says Fuseli,
rose the Patriarch of Poverty. So the gusto of Munden
antiquates and ennobles what it touches. His pots and
his ladles are as grand and primal as the seething-pots
and hooks seen in old prophetic vision. A tub of butter,
contemplated by him, amounts to a Platonic idea. He
understands a leg of mutton in its quiddity. He stands

wondering, amid the common-place materials of life,
like primæval man with the sun and stars about him.

Examiner, November 8, 1819; London Magazine, October 1822; Elia.

ELLISTONIANA

MY ACQUAINTANCE with the pleasant creature, whose
loss we all deplore, was but slight.

My first introduction to E.,[1] which afterwards ripened
into an acquaintance a little on this side of intimacy, was
over a counter in the Leamington Spa Library, then
newly entered upon by a branch of his family. E.,
whom nothing misbecame—to auspicate, I suppose, the
filial concern, and set it a-going with a lustre—was serving in person two damsels fair, who had come into the
shop ostensibly to inquire for some new publication, but
in reality to have a sight of the illustrious shopman, hoping some conference.

With what an air did he reach down the volume, dis-
passionately giving his opinion of the worth of the work
in question, and launching out into a dissertation on its
comparative merits with those of certain publications of
a similar stamp, its rivals! his enchanted customers fairly
hanging on his lips, subdued to their authoritative sentence. So have I seen a gentleman in comedy acting the
shopman. So Lovelace sold his gloves in King Street. I
admired the histrionic art, by which he contrived to
carry clean away every notion of disgrace, from the occupation he had so generously submitted to; and from
that hour I judged him, with no after repentance, to be a

[1] Robert William Elliston (1774-1831).—J. M. B.

person with whom it would be a felicity to be more acquainted.

To descant upon his merits as a Comedian would be superfluous. With his blended private and professional habits alone I have to do; that harmonious fusion of the manners of the player into those of everyday life, which brought the stage boards into streets, and dining-parlours, and kept up the play when the play was ended. "I like Wrench," a friend was saying to him one day, "because he is the same, natural, easy creature, *on* the stage, that he is *off*." "My case exactly," retorted Elliston—with a charming forgetfulness, that the converse of a proposition does not always lead to the same conclusion —"I am the same person *off* the stage that I am *on*." The inference, at first sight, seems identical; but examine it a little, and it confesses only, that the one performer was never, and the other always, *acting*.

And in truth this was the charm of Elliston's private deportment. You had spirited performance always going on before your eyes, with nothing to pay. As where a monarch takes up his casual abode for a night, the poorest hovel which he honours by his sleeping in it, becomes *ipso facto* for that time a palace; so wherever Elliston walked, sate, or stood still, there was the theatre. He carried about with him his pit, boxes, and galleries, and set up his portable play-house at corners of streets, and in the market-places. Upon flintiest pavements he trod the boards still; and if his theme chanced to be passionate, the green baize carpet of tragedy spontaneously rose beneath his feet. Now this was hearty, and showed a love for his art. So Apelles *always* painted—in thought. So G. D. *always* poetizes. I hate a lukewarm artist.

I have known actors—and some of them of Elliston's own stamp—who shall have agreeably been amusing you in the part of a rake or a coxcomb, through the two or three hours of their dramatic existence; but no sooner does the curtain fall with its leaden clatter, but a spirit of lead seems to seize on all their faculties. They emerge sour, morose persons, intolerable to their families, servants, etc. Another shall have been expanding your heart with generous deeds and sentiments, till it even beats with yearnings of universal sympathy; you absolutely long to go home and do some good action. The play seems tedious, till you can get fairly out of the house, and realize your laudable intentions. At length the final bell rings, and this cordial representative of all that is amiable in human breasts steps forth—a miser.

Elliston was more of a piece. Did he *play* Ranger? and did Ranger fill the general bosom of the town with satisfaction? why should *he* not be Ranger, and diffuse the same cordial satisfaction among his private circles? with *his* temperament, *his* animal spirits, *his* good-nature, *his* follies perchance, could he do better than identify himself with his impersonation? Are we to like a pleasant rake, or coxcomb, on the stage, and give ourselves airs of aversion for the identical character, presented to us in actual life? or what would the performer have gained by divesting himself of the impersonation? Could the man Elliston have been essentially different from his part, even if he had avoided to reflect to us studiously, in private circles, the airy briskness, the forwardness, and 'scape-goat trickeries of his prototype?

"But there is something not natural in this everlasting *acting;* we want the real man."

Are you quite sure that it is not the man himself, whom you cannot, or will not see, under some adventitious trappings, which, nevertheless, sit not at all inconsistently upon him? What if it is the nature of some men to be highly artificial? The fault is least reprehensible in *players*. Cibber was his own Foppington, with almost as much wit as Vanbrugh could add to it.

"My conceit of his person"—it is Ben Jonson speaking of Lord Bacon—"was never increased towards him by his *place* or *honours*. But I have, and do reverence him for the *greatness*, that was only proper to himself; in that he seemed to me ever one of the *greatest* men, that had been in many ages. In his adversity I ever prayed that Heaven would give him strength; for *greatness* he could not want."

The quality here commended was scarcely less conspicuous in the subject of these idle reminiscences than in my Lord Verulam. Those who have imagined that an unexpected elevation to the direction of a great London Theatre affected the consequence of Elliston, or at all changed his nature, knew not the essential *greatness* of the man whom they disparage. It was my fortune to encounter him near St. Dunstan's Church (which, with its punctual giants, is now no more than dust and a shadow), on the morning of his election to that high office. Grasping my hand with a look of significance, he only uttered, "Have you heard the news?"—then, with another look following up the blow, he subjoined, "I am the future Manager of Drury Lane Theatre." Breathless as he saw me, he stayed not for congratulation or reply, but mutely stalked away, leaving me to chew upon his new-blown dignities at leisure. In fact, nothing could be said to it. Expressive silence alone could muse his praise. This was in his *great* style.

But was he less *great* (be witness, O ye Powers of Equanimity, that supported in the ruins of Carthage the consular exile, and more recently transmuted, for a more illustrious exile, the barren constableship of Elba into an image of Imperial France), when, in melancholy af-

ter-years, again, much near the same spot, I met him,
when that sceptre had been wrested from his hand, and
his dominion was curtailed to the petty managership,
and part proprietorship, of the small Olympic, *his Elba?*
He still played nightly upon the boards of Drury, but
in parts, alas! allotted to him, not magnificently distributed by him. Waiving his great loss as nothing, and
magnificently sinking the sense of fallen *material* grandeur in the more liberal resentment of depreciations done
to his more lofty *intellectual* pretensions, "Have you
heard" (his customary exordium)—"have you heard,"
said he, "how they treat me? they put me in *comedy.*"
Thought I—but his finger on his lips forbade any verbal
interruption—"where could they have put you better?"
Then, after a pause—"Where I formerly played Romeo,
I now play Mercutio,"—and so again he stalked away,
neither staying, nor caring for, responses.

O, it was a rich scene,—but Sir A. C., the best of
story-tellers and surgeons, who mends a lame narrative
almost as well as he sets a fracture, alone could do justice
to it—that I was a witness to, in the tarnished room
(that had once been green) of that same little Olympic.
There, after his deposition from Imperial Drury, he substituted a throne. That Olympic Hill was his "highest
heaven"; himself "Jove in his chair." There he sat in
state, while before him, on complaint of prompter, was
brought for judgment—how shall I describe her? one of
those little tawdry things that flirt at the tails of choruses
—a probationer for the town, in either of its senses—
the pertest little drab—a dirty fringe and appendage of
the lamp's smoke—who, it seems, on some disapproba-
tion expressed by a "highly respectable" audience—had
precipitately quitted her station on the boards, and withdrawn her small talents in disgust.

"And how dare you," said her manager—assuming a

censorial severity, which would have crushed the confidence of a Vestris,[1] and disarmed that beautiful Rebel herself of her professional caprices—I verily believe, he thought *her* standing before him—"how dare you, Madam, withdraw yourself, without a notice, from your theatrical duties?" "I was hissed, Sir." "And you have the presumption to decide upon the taste of the town?" "I don't know that, Sir, but I will never stand to be hissed," was the subjoinder of young Confidence—when gathering up his features into one significant mass of wonder, pity, and expostulatory indignation—in a lesson never to have been lost upon a creature less forward than she who stood before him—his words were these: "They have hissed *me*."

'Twas the identical argument *a fortiori*, which the son of Peleus uses to Lycaon trembling under his lance, to persuade him to take his destiny with a good grace. "I too am mortal." And it is to be believed that in both cases the rhetoric missed of its application, for want of a proper understanding with the faculties of the respective recipients.

"Quite an Opera pit," he said to me, as he was courteously conducting me over the benches of his Surrey Theatre, the last retreat, and recess, of his everyday waning grandeur.

Those who knew Elliston, will know the *manner* in which he pronounced the latter sentence of the few words I am about to record. One proud day to me he took his roast mutton with us in the Temple, to which I had superadded a preliminary haddock. After a rather

[1] Madame Vestris (1797-1856), an Italian by birth, first known in London as a contralto, then as a dancer, next as an actress (especially in "breeches parts"), and finally as an enlightened and progressive manageress. On January 3, 1831, she had taken over the management of the Olympic Theatre where she was to stage a brilliant succession of extravaganzas known as "burlettas."

plentiful partaking of the meagre banquet, not unre-
freshed with the humbler sort of liquors, I made a sort
of apology for the humility of the fare, observing that
for my own part I never ate but one dish at dinner. "I
too never eat but one thing at dinner"—was his reply—
then after a pause—"reckoning fish as nothing." The
manner was all. It was as if by one peremptory sentence
he had decreed the annihilation of all the savoury escu-
lents, which the pleasant and nutritious-food-giving
Ocean pours forth upon poor humans from her watery
bosom. This was *greatness,* tempered with considerate
tenderness to the feelings of his scanty but welcoming
entertainer.

Great wert thou in thy life, Robert William Elliston!
and *not lessened* in thy death, if report speak truly,
which says that thou didst direct that thy mortal remains
should repose under no inscription but one of pure *La-
tinity.* Classical was thy bringing up! and beautiful was
the feeling on thy last bed, which, connecting the man
with the boy, took thee back to thy latest exercise of imagination, to the days when, undreaming of Theatres
and Managerships, thou wert a scholar, and an early
ripe one, under the roofs builded by the munificent and
pious Colet. For thee the Pauline Muses weep. In ele-
gies that shall silence this crude prose, they shall cele-
brate thy praise.

Englishman's Magazine, August 1831; Last Essays of Elia.

gallantry, where pleasure is duty, and the manners pe
fect freedom. It is altogether a speculative scene
things, which has no reference whatever to the wor
that is. No good person can be justly offended as a spe
tator, because no good person suffers on the stag
Judged morally, every character in these plays—the f
exceptions only are *mistakes*—is alike essentially v
and worthless.

The great art of Congreve is especially shown in t
that he has entirely excluded from his scenes—so
little generosities in the part of Angelica perhaps
cepted—not only anything like a faultless character,
any pretensions to goodness or good feelings wha
ever. Whether he did this designedly, or instinctiv
the effect is as happy, as the design (if design)
bold. I used to wonder at the strange power which
Way of the World in particular possesses of intere
you all along in the pursuits of characters, for w
you absolutely care nothing—for you neither hat
love his personages—and I think it is owing to this
indifference for any, that you endure the whole. H
spread a privation of moral light, I will call it,
than by the ugly name of palpable darkness, ov
creations; and his shadows flit before you withou
tinction or preference. Had he introduced a good
acter, a single gush of moral feeling, a revulsion
judgment to actual life and actual duties, the ir
nent Goshen would have only lighted to the disco
deformities, which now are none, because we
them none.

Translated into real life, the characters of his,
friend Wycherley's dramas, are profligates and
pets—the business of their brief existence, the un
pursuit of lawless gallantry. No other spring of a
possible motive of conduct, is recognized; p

ON THE ARTIFICIAL COMEDY
OF THE LAST CENTURY

THE artificial Comedy, or Comedy of manners, is quite
extinct on our stage. Congreve and Farquhar show their
heads once in seven years only; to be exploded and put
down instantly. The times cannot bear them. Is it for
a few wild speeches, an occasional licence of dialogue?
I think not altogether. The business of their dramatic
characters will not stand the moral test. We screw everything up to that. Idle gallantry in a fiction, a dream, the
passing pageant of an evening, startles us in the same
way as the alarming indications of profligacy in a son or
ward in real life should startle a parent or guardian. We
have no such middle emotions as dramatic interests left.

We see a stage libertine playing his loose pranks of
two hours' duration, and of no after consequence, with
the severe eyes which inspect real vices with their bearings upon two worlds. We are spectators to a plot or intrigue (not reducible in life to the point of strict morality), and take it all for truth. We substitute a real for a
dramatic person, and judge him accordingly. We try
him in our courts, from which there is no appeal to the
dramatis personæ, his peers.

We have been spoiled with—not sentimental comedy
—but a tyrant far more pernicious to our pleasures
which has succeeded to it, the exclusive and all-devour-
ing drama of common life; where the moral point is everything; where, instead of the fictitious half-believed
personages of the stage (the phantoms of old comedy),
we recognize ourselves, our brothers, aunts, kinsfolk,

allies, patrons, enemies—the same as in life—with an interest in what is going on so hearty and substantial, that we cannot afford our moral judgment, in its deepest and most vital results, to compromise or slumber for a moment. What is *there* transacting, by no modification is made to affect us in any other manner than the same events or characters would do in our relationships of life.

We carry our fireside concerns to the theatre with us. We do not go thither, like our ancestors, to escape from the pressure of reality, so much as to confirm our experience of it; to make assurance double, and take a bond of fate. We must live our toilsome lives twice over, as it was the mournful privilege of Ulysses to descend twice to the shades. All that neutral ground of character, which stood between vice and virtue; or which in fact was indifferent to neither, where neither properly was called in question; that happy breathing-place from the burthen of a perpetual moral questioning—the sanctuary and quiet Alsatia of hunted casuistry—is broken up and disfranchised, as injurious to the interests of society. The privileges of the place are taken away by law. We dare not dally with images, or names, of wrong. We bark like foolish dogs at shadows. We dread infection from the scenic representation of disorder, and fear a painted pustule. In our anxiety that our morality should not take cold, we wrap it up in a great blanket surtout of precaution against the breeze and sunshine.

I confess for myself that (with no great delinquencies to answer for) I am glad for a season to take an airing beyond the diocese of the strict conscience—not to live always in the precincts of the law-courts—but now and then, for a dream-while or so, to imagine a world with no meddling restrictions—to get into recesses, whither the hunter cannot follow me—

———Secret shades
Of woody Ida's inmost grove,
While yet there was no fear of Jove.

I come back to my cage and my restraint the fresher and more healthy for it. I wear my shackles more contentedly for having respired the breath of an imaginary freedom. I do not know how it is with others, but I feel the better always for the perusal of one of Congreve's—nay, why should I not add even of Wycherley's—comedies. I am the gayer at least for it; and I could never connect those sports of a witty fancy in any shape with any result to be drawn from them to imitation in real life.

They are a world of themselves almost as much as fairyland. Take one of their characters, male or female (with few exceptions they are alike), and place it in a modern play, and my virtuous indignation shall rise against the profligate wretch as warmly as the Catos of the pit could desire; because in a modern play I am to judge of the right and the wrong. The standard of *police* is the measure of *political justice*. The atmosphere will blight it; it cannot live here. It has got into a moral world, where it has no business, from which it must needs fall headlong; as dizzy, and incapable of making a stand, as a Swedenborgian bad spirit that has wandered unawares into the sphere of one of his Good Men, or Angels. But in its own world do we feel the creature is so very bad?—

The Fainalls and the Mirabels, the Dorimants and the Lady Touchwoods, in their own sphere, do not offend my moral sense; in fact they do not appeal to it all. They seem engaged in their proper element. They break through no laws, or conscientious restraints. They know of none. They have got out of Christendom into th[e] land—what shall I call it?—of cuckoldry—the Utopia

553 ON THE ARTIFICIAL COMEDY

which, universally acted upon, must reduce this frame of things to a chaos. But we do them wrong in so translating them. No such effects are produced, in *their* world. When we are among them, we are amongst a chaotic people. We are not to judge them by our usages. No reverend institutions are insulted by their proceedings—for they have none among them. No peace of families is violated—for no family ties exist among them. No purity of the marriage bed is stained—for none is supposed to have a being. No deep affections are disquieted, no holy wedlock bands are snapped asunder—for affection's depth and wedded faith are not of the growth of that soil. There is neither right nor wrong—gratitude or its opposite—claim or duty—paternity or sonship. Of what consequence is it to Virtue, or how is she at all concerned about it, whether Sir Simon or Dapperwit steal away Miss Martha; or who is the father of Lord Froth's or Sir Paul Pliant's children?

The whole is a passing pageant, where we should sit as unconcerned at the issues, for life or death, as at a battle of the frogs and mice. But, like Don Quixote, we take part against the puppets, and quite as impertinently. We dare not contemplate an Atlantis, a scheme, out of which our coxcombical moral sense is for a little transitory ease excluded. We have not the courage to imagine a state of things for which there is neither reward nor punishment. We cling to the painful necessities of shame and blame. We would indict our very dreams.

Amidst the mortifying circumstances attendant upon growing old, it is something to have seen *The School for Scandal* in its glory. This comedy grew out of Congreve and Wycherley, but gathered some allays of the sentimental comedy which followed theirs. It is impossible that it should be now *acted*, though it continues, at long intervals, to be announced in the bills. Its hero, when

Palmer played it at least, was Joseph Surface. When I remember the gay boldness, the graceful solemn plausibility, the measured step, the insinuating voice—to express it in a word—the downright *acted* villainy of the part, so different from the pressure of conscious actual wickedness—the hypocritical assumption of hypocrisy—which made Jack so deservedly a favourite in that character, I must needs conclude the present generation of playgoers more virtuous than myself, or more dense.

I freely confess that he divided the palm with me with his better brother; that, in fact, I liked him quite as well. Not but there are passages—like that, for instance, where Joseph is made to refuse a pittance to a poor relation—incongruities which Sheridan was forced upon by the attempt to join the artificial with the sentimental comedy, either of which must destroy the other—but over these obstructions Jack's manner floated him so lightly, that a refusal from him no more shocked you, than the easy compliance of Charles gave you in reality any pleasure; you got over the paltry question as quickly as you could, to get back into the regions of pure comedy, where no cold moral reigns. The highly artificial manner of Palmer in this character counteracted every disagreeable impression which you might have received from the contrast, supposing them real, between the two brothers. You did not believe in Joseph with the same faith with which you believed in Charles. The latter was a pleasant reality, the former a no less pleasant poetical foil to it. The comedy, I have said, is incongruous; a mixture of Congreve with sentimental incompatibilities; the gaiety upon the whole is buoyant; but it required the consummate art of Palmer to reconcile the discordant elements.

A player with Jack's talents, if we had one now, would not dare to do the part in the same manner. He would instinctively avoid every turn which might tend to unrealize, and so to make the character fascinating. He must take his cue from his spectators, who would expect a bad man and a good man as rigidly opposed to each other as the death-beds of those geniuses are contrasted in the prints, which I am sorry to say have disappeared from the windows of my old friend Carrington Bowles, of St. Paul's Churchyard memory—(an exhibition as venerable as the adjacent cathedral, and almost coeval) of the bad and good man at the hour of death; where the ghastly apprehensions of the former,—and truly the grim phantom with his reality of a toasting-fork is not to be despised—so finely contrast with the meek complacent kissing of the rod—taking it in like honey and butter—with which the latter submits to the scythe of the gentle bleeder, Time, who wields his lancet with the apprehensive finger of a popular young ladies' surgeon. What flesh, like loving grass, would not covet to meet half-way the stroke of such a delicate mower?

John Palmer was twice an actor in this exquisite part. He was playing to you all the while that he was playing upon Sir Peter and his lady. You had the first intimation of a sentiment before it was on his lips. His altered voice was meant to you, and you were to suppose that his fictitious co-flutterers on the stage perceived nothing at all of it. What was it to you if that half reality, the husband, was overreached by the puppetry—or the thin thing (Lady Teazle's reputation) was persuaded it was dying of a plethory? The fortunes of Othello and Desdemona were not concerned in it. Poor Jack has passed from the stage in good time, that he did not live to this our age of seriousness.

The pleasant old Teazle, King, too, is gone in good time. His manner would scarce have passed current in our day. We must love or hate—acquit or condemn—

censure or pity—exert our detestable coxcombry of
moral judgment upon everything. Joseph Surface, to go
down now, must be a downright revolting villain—no
compromise—his first appearance must shock and give
horror—his specious plausibilities, which the pleasurable faculties of our fathers welcomed with such hearty
greetings, knowing that no harm (dramatic harm even)
could come, or was meant to come, of them, must inspire a cold and killing aversion. Charles (the real cant-
ing person of the scene—for the hypocrisy of Joseph has
its ulterior legitimate ends, but his brother's professions
of a good heart centre in downright self-satisfaction)
must be *loved,* and Joseph *hated.*

To balance one disagreeable reality with another, Sir
Peter Teazle must be no longer the comic idea of a fret-
ful old bachelor bridegroom, whose teasings (while
King acted it) were evidently as much played off at you,
as they were meant to concern anybody on the stage—
he must be a real person, capable in law of sustaining an
injury—a person towards whom duties are to be acknowledged—the genuine crim. con. antagonist of the
villainous seducer Joseph. To realize him more, his sufferings under his unfortunate match must have the
downright pungency of life—must (or should) make
you not mirthful but uncomfortable, just as the same
predicament would move you in a neighbour or old
friend. The delicious scenes which give the play its name
and zest, must affect you in the same serious manner as
if you heard the reputation of a dear female friend at-
tacked in your real presence. Crabtree and Sir Benjamin
—those poor snakes that live but in the sunshine of your
mirth—must be ripened by this hot-bed process of realization into asps or amphisbænas and Mrs. Candour—
O! frightful!—become a hooded serpent.

O! who that remembers Parsons and Dodd—the wasp

and butterfly of *The School for Scandal*—in those two characters; and charming natural Miss Pope, the perfect gentlewoman as distinguished from the fine lady of comedy, in this latter part—would forego the true scenic delight—the escape from life—the oblivion of consequences—the holiday barring out of the pedant Reflection—those Saturnalia of two or three brief hours, well won from the world—to sit instead at one of our modern plays—to have his coward conscience (that forsooth must not be left for a moment) stimulated with perpetual appeals—dulled rather, and blunted, as a faculty without repose must be—and his moral vanity pampered with images of notional justice, notional beneficence, lives saved without the spectator's risk, and fortunes given away that cost the author nothing?

No piece was, perhaps, ever so completely cast in all its parts as this *manager's comedy*. Miss Farren had succeeded to Mrs. Abington in Lady Teazle; and Smith, the original Charles, had retired when I first saw it. The rest of the characters, with very slight exceptions, remained. I remember it was then the fashion to cry down John Kemble, who took the part of Charles after Smith; but, I thought, very unjustly. Smith, I fancy was more airy, and took the eye with a certain gaiety of person. He brought with him no sombre recollections of tragedy. He had not to expiate the fault of having pleased beforehand in lofty declamation. He had no sins of Hamlet or of Richard to atone for. His failure in these parts was a passport to success in one of so opposite a tendency. But, as far as I could judge, the weighty sense of Kemble made up for more personal incapacity than he had to answer for.

His harshest tones in this part came steeped and dulcified in good-humour. He made his defects a grace. His exact declamatory manner, as he managed it, only served to convey the points of his dialogue with more precision. It seemed to head the shafts to carry them deeper. Not one of his sparkling sentences was lost. I remember minutely how he delivered each in succession, and cannot by any effort imagine how any of them could be altered for the better.

No man could deliver brilliant dialogue—the dialogue of Congreve or Wycherley—because none understood it —half so well as John Kemble. His Valentine, in *Love for Love,* was, to my recollection, faultless. He flagged sometimes in the intervals of tragic passion. He would slumber over the level parts of an heroic character. His Macbeth has been known to nod. But he always seemed to me to be particularly alive to pointed and witty dialogue. The relaxing levities of tragedy have not been touched by any since him—the playful court-bred spirit in which he condescended to the players in Hamlet —the sportive relief which he threw into the darker shades of Richard—disappeared with him. He had his sluggish moods, his torpors—but they were the halting-stones and resting-place of his tragedy—politic savings, and fetches of the breath—husbandry of the lungs, where nature pointed him to be an economist—rather, I think, than errors of the judgment. They were, at worst, less painful than the eternal tormenting unappeasable vigilance—the "lidless dragon eyes," of present fashionable tragedy.

London Magazine, April 1822; *Elia.*

ON THE TRAGEDIES OF SHAKSPEARE

CONSIDERED WITH REFERENCE
TO THEIR FITNESS FOR STAGE-REPRESENTATION

TAKING a turn the other day in the Abbey, I was struck with the affected attitude of a figure, which I do not remember to have seen before, and which upon examination proved to be a whole-length of the celebrated Mr. Garrick. Though I would not go so far with some good Catholics abroad as to shut players altogether out of consecrated ground, yet I own I was not a little scandalized at the introduction of theatrical airs and gestures into a place set apart to remind us of the saddest realities. Going nearer, I found inscribed under this harlequin figure the following lines:

> To paint fair Nature, by divine command
> Her magic pencil in his glowing hand,
> A Shakspeare rose; then, to expand his fame
> Wide o'er this breathing world, a Garrick came.
> Though sunk in death the forms the Poet drew,
> The Actor's genius bade them breathe anew;
> Though, like the bard himself, in night they lay,
> Immortal Garrick called them back to day:
> And till Eternity with power sublime
> Shall mark the mortal hour of hoary Time,
> Shakspeare and Garrick like twin-stars shall shine,
> And earth irradiate with a beam divine.

It would be an insult to my readers' understanding to attempt anything like a criticism on this farrago of false thoughts and nonsense. But the reflection it led me into was a kind of wonder, how, from the days of the actor here celebrated to our own, it should have been the fashion to compliment every performer in his turn, that has had the luck to please the Town in any of the great characters of Shakspeare, with the notion of possessing a *mind congenial with the poet's:* how people should come thus unaccountably to confound the power of originating poetical images and conceptions with the faculty of being able to read or recite the same when put into words[1]; or what connection that absolute mastery over the heart and soul of man, which a great dramatic poet possesses, has with those low tricks upon the eye and ear, which a player by observing a few general effects, which some common passion, as grief, anger, etc., usually has upon the gestures and exterior, can so easily compass.

To know the internal workings and movements of a great mind, of an Othello or a Hamlet for instance, the *when* and the *why* and the *how far* they should be moved; to what pitch a passion is becoming; to give the reins and to pull in the curb exactly at the moment when the drawing in or the slackening is most graceful; seems to demand a reach of intellect of a vastly different extent from that which is employed upon the bare imitation of the signs of these passions in the countenance or gesture, which signs are usually observed to be most lively and emphatic in the weaker sort of minds, and which signs can after all but indicate some passion, as I

---

[1] It is observable that we fall into this confusion only in *dramatic* recitations. We never dream that the gentleman who reads Lucretius in public with great applause, is therefore a great poet and philosopher; nor do we find that Tom Davis, the bookseller, who is recorded to have recited the *Paradise Lost* better than any man in England in his day (though I cannot help thinking there must be some mistake in this tradition) was therefore, by his intimate friends, set upon a level with Milton.—C. L.

said before, anger, or grief, generally; but of the motives and grounds of the passion, wherein it differs from the same passion in low and vulgar natures, of these the actor can give no more idea by his face or gesture than the eye (without a metaphor) can speak, or the muscles utter intelligible sounds. But such is the instantaneous nature of the impressions which we take in at the eye and ear at a play-house, compared with the slow apprehension oftentimes of the understanding in reading, that we are apt not only to sink the play-writer in the consideration which we pay to the actor, but even to identify in our minds, in a perverse manner, the actor with the character which he represents.

It is difficult for a frequent play-goer to disembarrass the idea of Hamlet from the person and voice of Mr. K. We speak of Lady Macbeth, while we are in reality thinking of Mrs. S. Nor is this confusion incidental alone to unlettered persons, who, not possessing the advantage of reading, are necessarily dependent upon the stage-player for all the pleasure which they can receive from the drama, and to whom the very idea of *what an author is* cannot be made comprehensible without some pain and perplexity of mind: the error is one from which persons otherwise not meanly lettered, find it almost impossible to extricate themselves.

Never let me be so ungrateful as to forget the very high degree of satisfaction which I received some years back from seeing for the first time a tragedy of Shakspeare performed, in which those two great performers sustained the principal parts. It seemed to embody and realize conceptions which had hitherto assumed no distinct shape. But dearly do we pay all our life after for this juvenile pleasure, this sense of distinctness. When the novelty is past, we find to our cost that instead of realizing an idea, we have only materialized and brought down a fine vision to the standard of flesh and blood. We have let go a dream, in quest of an unattainable substance.

How cruelly this operates upon the mind, to have its free conceptions thus cramped and pressed down to the measure of a strait-lacing actuality, may be judged from that delightful sensation of freshness, with which we turn to those plays of Shakspeare which have escaped being performed, and to those passages in the acting plays of the same writer which have happily been left out in the performance. How far the very custom of hearing anything *spouted*, withers and blows upon a fine passage, may be seen in those speeches from *Henry the Fifth*, etc., which are current in the mouths of schoolboys, from their being to be found in *Enfield's Speaker*, and such kind of books! I confess myself utterly unable to appreciate that celebrated soliloquy in *Hamlet*, beginning "To be or not to be," or to tell whether it be good, bad or indifferent, it has been so handled and pawed about by declamatory boys and men, and torn so inhumanly from its living place and principle of continuity in the play, till it is become to me a perfect dead member.

It may seem a paradox, but I cannot help being of opinion that the plays of Shakspeare are less calculated for performance on a stage, than those of almost any other dramatist whatever. Their distinguishing excellence is a reason that they should be so. There is so much in them, which comes not under the province of acting, with which eye, and tone, and gesture, have nothing to do.

The glory of the scenic art is to personate passion, and the turns of passion; and the more coarse and palpable the passion is, the more hold upon the eyes and ears of the spectators the performer obviously possesses. For this reason, scolding scenes, scenes where two persons talk themselves into a fit of fury, and then in a surprising manner talk themselves out of it again, have always been the most popular upon our stage. And the reason is plain, because the spectators are here most palpably appealed to, they are the proper judges in this war of words, they are the legitimate ring that should be formed round such "intellectual prize-fighters." Talking is the direct object of the imitation here. But in all the best dramas, and in Shakspeare above all, how obvious it is, that the form of *speaking*, whether it be in soliloquy or dialogue, is only a medium, and often a highly artificial one, for putting the reader or spectator into possession of that knowledge of the inner structure and workings of mind in a character, which he could otherwise never have arrived at *in that form of composition* by any gift short of intuition. We do here as we do with novels written in the *epistolary form*. How many improprieties, perfect solecisms in letter-writing, do we put up with in *Clarissa* and other books, for the sake of the delight which that form upon the whole gives us!

But the practice of stage representation reduces everything to a controversy of elocution. Every character, from the boisterous blasphemings of Bajazet to the shrinking timidity of womanhood, must play the orator. The love-dialogues of Romeo and Juliet, those silver-sweet sounds of lovers' tongues by night! the more intimate and sacred sweetness of nuptial colloquy between an Othello or a Posthumus with their married wives, all those delicacies which are so delightful in the reading, as when we read of those youthful dalliances in Paradise—

> As beseem'd
> Fair couple link'd in happy nuptial league,
> Alone;

by the inherent fault of stage representation, how are these things sullied and turned from their very nature by being exposed to a large assembly; when such speeches as Imogen addresses to her lord, come drawling out of the mouth of a hired actress, whose courtship, though nominally addressed to the personated Posthumus, is manifestly aimed at the spectators, who are to judge of her endearments and her returns of love!

The character of Hamlet is perhaps that by which, since the days of Betterton, a succession of popular performers have had the greatest ambition to distinguish themselves. The length of the part may be one of their reasons. But for the character itself, we find it in a play, and therefore we judge it a fit subject of dramatic representation. The play itself abounds in maxims and reflections beyond any other, and therefore we consider it as a proper vehicle for conveying moral instruction. But Hamlet himself—what does he suffer meanwhile by being dragged forth as the public schoolmaster, to give lectures to the crowd! Why, nine parts in ten of what Hamlet does, are transactions between himself and his moral sense; they are the effusions of his solitary musings, which he retires to holes and corners and the most sequestered parts of the palace to pour forth; or rather, they are the silent meditations with which his bosom is bursting, reduced to *words* for the sake of the reader, who must else remain ignorant of what is passing there.

These profound sorrows, these light-and noise-abhorring ruminations, which the tongue scarce dares utter to deaf walls and chambers, how can they be represented by a gesticulating actor, who comes and mouths them out before an audience, making four hundred people his confidants at once! I say not that it is the fault of the actor so to do; he must pronounce them *ore rotundo;* he must accompany them with his eye; he must insinuate

them into his auditory by some trick of eye, tone or gesture, or he fails. *He must be thinking all the while of his
appearance, because he knows that all the while the
spectators are judging of it.* And this is the way to represent the shy, negligent, retiring Hamlet!

It is true that there is no other mode of conveying a
vast quantity of thought and feeling to a great portion of
the audience, who otherwise would never earn it for
themselves by reading, and the intellectual acquisition
gained this way may, for aught I know, be inestimable;
but I am not arguing that *Hamlet* should not be acted,
but how much *Hamlet* is made another thing by being
acted. I have heard much of the wonders which Garrick performed in this part; but as I never saw him, I
must have leave to doubt whether the representation of
such a character came within the province of his art.
Those who tell me of him, speak of his eye, of the magic
of his eye, and of his commanding voice: physical properties, vastly desirable in an actor, and without which he
can never insinuate meaning into an auditory—but what
have they to do with Hamlet; what have they to do
with intellect? In fact, the things aimed at in theatrical
representation, are to arrest the spectator's eye upon
the form and the gesture, and so to gain a more favourable hearing to what is spoken: it is not what the character is, but how he looks; not what he says, but how he
speaks it.

I see no reason to think that if the play of *Hamlet*
were written over again by some such writer as Banks
or Lillo, retaining the process of the story, but totally
omitting all the poetry of it, all the divine features of
Shakspeare, his stupendous intellect; and only taking
care to give us enough of passionate dialogue, which
Banks or Lillo were never at a loss to furnish; I see not
how the effect could be much different upon an audi-

ence, nor how the actor has it in his power to represent
Shakspeare to us differently from his representation of
Banks or Lillo. Hamlet would still be a youthful accomplished prince, and must be gracefully personated; he
might be puzzled in his mind, wavering in his conduct,
seemingly cruel to Ophelia; he might see a ghost, and
start at it, and address it kindly when he found it to be
his father; all this in the poorest and most homely language of the servilest creeper after nature that ever consulted the palate of an audience; without troubling
Shakspeare for the matter: and I see not but there
would be room for all the power which an actor has, to
display itself. All the passions and changes of passion
might remain: for those are much less difficult to write
or act than is thought; it is a trick easy to be attained, it
is but rising or falling a note or two in the voice, a whisper with a significant foreboding look to announce its
approach, and so contagious the counterfeit appearance
of any emotion is, that let the words be what they will,
the look and tone shall carry it off and make it pass for
deep skill in the passions.

It is common for people to talk of Shakspeare's plays
being *so natural*; that everybody can understand him.
They are natural indeed, they are grounded deep in nature, so deep that the depth of them lies out of the reach
of most of us. You shall hear the same persons say that
George Barnwell is very natural, and *Othello* is very natural, that they are both very deep; and to them they are
the same kind of thing. At the one they sit and shed
tears, because a good sort of young man is tempted by a
naughty woman to commit a *trifling peccadillo*, the murder of an uncle or so,[1] that is all, and so comes to an un-

---

[1] If this note could hope to meet the eye of any of the Managers,
I would entreat and beg of them, in the name of both the Galleries,
that this insult upon the morality of the common people of Lon-

timely end, which is *so moving;* and at the other, because a blackamoor in a fit of jealousy kills his innocent
white wife; and the odds are that ninety-nine out of a
hundred would willingly behold the same catastrophe
happen to both the heroes, and have thought the rope
more due to Othello than to Barnwell.

For of the texture of Othello's mind, the inward con-
struction marvellously laid open with all its strengths
and weaknesses, its heroic confidences and its human
misgivings, its agonies of hate springing from the depths
of love, they see no more than the spectators at a
cheaper rate, who pay their pennies a-piece to look
through the man's telescope in Leicester Fields, see into
the inward plot and topography of the moon. Some dim
thing or other they see; they see an actor personating a
passion, of grief, or anger, for instance, and they recognize it as a copy of the usual external effects of such passions; or at least as being true to *that symbol of the emotion which passes current at the theatre for it,* for it is
often no more than that: but of the grounds of the passion, its correspondence to a great or heroic nature,
which is the only worthy object of tragedy—that common auditors know anything of this, or can have any
such notions dinned into them by the mere strength of
an actor's lungs—that apprehensions foreign to them

don should cease to be eternally repeated in the holiday weeks.
Why are the 'Prentices of this famous and well-governed city, instead of an amusement, to be treated over and over again with a
nauseous sermon of George Barnwell? Why at the end of their
vistas are we to place the gallows? Were I an uncle, I should not
much like a nephew of mine to have such an example placed
before his eyes. It is really making uncle-murder too trivial to ex-
hibit it as done upon such slight motives—it is attributing too
much to such characters as Millwood—it is putting things into the
heads of good young men, which they would never otherwise have
dreamed of. Uncles that think anything of their lives, should fairly
petition the Chamberlain against it.—C. L.

should be thus infused into them by storm, I can neither believe, nor understand how it can be possible.

We talk of Shakspeare's admirable observation of life, when we should feel, that not from a petty inquisition into those cheap and everyday characters which surrounded him, as they surround us, but from his own mind, which was, to borrow a phrase of Ben Jonson's, the very "sphere of humanity," he fetched those images of virtue and of knowledge, of which every one of us recognising a part, think we comprehend in our natures the whole; and oftentimes mistake the powers which he positively creates in us, for nothing more than indigenous faculties of our own minds, which only waited the application of corresponding virtues in him to return a full and clear echo of the same.

To return to Hamlet. Among the distinguishing features of that wonderful character, one of the most interesting (yet painful) is that soreness of mind which makes him treat the intrusions of Polonius with harshness, and that asperity which he puts on in his interviews with Ophelia. These tokens of an unhinged mind (if they be not mixed in the latter case with a profound artifice of love, to alienate Ophelia by affected discourtesies, so to prepare her mind for the breaking off of that loving intercourse, which can no longer find a place amidst business so serious as that which he has to do) are parts of his character, which to reconcile with our admiration of Hamlet, the most patient consideration of his situation is no more than necessary; they are what we *forgive afterwards,* and explain by the whole of his character, but *at the time* they are harsh and unpleasant. Yet such is the actor's necessity of giving strong blows to the audience, that I have never seen a player in this character, who did not exaggerate and strain to the utmost these ambiguous features—these temporary deformities in the character.

They make him express a vulgar scorn at Polonius which utterly degrades his gentility, and which no explanation can render palatable; they make him show contempt, and curl up the nose at Ophelia's father—contempt in its very grossest and most hateful form; but they get applause by it: it is natural, people say; that is, the words are scornful, and the actor expresses scorn, and that they can judge of: but why so much scorn, and of that sort, they never think of asking.

So to Ophelia. All the Hamlets that I have ever seen, rant and rave at her as if she had committed some great crime, and the audience are highly pleased, because the words of the part are satirical, and they are enforced by the strongest expression of satirical indignation of which the face and voice are capable. But then, whether Hamlet is likely to have put on such brutal appearances to a lady whom he loved so dearly, is never thought on.

The truth is, that in all such deep affections as had subsisted between Hamlet and Ophelia, there is a stock of *supererogatory love* (if I may venture to use the expression), which in any great grief of heart, especially where that which preys upon the mind cannot be communicated, confers a kind of indulgence upon the grieved party to express itself, even to its heart's dearest object, in the language of a temporary alienation; but it is not alienation, it is a distraction purely, and so it always makes itself to be felt by that object: it is not anger, but grief assuming the appearance of anger—love awkwardly counterfeiting hate, as sweet countenances when they try to frown: but such sternness and fierce disgust as Hamlet is made to show, is no counterfeit, but the real face of absolute aversion—of irrec-

oncileable alienation. It may be said he puts on the
madman; but then he should only so far put on this
counterfeit lunacy as his own real distraction will give
him leave; that is, incompletely, imperfectly; not in that
confirmed, practised way, like a master of his art, or as
Dame Quickly would say, "like one of those harlotry
players."

I mean no disrespect to any actor, but the sort of
pleasure which Shakspeare's plays give in the acting
seems to me not at all to differ from that which the audience receive from those of other writers; and, *they
being in themselves essentially so different from all
others,* I must conclude that there is something in the
nature of acting which levels all distinctions. And, in
fact, who does not speak indifferently of *The Gamester*
and of *Macbeth* as fine stage performances, and praise
the Mrs. Beverley in the same way as the Lady Macbeth of Mrs. S.? Belvidera, and Calista, and Isabella, and
Euphrasia, are they less liked than Imogen, or than
Juliet, or than Desdemona? Are they not spoken of and
remembered in the same way? Is not the female performer as great (as they call it) in one as in the other?
Did not Garrick shine, and was he not ambitious of
shining, in every drawling tragedy that his wretched
day produced—the productions of the Hills, and the
Murphys, and the Browns—and shall he have that
honour to dwell in our minds for ever as an inseparable concomitant with Shakspeare? A kindred mind! O
who can read that affecting sonnet of Shakspeare which
alludes to his profession as a player:

> Oh for my sake do you with Fortune chide,
> The guilty goddess of my harmless deeds,
> That did not better for my life provide
> Than public means which public custom breeds—
> Thence comes it that my name receives a brand;

And almost thence my nature is subdued
To what it works in, like the dyer's hand.

Or that other confession:

Alas! 'tis true, I have gone here and there,
And made myself a motley to thy view,
Gored mine own thoughts, sold cheap what is most dear—

Who can read these instances of jealous self-watchfulness in our sweet Shakspeare, and dream of any con-
geniality between him and one that, by every tradition
of him, appears to have been as mere a player as ever
existed; to have had his mind tainted with the lowest
players' vices—envy and jealousy, and miserable cravings after applause; one who in the exercise of his profession was jealous even of the women-performers that
stood in his way; a manager full of managerial tricks
and stratagems and finesse; that any resemblance should
be dreamed of between him and Shakspeare—Shakspeare who, in the plenitude and consciousness of his
own powers, could with that noble modesty, which we
can neither imitate nor appreciate, express himself thus
of his own sense of his own defects:

Wishing me like to one more rich in hope,
Featured like him, like him with friends possest;
Desiring *this man's art, and that man's scope.*

I am almost disposed to deny to Garrick the merit
of being an admirer of Shakspeare! A true lover of his
excellences he certainly was not; for would any true
lover of them have admitted into his matchless scenes
such ribald trash as Tate and Cibber, and the rest of
them, that

With their darkness durst affront his light,

have foisted into the acting plays of Shakspeare? I believe it impossible that he could have had a proper rev-

erence for Shakspeare, and have condescended to go
through that interpolated scene in *Richard the Third*,
in which Richard tries to break his wife's heart by telling her he loves another woman, and says, "if she survives this she is immortal." Yet I doubt not he delivered
this vulgar stuff with as much anxiety of emphasis as
any of the genuine parts: and for acting, it is as well
calculated as any. But we have seen the part of Richard
lately produce great fame to an actor by his manner of
playing it, and it lets us into the secret of acting, and of
popular judgments of Shakspeare derived from acting.
Not one of the spectators who have witnessed Mr. C.'s
exertions in that part, but has come away with a proper
conviction that Richard is a very wicked man, and kills
little children in their beds, with something like the
pleasure which the giants and ogres in children's books
are represented to have taken in that practice; moreover,
that he is very close and shrewd, and devilish cunning,
for you could see that by his eye.

But is, in fact, this the impression we have in reading
the Richard of Shakspeare? Do we feel anything like
disgust, as we do at that butcher-like representation of
him that passes for him on the stage? A horror at his
crimes blends with the effect which we feel, but how
is it qualified, how is it carried off, by the rich intellect
which he displays, his resources, his wit, his buoyant
spirits, his vast knowledge and insight into characters,
the poetry of his part—not an atom of all which is made
perceivable in Mr. C.'s way of acting it. Nothing but
his crimes, his actions, is visible; they are prominent
and staring; the murderer stands out, but where is the
lofty genius, the man of vast capacity—the profound,
the witty, accomplished Richard?

The truth is, the Characters of Shakspeare are so
much the objects of meditation rather than of interest

or curiosity as to their actions, that while we are reading
any of his great criminal characters—Macbeth, Richard,
even Iago—we think not so much of the crimes which
they commit, as of the ambition, the aspiring spirit, the
intellectual activity, which prompts them to overleap
these moral fences. Barnwell is a wretched murderer;
there is a certain fitness between his neck and the rope;
he is the legitimate heir to the gallows; nobody who
thinks at all can think of any alleviating circumstances
in his case to make him a fit object of mercy. Or to take
an instance from the higher tragedy, what else but a
mere assassin is Glenalvon? Do we think of anything but
of the crime which he commits, and the rack which he
deserves? That is all which we really think about him.
Whereas in corresponding characters in Shakspeare, so
little do the actions comparatively affect us, that while
the impulses, the inner mind in all its perverted greatness, solely seems real and is exclusively attended to,
the crime is comparatively nothing.

But when we see these things represented, the acts
which they do are comparatively everything, their impulses nothing. The state of sublime emotion into which
we are elevated by those images of night and horror
which Macbeth is made to utter, that solemn prelude
with which he entertains the time till the bell shall
strike which is to call him to murder Duncan—when
we no longer read it in a book, when we have given
up that vantage ground of abstraction which reading
possesses over seeing, and come to see a man in his
bodily shape before our eyes actually preparing to commit a murder, if the acting be true and impressive, as
I have witnessed it in Mr. K.'s performance of that part,
the painful anxiety about the act, the natural longing
to prevent it while it yet seems unperpetrated, the too
close pressing semblance of reality, give a pain and an

uneasiness which totally destroy all the delight which the words in the book convey, where the deed doing never presses upon us with the painful sense of presence: it rather seems to belong to history—to something past and inevitable, if it has anything to do with time at all. The sublime images, the poetry alone, is that which is present to our minds in the reading.

So to see Lear acted—to see an old man tottering about the stage with a walking-stick, turned out of doors by his daughters in a rainy night, has nothing in it but what is painful and disgusting. We want to take him into shelter and relieve him. That is all the feeling which the acting of Lear ever produced in me. But the Lear of Shakspeare cannot be acted. The contemptible machinery by which they mimic the storm which he goes out in, is not more inadequate to represent the horror of the real elements, than any actor can be to represent Lear; they might more easily propose to personate the Satan of Milton upon a stage, or one of Michael Angelo's terrible figures.

The greatness of Lear is not in corporal dimension, but in intellectual: the explosions of his passion are terrible as a volcano; they are storms turning up and disclosing to the bottom that sea, his mind, with all its vast riches. It is his mind which is laid bare. This case of flesh and blood seems too insignificant to be thought on; even as he himself neglects it. On the stage we see nothing but corporal infirmities and weakness, the impotence of rage; while we read it, we see not Lear, but we are Lear—we are in his mind, we are sustained by a grandeur which baffles the malice of daughters and storms; in the aberrations of his reason, we discover a mighty irregular power of reasoning, immethodized from the ordinary purposes of life, but exerting its powers, as the wind blows where it listeth, at will upon the corruptions and abuses of mankind.

What have looks, or tones, to do with that sublime identification of his age with that of the *heavens themselves*, when, in his reproaches to them for conniving at the injustice of his children, he reminds them that "They themselves are old"? What gesture shall we appropriate to this? What has the voice or the eye to do with such things? But the play is beyond all art, as the tamperings with it show: it is too hard and stony; it must have love-scenes, and a happy ending. It is not enough that Cordelia is a daughter, she must shine as a lover too.

Tate has put his hook in the nostrils of this Leviathan, for Garrick and his followers, the show-men of the scene, to draw the mighty beast about more easily. A happy ending—as if the living martyrdom that Lear had gone through—the flaying of his feelings alive, did not make a fair dismissal from the stage of life the only decorous thing for him. If he is to live and be happy after, if he could sustain this world's burden after, why all his pudder and preparation—why torment us with all this unnecessary sympathy? As if the childish pleasure of getting his gilt robes and sceptre again could tempt him to act over again his misused station—as if, at his years and with his experience, anything was left but to die.

Lear is essentially impossible to be represented on a stage. But how many dramatic personages are there in Shakspeare, which though more tractable and feasible (if I may so speak) than Lear, yet from some circumstance, some adjunct to their character, are improper to be shown to our bodily eye! Othello for instance. Nothing can be more soothing, more flattering to the nobler parts of our natures, than to read of a young Venetian lady of the highest extraction, through the force of love and from a sense of merit in him whom she loved, laying aside every consideration of kindred, and country, and colour, and wedding with a *coal-black Moor*—(for such he is represented, in the imperfect state of knowledge respecting foreign countries in those days, compared with our own, or in compliance with popular notions, though the Moors are now well enough known to be by many shades less unworthy of a white woman's fancy)—it is the perfect triumph of virtue over accidents, of the imagination over the senses.

She sees Othello's colour in his mind. But upon the stage, when the imagination is no longer the ruling faculty, but we are left to our poor unassisted senses, I appeal to every one that has seen *Othello* played, whether he did not, on the contrary, sink Othello's mind in his colour; whether he did not find something extremely revolting in the courtship and wedded caresses of Othello and Desdemona; and whether the actual sight of the thing did not overweigh all that beautiful compromise which we make in reading—and the reason it should do so is obvious, because there is just so much reality presented to our senses as to give a perception of disagreement, with not enough of belief in the internal motives—all that which is unseen—to overpower and reconcile the first and obvious prejudices.[1] What we see upon a stage is body and bodily

[1] The error of supposing that because Othello's colour does not offend us in the reading, it should also not offend us in the seeing, is just such a fallacy as supposing that an Adam and Eve in a picture shall affect us just as they do in the poem. But in the poem we for a while have Paradisaical senses given us, which vanish when we see a man and his wife without clothes in the picture. The painters themselves feel this, as is apparent by the awkward shifts they have recourse to, to make them look not quite naked; by a sort of pro-

action; what we are conscious of in reading is almost
exclusively the mind, and its movements; and this I
think may sufficiently account for the very different sort
of delight with which the same play so often affects us
in the reading and the seeing.

It requires little reflection to perceive, that if those
characters in Shakspeare which are within the precincts
of nature, have yet something in them which appeals
too exclusively to the imagination, to admit of their
being made objects to the senses without suffering a
change and a diminution—that still stronger the objection must lie against representing another line of
characters, which Shakspeare has introduced to give
a wildness and a supernatural elevation to his scenes,
as if to remove them still farther from that assimilation
to common life in which their excellence is vulgarly
supposed to consist.

When we read the incantations of those terrible beings the Witches in *Macbeth*, though some of the ingredients of their hellish composition savour of the
grotesque, yet is the effect upon us other than the most
serious and appalling that can be imagined? Do we
not feel spellbound as Macbeth was? Can any mirth
accompany a sense of their presence? We might as well
laugh under a consciousness of the principle of Evil
himself being truly and really present with us. But attempt to bring these things on to a stage, and you turn
them instantly into so many old women, that men and
children are to laugh at. Contrary to the old saying,
that "seeing is believing," the sight actually destroys
the faith; and the mirth in which we indulge at their

phetic anachronism, antedating the invention of fig-leaves. So in the
reading of the play, we see with Desdemona's eyes: in the seeing
of it, we are forced to look with our own.—C. L.

expense, when we see these creatures upon a stage, seems to be a sort of indemnification which we make to ourselves for the terror which they put us in when reading made them an object of belief—when we surrendered up our reason to the poet, as children to their nurses and their elders; and we laugh at our fears as children, who thought they saw something in the dark, triumph when the bringing in of a candle discovers the vanity of their fears. For this exposure of supernatural agents upon a stage is truly bringing in a candle to expose their own delusiveness.

It is the solitary taper and the book that generates a faith in these terrors: a ghost by chandelier light, and in good company, deceives no spectators—a ghost that can be measured by the eye, and his human dimensions made out at leisure. The sight of a well-lighted house, and a well-dressed audience, shall arm the most nervous child against any apprehensions: as Tom Brown says of the impenetrable skin of Achilles with his impenetrable armour over it, "Bully Dawson would have fought the devil with such advantages."

Much has been said, and deservedly, in reprobation of the vile mixture which Dryden has thrown into *The Tempest:* doubtless without some such vicious alloy, the impure ears of that age would never have sate out to hear so much innocence of love as is contained in the sweet courtship of Ferdinand and Miranda. But is *The Tempest* of Shakspeare at all a subject for stage representation? It is one thing to read of an enchanter, and to believe the wondrous tale while we are reading it; but to have a conjurer brought before us in his conjuring-gown, with his spirits about him, which none but himself and some hundred of favoured spectators before the curtain are supposed to see, involves such a quan-

tity of the *hateful incredible*, that all our reverence for
the author cannot hinder us from perceiving such
gross attempts upon the senses to be in the highest degree childish and inefficient.

Spirits and fairies cannot be represented, they cannot even be painted—they can only be believed. But
the elaborate and anxious provision of scenery, which
the luxury of the age demands, in these cases works a
quite contrary effect to what is intended. That which
in comedy, or plays of familiar life, adds so much to the
life of the imitation, in plays which appeal to the higher
faculties positively destroys the illusion which it is introduced to aid.

A parlour or a drawing-room—a library opening into
a garden—a garden with an alcove in it—a street, or
the piazza of Covent Garden, does well enough in a
scene; we are content to give as much credit to it as it
demands; or rather, we think little about it—it is little
more than reading at the top of a page, "Scene, a garden"; we do not imagine ourselves there, but we readily
admit the imitation of familiar objects. But to think by
the help of painted trees and caverns, which we know
to be painted, to transport our minds to Prospero, and
his island and his lonely cell,[1] or by the aid of a fiddle
dexterously thrown in, in an interval of speaking, to
make us believe that we hear those super-natural noises
of which the isle was full: the Orrery Lecturer at the
Haymarket might as well hope, by his musical glasses
cleverly stationed out of sight behind his apparatus,
to make us believe that we do indeed hear the crystal

---

[1] It will be said these things are done in pictures. But pictures
and scenes are very different things. Painting is a world of itself, but
in scene-painting there is the attempt to deceive: and there is the
discordancy, never to be got over, between painted scenes and real
people.—C. L.

spheres ring out that chime, which if it were to enwrap
our fancy long, Milton thinks,

> Time would run back and fetch the age of gold,
> And speckled Vanity
> Would sicken soon and die,
> And leprous Sin would melt from earthly mould;
> Yea, Hell itself would pass away,
> And leave its dolorous mansions to the peering day.

The garden of Eden, with our first parents in it, is not
more impossible to be shown on a stage, than the Enchanted Isle, with its no less interesting and innocent
first settlers.

The subject of Scenery is closely connected with that
of the Dresses, which are so anxiously attended to on
our stage. I remember the last time I saw *Macbeth*
played, the discrepancy I felt at the changes of garment which he varied, the shiftings and reshiftings, like
a Romish priest at mass. The luxury of stage-improve-
ments, and the importunity of the public eye, require
this. The coronation robe of the Scottish monarch was
fairly a counterpart to that which our King wears when
he goes to the Parliament House, just so full and cumbersome, and set out with ermine and pearls. And if
things must be represented, I see not what to find fault
with in this. But in reading, what robe are we conscious
of? Some dim images of royalty—a crown and sceptre
may float before our eyes, but who shall describe the
fashion of it?

Do we see in our mind's eye what Webb or any
other robe-maker could pattern? This is the inevitable
consequence of imitating everything, to make all things
natural. Whereas the reading of a tragedy is a fine abstraction. It presents to the fancy just so much of external appearances as to make us feel that we are among

flesh and blood, while by far the greater and better part of our imagination is employed upon the thoughts and internal machinery of the character. But in acting, scenery, dress, the most contemptible things, call upon us to judge of their naturalness.

Perhaps it would be no bad similitude, to liken the pleasure which we take in seeing one of these fine plays acted, compared with that quiet delight which we find in the reading of it, to the different feelings with which a reviewer, and a man that is not a reviewer, reads a fine poem. The accursed critical habit—the being called upon to judge and pronounce, must make it quite a different thing to the former. In seeing these plays acted, we are affected just as judges. When Hamlet compares the two pictures of Gertrude's first and second husband, who wants to see the pictures? But in the acting, a miniature must be lugged out; which we know not to be the picture, but only to show how finely a miniature may be represented. This showing of everything levels all things: it makes tricks, bows, and curtseys, of importance. Mrs. S. never got more fame by anything than by the manner in which she dismisses the guests in the banquet-scene in *Macbeth:* it is as much remembered as any of her thrilling tones or impressive looks. But does such a trifle as this enter into the imaginations of the readers of that wild and wonderful scene? Does not the mind dismiss the feasters as rapidly as it can? Does it care about the gracefulness of the doing it? But by acting, and judging of acting, all these nonessentials are raised into an importance, injurious to the main interest of the play.

I have confined my observations to the tragic parts of Shakspeare. It would be no very difficult task to extend the inquiry to his comedies; and to show why Falstaff, Shallow, Sir Hugh Evans, and the rest, are equally

incompatible with stage representation. The length to
which this Essay has run will make it, I am afraid, sufficiently distasteful to the Amateurs of the Theatre,
without going any deeper into the subject at present.

The Reflector, 1811.

CHARACTERS OF DRAMATIC WRITERS CONTEMPORARY WITH SHAKSPEARE[1]

WHEN I selected for publication, in 1808, *Specimens of English Dramatic Poets who lived about the
time of Shakspeare,* the kind of extracts which I was
anxious to give were, not so much passages of wit and
humour, though the old plays are rich in such, as
scenes of passion, sometimes of the deepest quality, interesting situations, serious descriptions, that which is
more nearly allied to poetry than to wit, and to tragic
rather than to comic poetry. The plays which I made
choice of were, with few exceptions, such as treat of
human life and manners, rather than masques and Arcadian pastorals, with their train of abstractions, unim-
passioned deities, passionate mortals—Claius, and Me-
dorus, and Amintas, and Amarillis.

My leading design was, to illustrate what may be
called the moral sense of our ancestors. To shew in what
manner they felt, when they placed themselves by the

---

[1] Selected from those chosen by Lamb in 1818, for publication in
his collected works, from *Specimens of English Dramatic Poets Who
Lived about the Time of Shakspeare* (1808). A note by Alfred Ainger
(*Life and Works of Charles Lamb,* Boston: The Merrymount Press,
1888) states that Lamb's "prefatory words explain that he here se-
lects such criticisms as would be intelligible and interesting apart
from the passages to which they refer."—J. M. B.

power of imagination in trying circumstances, in the conflicts of duty and passion, or the strife of contending duties; what sort of loves and enmities theirs were; how their griefs were tempered, and their full-swoln joys abated: how much of Shakspeare shines in the great men his contemporaries, and how far in his divine mind and manners he surpassed them and all mankind. I was also desirous to bring together some of the most admired scenes of Fletcher and Massinger, in the estimation of the world the only dramatic poets of that age entitled to be considered after Shakspeare, and, by exhibiting them in the same volume with the more impressive scenes of old Marlowe, Heywood, Tourneur, Webster, Ford, and others, to show what we had slighted, while beyond all proportion we had been crying up one or two favourite names. From the desultory criticisms which accompanied that publication I have selected a few which I thought would best stand by themselves, as requiring least immediate reference to the play or passage by which they were suggested.

CHRISTOPHER MARLOWE

Tamburlaine the Great, or the Scythian Shepherd.— The lunes of Tamburlaine are perfect midsummer madness. Nebuchadnezzar's are mere modest pretensions compared with the thundering vaunts of this Scythian Shepherd. He comes in, drawn by conquered kings, and reproaches these *pampered jades of Asia* that they can *draw but twenty miles a day.* Till I saw this passage with my own eyes, I never believed that it was any thing more than a pleasant burlesque of mine ancient's. But I can assure my readers that it is soberly set down in a play, which their ancestors took to be serious.

Edward the Second.—In a very different style from

mighty *Tamburlaine* is the tragedy of *Edward the Sec-ond.* The reluctant pangs of abdicating royalty in Ed-ward furnished hints which Shakspeare scarcely im-proved in his *Richard the Second;* and the death-scene of Marlowe's king moves pity and terror beyond any scene ancient or modern with which I am acquainted.

The Rich Jew of Malta.—Marlowe's Jew does not approach so near to Shakspeare's as his Edward the Second does to Richard the Second. Barabas is a mere monster brought in with a large painted nose to please the rabble. He kills in sport, poisons whole nunneries, invents infernal machines. He is just such an exhibition as a century or two earlier might have been played be-fore the Londoners "by the royal command," when a general pillage and massacre of the Hebrews had been previously resolved on in the cabinet. It is curious to see a superstition wearing out. The idea of a Jew, which our pious ancestors contemplated with so much horror, has nothing in it now revolting. We have tamed the claws of the beast, and pared its nails, and now we take it to our arms, fondle it, write plays to flatter it; it is visited by princes, affects a taste, patronizes the arts, and is the only liberal and gentlemanlike thing in Chris-tendom.

THOMAS DEKKER

The Honest Whore.—There is in the second part of this play, where Bellafront, a reclaimed harlot, re-counts some of the miseries of her profession, a simple picture of honour and shame, contrasted without vio-lence, and expressed without immodesty, which is worth all the *strong lines* against the harlot's profession with which both parts of this play are offensively crowded. A satirist is always to be suspected who, to make vice odious, dwells upon all its acts and minutest circumstances with a sort of relish and retrospective fondness. But so near are the boundaries of panegyric and invective, that a worn-out sinner is sometimes found to make the best declaimer against sin. The same high-seasoned descriptions, which in his unregenerate state served but to inflame his appetites, in his new province of a moralist will serve him, a little turned, to expose the enormity of those appetites in other men. When Cervantes with such proficiency of fondness dwells upon the Don's library, who sees not that he has been a great reader of books of knight-errantry—perhaps was at some time of his life in danger of falling into those very extravagances which he ridiculed so happily in his hero?

AUTHOR UNKNOWN

The Merry Devil of Edmonton.—The scene in this delightful comedy, in which Jerningham, "with the true feeling of a zealous friend," touches the griefs of Mounchensey, seems written to make the reader happy. Few of our dramatists or novelists have attended enough to this. They torture and wound us abundantly. They are economists only in delight. Nothing can be finer, more gentlemanlike, and nobler, than the conversation and compliments of these young men. How delicious is Raymond Mounchensey's forgetting, in his fears, that Jerningham has a "Saint in Essex"; and how sweetly his friend reminds him! I wish it could be ascertained, which there is some grounds for believing, that Michael Drayton was the author of this piece. It would add a worthy appendage to the renown of that Panegyrist of my native Earth; who has gone over her soil, in his Polyolbion, with the fidelity of a herald, and the painful love of a son; who has not left a rivulet, so narrow that it may be stept over, without honourable mention; and has animated hills and streams with life and passion beyond the dreams of old mythology.

THOMAS HEYWOOD

A Woman Killed with Kindness.—Heywood is a sort of *prose* Shakspeare. His scenes are to the full as natural and affecting. But we miss *the poet,* that which in Shakspeare always appears out and above the surface of *the nature.* Heywood's characters in this play, for instance, his country gentlemen, etc., are exactly what we see, but of the best kind of what we see, in life. Shakspeare makes us believe, while we are among his lovely creations, that they are nothing but what we are familiar with, as in dreams new things seem old; but we awake, and sigh for the difference.

The English Traveller.—Heywood's preface to this play is interesting, as it shews the heroic indifference about the opinion of posterity, which some of these great writers seem to have felt. There is a magnanimity in authorship as in everything else. His ambition seems to have been confined to the pleasure of hearing the players speak his lines while he lived. It does not appear that he ever contemplated the possibility of being read by after ages. What a slender pittance of fame was motive sufficient to the production of such plays as the *English Traveller,* the *Challenge for Beauty,* and the *Woman Killed with Kindness!* Posterity is bound to take care that a writer loses nothing by such a noble modesty.

THOMAS MIDDLETON AND WILLIAM ROWLEY

A Fair Quarrel.—The insipid levelling morality to which the modern stage is tied down, would not admit of such admirable passions as these scenes are filled with. A puritanical obtuseness of sentiment, a stupid infantile goodness, is creeping among us, instead of the vigorous passions, and virtues clad in flesh and blood, with which the old dramatists present us. Those noble and liberal casuists could discern in the differences, the quarrels, the animosities of men, a beauty and truth of moral feeling, no less than in the everlastingly inculcated duties of forgiveness and atonement. With us, all is hypocritical meekness. A reconciliation-scene, be the occasion never so absurd, never fails of applause. Our audiences come to the theatre to be complimented on their goodness. They compare notes with the amiable characters in the play, and find a wonderful sympathy of disposition between them. We have a common stock of dramatic morality, out of which a writer may be supplied without the trouble of copying it from originals within his own breast. To know the boundaries of honour, to be judiciously valiant, to have a temperance which shall beget a smoothness in the angry swellings of youth, to esteem life as nothing when the sacred reputation of a parent is to be defended, yet to shake and tremble under a pious cowardice when that ark of an honest confidence is found to be frail and tottering, to feel the true blows of a real disgrace blunting that sword which the imaginary strokes of a supposed false imputation had put so keen an edge upon but lately: to, or to imagine this done in a feigned story, asks something more of a moral sense, somewhat a greater delicacy of perception in questions of right and wrong, than goes to the writing of two or three hackneyed sentences about the laws of honour as opposed to the laws of the land, or a commonplace against duelling. Yet such things would stand a writer nowadays in far better stead than Captain Agar and his conscientious honour; and he would be considered as a far better teacher of morality than old Rowley or Middleton, if they were living.

WILLIAM ROWLEY

A New Wonder; A Woman Never Vext.—The old play-writers are distinguished by an honest boldness of exhibition, they show everything without being ashamed. If a reverse in fortune is to be exhibited, they fairly bring us to the prison-grate and the alms-basket. A poor man on our stage is always a gentleman, he may be known by a peculiar neatness of apparel, and by wearing black. Our delicacy in fact forbids the drama-tizing of distress at all. It is never shown in its essential properties; it appears but as the adjunct of some vir-tue, as something which is to be relieved, from the ap-probation of which relief the spectators are to derive a certain soothing of self-referred satisfaction. We turn away from the real essences of things to hunt after their relative shadows, moral duties; whereas, if the truth of things were fairly represented, the relative duties might be safely trusted to themselves, and moral philosophy lose the name of a science.

CYRIL TOURNEUR

The Revenger's Tragedy.—The reality and life of the dialogue, in which Vindici and Hippolito first tempt their mother, and then threaten her with death for con-senting to the dishonour of their sister, passes any scen-ical illusion I ever felt. I never read it but my ears tingle, and I feel a hot flush overspread my cheeks, as if I were presently about to proclaim such malefactions of my-self as the brothers here rebuke in their unnatural par-ent, in words more keen and dagger-like than those which Hamlet speaks to his mother. Such power has the passion of shame truly personated, not only to strike guilty creatures unto the soul, but to "appal" even those that are "free."

JOHN WEBSTER

The Duchess of Malfi.—All the several parts of the dreadful apparatus with which the death of the Duchess is ushered in, the waxen images which counterfeit death, the wild masque of madmen, the tomb-maker, the bell-man, the living person's dirge, the mortification by degrees—are not more remote from the conceptions of ordinary vengeance, than the strange character of suffering which they seem to bring upon their victim is out of the imagination of ordinary poets. As they are not like inflictions of this life, so her language seems not of this world. She has lived among horrors till she is become "native and endowed unto that element." She speaks the dialect of despair; her tongue has a smatch of Tartarus and the souls in bale. To move a horror skilfully, to touch a soul to the quick, to lay upon fear as much as it can bear, to wean and weary a life till it is ready to drop, and then step in with mortal instruments to take its last forfeit: this only a Webster can do. Inferior geniuses may "upon horror's head horrors accumulate," but they cannot do this. They mistake quantity for quality; they "terrify babes with painted devils"; but they know not how a soul is to be moved. Their terrors want dignity, their affrightments are without decorum.

JOHN FORD

The Broken Heart.—I do not know where to find, in any play. a catastrophe so grand, so solemn, and so surprising as in this. This is indeed, according to Milton, to describe high passions and high actions. The fortitude of the Spartan boy, who let a beast gnaw out his bowels till he died without expressing a groan, is a faint bodily image of this dilaceration of the spirit, and exenteration of the inmost mind, which Calantha, with a holy violence against her nature, keeps closely covered, till the last duties of a wife and a queen are fulfilled. Stories of martyrdom are but of chains and the stake; a little bodily suffering. These torments

> On the purest spirits prey,
> As on entrails, joints, and limbs,
> With answerable pains, but more intense.

What a noble thing is the soul in its strengths and in its weaknesses! Who would be less weak than Calantha? Who can be so strong? The expression of this transcendent scene almost bears us in imagination to Calvary and the Cross; and we seem to perceive some analogy between the scenical sufferings which we are here contemplating, and the real agonies of that final completion to which we dare no more than hint a reference. Ford was of the first order of poets. He sought for sublimity, not by parcels, in metaphors or visible images, but directly where she has her full residence in the heart of man; in the actions and sufferings of the greatest minds. There is a grandeur of the soul above mountains, seas, and the elements. Even in the poor perverted reason of Giovanni and Annabella, in the play[1] which stands at the head of the modern collection of the works of this author, we discern traces of that fiery particle, which, in the irregular starting from out the road of beaten action, discovers something of a right line even in ob-

---

[1] *'Tis Pity she is a Whore.*—C. L.

liquity, and shews hints of an improvable greatness in
the lowest descents and degradations of our nature.

BEN JONSON

Poetaster.—This Roman play seems written to con-
fute those enemies of Ben in his own days and ours,
who have said that he made a pedantical use of his
learning. He has here revived the whole Court of Au-
gustus, by a learned spell. We are admitted to the
society of the illustrious dead. Virgil, Horace, Ovid,
Tibullus, converse in our own tongue more finely and
poetically than they were used to express themselves
in their native Latin. Nothing can be imagined more
elegant, refined, and court-like, than the scenes between
this Louis the Fourteenth of antiquity and his literati.
The whole essence and secret of that kind of intercourse
is contained therein. The economical liberality by which
greatness, seeming to waive some part of its prerogative,
takes care to lose none of the essentials; the prudential
liberties of an inferior, which flatter by commanded
boldness and soothe with complimentary sincerity.
These, and a thousand beautiful passages from his
New Inn, his *Cynthia's Revels,* and from those numerous court-masques and entertainments which he was
in the daily habit of furnishing, might be adduced to
shew the poetical fancy and elegance of mind of the
supposed rugged old bard.

GEORGE CHAPMAN

*Bussy D'Ambois, Byron's Conspiracy, Byron's Trag-
edy, etc., etc.*—Webster has happily characterized the
"full and heightened style" of Chapman, who, of all

the English play-writers, perhaps approaches nearest to Shakspeare in the descriptive and didactic, in passages which are less purely dramatic. He could not go out of himself, as Shakspeare could shift at pleasure, to inform and animate other existences, but in himself he had an eye to perceive and a soul to embrace all forms and modes of being. He would have made a great epic poet, if indeed he has not abundantly shown himself to be one; for his Homer is not so properly a translation as the stories of Achilles and Ulysses rewritten. The earnestness and passion which he has put into every part of these poems, would be incredible to a reader of mere modern translations. His almost Greek zeal for the glory of his heroes can only be paralleled by that fierce spirit of Hebrew bigotry, with which Milton, as if personating one of the zealots of the old law, clothed himself when he sat down to paint the acts of Samson against the uncircumcized. The great obstacle to Chapman's translations being read, is their unconquerable quaintness. He pours out in the same breath the most just and natural, and the most violent and crude expressions. He seems to grasp at whatever words come first to hand while the enthusiasm is upon him, as if all other must be inadequate to the divine meaning. But passion (the all in all in poetry) is everywhere present, raising the low, dignifying the mean, and putting sense into the absurd. He makes his readers glow, weep, tremble, take any affection which he pleases, be moved by words, or in spite of them, be disgusted and overcome their disgust.

FROM *Specimens of English Dramatic Poets Who Lived about the Time of Shakspeare*, 1808

A Short Bibliography

Works by Charles Lamb

Life and Works of Charles Lamb. Edited by Alfred Ainger. Boston: The Merrymount Press, 1888. Library ed. 12 vols.

The Complete Works and Letters of Charles Lamb. With an introduction by Saxe Commins. New York: The Modern Library, 1935.

The Letters of Charles Lamb. With an introduction by Guy Pocock. Everyman's Library, New York: E. P. Dutton & Company, 1945. Rev. ed., 2 vols.

Everybody's Lamb, Being a Selection from the Essays of Elia, the Letters, and the Miscellaneous Prose. Edited by A. C. Ward. London: G. Bell & Sons, Ltd., 1933.

Dramatic Works of Charles Lamb. With an introduction and notes by Brander Matthews. New York: Dodd, Mead & Company, 1891.

Biographies

Ainger, Alfred. *Charles Lamb.* New York: The Macmillan Company, 1926. Reprinted in English Men of Letters Series.

Anthony, Katharine. *The Lambs, a Story of Pre-Victorian England.* New York: Alfred A. Knopf, 1945.

Lucas, E. V. *The Life of Charles Lamb.* London: Methuen & Co., 1921. 2 vols. This is the standard definitive work on Lamb.

Winchester, C. T. *A Group of English Essayists of the Early Nineteenth Century.* New York: The Macmillan Company, 1910.

Critical Appraisals and Reminiscences

De Quincey, Thomas. *Literary Reminiscences.* Edited by Ripley Hitchcock. New York: D. Appleton Company, 1900.

Hazlitt, William. *Selected Essays.* Edited by Geoffrey Keynes. New York: Random House, 1930. See "On the Conversation of Authors"; "Of Persons One Would Wish to Have Seen."

————. *Table Talk.* New York: Oxford University Press, 1925. See "On Criticism."

Hunt, Leigh. *Autobiography.* With an introduction by Edmund Blunden. New York: Oxford University Press, 1928, World's Classics series.

Lucas, E. V. *At the Shrine of St. Charles.* New York: E. P. Dutton & Company, 1934.

Pater, Walter. *Appreciations.* New York: The Macmillan Company, 1927.

Saintsbury, George. *A History of English Criticism.* New York: Dodd, Mead & Company, 1911.

A selection of books published by Penguin is listed on the following pages.

For a complete list of books available from Penguin in the United States, write to Dept. DG, Penguin Books, 299 Murray Hill Parkway, East Rutherford, New Jersey 07073.

For a complete list of books available from Penguin in Canada, write to Penguin Books Canada Limited, 2801 John Street, Markham, Ontario L3R 1B4.

If you live in the British Isles, write to Dept. EP, Penguin Books Ltd, Harmondsworth, Middlesex.

A SHORTENED HISTORY OF ENGLAND

G. M. Trevelyan

In this brilliant chronicle one of the greatest writers of English history tells the story of the building of "this realm, this England," from the remote days of the Celt and the Iberian to the twentieth century. This exhilarating history of the British people has both pace and proportion.

ENGLAND IN THE EIGHTEENTH CENTURY

J. H. Plumb

This history of England in the eighteenth century is not a chronological narrative of ministries and wars, but a history of the development of English society; the ministries and wars have their place, but no greater a place than the economic, cultural, and social history of the time. The book has been divided into three parts: the ages of Robert Walpole, the Earl of Chatham, and William Pitt. These divisions are useful for analyzing those social forces that enabled these three great statesmen to stamp the impress of their personalities upon history. Yet a large part of this book is devoted to the hard and bitter lives of ordinary men and women, and to those men of genius and talent who made it a time of hope.

ENGLAND IN THE NINETEENTH CENTURY

David Thomson

The theme of this book is the major social changes that the people of England experienced during the period of "the great peace" between the Battle of Waterloo and the First World War. Political, economic, intellectual, diplomatic, and other "specialized" forms of history are drawn upon only insofar as they help to illuminate changes in mental habit or outlook or in social life and organization. The underlying motif is the remarkable accumulation of material wealth and power which the English people achieved—whence it derived, how it eventually diminished.

THE PENGUIN ENGLISH LIBRARY

The Penguin English Library series reproduces, in convenient but authoritative editions, many of the greatest classics in English literature from Elizabethan times through the nineteenth century. Each volume is introduced by a critical essay, enhancing the understanding and enjoyment of the work for the student and general reader alike. A few selections from the list of more than one hundred titles follow:

THE VIKING PORTABLE LIBRARY

In single volumes, The Viking Portable Library has gathered the very best work of individual authors or works of a period of literary history, writings that otherwise are scattered in a number of separate books. These are not condensed versions, but rather selected masterworks assembled and introduced with critical essays by distinguished authorities. Over fifty volumes of The Viking Portable Library are now in print in paperback, making the cream of ancient and modern Western writing available to bring pleasure and instruction to the student and the general reader. An assortment of subjects follows:

CERVANTES GEOFFREY CHAUCER
ANTON CHEKHOV SAMUEL COLERIDGE
STEPHEN CRANE DANTE
RALPH WALDO EMERSON WILLIAM FAULKNER
GREEK HISTORIANS THOMAS HARDY
NATHANIEL HAWTHORNE
THOMAS JEFFERSON
MACHIAVELLI MEDIEVAL READER
HERMAN MELVILLE PLATO
EDGAR ALLAN POE FRANÇOIS RABELAIS
POETS OF THE ENGLISH LANGUAGE
MEDIEVAL AND RENAISSANCE POETS: LANGLAND TO SPENSER
ELIZABETHAN AND JACOBEAN POETS: MARLOWE TO MARVELL
RESTORATION AND AUGUSTAN POETS: MILTON TO GOLDSMITH
VICTORIAN AND EDWARDIAN POETS: TENNYSON TO YEATS
RENAISSANCE READER ROMAN READER
WILLIAM SHAKESPEARE BERNARD SHAW
JONATHAN SWIFT VOLTAIRE
WALT WHITMAN OSCAR WILDE